I0761038

HERS TO KEEP

THE QUINTESSENCE COLLECTION I

SERENA AKEROYD

Created with Vellum

To my readers.
I'll always strive to bring you as much weird as I possibly can.
Serena
xoxo

PREPARE TO LOVE THE WEIRD

CHARMED BY THEM

Triggers:

- General violence

ONE

AS SASCHA DUBOIS pulled up beside the large end terrace house in Kensington, she did a little wriggle in her seat. Not only was she on time, but there was an empty parking space right outside. Luck was with her it seemed.

She took a deep breath and stared up at the massive house.

The address alone made her want this job.

Her vintage Caddy, cherry red and gleaming chrome, stuck out like a sore thumb in these very swanky parts, but she didn't care. That baby had cost her a fortune to import, but life in the UK would be very glum otherwise.

Dull weather, bland food… but the vibe? Jeez, nowhere compared. Especially London. It was a haven for all kinds of batshit craziness, and if anyone could embrace batshit, it was her.

As she swung her baby into reverse and parallel parked like a pro, the front door popped open. She cut her engine, and curiosity had her peeking through the window to spy the competition.

Another potential housekeeper, matronly as hell, was stomping out the door, a glower on her face as she toddled off, nose in the air, down the street. But Sascha wasn't interested in her. Her focus was on the hottie at the top of the stairs.

She popped her shades down so she could view him in full Technicolor, then wolf whistled under her breath at the sight of him.

Was this Sean Hayward?

The Sean Hayward? Eminent criminologist? Adored by the media, and the cops who, love Sean or loathe him, had helped solve some nasty crimes over the past two years?

She'd heard of him but only seen him on the news, and boy, had she missed out.

Black hair, blue eyes. Yep, *blue* eyes. They were like a husky's too. They pinned her in place because he'd finally spotted her, and as he caught her staring, he cocked a brow. They were dark, so not technically angel's wings, but damn, they framed those brooding eyes to perfection. His mouth was lush, wide and flared on the bottom, a pouting upper curve on the top—a woman would kill for those lips. His hair was smoothed back in a rough, tousled quiff, and the salt and pepper kissing his sideburns was divine. He had to be in his thirties, maybe even forties.

Yum. She did love an older man.

He wore a black tee with dark navy jeans. He was barefoot.

Her eyes flared at the sight, and she decided she was relieved she'd worn her red pencil skirt and a white, tightly fitting cotton blouse with the frilly lapels.

Sascha had a fetish for all things vintage. She spent more time looking like she belonged on the set of *Grease* than the twenty-first century. Though her tastes were unusual, she usually received interested looks, from both sexes, and not just because she dressed a little strangely, but because she rocked her outfits. It was all about having confidence, she'd found. It didn't matter if her own insecurities were eating her up on the inside, as long as no one else knew, she was doing A-Okay.

But now wasn't the time to think about insecurities.

She'd wanted this job before. Now that she'd seen one of her potential bosses? To have that kind of eye candy around, she'd better sparkle during the interview.

As she climbed out of the Caddy, locking it up behind her, she clutched her purse and popped the keys inside. With her cell tucked away for safekeeping, she strode on high stilettos around the car and headed for the bottom step.

When their eyes met, she smiled, slowly.

He broke off to check her out, and she let him. Not moving so he could take in the whole effect. Small waist, large boobs, long legs. She had curly auburn hair, bright green eyes, lips painted a cherry red, and cheekbones so high, Marilyn Monroe would have been jealous.

She was hot, and she knew it, but it wasn't like she had a big head or anything. She took care with her appearance because she enjoyed dressing up. It was fun, and what was life if not a chance to have fun and explore the various amusements that came one's way? After spending an adolescence drowning in being Ms. Average, once college had come, she'd reinvented herself.

Gone were the days where she was ashamed of her red hair or her too curvy body. Now, she embraced all the parts of her that weren't right for a society that wanted stick-thin blondes and brunettes, and made it her own.

"Sascha Dubois?" Sean asked, his voice deliciously low and rumbly.

She guessed she should think of him, even inwardly, as Mr. Hayward, but she'd never stood on ceremony. It wasn't her way, and thankfully, most Brits forgave her for it because she was American. They seemed to expect her to be outspoken…although, she'd found they were far more liberal than they expected she'd be.

"That's me," she said brightly, carefully climbing the six steps to the gorgeous Edwardian property.

It was large, and in London, large meant expensive. She knew he was famous, but she was surprised at this display of wealth. Three sash windows wide, and three stories high from the outside, but four if, and she guessed there was, a basement kitchen.

The place was like a mini mansion. Hell, for London, it *was*.

White moldings decorated the sides of the building, and dark stone clad the walls in a simple, elegant manner. London, in the rich parts, was one of the most beautiful places she'd ever had the joy of exploring.

In her most fanciful moments, she could easily envision ladies in Empire-line dresses roaming these streets. Beau Brummell, Britain's most elegant gent, striding to an appointment with the corpulent Prince Regent...

Sean held out a hand, breaking into her reverie. "Thank you for coming, Ms. Dubois."

"Sascha, please," she replied cheerfully, tucking her shades into her purse. "I don't stand on ceremony."

His lips twitched. "What if I do?"

"Then I guess we're better off stopping this interview now." She shrugged, but hid her disappointment. "I'm not that kind of girl."

"What kind of girl are you?" he asked, curiosity strumming through each word.

Her grin was like quicksilver. "I'm sure you'll find out if you hire me."

He ducked his head, but she knew it was to hide his smile. This close, he was almost better looking because she could see his flaws. He had a kink in his nose that spoke of a bad break at some point, and his stubble was at that point when it was feathery soft. Her palms itched with the desire to touch it, to feel it against her skin. He had a scar on his bottom lip that cut into the tender morsel, and a few more dotted around his face.

A bad beating?

She really hoped not.

"Please, come in," he invited but only after she'd looked her fill. His lips had been curved in a half smile all the while she checked him out.

Stepping inside, she whistled. "This place is gorgeous."

The door opened onto a small porch sectioned off from the hall with stained glass partitions. The hall itself was dark, and a grand staircase with a thick carved bannister that snaked in wide loops to account for the landings overhead. A rather dowdy but appropriate carpet, a kind of dark navy, made it a little hard for her to walk thanks to her stilettos.

The walls were lined with various achievements. And as she passed them, reading the names, she realized they weren't just for him.

Sean Hayward's degree was up there, framed, but so was that of a Sawyer Bennett, a Kurt Yeller, an Andrei Kirov, and a Devon Jerome. Not just degrees were there either, but certificates, various cut outs from newspapers, and academic memorabilia that confused her.

Was this some kind of office building? She'd thought it was a private home.

Maybe he saw her confusion because his eyes sparkled when he led her down the hall to a doorway that opened up into a sitting room.

High ceilings with ornate moldings caught her attention first. A hearth complete with a roaring fire and an Adam's fireplace took up a large chunk of one wall. Three chesterfield sofas were laid out in an open-ended square, a mahogany coffee table settled neatly between them.

One wall housed several tall, elegant windows that let in a glorious amount of daylight, while the other three had console tables lining them, each with a knick-knack upon them. A picture frame here, a trophy there. Overhead, a glorious chandelier hung pendulously. Large, delicately carved glass teardrops swayed and sparkled in the sunlight.

Sean headed for a sofa and waved a hand for her to follow him. She sat beside him, but he surprised her by lifting his leg and resting it on the cushion so that he could turn and see her better. It wasn't the most professional of stances, and from that alone, she knew this interview was going to be relaxed—just her style.

On the coffee table there was a tea tray with fresh cups and saucers, a Thermos, and a couple of bottles of water. Also, biscuits—she'd grown out of thinking of them as cookies now. After way too many discussions/arguments with staff in coffee shops over the confusion between biscuits and scones—and what looked like homemade Battenberg cake if the wonky squares were anything to go by.

She blinked at that, finding it hard to believe Sean was a baker, and he spied where her attention was and asked, "Would you like some tea?"

"I'd prefer some cake," she admitted sheepishly.

He grinned, but she knew she'd surprised him. "Help yourself. Andrei will be pleased to hear someone sampled his creation. Andrei's one of the men who live here, by the way."

"I'm the first to want cake?" she asked, astonished—what was wrong with the previous interviewees? She reached forward and using the cake slice, portioned herself off a too large piece and slid it onto a plate. She grabbed a small dessert fork and wedged off a bite with the edge. Sliding the morsel into her mouth, she moaned in delight at the rich almond-marzipan and creamy sponge. "That's delicious."

"Glad to hear it," he replied, beaming at her.

After swallowing, she murmured, "I noticed an Andrei Kirov's degree on the wall. I assume he and the baker are one and the same?"

"Well spotted." Sean nodded. "There are five of us here, Sascha. We all reside in this house full time, but we each head off on our various pursuits occasionally. Ninety percent of the time, however, we live here."

"So, I'd be keeping house for five men, not one."

He nodded. "I thought I'd explained it well to the agency, but they seemed to have misunderstood." He clucked his tongue with irritation. "Never mind. Though I do understand if the job doesn't suit you."

Slowly, she took another bite of cake, amused as he watched her mouth. After she'd finished, she asked, "Is this some kind of salon?"

"It's a living room. Parlor, I suppose is the appropriate term."

A snort escaped her. "I didn't mean the kind of room, silly," she said with a little giggle. "I meant in the intellectual sense. You all have rather impressive degrees and illustrious careers from what I saw… Is that why you live together?"

A salon was a select gathering of intellectuals where ideas were discussed, and concepts explored. They were rare in these times, but Sean seemed like he was a rare man.

An infamously famous criminologist who solved the nastiest murder cases and yet wore no shoes for an interview with a prospective housekeeper…

A guy who lived in the equivalent of a fancy-ass dorm house with his buds…

Yeah, this was no regular man.

His curiosity was piqued from her remarks. She could tell, could see it in his eyes, the intelligence brimming there as his gaze flickered around, seeing more than the image she portrayed. It made her wonder if he saw deeper, caught a glimpse of the real woman beneath the *Grease*-era get up.

Really, Brits seemed to think Americans were morons. She barely refrained from rolling her eyes when, slowly, he said, "I suppose it is in a sense. We all met at college. After, we stayed together. It suited us."

It more than suited them. Sean had to be nearer forty than thirty, she decided, now she had a chance to get a better look at him… which, if all the men were similar ages, meant they were approaching 'mid-life' as it were. For successful men to choose to live together like this, well, it was a tad unusual.

Or was she just being pedantic?

"Does the notion of looking after five men bother you, Sascha?" he asked, breaking into her thoughts.

"Not particularly," she replied. "What would my duties be?"

"The basics. I explained in the ad."

"I know, but I'd assume if the agency managed to make a mistake in one aspect, they may have made other mistakes, too."

"True," he conceded as he rubbed his chin. "We have cleaners who actually clean the house, so you'd manage them. We'd prefer you to handle our laundry, however. We eat three to four times a day, and hold dinner parties from time to time for work—we'd expect you to cook for us daily, but if it's too hard, you could find and manage the caterers for those special occasions.

"We'd give you access to a housekeeping account, and would expect you to manage the household bills. You'd need to see to any repairs, and negotiate with the council over them as this is a listed building so certain works require pre-approval."

"You'd expect me to play the role of housewife then," she said sultrily, enjoying how his eyes widened at her inappropriate comment—she was playing with fire, and wasn't entirely sure why that was.

He laughed a little, and his arm came to rest on the back of the sofa. Close to her arm. A hairsbreadth away. "I suppose so. You'd be better paid than a housewife though."

She grinned, liking the burn that came with teasing a living, breathing inferno of masculine hotness. "Would I have a day off? Vacation time? Do you expect me to work a set number of hours?"

"Now, this is the complicated part. Four weeks' vacation time a year, however, we'd expect you to agree to taking those days only in two or three-day chunks. It would be too much of an upheaval to do without you for even a week at a time."

Though that was a little exaggerated, she could understand. "I can see that," she confirmed, and was glad she did—the beam of a smile he sent her way had such wattage, her ovaries kick-started into hyperdrive.

"No particular day off in a week, but we don't expect you to work all the damn time. If you need time to yourself, we'd expect you to take it. A half day on Saturday and Wednesday morning, though."

She blinked at the strange requirement, then blinked even faster when he named her weekly salary. Coughing a little, she said, "Another mistake on the agency's part."

He frowned. "Really? What's the point in an agency if they make so many damn mistakes? I'm going to complain," he grumbled. "I refuse to pay for a service when they're not providing me with that service."

"I suppose they've taken their fees off the salary," she tried to soothe, while still reeling from the difference in wages. With that kind of money going into her bank account, she'd be debt-free before the year was up!

Sean scowled at her. "If you take the job, we can work out an agreement outside of the agency."

Her eyes widened. "That nulls my contract with them."

He shrugged. "If you take the job, we fully intend to make you happy enough you don't leave for a long time to come, Sascha." He shot her a wicked smile. "We can be persuasive when we need to be."

Her throat closed at the suggestion. Everything inside her tightening up in response to him.

How persuasive would he be? Sascha asked herself, licking her lips at the thought.

Swallowing, she reached for a bottle of water that was also on the tray and took a dainty sip from it. "I'd be interested in working for you," she said softly. "If the other members of the household like the idea too."

Sean's eyes gleamed. "They left it up to me. If I want you, they do too."

Jeez, she wasn't reading into *that*, was she?

Huskily, she asked, "I'd be living in?"

He nodded. "The attic has been converted into a small apartment."

"Do you have any questions for me?"

"I saw your resume. Called up a few of your references because I know the diplomat you kept house for three years ago. They were very pleased with you, and were sad you weren't willing to move with them to Dubai." He scrubbed at his chin. "I like you, Sascha. I think you'd fit in well here."

Her eyes widened. "I'm glad you think so."

"Would you be willing to work for us?"

Butterflies fluttered in her stomach. "Yes. I will."

AS THE SPARKLING Cadillac drove off into the murky distance of a grim, London day, Sean leaned against the doorjamb and watched her go.

He'd only seen cars like that the last time he'd visited Cuba. But they hadn't been in such good condition. Hers fairly sparkled, even in the dim sunlight the city was famed for.

Peering up at the sky, he grimaced, knowing rain was imminent.

To be fair, rain was always on the cards, but more than that, he knew because of his knee. He'd buggered the damn thing up back in university after too many rough games of rugby, and was paying the price now in his dotage.

Well, dotage was a little unfair, he reckoned. Especially if Sascha's response had been anything to go by.

She was twenty-seven according to her resume. Twenty-seven, and yet, she'd eyed him up like he was exactly her type.

Maybe she liked older men? Some women did, didn't they? Sean thought, his body stirring with the idea.

He was the eldest in the house. At forty-three, he'd felt every single one of those years separating him and Sascha when she'd walked up the stairs to the front door. Sixteen reasons why he shouldn't be attracted to her, and yet, he was.

But, with every step she'd taken, the mutual attraction had flared between them. Coming to life in a way that had made the tension between them tangible.

Somehow, he knew it took a lot to break Sascha's cool; she exuded a sensual confidence that spoke of the comfort she felt in her own skin, which was appealing in and of itself. The clothes she wore were a declaration to the world, one he'd heard and one that attracted him: she was not afraid to be herself, to wear what made her feel sexy. And sexy was exactly the word he'd use to describe her.

That, and *minx*.

Satisfied that despite her confidence, he'd managed to break Sascha's cool, and by the fact his morning hadn't been wasted on useless interviews, he closed the door behind him with the intention of heading for his study. Work awaited him. But when didn't it?

Murderers didn't have days off. They spent their time between kills planning and preparing. Even as the thought crossed his mind, he flinched at what that meant for the next victim.

No matter how many cases he worked on, Sean never got used to the soul-crushing agony of failure. Knowing that someone's death rested on his shoulders, because he'd been too slow, too stupid to find a pattern, was a fact he had to deal with on a daily basis. That burden was one of the reasons why he lived where he did.

Because, before he could let the tension eat at him, before the worry and the fury could coalesce and take over, Sean turned away from the door and saw them.

He should have known they'd be waiting for him.

Should have known they'd be there to guide him from the shadows and back to the light. Away from death and blood, murder and another man's madness.

That wasn't to say they didn't drive him around the fucking bend too. They did, but it was the healthier kind.

With them, there was no bleakness. Only the desire to bash his head against the wall when they pushed him on certain matters. And push him, they did.

God love them for it.

"Well? Is she staying?"

Andrei's voice was usually husky, thanks to his Russian heritage, but his question was doubly so, which told Sean the others had seen Sascha—undoubtedly from Sawyer and Devon's office two floors above—and that he wasn't the only one panting after her.

"Yes. She agreed to the terms."

Devon, sitting at the top step of the staircase, narrowed his eyes. "Doesn't she mind looking after five men?"

"Maybe?" Sean shrugged. "It didn't seem to bother her. Plus, it's not like she'll be scrubbing floors, is it? She'll have cleaners to help her out." He moved out of the porch and headed down the hall. Passing the lounge in which he'd interviewed Sascha, he huffed when he realized he had a Pied Piper's trail following him.

Heavy footsteps sounded behind him, and though he was tempted to shut the door in their faces, he didn't. His door was always open to them. But that didn't mean temptation didn't strike, so rather than do as he wished, he headed to the bay window where he'd placed his desk years before and took a seat with his back to the garden.

It was old fashioned, his study. Just like his bedroom. Walls lined with shelves, books everywhere. His desk was antique, and the banker's light was always on. Even in the early morning, the green-gold glow illuminated his work surface. A Mac buzzed into life as he switched it on, then peered at the men who took up too much space in his office.

Sawyer and Kurt had taken a seat in the armchairs opposite his desk, and though there was ample seating for when they all converged in Sean's office, which they did more often than not, Devon was standing in the doorway and Andrei was leaning against the dresser on the back wall where Sean had a silver tray loaded down with two glass decanters. Whiskey and scotch; his tipples of choice.

"What's wrong?" he demanded, casting his gaze over all of them.

"We want details."

Sean snorted at Kurt's question. "If you wanted details, then you should have sat in on the interviews with me."

He grimaced, folded his arms across his chest. "I was writing."

"You're not writing now," Sean pointed out. "I smell bullshit. Look, you all saw her resume, the same as I did. And we heard what Andrew and Celia had to say about her. She's more than qualified for the role." Andrew was the diplomat Sascha had listed on her resume. The man was a prized prick but he had high standards—higher than theirs.

"Do you think she'll like us?" Devon's question was loaded with a vulnerability that even after all these years, could still hit Sean in his gut.

All in their forties save for Dev, they were men, fully grown. Yet Devon somehow retained an air of innocence. Maybe it was his bipolar tendencies, or maybe it was the fact he suffered from insomnia so was always bug-eyed from lack of sleep... whatever it was, his vulnerability never ceased from reaching him where the others would never be able to touch.

The men in this room were more than just friends. They were brothers. Not necessarily in arms, although it felt like that.

Not one of them had a military leaning, but they'd found each other at Oxford, and ever since, they'd been a support system. From the dorm house where they'd lived together, over the years, they'd realized how that worked for them, and had never really moved out or apart.

As their personal successes increased their individual wealth, it never mattered. The collective was what counted. They worked as a quintet; protecting the group as a whole while ensuring each of them was safe, secure, and content. Devon was usually the priority—but each of them had their moments.

They were more than friends; they were family by choice.

Except Sean who had a consulting business in the city, and Andrei who commuted for clients from time to time, they worked from home.

Eight years ago, when that consulting business had necessitated he live full time in London, they'd moved here. All of them. They'd left Oxford and the dorm house they'd bought when Devon had made his first million behind, and made the capital their home.

It was an odd arrangement, to be sure. His mother, as well as Kurt's and Andrei's grandfather, were certain they were all gay and that it was a house of ill repute. But it wasn't like that.

Well, not for most of them. Devon and Kurt on the other hand… their oddities were enough to make a prostitute's brows rise.

"Well? Will she?" Devon demanded, breaking into his thoughts with all the finesse of a sledgehammer.

"You know we agreed not to look into that," Sean countered uneasily, running his hand through his hair and wishing like hell they could avoid this whole conversation. Being distracted from his latest case was one thing, talking about *this* was another.

Kurt shot Devon a look. "It's too much to ask of any woman."

"I don't see why. We could give her the world." His matter of fact tone always made him edgy. Devon was right. They could give their woman the world; if they could just fucking find her.

"As well as our dirty laundry," Andrei retorted, sighing and silently telling Sean that he agreed with Devon but knew what they wanted was too outré for most women to deal with.

"It makes sense, guys," Devon argued, as he often did when this topic cropped up. Which it did. Way too many times for Sean to even bother trying to remember. Or to forget.

"How does it make sense? You're only going on about this because she's hot. I notice the last one didn't get you going," Sawyer retorted, and if he was debating with Devon, then the topic had to be serious.

Those two were thick as thieves. But then, they worked together too.

Higher-order math was their specialty. Mostly, it flew over his head, but sometimes, he managed to understand something amid the algorithms and Fibonacci spirals.

"What woman wants to take on five men?" Kurt demanded, nudging a lock of dark blond hair away that had landed on his brow. His irritation was evident in his firmed jaw and the arms he crossed over his chest once he'd disturbed his hair.

Devon shook his head at their, what he often called, *myopic* stance. "You're arguing over something I know you all want."

Sean just stared at him. "What if we did, Devon? What good would it be? What use?"

"If you're open to the experience, then you don't know what the universe will allow you to attain."

"Not that *Secret* bollocks," Sawyer snapped. "Look, positivity will get you so far, granted. But it's not going to make a normal, everyday woman suddenly think it's A-Okay to fuck five guys at the same time. While all the guys live in the same house, and as all five are fully in the know about who she's spending the night with. It's too weird."

"Look, who said we wanted an everyday woman? I never said that," Devon snapped, his brow puckering with exasperation. "You saw Sascha's car, Sean. We all saw her outfit. Which part of her is everyday?"

"Just because she's retro, doesn't mean she'll take us on."

Devon lifted his chin. "I beg to differ. What kind of vibe did she throw off?" His gaze pinned Sean in place with laser-like focus.

Did he admit the truth? That attraction had flowed naturally between them? If he did, would that encourage Devon in a pursuit that went beyond the bounds of normal, decent society?

"Don't you dare say anything to her," Sean immediately stated, realizing that encouraging Devon would only end with him offending Sascha. "I was the one who had to suffer through all those bloody awful interviews this morning, not you. If she quits after a week, it's down to one of you to take up with the agency again." To Kurt, he said, "In fact, you need to cancel the contract with them."

"Why? What have they done?"

"What haven't they done? None of them were aware they'd have to look after five men. That's pretty much the entirety of our employment specs, dammit."

Kurt grimaced. "I'll call them when I get back to my office."

"Thanks. I'd do it, but I need to get to grips with this report. And Huey, Dewey, and Louis here are about as much use as chocolate teapots when it boils down to it." He shot Devon, Sawyer, and Andrei dirty looks, but they had the decency to look sheepish. To Devon, he demanded, "Don't frighten Sascha off, Devon. I know what you want… you tell us too frequently for us to bloody forget, and to varying degrees, we want it too, but even if she is mad enough to take us on—pushing her won't endear her to our desires, will it? And I know you. You'll push when you should tread softly."

"I'll keep an eye on him," Sawyer inserted.

"How? You're with him twenty hours a day, not twenty-four. You're not conjoined." Andrei retorted, brow quirked with amusement.

Sawyer flipped him the bird. "I'll make sure he doesn't scare her off," he repeated, and Sean nodded at him with gratitude.

"Right, now that's sorted, she'll be calling today to arrange for her things to be delivered here. She said she'll start by the end of the week."

"So soon?" Andrei asked, surprised.

"I think she needs the money." Not that she'd said as much, but her eyes had lit up at the salary they offered. Not in an avaricious way, but in a relieved way.

In this world, who didn't have debts, and who didn't money talk to?

Hell, even he, who had ample money for his needs, had moved to London for a job offer and displaced these bastards with him.

Everyone had a weakness, after all.

For him, it was these four sitting before him, not pounds and pennies.

Still, they were the exception not the rule.

TWO

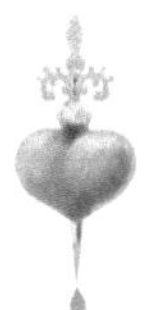

SASCHA PEERED over the bannister and whistled when she stood upright.

"That's a long way down," she said to herself as she eyed the vestibule below her. Up in the attic, in her new swanky little pad, she had to admit she liked the cozy nature of her room. The stairs, however, were going to kill her if she kept on wearing stilettos.

Plus, they'd damage the parquet flooring, which totally sucked. Beauty or damaging two centuries' old wooden flooring...? She'd love to be selfish, but it would be sacrilegious to deface any part of the property's antique touches.

Pondering whether platform wedges were a little too seventies for her mostly fifties' wardrobe, she shrieked when someone murmured, "A servant girl jumped to her death from that spot."

The ghoulish, macabre statement had her clutching her chest as she sought out the voice. She peered over the bannister once more and saw a man staring up at her from the shadows of the landing beneath her.

Jesus, he was gorgeous.

Creepy as fuck when it came to conversational gambits, it seemed, but like an angel or something to look at, albeit a dark one.

He reminded her way too much of Jamie Dornan, with his short-cropped hair, glinting chestnut eyes, and smiling mouth. His jaw was stubborn, his brow wide and crinkled a little with wrinkles, but hell, that crinkle had her swooning.

Even in sweatpants and a ratty tee, he stole her breath, and Sascha wasn't the type to start hyperventilating over a guy.

If this kept up, she'd need to start carrying *Ventolin* or something else for pre-asthma. First Sean, now this one? *There must be something in the water*, she thought.

Did the guys have to be ridiculously handsome as well as insanely smart to live here?

Jeez, she really hoped so. So much man candy would fuel her sessions with her Battery Operated Boyfriend, and make her one chilled chick.

"Excuse me?" she asked, more rhetorically than anything else.

Overhead, the domed skylight enabled her to see more of his face when he stepped out of the shadows and began to climb up the stairs to join her. His hotness just about melted her bones.

With that ratty tee clinging to his washboard stomach, and the comfortable sweatpants that were snug to his legs, he was anything but smartly dressed. Though pale, like he lived at his desk, he obviously worked out—his muscles were on display even in those loose clothes.

"I said, a servant girl jumped to her death from there. I heard what you mumbled under your breath. That it's a long way down. It is," he said simply.

She gulped. *Okaaaay.*

"I'm Sascha," she told him, deciding a change of topic was required.

"Devon." He smiled at her, and boy, did a choir of angels just start singing around him?

Christ, that smile packed a punch.

"It's a pleasure to meet you, Devon. Two down, three to go," she said brightly, trying not to sound winded from her reaction to his simple smile. "You're all very hard to pin down."

His eyelashes flickered. "You'd be surprised what we'd do if you asked."

Okay, first Sean, now Devon? Or was it just her? Was she so damn horny at the sight of her two sexy new bosses that she was hearing suggestive shit where there wasn't any?

"A lot of people have died here actually," he continued. *Definitely just horny and definitely one-sided,* she laughed to herself.

Blinking at him, and deciding a change of subject was imperative, she murmured, "Would you like some hot chocolate?"

So, a little random, but it was kind of her thing. After settling into her new post, and unpacking her shit, she always celebrated with hot chocolate. Homemade, of course.

He tilted his head to the side. "Is this some kind of American custom I don't know of?"

She snorted, amused at his utter bewilderment. "Not particularly. It's more of a 'Sascha' custom. Don't you like hot chocolate?"

"It's not that; it's just a housekeeper has never offered it to me before."

"Then they've done you a disservice."

He pondered that. "Really?" His hand came up to scrape over his chin, and as she heard no rasp, decided her eyes hadn't deceived her—his jaw looked like silk. She forced her hands to remain at her sides before she broke so many rules and reached out to touch him. "I've never had hot chocolate before."

His admission had her mouth dropping open. "What?"

He shrugged. "I'm not supposed to have sugar."

"Why the hell not?" She slapped a hand to her forehead, her distress too much to bear. "I don't think I could imagine anything worse. What about candy and cake?"

Another shrug. "I don't sleep. Sugar doesn't help."

"You don't sleep?" She frowned at him. "Do you have insomnia or are you just weird?"

He grinned. "A bit of both, I'm sure."

Well, that narrowed it down. *Not.* She pursed her lips. "Hot chocolate helps me sleep sometimes."

"Surely not at four in the afternoon though," he asked, peering at his watch.

Patek Phillippe? Or were her eyes deceiving her?

She wasn't sure why she was surprised. Just because he looked like a gorgeous stowaway at the moment, with a disreputable outfit that would do a vagrant proud, didn't mean he wasn't loaded and capable of wearing thirty-thousand-dollar watches with old jeans.

He lived here, after all.

"Maybe not at four. Not for me, anyway. But maybe it will help you."

His shoulders hunched. "I'm supposed to be sleeping," he admitted, but his tone was a little off. It was like someone had told him to sleep. Like a parent, or something. "Sawyer will be mad."

Sawyer? She remembered the name from the many on the wall. Why was another one of her bosses telling the other to sleep?

Weird.

"Well, I won't tell him if you don't," she conspired with him.

"You won't?" His eyes were hopeful, and she realized something… Devon was an innocent.

It was a bizarre realization to come to when she was drooling over him, and half believing that he was flirting with her, but he was. Genuinely.

Like *A Beautiful Mind* kind of innocent. Russell Crowe had been a superstar genius extraordinaire, but it hadn't stopped him from wanting to fuck Jennifer Connolly, had it? And hell, that character was based on a real guy, so that stuff happened in reality. *Right?*

Devon wasn't as awkward, but there was just something off about him. Like the world worked at a different pace to the one his brain functioned at.

Telling herself to slow down and not jump to conclusions, she told him simply, "I promise. Sawyer won't hear it from my lips."

He grinned, then held out a hand. She eyed it, then him, and seeing wistfulness had replaced hopefulness, she slid her fingers along his palm and clasped it.

The sensations that ricocheted through her were… in a word, stunning.

Her palm felt like it was on fire. Not in a bad way. A good one. Like pleasure and pain were getting mixed up with her nerve endings. The mixture collided and oscillated through her body, making her heart skip a beat as they descended the stairs together.

"Sean sleeps on this floor too, but this is where Sawyer and I live and work," he confided. "We're mathematicians."

Somehow, she thought that was an oversimplification, but she didn't say that. "How many rooms are here?"

"Three bedrooms and one large office. There used to be four bedrooms, but we converted the space." He shrugged. "We're partners."

She blinked, disappointment flooding her. *It figured he would be playing for the other team. All the good ones were gay,* she thought on an inner, distressed whimper.

"We're trying to solve one of math's greatest puzzles. P vs NP." He beamed at her. *So, not gay? Business partners?* She grinned, hope immediately replacing disappointment. "I'll have to show you our progress," he told her eagerly, and that eagerness was charming.

His excitement was contagious. And she, who detested math, found herself nodding to please him. Not because he was her boss, but because he looked at her with stars in his eyes at the prospect of her being interested in his work. In *him.*

Heady stuff, she thought to herself.

The back wall was covered in photo frames of Devon and another hunk. He had shaggy red hair, pale skin, and crystal green eyes. She could imagine him in a kilt, of all things. Standing on top of a heather-covered moor letting out a bellowing war cry to stop the English from invading his territory.

Be still her ovaries.

What was it with these guys? Were they sent from hell to torment her with their astonishing good looks?

Then, she spotted something that had her pulling him to a halt. "Is that the Nobel prize?"

Another beaming grin was aimed her way. "Yep. We won that five years ago."

"You won the Nobel prize?" she demanded a little breathlessly, astonished by not only the award's presence in the house but the fact she was standing next to an honest-to-God winner.

Sean had implied they were intelligent—but a Nobel prize?

Sweet Lord!

"It was quite easy, actually," Devon was informing her. "Our current research has far wider repercussions." He tugged her hand. "The next floor is where Kurt and Andrei live and work. There are five bedrooms though. Sean sleeps on this floor but his office is at the back of the ground floor."

"Kurt and Andrei's offices are attached to their rooms too?"

He nodded. "Andrei's an economist. He's a whizz with statistics. He's helping Sawyer and me collate our findings, actually."

"What about Kurt?"

"He's a writer. Quite a good one too. Just won a Pulitzer."

She blinked in astonishment at that nonchalant remark, then shook it off as they headed down to the ground floor. He pointed out various photos on the walls, articles and cut outs from papers he was particularly proud of. But his pride was unique—undoubtedly as unique as the man himself.

Devon wasn't smug or showing off his many admirable achievements. If anything, he was boyishly pleased with himself. Satisfied at a job well done, without his ego battering her in the side.

As they trundled down the corridor to the steps that led to the basement where the kitchen and utility were housed, she wondered if he realized how much she'd learned about him in that short trip.

Devon was unusual. And she *loved* unusual.

Sean, upon her arriving four hours ago, had given her a rudimentary tour of the basement and attic, and then had left her to unpack as he'd rushed out the door for a meeting.

It was quite handy having Devon pop up to guide her around, especially when he insisted on clinging to her fingers until he took a seat at the stainless-steel counter and watched her get to work in the kitchen.

It was a large kitchen. Surprisingly so, considering it was underground and natural light was almost nonexistent. The white cupboards and stainless-steel countertops were like ice chips among the warm lighting and copper accents. It was welcoming, and she immediately felt at home.

There were more appliances than she knew what to do with, and so many copper pans hanging over the white island glittering in the light she was in awe.

She took a peek in all the cupboards, but found the chocolate in the fridge—sacrilege, chocolate was always better at room temperature. Breaking up pieces, she grabbed some milk and a carton of cream and got to work.

As she bustled around, she felt his eyes on her. It was a bizarre sensation. She was used to being looked at; it came as part and parcel of wearing what she did. Not that she wore it for anyone else. But her tight pencil skirts, and Rita Hayworth hair always attracted attention.

Devon, however, was looking at her like an alien viewed a human. Or at least, that's how she'd imagine an alien would view a human. It felt like he was interested in some kind of probing too. Not necessarily of the anal variety, but still... She could sense his attraction, but also his bewilderment. At what, she didn't know.

"Do you like cinnamon?" she asked, throwing out the question into the silence that fell between them. It wasn't uncomfortable, just a little *off*. Like he was finding her measure and trying to figure out which language to talk to her in.

As if 'woman' was a foreign tongue. A thought that had her lips twitching in amusement.

"I don't know."

She scowled at him. "How don't you know?"

He shrugged, but before he could answer, another man appeared. This one was also tall, also freakishly handsome, but blond. Very, very blond.

"Devon doesn't concern himself with ordinary knowledge."

She blinked at the stranger with the sexy, lust-inducing voice. "And you are?"

"Andrei," he said with a smile, and then took a seat beside Devon.

Holy smokes, his accent? Sweet Jesus. They were trying to attack her from the waist down. It made her think of cold Russian winters, and steamy nights spent in bed. *She wished.*

In an attempt to get her thoughts out of the gutter, she half-mumbled, "I'm making hot chocolate. Would you like some?"

"If you wouldn't mind?"

"I wouldn't have asked if I did," she told him, trying not to gawk. She felt his eyes on her too. Tracing over her curves, filing away each nugget of information into his brain.

He was brawny. His muscles bulging through his, what had to be, tailored shirt. And the trousers, a thick silk blend with a fine pin stripe she'd like to follow with her tongue.

Bad Sascha! Bad, bad, bad.

Her cheeks flushed so she tilted her head down, letting her hair partially hide her face while she poured more cream into a pan and slowly, gently, heated the concoction.

When she was sure her initial blush had gone back to a normal, womanly glow, she tilted her face up to look at them both. As she chopped up more chocolate, she asked, "Why don't you concern yourself with ordinary knowledge, Devon?"

She peered at him through her lashes and saw his full attention was aimed at her. To be in the epicenter of this man's focus was enough to have her heart skipping a beat.

"I don't mean to. It just… it rolls off me like I'm waterproof."

Andrei smiled, clapped Devon on the back, and in a very masculine way, threw his arm over the brunet's shoulder and squeezed him. "You get used to his little oddities. He's the worst among us."

"The worst?" Devon repeated with a scowl.

"And you know it," came the unrepentant reply. To Sascha, Andrei said, "You're looking at this generation's Einstein."

Devon shrugged him off. "No, she's not."

"He's surprisingly modest." Andrei grinned. "His recent work is going to revolutionize the way we encrypt computers, and will, undoubtedly, make us all a bundle in the process."

Sascha's brows rose at Devon's pink cheeks. "You do it for the math?" she hazarded a guess when Devon looked displeased at the mention of money.

"Of course. That's all that matters," he said with a huff.

"You say that because you don't have to worry about petty things like bills." Sean's reappearance in the kitchen had her blinking in surprise. He'd trudged down the steps without her realizing, but rounded the counter and peered at her as she carried on making the hot drink. "Can I have some?" he asked, tone hopeful.

She grinned. Were these men or little boys? "Of course. Would Sawyer and Kurt like some too?"

There wasn't enough cream, but she could use more milk.

Sean asked, "Devon, is Sawyer at the gym?"

"Nope. He's upstairs."

"I'll call him." She watched him head for a phone she hadn't seen until then. He pressed a button she realized was an intercom. It crackled and spit on the speaker. "Sawyer," Sean asked when the buzzer stopped. "Do you want hot chocolate?"

"Not if it's that shitty powder stuff. You know I don't consume chemicals. You shouldn't drink that poison either."

Sean rolled his eyes. "It's homemade. You can meet Sascha, too."

"I'm coming."

"That's a yes," Devon said, beaming at her.

"I figured that out, sweetie," she told him, amused.

Sean rang the buzzer again.

"*Was? Ich arbeite!*" Angry German came down the line, startling Sascha into stillness.

"*Ja, das weiss Ich schoen, aber willst du Sascha kennenlernen?*" Sean asked, slipping into fluent German before her eyes—could he get any more delicious?

"Don't forget to ask about the hot chocolate," Andrei pointed out, plunking his head on his fist as he watched her work.

"Yes, please," came the quick retort through the speaker.

Totally changing the proportions of her little recipe, she bustled around grabbing more milk and chocolate. She found cayenne and cinnamon sticks in the cupboard too. Two of the latter she plopped in the cream to diffuse a little.

"I guess it shouldn't come as a shock that you speak German, huh?" she asked Sean. "What did you ask him? It was Kurt, right?"

"If he wanted to be introduced to you. And yes, it was Kurt."

"Do you all speak German?"

They nodded.

"Sawyer's accent is terrible though. He's Scottish, and it butchers his German," Devon said cheerfully.

God, he was cute.

She heard thundering steps and realized Kurt and Sawyer were on their way down.

"What about Russian?" she asked the kitchen's occupants.

Andrei shook his head. "Nope, they don't love me enough to try."

Kurt, overhearing this, started playing an air violin. "I, and my violin, weep for you."

Andrei flipped him the bird which gave her time to process how hunky Kurt and Sawyer were in the flesh.

Kurt was like a dark blond Ben Affleck. His eyes were hazel, framed by strong brows and a wide forehead that was crowned by a widow's peak like Sean's. Only difference was, he had ruffled mid-length hair that looked like he'd been tugging at it all morning.

His bedhead gave her dangerous ideas. Ideas that made her want to chuck the hot chocolate away and whip her libido into shape.

Sawyer was better in the flesh than he was in photos, which should have been an impossibility but wasn't.

How had their college coped having these five hotties on campus?

She imagined their bedroom doors had revolved over the years.

And were they single now? That couldn't be possible, could it? None of them wore rings, at any rate.

"I should have introduced them before I left, but I was running late. You've met us all now," Sean told her with a smile.

"I have. And you seem to like hot chocolate. Well," she tacked on, "we're about to see if Devon likes it too," she finished with a grin as she put the shards in the cream and let them slowly melt. With her back to the them, she stirred it a little, then looked over her shoulder as she spoke, catching them in the act of checking her out. Grin widening, she murmured, "My head's up here, guys."

"You have a very nice arse, Sascha," Devon told her, his tone earnest. "It would be a shame to ignore it."

She cleared her throat but then relinquished control on her voice box, and laughed out loud. "Thank you, Devon. My butt is very grateful for the compliment."

"It can't really have an opinion," he grumbled.

"She's being facetious." Andrei elbowed him in the side.

Deciding to change the subject, she asked Sawyer, "Do you have special dietary requirements?"

Sean clicked his fingers. "That reminds me. I've got a dossier on all our little quirks. There's nothing major; just likes and dislikes."

Sawyer studied her with an intensity that had her shivering as he murmured, "I don't eat anything processed. Devon doesn't either."

"So, if I make chocolate cupcakes, they'll be wasted on you."

Kurt snorted. "They'll be devoured in minutes. If you make them, they'll eat them. They just don't eat anything from the store."

Sean grinned. "Kurt cooks for us when we're without help."

"I slave away in this bloody kitchen because you're all too finicky to eat anything normal," he complained, suddenly sounding very German. His 'S'es were sibilant and over-pronounced.

"I bake. Sometimes," Andrei pointed out with a scowl.

"Twice. In twenty years," Kurt retorted, holding up two fingers that were more 'fuck off' than anything else. "It will be a relief to pass on the baton to you, Sascha."

"That's what I'm here for," she said brightly, and seeing that the chocolate had melted, added a teaspoon of honey, a pinch of salt, and stirred. "Where are the mugs?"

Sean, the only one not seated at the counter on the island, moved around her. The air around him was charged, and she could feel the heat coming off him as he squeezed past her—just barely brushing her body. He pressed the longest cupboard's door, and it released, revealing plates, mugs, cups, glasses, bowls. Everything she'd need.

He grabbed four cups, while she picked up the last two. With them on the counter, she poured out the hot chocolate, and asked, "Does anyone want cayenne pepper on theirs?"

"Why would you want that?" Devon asked. "Hot chocolate's supposed to be sweet, isn't it?"

"It adds a nice depth to it. Probably a little too adult for your tastes," Andrei snarked with a low chuckle. "I'll have cayenne, please, Sascha."

"Me too," Sean said, voice soft and close to her ear.

Nodding, and swallowing down a wave of nerves, she sprinkled a pinch on top of three mugs, then handed them all out to her rapt audience. *"Bon appétit,"* she said cheerfully, picking up her own mug, placing it on the counter behind her, then hopping up to sit on it. Five stools were behind the counter, with one on the kitchen side, but she preferred to be up high.

"That's not very hygienic," Devon pointed out.

"I'll be sure to use antibacterial detergent when I wipe the counters down," she assured him, lips twitching as he carried on frowning.

"Relax, Devon," Sean told him, as he came to stand beside her. He crossed his feet at the ankle, as he leaned back into the counter.

His proximity did things to her. Dangerous things.

Heck, they were all doing dangerous things to her, without even trying.

"This is very good, Sascha. Thank you," Kurt told her with a smile. The corners of his mouth were stained with chocolate, and she giggled at the sight.

"You're welcome." Their eyes clashed, held, and she swallowed; she felt as if she were drowning in those deep, dark-as-the-chocolate-he-was-drinking eyes.

His lashes fluttered down, bronzy colored wings that had her wondering why God gave men such lustrous eyelashes and left women with a mascara wand. The tiny act broke contact and she immediately stared down at her lap. Shoring her defenses, she asked, "Are any of you allergic to anything?"

"No. Only Sawyer and Devon are finicky about what they eat. I'm pre-diabetic, so I can't have too much sugar."

She squeaked at Sean's admission. "I just put honey in the chocolate!"

He laughed a little. "I saw, and you hardly used any. It's okay. I just have to watch my sugar intake, that's all."

Andrei grimaced. "We all should. We're middle aged now."

Devon huffed. "With the average life expectancy in this country at seventy-eight, we're past mid-life."

Sascha snorted—she couldn't help it. Sean sighed a, 'You see what I have to put up?' sigh. She patted his shoulder in commiseration. "I'm sure that by the time you're seventy-eight, the life expectancy will have increased."

Devon pursed his lips. "This is a distinct possibility, especially considering our financial status. We'll be able to afford the best health-care unlike most citizens in the country."

Andrei blinked and shook his head. "You do realize how gloomy this conversation is, don't you?"

The mad hatter frowned. "Why is it? It's factual."

"Exactly. We don't want to talk about facts. Facts are depressing," Sawyer pointed out, then, he turned to Kurt and asked, "How's the book coming along? From the state of your hair, not well, I'd say?"

Sean murmured, "Kurt's writing a kind of expose on life behind the Berlin Wall."

"You were an East German baby?" she asked, brows rising in surprise.

He nodded. "Just after. I'm not that old," he replied, his tone teasing in the face of Devon's earlier comments.

"Why are you having trouble with it?"

"It's fact-based but it's a fictional tale too. My characters aren't…" He huffed, took a sip of chocolate. "They're not behaving."

"Do you want me to critique it?" Sean asked quietly.

"No. Not yet. I know you're too busy."

"I wouldn't mind," Sascha inserted softly. "If you need me to sign, I don't know, an NDA or something, I will. Gladly."

Kurt tilted his head to the side. "That's very kind of you, Sascha. Fresh eyes might help."

"Only if they're green as grass?" Sean retorted, but he was amused, she could tell. "That reminds me, Sascha. I have a few contracts I need you to look over and sign before the week's up. It's just an employment agreement. But there's also an NDA, which would cover anything you read for Kurt. I'm afraid we all work on rather secretive branches of our field, and need those secrets to remain that."

She nodded, well at ease with his statement. "Of course. I expected no less." And she hadn't. With Devon as blunt as he was, an NDA was the least they needed.

She could imagine him sharing the intricacies of his mathematical discoveries just for the sake of being able to discuss them with her, uncaring that he might reveal something that should remain private.

As they drank their chocolate, an ease overcame them all, and the early strains of tension that came from having someone new in the fold, disappeared as they chatted among themselves.

It felt right to be here with them. *Comfortable.*

She was relieved to note that they didn't expect her to behave like a ghost. Whispering in and out of their interactions, expecting her to be silent in their presence. She spoke up when they broached a topic where she had something to share, and let her speak without interrupting as they processed her opinion.

When three of them headed back upstairs with effusive thanks for the chocolate, Devon and Sean lagged behind.

"There's no need to be lonely in this house," Devon told her with a beatific smile. "You can always come and visit any of us."

She smiled. "That's sweet of you to say, Devon. But I wouldn't want to intrude."

"We can always tell you to go away," came the earnest retort that had her snickering, because she could easily imagine him doing just that.

Sean pulled a face. "You're hopeless sometimes, Devon."

She shot him a grin, then surprised them both by stepping around the counter, reaching up onto tiptoe and kissing Devon, rather inappropriately, on the cheek. "Thank you, Devon. I appreciate that."

He frowned. "You're in a new place. A new home. I wouldn't want you to feel uncomfortable."

He said it so bluntly that she knew to take him at face value. It wasn't a suggestive remark, intended to enable him to seduce her at a later date. It was the truth.

She liked that. Liked him, in fact. He was sweet.

"I know where to come if I feel anything like that."

He nodded, seemingly content with her response, then shot Sean a strange look. She wasn't sure what passed between the two men, but it had Sean sighing and ducking his head. Devon headed upstairs, but Sean stayed leaning against the counter, his arms folded across his chest now.

"What was that about?" she asked softly. Her tone wasn't proper. Not considering she'd known the man less than a day, and the fact he was her new employer. But somehow, the walls of propriety had disintegrated over a cup of hot chocolate and a sniping session among her new bosses.

"You don't want to know," he told her, equally as softly, his gaze trained rigidly on hers.

She couldn't stop herself from licking her lips, and felt a thrill when his glance dropped down to watch the slow passage of her tongue. "I may not be a genius, but I'm infinitely curious," she informed him softly.

He cleared his throat, then stunned her by murmuring, "You need to sign the NDA first."

THREE

SHE REARED BACK AT THAT, and he couldn't exactly blame her.

Smooth, Sean. Real, real smooth.

Confusion hazed those emerald eyes, but she nodded slowly. "Sure. I'll sign it now. I'm not sure what one has to do with the other though…"

He grimaced—she'd find out soon enough from Devon if he wasn't careful, then said, "The papers are in my office."

"Okay."

Together, they traipsed up the stairs, down the hall, and to the back of the house where his study was located. He was, pathetically enough, excited about having her in his space.

Was he really about to make her sign the NDA so he could tell her something he'd already reprimanded Devon about?

But having seen her interact with Devon and the rest, as well as their response to her, hell, it was only a matter of time before something cropped up.

She was, to put it mildly, too hot to ignore.

There was no pushing this off, brushing it away. Attraction was attraction, and if they were adult about it, it needn't be a problem.

Of course, the five of them had a unique way of viewing the world. Women, they'd all found to their detriment, didn't see things the same way. But from how she'd responded to them, that had to bode well, didn't it?

He'd seen the definite reaction she'd had to them, and she hadn't shied away from their attention on her. When she'd caught them checking out her arse, she hadn't pretended to be peeved or called them chauvinist bastards. Instead, she'd smirked, made a joke of it.

The silence was killing him, but for the moment, it was the wisest option before he said something he might regret later.

The minute they entered his study, she inhaled sharply. "Wow, this place is so English."

He laughed, unable to do anything less. "It's in England. I'm not sure it could be more English."

Her nose crinkled at the bridge. "You know what I mean."

He grinned. "I do." Waving a hand at one of the chairs in front of his desk, he said, "Take a seat." He waited for her to sit, then headed for his own desk chair. When they were staring at each other across the expanse of his desk, he asked, "What do you think of the job so far, Sascha?"

She pursed her lips a second, then admitted, "I think I'll be happy here."

Relief unfurled through his churning stomach. How badly he wanted her to work for them stunned him. "Good. I'm glad to hear it."

"I wasn't sure how you'd expect me to behave. Like old-fashioned servants or as a part of the family. I like that you don't want me to bustle around you and hide."

He frowned, horrified by the notion. His parents were like that; and even as a child, the stilted atmosphere had choked him. It was why he could relax here—they needed staff, didn't have time to manage the day-to-day chores of running a house—but if things were formal, it would stifle the household. "Good God, what made you think we'd want that?"

"You're English, and you're rich." She chuckled at his disgusted expression. "I worked for a Marchioness before you. Well, you've seen my resume, probably checked out what she had to say about me? I did my job, and did it well, but there was a level of formality that always set me on edge. I could never settle in there. I worked for her for two years, but as soon as I could leave, I did."

"May I ask what made it so you had to stay there?"

She grimaced. "An ex. He lumped a lot of gambling debts on me. I didn't realize he was using my credit cards until it was too late."

"God, that's bloody unfair."

"I know. Tell me about it." Her grin was rueful. "Now, I make sure to keep my credit cards tucked away where no one can find them."

"Now I'm intrigued," he teased. "Surely everything can be found if you look hard enough?"

Her lips twitched. "My secrets shall remain my own. Unless, you'll sign an NDA too?"

He laughed, and it felt good. Really good to fling his head back and let the amusement flush through him.

She had a great sense of humor.

Another tick in the box.

She'd need it, with all five of them around. Even if they never went past an employer/employee relationship, humor was imperative.

Especially with Devon.

He had the unerring ability to say the wrong thing at the wrong time. Rather like a facetious toddler who knew the dictionary back to back.

"Maybe one day I will just learn your hiding place," he teased, eyes twinkling as he rustled through his papers, her words prompting him to seek out the non-disclosure agreement. He cleared his throat when he found it, and said, "It's standard, but feel free to read it."

When he passed it over to her, he let her read in silence. But he watched her, and she knew he watched her. A line of heat sparked between them, one that had his heart thumping and his blood thickening. He was suddenly aware of her every movement. The gentle rise and fall of her breasts which grew jerky in the prolonged silence; the gentle brush of her fingers as she flipped between documents. He watched her cross her legs, loved the whispering sound of her stocking-clad thighs brushing against the other.

Her eyes fluttered up to his every now and then, and within a very short space of time, she asked, "Do you have a pen?"

"You can't have read that properly," he chided, his voice as husky as hers.

"I'm a speed reader. I agree to everything detailed within the document." She shrugged, but the verdant fire in her eyes belied her calm demeanor. "With Devon roaming around, it's a wonder you don't NDA the cleaning ladies."

He grimaced, confessed, "We do. We didn't until a few years ago, when we realized he was discussing higher order math with our Polish cleaner. She didn't speak a word of English, mind, but that was more by luck than management." He passed her a pen and watched as she signed on the dotted line. He'd admit, relief flowed at the sight—the protection that document afforded would be used up within the next few minutes. "He's... well, his situation is strange. He takes on projects that can involve national security from time to time."

Her eyes flared wide. "Did you have my background checked?"

He nodded, sensed her discomfort by the idea and inwardly winced. "Standard protocol, I'm afraid. You came up clean."

"But you didn't know about the debts?" She frowned, and he could tell, the blatant disregard for her privacy pissed her off.

"I don't handle those checks, and I don't get to read the reports. I just have to phone a number, tell them your name and details, and they deal with that side of things. A few days later, I got the all clear, and knew I could hire you. Officially."

"But you hired me on the day," she whispered, confused.

"I know." He crinkled his nose. "A little premature, but we clicked, and I didn't want to lose you."

His words had her pupils dilating. He watched her throat as she swallowed. "Oh."

He smiled. "Oh." Reaching forward, he gathered the NDA documents, noted she'd initialed all the pages and had signed on the dotted line. Putting them back into their folder, he popped it into his desk drawer and continued, "Does the idea of having a background check freak you out?"

Her brow puckered. "Not now I understand why. Plus, it's less discomforting to know my private life isn't something you can read about in some report. When I moved over here, I got used to the various departments checking my background. Governments do what they have to do. But certain things, bosses should never know." She sank back into the small club chair and tapped her nails against the armrest. "May I ask a question?"

"Sure. Ask away."

"Why do you all live together?"

"Back in the day, gentleman's clubs weren't unusual. Nowadays, they are."

"But this isn't a club. And I know those kinds of places are still open. You're probably members to one or another simply because of your status in society here."

"You did some research on us."

It was her turn to smile, and it was that of a cat toying with a mouse. He didn't mind. If anything, her response was so felinely sensual he wished he had the right to kiss those smirking lips.

"I'd have been a fool not to, wouldn't I?" she told him.

"True. Five men in a house with a single woman. Tongues would wag."

"They still could."

"What do you mean?"

"Gossip spreads, even when rumors stir about staff."

He sighed, understanding where she was going with this. "You really did dig deep."

"Not really. I found it by accident."

"Janna James's stupid article." He huffed in disgust. Even saying the bitch's name had the power to irritate him.

"How true was it?"

"That was a long time ago, Sascha," he explained, then winced. What was there to explain? Hell, Devon wanted the same thing they'd had with Janna with Sascha!

And all that without having seen her or spoken to her.

He rubbed his chin, wondering what games the fates played to have stacked him with Devon Jerome in his world.

The man was irresponsible, utterly useless when it came to the ordinary aspects of real life, but he was also brilliant, charming, witty, and possessed the biggest heart of anyone Sean knew.

How to explain all that?

How to make her understand that Devon needed them to be together; that in this environment, he flourished. Could fulfill his potential, and that potential was so much more than any of them could jeopardize by destabilizing the household.

But this unusual living situation wasn't just for Devon. They all gained from it. Sean's work was dark and deep. The mindfuck that was his caseload was tempered by his brothers. By their humor, their care.

Their presence had the power to jerk him away from the void that beckoned when he failed, when someone was killed on his watch…

No, Devon wasn't the only vulnerable one of the lot of them. Nor was he the only one who flourished when they shared everything they had with one special woman.

"Devon collects people."

"Well, that doesn't sound creepy."

His lips twitched. "It did actually. I didn't mean in a serial-killer way." And if anyone would know, it was him. He'd profiled enough. "Let me rephrase. He sees the world differently to most, as I'm sure you've already noticed."

"I did. He's quite funny."

"Yes. Quite." He blew out a breath. "The smallest things can be like a magnet to him. He's attracted, beyond all reasonable doubt, and he fixates on it."

"What does the 'collecting people' have to do with the obsession?"

"Well, one helps explain the other. But I didn't say 'obsession', I said 'fixation.'" His collar suddenly felt too tight, and he tugged at his tie, then damned it to hell, and pulled it over his head once the knot was loose enough to allow the move. "The collecting… it's like friends. People are attracted to him and they flock to him because he's innocent and amusing.

"He can't lie. It's impossible. You can ask him what planet is closest to the sun, and he won't know, but if you want to know what a palindrome is, then he's your guy. It's… especially at college in our heyday, well, it was appealing to a lot of women. He had rather a following.

"Not that he was cruel about it or in any way sluttish. They seemed to recognize he was delicate in many ways, and they expected no relationship from him." He grinned. "We were all jealous as hell. With our conquests, we had tears and nasty calls and texts. But Devon? Nope."

"I can kind of see that," she said slowly, processing his words. "He's hot, but then open too. It's attractive."

Sean rolled his eyes, but he wasn't annoyed. Not really. They'd each stopped getting annoyed at how easy Devon found it with women. It was like getting pissed off at gravity—pointless. "See? Another one. I knew it when you kissed him on the cheek."

Her lips quirked in a smile. "It was rather… unintentional, I'll admit."

Sean shrugged. "It's nothing we're not used to. Anyway, one day, Janna is at our dorm house. She's been kicked out of her apartment, has nowhere to stay, and Devon, without asking us because that's Devon, lets her stay. It doesn't matter that we had an agreement with the landlord not to have another person living in..." He grunted. "Legal crap like that doesn't matter to Devon. His friend needed help, help that was within his means, therefore, help was given."

"That's how it started?"

Sean nodded. "Devon isn't capable of feeling jealous. He and Sawyer are very close. They've been together since they met at a kind of convention for young mathematicians." He waved a hand. "Ask them about it. They'll tell you. Anyway, Janna came on to Sawyer, they started sleeping together. Pretty soon, she'd worked her way around all of us, and we didn't mind. She seemed to enjoy herself, knew the score, and never expected anything from us. We were very appreciative of her extending her charms without fuss."

Sascha snorted. "Men. You're all the same when it boils down to it."

Sean pulled a face at the accuracy of her words. "Take pity on us. We were barely twenty at the time."

She conceded that with an eye roll.

"Anyway, we thought nothing of it. Enjoyed ourselves, and then eventually, she moved out. I can't even remember why. She was with us for nine months though. A long time. We didn't realize she'd taken pictures, why would we? Devon had told her he was working on something, and she, the clever, manipulative little bitch that she was and undoubtedly still is, realized the real-world implications of his work. She knew, someday, he'd be rich."

"She blackmailed him!" The astonishment lining her tone, as well as the disgust, appeased some dark need within Sean's nature.

He'd always hated that they'd left the situation with Janna as unresolved as they had, but with little to no choice, he'd just had to let it lie.

"Yes. She did. She blackmailed us in the end. Only, we didn't realize it, of course.

"Devon, having received her little demand, saw no reason to be ashamed of the fact she'd been sleeping with all of us. That the master creator of this incredible new algorithm that changed the way we deal with AI technology, had a kinky sex life was of no importance to him.

"It had happened, it was the truth, and if the rest of the world had a problem with it, tough shit."

"Oh dear."

"Yes." God, those days had been shitty. Just talking about them filled him with unease. "She went to the papers. We sued. Managed to get the story under lock and key though. Cost us enough. There was a small buzz at the time, but it died a death. Thank God. A year later, Kurt released his first book. I started consulting… etc. Etc."

"Okay, so I understand a little now."

He blew out a breath. "The truth is, Sascha, we liked living that way. Devon, especially. To him, we're family. He wants us to be happy. But, as they did back then, women get in the way. They demand things. They're over emotional.

"Of course, this is when it comes to us. Not with him. But he's witnessed that, and in his bizarre mind, has processed the thought that if we share a singular woman, one able to be with all of us, we will be happy, and, more importantly…"

"You'll always stay together."

He nodded, impressed by her perception. "More than anything, this… salon, as you called it during your interview, it keeps him stable. We're all clever men, Sascha. I won't lie to you about that. But Devon?"

"He's special. I know."

Sean shook his head. "He's more than special. He's unique. His intellect is beyond…" He grimaced. "The man solves impossible math puzzles for fun. What he develops for work will change the world as we know it. But, that comes at a price.

"Not only is he like a child in many ways…"

"A horny one, by the sounds of it."

Relief welled as he heard the teasing note to her tone. "Well, that too. But, he's an insomniac. He gets hardly any sleep. That's why Sawyer has him on this insane, chemical-free diet."

"He mentioned the 'no-sugar' thing. It's why I used honey for us all."

"Sawyer will comment upon that soon enough. He'll get you on Stevia or some shit like that." He grunted. "As far as I can tell, it's not helping Devon sleep… but, it makes Sawyer feel better, and because he's the main 'keeper' of Devon's sanity, we allow him full sway."

"Sawyer babysits him?"

"We all do to an extent, but we love him. We need him to be well like we'd need our family to be well. He's vital to us. Do you understand?"

She nodded, slowly. "I do."

His smile betrayed his relief. "He has episodes of paranoia, and can display symptoms of bipolar, but it's never been diagnosed." Devon *was* bipolar, but Sean's official opinion didn't hold sway considering their close friendship.

The state of Devon's mental health had been stable for a long time; thanks to the way they led their lives, Sean knew, so he'd never pushed Dev into getting meds or to going to a psychologist.

Sean, more than even Sawyer, monitored Dev for that.

"Wow, you're really loading this on me, aren't you?" she admitted on a low exhalation.

"Why do you think I needed you to sign the NDA?" he said ruefully. "I've just armed you with enough poison to blacken all of his research."

Her eyes flared wide with distress. "Seriously?"

"Seriously. I wasn't kidding when I said some of his work affects national security. If his equations are cast into doubt, then it would undermine everything. All the good he's managed to achieve."

"Jesus," she said on a gulp, pressing a hand to her chest.

"I know. It's a huge responsibility. It's why I let you sign the NDA first before the employment contract."

"So, I'd have an out?"

He nodded. "I warned Devon off. I told him not to broach the topic, but I could see today you were charmed by him, and even though he's incredibly blind when it comes to some things, he isn't where a beautiful woman is concerned."

She chuckled. "You charmer."

He shot her a grin, relieved that she was taking this so calmly. "The truth will set you free. Another truth: he'll see you're as attracted to us as we are to you, and whether I leash him or not, he'll talk to you about it. The idea of you being all of ours will be natural to him."

"Why?"

"It just… it works for us, Sascha. We're busy men. We don't have time to date. As a collective, we can all work to make sure our woman is happy. Individually," he confessed, "we're probably the shittiest boyfriends ever."

She processed that. "You said you leashed him… before today, I'll assume?"

He nodded again.

"But, I'd never met him, and the shot I clipped onto my resume, wasn't the best picture. How did it come about where you even had to think about leashing him?"

"He saw you from the car."

"Okay?"

"Sawyer said he likes your hair. That's enough."

"It is?" She gawked at him.

"To Devon, beauty is…" He shrugged. "I'm just a man. You're hot, Sascha. We both know that. From that little dimple in your cheek to the curve of your ass in those slinky skirts you wear. But, knowing Devon, you'll have a Fibonacci spiral somewhere and he'll adore you until the end of time because of it."

"Jesus." She let out a low laugh. "This is nuts."

He shrugged. "It's down to you whether you sign the contract, Sascha. And, it's imperative you understand… just because I've told you what Devon's wishful thinking is, doesn't mean that you have to want it. You can always say no. He would never force you. None of us would. That isn't how this works."

She stared at him a second, then whispered, "How many times have you done this?"

"Successfully?" Sean blinked. "And by that, I mean, excluding Janna?" At her nod, he said, "Three times. The first time, she had to move to the States, ironically enough. Our lives will always be here."

"Didn't you fall for one another?"

"In a sense, and when she left, we missed her, but she'd outgrown us. You must bear in mind, to a lot of people, this is almost like a sex game. They want to do it, check it off the list, and that's it. It isn't like that for us. The ladies with whom we shared a similar arrangement treated us that way." He jerked a shoulder. "That affects our responses to them."

A frown puckered her brow. "What if I fell in love with you?"

His eyes widened. "You think that would be possible?"

He loved the hectic color that stained her cheeks as she mumbled, "Well, I don't know. I'm just asking."

"Then," he told her easily, knowing he spoke the whole truth, "we'd fall for you."

"You can't guarantee that," she said huskily.

"Of course not, but you know that phrase… 'treat others how you wish to be treated yourself?" Her nod had him concluding, "If you treat us with love, that's how we'll treat you."

Sascha stared at him, and he could see a curious mixture of inquisitiveness, a tender vulnerability, and longing etched into her features.

Her cheeks were pink with emotions, her lips parted with desire, but her hands had a tight hold on the armrest.

"What will it be, Sascha?" he asked softly, studying her as intently as she studied him. "Are you going to sign the contract?"

SHE SIGNED.

How could she not?

The guys were nice, friendly to work with. The house was gorgeous. Her little attic bedroom beautiful, and the salary was insane.

All of those were definite pluses for the job. Then, throw in this… well, *unusual* background, and Sascha was more than just curious. She was intrigued.

Devon wanted her for her hair?

The notion was both charming and bemusing.

He was the lynch pin, she'd come to realize over the subsequent two weeks in 'service' to the men of the house.

In fourteen days, she couldn't say a lot had happened, save for them all falling into a regular schedule with one another. Sascha learned their quirks, and their habits. She quickly saw which dishes disappeared from the tables she laid out for them, and knew which one needed non-bio laundry detergent—Kurt. Not that he'd told her. She'd just watched him scratching at his collars and cuffs, and recognized the signs.

She baked, she helped clean. She did laundry.

In essence, she did her job.

None of them, not even Sean or, strangely enough, Devon, had brought up the topic of her being shared among all five of her bosses. She wasn't sure why. She'd expected Devon to bring it up in the middle of a very ordinary conversation, and had to admit to being disappointed when he hadn't.

Not that he hadn't let out some doozies.

Like when she'd taken a seat at the dining table—she sat at one head with Sean at the other—and he'd asked her if she had her period. Because, *get this,* her color was high, and she'd flinched when a cupboard door had opened too quickly and swung into her chest.

Not even her previous boyfriend of three years had realized she got sensitive boobs during her period. And Devon? The man who wasn't sure what cinnamon was, had figured it out in a matter of minutes.

The conversation had hushed at the table, all of them waiting for her response. She knew they'd been waiting for an explosion, but though she'd been a little bewildered, Sascha had smiled at him and told him, "That's none of your beeswax, Devon."

He'd scowled, looked set to argue, but Andrei had elbowed him in the side and told him to shut up.

Then, the next day, he asked if she had any tripe—because sure, every household had that lump of horribleness in their fridge. Perplexed by the request, she'd asked him if it was something he wanted to have in the house, but he'd wrinkled his nose in disgust. "I was researching last night. The average woman loses a cup of blood during menstruation."

She'd frowned. "What does that have to do with tripe?"

"It helps replace lost blood," he told her cheerfully. "I thought it might be wise for you to eat some."

Unsure whether to be stunned or offended at his interest in her uterus, she'd decided to just roll her eyes, pat him on the shoulder, and swiftly serve him his regular breakfast of scrambled eggs on home-baked rye bread.

Thankfully, the distraction had worked, and he'd left her and her ovaries alone. Well, apart from when he wasn't twisting them into knots when she caught him working out or scowling at the boards he had in his study as he tried to solve whatever immense calculation was vital to that day's research.

But hell, she was getting used to that all round. Sawyer had a habit of waking up, trudging down to the kitchen for breakfast shirtless, yawning, and barefoot.

Kurt somehow managed to get pen all over his face as he worked, and she loved licking her thumb and wiping it off his cheek or chin—and he didn't even mind the germs.

Andrei wore the sexiest aftershave that turned her on something fierce, and when she went into his bathroom to get the laundry, she near as dammit sniffed his dirty towels to inhale his scent because it went so far deeper than just the aftershave. It was him. He smelled like… Hell, she didn't know what but her nose sure as shit appreciated it. And she didn't even care that it was gross as fuck.

Sean was the most serious of them all. She wasn't sure why. Maybe it was because he had to deal with the nastier side of life? He was a criminologist.

Watching him in the throes of a breakthrough was like watching dancing flames. He had a board like Devon and Sawyer, but it was discreetly hidden in a cupboard when he wasn't working on it.

She'd brought him his afternoon tea complete with a slice of cake she'd made for the boys one afternoon, and had watched from the doorway as vitality whizzed through him, literally charging him with an energy that was both impossible to see but so present, it had made the hairs on the back of her neck stand upright.

When she looked back to that morning when she'd signed the NDA and her contract, she wondered if it had been a joke of some sort, because they'd never mentioned it since. But also, she realized that though the idea of being with all five of them should have terrified her and had her screaming for the hills, it didn't.

She wanted them.

There was no mistaking it.

Being around them was like having porn on in the background at all times. They didn't have to do anything to turn her on—Andrei had helped put away the groceries yesterday, and she'd nearly had an orgasm watching the play of his muscles in his tight shirt. Somehow, they managed to make the ordinary, extraordinary, and by being around them, it was like it rubbed off on her.

Jesus, she wished they *would* rub off on her. She'd totally be game for that!

Peering out of her bedroom window onto the dull day ahead, she grimaced, then wished for a bit of sun. From Arizona and accustomed to the shocking, searing heat of Tucson mid-July, this was the exact opposite.

A good old British summer's day meant rain, rain, and more rain, she'd come to learn over the last few years, and though she quite liked the glum climate because it made everything so green and fresh, it sucked at this time of the year.

Pressing her forehead against the cold window, she marveled over her new home. This wasn't just any home though. This place was in Kensington. Before she'd moved here, she hadn't understood how many different parts there were to London. How many rich parts there were, and how many poor ones too. But now she did? Oh, boy. She'd hit the jackpot.

Kensington was like the Upper East Side of Manhattan, except, there was a palace close by where real-life princes and princesses lived.

Yep, she was sharing a zip code with royalty.

Amused, she glanced over the small park in front of the house. She saw a few neighbors were huddled under umbrellas as they walked their dogs and saw a rather nice Lamborghini—far too flashy for this sort of neighborhood—whizz past on its way to only God knew where. An Arab Sheikh maybe? A rich footballer? Who knew? Still, it was fun to guess.

Turning away from the gray day, she looked at her bedroom and hugged herself. She'd lived-in on a few jobs, but nowhere had been as nice as this.

She had a king-sized sleigh bed with matching oak bedside tables. Two rather grand lamps illuminated a back wall that had a pretty mural on it of huge Calla lilies, where the rest were painted a pleasant duck egg. She had a dressing table, and a corner unit with a TV perched on top. Two doors led off her living space. One housed a connecting bath that belonged in a hotel, and the other an extensive closet for clothes and storage.

Underfoot, there was a thick carpet, but a huge rug covered a good two thirds of the floor, and her feet sunk into the shaggy sheepskin pile with delight. It was a weird British thing she'd come to appreciate over the years. Back home, she'd never had both. But here? Rugs over carpets was a standard she'd come to appreciate—maybe because it was always fucking freezing here. She didn't know, was just grateful for the extra padding.

She'd never lived anywhere like this, and knew she was being spoiled. Still, she did her best to spoil the boys back, so it was Even Stevens as far as she was concerned.

Eying the clock on the bedside table, she decided to do something she rarely did… head down to the kitchen still in her nightwear.

It was unprofessional and… she'd admit, provocative. It was a move she wasn't entirely sure why she was making.

Well. That was a lie, she admitted to herself as she blew out a gusty breath.

None of them were in anyway suggestive with her, and, truth was, that was starting to irk her.

Was she probing for a reaction? Of the verbal or physical kind? Sascha honestly couldn't say as she stepped downstairs in the faint light of the morning, not bothering to turn on any lamps, as she bypassed all the bedrooms and headed for the basement—stopping off only to gather the various papers and magazines that had been dropped off at the door pre-dawn—paper boys started early here.

Though only two weeks had passed, she'd made the kitchen her own. Rearranging the work surfaces so all the gadgets were on hand and reordering the cupboards so she knew where things were… this was probably where she spent most of her time. Cooking and baking, but also, the men tended to gather here. It was like an unofficial space for congregation, and as a result, chatter.

On the first floor, their ground floor—Brits had weird ideas about that—there were two living rooms. One a little formal, where she'd been interviewed, the other a man's paradise. Complete with a huge TV, several large leather sofas, and more comfort than anyone would know what to do with. And yet, they never used it.

Or never seemed to, anyway.

Shrugging off the thought, she got to work. They had a bread maker and a coffeemaker which were pre-programmed to start before she came down here. Thankful for the coffee, she served herself a large mug, took a sip, and inadvertently caught sight of herself in the reflective surface of the counter.

Biting her lip, she realized why she was doing this as she stared at her hazy reflection. This was a test. An unnecessary one, but still, vital to her.

Devon was attracted to her hair, Sean had told her. The men, it would seem, appreciated her quirky dress sense. But what about when she was raw? Naked. And she didn't mean what she looked like without clothes.

No make-up. No war paint. Her hair, neat, but not pulled into a tight chignon, and loose about her shoulders.

Without a bra, her large breasts were pendulous. Her waist, hips, and thighs, without her wonderful tug-it-all-in underwear, were rounded and thick.

They were attracted to the image she sold, but what about the woman underneath?

She wore a silky peignoir that covered a cotton nightdress that draped to the floor. It had inbuilt cups to support her breasts a little, but not a lot. On her feet, she didn't wear stilettos but comfy slippers, so she was four inches shorter.

The change would be radical, and the truth was, she needed to know what their reaction would be to this side of her.

It wasn't necessary. Not really. Not when a single one of them hadn't come on to her. But she'd seen the looks. The glances. Had noticed their eyes trained on her tits or, by spying them in a mirror, her ass. She knew they were looking but not touching. A fact, she would fully admit to herself, she was ready to change.

As she fried some turkey bacon, started scrambling eggs, pressed oranges for juice, and let the fresh bread cool down on a wooden board, Sascha asked herself if she was some kind of slut. What kind of woman was willing to take on not one, not two, not even three, but *five* guys?

But they were a unit. And though she knew how weird that sounded, it didn't change a thing.

She did want them. They attracted her in ways no other men had. They were intelligent, thoughtful. Their conversation was opinion-provoking and engaging. They looked at her like she was as smart as they, not just a housekeeper. They included her, involved her. She loved looking after them, and though it had never happened to her before, even after four years of working as a professional housekeeper, she realized she wanted more.

She didn't want to be on the outside looking in.

She wanted to be a part of the family.

The realization scared her a little.

She'd been here just over two weeks. How could she be making grandiose statements like that? This was still the damn honeymoon period… but, she knew. Sascha didn't know how she knew, granted, but that didn't stop her from feeling like she'd finally, after years of searching, found her place.

Steps echoed from upstairs, and she felt herself tense with the knowledge that Devon was on his way. He always came down first. Usually followed by Sawyer, then Sean, and Andrei. Kurt was *always* last. He usually was starting when everyone else was finishing up.

Hearing Devon heading down to the basement, she girded her loins, then shot him a smile as he rounded the staircase and made his way toward her. She passed him orange juice as he took a seat at the counter, and glanced over him a second.

He looked exhausted. Dark shadows were lining his eyes, and his shoulders were hunched. He didn't wear a shirt, so she could see and drool over his belly, then felt guilty because there she was, eying his happy trail, and he was busy trying not to expire from sleep deprivation.

She didn't wish him a good morning, not yet. Mornings were the only times he was quiet, she'd come to learn. Only after he'd finished processing the orange juice, had sorted through the magazines and papers for his own, would he even say a word.

Today, of course, had to be different.

"Your hair's down."

She jolted at the sound of his voice; Sascha was quite comfortable with the silence and liked knowing they were relaxed enough with each other for her to work on his food while he woke up. "Yes."

Magical, Sascha, she chided herself, but nerves held her tongue.

She readied his bread, turkey bacon and eggs, and placed the plate before him. As she turned away, getting ready to make the deconstructed and barely-spiced chorizo Sawyer favored for breakfast, he grabbed her wrist. She jerked to a standstill, then looked down at his fingers which clutched at her.

Though he was pale, he was darker than her. His fingers were almost like gold glowing against her creaminess.

She peeked up at him, her gaze switching from his hold on her and slowly rising to look into his eyes. When she did, she saw he was smiling.

"This is you."

Sascha cleared her throat. "I was tired this morning." Lies. But, she had to have some explanation.

He shrugged that off though. "I wondered what you looked like without all the make-up." He beamed at her, let go of her wrist, but with that same hand tapped her nose in the least sexual way imaginable. "Beautiful."

His choice of words far outweighed his actions, but she should have figured that would be the case with Devon.

Stepping back, she let him start to eat, and within minutes, she heard more footsteps. Deciding that the best way to ride this test out was to stay cool and calm, and not like she was out for a reaction, she didn't look up as a steady swathe of hungry breakfasters appeared in her domain.

They greeted each other with grunts and only truly greeted her when she placed their breakfast before them. For Sean, granola and yogurt. Andrei had porridge with honey or jam. Sawyer, his chorizo with eggs. All of them helped themselves to the freshly baked loaf.

Truth was, their reaction to her outfit was kind of disappointing. But then, they were men. Capable of remarking on something to cause unintended offense, then completely blind to the obvious.

As she fried some ham for Kurt and set it out with poached eggs and beans as he trudged down the stairs, she asked herself if they, aside from Devon, had even noticed she was underdressed.

With the five of them eating, she staked her own place out at the back of the counter, where she ate her own breakfast of cereal and some toast. They were all quiet first thing, and she liked the continued ease so even though she'd have easily chatted with them, the peace was nice too.

As she snickered at something she saw on Facebook, Sean cleared his throat. "Are you feeling okay, Sascha?"

She peered over her cell just in time to catch all five of them shooting looks at one another, and a whole lot of nudging-their-neighbor-in-the-side going down. Blinking, she replied, "Of course."

"W-We've never seen you out of a pencil skirt," Kurt said roughly, his accent heavy first thing.

Devon's voice was ever bright as he said, "I often wonder if you do the laundry in a pencil skirt. But then, I realize that can't be the case because surely the seam would split if you're always bending over."

Sean let out a little groan, but she shook her hand at him, well aware he was about to make Devon apologize. Amused at Devon's lack of delicacy, she said, "My skirts aren't that tight."

"They are. If you bend over a certain way, we can see your thong through the fabric."

Laughter burst from her at that, and shaking her head, she grinned at him. "I suppose I should be flattered you noticed."

"I'd have to be blind not to, Sascha. Your butt is as delicious as the cakes you bake." He beamed at her again, in that way he had. One that combined sexy man with demented toddler—a mix that shouldn't have been as appealing as it was. "And they're better than any cakes I've ever had."

Her nostrils flared as she rolled her lips inward. His earnestness didn't deserve to be mocked, though she could see the other four were groaning at him. "Well, I'm glad you think so."

Devon's brows lowered. "In fact, I think I'd prefer you to dress like this for breakfast, Sascha. I can see more of your boobs. Would you be willing to always cook this way on a morning?"

Uncertain of what to say, her mouth worked dumbly until... "Sexual harassment alert," Andrei grumbled under his breath, but he was studying her with the same intensity as the others. Well, studying her *tits*.

Immediately, she peered down at her chest to make sure the girls were contained, then frowned when she saw they were—their reaction to her more than stunned Sascha. It was like she was flashing her breasts when they were respectably covered.

Devon, of course, saw the direction of her glance, waved a hand, and murmured, "In fact, I know why I prefer this look. You look like you've just had sex."

As one, the other four men covered their faces with their hands. Devon truly was hapless, and it was genuine. Not feigned. He looked at his friends and frowned at their stances.

Before he could say anything, or could even think to back off from his statement, she asked, "How do you know what I look like when I've just had sex?"

Tension shot through the kitchen at her words, and she almost reveled in the reaction.

"I don't. But I'd imagine that's how you look."

"And you've imagined my post-coital glow, have you?" she teased.

He nodded, and quite bluntly admitted, "Yes. Often. Last night in the shower, actually."

At that, her mouth dropped open, and Sawyer gritted out, "This is totally inappropriate, Devon. She doesn't want to know about you wanking off in the shower."

Sean grimaced. "Thanks for painting more of a picture, Sawyer. Jesus." To Sascha, he murmured, "Sorry about that, Sascha. It was uncalled for."

She waved a dismissive hand. "If I didn't want the answers, I wouldn't have asked the questions."

Kurt frowned. "I don't understand."

"I'm sure you do. If you really think about it." She smiled at them, then clambered down from her stool. "I'm going to get changed," she informed them all. "If you need anything from the store, write it down. I'll be going out shortly." As she rounded the counter and headed for the stairs, Sean snared a hold of her arm.

His eyes were loaded with confusion as he asked, "Devon didn't offend you?"

The man in question huffed. "Why do you always think I offend her? She laughs more at me than she does at you." He sounded quite proud of that very truthful point.

"Because you say the most ridiculous things," Andrei retorted. "Rude things too."

To Sean, she said, "I'm not offended. I'm a big girl, Sean."

His brow puckered, and with his free hand because he was keeping her in place with the other, he reached up and trailed a finger along her cheek. Heat welled, pooling in great swells that had her tilting her head and leaning into his caress.

"Be careful, Sascha," he whispered softly. "We're not the sort of men to play games with."

Her eyelashes fluttered to a close. "I'm not the sort of woman who plays games."

Silence dropped at her statement, and she sent him a sleepy kind of smile before pulling away from his hold and heading on her way to the stairs.

She'd dropped the baton. Now, she just had to wonder if any of them would bother to pick it up.

"WAS that what I think it was?" Kurt wasn't alone in his confusion, Sean realized. They were all a little dazed and a lot bewildered.

Save for Devon, of course.

He was back to tucking into the bread Sascha made for him specially and loading up his slice with butter and honey.

If he didn't love Devon like a brother, the bastard would have irritated the fuck out of him.

As it was, he *did* love him, but still fantasized about slamming his head down into the counter a time or two. Hell, nobody was perfect.

"She was coming on to us," Devon pointed out before he took a bite of his breakfast. "I told you she was cool."

"There's cool and there's cool," Sawyer muttered. "She can't have been coming on to us. That never happens."

Sean grimaced. His friends were right. Well, Devon *wasn't*. Not unless Sascha was totally fucking with their heads.

In all the other instances, they'd fallen into an abstract sort of relationship. Hooking up here and there.

Sascha had almost thrown down the gauntlet, and considering she knew what they were interested in, considering he'd explained it all to her so there was no bloody misunderstanding, that had to mean…

He toyed with his spoon, wishing for a huge bowl of the cereal Sascha had been eating for breakfast. "We must have mistaken her intent."

"What's the woman got to do?" Devon grumbled after gnawing down a huge chunk of bread. "Come downstairs naked? She almost was today."

"Is that a complaint?" Sawyer mocked.

Kurt groaned. "I had to look twice this morning when I came down here. I thought an angel had taken over her kitchen."

Her kitchen. Kurt was right on the money. She'd barely been here two minutes, and already it felt like forever. She blended in so perfectly he could barely remember what it was like without her.

After a *fortnight!*

What would it be like after a month? Six months? A *year?*

The stamp she'd made on this place concerned him.

She was too integral, too soon, and yet, he couldn't stop it. Couldn't stop her from doing whatever it was she was doing.

"You're such a writer sometimes," Andrei remarked with a quick grin, shattering Sean's train of thought. "But I know what you mean. Her ass was…"

"Divine," Devon pointed out.

"That's one word for it," Sean confessed. Hell, he'd noticed just as much as the others had.

In the silky peignoir with the linen-cotton nightdress underneath, she'd looked like a movie star of old. In fact, there was an old-world kind of charm to Sascha. It was in everything she did. Even when he saw her bending over to pick up dirty laundry—and he knew for a fact, her seams didn't split because he'd watched—or covered in a light dusting of flour when she was baking, she did it with a kind of elegance he knew couldn't be bought.

With the silk clinging to her every curve, the cotton imbuing her with an innocence that belied the sweet sensuality of her appearance, he had to admit, he'd been rocking a hard on since he'd come down for breakfast.

"What do we do, guys?" he asked softly. Then, pre-empting Devon, stated, "Everyone but you, Devon." When he grumbled, Sean hid a smile behind the glass he was sipping from.

Andrei murmured, "I think we can't mistake her intent. She was quite blatant."

"Now who's making things sound bad?" Devon argued. "I came down to breakfast dressed in what I went to bed in. We all are apart from you and Sean. You're making it sound like she's easy or something."

Surprised by Devon's defense, Sean murmured, "I don't think he meant that, did you, Andrei?"

"No, of course not." The Russian sighed. "You're sensitive where she's concerned, Devon. I noticed that before."

Devon shrugged. "I like her."

"You like everyone," Sawyer scoffed.

"No. I really like her. *Really.* She's nice. Her bread is phenomenal, and if I eat my dinner, she usually kisses me on the cheek like I'm a good boy."

Sean shook his head at his complex genius of a friend getting off on being treated like a kid. "You'll be grateful if she ruffles your hair next," he complained.

"No, I don't mean it that way. She's not like the others."

"How do you know? She's only been here a fortnight," Kurt argued softly.

"She treats us differently. If you haven't noticed that yet, then you're blind. All of you."

"We're blind," Sean said gruffly. "Point it out, Devon. What have you seen that we haven't?" Devon, so incapable of seeing the bigger picture, could see the minutiae. Sean, for one, wanted to know exactly how Sascha had made it seem she'd been here forever.

"Andrei, when you're working, have you noticed that there's always a fresh tray of coffee on the dresser in your study."

"Well, yes." He blinked. "I guess that's right."

"Yeah, because she sneaks in with fresh pots for you. And it's that disgusting stuff you like too. She brews it specially for you, not that you even noticed," Devon said with a huff. "Kurt, she changed detergent twice because you kept itching every time you wore something clean."

Kurt frowned at Devon. "How the hell have you noticed this stuff?"

"I like watching her. She's interesting."

He narrowed his eyes at his friend. "How interesting?"

Devon scratched his chest. "Poincaré conjecture interesting," he replied.

Sawyer choked on his coffee. "No fucking way." When Sean, Andrei, and Kurt just stared at Sawyer blankly, he explained, "You know we're working on P vs NP, right?"

"One of those Millennium Prizes, no? If you solve it, you'll get a million bucks?"

At Andrei's explanation, Devon sniffed. "Like the money matters."

Andrei just rolled his eyes.

"Well, the Poincaré conjecture was another of those prizes. It's the only one that's been solved thus far, and Devon's been studying it recently. He thinks it can help with another of his pet projects."

Sean's eyes widened at the explanation. If Devon thought Sascha was as or *more* interesting than math, then God help her, she was going to be bearing the full brunt of his focus. Nothing would slip by him.

Though he knew it was childish, he murmured, "What does she do for me?"

"Your cupcakes are with a special sweetener." He rubbed his chin again. "I can't remember what it's called, but it's made from birch sap."

Despite himself, he was touched. "Because I'm pre-diabetic?"

"I'd hope so. Otherwise she's trying to poison you," Kurt teased.

"What about me?" Sawyer asked, apparently not wanting to be left out.

"That disgusting chorizo you eat. She doesn't get it from the deli."

"She makes it?"

"Yep. Plus, she puts the extra creases in your pants like you want."

"Well, that's it. We need to marry the girl," Andrei mocked, but Sawyer elbowed him in the side.

"Don't mock. Devon's right, she's not behaving like a housekeeper."

"Housekeepers do no more or less than their duties. They don't go above and beyond," Sean added quietly.

"You said you'd talked to her about Janna?"

Sean winced at Andrei's question. "Yeah." He shot Devon a look, but he was looking down at the bread he was buttering. Trust them all to figure he'd be the most sensitive where Janna was concerned, when he didn't actually give a shit. "She'd seen something online."

"Was she… what was her reaction?"

"It wasn't negative," he said softly. "I think she was curious."

"Because that's exactly what we want. To be treated like a freak show," Sawyer said gruffly.

"No. It wasn't like that."

"What was it like then?"

"I don't know. It was like she was pensive and pondering what I told her."

"Which was what exactly? Just the bare bones of that particular situation or something else?" Kurt demanded, his tone suspicious.

"I said that she should probably expect Devon to approach her about our tastes."

The man in question, rather than appear offended, looked quite proud. "See, you were wrong. I behaved. I didn't say anything."

"No, you just brought up her period and tried to get her to eat tripe," Andrei said with a snort.

Sean, recalling those horrendous conversations, rubbed his eyes. "It's a wonder she hasn't run screaming from the damn house."

"She's happy here," Devon said softly. "She sings when no one's down here and she's baking."

"She's been here two weeks," Kurt pointed out again. "Even if she was interested by the idea, she's barely been here long enough to know what she wants."

"He's right," Sawyer stated quietly.

"Maybe he is, maybe he isn't. Sometimes, the connection is there. What are we supposed to do? Ignore it just because normally, things don't develop for ages?" Devon snorted. "In my experience, women are always far more proactive than men. I'd dither, they pounce."

Sean grumbled, "That's because you're a lucky bastard."

"I wouldn't say that. I'd say I'm receptive, and they know it. It's appealing to them."

"Okay, so let's say *she's* receptive. What's the next step?"

"I think there shouldn't be one. Not for a while yet. Let's make sure she's happy here before we take this any further."

At Kurt's suggestion, Devon groaned. "You lot are so fucking boring sometimes." He huffed and climbed off his stool. "I'm going shopping with Sascha."

"Since when do you go shopping?" Sean demanded, gawking at the friend he'd known for close to two decades, and who had never entered a supermarket in that time.

They were enablers. So, sue them.

"Since I'll be going with Sascha and in her Caddy." He grinned, then mumbled under his breath, "I wonder if she'd let me drive it."

And with that, he left, heading for the stairs with a speed that surprised the men he left behind.

"He'll fuck this up for us," Andrei predicted.

"When has he ever done that?" Sean asked. "He's usually the catalyst."

"He's being weirder than usual. Am I the only one to notice?" Andrei countered.

Sawyer grimaced. "He's definitely keen on her. I didn't know where to look when he started talking about her being bloated the other day."

"She seems to find him amusing."

"It's probably because she's American. You know they think we're being funny when we're being serious."

Sean snorted at Sawyer's en pointe retort. "Let's be thankful for small mercies." He cleared his throat. "I propose we let this take its natural course. If Devon's right, and she pounces… as he phrased it… then I think we should go with the flow."

"The flow…" Andrei chuckled. "Like we wouldn't pounce right back?"

Sean blinked, then grinned. "True. I'm just stunned that's all. When I hired her, I thought she was hot, but I never imagined we'd be having this conversation. Not after the last debacle."

Kurt shrugged, then after he took a sip of his coffee, murmured, "She's witty, charming, warm-hearted, and beautiful. It's no wonder we're hooked. The question is why *she* would want to be with all five of us."

And that, as was always the way, was the question.

FOUR

"WHAT ARE YOU DOING?"

Sascha frowned over at the door to the living room, where she saw Andrei standing, watching her.

"Knitting." She had needles in her hand and a big ball of wool. "What does it look like I'm doing?"

His lips twitched at that. "Somebody's prickly today."

If her nose lifted into the air, then that wasn't her fault. "Don't ask me if I've got my period. I've had enough of Devon with that."

"He is rather obsessed, isn't he?" Andrei said blandly, and she shot him a look. Unsure if he was laughing at her or not.

He was an odd one, Andrei. Quick to mock, but quicker to laugh at himself. He didn't share all that much about himself, and was usually the quietest of the bunch.

"May I sit?"

"Of course," she mumbled. "It's your house."

He snorted as he took the seat beside her on the sofa opposite the huge TV set. "If you haven't figured out we're not like that in the two months you've been here, then there's no hope."

Two months. How had that happened? Where had those sixty days gone, and why hadn't she gotten laid in a single damn one of them?

"Well, that's true," she conceded. "But if I'd wanted to be alone, I'd have stayed in my room."

"Since when did you start knitting?"

Since she'd read it was great for relieving sexual frustration. She wasn't entirely sure if it was working. She was still frustrated, just not at being able to knit, which seemed counterintuitive to her.

Not that she could tell him that.

If she dropped any more hints, she was going to look desperate. And that was the last thing she wanted.

She'd never been blatant with her hints, so it was either that they were ignoring them willfully or she'd been too discreet.

"Since I read an article about how good it is for the brain," she lied, making the story up on the spot. It was either that or beg him to go down on her. Oh crap. If he did and talked to her in Russian at the same time? She knew she'd melt for real.

"Seriously?" He pursed his lips as he tucked his hands into his trouser pockets and watched her as she tried to do the whole loop and knot thing. "My grandmother used to knit. And crochet. I loved watching her."

She smiled. "You can watch me if you want. I'm sure the TV is more interesting though."

He snorted. "I don't watch much TV."

"I noticed," she said wryly. "I think I'm the only one who uses this room. Which makes no sense, considering someone had to buy the stuff in here."

Andrei cast a glance around the lounge and shrugged. "It was either that or just have an empty room, which would have freaked Kurt out."

"Why?"

"Haven't you noticed? He's a packrat."

She blinked. "I just thought he was messy."

"Well, that too." When she chuckled, he grinned at her, then focused on her hands once more.

"Are you okay, Andrei?" Sascha asked quietly.

He tilted his head back against the sofa, then yawned. "I have to write a speech for a gala I'm attending. It's not going well."

She cocked a brow. "No? Can I help?"

"I wouldn't bore you with it," he said dismissively. "I hate galas and I hate speeches."

"If they've asked you to speak, then that's an honor, surely?"

Who was he going with? She longed to ask. Wanted to know if he had a date, but she couldn't. Could she?

In all the time she'd been here, not a single person with XX chromosomes had crossed the front door.

What was wrong with the women in this country? Were they fucking blind?

"It's an honor, but it's still tedious."

She snorted. "You're all so dismissive of your talents. I've never known men so humble."

Andrei rolled his eyes. "You live with Devon long enough, it's hard to feel like you've a lot to boast about."

"I can see why you'd feel like that," she confessed.

"When someone's so brilliant," he continued, "your own glitter seems dull in comparison." He smiled. "That sounds self-piteous, but it isn't. I think Devon saves us all from believing our own press. How he's not an arsehole about it too, I'm not sure."

Devon was the least big-headed person, she knew. Apparently, Andrei too, and he, Devon, and Sawyer seemed to work within the same sphere.

Andrei was into economics and statistics more than the other two, who seemed to focus solely on theoretical math, but hell. Who was she to say? When they talked about Gödel's theorems and Cantor's diagonalizations, she had no idea what they were talking about, but it got her wet.

Seriously wet.

Like, disturbingly so.

She'd never realized until now that she found intelligence attractive. Her dumbass ex had been a gambler for a living—he'd worked in the City on the Stock Exchange. At the time, she'd known he was smart. But after being with these five?

They were hard to live up to.

"Do you know what a sapiosexual is?" she asked Andrei, tone curious. Sascha thought it wasn't wise to ask, but she liked to stir shit up from time to time. Especially when they were being so goddamn dense.

How could Sean raise a topic because he believed it would come to a head soon, then… *nada.* It was like the biggest pussy-tease going.

She'd been prepped, all engines revved and raring to go, but it was for nothing.

Was it any wonder she wanted to stir things up a bit?

When he cleared his throat, she had to bite back a satisfied smile. *He knew.* A sapiosexual was someone attracted to intelligence—and boy, did she have an endless source of that wafting through the house.

"Why do you ask?"

"I just realized recently that I am one."

Andrei was paler than the others. She wondered if the cold Russian winters had bleached him white, but it came in handy at times like these. The tips of his ears turned pink, and his cheeks flashed with color for a second at her pursuing the conversation.

If anything, it enhanced his appeal. She liked knowing that she could have them on edge.

Truth was, it would be easy for her to feel like they were toying with her in some way. These guys were rich, powerful, intelligent, and so freakin' gorgeous, she didn't understand why they didn't have women trying to slip through the cracks in the door to get to them.

Yet, they didn't, and she was still unable to believe that not one woman had visited, called, or done anything in any way normal with the hunks she lived with.

Either they were totally ignoring the chicks who were coming onto them, or British women the city over were blind.

Could it be they were selectively weeding out the women who wouldn't accept their unusual household?

It was a question to ponder.

Andrei had remained silent at her comment, but his ears were still burning. She liked that she could embarrass him, which she knew made her sound cruel. But Andrei's humor was a little cutting. Even mean, at times. Especially with Devon.

There was definitely a bromance aspect to their friendship, but if anyone would call Devon out on any shit he was spouting, it was Andrei. He was, for example, the first to leap to her defense when Devon spewed his usual twenty questions at her as soon as they were seated at the dining table. In a sense, he protected her from Devon's total lack of filter, and though she didn't need it, she was charmed by it regardless.

When he didn't seem willing to take the bait, she sighed wearily. She'd expected to be overwhelmed by them peppering her to let them share her. She *hadn't* expected having to goddamn beg for it!

Pissed, and more curious now than ever, Sascha asked, "Are you attending this gala alone?" If her work grew a little sloppier with her exasperation, then it was tough shit.

He cut her a glance. "Yes."

What? She shook her head at the stupid British women in the area. "Why?" She wondered if her bewilderment bled into her voice, but if it did, he barely reacted.

"I didn't want to ask anyone." He grimaced. "I don't want to bore them. It's not exactly going to be a barrel of laughs."

"I'm sure I'd find it interesting. Would you like me to come with you?"

"Why would you want to?" he asked, sounding perplexed. "It will be boring," he repeated.

"I think it sucks that you're going to go to an event alone, when it seems to me like you're being celebrated for something. You should have someone there to clap for you."

His brow puckered. "You would do this?"

"Of course."

"It will be boring," he stated again, as though trying to reiterate that she would not be having fun.

"You said that already. About four times?" she teased. "I can cope with a few hours of boredom. I do your laundry for a living, don't I?"

He chuckled. "True. Monotony is separating whites from darks."

"Exactly," she said with a grin. "Is it a very formal event?"

"Yes. Will you have something to wear?"

"I can find something I'm sure."

He frowned. "I don't want you out of pocket on this. Has Sean given you the household credit card yet?"

"Yes. A month ago." She'd not realized there was a 'household credit card' until Sean had given it to her. For the first four weeks, she'd paid for everything out of petty cash. Once they seemed to realize she was around to stay and could be trusted, Sean had handed her the card with an ease that had warmed her.

She knew the card represented their faith in her, and knowing them, the limit was probably for an ungodly amount, so that faith was even more invaluable. She'd actually hoped it was a sign that one of them would come onto her.

They hadn't.

It was nice knowing they were gentleman, but that didn't help the situation in her panties.

What was it about them that hit her in all the right spots?

She wished she knew. She'd never experienced these kinds of 'deviant' desires before now. It was like discussing it with Sean, allowing the idea to percolate and be given room to breathe, had been all the encouragement she needed. And now, they weren't taking the damn bait!

"Well, this event will be designer fancy," Andrei told her, breaking into her brooding thoughts. "Use the card to buy a dress. Anything else you need too. Shoes or whatever. I'll explain the extra expense to Sean."

She blinked. "Are you sure?"

"Of course."

Carte blanche with a credit card and permission to go wild in 'designer fancy' stores?

She grinned at him. "You totally made up for any boredom that's to come."

He snorted. "Like shopping, do you?"

"When I can buy whatever the hell I want? Yes! Who doesn't?"

"I hate shopping."

His glum retort had her snickering, then, she leaned over so that she was resting against his side. "If you come with me, you could always help me zip up the dresses I try on."

Her words had his nostrils flaring. "Sascha…"

"Yes?" she pounced.

He licked his lips. "I don't think you understand what it is you're inviting here."

"I think I should be the one to judge that," she retorted, equally as softly.

Andrei turned his head away from the TV and peered at her from under thick, dark gold lashes. The man made Chris Hemsworth look ugly. Yeah. Impossible, she knew, but Jesus Christ, he was hardwired into her hormones. His smell? Fuck! She had no idea what was going on that turned her into a horn dog around these five, but God, if she didn't get some action soon, she'd be assaulting one of them.

Devon, probably.

He'd probably find the experience enlightening.

"You can't turn us against one another," he told her softly, and their faces were so close, his breath brushed her lips.

Her scowl was like quicksilver. "Why would I do that?"

"A couple have tried in the past."

"I have no intention of doing anything of the sort," she said with a huff, her knitting needles clacking as she dumped the mass of poorly woven fabric into her lap. "These feelings I have… you all inspire them."

"Why?"

And there was the million-dollar question. *Why?*

She hesitated, not because she didn't want to answer, but because she wanted to explain this to him, and to explain it well. Which, considering she didn't really know the truth, was hard going.

When she stayed silent, he cut her a look. "I think we should change the subject."

Sascha's hand came out to grab his arm. "No."

"No, what?"

Her tongue peeped out to wet her suddenly very dry lips. "Sean explained to me about your predilections," she started softly, casting her gaze down onto the mass of wool in her lap.

"I know he did. He told us. He also said that you were already aware of our tastes. You'd researched us."

She snorted. "I did a Google search. I didn't exactly hire a private detective."

"Glad to hear it," he said gruffly, but she could tell her snark amused him. "We were surprised you came back for the job once we knew you'd learned about our past."

"Why? It's not like you're perverts."

He shrugged. "To some we would be."

She licked her lips again, knowing full well his gaze was trained on her mouth. "Not to me."

"And there it is again," he told her, whisper soft. "Why? Why, Sascha?"

"Can't you just be happy that I don't feel like that where this topic is concerned?"

"No. I need to understand. *We* need to understand."

She huffed again. "Most men would just pounce. You do know that, right?"

"We're not predators," he countered. "And you're not prey. That's not how this works." He scraped his chin with a hand. She noticed his hands were neat, his nails manicured. None of them were metrosexuals, but they were all clean cut. Tidy in appearance if not in mind.

"When Sean explained, the idea appealed to me," she mumbled.

"Have you wanted to engage in polyamory before?"

Now, it was her turn to flush. She really didn't appreciate having the tables turned on her, but she guessed she deserved it after provoking him. "No."

"Then why did it appeal to you?"

"Because you're all you."

He frowned. "What does that mean?"

"It means," she admitted softly, "You're all special. That very first day, I knew that. I mean, you radiate it. And you're so attractive, kind and interested in me. You come as a group, I get that. I'd be happy with one of you, but it's like the group is a single entity." She groaned. "Shit, that's a crap explanation."

"No, it isn't. Carry on," he directed her softly.

She peeked over at him and gulped. He was interested. She could tell. Open and receptive to what she had to say. Hesitantly, she murmured, "You work as a unit. I saw that from the beginning. Being with one of you is like an extension of the others. I don't understand how it's possible, but it's true. You're so different, but streamlined in the same way.

"Then, there are the individual quirks that make you unique.

"I'm your housekeeper," she said bluntly. "But you don't treat me like that. None of you do. I don't understand it, but it's the truth. You defend me and shield me from Devon's prying. He teases me, makes me laugh with his batshit questions. Sean supports me… I mean, I'm just your employee," she gritted out. "But guess who bought this stuff for me?" Sascha pointed down at her lap. "Sean. He heard me talking about it to Devon. 'Lo and behold, today, I have a 'How-To' magazine with the basic kit. He *listened*. Do you have any idea how attractive that is?

"Then, there's Kurt. He checks up on me. Makes sure I'm okay. That I've eaten. If he sees me stressing over the household accounts, he's there with coffee and a hug—when I should be the one giving *him* coffee.

"And Sawyer? When I told him I was thinking about working out again? He created a plan for me. Worked it out and everything. We're starting jogging together when the weather gets better." She blinked at him, wondering why he was surprised at why she *needed* more. The glimpses of how a relationship would work with them was more than she could take.

"Can't you see, Andrei?" she half-pleaded, hating herself for sounding desperate, hating the tears that burned in her eyes with the sudden desire she had to be *theirs*. "I want all of that. But I want it for me. As mine. Not as a woman who works in your house; which, to be fair, wouldn't change if we were... *together* like that, you know? But, the way you treat me... I crave more. Can you blame me?"

Her admission had him blowing out a breath. "You feel loved."

She bowed her head. "Yes." Her fingers tightened on the wool, clenching to the point of pain. "Maybe at first, the notion was exciting. Kinky, even. You're sexy, and I have eyes and hormones like anyone. You all get me hot under the collar. But now? It's more. *I* want more."

His hand came out, and she sighed when he cupped her chin and tilted her face. Before she could say anything more, ask him anything else, he connected their mouths.

Finally!

Etta James' *At Last* boomed in her head, complete with orchestral accompaniment, but he knocked the sultry jazz from her memory banks by robbing her breath and stealing it for himself.

She moaned against his lips as the taste of him, the scent of him, flooded her senses. Her whole body quivered beside him as he carefully explored all she had to give.

With a shudder, she opened her mouth and let him in. His tongue tangled with hers, entwining around it before tracing tiny circles that had her whimpering as sensation flushed through her. He didn't thrust it into her mouth like he was tongue-fucking her mechanically. He enticed. *Teased*.

She placed her hands on his shoulders, before letting them sweep up to circle his neck. He grabbed a hold of her waist and tugged her into him, until their torsos were flush, and they were as close as could be. He tilted her back, angling her head so she could accept all his kisses, and she let him. Not needing to take charge when he had the power to make her feel like this with just his mouth.

Pulling back to nip at her bottom lip, he chuckled when she moaned and pouted. He traced the curve of her mouth with the tip of his tongue before diving back in and taking her to a whole other world.

She moved a hand, grabbed one of his and pressed it to her breast.

Arching into him, she silently pleaded with him to touch her more. God, she needed.

How she needed.

It was like a gnawing toothache deep in her belly. She couldn't control it, couldn't stop it. She needed him to control and stop it for her. She shuddered when he caressed the mound of her breast, plucking at the tip blindly through her shirt. She whimpered when he pulled away and dotted tiny pecks around her mouth, then her chin, jaw, and throat were anointed with the same caresses.

Her skin felt on fire with tingles. She mewled as his tongue played with the sinews of her throat, tracing small patterns on one of her sweet spots. She clung to him as he teased her, before he dropped down to the V of her shirt and kissed the plump mounds of her breasts.

Letting her head fall back against the sofa, she ran her hands through his hair and held him in place as he palpated the tender flesh with his lips. He reached for the hem of her shirt and as he dotted more kisses here and there, she sucked her gut in so he could tug the fabric out of her high-waisted skirt and start to pull it up over her chest. He didn't stop until it was high above her breasts and her bra was exposed to him.

"*Yebat-kopat,*" he said gruffly in Russian. The heavy syllables just fucked with her head. He sounded so sexy that she wished the skirt she wore wasn't tight to her hips. She'd have spread her legs and begged him inside her for that voice alone.

He carried on whispering, in a low grating voice that spoke of his need. Of his want, and it stoked the fire in her. Embers became a small flame, those few flickering flames became an inferno as he ducked into one cup and began to squeeze and torment one breast while he suckled the other.

The whispers against her tender flesh drove her nuts, and she dug her nails into his scalp. Each time she did that, his voice deepened, until the rumbles vibrated against her skin, adding to her torment.

"I need to touch you," she told him thickly, her hands releasing the hold on his head to tug at the back of his shirt. He moaned against her breast, then peered up at her. Ice blue eyes danced with wicked intent and she let out a yelp when suddenly, she was no longer perched up against the sofa, she was lying flat out. Her hips dragged down so he had more access than ever.

At his chuckle, she grinned, but the grin died and was replaced with a moan when he began to ruffle up her skirt, dragging it up over her knees, then her thighs. The instant she could, she spread her legs wide, and he groaned as she grabbed a hold of his hips with her calves and pulled him close.

His cock was hard against her pussy. She felt every inch of him, that delicious pressure, the force of his passion for her, and needed to feel it without anything separating them.

The desire he inspired in her was so beyond insane, she wasn't sure if she'd be insensate by the time they actually got past third base. She rocked her hips, loving when he thrust against her. His hardness nudging her clit on each strike as he went back to work on her tits. Nibbling and nipping at her nipples, squeezing the other as he tongued her tender parts.

Her hands scrabbled at his hips, tugging and plucking, desperate for him to rise up, to let her feel more of him. She loved that he was in charge, loved that he was in control, but she needed to feel him bare against her.

It was hot that they were still dressed. It spoke of their urgency, their desperation, and God, she felt both. He somehow arched his hips, so she could scramble underneath, and within a few moments, his belt was unfastened, his fly unbuttoned, and his zipper down. With all the delicacy of an archaeologist who'd just found a precious artefact, she burrowed within and reached for his shaft.

The silken flesh against her palm made her skin tingle, but the slick tip was a wet kiss against her fingers, one she wanted to taste, and to savor.

With a moan, she pulled him free and loved the new angle, how he could rock against her harder, how she could feel his wetness against her.

"I'm on the pill, and I'm clean," she gasped as her hand squeezed his base and his mouth bit her nipple with enough force to have her yelping.

Her words were the sexual equivalent of 'open sesame,' because he slid a hand between them, pulled her panties aside, and gritted out, "Let me inside you."

Her eyes widened, and a whimper gathered in her throat as she pressed his tip to her gate. Feeling his thickness in her hand was one thing, against her panties-covered crotch another. But against her *bare* pussy? That was a whole other ball of wax.

She whimpered as he stretched her fully with just an inch, his voice was a growl as he gritted out, "Ready?"

A mewl of assent was all she was capable of, and as he rocked his hips, thrusting into her with a care that touched her, she had to moan with delight as he slowly claimed everything she had to give.

Her hands ran up and down his back with an urgency that came from his size. She was so utterly on edge that she pulled and tugged at his shirt, dug her nails in spots and raked them down his spine in others as he found his way fully inside her.

She clutched his hips as she let out a long, deep gasp when he was there, all of him, claiming all of her.

"*Pizda rulyu. Nu naher,*" he whispered against her throat, then loomed over her so their eyes were caught in each other's gaze as he pulled his hips back and slowly retreated. Tender tissues sparked to life at the move, and she dug her nails deeper into his back in response.

She didn't have a clue what he'd said, and at that minute, didn't give a flying fuck. In one swift stroke he returned, filling her so full she thought she'd choke and any thoughts of translations definitely did a disappearing act.

She stared deep into his eyes all the while. Trapped in his attention. Ensnared by his desire.

And she loved it.

She loved all of it.

He taunted them both at first. Dragging it out so that each thrust felt like both a wet dream and a nightmare. And then, he grabbed her thighs, spread them wider, and as he clutched her ass, he began to fuck her. Each move had his pubis rubbing against her clit in a way that had her seeing sparks. She cried out with the first thrust, and then each one thereafter had an endless litany of, "Ohmigod, ohmigod, ohmigod," spilling from her mouth.

Now, she looked at him blindly. Not seeing him but the fireworks his fucking brought to life behind her eyes. She clenched them shut as they reached climax. The burning so fierce she knew she'd be seeing stars for hours after they were no longer joined.

And that was exactly what they were.

Joined. United. Bound.

It was scary, and it was hot. It should have felt more relaxed, less powerful, but it didn't.

He claimed her. With each thrust, he made her his. He made her one of theirs.

The door squeaked, and her eyes flared open at the sound. Blindly, dazedly, she stared at the doorway, and saw Kurt standing there.

She about expired at the sight of him. His hot gaze taking in what they were doing and loving it.

It felt right him being there. Andrei claimed her for them, but Kurt was backing it up. Reminding her, reminding *them* that she belonged to them.

And then, he grabbed a hold of his cock through his pants. Her eyes dropped to his clutching grip, and she moaned at the sight.

Inspired by that moan, he pulled his shaft out and began to jack off. Staying in the shadows. Letting her know that this was her time with Andrei, but that he was grateful she wanted him to be a part of this. Her vision grew hazy as her senses tried and failed to process the stimuli.

It was impossible.

She couldn't.

She'd needed them, and they'd provided. Her pussy clung to Andrei's, her body clamored for Kurt's, and when Andrei gritted out something that sounded like a swear word in Russian, a sharp gasp escaping him as her muscles clenched down on his when he pounded into her hard and fast, his own needs raking at him, she came.

It exploded from nowhere. Filled her senses to overfull. She was blind and deaf to everything around her for a handful of seconds, until her heart suddenly pounded back to life. And with that, sensation returned, and it was too much.

The double blow had her gasping, her back arching as the glory of the moment ricocheted through her like a wild bullet.

And the magic of the moment came when she felt Andrei come, his cock hardening and pulsing inside her. And when Kurt gasped, a moan escaping him as he too found his release.

But that was all she could handle, until her body took over, regained control from Andrei, and pushed her over the edge into an oblivion that was tinged with the bright glitter of stars.

FIVE

FLICKING the switch in his dark study, Sean jumped a little at the sight of Andrei who had his head tilted back against the corner wing of the club chair in front of Sean's desk.

He was relaxed, at ease, Sean thought, but there had to be something wrong for him to be sitting in the dark, alone, as he waited for Sean to return home.

When the light flared on, he didn't open his eyes fully, just slitted them to stare at him.

"What's wrong?" Sean asked, curious now. Andrei wasn't necessarily a talker, but he usually sought Sean out when there was something going on with him.

As far as he was aware, the only thing that could be at the moment was Sascha.

She'd been restless these past few weeks. *On edge?* He knew she was content with her position here and could only assume her restlessness stemmed from being on edge around *them*. Thus far, they'd decided to wait her out. To see if she truly meant it when she spoke of them sharing her. Of course, not that she phrased it like that, but it's what it boiled down to.

"Sascha and I…"

Sean cocked a brow, then as realization struck at Andrei's

continued silence, he blew out a breath, rounded his desk, and sank heavily into his wide leather desk chair.

"Really?"

"Yes."

"Why?" Only between them would that question make sense.

What man would turn a willing woman down, after all?

But in this, there was so much more going on, so much more at stake.

"She was flirting with me, and then being quite serious. I asked her what she thought she'd achieve from being with us in that way, and her explanations… they were as serious as her mood at that moment.

"She wants to be with us, Sean," he finished, his words soft but his tone heavy.

"Why do you look like someone just told you your dog has died then?" Confusion filtered through his words. That she wanted them, that Andrei believed her, was something to celebrate, wasn't it?

"Because she could hurt us," Andrei confessed thickly, his eyes somber and bleak.

"They all hurt us," Sean told him matter-of-factly.

It was sad but true. Every time they'd done this, had tried, it had blown up in their faces. It was why he'd told them he refused to try again, but with Sascha and Devon getting on so well, then her fitting in like she was made for them… it had been hard not to get excited. He'd held back, intent on playing a waiting game. Desperate to see if she'd stay the course before they got involved. Because, when the women grew bored, the men were devastated when they left.

The world seemed to think it was only women who could be hurt in a relationship, but that wasn't the case.

"I know," Andrei murmured. "I ask myself why we do this, and then, I remember."

"The bond." There was nothing like it, nothing could compare to it, and they'd only held the shadow of that bond. None of Sascha's predecessors had ever wanted it to develop fully.

But the connection was something they'd strived to attain for years. That feeling of their household being complete, of their unit being solid and impervious to threat—it was unsurpassable.

One woman, loving them. Them, loving one woman. Providing for her, caring for her, giving her what they couldn't give her individually…

Andrei released a shuddery breath. "She spoke of it too. It's why I kissed her. I had no intention of taking the next step, but the way she spoke? It was everything I needed to hear. She meant it. Every word."

"They all do," Sean countered, trying to be realistic.

"Not like this. She spoke of… family." Need flashed through him, and Andrei must have seen the spark because he whispered, "The way she talked, it was like she'd read our minds."

"We should talk with her again."

"No. There's no need."

"Why?"

"Kurt walked in. He watched."

"Perv," Sean said without any heat. They all knew his predilections for watching, and had grown accustomed to them over time. "How did she react?"

"She climaxed."

"Well, that's a good sign," Sean retorted with a quick grin.

"That's what I thought too," he murmured.

"Where is she now?"

"Kurt carried her to the bedroom."

"When was this?"

"About an hour ago. She was fast asleep. Didn't even stir when he righted her clothes and tugged her into his arms."

Sean rubbed a hand over his face. He felt weary, but hope was bleeding through, and he'd learned over the years how dangerous hope was. "I want to…"

"I know. It's hard to rejoice when you feel like the other shoe's about to drop."

Because his friend understood entirely, Sean relaxed back into his seat. "What do we do?"

"Integrate her. She wants to be family. Let her experience it."

"She's been with us two months," Sean argued. "How can we—?"

"We just do. We have to see if she likes it." He paused, seemed to savor the words as he whispered, "She's different, Sean. I can feel it."

The ramifications of the evening's events would be far-reaching, they both knew. But it was the next step that was hardest to discern. How to behave around her. How to interact with her. If they threw her in too quickly at the deep end, she might become uneasy. Scared, even. If they took it too slowly, she might be frustrated. Grow bored.

"I think we should let her sleep the whole night through. She's coming with me to that gala of mine next week. I said she should buy a dress on the household credit card."

Sean nodded, and rubbed his chin. "I'll go with her."

Andrei cocked a brow. "Why?"

"We should talk. She's used to talking to me about these things now."

"She should be at ease discussing them with all of us," he argued.

"Eventually, but you know that's not how this works. She'll come to us for different things, until those lines blur."

Andrei blinked, sighed. "You're right."

Sean grimaced. "If it makes you feel better, I'm not looking forward to it."

He snorted. "You're a fool then. She'll probably let you zip her up in the changing rooms."

"She said that?" he surmised from the wicked gleam in Andrei's gaze. When the other man nodded, Sean chuckled. "Okay, so it might start off a little rough, but it could have a happy ending."

Andrei grinned, then his grin skewed. "I think Kurt intends on napping with her."

"So?"

"That means you, Sawyer, or I need to cook dinner."

Sean, understanding this dilemma, grimaced. "Pizza?"

"Pizza."

THE LIGHTS WERE off when she woke up, and she was alone in bed. She'd stirred a few times, had realized Kurt was by her side snoozing away, and had snuggled back under the covers—amazed that he'd had the strength to carry her up three flights of stairs.

Hadn't that made her feel petite and delicate when she'd always felt big and chunky all her life?

Now, though, she felt the other side of the mattress was cold, and rather than be affronted that he'd made the decision without her to sleep there, she wished he was back, and wished she wasn't alone.

If it weren't for the ache between her legs, this evening might never have happened, and she didn't want that to be the case. Even though she was sore—it had been a *long* while since she'd last had sex, and

Andrei was bigger than her ex—it was with relief that she felt the dull ache because it was proof.

She hadn't dreamed it.

Her needs had come to fruition and she'd reveled in every moment of it. Hell, more than that. It was everything she'd imagined and more.

With a sigh, she wriggled and then realized her skirt had caught the 'wet' patch. Having felt the slickness against her skin, she could no longer snuggle under the covers and quickly traipsed over to the bathroom to take a quick shower.

Once clean and dry, as well as dressed in a thick and fluffy bathrobe, she decided she was hungry. Only trouble was, Andrei had to have told the others they'd had sex… She gnawed her lip at the thought. Was that a bad thing?

She wasn't sure.

Hunger urging her on, she headed down the stairs and as she did, saw most of the doorways to the men's room had lights running beneath them.

She could sneak down there, but was that the wisest option? Wasn't it better to take the bull by the balls and brazen it out?

That had worked so far for her in her dealings with them, right?

Well, kind of.

Knowing that Devon would probably amuse her rather than embarrass her, she knocked on the door. At her tap, he called out, "Come in, Sascha."

She stepped inside. "How did you know it was me?"

"Your knock's gentle. Plus, you actually knock. The rest of the barbarians just barge in."

He peered up from his work, appearing like some kind of hobbit surrounded by his files. The room was chaos, and the one place she was allowed only to dust and empty the trash. No cleaners were permitted to enter—considering the disaster with the last cleaner, the one Devon had spilled state secrets to—that was probably wise.

When she stepped into the room, he rocked back in his chair and murmured, "You look relaxed. The others always said Andrei was good in bed." He pursed his lips in consideration, then nodding, more to himself than her she thought, advised, "You should get him to go down on you and speak in Russian. Janna always seemed to appreciate that."

Sascha winced. "We're not really having this conversation, are we?"

Her cheeks were pink from his usual bluntness, but she had to admit… he amused the hell out of her without even trying.

She wasn't sure why he didn't offend her. If anything, his comments were rude and far too personal, but it was just Devon.

Like a toddler might paint on the walls with his crayons, she expected Devon to come out with something that most would find offensive.

Because she was prepared for it subconsciously, she rolled with his verbal punches, and found herself tickled pink more than three-quarters of the damn time.

"You're very beautiful post-sex," he remarked. "Why wouldn't I talk about it when it's very noticeable?"

She rolled her eyes. "The just-fucked look suits every woman according to every man."

He snickered. "True. Anyway, what can I do for you?"

Well, that was frank. Had she expected any less though. Awkwardly fiddling with the belt of her dressing gown, she peered down at her bare feet and mumbled, "I thought I might sit with you."

"Why?"

Her eyes darted over to him at that particular question. "Why not?" When he just tilted his head in question, she sighed. "I want your company." Okay, so she was hungry too but who didn't hate eating alone? Maybe she could convince him to take a break?

A girl could only try.

He beamed at her. "Take a seat."

She eyed the chaotic spree of chalkboards, whiteboards, papers, books, and file folders that were the sum total of the room. There were more filing cabinets here than in a government office she felt sure, and more boards than a classroom. It was a fugly room, but… there was magic in here.

Call her crazy, hell, she regularly did, but what these two worked on? It was life-changing, mind-boggling, world-affecting shit. Who wouldn't be impressed by that?

She stepped over a small hillock of paperbacks that hadn't been there earlier in the day when she'd done a quick tidy up of the area, identified Sawyer's desk chair under a pile of papers, pushed them into a stack and then shuffled them onto the floor. It was old fashioned; wide and broad, made from leather, and so close to being an armchair, she knew she'd be comfortable.

"Sawyer at the gym?"

He hummed a 'yes'.

As she bustled, she was aware Devon was watching her. Again, it amused her that he didn't offer to help. Just eyed her like she was a visiting alien in his wonderland.

She curled her legs underneath her, settled down into the crinkling leather, and pulled her cell out of her pocket. Resting her head against the wing, she began scrolling through her social networks. It was the only way she really kept in touch with friends and family in the States. Not that she had many left.

Her mother had died when she was ten, and her father had remarried by the time she was fourteen. Sascha and Linda had never seen eye to eye, and it had been a relief when she flew the nest and went to college. The distance, both physical and emotional, between her father and herself saddened her, but she didn't think there was any point in being upset about something she couldn't change.

Linda's claws were buried far too deeply into her dad for him to see the light, and she had to deal with that or let it really work its poison on her.

"You don't want to talk?"

Devon's question had her peering at him. "No."

"Why come here then?"

She bit back a smile. "Company. I told you."

He pondered that. "You can talk. If you want."

"I don't want to."

"Why not? Women talk."

"And men don't?" She snorted. "You guys talk all the time."

"Yeah, but women…" He grimaced.

"You mean, the ones you've had in the past?" she said, borrowing his lack of delicacy and using it against him.

Devon frowned but nodded. "Why don't you want to? Aren't you comfortable?"

"You're overthinking this, Devon," she teased gently. "I'm very comfortable. That's why I don't have to talk to you. And I don't want to because I'm tired, and still a little sleepy."

"Do you want some pizza?"

She cocked a brow. "Do you have some?" The promise of grease made her belly rumble.

"We ordered in, so you could sleep."

Sascha refused to blush. "Oh. Thank you."

He shrugged. "It was Sean and Andrei's idea. You and Kurt were asleep, and you're the only ones who can cook."

Giggling because he wasn't wrong—she'd tasted Sean's idea of toast, and who the fuck could ruin toast?—she got to her feet when he rustled some more papers to reveal a pizza box.

"I'm surprised Sawyer ate it." She knew his opinions on foods that weren't home-made. Chemicals and E-numbers were his personal enemy.

"He didn't. He went to the gym instead. Said he'd eat at the kitchen there." Devon handed it to her, and asked, "Do you like pepperoni?"

"Love it."

"You're okay then. There should be more downstairs if that's not enough."

She snorted when she opened the box. The two huge pieces were enough even for her rather large appetite.

"This will suit me to a tee," she said grandly, shooting him a happy smile as she trekked back to the armchair, crossing paper rivers and book mountains to get there. Once settled in Sawyer's chair again, she munched and went back to Facebook.

"Do you have a lot of family in America?"

She blew out an exasperated breath. "Devon, you don't have to talk to me. I didn't come here to interrupt you."

"You're not interrupting," he denied.

"Were you working before I came in?" she argued.

"Well, yes, but I'm working all the time. My brain doesn't stop. That's why I can't sleep."

She frowned. "We need to work on that."

"How?"

"Oh, I don't know. We could do yoga together? Something like that? Meditation might be good."

He wrinkled his nose. "I was hoping you were going to say sex."

Laughter gurgled from her. "That too. Not tonight though." She matched him; her nose wrinkled too as she confessed, "I'm sore."

With a commiserative grimace, he nodded. "We're all quite big I'm afraid. It might take you a while to get used to us."

She laughed. "I guess it's gone around the house by now then, huh? What I want?"

"I told them from the start," he stated crossly, folding his arms across his chest with a huff. "They wouldn't listen. They're all scared you're going to walk out on us."

Stilling at that, she asked quietly, "Why do they think that?"

"Everyone leaves us," came the simple and painful answer, but his tone was matter of fact. Like the statement was about everyone else, and not him.

"Surely not everyone?"

He shrugged.

"You mean women."

"I mean everyone. It can't have escaped your attention that no one really contacts us outside of work."

"I had noticed you don't seem to have much family."

"We have family, they just don't talk to us all that much."

"Why not?"

"They have their reasons."

"I guess I can understand that. I don't talk to my dad as much as I'd like because of my stepmother." She held up her phone and shook it. "I see most things on here. It's my connection to home."

"How long have you been in England?"

"Don't you know?" She eyed him curiously. "I thought you'd have seen it on my resume."

He snorted. "Do I look like the sort of person who reads CVs? I leave that boring stuff to Kurt and Sean."

Her tone was gravelly as she murmured, "Yes, that was silly of me." God, he was too freaking cute sometimes. "I've been here six years."

"Why did you move?"

"For a boyfriend. He got a job here, and I didn't want to leave him, so I came with him." She sighed. "That didn't last long. The move was stressful, and his job took up more of his hours. I was kind of lonely, found it hard to adapt here, and was homesick… he started having an affair with his PA. I left and found a job with an agency. Fell, by chance, into this line of work."

"You haven't always been a housekeeper?"

She chuckled. "I'm not sure it's one of those types of professions, Devon. But no. I majored in hospitality and management, but I didn't want to work in a hotel or anything like that. When the agency saw that on my resume, they said they had a client who wanted someone to 'manage' their household. I did, liked it. Carried on with it."

"Why did you leave?"

"They moved to Dubai."

"You didn't want to go?"

"I could have gone. They asked. But I like London now." She smiled. "It's home."

"You called the States home."

She jerked a shoulder. "I have two homes. One where my old friends and family are, then here, one of my choice and a life of my own making."

"Would you move back?"

"Are you asking because you think I'll leave?"

"Everyone leaves us," he repeated.

"Don't give me a reason to, and I won't."

"What kind of reason?"

"I don't know, don't be jerks. Don't treat me like shit. Don't under-appreciate me."

He rubbed his chin. "That seems very basic."

She snorted. "Women are basic creatures. Pet us, keep us warm, feed us, love us and tell us you do, then we're happy."

"I should probably write that down."

Sascha chuckled. "I'll remind you. Don't worry."

"Do," he directed with a somberness that had her eyes widening; it was unusual for him to be so serious. "I don't want to mess this up, Sascha. I like you."

Her smile grew slowly. "I like you too, Devon."

"Good. That's a start, isn't it?"

"It's a great start."

"You like us all?"

She nodded. "I wouldn't have…" She placed the pizza she'd been chomping on back in the greasy box. As oregano and tomato assailed her senses, she confessed, "I wouldn't have started something if I hadn't thought I could finish it."

"You mean, you wouldn't have slept with Andrei if you weren't willing to take us all on?"

"Say it like it is, Devon," she teased. "But yes. Right on the nose. I want to be a part of your family. Does that sound weird?"

"I suppose it does. Well, to average people, but average people are so boring, aren't they?" he asked conversationally. "Their opinions don't matter."

"Well, I'm not sure that's wholly accurate," she countered with some tact.

"No. It is. What you just said makes perfect sense. You're happy here. You fit in with us, and you make us happy too. What could be better than embracing it and letting it form into something unique that will brighten our lives?

"How could that be a bad thing?

"And yet, to average people, who can't understand anything outside of the pigeonhole of their boring worlds, what we have is wrong. *Alien*. Not to be allowed." He pursed his lips and rocked back in his more modern ergonomic monster of a chair. "How can that be right?"

When he put it like that, what could she say but, "It isn't."

He nodded. Apparently satisfied by her concession. "Allow yourself to be happy with us, Sascha. Don't worry about the outside world. The others did," he said with a grunt. "I tried to talk to them. Make them see what society wanted wasn't important, that that wouldn't keep them warm at night. They didn't listen." He pressed his head back against the rest. "Why do you want to be a part of our family?"

She stared at him, astonished by his wisdom when he was more like the Rain Man sometimes than a living, breathing man with a heart and soul. That probably sounded cold, but Mr. Calculator was capable of a clinicalness that was quite astonishing.

"I like how you interact."

"Explain."

"Your dynamic, it suits me." When he cocked a brow, she knew he wasn't going to let this drop. "I get bored, Devon. It's a nasty fact, but I do."

"Bored about what?"

"Just... everything. I'm quite smart," she confessed. "Nothing like you."

"That's relative," he immediately countered. "Intelligence is a bottomless pool. I'm capable of making millions but paying the electricity bill? It's beyond me."

"True," she conceded, liking and appreciating his instant defense of her. Protecting her from herself... it warmed her. "Housekeeping doesn't really excite me, but it keeps me with a roof over my head and puts food in my belly."

"That's enough?"

"There's not much of a challenge."

"Do you want a challenge?"

"Sometimes." She pursed her lips as she put the pizza box on the floor, trying not to stain anything too important with grease from the oily base. "I'm lazy. I don't know what I want."

"Maybe it's enough for you to be... domestic."

With anyone else, she'd probably have bristled at that, but he didn't mean it offensively. Well, he never did. But in this, it was a simple suggestion. "I think sometimes it is, but then, when I check Facebook and see my friends are all achieving so much? I feel badly."

"Don't compare yourself to them. You're living in London, one of the world's most expensive and most beautiful cities. You've already achieved more than they ever can. Living in foreign countries broadens the mind in ways you can't even begin to imagine."

"You sound like you've lived elsewhere?"

His eyes shuttered a little, a realization that interested her because she'd never seen that before. Never seen him physically react to anything she said. "When I was a child, I lived in Germany for a few years. My father was in the army, and we have bases there. I also lived in Italy for a time."

"Wow, that's awesome."

"Not really. But I remember, and my time there changed me."

"For the good?"

"Not necessarily, but not for the bad either."

"Why do I feel like you're talking in riddles?"

He just looked at her. "I don't know. Why do you?"

Realizing she was facing a verbal wall, she filed that information away, knowing she'd ask one of the others about this topic of conversation. It was unlike Devon to filter himself. But he was. Without question.

When silence fell between them, she was uncertain of what to say. He was studying her, and she wriggled uneasily in her seat until he asked, "Would you like to go back to school?"

Her brow puckered. "To study what?"

He shrugged. "Whatever you want. Pottery. Archery. Fencing?"

She blinked. "Why would I want to?"

"Challenges don't have to be career-oriented. It's just this crazy world that makes it seem like that. We're all rats in the race," he informed her sadly. "But you don't have to be one."

"You're not a rat," she scoffed. "None of you. As far as I can tell, you all work for the fun of it. For the challenge," she accepted with a nod of her head.

"To some extent. We're all passionate about what we do that's for sure. I don't have a choice, and because I don't have a choice, Sawyer usually bustles along with me." Sadness seemed to line his features for a second before it flashed out of existence. "If it would make you happy, then feel free to look at courses or classes."

"That's not fair," she said softly. "I didn't decide to start this so I could take advantage of you."

"I never imagined you did. But you have, and things will change as a result. You're no longer just an employee, Sascha, and we're no longer employers. Surely you can see that?"

She blinked at him, realizing he was right. She'd inadvertently tipped the balance, and though it wasn't something she'd ever regret, she hoped they could work together to restore equilibrium because the last thing she wanted was for their dynamic to change.

Sascha wanted to merge into their world. Not alter it.

That realization was probably more confusing than anything else that had happened that day, and she didn't even know why.

SIX

"I'M SURPRISED."

"At what?"

As one of his favorite songs—Muse's *Feeling Good*—played on the radio, Sean watched as Sascha pulled a fancy U-turn in the tight parking lot, then made a few more moves as she parallel parked in a space he wouldn't have tried to get in with a Mini. She did it with an ease that bemused him.

"Most men don't like it when women drive them."

He huffed. "I'm not most men." He craned his neck, watching as she effortlessly straightened the large Caddy, then with a flourish, shut off the engine and put on the handbrake. "You did that like a pro." Hell, she drove better than he did.

She beamed at him. "This baby handles like a dream. She drives me."

"No." He shook his head. "This space is tiny. I wouldn't have dared."

"You're a wuss," she teased as she started to climb out of the car, but he grabbed her arm, and stopped her.

"Are you okay?"

She blinked at him. "I'm fine."

"Are you sure?"

Her gaze softened, and she stunned him by reaching up and

cupping his cheek. Her thumb caressed the bridge of his cheekbone, and he tried not to melt at the simple, affectionate touch. "I'm very sure."

"I still think this is all starting far too quickly," he said, annoyed by his fretting tone, but accepting it nonetheless...he *was* fretting, and he didn't care if that made him a pansy to admit to that or not.

She didn't know it, but she had the ability to destroy their ordered world.

The fall out of her leaving would have repercussions she'd never foresee, never imagine. Why would she? She didn't know how delicate Devon's mental health was. How Kurt's was just as precarious.

They were men, and it seemed the world thought they were infallible because they had a dick.

No one was infallible. It was folly to think otherwise.

Even dicks hurt.

"It didn't start quickly enough for me," she confessed softly. "I wanted you from the start."

"You think I didn't?" He shook his head. "I wish things were simpler," he told her softly, tilting his head a little so he could press a kiss to the base of her hand.

"Things are never simple. Haven't you realized that?" she whispered, and he saw she'd closed her eyes at his gentle kiss.

"Did you spend the night with Devon?"

She smiled and nodded, all with her eyes shut. "He's a bed hog."

He chuckled. "Comes as no surprise. He's a spoiled brat."

"Hardly." She winked at him. "He's just unique."

"For unique read brat," he huffed. "Did he sleep?"

"Yeah."

"He'll probably hog you too if you can help him sleep better." His lips twitched. "Although, considering we're usually worried about him not sleeping enough, that will take a weight off our minds."

She smiled a little. "You see? How can I not be charmed by this world of yours? You care. I feel like..." A shake of her head told him she was finding it hard to put the words together. "Well, like nobody cares anymore. I can stay close with my friends in the US, but do you know how few people I know here? Even after so many years here?"

"You're lonely?"

"I-I guess. The way you live, it's like a dream. You all care for one another. I love that. It's how I want to be. Where I want to be."

"You don't know all the facts," he said softly. "They might change how you feel."

"Tell me them, and let me decide for myself."

"They're not my secrets to tell, and they're deep, Sascha. Not facts I can just lay down in black and white. They need to be entrusted to you."

"Well, isn't that how relationships work? You don't just blurt out your deepest darkest secrets to people you don't know."

"I suppose you're right."

"There's no supposing about it," she teased. "Can't we just let this go with the flow, Mr. Micromanager?"

He grinned. "I am, aren't I?"

"You're trying to," she asserted, "but there's no point. This has to form naturally. If it doesn't work, then we'll all be sad I'm sure, but if we don't try, then there's nothing to work with, no?"

"Does that mean you'll let me zip up your dresses in the changing rooms?"

Her laughter warmed his heart. "Didn't realize you were like Kurt."

Sean's grin turned sheepish. "I still can't believe he did that."

"What? Watched me climax with another man?" Her laughter morphed into a hoot. "It surprised me more, let me tell you. Still made me come though. Hard, too. It was hot as hell." She peered at him through her lashes. "He does that often?"

"From time to time."

She reached forward, stunning the hell out of him by pressing a kiss to his nose. Before he could do more than process the ease with which she touched him affectionately, she was out of the car. Ducking down to stare at him through the driver's door, she chided, "Come on, then. I have dresses I need you to help me into."

Though he laughed, his cock stirred not only at the notion but at her tits, which—in her tight V-neck blousy dress, a first for her as he usually saw her in skirts—were dangerously close to falling free from the neckline.

"My eyes are up here, Sean," she teased, then she grabbed both of them and squeezed. "I'll let you play later."

The heat in her eyes matched the heat in his body. He chuckled. Somehow feeling a thousand pounds lighter because of her jovial ease as he climbed out of the car and studied her parking job while her swaying hips attached to that fine ass of hers headed to the parking meter.

Upon her return, he admitted, "You did a damn fine job."

She curtsied, pulling out her skirts then letting them flutter around her calves. "I always was good at the maneuvers," she told him conversationally. "I just couldn't stop crashing into things."

His eyes widened as she displayed the ticket on the dash, and then locked up the car, stacking the keys in her purse which she tucked under her arm.

"What are you gawking at?" she asked, brows high.

"You. You crashed into things? In a moving vehicle?"

"Well, I'm not a genius but without motion, there is no crash." She blinked prettily up at him. "Now who's the smarty-pants?"

He grunted. "How many times did you crash?"

"I totaled a couple of cars," she admitted, no shame to her tone, mind. Which had Sean's heart clutching with terror. "My dad kept getting mad, especially at the insurance premiums so he bought me the Caddy. He knew I loved vintage cars as much as I loved everything else vintage. He figured, and he was right, I'd learn to be more careful in a ride like that."

"That was a lot of faith he had in you," Sean said cautiously as she tucked her arm through his and they stepped off the side road where they'd parked, and headed for Regent's Street, which was barely a street away. They were approaching from Langham Place, and just around the corner, the delight that was Regent's Park was near to hand.

Though Regent's Street was probably where she usually shopped, he knew he'd have to direct her to Mayfair. The event Andrei was going to attend was… well, it called for a gown from one of London's most expensive districts.

As they headed onto the curving road with its tall and looming Victorian architecture, he grimaced at the sight of the crowds. Even this early in the morning, there were heaps of people.

Tourists, residents, workers alike.

They all bustled to and fro, adding to the mania of the moment. The busy streets teamed with cars, and bright red double decker buses were an incongruous sight as they married modern city living with history. Black cabs darted in and out of traffic, and bells from bicycles rang and hooted as people darted across the street without looking both ways first.

All in all, it wasn't hard to remember why he tended to buy things in bulk from his tailor on Savile Row. Shopping wasn't, and never had been, a fun pastime for him. Not so for Sascha, he could see though.

The teeming humanity had distracted him. Enough to realize he was waiting on a response from her. She jolted him from his thoughts as he tried to maneuver around an old man in a disability scooter who was intent on crashing into their ankles.

"Dad always believed in me," she murmured softly, tone just sorrowful enough to have him flashing a concerned glance at her. To be honest, he'd thought she wasn't going to reply, had mistaken her silence for avoidance. "He just didn't believe in me enough to allow our relationship to grow after my mother died."

Hearing her sadness at that, a sadness he felt for her, he murmured, "I'm sorry."

"Don't be. It's not your fault." She tightened her hold on his arm and straightened her back. "Thank you though. What about you? Your family? Devon mentioned something last night, and it made me wonder..."

"What did he say?" Sean asked, bewildered at the notion of Devon even mentioning anything to do with his kin. He loathed his father, and Sean couldn't blame him.

"He told me that he was basically an army brat. That he lived in Italy and Germany. But he also said that you were all so close because, and I quote, 'everyone leaves.'"

He grimaced. "Devon takes things too literally sometimes."

"You don't have to tell me that," she pshawed. "I was just wondering what he meant."

"They all believe we're gay and living in some kind of London-gay-*Big Love* household. Kurt's mother gets pissy about his living here, they consider it a kind of defection."

"Jesus. What year is it? 1958?"

He snorted. "They're old fashioned. And, to be honest, old. He was a late baby. It's sad though. He wants to visit from time to time, but they won't see him." Not since Kurt had divorced, at any rate.

Her grip on his arm tightened. "That's sad."

"It's how they want it."

"Does he get upset about it?"

"Not that you'd know." Sean shrugged. "You'll find that we'll share different things with you that we won't tell the others."

She turned her head up to look at him. "What are you trying to say?"

"That most information is issued in confidence. Just because we're a unit, doesn't mean the individual's needs are any less important."

"You mean don't tell Sawyer about something Andrei said, just in case he tells me something he's never shared with him before?"

"Yes."

"Makes sense," she remarked, her attention turning to the gleaming shopfronts as they finally headed onto one of London's biggest and brightest shopping hotspots. "I'll only discuss something another one of you said if I'm concerned. Like, what Devon told me, concerned me. I know something is going on, but I can see you're not going to tell me."

"He'll have to," was his immediate retort.

She sighed. "I knew something major had happened to him."

"There's a reason he's the way he is," was all Sean said.

"And what about you? What makes you tick?"

He grinned. "Me? I'm a simple man, Ms. Dubois."

"I doubt that," she chuckled.

"That's where you're wrong," he chided. "All this? The money, and the name… it means very little in the long run." And he wasn't lying. Over the years, he'd come to realize it was all bullshit.

The five of them were in very different spheres, and yet, the same bullshit came at them all. People were the problem, he'd come to realize. It was why, outside of their collective, they led solitary lives.

The fewer people they had around, the less aggravation there was in the long run.

They'd had many lessons over the years. Janna hadn't been the first, but she was the biggest reminder they'd had about being cautious with the women they shared. Kurt's mom's meltdown over his being gay had been another. Then, there were the rest of the parents. None of them really understood why they all lived together, with his own mother dismissing it as a 'bizarre kind of fraternity'.

With that kind of background, sharing anything of importance wasn't easy. Trusting someone not to judge, to just be a willing ear was difficult. After all, if one couldn't trust family, who could one trust?

And friends? They were transient, save for the four back at home.

They were family by choice, he knew. Kin, he'd discovered when he was young, and had no intention of leaving.

Devon wasn't alone in his desire for this situation with Sascha to become permanent. It was simply that he feared the repercussions less because he didn't have to deal with them. He'd dive into work, so deeply that they'd almost lose him... The last time...

Sean swallowed down the memory.

He had to make sure Devon was okay. That his family was.

None of them were blind to the harsh realities of life. Andrei and Devon had been touched by harshness at far too young an age, but Sean dealt with it on a daily basis. It was his stock in trade.

Maybe it made him a control freak, but he protected those close to him because he knew the pain of loss and couldn't bear the thought of losing one of his brothers. Especially not because a woman had fucked with their heads and had knocked them for six.

"I lost you for a moment," she said softly, squeezing his arm.

"I was just thinking about why we are the way we are."

"Oh? Come up with any great pieces of wisdom?" she teased, then added, "Kemo sabe."

His lips twitched, amused by the notion of her watching the old-school show that had been his father's favorite. "You're too young to even know what the *Lone Ranger* is."

"I've got Wikipedia like anyone else. Plus, they remade it with Johnny Depp," she chided, then tugging at his arm, asked, "Go on. Tell me. Remember, we're learning about each other, aren't we?"

He stared down into her bright green eyes and wished it wasn't so easy to get lost in them. They sparkled in the grim sunlight of a dark London morning, and even the splendor of Regent's Street, with all its glitter and glamor, couldn't match the deliciousness of her gaze.

"We're all quite reclusive."

"I've noticed that without your help," she retorted with a pout. "Tell me something I don't know."

"Doesn't it bother you?"

"No. I'm not exactly one for going out, am I?" At his blink, she gritted her teeth. "I'm not mocking. I mean it. And you're not reclusive. Well, most of you aren't. *Kurt* is. Devon too."

Sean nodded. "Kurt's been anti-social since he got divorced," he commented grimly; that particular period in Kurt's life had been disastrous from the get-go. But then, Katrin had been the wife from hell.

"He was married?" she demanded, gawking at him and pulling on his arm until he came to a stop.

Smiling down at her, he reached for a russet lock that had fallen from her loose but sexy topknot. Tucking it behind her ear, he then proceeded to tap her on the nose. "You'll have to ask him about that."

"I will," she huffed, stifling her inquisitive nature with a pout of her sulky bottom lip. "But, like I was saying, you're not reclusive, you're just selective."

He laughed. "I think you're splitting hairs."

"Maybe. But I can, can't I?" She winked. "You're busy men. It's not like you have time to go out dancing until dawn."

He cleared his throat, then cupped her chin. "If you want to go dancing until dawn, one of us will take you." He'd never been a lover of dancing, but hell, that didn't mean he wasn't willing to give it a try.

Her grin grew. Slowly. And her reaction made him grateful he'd stepped outside his comfort zone. "Seriously?"

He nodded, blew out a nervous breath. "This… it works both ways, Sascha."

"I guess it does," she said slowly, but if her smile was anything to go by, she was happy about that particular fact.

"You want to go dancing until dawn?" he asked, cocking a brow at her in question and wondering which poor sap would suffer through that for her benefit.

"No. But Devon said something last night that caught my attention."

"Oh?" he asked warily.

"He said if I wanted to, I could go on courses and things."

"Sure, that's not a problem. Whatever you want to do, there's always time for you to do it." His tone brightened at the prospect of not having to spend hours in sweaty clubs.

She pursed her lips. "I'm not a kept woman, Sean. I can pay for things myself… I'll even pay for whoever comes with me."

Wary once more, he asked, "Comes with you where?"

"To tango classes."

He coughed, then snickered. "Ask Andrei," he murmured, his voice a little hoarse. "He'd probably enjoy that."

"Why do I think that's a big lie?"

"Please. Just ask him. And make sure I'm there while you do."

She grinned. "Okay. I will. But, seriously, who would do that with me?"

"I would. Or Kurt." He wriggled his head from side to side. "We're both used to being in the public eye. It can't be too bad making a fool of yourself on a darkened dance floor."

"I don't know," she teased, then surprised him by curling around him, and in front of Regent's Street and God himself, grabbed a hold of his hips, and did a little shimmy against him. "You look like you might have rhythm."

"You're incorrigible," he informed her, his tone raked with gravel to hide his amusement.

She winked. "Maybe."

Before she could sneak away, he pressed a hand to her lower back, pulled her close, and with his lips hovering above hers, whispered, "You're playing with fire. You do know that, right?"

Her grin was wide, and dammit, youthful. How could she make him feel every one of the years separating them, and yet, make him feel young too?

The growing phenomenon that was Sascha Dubois, he supposed.

"I like fire," she whispered, smooth as silk, then leaned up on her stilettos and joined their mouths.

He wasn't sure who led the dance. Whether it was him or her. Just knew that at that moment, everything stopped. The whole world came to a standstill.

It was crazy, insane, and yet so fucking perfect, he knew the moment would stick with him for the rest of his life.

Probably longer than she'd stick with them, because Devon was right. Everyone left. But, she'd leave this memory behind, and he'd embrace it with all he had.

He supped from her, sipped at her essence, and returned it twofold. Her lips were soft, tempting morsels that invited a man to sin, and it was with a gusty sigh of delight that he fell into temptation.

She tasted of mint and coffee, with a dash of honey from that morning's granola. Her tongue explored his with an intensity that had his cock hardening, and he dragged her up against his chest, pressing her hips harder into him so her little wriggles would do more than just tease.

A throat cleared, and the sound jerked him from the dazed bubble she'd dragged him into. They pulled away from each other, softly caressing each other with intense eyes until a prune-filled voice stated, "You should be ashamed of yourselves. This is a public place."

He turned to face the onlooker. She looked as much of a prune as she sounded. "You don't like the show, you don't have to pay for the ticket."

The old woman gasped, pressed a leather-clad glove to her Hermes scarf-covered throat and strode off in umbrage.

Sascha grinned at him. "That was *not* how I thought you'd handle that."

"Maybe your American-laxity is getting to me," he joked. "Soon, I'll be word vomiting all over passersby who dare to watch us kiss."

She snorted, reached up again to dot a kiss to the corner of his mouth. "Word vomiting, huh?" She shook her head, but he could see her smirk. "You taste good," she breathed against his lips before dancing away, back to his side.

He peered at her as they started off down the street once more. "You're bright and breezy today."

"When aren't I in comparison to you guys?" she teased. "I'm not the major hotshot in my field."

"I don't know, you bring a certain spice to these hotshots' lives." He snorted at the phrase.

Is that how she saw them?

He'd admit to preening a little at that. Having always considered himself a bit of a geek, it felt rather enticing for her, this dazzling creature, to see them as something that sparkled.

"Now I'm on the inside looking out, I'll be certain to make things more Vindaloo than Madras."

"Now I know you've been living here too long," he jibed. "I doubt most Americans know what those dishes are."

She tapped her nose. "I've been to several 'Curry Miles' here, I'll have you know," she informed him, referring to streets filled only with yard after yard of Indian restaurants. Most cities had a 'Curry Mile'.

"We've anglicized you."

"I hope to be further anglicized," she retorted with a grin, then grabbing his hand, squeezed his fingers, and tugged him into walking down the street.

Their hands swayed with a swinging motion started by her, and her childish glee at what was going on around her charmed him.

She squealed with delight when she saw a large 'SALE' sign in a window, and braked to a halt to glance over the goods in the store.

"You don't have to buy everything on sale, you know?"

He'd admit to being amazed at how she darted here and there without ever really leaving his side. She tried on shoes, experimented with clutch purses, but only ever with items on sale.

He'd have stayed silent, but she did it with the first five shops they went to, and it looked set to be the trend of the day. A trend he was determined to put a stop to.

"Not all of this is for the gala," she told him absently, as she peered at a pair of stilettos that made his cock hard by what they did to her arse.

Sweet Jesus. The globes of her bum, so round and peachy, tautened up even more in those five-inch beauties.

"Can you walk in them?" he asked, eying their height doubtfully.

She grinned, dared him, "Catch me if I fall?"

He snorted, moved over ten steps away, then held out his arms. "Walk to Daddy."

The sales assistant's eyes flared at the comment, but he ignored it, ignored the rest of the store to watch her, giggling, as she swayed toward him with just enough sass that he wanted to take her to a changing room and fuck her right there and then.

She snuggled into his arms when she reached him, and demanded, "What do you think? Can I walk in them?"

He jerked his hips forward. "Have your answer?"

Her laughter was low, sultry this time. Not gleeful as it was before. "Glad to hear it." She slipped her hand between them and stunned the shit out of him by patting his cock. "The next store we go to had better have a decent changing room."

With those words, she hustled off, but she shot him a glance over her shoulder that had him panting.

The need to adjust himself was urgent, but instead, he positioned the bags he was carrying over his lap as he took a seat and watched her deal with the assistant.

Janna would have taken the card and bought everything in sight. Whether it was for the event or not. Helen, another ex, would have sniffed at the idea of going to a boring event, and would have refused to go. Kelsey would probably have agreed to go, would have dressed up, but in the end, would have cancelled. She'd been flaky. Irritatingly so.

He knew it wasn't right to compare her to past girlfriends, and he wasn't. Not really. She was different. He was just trying to ground himself, figure out exactly how she was different and make sense of it, so that he could rationalize this in his head.

Sean had to rationalize everything—even if it was to his own detriment. Only when he understood a situation, could it be categorized.

Sawyer said he was a nitpicker, but it was why they counted on him. He was the unelected 'head' of the household because he made sure all the I's were dotted and all the T's were crossed.

So, while he *knew* she fit them so perfectly, he had to ask *why?*

Seeming to know that Andrei actually did need a date but had no one he wanted to ask. Understanding that Devon needed to sleep more, so she'd slept with him last night, encouraging him to rest when he'd have stayed at his desk until morning—he had no doubt she'd been the one to encourage 'bedtime'.

Small examples, but important ones.

With narrowed eyes, he watched her brash American charm come out to play with the snooty assistant.

He didn't like the woman's snootiness, but understood the nearer they got to Mayfair, the more it would make an appearance.

Still, it pissed him off.

He could see the assistant judging her outfit, her very non-designer clothes, as well as the fact Sean was her companion and most definitely the wealthier one in the partnership.

Feeling a bit like Richard Gere in *Pretty Woman*—a movie he'd suffered through for his sisters—he got to his feet, strolled over, and retrieved a credit card from his wallet which he handed over to the assistant.

When she saw it, the exclusive card that only vendors in this particular area were accustomed to seeing, her attitude changed entirely.

From snotty to obsequious in less time than it took a Ferrari to hit sixty miles an hour.

Sascha grabbed his arm, hissed in his ear, "You're not paying for this."

He tugged her aside, bent down and murmured, "I want those stilettos around my ears, Sascha. They're my treat to myself."

Her mouth had dropped open at his words, and he congratulated himself on shutting her up and shocking her.

"B-But…"

"I know, you're not a kept woman. But like I said, they're my gift to me. Let me be selfish."

She gulped. "Around your ears, huh?"

"And digging into my arse."

"That can be arranged," she whispered, and he loved how the need he'd inspired made her tone raspy.

He winked. "I'll look forward to it."

She licked her lips, not to entice but out of self-defense, and blinking, stepped back toward the counter. The assistant had wrapped up the few items Sascha had bought and was waiting with a bright smile for Sean's PIN. The money she'd spent was negligible to him, but not to her. It charmed him that she hadn't expected him to pay. If anything, it made him want to spoil her.

Talk about inadvertent reverse psychology.

Smiling at his own folly, he grabbed the bag, added it to the collection in his hand, after he tucked his card back in the slot in his phone case.

"Ready?" he asked, ignoring the flirtatious smile sent his way by the attendant.

Sascha shot the other woman a cocky glance, held out her hand for his, and murmured, "Definitely."

As they headed back down the street, she stated, "She was totally checking you out." Then, Sascha sighed. "I can't blame her. You look hot today."

He cocked a brow at that. "I do?" He was wearing jeans and a T-shirt with a leather jacket. Hardly anything über sexy.

"Oh yeah. You make James Dean look like he's learning how to brood."

"I look brooding?" Now that came as a shock.

She smirked. "Your face is a card."

He chuckled at her teasing, liking how she made him lighten up. How she made the whole house sunnier. More buoyant.

Jesus, he hoped he wasn't putting too much into this. Into her.

Sighing, knowing that it was too late already, *fait accompli*, he asked, "Do you want something to eat?"

"Bored already?" she ribbed, then leaning into him, murmured, "I thought we were going to find a nice, sturdy changing room?"

He gritted out, "You were being serious about that?"

Her laughter was lighter than air and just as energizing. She grabbed his hand tighter. "I was being serious about that. Deadly serious."

"Fuck, we need to find somewhere. Now."

"Hard, baby?" she asked huskily as he half-dragged her down the street.

Before he could tell her his cock was so hard he could hammer nails into wood, she pulled him to a halt and jerked her hand from his.

When he looked down, wondering why she'd disconnected their fingers, she'd already gone like an ethereal sprite who darted into his life, snatched his heart from him, then took off into the night.

He blinked, sought her out. Saw her whizz to the right. Straight into the road where a car was heading directly for her and the little boy who was too busy trying to pick up something shiny from the asphalt.

A woman screamed, "Lewis!" as Sean cried, "Sascha! Wait!"

Leaping forward, he tried to grab her, tried to pull her back and get to the boy first, but he was too late.

He was always too fucking late.

His stomach didn't even have a chance to leap into his throat before the car struck. The boy, pushed out of the way by Sascha, started sobbing as he made it into the central line of the road to relative safety.

But Sascha wasn't safe. The vehicle glanced off her, tossing her into the air like a rag doll, knocking her down, and with it, breaking Sean's fucking heart…

HEALED BY THEM

SEVEN

"ARE you certain this isn't someone targeting you again?"

Sascha opened her eyes and immediately regretted it once the dim light pierced her retinas.

"Oh sweet, Lord," she gasped. Agony had words tumbling from her lips in an indecipherable torrent. She made to sit up then yelped when a sharp pain radiated up her right arm. Her *throbbing* arm. Her *'oh, my God, what the fuck is wrong with me'* arm.

What the hell?

The left arm wasn't much better she found. Her shoulder was creaky on that side, but the pain wasn't so intense. Still, she guessed that made up for the fact her entire body felt nothing more than a bag of bones.

A big bag of *aching* bones.

And why did her mouth taste like vomit?

When the hell had she puked?

"Sweetheart, it's okay. You're fine."

Sean.

She blinked, then regretted it when it felt like sandpaper scouring over her eyeballs. Pressing her fingers to her temple, she winced when she felt the bandage covering her forehead, and the soreness underneath. "Sean?"

"We're all here, baby."

Kurt.

She tried to focus for the tenth time and finally succeeded when her bedside came into view. Her very full and jam-packed bedside.

Before she knew what was what, a crowd surrounded her. Kisses were pressed to her cheeks and hair, her knees were squeezed, and someone cupped her foot.

After that exuberant greeting, she blinked blankly around, then wrinkling her nose, murmured the first thing that popped into her head, "This isn't an NHS hospital."

It most definitely wasn't a hospital in Britain's national healthcare system. She'd been in one before. They were all avocado green lino and stinky rooms.

This place was... *fancy*.

Yeah, a word not often associated with hospitals but this one was definitely overachieving in the looks department.

And the lack of bleach and cabbage odor in the air? *Bliss.*

"You're on the household plan," Andrei told her, his dulcet Russian tones the only soothing thing about this mad moment.

"The household plan?" she asked, dumbly.

Sean snorted. "I knew you hadn't read that contract thoroughly."

"Now probably isn't the time to be mad at her lack of critical reading skills," Kurt pointed out wryly, and she sent him a grateful glance which had him squatting down beside the bed, and reaching for her non-sore hand.

Oh! That reminded her. What the hell was going on with her hand?

She peered down at the cast with some astonishment. "What happened?" And why did her mouth taste gross?

"You don't remember?" Sean asked, concern lacing his tone.

She was grateful to remember anything with this banging migraine. Jesus. The pain.

As it stood, she was more than grateful to remember all their names.

Before her, in their looming gorgeousness stood her five bosses. She was their housekeeper of two months and lover of... well, it depended on how long she'd been in the hospital.

When did that even happen?

Huffing out a breath, she asked, "How long have I been here?"

"An afternoon?"

"That's it?" she squeaked, gawking at Kurt.

He nodded. "Feels a lot longer from our end, I promise you."

Sean let out a deep sigh, and she watched him sink heavily into a guest armchair. "I second that. You scared the hell out of me, Sascha. Fuck. Don't ever do that again."

He looked angry. Stern. At some point, he'd mussed up his black hair, the scowl splitting his forehead had her blinking at him in astonishment.

"I don't understand. What happened? What are you so mad about, and what the hell happened to my arm? It's aches like a bitch," she complained with a pout.

She understood that, for whatever reason, they'd been worried about her, but it wasn't fair for them to be all pissy with her when she didn't even remember what had happened.

Talk about unfair!

"You don't remember any of it?" Devon demanded, folding his hands on top of his taut belly. She really shouldn't have noticed that, not with her head aching the way it was, but Jesus, migraine or not, she was still a woman.

And boy, what a man he was. Nobel prize-winning, genius mathematician to boot.

"Obviously, there's something worth remembering. But whatever it is, it's a blur. Should I be concerned?" She frowned. "More than normal, I mean. A radioactive spider didn't bite me, did it?"

Sawyer snorted, and though his next words were mocking, his Scottish brogue was deeper than usual, rougher. He was worried about her. "She's okay. If she's well enough to be glib at the same time, I think we can chill out."

"Hey," she complained. "Where's my tea and sympathy? I thought Brits specialized in that shit."

Kurt chuckled. "You're on a losing streak with me, sweetie. Germans aren't exactly renowned for their softer sides." His deeds contradicted his words, however. He reached down and cupped her foot. Before she knew what was what, he'd dug his thumb into her arch, and headache be damned, nearly had her wriggling in the bed like a damn puppy as pleasure soared through her veins in response.

She released a whispering moan. "Screw the tea and sympathy; I'll stick with the German version." Close to panting as he massaged a sensitive part, she let out an honest-to-god whimper.

"I think she likes that, Kurt," Devon pointed out, with the clinical blandness of a doctor taking notes on a case.

She rolled her eyes because even though she was two seconds away from climaxing, broken arm and what she figured was a concussion be damned, Devon still had a way of amusing the fuck out of her.

"Which parts gave it away, Devon?" she egged on. He was making her worse, she knew. Her already sarcastic nature came in handy around the man who made Einstein look normal, but if you believed sarcasm was the lowest form of wit, then she wasn't the best person to be around.

Devon rubbed his chin, and taking her question seriously, studied her too hard. No longer feeling the whole doctor-patient vibe, but like bacteria in a petri dish, she groaned out an exasperated breath when he explained, "Your color has improved. You were looking a little green around the edges. But now, you're bright pink. Plus, you keep rocking your hips. Classic signs of arousal."

Andrei laughed, shaking his white-blond head in disbelief. "Like you'd even know! Most women come on to you, don't forget. I truly think you don't even need to touch their clit. They probably just listen to you speak a load of math, and climax instantaneously."

Devon blinked. Turning his topaz-blue gaze from his Russian friend, he pinned Sascha in place. "Is that possible?"

Around him, they all chuckled. He didn't seem offended, just confused. Which, she knew, was pretty much par for the course. While he could understand complex mathematical formulae, ask him to figure out the toaster, and she'd be better off asking the neighbor's cat, Tiddles, for help.

"What? What did I say?" he demanded, peering around the group.

Sawyer, standing behind him, squeezed his shoulder. "Well done, mate. You managed to lighten the atmosphere."

"I did?" His brow puckered. "How did I do that?"

Sean snorted. "Don't worry about it, Devon. But to answer your question, no, math doesn't cause spontaneous orgasms. Does it, Sascha?"

She grinned. "I don't know, Sean. Maybe Devon will have to try it out on me sometime."

Andrei nudged him in the side. "You're on a promise there, Dev."

"I am?" Devon eyed her. "What kind of promise?" he asked, his tone suspicious now.

"One that ends with us sweaty and satisfied. How about that?"

He beamed his kilowatt smile at her. "Do you go back on your promises?"

"Nope. Cross my heart. Ooh, and I'll throw in Scout's Honor. Now, back to the subject at hand. I can remember Tiddles, but I can't remember how I broke my arm. What's going on?" Something had to explain the nagging aches that were covering her body.

Had she fallen down the damn stairs? Was that why her head was banging harder than a heavy metal fan's in a mosh pit?

Kurt, now perched on the side of her bed, carried on massaging her foot, and told her, "You're a hero."

"Technically, a heroine," Devon corrected. "She's female, Kurt."

"This totally escaped my attention," Kurt retorted, turning around to roll his eyes at Devon. "Anyway, before we get sidetracked. *Again.* You saved a little boy's life."

Stunned, she blinked at him. "I did?" Why didn't she remember any of that?

Sean leaned forward in the mauve armchair which was part of a set in the private hospital room that belied the fact she was in a clinic at all. Hell, there was more thought and care taken with the décor in this room than there'd been in her last two apartments.

"He rushed onto the road to pick something up. You saw him, saw the car, dashed off before I could stop you. You pushed him out the way until he was in the middle of the street, but the car clipped you." He hunched his shoulders. "By the time I realized what you were doing, I didn't have a hope in hell of making it to you in time."

"I ran into the road?" she asked weakly, sinking deeper into the pillows cushioning her back. "I don't remember any of it."

Kurt gently rubbed her foot with his fingers. "That's perfectly normal according to the doctors. Luckily, there's no damage to the skull. You really must have a hard head," he teased softly, "But you've broken your arm."

"Her radius is broken," Devon corrected, making Kurt blow out an exasperated breath. When Andrei elbowed him again, he blurted out, "What? The radius is her wrist, not her arm!"

"Shut up," Sawyer said on a low hiss.

"No, it's okay. He's just trying to make sure I know all the details." When Devon preened at her defense, the rest of them either gritted their teeth, grunted in exasperation, or rolled their eyes.

"See," he said proudly, sending her the smile he should patent because it never failed to get her knickers in a twist.

Well, her panties.

Shit, the more time she spent over here, the more her English was being corrupted by the weird shit the Brits said.

Clearing her throat, she asked, "It's a regular break? Nothing complicated?"

"A simple fracture. Six weeks with the cast. Everything else... you're very lucky, we've been told." He shuddered. "While the doctor's idea of lucky differs to mine, he did say the hit to your head has given you a moderate concussion and they want to keep you in because of that.

"Kurt's going to spend the night with you while you're under observation. But you should be home tomorrow," Sean explained softly. He rubbed his nose. "If anyone asks, I'm your fiancé. I had to tell them that or they wouldn't have given me any information at all."

Fiancé. Boy, did that sound nice. As well as premature.

Waaaaaay too premature.

She bit her lip and peeped up at Kurt. "You don't have to. I'm sure you have better things to do."

He frowned. "What things could be better than making sure you're okay?"

She frowned back—and even that hurt, dammit. *Ouch*. The scowl pulled at whatever the hell was going on with her forehead—and had they taped some of her hair to the bandage too? *Fuck*. "I thought there were visiting times to abide by? And isn't it weird my fiancé isn't the one spending the night?"

"There are visiting times, but they don't count with us. A few of the rules can be stretched a tad where we're concerned."

"Why?" she demanded. "That's a bit unfair."

Sawyer snorted. "The nurses like us. Devon pays for their Christmas party every year."

That had her blinking in surprise—whatever she'd expected, it wasn't that.

Devon elbowed Sawyer in the side. "Shut up."

Before they could start bickering, Sean heaved out a sigh. "Anyway… Andrei and I have meetings, and Sawyer and Devon have to make a pitch to their board as well. We'll be in and out around those appointments, but Kurt's staying the night."

Kurt grinned. "I'm the wastrel writer. My time is the least precious."

Sean snorted. "Get out your violin, Andrei. I hear bleeding hearts."

Chuckling, Andrei hummed a quick tune under his breath. "We pity you, Kurt."

"Good," he retorted. "I deserve the pity. Just because I'm not changing the world one algorithm at a time," he finished with a very masculine pout. When she choked out a laugh, he winked at her. "But no, Sascha. It will be my pleasure to sit with you and make sure you're okay."

Warmth flushed through her because his look wasn't disinterested or irritated as her ex would have been at the prospect of spending the night in a hospital room—even one as swank as this one.

In fact, that they were all here was telling.

They give a crap, she realized.

They hadn't shoved this onto one person to deal with. All of them had taken times out of their horrendously busy schedules to come here and be with her until she woke up.

Even though she knew it was stupid, tears welled in her eyes. As one, they all noticed and froze in place. She gnawed on her cheek to stop the drops from falling, but she couldn't. They spilled forth regardless of her attempt to hold them in.

"Hey, we'll stay if you need us," Sean immediately told her, reaching over, he pressed a hand to her knee and gently squeezed.

"Of course."

"I can rearrange things..."

Agreements came in a four-strong variety, but she shook her head. "That's not why I'm crying. You need to go and do your stuff; that's fine with me. Having Kurt here is more than I expected."

"Then why are you crying?" Devon demanded, having gotten to his feet, his hands were stacked on his very trim hips, and his eyes were narrowed mulishly. She had to admit, he not only looked cute as hell but more confused than he'd been earlier regarding their conversation on trigonometry-based orgasms.

"Because I'm touched, silly," she whispered, a frog in her throat as well as the tears still prickling her eyes.

How could she not be?

All five of them had instantly reacted to her supposed upset and had told her they'd rearrange their lives for her... No one had ever done that for her before. Not since her mom had died.

And hell, she could remember enough to know that only yesterday, they'd consummated this strange relationship of theirs. Andrei had taken her on the sofa while Kurt watched, and she'd slept—actual REM sleep, not of the orgasmic variety—with an insomnia-stricken Devon.

Yesterday had been the first day of the rest of their lives together. For however long that life may be, and yet, here they were. Like they'd been together a decade. Their concern shrouding her in a comforting embrace that made her feel loved. Cherished. *Wanted.*

Gulping, she whispered, "Thank you for being here for me."

Sean sighed, and she could feel his relief that she was okay. "You're a priority, Sascha. That's how this works now."

She blinked, taken aback by the simplicity of his belief when that belief circled upon something that was so intrinsically complicated, very few people would ever be able to understand its dynamic.

Five men. One woman. The math was something only Devon and Sawyer would be able to theorize, because to everyone else in the world, she knew it would make zero sense.

But to the people in this room, herself included, it made perfect sense.

Perfectly, wonderful sense.

"I just wish I'd been in time to stop this from happening at all." He ran a hand through his hair, disheveling the already messy, silver-streaked chestnut locks.

She wondered if he looked like that after sex, or if he was more rumpled... Sascha couldn't wait to find out even as she was inwardly gawking at herself—these guys had her sex drive on overload even when she felt as shitty as she did!

Is that a good portent of the future or not? she asked herself.

"How could you have known?" she asked, dismissing thoughts of her weird sex drive as she sensed Sean's genuine distress and attempted to ease it. "It was an accident. Accidents can't be accounted for. Plus, if the car just clipped me, it would have driven straight into you." She shook her head—bit back a whimper as her brain rattled inside her skull. "Thank you for trying, but I'm glad you're safe," she tacked on hoarsely.

His smile was wobbly. "Just... What you did was amazing, but don't do it to me again, please?" He blew out a long, shaky breath. "I think you took about ten years off my life. Watching that car come for you was... Well, let's say it's something I won't forget in a hurry."

"I wish I could hug you," she told him quietly. "To apologize."

"Jesus, there's no need to apologize," he countered instantly. "But I do wish you could hug me too. Things were just getting interesting when you took a dive under a car."

"They were?" She grinned, the burn of tears disappearing at his statement. Sitting up with excitement, she winced as her head immediately began to pound. Pain had her curling in on herself a little, her shoulders hunching, but even as she was trying to remind herself to move as little as possible, Sascha demanded, "How? What were we doing?"

"We kissed, and we were about to have sex in the changing rooms."

"Shit." She pouted. She'd almost seen if that tousled hair got even messier in the post-orgasmic glow. "Raincheck?"

He snorted. "Without a doubt." Chuckling, his tone became somber as he asked, "Is it just this morning you don't remember?"

Trying to figure that out had her head aching harder, and though the act had her wincing, she scoured through her memory banks to hesitantly comment, "I think I remember why we were out. Andrei has a gala sometime soon, right? We were shopping for a dress I could wear there." She squinted as mining for thoughts triggered a sharp bolt of pain that sliced into her skull with the accuracy of an ice pick. "Ouch," she mumbled. "That hurt. But, I remember parking Baby close to Regent's Street. Just not much else after."

"Baby? Who the hell's Baby?" Devon demanded.

"Her car, idiot," Andrei pointed out with a scowl. "I'll cancel your RSVP at the gala, Sascha. You don't need to worry about something as unimportant as that."

She dropped her shoulders. "No way! I'll be fine by then. That is, if you don't mind me turning up with my cast! I think that's kind of non-negotiable." She crinkled her nose. "Not the swankiest of accessories, but I want to be there."

He leaned into the bed, his hands wrapping around the foot rail. "Are you sure?"

"I'm more than sure," she retorted stoutly. "It's happening."

Andrei's smile was—in a word—boyish. It morphed into a grin. "Does this mean I can pick the dress?"

She eyed him owlishly. "Do you really want to?"

Sean cleared his throat. "You do need to rest, Sascha. It's on Monday night, isn't it, Andrei?" When he nodded, Sean carried on, "I got a sense of your taste today. I could help him pick something out."

"Seriously?" She bit her lip, but couldn't stop her wide grin from blooming. "Okay, challenge set. Let's see if you can pick something I'd like." Not that she thought he'd lose.

Unlike her ex who'd barely noticed she tended to wear stuff with a vintage style, she highly doubted Sean, renowned and celebrated for his attention to detail, would have failed to spot she liked things kooky.

He rubbed his hands together, and she was relieved to see he looked less green around the edges than earlier. "Challenge accepted."

THE WARD WAS quiet when the other four left. The instant the door closed, Kurt settled in the armchair Sean had vacated to watch Sascha sleep.

Those last few moments; her eyelashes had been fluttering as she fought to stay awake. Only when they'd closed and stayed that way for a handful of seconds had the guys gone.

He'd been watching her ever since, but it was hard to sit beside her and not hold her.

The bruises were literal stains against her skin. Sharp and dark, they highlighted her creamy fragility, and made him want to rage on her behalf. She'd done a good deed; a little boy was alive because of her, and yet this was how she'd been thanked.

Bruises to her temple, across her cheek. Her jaw was swollen and red, and her left cheek had road burn on it.

He wanted so badly to wrap her up in his arms, and knowing she wouldn't reject his touch augmented his need all the more. Her acceptance of their unusual predilections had been confirmed the night before.

She'd slept with his friend while Kurt watched. She'd accepted comfort from them all, gentle kisses to her mouth as her relieved men greeted her upon awakening…

She was willing to be theirs, and he wanted to treat her as such.

Among themselves, they were ebullient, crass, but always friendly.

Though there were celebratory handshakes, half-hugs, and slaps on the back, they were, at heart, all men. Men's men, too.

Just because they shared a woman, and got off on it, didn't mean they wanted one another. Despite the heartfelt disbelief his mother had on that particular topic, he was straight. Ever since his divorce, he'd had very few relationships though, and he missed the advantages being in a relationship had.

Simple kisses, holding hands, hugs… Basic touch. Affection.

He'd felt the lack recently, and he wanted to make up for it. Especially considering her current battered state.

The need to hold her was one he was finding hard to fight. Though their own relationship hadn't developed that far, he wanted it with an eagerness that surprised him.

Finding one woman who suited five men should have been a statistical improbability, and yet, they'd not only found that one special lady who had fit in among them, they'd found a handful over the years.

Sascha, though, was different.

Of course, Sawyer and Andrei—ever rational—would tell him he was being a romantic, and maybe he was. There was no harm in that, was there? But she felt different.

Explaining that was harder than it should have been for a celebrated writer. But creating and weaving a tale around some of Germany's darkest days was easier than understanding his own heart.

Perhaps not to others, but to Kurt… He'd prefer to stick pins down his nails.

Digging into his pocket as he kept an eye on Sascha, he retrieved his cellphone. Within seconds, he'd opened up his WIP—work in progress—and was reading through the last few pages.

He'd been stuck on this part for the past three weeks. It wasn't like him to experience writer's block, but where this book was concerned, and the previous two in the series, he found the novels inordinately difficult to write.

After the fall of Hitler, within the power vacuum left behind, a force had risen from the dark into the light. As an organization, it had only ever belonged in the dark. The German Democratic Republic, or East Germany as many had known it, was a nightmare no one could dream up.

Why was it, he wondered, that the most extreme of parties always had the most liberal of names?

National *Socialism*. German *Democratic* Republic.

Two entities that were neither socialist nor democratic.

He rubbed his chin as he skimmed through the torture scene he'd been crafting for days. The knowledge that his grandfather or father might have been subjected to these techniques was more than he could handle at times.

Kurt often asked himself why he put himself through this personal form of torture. But using that word in this context often made him feel like a coward. Reliving this horrendous history through words… how could that in anyway compare with what his parent and grandparent had endured?

The comparison, as always, succeeded in making him feel nauseated. The text ended, leaving behind a white blankness that surprised him with its power to intimidate.

How could space be intimidating? But it was.

Blowing out a breath, he frowned as he clicked on the screen and started a sentence.

His editor had been ragging him for the past three weeks for the first half of the manuscript, but he was barely a quarter of the way through the intended plotline he'd formulated for the novel.

Pressure normally inspired him. He had a way of working well when stress was bogging him down, but this time, it wasn't doing anything other than making him nervous.

It was an odd admission to make but he kind of wished he hadn't won the Pulitzer. Then, he felt like a dick, because that Pulitzer had highlighted his work, brought more of the horrors that had been everyday life in East Germany to the twenty-first century. People forgot, seemed to view it as a kind of divine punishment for the Second World War, but what had replaced the Nazis had been a tyrannical power that the world needed to know about.

How could he regret shining a light on that?

Yet, he did.

And it made him feel selfish as hell.

Grimacing, he stared at the document, trying to magic up the next line, another paragraph, one more page worth of stimulating and engaging narrative… Instead, he jolted in his seat as his phone buzzed in his hand with an incoming call.

"*Scheisse,*" he spat under his breath, then grinned at himself for jumping like a little girl. Shooting Sascha a look, and seeing she was out for the count, he accepted the call. Deciding to speak in English so that the harsh and alien German wouldn't disturb Sascha's sleep, he murmured, "Katrin? The Decree Nisi came through three months ago. I was hoping you'd deleted my number."

"Like you'd deleted mine?" came the purred retort that had him rolling his eyes. Katrin seemed to believe that she was a sex Goddess. Her sole duty on Earth to spread the love around. Hence the forty cases of adultery he'd used in his divorce suit against her.

"Forewarned is forearmed. I can't screen call if I don't know who's calling, can I?" he retorted.

She still had the power to irritate him, something that angered him more. She meant nothing to him. Hadn't for a long time, and yet, here she was, disrupting his day.

With his eyes on Sascha, he had to shake his head. Katrin was old world elegance. Sascha was vintage charm. Like him, Katrin came from old money, so she could afford to be elegant. It was a state she cultivated. Sascha was far more innocent, far more naïve.

He doubted she'd agree with that statement, though.

Like he wielded the word as a sword meant to cause offense, he thought with an inner smirk. If anything, it was a compliment.

After his ex, the last thing he wanted was contrived interaction with yet another woman.

"I'm hurt, *Liebchen,*" she remarked, a genuine note of sorrow to the endearment.

"Yeah? That's a first. I didn't manage to wound you in all the years we wasted together."

"All the years?" she snorted. "We lived together for maybe a full year of those six we were officially wed. The rest of the time you spent with *them*."

Kurt sighed. *This* was what had fed his mother's horrified belief he was gay, and that the house where they lived was the scene for nightly orgies and unchristian acts of debauchery.

Katrin fed it, and fed it well. If he had one regret about his marriage, and the truth was, he had many things to regret, it was the fact Katrin had grown so close to his mother. It meant she listened to the shit Katrin spilled. Still, to this day, Margritte couldn't understand why he'd divorced her. Even though he'd had proof of over four dozen acts of adultery.

Considering Katrin knew his taste for watching, that she'd chosen to cuckold him without letting him join in, her affairs spoke a lot for her intentions.

Sighing again because this conversation was an old, oft repeated, and damn boring one, he asked, "What do you want, Katrin?"

"Your help."

"Why?" He frowned. She'd never needed his damn help before.

"Andrei won't return my calls. I need him to look into my investment portfolio. I think my hedge fund manager is… Well, I don't know what's going on. I just don't trust it."

Kurt let out an amused laugh. "This has to be a first, Katrin. Are you on bended knee asking me?" he mocked. "I'd like to see that." The ways in which she'd verbally castrated him over the years, he'd probably snapshot the scene just to relive it.

Well, maybe not.

His bitterness *was* fading. In fact, he'd barely thought about Katrin since Sascha had entered their household. She had a way about her…

When Snow White used the forest creatures to help her clean up the Seven Dwarves' home—that was Sascha. Well, without the dress. More like a pencil skirt so tight it looked like the seams could split at any moment—a sight he'd pay to see, and one he'd take immediate advantage of—and a blouse fitted to her waist with such tight tucks, her breasts looked like they could spill out.

Plus, Sascha was a redhead, not brunette. Shit comparison, he guessed, but that kind of bouncy joy Snow White had seemed to emanate? That was Sascha too.

She'd come into their lives, and with the help of bluebirds and fucking squirrels, managed to sweep out the shit.

Katrin broke into his thoughts with a huff. "Kurt! Are you even listening to me?"

He cast a look at Sascha, studied her peaceful expression and felt a smile curve his lips. "I don't have to anymore," he told her, and he knew he should be ashamed at his gleeful tone, but he found he couldn't be.

"I need your help, Kurt. How can you be so cruel?" Before he could answer, tell her that she'd know because she was the queen of cruelty, she inserted, "I could ask Margritte."

He snorted. "I'm usually in my mother's bad books, Katrin. You throwing me further into the shit won't do me much harm. No more than you've already done our relationship anyway." Though his tone was mocking, that was only for her benefit.

His at-odds relationship with his mother was a constant source of pain.

He'd lost his father at a young age to a Stasi prison cell. She and his paternal grandmother had been all the family he'd had left. Though his father had eventually returned to the family home, what had happened to him had changed him forever. However he'd been tortured, it had damaged him permanently. Now, with *Oma* gone, and his father a living ghost, Kurt wished he and Margritte were closer.

He'd tried and failed to please her over the years. Marrying Katrin had been one such attempt, but the divorce had been the final straw for Margritte; not only from the shame but because he'd moved back into the Kensington house. As a result, he hadn't heard from her in two years.

The saddest thing was, he didn't miss her. She was too demanding, too invasive and insistent. Life was easier without her in it, and he hated that. Wished it weren't so.

"Please, Kurt," she whispered, her haughtiness fading in a way that told him she was genuinely concerned. "Speak to Andrei. I need him to investigate."

"Sean's the investigator," Kurt retorted, reshifting his phone against his ear so it was more comfortable and kicking his legs out, so he could cross his feet at the ankles.

"You know what I mean," she spat. "I need Andrei. He's a quantitative analyst. I need him to look into this situation, see where my money has gone."

He clucked his tongue. "Always about the Euros, Katrin."

She hissed, and he could imagine her stamping her foot against the ground in exasperation. Yeah, she really was that big of a brat. "This is about theft, Kurt! You know that. Please, speak to Andrei. I know he hates me. But we don't have to meet in person. I can send the files over."

Kurt rubbed his chin, but as he deliberated his answer—genuinely unsure as to whether or not he'd help—she whispered, "Kurt, you have every reason to hate me. I wouldn't ask you if I wasn't scared. And I am."

Though Kurt's family had wealth, that was nothing to Katrin's—a fact that might have changed with his recent success with his writing, but either way, he'd never sought out an alimony payment. Had been grateful to get out of the marriage with his balls intact, his manhood dented only slightly rather than sliced through.

Her fear was the only thing that would probably pierce the armor he'd developed over years of dealing with her.

That she was worried enough to feel fear, had him wondering how much she'd lost. It must have been a lot. Millions. Maybe even tens of millions for her to sound this overwrought.

"I'll talk to him."

With that, he cut the call. Blowing out a breath as the screen reverted to his Word document, he was about to save the paltry few words he'd written, when Sascha murmured, "I didn't think you were going to help her for a moment."

His gaze cut to hers. "Hey. I thought you were sleeping."

"I was," she said with a smile. "Now I'm not."

"I'm sorry if I woke you," he told her regretfully.

"You didn't. The pain was bad. Anyway, they'll probably be waking me up soon to check on me if I have concussion."

He looked at the clock on his phone. "Another ten minutes. You'd only been sleeping for about three-quarters of an hour."

"Really? Feels like I was asleep for hours." She studied him a second, a tension to her face that had nothing to do with the pain she was in. "Who was that on the phone?"

"My ex-wife."

She tilted her head to the side. "Acrimonious split by the sounds of it?"

He grunted. "What gave it away?"

"I heard her side of the conversation. At the risk of sounding like a Mother Hen, you have your phone set way too loud than is good for your hearing." Her teasing smile fell off the mark. "I didn't hear the start of the call though, what did she want?"

"To use me again," he told Sascha without bitterness.

She pleated the blanket between her fingers. "It sounded like she was genuinely scared."

"You have good ears," he murmured wryly, watching her concede that by wrinkling her nose. "That's the only reason I said I'd help her. Katrin is… she's very good at manipulating people. I escaped that wonderful fate a long time ago. I have no desire to be embroiled in it again."

"So why have you?"

"Technically, I've embroiled Andrei in it, and he can always say no. He's under no obligation to help her—not after the way she treated him. But, in all the years we were together, I've never heard her scared." He shrugged. "I don't have to like her to behave with basic human decency."

She shuffled about on the bed. "Dammit," she grunted out after a few minutes of shuffling. "Can you help me sit higher?"

His lips twitched. "The remote is beside your good hand. I put it there earlier."

She cast him a grateful, all be it, shamed glance. "Sorry for snapping."

"You didn't. You're uncomfortable, in pain, and in a hospital ward… I'd expected you to behave worse than you've done so far." He grinned. "I'd have offered to help, gladly, but I didn't think you'd want me panting over you."

The bed began moving at the start of his remark, but by the last comment, it froze as her finger slipped off the button. Their eyes caught and held as they'd done only yesterday when he'd watched Andrei fuck her in the living room.

She licked her lips, but her eyes—already heavily lidded after the day's events—seemed to fall into a deeper half-mast. "I'm not up to word games," she said hoarsely. "My head aches too much."

He wrinkled his nose. "They say orgasms are good for pain management. In a few days' time, feel free to test the hypothesis out on me."

Sascha snorted, then plucked at the sheets, settling them on her lap as the top half of the bed shifted higher so she wasn't lying flat. "I might do that. My head doesn't appreciate the banging, but my pussy probably would."

A laugh escaped him. "And you said you weren't up for word games."

She winked at him, making his laugh deepen. "That's as much as I'm capable of." A heavy breath escaped her. "I'm not sure if I'm horny now or hurting." With her good hand, she rubbed her temple then let out a little grunt. "Wow, it hurts. And I think they caught my hair under this stupid bandage." She gently fingered the gauze on her forehead. "What's even under there? Can I take it off?"

"One of many cuts and bruises, and no. They wouldn't have put it on there, silly, if it wasn't necessary. Do you want the nurse to adjust it or to grab you some pain meds?" he asked, sitting up, preparing to head out and seek help if she needed it.

Sascha held up her hand—cast and all—then as pain crossed her features at the jerky move, gritted out, "No, it's okay. Women can go through childbirth without an epidural. I can deal with a headache. I'd kill for some water though."

He blinked at her even as he passed her a bottle he had at his side. "Okay. I'm not sure what one has to do with the other. And don't drink too much. You've already been sick a few times. There's a reason you're being monitored."

"I didn't expect you to understand the correlation between labor and my headache," she said with a snort, then moaned in delight after she took a small sip of water. "Anyway, they won't give me anything. Not with a concussion." She winced. "I'll just have to put up and shut up."

He frowned, remembering something the doctor had said—that the headache might last for days. "I should tell Andrei to cancel your RSVP for definite. You might still have the headache when it comes time for the gala."

"Don't you dare," she snapped, half sitting up, then letting out a shriek of pain before she sank back against the covers.

He leapt up, hovered over her. Hating that he couldn't help her, hating that he was fucking useless. "What can I do?" he demanded.

She gulped. "Nothing. Just…" Blowing out a breath, Sascha whispered, "Just don't cancel the RSVP."

"Why?" he asked, a confused scowl puckering his brow. "What's so important about the gala?"

"Andrei was so… I don't know, dismissive? When we were talking about the gala. But he said it was a big deal. He shouldn't be alone when he makes a keynote speech."

Touched on his friend's behalf, his smile grew slowly.

This.

It was *this* that made him think of her as their Snow White. She'd bounced into their world, intent on making things right in ways that no one had ever tried. Even going so far as to attempt to fulfill their kinky needs.

Of course, she had to share those kinks for it to work, but he knew this was the first time she'd ever contemplated sleeping with five guys at the same time. Sean had said as much, anyway.

Still, with the other lovers they'd shared, no one had given a fuck about their career. Well, outside of the prestige of their positions, that is.

Devon's girlfriends usually fell for his brains, sure, but it helped that his Rain Man tendencies were softened by a bank balance that could cushion any verbal slight he had a habit of inflicting upon people. With the rest of them, they all held positions of power, and he didn't doubt that the women they'd shared had known and appreciated their status. They'd had careers of their own. It wasn't that they were solely after their money, he conceded with ease, but nothing like this.

They hadn't *cared*.

The difference was enormous.

"Why are you looking at me like that?" she asked crossly as she rubbed at her temple again.

"Thank you," was all he said.

"For what?"

"Giving a shit."

She blinked at him. "Oh."

His smile was warm. "Yeah. *Oh*."

EIGHT

MOVEMENT HURT.

Seriously.

Jesus, she was supposed to dance tonight too. Well, okay, Andrei hadn't mentioned dancing. He'd just mentioned a speech. And he was an economist. Or, if what she'd heard on the other end of a phone call the other day was right, a quantitative analyst.

Even googling that hadn't clarified things.

Maybe she was still a little dumb thanks to the whole being hit with a car thing, but humanities people never gelled well with math people. At least, she was going to use that argument and defend her dumbness with every ounce of her being.

Someone had to take a stand against all the geniuses in this damn house.

Sinking into the sofa with a grimace, the sofa she'd been fucked on by her date a mere four days ago, she rested her head against the plush cushion, and tried to get comfortable.

Of course, it was impossible. Her head was… She didn't know what it was. Equal parts concrete and mush, she felt sure. Nothing was soft enough for it, and after seeing footage of what had happened that day at Regent's Street, she could understand why she was feeling so delicate.

Fortunate was an understatement, she knew. In fact, it was more than that. She had a guardian angel or somebody watching out for her. That was the only explanation as to why she'd come out of that scrap with a broken wrist and a sore head.

Okay, sore was an understatement. Tits in a meat grinder probably ranked lower on the list of how badly her head ached. The nausea it triggered was adding to her woes, but after being flung through the air like a goddamn Raggedy Ann doll-gone-trapeze-artist, it was still hard for her to believe she was all in one piece.

The car on the opposite side of the road had been scant seconds away from running over her damn head. *Tits through a meat grinder* was probably how her noggin would have looked if that had happened.

"You look uncomfortable."

She blinked—even that hurt today—but didn't bother tilting her head to see who spoke. She recognized the voice—though he used it rarely, as he was probably the quietest housemate here, Sawyer's voice nevertheless packed a punch.

He had a kind of brogue that did things to her insides that insides had no place feeling; especially when she was as wrecked as she was.

His Scottish accent had him rolling his Rs and calling her things like 'lass'.

Be still my quivering heart, she thought wryly.

"I *am* uncomfortable," she admitted, voice hoarse with the truth of that as well as her body's response to his gorgeousness—the timing of which was nothing short of inappropriate.

He sighed, a pained look crossing his face at her words, then stepped into the room. She'd noticed he was often ill at ease when Devon wasn't around, which kind of saddened her. She felt like she was learning them all, bit by bit, but Sawyer was the hardest to crack if she was being honest.

Devon was, in his own way, a loudmouth. Used to blurting out whatever shit came into his head at whatever moment—didn't matter if that moment was appropriate or not.

She figured Sawyer was so used to trying to calm situations down that Devon riled up, he allowed himself to fade into the background.

He was a watcher.

Just not the same kind of watcher as Kurt, she thought with a snort. A snort that had her whimpering a little as the tiny vibrations made her eyes ache.

When he settled beside her on the couch, she carefully tilted her head to look at him.

"You doing okay there, lass?" he asked, tone gravelly with a concern that made her pussy ache.

Bad pussy!

Talk about her body giving out mixed messages!

"No, not really," she said, hoping she didn't sound as pathetic as she felt.

"Would a massage help?"

"Is one in the cards?"

His lips twitched. "Aye. It can be."

Aye? Ugh, Jesus. If he spoke any more archaically, she'd spontaneously orgasm. Headache be damned. "Do you speak Gaelic?" she asked, ever hopeful.

Her out of the blue question had him blinking. "It's a dying language."

"So? If anyone was weird enough to learn a dying language, it would be someone in this house."

He smirked, and the cocky, megawatt grin was capable of challenging Devon's beatific smile to a game of rock, paper, scissors. And God only knew how Devon's affected her… She wasn't sure whose smile would win in such a contest, was just grateful their lips belonged to her for the foreseeable future.

Sheepishly, she thought, he admitted, "I speak Gaelic."

That whole emoji with hearts for eyes thing? Yeah, that was her right then. "Damn. You need to speak to me in Gaelic."

He chuckled. "Maybe when you're ready to be bowled over."

"Bowled over into bed?" She considered that and his nod. "You're right. What with you and Andrei, you could probably make me come from words alone."

"I thought Devon was supposed to wreak that particular miracle."

"Between you and me, math doesn't compare to Gaelic and Russian."

His chuckle deepened. "You're crazy, you know that, right?"

She winked—regretted it after, and made a note not to do *that* again today. It would seem even her eyelids hurt. "Takes one to know one."

"What about Kurt?"

"German doesn't do it for me. Although, his accent is cute. I like when he swears in German. *Scheisse* and *Arschloch* sound so much worse than shit and asshole."

He rubbed his chin and confessed, "Never thought about it, lass, if I'm being honest."

"That's because you're a math guy. Math people don't think about things like this."

"Is that right?" he asked, sounding amused. She was used to that though.

In a way, she and Devon were kindred spirits. She had *some* decorum. But her thoughts rarely ran along lines that could be considered 'normal'.

"Aye, lad, that's right," she mocked, pronouncing 'right' like 'reet'.

He winced. "Jesus. Stick to the American accent, Sascha."

Her lips pursed into a pout. "You're supposed to be nice to me. I'm hurting," she whined.

"I offered a massage, didn't I?"

It was her turn to wince. "I'd love one, but I don't think I could." Biting her formerly pouting lips, she whispered, "Promise you won't say anything?"

He cocked a brow. "To who?"

"Anyone in the house."

Curious, he asked, "Okay. I promise."

"I'm not sure how long I'll be able to stay at the gala tonight, but I refuse not to go."

His frown was so loaded with concern, she couldn't cope. These guys… what was it with them?

Hell, her dad had barely looked up from his paperwork when she'd told him she'd broken her foot back in high school. The stepmother from hell had actually shown more concern.

Yet these men?

It was like she was the center of their world, and Jesus, was it potent. And addictive.

How had any of the women before her learned to do without it?

It was overwhelming, sure, but at the same time, it was empowering. It made her feel like she could do anything, *be* anything because these five insanely intelligent men saw something in her, something that made her special enough to be able to be with them.

Not just one of them, but all of them.

She'd have shaken her head at her thought process if she hadn't known the agony triggered by that particular mistake—one she'd made too many times in the past few days.

He rubbed his jaw at her words. "I'm not going to convince you not to go, am I?"

"Nope," she retorted stubbornly. "I'm going to be there even if it means I need to get high on Ibuprofen first."

He grunted. "Let's see if we can make you feel better with a massage, huh?"

She blinked. "Everything hurts. I can't see how you massaging it will make the pain go away."

"I can be gentle," he retorted with an eye roll. "Come on. If you're going to be stupid and do what you want regardless of your own health, something every single one of us would cherish more than a visit to a damn gala where we're keynote speaker, let's try to make you feel better first."

She scowled at him. "He should have someone there with him."

Her statement had him grunting, but otherwise, he ignored her as he maneuvered himself so that he could slide his hand under her knees then the other behind her back. "I'm going to lift you, when I do, move your good arm and support your head."

"You won't drop me, will you?" She eyed his brawn with concern.

"I'm offended," he said with a snort.

She huffed. "Everyone knows that bodybuilders actually have very little muscular strength."

"Yeah, well, I'm not a bodybuilder." He huffed back at her. "Ready? Three, two, one…"

Flinching when he lifted her, but managing to hold and support her head with her hand, he carefully moved away from the sofa, then gently stepped towards the door.

Gulping, Sascha murmured, "This is such a bad idea."

He cocked a brow at her as he maneuvered her through the door. "It is?"

"Yeah. I'm not ready to have your hands on me. I'm going to want to cum, and even though that will feel great, the aftermath won't be worth it."

Her words had him freezing in place. Then, hissing out a breath. "Jesus Christ. You're as bad as Devon."

Because her thoughts had run along similar lines earlier, she had to smile.

"Stop looking so proud of yourself," he retorted, returning to the earlier caution with which he'd moved as he carried her down the hall.

"Why? I managed to stun you. I don't think that's something that happens often without Devon around."

"No. You'd be right on the mark there, lass." His grunt was more from disgust than from effort as he, *effortlessly,* carried her up the fucking stairs. To the fourth floor in the five-story house.

Okay, if that wasn't enough to make a woman melt, she didn't know what could do it.

By the time they made it upstairs, all thoughts of arousal had dispersed to dust. "Ow," she whimpered as he carried her into his bedroom.

She'd tidied his room when on the hunt for dirty laundry, so she knew what it looked like. But it was the first time she was there in anything other than her 'official' capacity.

Amazing, wasn't it, how the same object could appear totally different when she was changing the sheets, and now, with the prospect of laying atop it, it could feel like another bed? Another bedroom, in fact.

The bedroom was one of the plainest in the house. A bed, two bedside tables, and a large armchair nestled by a bay window that overlooked the back yard. That was it.

She loved it on her rounds. It was the easiest to pick up after. Now, there was a comfort in the white walls, the white sheets she'd pressed herself… it was clean, calm, soothing. Quiet in more ways than just the nonexistent décor.

With a wince, she allowed herself to be pressed onto the firm mattress. It was one of those space agency ones, where the minute you pushed your butt into it, you were glued there for all eternity.

This time, however, she quite liked the sensation. It was supportive on her weary bones. Just because she hadn't broken anything else, didn't mean the rest of her wasn't bruised and sore from being hurled against the ground by a moving vehicle.

"You need to roll over, Sascha," he murmured, his voice so low it was like a hum. When she grimaced, he asked, "You need help?"

A sigh escaped her. "I think I do. Jesus, I hate being so incapacitated."

"It won't be for long," he reassured her, carefully supporting her neck as he helped guide her onto her front.

With her face smushed into the sheets, she groaned. "Shit. We didn't take off my shirt."

Silence followed her words.

"Sawyer?" she asked, more into the sheets than at him.

"You wanted to be naked?"

"Well, half-naked," she retorted with a quick smirk that he couldn't have seen anyway. "Isn't that how massages work?"

He cleared his throat. "True. But it's okay, I can pull it off just as easy like this."

She wasn't sure how that was possible, was just grateful that she wore a baggier than usual man's shirt.

Hearing him moving around, curiosity almost got the better of her. But she stayed in position, appreciating the change from laying on her back, and having different muscles aired and others supported.

The sound of his shoes clicking against the floor as he toed them off was one she immediately recognized. Another, a drawer whistling open then closed before he retrieved something that clunked against the white enamel bedside tables. She felt and heard the mattress squeak as he climbed onto it, and she'd admit to being too exhausted and downright weary to feel anything more than relief at the prospect of having some of her aches massaged away.

A few days ago, pre-car crash, she'd have been too busy humping Sawyer's leg to wait for him to dally around doing God knows what. Now, she had no choice but to be patient, because her body wasn't going to let her do anything else.

His hands came to rest on her waist. She felt his knee settle in a kneeling position beside her left thigh, the heat from his body radiating against her skin. His fingers were strong, warm. That warmth seeped into her bones, and she nestled deeper into the sheets, knowing she was about to enjoy this.

He tugged at the hem of her shirt and she pulled her stomach in and raised her butt to release any pressure on the fabric. It wasn't too hard for him to work the shirt up to her armpits, baring the majority of her back.

"You can try to pull it over my head," she told him. "I'll deal with the pain if it means you working at my shoulders."

He snorted. "You're a bossy little miss, aren't you?"

She sucked in a breath when he did as she'd asked; quickly lifted the fabric over her shoulders and head. When she settled back into the plush comforter, Sascha would admit to feeling dizzy and sick with the movement. It took her a few seconds to whisper weakly, "Sometimes. Not always for my own good though."

"I'd never have guessed. Need a keeper," he commented gruffly, but before she could reply to that cheeky remark, she let out a gasp as cold liquid suddenly pooled at the base of her back. The scent of sandalwood, oranges and cloves whispered through the air, perfuming her skin and the bedroom with its seductive scent.

"You could have warned me," she grumbled, but sighed happily as he made a 'W' with his hands at the base of her back by resting his thumbs together, then dug them into the muscles.

"No point. You'd have tensed more." As he worked his fingers into knots she hadn't known she'd had, making her force herself to stay still so as not to wriggle and cause a deeper headache, he murmured, "Jesus, the bruises on you, Sascha. You look like we've been beating you."

"You just try it, buddy," she warned him drowsily, moaning as he ran his thumbs along the side of her ribs, letting his little fingers drag against the plumped edges of her bared breasts. She knew going bra less had been the best decision today. "I know how to defend myself."

He chuckled. "You do, do you?"

"Aye, I do," she said in a mock brogue. "My dad's a cop. He busted enough pedos, rapists, and pervs to scare me into learning how to protect myself from predators. Now, I can prey on them. How the world turns," she finished triumphantly.

"I'm certain it does, lass. Not much use against a car, though, was it? You're black and blue. No way you can wear that dress tonight, Sascha."

"Dress?" She popped an eye open with interest, but it wasn't enough to induce her to tilt her head or to turn around to look at him. "Sean picked a dress for me?"

"He did. A few. But the one we all settled on, no way you can wear it."

She blinked, charmed by the notion of five guys choosing her dress. Maybe she shouldn't have found it as amusing as she did. It was a decision made for her, when she was more than capable of making it for herself.

Totally unnecessary because she'd been a big girl for a long time, after all.

But, Sascha couldn't find it in her to take offense. Like five boys arguing over baseball stickers or Pokémon cards, she likened them to discussing the pros and cons of her outfit.

Which had the easiest access?

Which showed more of her boobs?

Which would frame her ass?

They were questions that stirred her up inside in more ways than one.

She wriggled her butt at the thought, and he tapped her gently on the curve of her ass, making her eyes widen in response. "Don't move. You'll make your headache worse."

Sascha cleared her throat. "Is the dress sexy?"

"With five guys in charge, what do you think?" he retorted, but she could tell he was teasing. His voice was always so serious. Like he rarely had time for laughter.

But then, they were all like that. Like their work was a weight that shrouded their lives, and didn't give them much escape.

Of the five, she knew Devon was the smartest. Of course, they didn't care about rank, but she did. Not because of any kind of 'status', but because she'd realized the men treated the cleverest in an unusual way.

Devon, they usually helped, chided, or chivvied. They moaned over his antics, grimaced at his responses, and tried to save him from himself if he, for example, accidentally set fire to the curtains—a failed attempt at lighting a fire in the hearth, or so he'd told her. More like he'd been in a fit of pique over some of his work and had tried to burn his workings out!

Andrei and Sawyer came next, she knew.

Sean and Kurt had their own smarts. They were more than just highly intelligent. They too were, without a doubt, geniuses. With reputations to match, and prestigious peers who spoke of them with great regard.

But Sawyer, who could keep up with Devon—just the thought beggared belief—was sensitive, she'd come to realize. His quiet nature reminded her of a still lake. The surface didn't ripple with movement, but underneath, so much was going on, so much that onlookers could only guess at.

Behind his shamrock green eyes, she felt certain there was a whirl of activity going on, and she for one wanted to mine it.

His hands ran along the length of her spine, stopping at her shoulders. When he began to work on those muscles, she nearly sobbed with both pain and relief. Every time his thumbs accidentally swept up into her neck, she had to withhold curses, but as he worked, sometimes gently, sometimes with a pressure she felt certain would have her bones caving in—ouch—she realized she wasn't so tense.

She felt pink. Hot and flushed. But the nausea had gone, as had the dizziness. The pain in her head was a dull throb, but nothing she couldn't handle, she realized with astonishment, and as she processed that, another realization came to her.

She was horny.

Really, really horny.

Fuck.

If he slipped his hands down the loose fabric of her sweatpants, she knew what he'd find, and Sascha found that she didn't give a damn. If anything, she wanted him to touch her.

"How's that, sweetheart?" he asked, breaking into her dirty thoughts with a huskiness that warmed her.

Either he was as affected by this as her, or the huskiness was just a manifestation of his affection.

She liked the idea of both options, truth be told. Sascha wanted him to be turned on, but she also loved the prospect of his voice being weighed down by caring.

"It's much better," she admitted, stunned by her own voice which was sounding a little raw and a lot needy.

She felt the bed shift, the pressure points where his knees were pushing into the mattress moving with him as he bent down and touched his lips to the back of her head.

"There anywhere else you need massaging?"

Oh Jesus, that was practically an invitation, wasn't it?

Swallowing, she whispered, "A little further down?"

He froze above her. She wasn't sure if it was in rejection or just surprise, then a husky chuckle sounded from behind her, and the bed shifted once more as he bent over her, and against her ear, whispered, "You feeling needy, lass?"

Sascha blinked. *Needy*? That wasn't a word she particularly appreciated, but was now the right time to tell him when he might make her cum?

Decisions, decisions.

Correct him on his poor word choice or potentially get an orgasm.

No contest.

With a grunt, she carefully rolled over—knowing full well she'd hate herself later on when it came time to laundering these sheets and trying to get the damn oil out of them—and lay flat on her back without too much stiffness working against her. His looming over her enabled her freedom of movement, and she watched his throat work as his gaze dropped down to look at her breasts with covetous eyes.

"Fuck," he said thickly, resting his weight on one hand so he could grab hold of one and begin to squeeze it.

She groaned as the oil started to heat, and she realized it wasn't just from his hands but from the liquid itself.

As he plucked at her nipples with his slick fingers, she groaned again as his touch sent shivers through her. He reached behind him, palmed the bottle, and poured some between her breasts. She peered down, watched the oil and gravity start playing, as he lifted a leg and straddled her thighs.

With a shuddery breath, their gazes connected all the while, he reached down and began to rub the oil into her torso. Without leaving an inch untouched, he rubbed the liquid into every part of her upper body, making gooseflesh rise and fall in the sexiest Mexican wave imaginable.

Gulping when he carefully traced his fingers around her nipples, getting close to but never touching them outright, she released a moan as he plied the mounds, gently squeezing before ignoring them altogether and moving onto her stomach.

She wasn't the skinniest Minnie in the world. Had silvery stretch marks that ran around her belly button and down to her hips, some from being plump as a kid, others from growth spurts, but the desire in his eyes burned away any embarrassment she might have felt about them.

He looked at her like she was a Goddess.

That level of intensity was more than exciting, it made her heart thud in her throat.

"Jesus," she whispered thickly.

He swallowed as he carefully massaged her belly, ran down to her sides where she was a little ticklish. Sawyer's smile about broke said thudding heart, because he looked so boyish at that moment, so playful and not his usual intense self, that she wanted nothing more than to be as close to him as two people could be.

Biting her lip, she reached for his left hand with her good one. Bridging their fingers, she nudged at the lip of the waistband of her sweatpants, and whispered, "Somewhere else needs massaging."

Fire burned at the backs of his eyes, and she let out a throaty sigh, head falling to the side as he slipped his fingers free from hers, shoved his hand down her pants, and sank three moist fingers down the line of her slit.

The digits were oily, greased, and they slid around her cunt like a teenager on coke while ice skating. She immediately separated her thighs, parting them as wide as she could to allow him all the access he needed. The movement seemed to open up her pussy, giving him more freedom to touch her how he wanted—*thank God for sweatpants.*

"You like that, lass?" he asked softly, his fingers caressing her clit. It wasn't how she would touch herself, but with the slip and slide of the oil, his movements were actually softer than hers usually were. That soft swiftness had her tensing up at a ridiculous speed.

She rocked her hips up, aware that this could be the quickest orgasm she'd ever had in her life.

That is, until the bastard moved his hands away.

She glowered at him, made to reach for him, then whimpered as pain shot through her head and arm at the jerky movement.

He glowered back. "Still yourself," he growled "I'm not going anywhere. Just making you more comfortable."

A moan escaped her by way of response, and the sound lessened his glower into a glare of irritation—an irritation that was aimed at the pain she'd caused herself.

Embraced once more by his caring tenderness, she allowed him to maneuver her. He was careful not to jostle her further as he pulled down her pants, and he let out a hissed breath, as he whispered, "No bra, no panties, dear God, if this is how you usually walk around, I'll have a constant hard on."

She chuckled a little, but it was breathy and weak. "No. I usually wear thongs, remember?"

His eyes flared with remembered amusement. Devon had pointed out in his regular unsubtle way that the lines of her thong were perfectly visible through her skirts.

"Aye, how could I forget?" He sighed as he looked her over.

Though she could see the many flaws, he shoved that aside and murmured, "Jesus, Sascha, you're beautiful."

Gulping, she whispered, "You're too far away." With her good hand, she reached down between her legs and touched herself. Rubbing her clit in the way she liked, a movement he took note of if his narrowed eyes were anything to go by, she moved her fingers down to her gate, and slipped two into her pussy. "I want you here."

He cocked a warning brow at her. "We can't do anything too rough. Not with your head and arm like that."

A deep groan escaped her, not just from disappointment at his words, but also from the need his touch and hers had inspired in her.

"I need you," she whispered throatily, loving how his already narrowed eyes turned into desire-loaded slits.

His hands were still greasy, worse, they had her juices on them—because boy, was she wet. Her fingers made noises as she fucked herself, but she didn't have it in her to even care all that much—but that didn't stop him from running his fingers through his hair in a gesture of exasperation.

"I need you too, lass, but I need your head to stay glued to your neck more."

"Isn't there a way?" she asked with a pout. "I didn't even think I had it in me to feel horny, Sawyer, but I might just explode anyway. How about on my side? I feel so empty…"

She watched as a pained expression glanced over his features. "It would still rock your head."

"Just go slow." Huskily, she whispered, "I want to feel your cock, Sawyer. Deep inside me."

He gulped, and finally, moved his hands to his fly. Within seconds, his cock was in his fist. Mouth watering at the sight, she explored him with her eyes. He was fully dressed, and she was nude—what was it with these guys? First Andrei and now Sawyer?

This needed to stop right here and now.

"Take off the rest of your stuff," she commanded, feeling queenly and in charge now that he'd complied with her other request.

"Yes, your highness." The look in his eyes told her she was playing with fire, and she fucking loved it.

A grin curved her lips because their thoughts were running parallel in regard to her regal status upon this mattress. Plus, her entire form which had been one big ache just twenty minutes ago, felt lighter than it had in ages.

She was ready for this, she realized. Even though she could see the trace of guilt on his features, knew he didn't want this for her sake, *she* did. She knew her body, knew what it needed—he'd learn to have faith in that in time, and time was a luxury they had on their side.

"I'll make you bow and scrape next," she told him with a smirk, feeling cheeky and knowing he'd let her get away with it.

Rolling his eyes, he climbed off the bed with a care that touched her, pulled off his plain tee by grabbing it from the back of the neck—*was there a sexier and more impractical way of stripping down?* Sascha asked herself—and revealed a body that was made for sin.

Her tongue cleaved to the roof of her mouth as she looked at the flat, dusky peach nipples, the thick pecs, the solid abs… He even had that whole V thing going down to his cock, and a happy trail she'd willingly hike any day of the goddamn week.

The moan that escaped her was one she couldn't contain. It fell from her lips as he shoved down his jeans and kicked out of them, baring thick thighs that were made for rugby. His body was covered in a fine layer of golden hair that flecked against his semi-tanned skin. On his chest, there was more of a pelt, but nothing too Neanderthal. Nothing that would have her giving him a body shaver for Christmas, anyway.

"Like what you see, lass?" he asked, more from amusement than arousal she thought. And he certainly didn't expect an answer—good job, because she was speechless at the sight of his raw beauty.

His wicked grin was inspiring, she thought, as he reached down and jacked off his cock for a few strokes. Her fingers curled in, making her have to hide a wince of pain as she moved the ones on her bad hand too.

He must have seen though. Damn him and his observational skills.

"We shouldn't do this," he retorted with a grimace, but she noticed the fist about his cock tightened to what had to be the point of pain. "I can get you off, lass. There are ways and means."

"We should. I'm hurting, yes, but I'm aching more between the legs." She flared her eyes at him. "Just... be careful."

He huffed. "How can I be careful? Sex involves movement. Your body needs stillness."

She began to fuck herself with her fingers. It was better to do that than to answer in any way that would have discouraged him from climbing onto the mattress and fucking her how she needed to be fucked.

Heck, she'd gone two years without sex. It had been that long since she'd split up with her dick of an ex. No sex in all that time save with a BOB, and she'd been fine.

Now, she felt more starved than she ever had.

He needed to be inside her. Stat.

With a groan, he climbed onto the bed. "You're a temptress," he growled out. "Either that or a fucking pricktease."

"Prickteases don't come through with the good stuff," she retorted primly, then spoiled it by letting out a mewl as pleasure cascaded through her when she accidentally nudged her clit with the edge of her wrist.

"True," he conceded, then gritted out, "Stop touching that pussy. It's mine to touch, not yours."

"It's between *my* legs, Mr. Bossy."

"In this room, it's mine," he growled, then with a care that belied the edge to his tone, he helped roll her onto her good arm. When he moved away, she started to sit up, fearful he was leaving her, but he shot her a narrow look that had her freezing in place.

Huffing, because who knew he was so bossy, she watched as he grabbed the pillows at the head of the bed—six in all—and began to place them beside her. Three along her torso, with one so she could rest her forehead on it, another at the back of her neck to keep her head as still as possible. He lifted one leg up and stuck a pillow between her knees. The move had a little whisper of air running along the length of her slit, which made her shiver in response. The final pillow he tossed back to the headboard.

"How do you feel?"

"Like I'm in a padded cell?"

He grunted. "Padded cell inmates wished the view was this fine." He wafted a hand in front of his body, then stunned the shit out of her by winking.

She barked out a laugh. "Now who's got a big head?" she teased.

He grabbed his cock. "You'll have to tell me in a minute."

Snorting with amusement, she watched as he moved around her, curling onto his side at her back. She hadn't expected him to have a bawdy sense of humor, and she'd admit that she loved it. He was so damn serious all the time, so having him tease her like that was just the cherry on the goddamn cake.

Pressing his head to the pillow he'd propped at the back of hers, he cautiously approached her. When her back met his chest, she whimpered because the movement put his cock between her ass cheeks.

"I can't wait to fuck you there," he murmured roughly, as he placed his hand on her belly and pulled himself closer to her, so they were as tightly pressed together as could be.

"Where?" she teased.

"Your arse," he retorted, reaching down to nip at her oil-slick shoulder. "When your head's better, I might just treat you."

"Treat me?" She growled. "I've never had anything down there, buddy. It's a treat for you, not me."

"When you come so hard your head really does come off, you'll be grateful then."

"How does it get reattached?" she demanded. "As far as I'm aware, you're all Messrs. Smarty-Pants, but not a one of you is a doctor."

"One of us will Frankenstein something up," he retorted, chuckling as he began to rub his hand in a circle over her belly.

She pouted. "You're touching too high up."

"I'm touching where you need to be touched," he countered, rubbing his nose behind her ear and flicking the lobe with his tongue. The simple act had her shuddering in unexpected delight.

She felt certain there was more gooseflesh on her body than was humanly possible. What with the oil and his massage, she was already hypersensitized. Throw in the need that was starting to make her burn up, Sascha wasn't sure why she hadn't already spontaneously combusted.

With a groan, she rocked her hips into him, but he grabbed her side and stilled her with a force that had her lips pouting. "If you move, I won't give you what you need," he whispered into her ear, teasing the lobe again by sucking it between his lips. "I'll leave this bed so quickly you won't even see me move, and after, I won't help you get off."

"Bastard," she hissed, then hissed again when his hand finally slid down between her legs. His fingers dove straight for her clit, and when instinct had her rolling her pelvis forward, he immediately pulled away.

"What did I tell you?" he demanded.

Panting because he'd taken her far closer with those few touches than was good for her sanity, she whispered, "I'm sorry. I'm trying. I promise."

He grumbled, but her apology must have worked, because he returned to her, giving her what she needed. Sharp cries escaped her as he worked her clit as she'd done moments before. His observational talents came in handy from time to time it seemed. Hard and fast, he frigged the nub. A low hum seemed to buzz around the insides of her skull, and with a hoarse yell, she came.

Like that. As quick as you like, and as unexpected as fuck.

It rammed her in the belly like a freight train, and only the promise of losing his cock had her managing to stay still. She wasn't sure what the miracle was here. The fact she'd climaxed so quickly or managed to do so without moving.

Truth was, the fact she couldn't move, intensified the sensation. It felt like an A bomb had exploded inside her core, and before she could do little more than moan with delight, his cock was there. He ran the tip along her slit, lubing it up with ease—fuck, she was so wet. The noises the rubbing made should have embarrassed the fuck out of her, but it didn't.

She fucking loved it.

"I'm clean," he told her softly, whispering the words into her ear.

"Me too. On the pill as well," she replied, excitement thrusting her into another fucking realm, because she wanted him inside her so damn badly, she thought she'd go nuts.

He grunted at her words. "Good." He nipped at the earlobe, then with one hand on her tit, which he squeezed, before finally trailing his fingers to her nipple and teasing the nub. Pinching it, he notched his cock against her gate, and slowly, carefully pressed into her.

He was thick. Hard. Big. So big.

Apparently, to be a part of this household, you needed huge cocks, because she'd seen three so far, felt Sean's, and they were all a lot bigger than average.

Her eyelashes fluttered as his cock thrust against her sensitive walls, raking nerve endings to life in a way that had her nuzzling her face into the pillow and biting down against the feathers inside.

She let out a sharp moan as he bottomed out, her butt touching his belly. With a final squeeze to her greased-up nipple, he rubbed a path down to her pussy and pressing a hand between her legs, putting a distinct pressure on her clit, he held her against him.

His thrusts, when he moved, were agonizing in their speed.

Slow. So fucking slow it almost hurt.

Deep, so goddamn deep she wanted to sob.

It was intense. More intense than she'd ever thought possible. It was the hottest fucking she'd ever had because it felt more like making love.

"I wish I could see your eyes," she whimpered, ceasing to bite down on the pillow to whisper that to him.

He grunted. "Another time, lass." Pressing his lips to her throat, he began to suckle the skin there. Later, she knew she'd curse him for marking her because no amount of foundation ever hid a hickey, but then and there? It fit. She needed him to mark her. Inside and out.

It took all she had not to move, to rock her hips to encourage him to speed up, but the threat of losing that delicious fullness, of losing him, had her staying in place. She was well aware that this was for her. All for her.

No man wanted to go this slow. He practically trembled with tension at keeping still while working his cock into her. It was heaven for her though. She trembled with the intensity, and with the pressure on her clit working against her, she could feel an orgasm coming again.

It tightened her inner muscles in a way that had Sawyer hissing, "That's it, lass, give it to me. Give yourself to me."

With a groan, she focused on the hazy goal ahead of her. He tilted up, rocking into her a little swifter, and a hoarse cry escaped her this time as the haziness disappeared and was replaced with a fully formed 'finish line'.

The cry turned into a shriek as he cursed under his breath, his fingers biting into her hips, as he groaned out his own release against her throat.

Feeling his cum deep inside her should *not* have been as big a turn on as it was, but it didn't matter. His release rammed hers into the stratosphere. The slickness deep inside her facilitated his final, deep, wet thrusts, and she knew that the stars she was seeing were ones she'd gladly visit time and time again with this man as her tour guide.

"SHOULD YOU REALLY HAVE DONE THAT?"

Devon's voice woke her up, and with bleary eyes, she peered at him. He was backlit by the windows and perched on the side of the bed like he'd joined them at the dining table, not on a mattress where sex had recently just been had.

Plus, she was naked. Sawyer too. Yet he was sitting there, scowling at them, like they'd met up at the park or something.

Odd thing was, she had no desire to hide her nakedness from him. There was little point.

Sometime in the future, he would see her like this. His cock would be nestling between her asscheeks as Sawyer's was. Why hide from what was going to happen anyway?

She squinted. "Why shouldn't I?"

"I wasn't talking to you," he told her with a huff.

Watching as he sank back against the only pillow not being used to support her, then lifted his legs and crossed his feet at the ankles damn close to her boobs, she murmured, "Sawyer's asleep."

"No, he's not," came the grumble, and his brogue was so thick at that moment, her exhausted pussy fluttered to life once more. "He was, until someone interrupted."

His yawn stirred the hairs at the back of her neck, and the intimate touch made her smile. "My head isn't aching," she told them both, her intention to reassure Sawyer, as well as to inform Devon that she was okay, and that there was no reason to blame Sawyer for any of this. "Plus, I wanted it."

"And what you want you always get?" Devon asked, sounding curious.

She grinned. "Not usually, but I have a feeling that's how this is going to work here."

Sawyer chuckled. "Probably. You'll get spoiled."

"Spoiled? That's bad, isn't it?" Devon asked, rubbing his chin in contemplation.

"It can be," she answered, nestling her forehead into the feathers of the plush cushion Sawyer had stacked there earlier. "I won't let it go to my head though," she teased.

"Janna was spoiled," Devon said, his tone reflective.

"Aye, she was. She was also petulant and a pain in the ass who didn't have a sense of humor. Fine tits on her, mind." He nipped Sascha's shoulder. "Not as fine as these beauties though," he told her, squeezing her boob as he spoke.

She snorted. "Thanks for the backhanded compliment."

Sawyer chuckled again. "You'll get used to that too, don't worry. You can't help it with him around. Also, get used to inappropriate conversations. Like talking about exes in front of the new lady in your life, while your best friend's cum is still leaking out of her."

She blinked. "Ewww." Though her cheeks grew pink, she'd admit to liking his crudeness.

Sawyer was very raw. She liked that. It made her feel very feminine at his side.

The human psyche was all kinds of fucked up, she realized with an inner snort of disgust at herself.

Devon shrugged. "Better out than in."

"What? His cum or are you talking about the inappropriate conversation?"

Sawyer's chuckle deepened into a rough laugh. "She's got you there, Dev."

The man in question just frowned. "I suppose both." Another chin rub. "Although, if I was to seduce you now, it would probably feel like heaven."

"Devon likes sloppy seconds, don't you, bud?" Sawyer asked, sounding very affectionate.

"Okay, that's weird," she confessed with an eye roll.

Devon grinned, apparently liking that she was squicked out. "It's not weird at all. You'll see."

"Oh, I will, will I?"

"Can't be helped with him around," Sawyer mumbled, sounding like he was dropping off to sleep once more. Then, he stilled. "You meant it before?"

"Meant what?" she asked, a little alarmed by his stillness.

"About your head? Your arm?"

Ah, that. She purred, "I feel like a new woman."

"Literally, an impossibility," Devon instantly countered.

Sawyer ignored him and leaned up so he could look over her shoulder and see some of her face. "Promise?"

"Promise. I'll pinky swear if it makes you feel better," she joked.

He rolled his eyes. "I can do without it. You should get some sleep," he advised as he settled behind her again. "You'll need it for tonight."

As bright as can be, Devon inserted, "Oh, you don't have to go out now, Sascha. That's why I came looking for you. The gala's been rescheduled."

She blinked blearily at him. "It has? Why?"

With his gaze fastened to her breasts, he reached forward and flicked the tip of her nipple. Studying it as the bud tautened, he murmured, "What?"

She smacked his hand away and tried not to be amused. "Devon! *Focus.*"

"On what?" he asked.

"For God's sake, Dev, why the hell has the gala been rescheduled?" Sawyer demanded, the words whispering against the back of Sascha's neck. That little stimulus and Dev's focus on her body had her heating up inside, and she really couldn't go for round two.

Even if her pussy was all for it.

Before she could even contemplate what it would be like to be in a Devon and Sawyer sandwich, before she could even wonder what the hell had happened to her where such an idea made her melt instead of scandalizing her, Devon shattered her arousal with a single, blunt statement:

"The venue was blown up."

NINE

"DO THEY KNOW WHO DID IT?" Kurt demanded, pinning Sean in place with a glare that wasn't aimed at his friend, but the fuckers behind the explosion. "Do they know why?"

"No. But I've heard leaks that it went off earlier than it was programmed to. They don't know why yet."

"You mean it should have gone off when the gala was on?"

Sean's tone was gruff as he admitted, "Maybe. Like I said, it's just chatter I've heard." He looked at his watch. "The Chief Commissioner has asked me to attend a meeting in twenty minutes. I need to go if I'm going to get there on time."

Kurt grimaced. "Keep us updated."

Before Sean could even move out of his chair, the door slammed open, hitting into the back wall. "A bomb?"

Sascha's squeak had him wincing, but her terror was plain to see.

Sean nodded grimly.

"How many people were hurt?" Sawyer demanded from behind her.

Kurt's eyes widened as he realized they were looking rather rumpled. Had they just fucked?

No, surely not. Not with Sascha's head as delicate as it was?

The thought had him glowering at Sawyer, whose nostrils flared as he ducked his head with guilt.

"Numbers are still coming in. So far, it's staff caught in the blast. They were organizing everything for the gala tonight," Sean murmured. "But I have to go. I'm needed in a meeting."

"About this?"

Sean nodded at Sawyer's question. "The Commissioner said he needed my help on this one."

"Why? There have been terror attacks before and you weren't called in."

His shrug said it all, but the uneasy look on Sean's face caught Kurt's attention. "They don't think it was the usual suspects," he stated rather than asked.

Sean grimaced. "You're too perceptive by half, Kurt," he grumbled. "They don't know, but the chatter says not."

"Chatter? What chatter?" Sascha asked, scowling and leaning back into Sawyer as though needing his support. Sawyer's hands came up to cup her shoulders; a move that caught both his and Sean's attention.

Of them all, Sawyer was the least affectionate. Though Janna, their first shared lover, had hurt each of them, she'd hurt Sawyer the worst.

He'd never trusted any of the other women in their life since, and that lack of trust came in the shape of only fucking them, only touching them when it boiled down to sex. Nothing more, nothing less.

Clearing his throat to shake off his surprise, Kurt murmured, "Sean has a lot of fingers in a lot of pies."

"It helps when it comes to situations like this one."

She lifted a shaky hand and rubbed her forehead. "Okay. Where's Andrei? I know he wasn't there, but does he know about this?"

Kurt shook his head. "I doubt it. He's been in a meeting since eleven. Locked down."

"Locked down? Why?" Sascha held up a hand. "Let me guess. He was talking to some Chancellor or Minister or somebody."

Sean's lips twitched. "You're dealing with a different sort of person now, Sascha. We're not builders or bakers."

"Last time I looked, I wasn't a candlestick maker either," Sawyer quipped, and Devon, at his back, and Sean, immediately chuckled.

Sascha scowled. "You think this is funny."

"No, of course not," Sean placated. "It's just a saying. Butcher, baker, candlestick maker."

"What does that have to do with any of this?" she demanded, settling deeper against Sawyer.

Kurt, noticing this, murmured, "You should be in bed." Before she could argue, he moved toward her, bent down, and carefully swept her into his arms. She moaned a little but nestled into him as he carried her over to one of the many armchairs in Sean's study. Sinking into it, he let her rest against him.

"Thank you," she whispered weakly, pressing her forehead against his shoulder.

He couldn't stop himself from pressing a kiss to her temple. "You looked shaky."

"I was. This is all so much."

She looked ridiculously frail in his arms, and when he looked up, he saw Sean, Devon, and Sawyer were all staring at her with concern.

"Maybe you should go to bed, Sha. You probably need the rest."

Peering at Sean through her lashes, she grinned. "Sha?"

He winked. "You ready for me to call you 'honey'?"

"I think I'd prefer that to Sha." She wrinkled her nose, then lifting her hand, she mocked him by holding her chin in her fingers, in a total Sherlock Holmes pose, and murmured, "Although, you might be able to persuade me."

He barked out a laugh. "If anyone could, I'm sure it's me."

Kurt smirked. "Speak for yourself. I'm the wordsmith here."

Sawyer hooted. "If you can get him to talk about his feelings, Sascha, then you're a miracle worker. You think I'm reticent? Jesus, the man's more sewed up than a Cabbage Patch Doll."

Ignoring the eye roll Sawyer sent his way, he pressed back into the armchair more. She was a comfortable armful, he'd have to admit, and the way she'd cuddled into him, he wanted to enjoy it.

Devon moved away from the doorway and came to squat down in front of the armchair. He leaned against Kurt's legs as he raised his knees, then rested his arms on them. The move had his head pressing against Sascha's calves, and at the touch, she reached down and hesitantly ran her hand through his hair.

"Is this a private love in? Or is anyone invited?" Sean asked, apparently amused at the tableau before him.

Kurt grinned for the sheer joy of just being fucking happy. At that moment, he really was.

Sascha was in his arms, at peace and comfortable enough with him to melt into his embrace. One of his best buds was at his side, and another two were in the same room, under the same roof.

Trouble was always around the corner. Whether it was this issue with Andrei or Katrin's money problems... With five people in a house, each with their own circle of friends and family, strife often knocked at their door.

Even as solitary as they were, unsociable to boot, people still waited in the wings.

Devon, of course, murmured, "Love in? I think she's too tired after doing the nasty with Sawyer."

Sascha snickered. "Who said it was nasty?" To Sawyer, sweet as pie, she told him, "I thought it was very nice."

Kurt watched on in amusement as Sawyer cocked a brow, folded his arms across his bare chest, and leaning against the doorway, murmured, "I wasn't doing it right if it was nice, lass."

Her snicker turned into a laugh. "Well, you did have certain parameters to work within."

"He's very good with direction, isn't he?" Devon added conversationally.

Sawyer's eyes widened. "Jesus, Devon. Keep your trap shut."

Sean swiveled in his chair to better look at Sawyer, who was blushing in the doorway. Surprised, he murmured, "Since when were you good with direction?"

If he'd been wearing a shirt with a collar, Kurt knew Sawyer would have tugged at its choking confines. As it was, his glower darkened. "Devon's heading up the project we're working on."

Sean snorted. "Yeah. Sell me another one."

Sascha, apparently taking pity on him, changed the subject by asking, "When's Andrei coming home?"

"When he's out of the meeting," Sean immediately answered, but his gaze was still pinned on their discomforted friend.

"I swear. You guys are so literal sometimes. *When* will that be?"

He blinked. "Six? Seven?"

"Seriously? He scheduled that meeting when we had to be at the gala at eight?"

Kurt laughed. "We don't primp, Sascha. Ten minutes, and we're usually ready."

She scoffed. "It's a gala! You have to primp."

"If you're female or gay," Devon told her disgustedly.

"Less of the attitude, buddy. You can judge when you get your hair cut."

He half turned to glower at her. "What's wrong with my hair?"

"It looks like someone put a pudding bowl on your head and cut around it. You're lucky you have such a pretty face and that your hair's so wavy you can't tell it's a straight cut," she retorted.

"What's wrong with cutting it that way?" he immediately defended, making the other men in the room chuckle. "It's practical. Takes two minutes."

She gawked at him. "I was joking. Jesus Christ, Devon. You don't seriously cut your own hair?"

He blinked at her. "Why not? When it gets too long, it drives me insane."

"Fuck. I swear, you guys need a goddamn keeper. Not one for the *house* either," she finished before Devon could say it—his lips were pursed to do just that. With a huff, she told him, "Next time it needs cutting, come to me. I'll sort it out." She glared at her cast. "If it wasn't for this, I'd do it now."

Devon pouted. "I like it."

She gawked at him, then a shifty look etched itself onto her face. "We'll see."

Kurt cleared his throat. "He doesn't work well with threats."

She cocked a brow. "Who said I was threatening him?"

Sean laughed. "I think you might have met your match, Devon. And I don't mean with math either."

"I think we're getting off topic," Sawyer inserted gruffly. "And you need to go to that meeting, Sean."

"Shit." He grunted. "I do. Are you guys going to be okay?" The question was aimed at everyone, but his gaze was on Sascha.

"I'm fine. I promise," she assured him.

"Good. I'll be on my cell if something crops up, okay?"

A round of nods was his response, and he got to his feet, grabbed his briefcase from under his desk, and shoved some papers in it from the organized chaos on its surface.

When he circled the desk one-eighty, Kurt expected his next action, but he could sense Sascha hadn't. She froze, then melted into him when Sean bent over and pressed a kiss to her forehead.

Arching her throat a little, she whispered, "Aim lower."

He gave her a quick grin, then did as bade. Their kiss was short, and unsatisfactory if both of the grunts they made when they parted were anything to go by.

Kurt felt the heat between them, and as was usually his way, responded to it. He was a watcher in all things. It was probably what made him love writing. But in this, he felt the visceral scorch of their arousal, and his body turbocharged it a thousand times more.

His cock stiffened, and he knew she felt it when she shifted her butt slightly—not away from his erection, but against it, almost like a whispered greeting.

Of course, that gentle, barely there touch was translated poorly by his cock; it hardened fully. Her lips twitched, but that was her only reaction as her gaze was still caught in the visual fucking going down between her and Sean.

Devon glowered up at him. "Jesus, Sean, fuck off. You're crowding me."

Sean snorted, blinked, and the heat was cast off. "God forbid I crowd you, Devon, eh?"

"Until later," he told her, before shooting her a wink and stepping toward the doorway. He nodded at Sawyer then headed out into the big, wide world.

Devon was the first to speak when he'd gone. "If the usual suspects weren't to blame, why would anyone target a gala celebrating an economist?"

"I don't think we should talk about this when Sascha's here. She's still not feeling well."

At his words, she shook her head—immediately regretted it if her grimace was anything to go by—but stated, "No, I'm okay, Kurt. I promise. It was just the shock. That's all."

"Are you sure?"

"I'm positive. Devon's right. It's not exactly an event worthy of much note, is it? Well, save from within that particular community, I mean."

Sawyer stepped into the room and perched his ass on Sean's desk. Gripping the edges with hard fingers, he retorted, "There were a lot of important people invited. Andrei was telling me about it the other night."

"Like who?" Devon demanded.

"Politicians. Some very big entrepreneurs. You know Edward Jacobie?"

"The tech mogul?" Sascha drummed her fingers on her knee.

He nodded. "More than that. He's the next Zuckerberg. Shits money twice a day."

Her nose wrinkled. "Great image."

"It worked though, huh?" he told her with a chuckle.

Kurt, aware the conversation was approaching devolution, slotted in quickly, "Why was he going to be there?"

"Andrei helped him with a new piece of software. He was going to be there to introduce Andrei."

Sascha blinked. "Well, he's probably the target then, right?"

Sawyer shrugged. "Maybe. Who knows with these fucking whackos. Let's just be grateful the bomb went off too early."

She shivered in his arms. "I'll be glad when he gets home."

"He won't know anything about it until his driver tells him," Kurt tried to reassure her. "So, don't think he'll be freaking out about this."

"Like he would anyway," Devon retorted with an amused chuckle.

Sascha scowled. "Why wouldn't he be freaked out about a bomb going off at the gala he was supposed to be attending tonight? I know I'm freaked out."

"Devon, now isn't the time, dammit," Kurt snapped, annoyed at his friend's lack of care.

Hell, it wasn't like he wasn't used to Devon spilling his thoughts at the fucking drop of a hat but when it came to this? Seriously.

Even Sawyer looked pissed. He growled, "Devon, we should get back to work."

"Wait a minute," Sascha immediately argued. "I want to know what's going on."

Devon, sensing he'd fucked up for once, cleared his throat. "I think it's best if you ask Andrei, Sascha."

She narrowed her eyes as he climbed to his feet.

Though Devon was most definitely a skin and bone man, at times, he was pretty much the tin man. When he bent over to kiss Sascha, Kurt knew he was mimicking Sean's gesture. Not out of a need to compete, but how AI mimicked real life.

Feeling rotten for comparing his best friend to a robot, Kurt sighed out his irritation with the man.

It wasn't Devon's fault his father had been a complete and utter bastard, was it? If a boy wasn't shown love and affection as a child, how could he understand it as a man?

As Devon headed out the office, Sawyer also came over to kiss Sascha before he too departed. Leaving them both alone.

"Are you comfortable here?" he asked. "Or do you want to go to another room?"

His aim had been to change the topic, but she pinned him in place with a narrow look. "Explain."

"Andrei's seen things no one should have to see, Sascha." He shrugged. "Devon's right. He wouldn't be afraid of what happened today. Take comfort in that."

Her head tilted to the side as she studied him a second. With more gravitas than he'd have liked, one that told him she'd heard and understood the unintentional undertones to his words, Sascha asked, "What did he see?"

Kurt cleared his throat. "He should be the one to tell you."

The instant he said it, he knew she'd have a problem with it. Not because she was nosy, but he'd concerned her.

She was concerned for Andrei.

His heart skipped a beat at that. All the other women in their life had been there for the sex. With the worry in her eyes, the pinched tightness around them, and the serious set to her mouth, he saw as well as felt her distress at what he wasn't saying out loud.

"I want you to tell me," she retorted, prodding him in the chest with her good hand. "Sean warned me about this," Sascha confessed.

"Said there were secrets that belonged to each of you, and that I wasn't supposed to pry. That I was supposed to wait until you, as individuals, came to me and shared your secrets, but this is too important… I know you're not telling me something." A small sigh escaped her. "And that's okay; or it would be if I didn't feel like we were actually discussing something major. And I don't mean an emotional boo boo."

Ordinarily, he'd have told her to ask Andrei. To go to the source; no one had the right to make this revelation save for Andrei, and yet…

She was hurting for Kurt's best friend.

And knowing how sensitive this topic was for Andrei, how could he not share something that would only drag up a past left buried?

As he worked through a way to soften a harsh truth, he knew there was little point in wasting too much time on this as it was impossible to gentle something so heinous.

With a deep sigh, he admitted the nasty reality.

"Andrei's mother was killed in front of him."

TEN

"ARE you supposed to be down here?"

The statement, complete with Russian accent, had her jolting in place. Not only because she'd had her back to the staircase but because she'd been lost in her thoughts. Thoughts that centered around the man currently infiltrating her kitchen.

How was she supposed to act around him?

Like she didn't know? Like everything was normal?

To him, it was. After all, he wasn't to know Kurt had told her the truth about his family, and wasn't that for the best? She knew Kurt had only told her because… Well, she wasn't sure why. She got the feeling he'd been on the brink of telling her to go and speak with Andrei, but he'd stopped. Had studied her, then had revealed a nasty truth.

Had he sensed her concern? Her anxiety for this, the first man in their household who had touched her? Had he felt her panic when she'd read deeply into his words, sensing the undertones led to a grim reality?

She jolted when a gentle brush of her arm brought her attention back to the matter at hand. Looking up at him and sending him a quick smile she hoped didn't convey her sudden unease, she mock-grumbled, "Not you too? I wouldn't be in here if I wasn't well enough."

He snorted, seemingly amused. "Had a lot of that today, huh?" he asked. Before he headed toward the fridge, he bent down and kissed her softly on the temple. She smiled into the kiss, loving this new habit they were all adopting. "We can't help but be concerned about you, Sascha. It was too close a call—" His jaw clenched as his words broke off.

She pressed her hand to her mouth and watched as he retrieved a beer from the fridge. He saw her gesture, tilted his head at the sight of it, then, his lips twitched.

That was the only indication he'd noticed.

"Are you okay?"

She shrugged. "I guess. It's weird thinking we might be in a hospital or the morgue right now."

"Cheerful thoughts," Andrei teased after he took a deep sip of beer. When the alcohol hit home, he let out a deep sigh.

"I thought Russians only drank vodka."

He rolled his eyes. "Want me to do the mazurka too?"

She smirked. "I'd probably pay to see that if I'm being honest."

"Why do I believe that?" He laughed, then, growing sober, he murmured, "I'm sorry if what happened today frightened you."

She watched him lean back against the counter, propping himself up with an elbow like he didn't have a care in the world.

Maybe he didn't, she pondered.

He'd watched his mother being murdered. Aged seven. *Seven!* Once a person had seen that, could anything else shock them?

Goddammit, *seven!*

She still couldn't grasp it. Couldn't comprehend how this wonderful man had seen such violence, such horror.

Kurt hadn't told her much, just enough to quench the need she had for answers, but those answers hadn't eased her worry. If anything, the revelation had made it a thousand times worse.

The need to touch him, to connect with him, overwhelmed her. She moved away from the counter where she'd been prepping for dinner and hobbled over to press her hand to his, then asked, "Aren't you frightened?"

He diverted his gaze to the mouth of the bottle in his hand. "No."

"Why not?" she asked, trying to urge the truth from his own lips rather than Kurt's. Regret formed a hard knot in her chest. Why had she badgered Kurt for this particular secret? Why hadn't she waited?

Her only defense was concern. Worry for Andrei, a desire to know him more, to understand him better.

"Because I'm a mathematician."

"Does that make you the tinman?" she teased.

"Sometimes," he admitted with a sheepish grin. "In this, I just know we weren't caught in the blast. I'm… pleased about that."

"Pleased?" She bit back a smile. "You astonish me with your effusiveness." Mad that he hadn't divulged a damn thing, she switched on the mixer to drown out her thoughts and anything he had to say.

"What are you making?" he asked when she switched off the power.

"Cookies."

"What kind?" he asked, moving away from the counter to approach the cookie dough with eager eyes.

She laughed as he scooped some of the mix out onto his finger. "It will be better baked. I promise."

"I'm sure," he teased. Then, pressing his clean hand to the small of her back, he asked, "How are you, really?"

Knowing he meant her injuries, not emotionally, she murmured, "I'm fine. Sawyer gave me a massage so I feel better."

He snorted. "Devon informed me about the massage."

"He did?"

"Yes," he said with a snicker. "I had one call about the blast, and the next thing I read was his disgust at Sawyer's having seduced you."

"I seduced him," she confessed lightly. "A girl doesn't always have to take no for an answer."

"True," he conceded. "But, I thought you'd still be under the weather?"

"I am. We were careful." She studied him a second. "Can I ask a question?"

"Of course."

He answered freely but she sensed his wariness. "Did Katrin, Kurt's ex, call you?"

His eyes widened, and she knew she'd surprised him. "You know about her?"

She jerked a shoulder. "Sure. Sean told me, and she called Kurt when he was sitting with me at the hospital. Did he talk to you about her?" When he nodded, emanating more wariness than before if that was even possible, she asked, "Did you speak with her?"

He rubbed his chin. "She's on my to do list."

"You haven't called?"

"I don't like her."

"Why?"

"She treated Kurt like shit. I'm surprised he asked me to help her out if I'm being honest. She destroyed him. It took him a long time to come back to us."

"In what way?"

He hesitated. "He drank. A lot. For quite a while. He's got it under control, and while technically he wasn't an 'alcoholic', he was certainly dependent."

"You all drink around him," she chastised.

"He drinks too. With no issue at all. That was then. This is now."

"She sounded desperate. It surprised him."

"He's a better man than I. Did he tell you she cheated on him enough times even the divorce court judge was surprised? They had forty cases documented. God only knows how many went *un*documented."

Bug-eyed, she repeated, "Forty?"

He nodded. "See why I don't want to help her?"

"A bit." She nibbled at her bottom lip. "She *did* sound scared."

"Why are you defending her?" he asked, sounding more curious than anything else. "I'd have thought you wouldn't want us to have anything to do with her."

"I don't. But closure is important."

"This isn't closure. She calls him every now and then. Gets him to do things." He shot her a look she didn't particularly understand—Andrei was hard to read sometimes. She thought she sensed self-deprecation, but that didn't make much sense. "Regardless," he continued, "you have zero reason to feel jealousy. I think he'd rather fuck that cookie dough than Katrin. Cold bitch. I don't understand how she strong-armed forty poor bastards into fucking her. It's a wonder their cocks didn't drop off from the deep freeze."

She snorted, raked her teeth over her lip to hide her amusement. "That's not kind, Andrei."

He shrugged. "Who said I was kind?" With a wink, he reached down and pressed a kiss to her temple. "I have some work to do. Call me when the cookies are ready?"

"I will," she confirmed, watching as he walked off, beer still in hand.

Would she ever understand these men?

Their intelligence shouldn't have made them seem otherworldly, but in many ways, they were. The way they dealt with things was unusual. It made living with them feel akin to dodging mines on a grassy lawn—outwardly pretty and neat, inwardly deadly and dangerous.

Not that she felt like she was in peril around them. God, no way. Nutjobs were everywhere, after all. What had happened today could have happened at any other time too.

She had no real right to feel shaken up about something that hadn't happened to her, when a lot of people were currently being nursed in hospital. Well, the lucky ones. The unlucky…

She bit her lip as she spooned out dough onto a lined baking sheet.

Four days ago, she'd almost been killed in an accident.

They could have died tonight, but instead, they were both alive.

Sascha really hoped this kind of shit didn't come in threes. Or if they did, then the third time *wasn't* the charm.

"WHAT'S GOING ON, SEAN?" Andrei made the demand with a growl as he headed through the door to his study.

Kurt shot him a glance, and saw that Devon and Sawyer were eying him warily as he flung his coat onto his vacated armchair. Sean merely pressed his fingers together in a contemplative pose. "There was a bomb."

Andrei's nostrils flared. "I know there was. Devon told me. He also said that you were looking into this."

"I am."

Kurt heaved out a breath. "Sean. Come on."

Sean sighed. "There's more to this than we think."

"Of course there is. A bomb went off in the capital tonight, Sean. There's definitely more going on than meets the eye."

"No. I mean with Sascha."

Kurt narrowed his eyes. "What are you talking about?"

"She's being targeted."

Sawyer's hand slammed down against the armrest of his chair. "You have to be shitting me."

"I wish I was."

"Tell us what's going on, Sean," Andrei demanded. "Are you trying to tell me that you think the bomb was for her?"

"No. I'm trying to tell you there's a correlation between her being hit by a bloody car and this attack tonight."

"What kind of correlation?" Devon asked quietly, his eyes trained on his phone. Kurt knew it wasn't because Dev wasn't interested, it was because he worked on different levels. His attention split off in so many ways, his brain had to be like a rainbow. "There can be no connection. It makes no sense. What happened to Sascha was happenstance. That boy was in the street, she saw him, and rushed to get him out of the way of oncoming traffic. There's no way in hell anyone could predict that."

Sean sighed and rubbed at his temples like an ache was gathering there. Kurt could understand. A storm was brewing in his head too.

"She was hit by that car by accident. But it was intended as more."

Sawyer scowled at him. "Stop talking in circles, man. How can an accident be anything other than an accident?"

"The driver who rammed into her… he's confessed to being paid to run her down."

Silence filled the room, but Sawyer put it succinctly, "Fuck."

Sean's smile was grim. "Yeah. Exactly."

ELEVEN

"MEIN GOTT. WARUM KANN ICH NICHT..." He blinked, jolted from his anger at the knock on the door. "*Was*?" he snarled, then remembering where he was, *England*, grunted. "Yeah?"

Sascha's head popped around the door. "Everything okay?"

He pursed his lips and tried not to be charmed by her bright-eyed concern. Jesus, she had no right to be so distractingly beautiful. Not when he needed to concentrate.

"Not really," he admitted, glowering at his computer screen. "The story I plotted isn't working. It's going in a whole other fucking direction."

"May I come in?"

Her hesitance was probably the only thing that could penetrate the density of his writer's cave. Blinking at her, he murmured, "Of course. You don't have to ask."

She grinned. "Ever? I think that's a rule you want to nip in the bud right from the start."

He shook his head. "Is your door closed to us?"

Sascha tilted her head to the side. "No, I guess not. You'd only go up there if you had a reason, and that reason would be enough for me to understand why you'd interrupt my alone time."

He smirked at her. "Exactly. Now, what's wrong?"

She laughed. "Nothing. I just heard you cursing in German.

Wanted to make sure everything was okay, and if it wasn't, could fresh baked pumpernickel make it better?"

He knew his eyes lit up when her laugh deepened. "For me?"

"For you," she teased. "You're the only one who eats it."

Touched that she'd thought of him, he shoved away from his desk, eager to taste his treat as well as get away from his computer.

Sliding his arm around her waist, he pressed his hand to the base of her spine. "How are you feeling today anyway?"

"Fine," she said. "Which you'd know if you'd come down for breakfast."

He sighed as they walked down the steps, the kitchen their end goal. "I was writing."

"You sure you weren't hiding?"

"Hiding from what?" He snorted for good measure at the preposterous idea.

"I don't know. You've been weird ever since you told me about Andrei's mother."

"I haven't. Or, that was never my intention." He rubbed his chin. "Truth is, this book is a fucking nightmare. I don't know why I started it in the first place."

"Can I help at all?"

"Just being here is a help," he told her earnestly.

"Why? Because I cook so you don't have to?"

Her light tone was one that invited him to join in, but he couldn't. "No, because you make this place brighter."

She turned her head to stare at him in surprise, and he noticed her flushed cheeks. "You always make me blush," she whispered, laughing a little, at herself this time though.

"Why?"

"Your intensity—it's more than I know how to handle sometimes."

He tensed at that. Did she think he was desperate?

Before he could even think of what to say, she whispered, "I want to believe everything you say, but sometimes I can't."

He stared at her, then realized they were hovering on the staircase. Though it had been over a week since her accident, and five days since the bomb, she was still delicate. Could move around more, had started cooking more complex meals with the help of a food processor and a slow cooker, but wasn't strong enough for her other duties just yet.

Not that they mattered, save for her restricted mobility. It was beginning to drive her crazy.

They'd all noticed she was more snippy than usual. Which, considering she had to be in pain, not only from her head but her wrist, was more than understandable.

"We should talk about this around some snacks," he decided, smiling at her encouragingly. Gently pressing his hand against her back, he led her downstairs to the basement kitchen.

The space was a white, colorless haven. She'd brightened the place up with flowers and potted plants, but for the most part, it was the same white and copper as it had always been.

Adjacent to the breakfast bar, there was the dining table where they usually ate every meal save breakfast. It was placed in front of a set of patio doors that overlooked the yard. The day was dull. The sun barely gleaming through heavy set clouds that looked gray with the promise of rain. In the barely there light, the green grass, though rich and verdant, looked pallid and tired.

He sighed at the bleak view—it wasn't exactly inspiring. "It's a good thing I'm German."

A laugh escaped her as he grabbed a tray she'd loaded down with the fresh bread and the butter she bought for him—it had Himalayan rock salt crystals in it, and was his new favorite food. He noticed, with interest, that she'd also put a small mason jar of hummus on the tray too, as well as a few chunks of cheeses and pots of different vegetable and fruit chutneys.

"Why is it a good thing?" she asked.

"Because I'm used to this miserable weather. It must drive you crazy. I've been to Arizona. It's sunny. All the time. I needed sunglasses at night."

She snorted. "That sounds about right." Hunching her shoulders, Sascha confessed, "I guess I miss it sometimes. But not too much. It's a different kind of home to me now."

He watched as she retrieved a bottle of fizzy water from the fridge, and got to his feet to collect two glasses for them.

When she'd settled at the head of the table, her unofficial place with Sean who was seated opposite her, he reached for their plates. Putting them in front of him, he grabbed the loaf and hacked into it.

"You're slaughtering the bread," she grumbled, but her lips weren't curled downward.

"Then you should tell your wrist to heal already. There'll be more slaughtering before the months' out."

She huffed. "I don't know if I can stand it that long."

"You have no choice," he chided, cocking a brow at her.

"Not with my head aching the way it is." She pressed her gentle fingertips to her forehead. "I can't believe the pain's still there."

Sympathetic, he put down the knife and rubbed her upper arm. "It will stop soon. We've all seen the footage." He shook his head at the memory—one of Sean's police contacts had sent him the link to a video some sick fuck had put on YouTube, and they'd all watched it in a vain attempt to try to understand why the bastard behind the wheel had been targeting her. "It's no wonder you're aching so badly with the tumble you took." Tumble was an understatement. Seeing her flying through the air like a movie stunt gone wrong still had the power to make him feel sick—God only knew how Sean felt after seeing it in the flesh.

"I guess. I'm just tired of it already. It went away after..." She cleared her throat. "You know, with Sawyer and me? But ever since, it's just been making me grouchy as hell."

He grimaced on her behalf. "I'll bet. Now, do you want hummus or cheese?"

"Hummus. The cheese is for you."

"You know me so well."

She grinned. "I'm getting there."

He slapped hummus onto the bread and placed a few slices on her plate, then began serving himself.

As she picked at her snack, her words came back to haunt him. Because he wanted to know if his manner pleased or displeased her, he asked, "You were saying on the steps that I'm intense?"

He watched her fingers as she toyed with a breadcrumb. "Sean's the same. It's like both of you know exactly what to say to turn me to mush. It freaks me out."

Her words had him frowning. Taking a bite of the bread, he moaned at the deliciousness of the treat baked solely for him and pondered her words. "So, it's your reaction to the words that freaks you out, not the words themselves?"

"I guess."

"Why?"

"Do you know how many men have bullshitted me over the years just to try to sleep with me?" She cocked a brow. "I'm scared that this is all just going to turn out to be like that. And I really don't want it to be. I…" She sucked in a breath. "I like it here. I…" She ducked her head, and he realized that for the first time, he saw her truly vulnerable. "I like you."

"You're frightened the floor is going to fall out from under you?"

"Yes," she whispered, awkwardly pulling off a piece of bread and shoving it in her mouth.

"Do you think we want to hurt you?"

"No. But it doesn't mean it might not happen anyway."

He pursed his lips. "Has any of them spoken to you of my marriage?" She fidgeted a second, which was an answer in itself. He smirked a little. "It's okay," he told her. "In our own way, we share things we shouldn't to help each other out."

"Andrei told me Katrin cheated on you." She cleared her throat. "A lot."

He nodded. "A lot."

"I'm sorry."

"Don't be. But, if you think you're the only one scared of being hurt, you're wrong."

"You're scared?" she asked, her eyes wide.

For some reason, her shock amused him more than offended. "Men get scared, too," he told her wryly. "We just don't admit it all that often."

She bit her lip. "That doesn't make me feel better."

He barked out a laugh, amused again, despite himself. "It wasn't supposed to make you feel better, per se. Just to open your eyes to the fact you're not the only one who wants this to work."

Her frown discomforted him, but she seemed to be pondering his words. "I guess there's never any certainty when it comes to things like this."

His stomach plummeted at that. "No. Sadly, there isn't."

"That doesn't make me feel better either," she confessed again, making him snort this time.

He reached for her hand, bridged his fingers with hers complete with hummus on hers and butter on his, and murmured, "We can only try."

"I-I really want it to work. Sometimes, when you say the things you do, it's like a reminder of why this should all be impossible. It's like you know what I need to hear. But I don't want that. I want you to mean the things that you tell me." She sighed. "Sorry. I'm rambling."

"Maybe a little, but I know exactly what you're saying." He smiled. "If you hadn't noticed already, we're all very honest around here."

"True that," she retorted with a huff. "Jesus, if you guys get any more honest, I don't know if I'd be able to cope."

"I don't just mean Devon," he replied, knowing exactly what she was talking about, or *whom* was more precise. "We all are. We're not in the habit of saying shit just to get you to pull your panties down."

"Wow. That was blunt," she remarked, smirking a little as she tightened her fingers on his. "And dirty too."

"You like it dirty?" he asked, cocking a brow at her.

She grinned, then scowled. "I do usually. I can't wait for normal service to be resumed. Do you realize how hard it is living with five sex Gods, knowing you can touch them any time you want, and not being able to for fear of giving yourself the migraine from Hell? It makes me so mad."

A thought occurred to him. "Is that why you're so pissy at mealtimes?"

Her scowl deepened. "I'm not pissy."

"You totally are."

She huffed again. "Well, it's hard not to be a touch angry when the only dishes you want are the ones you can't have."

He grinned. "We're a smorgasbord just waiting to be sampled," he teased. "Delayed gratification is good for the soul."

"But not for my pussy or your cock," she retorted waspishly, then she wailed, "A girl has needs, you know?"

"She does, does she?" he asked, lifting a brow at her.

"I'd nod repeatedly here, but if I do, that counteracts the good in sitting still," came her glum retort.

"Think you can lie back on the table without moving your head too much?"

Her eyes widened, and she gawked at him.

"I fancy a snack that isn't on the menu."

Before he could say another word, she shot up out of her seat with enough haste to make him chuckle, then wince when she clutched her head and whispered, "Jesus H. Christ."

"Slowly, Sascha. There's no rush," he chided, watching as she, whimpering as she moved, perched on the edge of the table.

Uncertain if she needed to be carried back to bed, he watched on in amusement as she carefully, slowly enough to make him pause, lowered herself against the table.

Hell, she really did want to be eaten out.

He hid his smile at the thought, because she looked so uncomfortable, he wouldn't have blamed her for snapping at him. "We can do this in bed," he advised, eying the tension in her frame. This was for her, not for him. She'd said that sleeping with Sawyer had helped her head, after all.

Plus, he'd get a taste of her. At last.

"No," she countered. "I want to cum on this table. It will stop me from being pissy later."

"There's no way you'll cum all tense the way you are."

"You get that tongue working on my clit instead of on words, I'm sure I'll relax," she retorted, then, her waspishness disappeared. Grinning, she said, "I'm really glad I wore a skirt today."

"Not as glad as I am," he retorted, sinking down onto the seat she'd just vacated. Her butt was halfway down the central line of the table, so she was positioned perfectly for his needs.

Lifting her skirt, he dragged the hem over her thighs, letting his palms scrape over the tender skin. Watching her every move, both the voluntary ones and the involuntary ones, he saw gooseflesh rise on her legs, and smiled at the reaction.

Laughter barked from her all of a sudden. "I'm just trying to imagine what Devon would say if he caught us."

His lips twitched. "I wouldn't worry about Devon." Then, he focused on his prize. "Will it hurt if I spread your legs?"

She snorted. "Even if it did, I'd tell you to spread them."

"Good to know," he retorted, chuckling as he parted her thighs and groaned at the way her thong was digging between her ass cheeks. He pulled at the fabric, tugging it higher so that it went all the way down between the lips, and added pressure to her clit.

A muffled groan escaped her, and he saw she'd rested her forearm over her eyes. The move was a curious one. Defensive? Was she hiding?

He decided to leave her be. She was already uncomfortable enough without him pointing something of that nature out to her.

He tugged up again, liking how her hips jerked with the move, before pulling the fabric away from her cunt entirely. With a groan, he sank between her legs and devoured her.

There was no finesse, he was as hungry for her as she was for him.

He didn't enjoy oral sex all that much. Hadn't done it often since Janna had basically ruined it for him, but considering this was the only way he could get her off without moving her head in the process, it was the least he could do.

But he should have realized everything would be different with Sascha.

Because, Jesus, her *taste*.

It got to him like the finest whiskey.

And the sounds she made, her natural responses and the gentle rocking of her hips, were enough to have him reaching down and grabbing his cock in his fist.

Janna had laid there like a limp rag. Her lack of passion had turned him off oral sex, had, if he was being honest, eaten into his confidence. But a simple flick of his tongue had Sascha reacting like she was on fire, and in response, he wanted to devour her. To taste all she had to give. The pressure of his fly was uncomfortable, and he quickly unzipped himself and began to wank his dick as he slurped up her juices.

Exploring her outer lips, he sank onto her clit, suckling the nub until she was shrieking, the fingers of her good hand burrowing into his hair in a way that told him she was loving his mouth on her as much as he was loving having it there.

He smiled against her pussy, and she must have felt it because she screeched, "Bastard!"

"Why am I a bastard?" he teased, muffling the words against her clit. It was hard not to laugh when she let out a shriek.

Her legs rose up onto the table, and her toes curled around the edge before she let her knees sink down once more against the surface.

Her tension had changed as she'd predicted. No longer was she rigid with pain, but with the pain of pleasure. He loved that he'd done that for her, and with little more than his lips, teeth, and tongue.

The thought had him gripping a tighter hold on his shaft and pulling in tandem to the pace of his tongue as he fucked her pussy with it.

With his other hand, he pulled her lips apart to bare her clit to the air, before he pinched it.

She went off like a rocket. He hadn't expected that reaction. Her hips jerked up into the air, her butt wiggling as she howled before slamming her legs closed and turning half onto her side. Certain he'd hurt her—but shit, the pinch hadn't been that hard—he watched as she panted, moaned, and groaned her way through what had to be one of the hottest fucking orgasms he'd ever seen in his life.

He couldn't help it. He had to be a part of this.

He grabbed her legs, pulled them apart again, then grabbed his cock and jacked off. The sight of her flushed face, slick and juicy cunt… it took embarrassingly little to have him shooting his wad. He aimed for her pussy, and wasn't disappointed when he saw the flecks of his seed coating her most intimate parts.

His head fell back for a second as his own pleasure kneed him in the balls. With a deep breath, he tilted his head forward again, and saw her watching him as he'd watched her.

"That was hot," she whispered. "And unsanitary. I'll have to tell Devon I didn't use antibacterial soap on the table." A snicker escaped her.

He blinked, caught off guard by her words. Then, he chuckled. "You do realize you'll have him hovering over you with the *'kills 99% of all germs'* spray, right?"

"Fuck. I'm better off not teasing him then."

Grinning, he leaned over and pressed a kiss to her knee. "Feel better?"

Her eyelids fluttered, and a dreamy cast overtook her features. "I'll feel better if you kiss me."

He frowned. "But I'm…" He wafted a hand at his lips, which were wet, slick from her juices.

She licked her own and curled her finger at him. He eyed the table, unsure if it would hold both their weight. It looked solid enough. Ish. Damning it to hell, he climbed atop it, crawled over her, and bowed his head so their lips could touch.

Her moan vibrated in his mouth, and he let her sup from him as he'd just supped from her. She suckled his tongue, tasted herself on him. Explored his lips and bit down hard on his bottom lip.

"Thank you," she breathed against his lips. "That was so hot watching you come like that."

"I made a mess," he confessed ruefully.

"A hot one," she whispered, the words close to a rasp.

He nuzzled her cheek with his nose and slipped his hand down between her legs. He rubbed his cum into her pussy, her lips and clit. Anointing all of her with all of him.

"I dare you to stay like that until after the evening meal."

She smirked, unabashed. "You should have asked if I was on the pill before you did that."

He cocked a brow. "Word's spread. We can go in bareback."

"Wow, romantic. And I thought you only said words I wanted to hear?" she snarked, cocking a brow at him.

He chuckled. "I can't be Prince Charming all the time."

"Why not?" she complained, but reached up to cup his cheek. "Dare accepted."

His eyes flared at that. "Seriously?"

"Yeah." She grinned. "Why not?"

"Next time, remind me to come on your face."

She bit her lip, but he could see in her eyes, the idea didn't revolt her. If anything, it turned her on. Now, wasn't that a revelation.

Their Sascha was a dirty minx.

And he hadn't thought she could be much hotter.

TWELVE

"DAD?"

She guessed answering the phone with a question was indicative of their relationship. Which was kind of sad.

Okay, fuck 'kind of'. It was very sad.

She wished it was rectifiable too, but there was no way that was possible when her stepmom insisted on destroying bridges rather than constructing them.

"Hey sweetheart," her father murmured softly. His voice was weird though. Raspy.

"You doing okay? I didn't expect your call."

When she'd first moved over, he'd called every couple of weeks. That had drifted down to once a month, now she was lucky if it was three times a year. Sure, she could call him, but his schedule was fucked. He worked so many hours she worried for him, so the last thing she wanted was to ring him and wake him up.

He sighed. "Just wanted to hear your voice, baby girl."

"Okay." She drew out the syllables, unsure of what to say now. *Oh, the irony,* she thought. The man called to hear her voice, and said voice went silent on her. She cleared her throat. "How's things at home?"

"Weird. Tough times here. Makes me glad you're in England if I'm honest."

She blinked. Her dad was an ardent patriot. "Really?"

"Yeah."

His somberness wasn't too unusual, but she sensed something else was going on other than a disagreement on their homeland's politics. "Are you okay, dad? You sound weird?"

He gulped, the sound audible. "Linda's left me."

Her mouth dropped open. "Linda left you?" she squeaked, repeating him because that was all she was capable of.

Jesus H. Christ.

Linda had spent the last nine years of her marriage practically supergluing herself to Sascha's father. What the hell had changed? She let out a squeak of shock.

"I'm so sorry, dad."

"No, you're not," he answered, but without malice. "You two never got on. More on her part than yours. You tried a lot at first, I know, and she just played at it. By the time I realized that, it was too late. We were engaged and… I-I loved and missed your mom terribly so I made an even stupider mistake by going through with it just to... Jesus, I don't even know anymore. It made sense at the time."

Her eyes widened. *Were they really having this conversation?*

She turned on her side, away from Sean who was sleeping beside her. She'd crawled into his room last night when a migraine had her sobbing into her pillow. The accident had happened three weeks ago, and the pain was unbearable sometimes. Especially at night with nothing to keep her occupied.

The only relief came when the guys attended to her. Who knew? Orgasms were better than Ibuprofen. But they were scared of hurting her, scared of making it worse, so they barely touched her.

She felt certain she was going to go mad.

They kept trying to make her go to the doctors, too. But the truth was, she was frightened. What if something was really wrong with her?

Sean had nearly jolted out of his skin when she'd climbed under the sheets with him, but he'd soon settled down and had curled about her with an ease that really shouldn't have existed between them.

It was like they were lovers, but they weren't.

Not yet anyway.

Only because *he* wouldn't. *She* was more than ready.

Lowering her voice because she'd managed not to disturb Sean's sleep with her shrieking, she whispered, "It's okay, dad."

"No, it's not. I should never have allowed that to happen. You're *my* baby girl," he muttered fiercely. "You should always have been my priority. If you had, you wouldn't be in another goddamn country right now."

"Hey, you were pleased I was here a minute ago," she tried to gently tease, but the words sailed overhead. She heard a faint slur, and asked, "Have you been drinking, dad?"

There was a long silence. "Maybe."

She sighed. Her father was the worst drunk ever. He either sobbed out his misery or shouted out his rage. For that reason, she'd always been grateful he preferred maintaining a firm hold on his self-control than to succumbing to the demon's drink.

"You need to dose up on Alka-Seltzer and get into bed, dad," she ordered him. "You know you and beer aren't friends."

Her warning didn't do much good. He began sobbing. Though she knew the tears were more alcohol-fueled than anything else, it still hurt to hear her dad crying. It was like his world had ended, and she guessed that in a way, it had.

Linda was one of those Stepford Wives' types. She'd kept a clean and tidy house, had fed her father well, and had probably scheduled sex in both their diaries to make sure he never strayed.

Yes. She was that weird.

Truth was, she felt sadder at her dad's misery than the fact that Linda had left him.

Of course, that increased her guilt.

"Dad, please, don't cry. Just go to bed and get some rest. Call me in the morning. We'll talk. Properly."

"You promise?"

She blinked. When had she never answered a call? Even when it was four in the morning like now, and she had a man in her bed...

Sighing, she whispered, "I promise."

"Night, baby."

"Night, dad."

He cut the call first, and she bit her lip, wishing she could have someone confirm he was stumbling into bed.

"Everything okay?"

Sean's voice was a sleep-deprived rasp that had her wincing guiltily. "Yeah. Everything's fine. Go back to sleep." She set her cell phone back on the bedside table, and settled into a comfortable position.

"You don't talk often, do you?"

It took her a while to admit, "No."

"How come?"

"We just don't get along."

"Why not? You seem really laid back and chilled with most people. Why not with him?"

She sighed. "He just called because he split up with his wife. His wife is why we don't get along all that well. Ex-wife."

He rolled onto his side, and as he did, he tucked his arm under his head. She saw a small tuft of hair peeking out from under his arm, and had to smile. She'd never liked those metrosexual guys who shaved everything, and were all neat and tidy. Give her a little rough and ready any day of the week.

"What are you smiling at?" he asked roughly.

"Nothing in particular. Just… I don't know. You're hot."

He grinned. "Thanks. I think. If that's a compliment, that is?"

A snort escaped her before she could withhold it. "When is 'you're hot' never a compliment?"

"True. You just looked at me weirdly. I thought maybe I felt feverish to you or something."

"I look at most of you weirdly. You're all weird in comparison to me. I'm like the only one normal here."

"I'll give you that."

She wished she could mirror his position, but that would have involved lying on her bad arm, which wasn't going to happen.

Not unless she wanted to be sobbing within the next ten seconds.

"How could you not?" she teased. She rested on her back but turned her head to the side so she could look at him properly. "Things weren't great before they married, and then after? It just got worse.

"When I was in college I met a guy who had to move over here for work, and I came with him after I finished my degree. It wasn't hard to leave home, because home hadn't been *home* since my mother died."

"I'm sorry," he said roughly.

"Not your fault," she replied with a smile. "What about you? What about your family?"

He shrugged. "Mother, father. Two sisters, and a brother."

"That it? What about the skeleton in the closet?"

He grunted. "That's me. I'm the skeleton they try to avoid talking about."

That had her immediately scowling. "What the fuck? Why?"

"Hey, it's okay. I came to terms with it a long time ago."

She blinked. "No fucking way is that something you can accept with ease." Rage flushed through her, her cheeks were growing pink in reaction. "Holy crap, I'm so fucking mad right now, I don't think I can stand it. How dare they judge you! And for what? You're brilliant, generous, gorgeous in looks and nature. What do they have to complain about?"

"For one, they think this set up is weird."

"It is. *Weird*, I mean. But, so what? If it makes you happy, that's all that should count."

"Seriously, I've had a long time to get used to it. There's no need to be so concerned for me." He reached forward and traced a finger down her arm. "Thank you though. It's nice knowing you have my back, sweetheart."

"Why are you the family skeleton?" she asked, ignoring the words spoken to soothe her—she didn't need fucking soothing. She had no need to be pacified. She wasn't a baby. What she was, was totally, and *righteously* furious on Sean's behalf.

"Why wouldn't I be?" he answered with a sigh, and by God, it annoyed her to see how accepting he was of his family's shitty attitude. "I live with four men, and I share a woman with them, Sascha. What part of that is normal?"

"But they don't know that, do they?"

"Well, they do about the four men part. Not sure if it's even possible to hide Devon. Although maybe I should have tried a long while ago."

She snorted. "Yeah. That's not possible. His big mouth gets him into too much trouble."

"I don't know. He's actually pretty good with certain stuff. It's just a matter of whether he can understand the importance of it. Like, he would see no reason to hide why we're all living together. What society thinks, he doesn't give a damn about, and as living this way makes us happy, it makes even less sense to him to hide it. He only does because Sawyer would go crazy, and Devon tries not to anger him if possible."

She pondered that a second, then murmured, "It's kind of a nice attitude to have really, isn't it? It cuts out all the bullshit and makes life so smooth, because if you don't care what your peers think, then there's no pressure save for what you put on yourself."

Sean jerked a shoulder. "In theory, yes. That's how it works. The reality is often much different."

"Why? Because the reality involves you almost getting punched every time you open your damn mouth?"

Sean snickered. "Yeah. There's a reason Devon has a Sawyer-shaped keeper."

She grinned. "Cerberus, thy modern name is Sawyer." A thought occurred to her, and though it was a sensitive question, she asked it anyway, "Doesn't it offend you that they don't support your choices?"

"Of course, it does. But hell, what can I say? They're my family. I love them. They love me even if they don't understand me." His chin tilted up. "Would you tell your dad?"

"About you guys?" She pursed her lips. "I don't know. Maybe?"

"Depending on what?"

"If we were serious. If I got pregnant. I don't know. Something like that. Bearing in mind I didn't tell him I was in the car accident, Sean… that tells you how open I am with him."

His mouth dropped open. "You didn't tell him about the accident?"

She shook her head. "What good would it have done? He'd have just freaked, and there was no need."

"You need to give me his number and details, so I can keep him in the loop. Jesus, Sascha," he breathed, sitting up a little. "There's some shit family just needs to know."

She grimaced. "If you say so."

"Would you?" he asked, after silence fell between them. It wasn't an uncomfortable silence though, if anything it was relaxing. She liked being with them, she realized. They all brought equal parts peace, humor, and irritation to her days.

The perfect trifecta. *Well, more like my perfect Quintecta,* Sascha thought with an inward giggle.

Plus, if one of them pissed her off, one of the others could usually persuade her out of her funk.

Like yesterday when Devon had, with genuine confusion, asked if she'd meant to wear a bra that had her breasts almost falling out of it.

Because sure, she often did that just for the fun of it.

She snapped at him that being stuck in the same position wasn't great for keeping in shape, and that her tits were bigger because they were all too busy stuffing food in her face.

Kurt had been the one who'd brought her out of her mad on that occasion. He'd given her his manuscript to read. A quarter through, he'd asked her to give her opinion on what he'd written so far.

Smart didn't mean *smart* she was coming to realize. Baiting a bear with a literal sore head, Devon had no idea when watching his mouth was the best option.

"Would I what?" she asked, cocking a brow at him and the enigmatic question he'd thrown at her.

"Would you have a baby with us?"

"Are we really talking about that?" she answered softly. "When I haven't slept with you or Devon, and poor Kurt got off while he went down on me?"

He snickered. "You keeping a tally?"

"Inadvertently," she retorted with a huff. "The pussy is willing, as is the mind, but the body sure as shit isn't. I am so freakin' horny you wouldn't believe, but every time I try something, none of you will touch me. Even though it makes me feel better," she whined. "It's freakin' hell."

He blinked at her. "You know that's not an issue, right? I mean, yeah, there are five of us, but nowhere does it say you have to—" He grimaced. "Service us."

She stared at him a second, then let out a hoot for a laugh. "You did not just say that."

"I did just say that," he told her, tone serious. "And I mean it."

"How can you mean that? It makes no sense. Why would you want me to be a part of the household, as your girlfriend and partner more than just a housekeeper, if we didn't fuck?"

"Now you're purposely misunderstanding me," he retorted. "I'm saying that there's no pressure on you to do anything you don't want to do, or *can't* do. Okay? You don't have to think about the fact we haven't shagged yet. That's not an issue. The tally is on you, not us."

"Don't you want to fuck me?"

He rolled his eyes. "I've had a hard on since you sneaked into bed with me, Sascha. What do you think?"

"I think you're nuts."

"Why? For being considerate?"

She grimaced. "Maybe." Then, she admitted with a grunt, "Okay,

okay. That's not fair. I'm just not used to considerate guys, I guess. It's hard not to feel like there's some kind of pressure from you."

He stared at her, utterly aghast. "No way. That's not how this works."

She whispered, "Really?"

"No. We're a unit. A family. I thought we spoke about this before, thought you understood that?"

"I do. But the reality doesn't always gel well with that understanding. You're men. You have needs."

"Needs which we mostly ignore," he retorted with a little laugh, which charmed the freakin' life out of her.

"When was the last time you had sex?" she asked curiously.

"Do you really want to know?"

"Yeah. I do. Wouldn't have asked otherwise."

"Okay. I'll answer. Only if you'll answer mine."

"About the pregnancy thing?" At his nod, she sighed. "I would. If things were serious."

"What constitutes serious?"

"I don't know. I feel like I'd know more when the time came. I'm not waiting for anything, just… a click? A moment in time, I guess. It's different because this is unlike anything I've ever done before, so it's hard for me to say. But," she paused to contemplate her words. "you know when a guy proposes?"

He blinked, but nodded at her. "Yeah. I do. I've never been in that situation myself though, so I don't have practical experience of that."

"It doesn't matter. You get the concept. But the moments that lead up to that proposal? *That*. The nervousness, the hesitation. Will she, won't she? Asking if it's the right thing to do, then figuring it out it is… That's what I'm looking for. Aren't you?"

"I guess I am," he answered softly, seeming to process her words so he could fully understand them. "I never thought of it like that."

"So, why ask?"

"I don't know. You just mentioned it so flippantly. It gave me pause."

"Do you want kids?"

He nodded. "At some point, it would be nice. Just never looked like it was on the horizon."

"Because of the whole five guys/one chick thing?"

He snorted. "Yeah. That thing."

She grinned. "Didn't you ever think about doing what Kurt did?"

"Maybe. There were a few women over the years who made me think about a regular lifestyle, but things never worked out. Even if I couldn't have *this* with them, I wanted them in my life. They're my kin. Not by blood, but by bond. That matters. But it never did to any of the women who were important to me." He sighed. "They always wanted me to push them aside. Stop making time for the guys, and dedicate all my private life to them.

"I guess, looking back, they weren't asking for the Earth, but it was too much then. It would be now. Then, Kurt got divorced and there was a whole shitstorm there, so that totally discouraged me. We all came together again when he moved back in here, and Devon started going on about wanting this kind of lifestyle once more. The rest, as they say, is history."

She blinked. "So, when did you last have sex?"

"About eight months ago."

"Eight months?" Her mouth dropped open. "No way."

He laughed. "You don't believe me?"

"Nope."

"Why not?"

"Because you're too hot not to have every woman in the area trying to hump you."

"Well, the humping is an occupational hazard, but I manage."

She snickered. Reaching over to cup his cheek, she whispered, "I could fall in love with you so easily." The words had no right to slip from her lips, but she couldn't contain them. Couldn't stop herself from uttering them because they were the truth, and Sean, for whatever reason, always inspired her to speak the truth and nothing but the truth.

So help her God, she tagged on with an inner snort that made it easier for her to lighten up.

He cleared his throat at her declaration, but not because he was embarrassed. If anything, it was the opposite. He hadn't tensed up in reaction to her statement. Hadn't done anything save for settle deeper into the bed.

"You really mean that?" he asked her softly, but though his silence had been intense, it hadn't scared her.

"I'm not in the habit of saying things I don't mean. Isn't that what you told me when I first started here?"

He grumbled, "Jesus, I love having my own words repeated back to me."

She chuckled. "It's a pity for you that I have a great memory."

"Pity? I'm sure when I'm old and gray, I'll be grateful."

His words had her biting her lip. "You mean that?"

"Want me to repeat my own words again?"

Smiling, she shook her head, then whispered, "Kiss me goodnight."

He reached over, pressed his lips to her temple, and whispered, "I could fall in love with you too."

And those words were like a charm for her.

The madness of her feelings couldn't be total insanity if he was in as deep as she was, which meant she was safe. If he felt this way, then she wasn't in this alone.

She closed her eyes and sighed happily. What more could she ask for if not that?

"WELL?"

Was it stupid to admit to being nervous? Stupid or not, it was the truth. He *was* nervous. He wanted her to like his work, even if he wasn't pleased with it himself.

Or maybe it was *because* of that.

Which was totally fucked up.

"Are you going to kill off Herr Gruber?"

He blinked, taken aback by the question. "Maybe. Why?"

"Just answer the question," she retorted, her eyes wide with a curiosity that stunned him. "Does he die?"

"I haven't decided yet," he told her, rocking back into his desk chair, and watching as she folded a leg underneath her and took a seat opposite him, the manuscript still in her hands. "In the original plot, no. But the story hasn't worked out the way I'd thought it would."

"He has to die. If you don't kill him, dear Lord, I will never give you a blowjob. Like ever. That sick son of a bitch!"

He blinked, then grinned. "No blowjobs ever?"

She pouted. "I hate him."

"You're a brat."

"Maybe. Devon warned me about getting spoiled," she mocked, then grumbled, "but this isn't about being spoiled. It's about justice!

Dammit. He can't live. After torturing all those people in the secret police prison? He needs to go."

"You do know this is based on a real story, don't you?" he asked slowly, curious if she was aware of the backstory. He'd thrown the book at her the other day, not having forewarned her with the first novel in the series which came with a whole explanation as to the background.

"Yeah. I know about East Germany, and the secret police that helped keep it communist. I just… I knew about it, but nothing like this."

"To be fair, a lot of people your age don't know about the depths of depravity the Stasi sunk to in their desperate attempt to maintain order and control."

She blinked. "Seriously?"

"I'm sure it's the same in the U.S.," he said dismissively. "Guantanamo Bay ring any bells?"

"Sure, but we know about that one."

"What about the ones we don't know about?"

She blinked, shivered. "True." Another shiver. "This is creepy."

He snorted. "Good. It's supposed to be."

Staring down at the mass of paper in her hands, she flipped through the sheets and asked, "Why are you finding it so hard to finish?"

"Because of Gruber," he admitted. "In real life, he survived and went on to become a politician." His smile was bitter. "I'm fighting my inclination to do as you say, create justice through my pen."

"I know a lot of ex-officials for the East German government went on to have other careers, but they were found out and shamed, right?"

"Some of them," he confirmed.

"Was he?"

Another bitter smile. "No."

She hissed. "I'm so angry."

He grinned. "Well, I'm glad my book inspired something in you."

"It did. I feel all kinds of messed up. Especially because the ending is nowhere near ready. Okay, how about I give you all the blowjobs you need if you'll just write the damn book already?"

A chuckle escaped him. "How's the head?"

She pouted. "Too sore to be bobbing up and down," she admitted. "How about a throat fuck?"

Of course, she had to pick that exact moment when he slurped down some coffee to make that particular comment. It sprayed out of his mouth, and he pressed a hand to his lips in amused dismay.

"Jesus, Sascha, you really know how to pick your moments."

"I certainly do." She grinned. "Have I convinced you to get working or not?"

He smirked, ridiculously pleased that she liked his stuff. Changing the subject however, he asked, "Did Andrei tell you the gala's been rescheduled?"

"Of course he did. After last night's dinner."

Kurt rubbed his hands together. "I can't wait to see you in the dress we picked out."

Her nose crinkled. "I'm relying on men's taste in clothes. I must be crazy."

"You're probably certifiable if what you've shown me so far is any indication."

"You're a charmer. Jesus, I'm surrounded by them."

He grinned. "Come here."

"Why? Do you want some sugar?"

"Does a kiss constitute as sugar?" he asked, infinitely curious.

"It does. It could also constitute as something else if I was feeling one-hundred percent."

He sighed. "*Liebchen,* you need to go to the doctor."

She swallowed, ducked her head. "Next week. If things aren't better."

"I'll go with you," he promised her. "I'm sure nothing's wrong. It's just been so crazy around here lately that's all. It's the stress."

"But that's just it. I'm happy," she told him sadly. "I don't understand why the headaches are reoccurring so much. I know that whole bomb thing was scary, but aside from that, everything's been normal again, hasn't it?"

He nodded quickly. "It has."

She huffed out a breath. "I'll make an appointment. I really need to get back to doing regular stuff. I hate this. I feel like such a leech, too."

Though he was relieved his agreement hadn't aroused suspicion, he wasn't pleased with where her thoughts had led her. "Do you think if you hadn't fallen into this relationship with us we'd have made our housekeeper resume 'full' service after what you went through?"

"I don't want you to think I'm taking advantage of you."

"I think we'd know if you were."

"You wouldn't. I'm a great actress."

"Not that great," he said softly. "I can see the pain in your eyes. Why you've waited this long to go is beyond me."

"I hate doctors."

"Well, no one is a fan of them, Sascha."

She wriggled her shoulders. "I hate them more than most. I have since my mom died," she confessed uneasily. "She had cancer and had to spend a lot of time in the hospital. I feared losing her, so I was almost glued to her side through the treatment. It terrified me being away from her.

"I spent so much damn time at hospitals when I was a kid that I think now, I just can't face going back there. Even to clinics."

"You trust us to take care of you?"

"I know I shouldn't, not so quickly, but I do."

He smiled. "Good. So, if your head's still sore next week, we'll go to the clinic then, hmm?"

She bit her lip, but nodded. Her face was clouded with a misery that made his heart ache.

His gaze darted to the clock on the lower right side of his screen. "It's still early. You could take a nap."

"I have dinner to make."

"I can make dinner tonight if your head's bad."

"No. I'd prefer you to write Gruber's demise."

He smirked. "I can do both. Not only women multitask, I'll have you know."

She chuckled. "I've seen that in real life. I know you can do two things at once."

His smirk deepened into a genuine smile. For all its genuineness, however, it was utterly filthy. "I forgot. You have seen my marvelous skills at doing two things at the same time."

She winked, then admitted, "Thanks for the offer, babe. But I'll be fine. Anyway, I like cooking. It's relaxing."

"If you're sure?"

"Course I am." She beamed at him. "Wouldn't have said if it wasn't so." Their ritual now was that whenever they left the room, they kissed her farewell, or she came to them.

Pleased when she did just that, he watched her curvy ass sashay out of the room. Grunting a little at the sight of her butt, he adjusted himself, amazed anew at her ability to give him a hard on with barely any interaction.

Only when she'd closed the door, did he reach for his cell phone. "Any news?"

Sean sighed. "I can't really talk about this now. I'm in a meeting."

"It's important," Kurt argued. "Sascha was just talking about this with me, Sean. We need to give her some semblance of closure."

"Fob her off."

"I did, but she's not stupid. The only reason she hasn't asked sooner is because of the way her head has been aching."

"We need to get her to go to the doctors."

"I know. I convinced her. We're going next week if the headaches haven't stopped. But, though I don't want her to suffer, they're the only thing keeping this on the downlow."

"There's nothing to tell her. Not yet, anyway."

"Of course, there is," he snapped. "We can't keep on keeping this shit from her. It won't do us any good in the long run."

"No, but in the short run, it buys us time. I could be wrong about this entire situation."

"You're never wrong," Kurt argued. "You wouldn't have mentioned any of this to us if you weren't close to certain that Sascha's being targeted."

He blew out a long breath. "That's because it's insane. Why would anyone try to mow down a housekeeper and then blow her up? It doesn't make any sense."

Kurt gritted out, "Don't backtrack now, Sean. We both know you think there's merit to this supposition."

"I must have been crazy bringing it to you."

"Maybe. But sometimes the truth is stranger than fiction. Tell me, how's the investigation going?"

"Poorly. We've managed to ascertain…" He broke off. "I really can't discuss this, Kurt. Not here, and not *now*."

"MI6 beckons, huh?" he joked a little.

"You jest, but yeah." He blew out another breath. "I'm just trying to prove anything other than the fact Sascha is in danger. I want to be wrong where this is concerned."

"Of course, you do. Dammit, Sean. I never thought otherwise."

"I have to be wrong, don't I, Kurt? Why would anyone want to hurt her?"

"You've seen her background profile," he replied quietly. "You know what the security agencies know. Is there anything there?"

"No. The only thing that leaps to attention is the fact that her father is a cop, but he's a desk sergeant. It's not like he's active on the streets. He works a desk—in the U.S. nonetheless."

"He didn't always though, surely?"

"No. But he worked mostly traffic back in the day, and a beat that wasn't the most dangerous."

"It has to be because of him though, doesn't it?"

"That's the only thing that makes sense, but when I look into him, I see nothing that jumps out. Unless he took a bribe from the wrong person…? That's not going to be documented. But why wait until now? Why wait until she's with us to start targeting her?"

A puzzled frown puckered Kurt's brow. "What about her mom? Her grandparents?"

Sean let out another sigh. "There's very little on her mother. She was an immigrant though. Gained citizenship here when she was very young."

"From where?"

"Russia."

"That can't be a coincidence."

"Just because Andrei's past is a shitstorm over there, doesn't mean hers is."

"Bullshit. You know who Andrei's grandfather is, Sean. What if her mother's family knew Andrei's? They're the only ones psycho enough to do any of this shit."

"But why? It doesn't make any sense."

Kurt shrugged. "Just because it doesn't make sense to us, doesn't mean that's not the answer. We're missing so much information, there's actually very little point in hypothesizing.

"But, the truth is why else would Sascha be in danger? Her past is innocuous, but Andrei's isn't. And throw in the bomb scare? Maybe she's being targeted because of us. That's the only thing that makes logical sense."

"It falls back on why, Kurt! Why would anyone target Andrei, first off, when he's been out of Russia all these years? Why would anyone use Sascha to hurt Andrei when there's no reason to target him in the first fucking place?" Exasperation had him letting out an irritated hiss. "It's not like any of us need security; we've received no threats or warnings that would put us on our guard. And if Andrei's grandfather feared for his safety, you don't think the old bastard would have called?"

Kurt shook his head. "No. I don't think he would. He'd have handled it himself, in house. He knows Andrei would get the police involved, and Vasily never wants that. No matter how 'retired' he's supposed to be."

Sean sighed. "You're right on that score, I guess. But there has to be some link to connect these dots. All we have so far is that the SOB who hit Sascha was paid to mow her down. Without that, the bombing could be a coincidence. We wouldn't even be worried about her being targeted if it wasn't for his confession."

Kurt pulled his bottom lip away from his teeth and played with it as he thought. Sean wasn't wrong, but at the same time, Kurt had plotted enough mysteries to realize they were missing some pieces to the puzzle. "Has the driver spoken yet? Told the police anything else?"

"No. He's staying quiet. Not breaking after he misspoke that one time."

"Misspoke," Kurt commented with a snort. "Like admitting to being willing to ram into a crowded sidewalk isn't a huge fucking problem."

Sean grunted. "It isn't to these bastards. They have a target and a task, and they want to see it fulfilled. It's all about the money." He sighed. "It's always about the money."

Kurt heard his friend's weariness, but said only, "It's a messy way to go about it."

"Is it? Really? You can target someone in a crowd, and it looks like a regular terror attack—especially if you take into consideration the fact we were on Regent's Street, and it was busy. Plus, think about the bomb. With Jacobie there, it's plausible that he'd be the target. Why would the last-minute addition to the guest list cause question?"

"Do we know if Andrei specified who his guest was?"

"They needed her details to add her name to the table."

As the little information they had coalesced into one big mess in his head, Kurt whispered, "Fuck. This is messed up."

"Yeah. It is. Now you know why I want to be wrong."

"I always knew you wanted to be wrong, Sean. I'm not a fool. I just don't think putting blinders on is going to do any good."

Sean murmured, "I need to go now."

"MI6 is really looking into this?"

"Of course. It was a potential terror attack in the capital, Kurt. Jesus," he said on a tired sigh, "this is all kinds of fucked up."

"You're lucky you have the clearance to be dealing with this case."

"Yeah, *real* lucky. After I helped out on that situation in Malta, I figure they realize I'm good," came his wry retort. "I'll see you later. If she asks, just try to maintain the fact there's no information as yet. That's all we can do. And it's not really a lie."

"Okay. See you later, Sean. Good luck."

"I need it, mate."

When he cut the call, Kurt stared at his screen then down at the notes in front of him. As he flickered through the manuscript, he realized she'd made very competent annotations down the side of the MS.

Head tilting in surprise because she'd caught things his editor wouldn't have, he rubbed his chin, contemplating ways to keep her occupied but also, curious about her insight.

He had another manuscript he'd been working on. A 'secret' project that his publisher was unaware of. One that he was scared for anyone to read.

It was too raw. Too real.

But, it would keep her mind off the bombing. Keeping her mind off that was the priority, and with every note he read, he realized she was more than capable of reading his work in a way that most readers never would be able to. Editing a manuscript was more than just tough. There were levels to the process. Levels, Sascha seemed to be able to manage.

Ducking into the bottom drawer of his desk, he unlocked it with a key he kept in another drawer—it wasn't difficult to find, his intention wasn't to secure it but have it act as a deterrent—Devon had a habit of going through the house on the hunt for blank paper if he'd run out and Sawyer was at the gym. The man went through paper like a chain-smoker blasted through a packet of cigarettes.

As he retrieved the thick wad of the file, his cell rang. Spying his ex's Caller ID, he rolled his eyes. Katrin wasn't giving up. But the truth was, he'd spoken to Andrei already. What more could he do if his friend wasn't willing to help?

It wasn't like he could force Andrei to sit there and work through Katrin's problems like he was some kind of embezzlement detective. The man wasn't a math bloodhound.

Deciding to ignore the call, he grabbed the manuscript and headed for the kitchen.

As he made it downstairs, he realized she was listening to Erik Satie's *Trois Gymnopedies*. Three delicate piano pieces that would probably soothe her as she got to grips with the day's meal, and that echoed around the perfect acoustics in the kitchen.

She must have heard him coming down the steps because she smiled over at him. "Couldn't stay away, huh?"

A laugh escaped him—her humor was just one of the many things he found charming about her. "I come bearing gifts."

"You do?" She cocked a brow at him. "What kind of gifts?"

"A manuscript."

"You lied? *Black Blood II* is finished?" She squealed, then winced as the squeal obviously hurt her already pounding head. Pressing a hand to her temple, she turned eyes that were bruised with fatigue. "You're mean," she chided, her voice a little hoarse. "Gimme." The arm in a cast shot out, and she groaned. "I am so sick of this fucking cast."

Feeling guilty at the double whammy of pain he'd inadvertently caused, he murmured, "No. This isn't *Black Blood II.*" He tutted at her. "As if I'd lie to you about something as unimportant as this."

When she rolled her eyes at him, he shook his head—it was suddenly imperative that she know that. They were only keeping the truth of the bombing and her accident back because they didn't want to frighten her or cause unnecessary worry while she was still reeling from the concussion. All Sean had at the moment was a 'supposition'. That wasn't fact. Why scare her with hypotheses?

"I mean it, Sascha. I wouldn't lie to you unless it was imperative."

She tilted her head to the side, obviously questioning the severe tone he'd used. "I was only teasing, Kurt," she told him gently.

"I know, but I mean it. Lying to you isn't a habit any of us will ever adopt. For this to work, as complicated as it is, we must all be open with one another." That was one of the reasons why withholding the whole truth hurt him and made him feel like a hypocrite of the worst order.

"You really mean that, don't you?" she asked softly, her tone a little wondrous. "I mean, the fact you want this to work."

"Of course, I do," he retorted, surprised at the fact that was what she'd picked up on in this conversation. "We all do."

She reached for the coffee pot, placed it on the counter, then a tray came next, upon which she placed cream, sugar, and two mugs. Sensing where she was going with this, he grabbed the tray when she'd finished stacking things on it, laid it on the table, and watched her round the counter to come and sit beside him.

Playing mum, Sascha poured them both a coffee and dosed it up the way he liked. After sipping at the brew, he asked, "What's wrong?"

"Why do you want this? Explain it to me, Kurt. Why don't you want me to yourself?"

He blinked, because the answer was obvious to him, but he guessed, at varying levels, she'd ask them all this at one point or another.

"Because we work best as a team."

Her eyes widened at that, and she smiled. "Tag teaming FTW, huh?"

He snorted. "You know what I mean. My marriage failed because I was used to living with these four. Used to working with them, interacting, being a part of this…" He shrugged. "I don't even know what to call it."

"On my interview, I called this place a salon."

He grinned, shot her a wink. "That's actually quite accurate. Very perceptive of you." Fiddling with the coffee mug, he murmured, "You know when you realize something just works?"

"I do."

"I found that when we were with Janna. Everything made sense. To others, it wouldn't. But we were all busy. All had insane schedules. Sean had already come to the attention of several security agencies, and was being headhunted. Devon and Sawyer too. Living as we were, we all knit together. Each providing something the other needed." He shrugged. "It wouldn't work for many, but it does with us."

"Why did you get married then?"

"Because my mother introduced me to Katrin, and I didn't want to displease her."

"Bullshit!" she chortled. "Who marries someone because their mommy wants it?"

He rolled his eyes. "Let me explain," he chided. "My mother has never appreciated the 'Salon' as you call it. Thinks it's a cover for us all being lovers. She went through a phase where she tried to set me up with as many women as she possibly could. Katrin is a beautiful woman, and I'm a man. She was temptation itself, and I fell under her spell.

"Then, I realized a few things about myself. She took advantage of the situation, of me. Lied to me. Made me see I couldn't trust her. The day that happened, I was looking for an opportunity to divorce her."

"What did you realize about yourself?"

His grin was sheepish. "Things that if you ask the others, they knew long ago." He rubbed his chin. "You sure you want to know?"

Her eyes twinkled. "I'm sure. I'm a big girl. I can cope."

"Janna liked being shared. I used to love watching her being worked over by Sawyer and Devon. It was hot as fuck. They let me. So did Andrei and Sean when they were with her too, although, they never shared Janna that way. I didn't really put a name to the need until I married Katrin.

"She suggested it one day."

"*She* suggested she sleep with another guy?"

He nodded. "Yeah. I don't know how she figured it out, but she knew what got me off."

"Wow. That's beyond weird."

"I guess. I later learned that she only married me because she had a trust fund she wanted access to. She likes to have many lovers… this way, she could be married to me, and facilitate that need."

"That's a bit sick."

He snorted. "Fine words, Sascha."

"What?" she grumbled. "It is."

"It's not. It's just what she wanted. At the time, I was more than happy. Don't forget, my kink is to watch. But, then I realized she was doing it without me there too, and my eyes were opened.

"I hired someone to tail her, gather evidence. There was a lot of money riding on the divorce, hers and mine. I needed the leverage to make sure we both left with our own assets intact. She's bitter enough to have taken as much from me as she could even though she's the wealthier of the two of us."

"She's lucky you answered her call when we were at the hospital."

He grinned at her waspish remark. "She bruised my ego, not my heart, Sascha."

"Why?" She cleared her throat. "Not that I'm not glad she didn't hurt you too much."

"At the time, it hurt. But now, looking back, it helped me learn a lot about myself."

"So, I should expect to frequently find you jacking off while watching me and one of the guys at some point in the future?"

His cheeks pinkened at her blasé tone. "Would that disturb you?"

Her lips pursed, and her gaze dropped to her coffee. "No. If it had, I wouldn't have let you watch me with Andrei." More to the coffee than him, she whispered, "Knowing you were watching was hot."

Inside, his nerves scrambled away to dust. *She understood!* He blew out a breath. "I don't have to, if you don't like it."

She cut him a look. "I just said I did. Don't push your luck."

His grin was quick. "I won't."

Propping her chin on her good hand, she studied him. "So, being married helped you realize you wanted what you'd lost with Janna and the others?"

"Yes. Being with a woman is surprisingly demanding work."

His earnestness had her laughing. "Thanks."

He crinkled his nose. "I meant no offense."

"I know. I'm developing thick skin."

"Probably wise with Devon around."

"You blame him, but you're all as bad as each other sometimes. You take honesty to the millionth degree."

He winked. "At least you'll always know where you stand with us."

"True," she ceded. "Anyway, you were saying…"

Nodding, he carried on where he'd broken off. "It truly is hard to satisfy a woman fully if you're a busy man. Which we all are. Yet, one of us can always be there for that woman who matters to us.

"Look at now; Sean and Andrei are out in meetings, and Devon and Sawyer are working upstairs. Yet, you need not be lonely or feel like we've forgotten you because I'm here."

She blinked. "But you don't have to worry about that."

He shrugged. "It's not a worry, per se. It's just a concern to us. We get very involved in our work. You haven't seen me when I've been working manically. It hasn't happened yet as I've been having trouble with *Black Blood II*. You have me here now, but I might not be here if that was the case. One of us would adjust to suit."

"So, basically, you like this lifestyle because you can manage me?"

His eyes widened. "No! Nothing like that!"

She frowned at his vehemence. "Okay. Then what?"

"We want you to be happy. That matters more than anything. Our being absent detracts from that. We can work as a team to satisfy you."

Sascha blew out a breath. "I'm not sure if you're digging yourself into a deeper hole here or not," she said with a chuckle. Running a hand through her hair, she disheveled her loose topknot and sank back into the leather dining chair. It rocked with her movement, which in turn had pain shadowing her eyes.

"How can I explain this to you?" he asked himself irritably. "Sawyer's right. I can write what I do, but find it difficult to talk about my feelings."

"I don't know," she countered. "You've been doing a damn good job of it so far."

He eyed her. "Are you being sarcastic?"

She grinned. "Maybe." Holding up her hand, she pinched the air between pointer finger and thumb. "Maybe just a smidgen."

Her wink shouldn't have set his heart alight, but it did. As a result, he was far too earnest as he admitted, "I could fall for you so easily."

Her grin died as a soft breath escaped her lips. "Oh, Kurt. Me, too."

He reached for her hand, and like a courtier of old, pressed his lips to the backs of her fingers. "Then we're on the same page?"

Kurt wouldn't lie—he was stunned to see the moisture in her eyes, but relieved too.

"We are."

THIRTEEN

DEVON WAS the first down for dinner, which stunned her as he was usually the last. First for breakfast, last for dinner.

"What happened? Someone set fire to your desk chair?"

He blinked. "Huh?"

With a grin, she repeated the question.

"No, there's no fire. I would have called the fire department if there was," he told her earnestly.

"I'm surprised you know the number."

"Numbers are my thing," he told her, with all the sagacity of Dumbledore parting wisdom to Harry.

"They're not, are they?" she pretended to gasp.

He frowned. "I'm concerned, Sascha. Has the concussion made you forget even the basic things?" Before she could do more than snicker, he continued, "I noticed that you put a flower on my desk. I looked that up online, but I can't see why you'd do something like that unless it's because you're sick."

Withholding her chuckle was impossible. "It's not a flower, Devon. It's a cactus."

He wafted a disinterested hand. "It wasn't listed on the symptoms of concussion I found online."

"It has nothing to do with my having a headache." She tutted under her breath. "I wanted you to have some green in your room."

"But why?" he demanded, sounding bewildered.

Stepping further into the kitchen, he took a seat opposite her at the counter. "Because your room is chaos. So, I've decided I'll be adding more things to your office," she warned. "You need more oxygen in there."

"There's plenty to go around."

"You won't let me open the windows in there. It stinks."

"How can it stink? We don't do anything in there apart from work."

"It smells like there's no fresh air in that room," she retorted. "Fresh air is good. Stale air is bad."

He glowered. "I like it that way."

"Well, I don't. I've been researching which flowers and houseplants bring more oxygen into a room. I'm warning you ahead of time. There'll be more coming your way."

"I won't water them," came his staunch reply.

She snickered. "Honey, if I'd expected you to water them, I might as well expect to pick the winning lottery numbers tomorrow."

"Now you're being sarcastic."

"Good job for picking up on that," she congratulated him as she moved around the counter with a dish in her hand. It charmed her when he got to his feet immediately and met her more than halfway.

He could be a forgetful clod most of the time, but he was as debonair and gentlemanly as the rest of them.

He grabbed the platter and tutted. "You should have asked me to get the dish. It's too heavy for you." Before he returned to the table, he said, "Sorry. I forgot." And bent down to kiss her softly on the lips.

Breathily, taken aback by his kiss although she was getting used to their new habit of greeting her this way, she replied, "I could get used to being waited on by you guys," she murmured softly, smiling as he placed the dish in the center of the table just so—bang in the middle of the round mat so that there was equal distance all around it.

She often wondered what he saw when he looked around the world.

Whatever it was, it wasn't what she and the rest of them saw. For all their brilliance, Devon worked to a whole other scale, and that was a part of his charm if she was being honest.

"I didn't hear any noise down here, and your hair looks normal," he commented as he reached for a few more dishes she stacked on the top.

Dinner consisted of a large bowl of pasta, another of an Amatriciana sauce complete with large chunks of tender pig cheek and sweet tomatoes, a dish of slivered parmesan cheese, and a long breadboard with garlic bread on it.

"Why would you? I was cooking. And what does my hair have to do with anything?" she asked, perplexed with the segue.

"You and Kurt were down here."

"So? And that was ages ago." She took a seat at the head of the table and asked him to, "Hit the intercom again, please. It's getting cold."

He wandered over to the intercom at the other side of the kitchen, pressed it, then said, "If you don't come down now, I'll eat your portions."

She tilted her head to the side as he came back to her and sat next to her. "Aren't you getting enough food?"

Eying the pasta dish which contained over a kilo of dried spaghetti, as well as the large tureen of sauce, and the four loaves of garlic bread, she mentally calculated how she'd make their portions bigger. Of course, that was unnecessary, because he shook his head.

"Nope. You feed us enough," he told her with a smile as he began to serve himself. "I was just making an empty threat."

"We should wait for the others."

He shrugged. "I'm hungry, and on time. You snooze, you lose."

Grinning at him, she watched him dish up, and then remembered what he'd said. "Oh yeah, you were saying something about Kurt and I being downstairs in the kitchen earlier?"

He blinked. "I thought you were having sex that's why I didn't come down for cookies."

Her mouth dropped open. "Why would you think that?"

"I heard you the other day, and Kurt likes to have sex in odd places."

A snicker sounded from behind her. "What a glorious time to arrive at the dinner table."

She shot Andrei a quelling look, which had him shrugging before he bent down and kissed her temple. "What? It Is!"

As he took a seat, Devon peppered him, "Am I right or wrong, Andrei? Doesn't Kurt fuck in weird places?"

Andrei served himself too, and as he loaded sauce onto the dish and grabbed bread, he nodded. "Yes. Expect to get used to feeling things sticking into your ass."

"See, I told you," Devon said proudly. "And don't worry," he confided. "I sprayed down the table after you had sex on it." He patted her hand.

She choked at that.

"Do you need some water?" he asked, innocently.

"No," she retorted, feeling a little hot under the collar at his line of thought.

Andrei, spying this, grinned. "It's nice to know the whole house will be disinfected from time to time."

Glowering at him, she retorted, "I expect this from him, not you."

He shrugged, but shot her a wicked grin which slowly and tenderly morphed into a gentle smile. "How's the head?"

"Bad."

The confession had Devon frowning. "When are you going to see the doctor again?"

"I don't want to talk about it." Jesus, she hated going to clinics.

"That page I looked at says headaches are common for a while after the concussion," he tried to reassure her which was the cutest thing ever. As well as the fact he'd thought of her while he was in super-math-genius mode.

Was there any other way to melt around these guys than the many ways she had already?

Andrei shook his head. "Doesn't mean she shouldn't go to the doctor anyway. Kurt said something about you agreeing to go next week?"

"Only if things haven't improved," she retorted, a tad stubbornly.

Andrei cocked a brow at her, but before he could say anything, Sawyer and Sean made their way down the stairs. Before heading for their respective seats, Sawyer kissed her on the cheek, Sean on the lips.

Jesus, was she the only one feeling flustered around here or what?

Fanning herself would have been too obvious, so instead, she took a drink of ice water and hoped it would stop her from melting.

"What hasn't improved?"

Andrei looked at Sean. "The headache situation."

Sean immediately scowled. "Why haven't you gone to the doctor's, again?"

She huffed. "Because I don't want to. We've already had this discussion."

Sawyer, as he loaded himself up with spaghetti, murmured, "I'll go with you, lass. I hate doctors too. They give me the willies."

She blinked at that, then snorted. Even though she was uncomfortable with the topic of conversation, she had to laugh. "The willies? What the fuck are they?"

"Not penises," Devon informed her. "It's a phrase."

Andrei clicked his fingers. "I know this one. Heebie-jeebies?"

She chuckled. "How do you know that?"

"A misspent youth watching too many *Home Alone* movies on repeat."

Snickering at the precision of his comment, she turned to Sawyer and said, "You'd really go with me even though doctors give you the willies?"

He shrugged. "Course."

Touched to the point where her stomach churned with excess emotion, she whispered, "Thank you."

Apparently uncomfortable with her regard, he shifted in his seat. "You don't have to thank me."

"Sure I do." She cleared her throat, overwhelmed by the knowledge he'd go to the clinic with her even though he didn't like it.

But, wouldn't she do the same for any of them?

And, if they were experiencing headaches as fucking painful as the ones she was having, wouldn't she make them go, and sit with them, too?

Fuck.

Overwhelmed wasn't the word, as she realized exactly how far along her feelings were for these men. Was it possible to fall in love when you were halfway to the ground already? Wasn't that more a case of '*fallen*'?

The intercom buzzed, and she embraced its meaning with relief. Jerking upright, then wincing as her head throbbed after the too-swift move, she stated quickly, "I'll get the door."

Sean frowned. "You should sit down. I'll go."

"No. I'm good. Eat. You're growing boys," she tried to tease, and wasn't sure she'd hit the mark when they all looked at each other uncertainly—shit, she must look like hell if they were studying her the way they were.

"If you're sure?"

"Positive," she retorted, already on the stairs and on the way up to the first floor.

Each step she took had her head pounding, and she couldn't contain the slight groan that fell from her lips. Leaning against the wall, she gathered her breath, then stepped on toward the front door.

Opening it, she blinked at the woman standing there. "Yes?" she asked, when the stranger looked her up and down.

"Let me in," came the snooty retort.

"Excuse me?" Sascha demanded, rearing back at the sharp command, her dizziness forgotten. "Who are you?"

Behind her, the sound of footfall coming down the stairs had her turning around. As she did, she saw Kurt was on his way, looking harried—he must have thought the second buzz of the intercom was the reminder for dinner, and he knew she hated it when they let their food go cold.

She wasn't sure if the men needed a housekeeper and a lover, or a mother sometimes.

The way she moved, however, gave him a perfect view of the woman at the door. His eyes widened at the sight, and he froze in place.

"Katrin? What the fuck are you doing here?"

WORSHIPPED BY THEM

FOURTEEN

WITH A FROWN, Sawyer looked at the woman sitting in his friend Kurt's seat, and wondered what it was the idiot had seen in his ex-wife, Katrin.

She was a hard-faced bitch. And that wasn't just because he knew all the shitty things she'd done to Kurt. Her malice and lack of interest in anyone other than herself was evident from every angle on her face.

From the constant purse of her lips, to the dissatisfied narrowing of her eyes, it was as though everything around her wasn't worthy of her attention. She was haughty, dismissive, and high-maintenance—and the day Kurt had divorced the cow had been a day Sawyer had let his inner Scot out by doing a jig.

Somehow, she managed to pack the sly wickedness into a pretty package. The bitch was beautiful, he wouldn't lie, but he'd rather stick his dick into a vat of liquid nitrogen than Katrin.

Although, fucking her would probably be like fucking the freezer anyway—the woman made frigid seem positively tropical. Rubbing his chin, he watched as the skinny blonde invading his kitchen shed crocodile tears and put on an act worthy of an Academy Award.

"Oh, for God's sake. How long do we have to listen to this bullshit for?" he snapped, tired of her games, and, call him mean, but bored of her. She was Kurt's ex-wife. Ex being the most important word in that sentence.

The woman only gave a fuck about herself. That was it. She was *numero uno*. It didn't matter that Kurt might have a new woman in his life, that they all might have something going on that didn't involve her troubles—hadn't she come here just in time for the evening meal? When she knew they'd all be there?

All that mattered was Katrin.

Not them.

Just her.

The others shared uneasy glances. None of them were interested in anything Kurt's ex had to say, not even the man himself. He was looking more awkward than all of them put together, but Katrin had come here, and was making no move to fuck off.

"Sawyer! It isn't bullshit," Katrin cried, her German accent thicker than Kurt's. Although, while Kurt's had an attractive, polished air – hers was nothing more than angry noise.

"It is. Or at least, the tale isn't, but the tears are. You don't give a shit about what happened to your hedge fund manager. You just want to know what happened to your ten million."

Her eyes flared with irritation—she'd never liked him. It was a mutual dislike, so he wasn't exactly weeping into his porridge, but still, her distaste for him was as plain as the nose on his face.

Of them all, he was the only one with humble beginnings. The rest had silver spoons in their mouths from birth. Not that he held that against them. Never had, either. Even when they'd first met, and he'd thought them smug dicks, he'd gradually grown to like them—silver spoons and all.

Sawyer, unlike the rest—even Devon—had worked insanely hard to get to where he was in this world, and Katrin didn't appreciate that. Why would she? She hadn't had to work for a damn thing in her life. She constantly looked down on him, and he wasn't willing to cower like other mortals would have done in her *divine* presence. He sure as shit wasn't going to kiss her fucking feet.

A small wail of German had them wincing—they all spoke the language. "Can you blame me?" she demanded. "Ten million isn't like ten pounds. It's a lot of money. Money nobody could afford to lose!"

He shrugged, disinterested. "And this is our problem, why?" When she glowered at him, he glowered back. "Why haven't you gone to the police?"

"I have. They're not listening." Her lips flatlined with disapproval.

Sawyer narrowed his eyes at her, and declared, "If I needed more confirmation that this was bullshit, I've just had it. If a woman with as much clout as you can't make the authorities listen, then there's nothing going on."

Sean cleared his throat. "Sawyer's right, Katrin. You pull a lot of punches in Bavaria. If you can't get someone in Munich to listen, then why should Andrei be able to change things?"

"I don't want Andrei to pull strings, I want him to look into the books."

"Since when was I a forensic accountant?" he retorted coolly. He was the only one who'd continued eating throughout Katrin's performance, almost as though the pain in the arse hadn't interrupted their meal. He'd always had a fucked-up idea of what the word 'drama' represented.

Truth was, Sawyer was starving, but her nonsense put the distinct stench of BS in the room, and *that* was off-putting. Still, he felt guilty. Sascha had slaved over this food, and they were letting it go cold. He hated waste too.

Cutting her a glance, because in his irritation, he'd not checked in with her—even visually—he saw she was looking faintly shell-shocked as well as tired and a little bruised from fatigue.

She didn't need this shit.

But none of them did.

Just under three months ago, Sascha had entered their world as their housekeeper. She'd since become their lover.

She was sinful and sexy, vivacious and earthy. She was everything he'd never realized they'd been looking for, and if Katrin, the bitch, thought to mess with that, Sawyer would stop any of her crap in its tracks.

He'd seen the looks Katrin had been shooting Sascha's way. *Friendly*, they weren't.

Three weeks ago, Sascha had been in a car accident. Well, what had appeared to be an accident. A kid had wandered into the road to pick something up, Sascha had pushed him out of the way, and had been clipped in the process. She'd been diagnosed with a moderate concussion and a broken radius.

Ever since, her headaches had put her down for the count. She was suffering; and that suffering was more than visible on her face. Dark shadows lined her eyes, and the lids were heavy, almost swollen with her fatigue.

It killed him to see her like that. It killed him more to think that the accident hadn't been an accident at all.

The driver had confessed to a 'plot' to kill Sascha by mowing down a wave of pedestrians just to cover up her death. That particular confession had come hours after the crash, and ever since, the driver had stayed quiet. The only thing they knew now was that the bastard wasn't talking. About anything.

Not why Sascha was the target.

Not who had paid him to take her out.

Nada.

Then, there'd been the bomb at an event where Andrei and Sascha were due to attend.

The police had concluded it was related to the presence of a software mogul of Zuckerberg proportions—only one better at keeping out of the spotlight. The authorities had figured the threat was aimed his way, but the driver's confession had prompted Sean into seeking a connection between the two events, and thus far, he hadn't come up with much.

Trouble was, Sean's hunches were always right on the money.

It was why the bastard had reached the lofty heights he had. A man didn't consult on cases with MI6 without having earned himself a reputation. And Sean had several notable cases that had found him in the papers.

The Lancaster Bomber was behind bars thanks to Sean, and that sick fuck who'd murdered eight women, and made a game out of it with the cops? Sean had solved every single one of those riddles. If the idiot police had listened to him ahead of time, instead of doubting the man's genius, a few of those women would still be walking around today.

Because they hadn't, Sean had their deaths on his conscience. The shadows in the man's eyes ate at Sawyer. He loved Sean like he was a brother, and to know the man was in pain all because some dickheads in uniform hadn't listened when they should have, was a knife to the gut.

It was why Sean worked so goddamn hard now. The man burned the candles at both ends, and considering Sawyer was accustomed to

Devon, who worked like night and day were the same concept, that was saying something.

"Why are you letting them talk to me like this, Kurt?" Katrin demanded haughtily, resting her elbow on the edge of the dining table. The move drew the full plate in front of her to her attention. She wrinkled her nose and pushed it away like she was shoveling horse dung out of her path.

"You're no longer my wife, Katrin. They can talk to you any damn way they see fit. I'm not their keeper."

Sean sat at the head of the table, Sascha at the other end. Behind Sean, Kurt was leaning against the wall, his arms folded, and his expression one of disinterest.

Katrin's nostrils flared with outrage, her eyes flickering to each man in the room. "You can't be serious."

"Can't I?" Kurt cocked a brow and sniffed his lack of regard for her delicate *sensibilities*.

But then, Katrin wasn't here for Kurt. They knew that. Well, Sawyer figured, everyone but Sascha seemed to know that.

Her confusion hurt him, and he wished he was sitting beside her. If he was, he could have held her hand, squeezed it to reassure her. But Devon was next to her, eying Katrin the way he eyed their chalkboard when they were in the middle of a problem they needed to solve.

Not that Katrin was that hard to figure out.

Devon just saw things differently.

Having never been inside his best friend's head, he couldn't imagine how the world looked to him. But… knowing him as well as he did, Sawyer could easily picture it where, hovering over everyone's head, there was a bubble.

Above Sawyer's, it probably said 'math friend—love—give beer, friend for life'.

Over Sascha's, 'Friendly—makes good cookies—sexy—will sleep with me if I'm not too weird'.

Then, over Katrin's, 'Avoid—hurt Kurt—makes too much noise—slam door in her face'.

The latter was less of a guess.

During Kurt's marriage, they'd had a huge problem convincing Devon to let Katrin into the house if she ever knocked on the door. Sean had solved it by telling Devon he was never to answer the door again. But before that dictate had sunk in, any time Katrin had knocked and Devon had been the one to open the door, he'd closed it swiftly afterward.

Even Kurt had found that funny, and he'd been the one who'd gotten shit for it later from the old lady.

With thoughts of the very recent past swimming in his head, a past where Kurt had been more miserable than Sawyer had ever seen him, he eyed Katrin with as much distaste as Devon. She was only there to sway Andrei to her cause—hadn't even come for Kurt's help, just Andrei's.

Andrei had, for some weird reason, always been attracted to Katrin. Kurt had even invited Andrei into the marital bed, and the idiot had accepted. Ever since, he'd trod carefully around her. But, since the woman's surprise arrival, Sawyer had to admit he hadn't noticed any lingering glances between them. If anything, Andrei was as concerned about Sascha's pallor as the rest of them. His interest flickered between his plate and Sascha, that was it. It was almost like Katrin wasn't there —a fact that had to stick in the bitch's craw.

When Katrin began bickering with Kurt in German, a language they all spoke but Sascha, Andrei reached over and cupped her arm, softly asking, "Sascha, sweetheart, are you feeling okay?"

She blinked, her gaze shifting away from the argument going down in front of her and moving to the hand Andrei pressed to her knee under the table. "I'm fine."

"You don't look it," Sawyer countered, willing to say that much and little else.

He was uneasy with Sascha, that he'd admit. She turned him on something fierce, and his body was more than willing to overcompensate for the fact his brain was at a loss.

Sascha made him think about things he'd never thought about before. Hell, she even made him feel shit he'd never felt. In his fucking forty-one years of existing, God help him.

If he was being honest with himself, he knew he clamped down on his reactions to her. Especially in front of his friends. Alone, it was easier to come to terms with the strange way she made him feel. Not by much, but some.

Trouble was, he didn't seek her out enough to get used to the way she made him feel. A fact he knew he needed to change.

"They're right," Devon murmured, as usual sticking his foot in his mouth. "You look a bit crappy."

Sawyer hissed out a breath. Could the man never hold his goddamn tongue?

Jesus. He loved Devon like a fucking brother, but sometimes, he'd love to deck him and knock him the fuck out.

For whatever insane reason though, Sascha rarely took offense. Most of them took that as divine providence. If she could accept Devon's inability to say the right thing at the right time, then she was heaven-bloody-sent. And in this, there was no change, because at his words, she chuckled.

"Say it how it is, Devon, why don't you?" She reached forward and, with her good hand, pressed her palm to his cheek. "I'm fine," she told him, then turned to look at them both. To Andrei, she shot him an earnest smile, and pressed the fingers half-shielded by a cast against his.

Sawyer scowled. She was lying. Why though?

Her attention immediately returned to the bickering Germans down the end of the table, and he had to wonder if she was jealous. But she couldn't be, surely? Not when they were arguing the way they were.

Kurt and Katrin had never been blissful, and right now they weren't even remotely trying to get along.

Because he could sense the argument was upsetting her even though he could sense she didn't want to miss out on what was happening, he barked out, "Enough, you two." To Kurt, he quietly reminded, "Sascha's head."

Katrin's jaw flexed with irritation, but Kurt shot him an understanding look before he too studied Sascha.

It was amazing how the diminutive American had entered their lives and taken over. They hadn't been looking for another partner, but it was what they'd found when she'd agreed to work for them. A notion that had even Sean flabbergasted, and that man was pretty difficult to surprise.

Kurt strode away from the wall and headed for Sascha's side. He crouched down in front of her, and softly murmured, "Want to go upstairs?"

She bit her lip, peered over at Katrin. On the brink of her refusal—

she looked like she'd stay put through an air raid—Sean murmured, "Everything will be all right, Sascha. I promise. You go get some rest."

Sascha's eyes met his, then she slowly nodded. Sean was the *de facto* head of the house. They all deferred to him. Even Andrei, who probably held it together better than most of them. It came as little surprise that Sascha's reaction was proof that she'd follow their lead.

Kurt, completely ignoring Katrin, stood up, helped her to her feet, then carefully hefted her into his arms. They were gradually growing accustomed to doing things very slowly where she was concerned.

She'd had the concussion for three weeks, and it didn't look like it was going anywhere soon. With every flinch and wince, groan and whimper of pain, Sawyer had to admit, he was going nuts for her.

Who the fuck had done this to her? Who was plotting to hurt her? Sawyer wondered. Hating that she was in danger and hating it even more when he knew they had zero idea why or from whom the peril was sourced.

She let out a little moan when she was in Kurt's arms, but settled into him with an ease that spoke of a deep intimacy. There was no way Katrin could fail to see that, and after he watched Kurt carry Sascha up the stairs, Sawyer looked at the ex-wife from hell and saw the calculating look in her eye.

"Katrin, you have less than five minutes to leave the house."

His order had her eyes widening, mostly because Sean was usually the one who'd issue such a dictate. Around him, he felt the unease his friends felt. They were family, and he loved them, but from time to time, they could be pussies.

He was, in his own way, a gentleman. He believed in caring for the women in his life, opening doors and all that shit. But when it came time to deal with bitches like this one, he knew when to back away from the chivalry and get down to brass tacks.

Katrin was a manipulator and a user. Having a pussy didn't suddenly make that acceptable. She was toxic, and she needed to go. Stat.

The others, though they knew it, were too well bred and kindly to spring into action.

"I need your help," she argued, a beseeching tone to her voice.

Trouble for her was, with that thick accent, no way could she ever pull off beseeching. "I'm sure you do. You can call at office hours."

She snorted. "Since when have any of you held office hours?"

Sean sighed. "Since forever. Now, as you can see, it's time for the evening meal. Sawyer's right, Katrin. It's time to leave."

"I can't leave."

Devon frowned. "Technically, there's no such word as can't."

Katrin narrowed her eyes at him. "Don't be pedantic, Devon."

"Sascha says it's what I do best," came his proud retort, a reply that had all their lips twitching in varying degrees.

Sawyer had a feeling that over the coming weeks, the longer Sascha lived with them, and the more they got to know her in the Biblical sense, they'd be hearing that more and more often.

'Sascha says.'

Had Katrin not been here, he'd have mocked Devon, and from Andrei's smirk so would he, but with the bitch present, there was no way they'd break ranks.

Her narrowed eyes became all the narrower. Jesus, she was practically squinting at them as she murmured, "She's another one of your whores, isn't she? *Mein Gott*, are you so desperate you're hiring the women in now?"

Slamming his palm against the table, uncaring that the plates rattled, he spat, "You say another fucking word, Katrin, and I'll toss you out rather than let one of the others escort you."

She went from squinting to gawking in less than a millisecond. "You wouldn't dare," came the huffy but wary retort.

"Just try me."

She pushed her shoulders back a tad, then murmured, "I can't leave. I have nowhere else to go."

Andrei frowned, but as he asked, "Why not? Never heard of hotels?" Sawyer noticed he didn't look at the woman.

"I don't have enough money for a hotel."

The five of them froze in their seats. Kurt's family wasn't exactly super rich, but they were damn wealthy. Katrin was wealthier still. Her grandparents had more fingers in more pies than a freakin' baker back in their heyday. A wealth her father had increased exponentially.

For her to say that? It was beyond fucked up.

"How is that even possible?" Sean asked, his tone showing the bewilderment they were all feeling.

"I told you. My financial advisor is embezzling from me."

"That's more than embezzling if he's left you with nothing," Andrei snapped. "What's going on, Katrin?"

For the first time, Sawyer thought he saw genuine emotion on her face as she blinked at him. "I truly don't know. I just… a few weeks ago, I tried to withdraw a large cash sum, and was denied. I looked into it, then tried calling you, Andrei. When you wouldn't answer, I contacted Kurt, and now I'm here because I have no money in any of my accounts." She swallowed roughly, as though she was trying to compose herself, then wailed, "I-I'm poor."

"WHAT'S SHE DOING HERE, KURT?" Sascha asked, her tone less strident than she'd have liked. But hell, she was feeling weak. Weaker than she'd done since the car accident itself.

Maybe she *did* need to go to the doctors? She wasn't used to feeling anything less than hale and hearty, so to be shaken up by this rattlesnake's appearance in her world was unsettling.

From what she knew of the woman, she was predisposed to dislike her. Then, Katrin had done nothing but peer down that too big a nose of hers and treat Sascha like she was dogshit on those Blahniks she wore…

Yeah, predisposed, my ass, she thought wryly. With or without the accident, she wouldn't have appreciated such a toxic presence in her house.

And she totally knew how presumptuous it was of her to say that but say it she would—to her damn self, at any rate.

Before her brain started on overtime at what Katrin's true purpose was here, she had to smile as Kurt began tucking her into bed. He'd had to pull the covers off one side so he could set her down on the sheets, and the awkward position had her giggling when she'd nearly fallen out of his arms.

Not that she'd have been giggling in the aftermath. Christ, she didn't even want to think of how badly her head would have pounded if he'd actually dropped her. Still, she'd felt secure in his arms, hence the giggle.

Keeping her safe was their top priority… was it any wonder she was getting addicted to them? To their care and cosseting?

Talk about living the dream.

With a sigh, she watched as he tucked the covers around her so tightly she wouldn't be able to move during the night. Not that she complained or anything, but still, it was cute.

"I don't know," he said after a few moments. "Katrin's actions rarely match up with what she has to say."

She frowned, unsure if he was saying it how it was or simply being cryptic. "What do you mean?"

"She says she's here for Andrei's help." He shrugged. "Undoubtedly, there will be another reason. A reason I'm not interested in."

Feeling stupid for being insecure, she nevertheless had to ask, "Do you still care for her?"

He froze in place, his hands stilling with the bedsheets in his clasp. Turning to her, she saw amusement buried in his gaze. "Yes, Sascha. I do. I'm so madly in love with her that I'd walk into the path of an incoming bus for her."

She pouted. "There's no need to tease."

He rolled his eyes. "There's no need to ask if I still have feelings for my ex. I'd prefer to spend time with a snap-happy cobra than her, Sascha. I mean that. The minute the divorce came through, I was a very contented man."

"Sean said you were depressed."

"Of course, I was. I'd just wasted years on a witch of a woman to whom I meant nothing." He shrugged. "I felt like a fool. So stupid for having put up with her, with the shit and drama she brought into my life, but even more of an idiot for having listened to my mother and having allowed her to interfere. Plus, my ego was hurt. My pride, too. I am but a man, Sascha darling."

He bent over to press a kiss to her forehead. "Now, I should go and see what her game is."

As he made to stand, she grabbed his hand with her good one, and pleaded, "Stay. Please."

His brow puckered. "There truly is no reason to fear my being with her. I doubt she'd try to seduce me to help her, but even if she did, I wouldn't act on it, Sascha. I truly have no feelings for her anymore." He rubbed his chin. "If she seduced anyone, it would be Andrei, but he wouldn't touch her either. I can promise you that."

Something inside her settled at his promise, but she whispered, "It's not that. I don't want to be alone."

The frown deepened. "Your head is that bad?"

She swallowed. "Yes. It's..." Her eyes fluttered shut, unable to think of a comparison.

"You need to sleep."

"I know. But I don't want to sleep alone."

He let out a soft sigh but toed out of his shoes. "I will leave when you drift off, okay?"

"I'd nod, but it would make it hurt more," she teased, still capable of humor even if it felt like her skull was caving in. "Why would Katrin try to seduce Andrei? Just to get what she wants?"

His grimace had her narrowing her eyes. "We had an open marriage, remember? I invited him to..." He cleared his throat.

"He slept with her while you watched," she clarified blankly. When he nodded, she squinted at him. "That's why he was okay with you jacking off the first time he touched me, isn't it? He's used to it." And from what Andrei had once told her, she'd thought Katrin had disgusted him.

Hmm.

She was almost amused at the sudden sight of the pink cresting his cheeks as he admitted, "They're all used to it. But yes, Andrei more than most." His knee came up to the side of the bed, and he cocked a brow at her. "Do you still want me to rest with you?"

"Of course."

"You're not mad?"

"How can I be mad about a past that didn't involve me?" she asked, trying to be rational when deep down, she was feeling anything but. Still, it wasn't his fault Katrin was... well, perfect. Goddamn perfect. So tiny and freakin' blonde... and skinny, let's not forget skinny. The Bitch. Totally deserving of a capital letter too because the sexy package wrapped up the heart of a boa constrictor.

Kurt eyed her warily, like he expected her to pounce, but climbed onto the mattress. "If you say so."

He settled beside her with a care that had her throat closing up. Nervous, she might be when it came to the human-sized Tinkerbell sitting in her kitchen—because, dammit, it *was* her kitchen—flirting with her men, but Sascha could never doubt the care and attention they gave her.

In the face of that, her petty jealousy and stupid insecurities were ridiculous.

Hadn't she caught each of them studying her when she'd been

absorbing Katrin's diatribe? Each of her men checking in on her, making sure she was okay. Somehow knowing that exact moment when the headache had devolved into a migraine, and taking her away from the situation to get some rest.

She was fortunate. It was time to embrace that fact and shove aside anything else. Because, jealous or not, it was irrelevant. By word and deed, they showed her what she meant to them. Just because Katrin probably weighed as much as the left side of Sascha's body didn't change that.

"Thank you for this," she whispered, when he rolled over, curling his body about hers.

"You don't have to thank me. I'm touched that you trust me enough to be here."

Carefully turning her head to look at him, she murmured, "You really mean that, don't you?"

He snickered. "Of course, I do."

"I was very lucky the day I got the call from the agency for this interview."

"Not as lucky as we were," he said softly. Reaching over, he carefully began to stroke her hair away from her face. It had been in a topknot earlier, but she'd loosened it when the pain had begun to pound at her skull and the pressure had grown with it. "You'll be fine, Sascha. When we go to the doctor, whatever they say, you'll be fine."

Her eyes widened. "How did you know I was scared?"

"Because you asked me to rest with you." He cocked a brow at her. "I might not be the smartest man in the house, but I'm not a complete fool."

"Never thought you were," she replied, closing her eyes when he began to trace his fingers over her face in gentle swirls. It should have been ticklish, but if anything, it was soothing.

She wasn't sure why they cared for her so much. Sascha knew she was nothing special. And yet, she'd wormed her way into their lives, and they didn't seem to want her to worm back out again.

The five men in this house were beyond brilliant. When Kurt said he wasn't the smartest here, it was because Devon was off the charts, batshit brilliant, where Kurt was only another literary genius. When you had that kind of comparison going down, being smart was a relative concept.

She'd always considered herself of average intelligence. More than most, but not cray cray. Yet, though she was way less smart than they, they never made her feel like she was an idiot or stupid.

She was falling for them, Sascha knew, and as she tumbled into sleep, couldn't find it in herself to be scared about that.

If anything, she was excited, and that was probably way more dangerous.

FIFTEEN

"I CAN'T BELIEVE we're letting her stay," Sawyer growled.

"It's only on the sofa," Sean retorted, folding his arms across his chest. Even though he defended their agreement to let the Wicked Witch of West Germany spend the night, he wasn't happy about it either.

"You tell that to Sascha tomorrow. Because I'm not going to," Andrei retorted easily, sinking back into the dining chair with a topped-off cup of coffee in his hand. It was the disgusting glop Sascha made specially for him, and Andrei never wasted a drop.

"She'll understand." When no agreement was forthcoming, Sean tugged at his collar. "Won't she?"

They shared uneasy looks, and Sean, conceding defeat, stopped pulling at the top button of his shirt and finally unfastened it.

After Sean had led Katrin to the living room, telling her she could stay a night and, in the morning, he'd arrange a hotel room for her, the rest of them had stayed down here in the basement kitchen once she was sequestered upstairs.

Usually, they congregated in Sean's room.

Why?

Sawyer guessed it was more habit than anything else.

Not only did he have the largest office, with more seating—intentional or otherwise, he didn't know—but Sean was the unofficial head of their little household.

He dealt with most of the administrative matters. Well, either him or Kurt. Mostly because if it was left to the rest of them, they'd never have any electricity and the food in the fridge would only be a shade of green.

"She'll understand," Sean reasoned, his tone firmer, though he still looked uneasy.

"Will she? Females tend to be irrational when it comes to things like this," Devon retorted, biting into a cookie Sascha had baked earlier for dessert.

"*Females*? I'm sure she'll appreciate being called that more than having the ex upstairs lodging with us," he said with a scoff, trying and failing to ignore the fact Devon was eating the wrong set of cookies—there were ones baked with Stevia and others with sugar.

Devon peered at him as Sawyer snatched the treat out of his hand, replacing it with the oatmeal and raisin Sascha prepared for Devon, who didn't need the sugar messing with his constantly sleep-deprived self, and pre-diabetic Sean. Though he studied the new cookie in his hand, he didn't comment on it, just asked, "Why? What's wrong with females?"

"She's a woman."

"I don't understand why we can't call them ladies anymore," Andrei grumbled, reaching for a cookie and taking a bite. "Woman sounds so harsh."

He shrugged. "Women's lib. That's how they want it."

"We should ask, Sascha. She usually has the opposite opinion to what we imagine. I bet she'll prefer females," Devon remarked, sliding his chair from the table to get to his feet.

Frowning, Sawyer grabbed his arm and kept him in place. "Where are you going?"

"To ask her which word she prefers."

With a sigh, because he really shouldn't have to explain shit like this, Sawyer rubbed his temple and said, "Devon, you saw her earlier. Didn't she look tired and uncomfortable? She needs to sleep."

Devon tilted his head to the side. "But she always answers."

"You mean you do this a lot?" he asked, aghast. Completely unaware that Devon had been pestering her over the random shit that popped into his head, guilt filled him but there was only so much he could do. Only so many hours in a day he could keep Devon on a leash.

It didn't help that his best friend rarely slept, while Sawyer did. That mean there were hours where Devon could get up to only God knew what kind of trouble.

And it wasn't aided by the fact that Sascha found him amusing and, as a result, let him get away with murder. She'd have to nip that in the bud if she didn't want to be peppered with questions for the rest of her life.

His eyes widened at the thought.

The rest of her life?

Quickly swerving away from thoughts of that nature, he waited for Devon to sheepishly admit, "Well, yeah. She never minds."

"It doesn't mean that you should do it," Sean pointed out. "She needs rest and down time too, Devon."

He shrugged. "I make her laugh."

"You make us all laugh," Andrei retorted. "Doesn't mean I want you buzzing me on the damn intercom 24/7."

"Well, I don't do it at night. I do have some consideration," he stated with a huff as he plunked himself back in his seat. "I bet she wouldn't mind," he muttered, more to himself.

"I bet she would. She looked close to sleep before Kurt led her upstairs," Andrei commented, frowning a little at his own words. "What do you think's going on with her?"

Sean questioned, "Who? Katrin or Sascha?"

"Sascha, of course," Andrei said with a huff. "Like I give a fuck about Katrin."

"You're not going to help her?" Sawyer asked, curious. Andrei and Katrin were tied in more ways than the Russian would probably appreciate. That would either help her lead him down the garden path, or it would encourage him to stay the fuck away from her.

A male Black Widow spider who escaped, didn't tend to go back for second helpings. At least, he didn't think they would. Evolution at its finest, he thought with an inner chuckle.

Andrei grimaced at his question. "I'm going to look into it and have a few of my assistants tackle the situation. I want her hanging around as much as I want Devon buzzing me on the intercom asking me shit about the meaning of life."

"I don't ask her about the meaning of life. Just things I think she'll know the answer to," came the immediate argument from Dev.

"Like what?"

Sean's interested question had Dev shrugging. "Like why brown sugar is brown? How come women have to wear bras? That kind of stuff."

"You have heard of Siri, right?" Andrei demanded, shaking his head in disgust.

"It's not accurate. I like her take on things." He hunched his shoulders. "Plus, she's always patient with me."

Sawyer, feeling guilty—again—clapped a hand on Devon's back, then slid his arm around his shoulders. Tugging him into a half hug, he stated, "I'm patient with you. Don't hear me shouting at you, do you?"

Devon peered up at him, and as always, that look had Sawyer feeling both uneasy and amused. Since he was sixteen, he'd had Devon looking at him that way. He was more used to being with him than being without the massive pain in the arse.

Sometimes, it was like being a friend, father, brother, and caretaker. Devon was a huge responsibility, but he did it because he loved the bastard. Devon wasn't retarded, or anything like that. He was neuroatypical, and as a result, said whatever was on his mind whenever it cropped up. But it had gotten them both into a lot of trouble over the years.

Not that he'd change that. They were kindred souls, after all. It was why Sawyer looked after him—he understood the obsessive need to work, understood Devon's drive like no other. And, as a result, recognized how truly rare his friend's intellect was. *That* was why he was like his damn shepherd. Devon needed to be protected. At all costs.

As bizarre as it was to even think it, Sawyer knew Devon was far too precious for the world to lose.

Just because a mind was great, didn't mean it wasn't weak too. The world had lost way too many geniuses before their time, and Sawyer was hellbent on making sure Devon wasn't another Nikola Tesla waiting to happen.

"You don't know why women wear bras though, do you?"

His lips twitched—had Tesla asked such a question, he wondered. "So, she's the female version of me?"

Devon nodded, beaming at him in approval at his understanding.

"Exactly. You wouldn't know why brown sugar was brown, would you?"

"True. Although, it's probably something to do with molasses."

Devon's mouth dropped open. "She said that." He looked at him like he was Yoda. "You knew!"

"I did," he retorted with a grin. Then, squeezing Devon's shoulder, he turned to Andrei and stated, "You remember that year when I had four concussions after playing rugby?"

Sean chuckled. "How could we forget? We had to keep waking you up, and every fucking time you woke up, you came out fighting."

His grimace was rueful. "Aye. I remember. Did I ever apologize for that?"

Andrei snorted. "No."

Sawyer cleared his throat. "Sorry."

Sean chuckled. "Forgiven. Anyway, what was your point?"

"I got bad headaches for months after that last concussion. I had to stop playing rugby because of it." He shrugged. "I'm not saying she shouldn't go to the doctor's, but I'm saying I don't think there's cause for concern."

"Before the accident, she hadn't had the shit kicked out of her on the rugby pitch," Sean pointed out.

"No, but we've all seen the footage." Some bastard had uploaded a damn recording onto YouTube. Sick shits.

"I saw it in live action. Replaying that isn't on my agenda," Sean said with a grimace.

"I know," Sawyer immediately conceded, because he hadn't wanted to watch it either, but Andrei had, like the robot he could be from time to time, declared that statistically four of them watching that horrendous shite was better than one. And they'd gritted their teeth through the forty second nightmare just to make sure nothing had slipped their attention at the crime scene, "but I just mean, she landed hard on her head. She's lucky there was no major damage. In fact, it's a miracle there isn't."

"All the more reason to make sure the doctors at the hospital didn't miss something," Devon pointed out softly, and as usual, managed to get to the heart of the matter with the precision of a laser.

Neuroatypical people were often thought of as naïve. But Devon wasn't. He seemed it because of the questions he'd ask, and the responses he'd give when prompted, but he was sharper than a scalpel.

Put Devon in a room with a stranger, and he'd figure out if that person was like him or not. Read them, know them, *see* them, for what they were at their core.

It was for that reason he kept to himself.

When they'd interviewed housekeepers for Sascha's position, it would have been useful to have Devon sit in. He saw past the bullshit people spoke on a daily basis. Cut through the swathes to the person underneath. It was an ability he'd honed over the years. Tweaked with every betrayal. What he found now when he met new people, he rarely liked. Hence his unsociable nature.

Rubbing his chin, Andrei murmured, "We must make sure she visits a clinic next week."

Sean nodded. "I'd already put it in my diary."

"Good," Devon inserted grimly. He swirled his finger amid the cookie crumbs in front of him. Quickly forming the 'root square' symbol, he demanded, "What news from MI6, Sean?" He shot him a look. "And no BS. My security clearance is probably higher than yours."

"They're still linking the bomb attack with the car accident."

Kurt snorted. "Only because you put them onto the potential connection."

Sean just rolled his shoulders—the man never took credit for his smarts.

That said smarts were going down that particular direction, however, had Sawyer scowling.

"But why? Why would someone target Sascha? She's hardly a wanted criminal or drug kingpin. She had a security check before she came to work for us; something would have cropped up then, wouldn't it? If she had some kind of dodgy past?"

Sean nodded, reached for his glass, and took a deep sip of the red Sascha had served with dinner. "Of course, it would. And yet, we have a man in custody who admits to having been paid to kill her, and to make it look like an accident. An accident that follows the MO of recent terror attacks in the capital. Then, we have a bomb scare two nights later. At an event she's supposed to attend. Whether or not it makes any sense, coincidences like that rarely exist."

"Don't talk to me about probability," Devon snapped. "I want to know that she's safe."

"We'll figure this out," Sean assured him.

"When? After she's been attacked a third time?" Devon shook his head. "That's not good enough."

"The nation's finest is working on this, Dev," Andrei pointed out. "Not just the city police, but the country's. Plus, Sean's been brought in to consult… They'll figure out what's going on soon."

Devon pursed his lips. "What are we going to do about her?"

Sean frowned. "This is getting confusing; who her? Sascha?"

"Of course," Devon said with disgust, like thoughts of Katrin were way beyond him. Which, Sawyer knew, was true.

There was a whole class during their second year at Oxford, Devon had completely erased. Like, completely. Bad memories, he tended to delete like he was some kind of 'Windows' program. If he kept them, it was for a reason. Never a good one either.

Andrei's lips twitched, but answered, "Good question, Dev," He rubbed his chin. "What are we going to do about Sascha?"

Only Sean didn't seem to understand where they were going with this. "Can someone give me a clue what we're talking about here? We just said we'll make sure she goes to the clinic."

Devon huffed. "And Sawyer says I'm slow. Look, she's different." He looked at them, individually studying them before he said, "You know it, I know it."

"He's right," Sawyer stated. "I… I don't want her to go anywhere."

Sean stilled, sensing that that was as deep as Sawyer would go. "I don't want her to leave either."

"Me too," Devon chimed in.

"Nor I," Andrei whispered.

They shot one another a look; their euphemism for her 'not leaving' meaning they were falling for her. Hard. And they each knew it.

Sawyer reached for his wineglass. "What do we do?"

"There's nothing we *can* do. We just have to go with the flow. She feels as much as we do for her; I'm sure of it," Andrei pointed out softly.

"I know she does," Devon retorted.

"Then, we have nothing to worry about, do we?"

"Nothing save for a bomber," Sawyer answered Sean glumly.

He drew in a shaky breath. "I'll get on it." His chair scraped against the stone floor. "Devon, let her sleep," Sean intoned, before he headed upstairs to his office.

"We should clear this up," Sawyer said as he too got to his feet. "Last thing I want Sascha seeing is this mess when she wakes up."

Andrei stilled, then let out a chuckle. "Now I know you're in love. Actively willing to do chores? It's either love or a miracle."

"Or a head injury," Devon pointed out. "Maybe it's that concussion coming out to play?"

Flipping them both the bird, he asked, "You going to help me or not?"

SIXTEEN

TURNING ON HER SIDE, *the wrong side*, woke her up immediately. The agony that speared through her, radiating from her wrist, was just another walk in the park. Truth was, that was nothing to the headaches she'd been enduring of late. But on a brighter note, no headache at the present moment.

Opening her eyes, she realized she wasn't in her bedroom. But Devon's.

When had that happened? she thought.

His room was surprisingly spartan, considering the mess within his workroom. He and Sawyer seemed to share the same design mentality.

Less was more.

Only difference was, Sawyer went for metal whereas Devon went for natural materials. Sawyer's bed had a cast iron frame. Devon's was made from a very nice piece of mahogany. Apart from the bed, the room was furnished with two rugs which lay either side, and a large mirror which covered one wall and was actually the doors to a built-in wardrobe. It was fabulous to clean because of its simplicity. This was not a room meant for clutter of any kind.

She squinted though, surprised to be here when she was sure Kurt had carried her to her bedroom last night.

"You climbed in with me last night."

The voice had her eyes blinking open properly instead of squinting around.

It came from the ground, where, when she peered over the side of the bed, she saw Devon in a yoga pose. She'd mentioned it to him once, suggested that it would be a good way for him to relax—he had insomnia, and slept less than a hamster on LSD. He'd never mentioned that he was a damn near yogi.

It astonished her that a man with a concentration that ran somewhere between a gnat and a mathematician, chose yoga to relax.

Not that she was going to complain. Not with his ass in the air like it was… Even she recognized downward dog.

Looking at him through his legs, and checking out his ass along the way, she murmured, "I don't remember coming down here."

He shrugged mid-asana. "You had a nightmare."

"I did?" She rubbed her temple. "I don't remember."

"I think you took some medication. Well, it sounded like you were on drugs at least," he explained after a moment, when he breathed long and low through a series of asanas that had her wanting to hump him like she was the dog and he was the bitch in heat.

The notion had her grinning, which in turn, had him cocking a brow at her. Of course, the gesture held less merit because he was upside down. "Want to share the joke?"

She chuckled. "I was thinking I'd hump *you* rather than the other way around."

"I've been told I have a very hump-able butt."

"I can confirm this," she told him, just as deadpan as he. "It's also bitable. Next time you do yoga in front of me, I encourage you to do it naked."

"Dicks aren't made for yoga. They flop about."

"And there goes my sex drive," she teased.

He chuckled. "I should teach you yoga. We could have sex in interesting positions."

"I think we should stick to the regular positions first considering we've not done those together yet." She curled her finger at him, trying to beckon him to come to her. "In fact, my head feels fine for once."

He shook his head. "You're high on pain meds."

She snorted. "No. I'm not."

He scowled at her. "How do you know?"

"Because my arm hurts like a bitch," she explained, "but for me to fuck you, I don't need my arms."

"You to fuck me, huh?" he asked, going through another wave of asanas that had him in all kinds of weird postures that gave her a better view of his ass and defined every single muscle in his back.

Jeez, the man was hot.

He was sweating faintly. Not grossly, just enough for his bronze skin to have a sheen on it. A sheen she wanted on her.

Before these guys, the notion of being sweated on by a dude was the most revolting prospect she could have imagined. Even during sex, she wasn't enamored of the idea. Now? She'd take them anyway she could get them.

It was like, after years of shitty sex, her body suddenly realized great sex was in the vicinity, and it wanted it all, and it wanted it right now.

Of course, the broken wrist and concussion weren't facilitating that, so she was randier than usual. Well, when she wasn't feeling like she had the Seven Dwarves digging around in her skull.

By the time she was feeling warm, and panting over the way the muscles in his arms and back bulged with each move he made, he was back on his feet.

"I need to shower," he told her, perky as ever. "I don't want to get into bed sweaty."

"I'll make you sweatier," she promised.

He pulled a face, then said, "Will you change the sheets afterward?"

A snort escaped her. "And they say romance is dead."

"They do?" He frowned at that. "I hadn't heard."

Huffing out a chuckle, she murmured, "It's a rumor that's been going around for quite a while. I think we could prove them differently though."

"We could?" He pondered that. "How?"

"Do you want to romance me?" she asked, both amused and charmed by the earnest look on his face.

"I want you to be happy," he explained. "There's a difference."

She cocked a brow at more earnestness being aimed her way. Could he get any freaking cuter? Damn his delicious hide. "There sure is."

"Would being romanced make you happy?"

"I suppose." *Being fucked would make me happier still,* she thought ruefully.

"I have no idea how to romance someone," he continued. "This presents a problem. I wonder if Sawyer knows."

Considering Sawyer was earthy and gritty, she doubted it. "Ask Andrei or Kurt," she advised. They were charmers. Andrei with his warm smiles and eyes that could melt her with the looks he shot her way, and Kurt's tender affection, his cosseting… the two of them could train Devon to be a pro.

"Andrei or Kurt?" He put his hands on his hips and stared at a point right above her head. She looked up, wondering what he was gawking at, then she realized he was just processing what she'd said.

Jesus, the day she understood what the fuck was going on in his mind, she knew she'd have to check herself into the looney bin.

After thirty-seconds of processing, he murmured, "I'll do that. I'm surprised you didn't say Sean."

"Sean's romantic. Just in a unique way."

"What kind of way?"

"He's competent."

Devon scowled. "That doesn't sound romantic."

She snorted. "That's because you've never lived in a chaotic household before."

"True. My home was always ship shape and Bristol fashion. Although, that's more for the Navy than the Army," he conceded. "When was yours chaotic?"

"When my mother died. After, my dad went to pieces."

"Understandable."

"Yes, it was. It was just a lot to go through at the time. My mom was used to keeping things organized so dad didn't have to. Without her, everything fell apart, and dealing with losing her, as well as the nuttiness of the household was a lot for me to handle at the time."

"Is that why you became a housekeeper?" he asked softly, coming to sit on the edge of the bed at her side.

She reached for his hand with her good one, pleased when he entwined their fingers. Though he was a little robotic in some things, he needed affection as much as anyone. She'd noticed that as he grew more comfortable with her, he touched her more.

Especially if she made the first move. Once he knew she wanted his touch, it was like he'd been given permission to be affectionate.

She hoped that, in time, he'd feel enough ease with her to just throw his arms around her and hug her first. But that was asking a lot after she'd only really been with them like this for a month.

With their fingers bridged, she answered his question, "I think maybe it is. The money's pretty good too, and when I first started this housekeeping gig, I didn't have to worry about making rent, which in London is fucking insane."

"You didn't have to live in the city. You could have gone elsewhere."

"I know, but I didn't want to."

"Why not?"

Sascha shrugged. "I like it here. It's so different than America, yet just as fast paced and busy. It's alive in a way that I like. But, when you're a housekeeper, you tend to live in the swankier parts because only the rich can afford someone like me. Look at this place. I get to live here. In the middle of Kensington, for God's sake. Not everyone can live somewhere like this and for free."

"But you have to work hard to live here."

She wrinkled her nose. "You really think what I do is hard? When you have to calculate crazy math the way you do?"

He mused upon that for a second, then explained, "You know when you breathe?"

She blinked. "Quite well. I do it a lot."

Devon, her sarcasm going way over his head, just nodded. "Math is like that for me."

"Like breathing?"

He nodded.

"Wow. That's very sexy."

His eyes widened. "It is?"

She grinned. "To me, sure. Do you see symbols and shit everywhere you look?"

"No." With his other hand, he rubbed the back of his neck. "It's not like that. It's just…"

Seeing he was finding it hard to explain, she murmured, "Hey, it's okay, Devon. I don't need to know."

Relief had his shoulders slumping. "I didn't want to be unromantic by refusing to answer."

She snorted. "Math is never romantic, so we're good."

"Of course, it is. Everything's romantic. Rose petals develop in the Fibonacci pattern. Even I know roses are romantic."

Impressed despite herself, she winked at him. "Color me stunned." Then, at his confused look, and well aware he was on the verge of asking how he could color her in, she murmured, "Do you know what would be more romantic than a dozen roses?"

"What?"

"If you made me cum."

His eyes narrowed. "We agreed. We wouldn't touch you again until you healed."

She immediately scowled. "When did we agree that?"

"Not you, *we*," he retorted.

"Well, I think I'd like to be the one who takes control of my own body, thank you very much. And a couple of orgasms would suit me greatly." She could really do with the pain management.

Climax=no migraine for at least four hours.

That was her kind of deal.

His lips twitched. "A couple, huh?"

"Think that can be arranged?"

"Your head isn't aching now because you took meds last night. That doesn't mean you won't pay the price later," he counseled.

"I already told you; I didn't take meds last night. I must have just had a nightmare." She jerked his hand and pulled him toward her. "I want to feel your body against mine," she told him, her voice a husky whisper. "I want to feel you inside me. I want to know all of you."

She studied him, wondering if he'd react to the same stimuli as all men—because one thing she'd learned during her time here, Devon was *not* all men—and when his jaw clenched, his nostrils flaring slightly, Sascha was quite relieved to note that yes. He was.

He ran a hand through his already disheveled hair, rubbing the thick, glossy onyx strands until they were more tousled than before.

"You shouldn't tempt me," he chided her.

She peered down at his lap and the bulge tenting his fly. "One part of you appreciates the temptation."

"That part doesn't listen to reason." He let out a deep breath. "I'm trying to think of you here."

"I know, baby, but I don't want you to. I want you inside me, Devon," she told him, her voice low. She rocked her hips; her words and his tension making it easy to imagine him deep in her pussy.

With a sigh, she dragged their bridged hands to the apex of her legs, and through the duvet, pressed it against her core when she spread her thighs under the covers. The pressure wasn't right, but it was better than nothing. She let out a moan as she tilted their fingers, so a knuckle landed in a good spot, and tilted her pelvis up for better friction.

"What are you doing?" he asked, his voice thick, his gaze glued to their hands.

"What does it look like?" she retorted, gasping before she could whisper his name.

He licked his lips and swallowed hard as though refusing her was a temptation he couldn't avoid.

Good.

"Please," she pleaded sultrily, watching his eyelids droop at her words. His breathing changed. Becoming deeper, faster.

His hand tightened about hers, and then he began to pull away. About to complain, she watched as he planted one hand beside her head, then the other at her shoulder. Within two seconds, he was looming over her, after he'd tugged the sheets away, baring her totally unsexy flannel pajamas—since the accident, comfort had counted for more than damn silk.

He didn't look at her as though she was wearing flannel though. He looked at her like she was a Queen. A Queen he wanted to fuck.

She shivered, caught in the net of his attention as his bright blue eyes pinned her in place beneath him.

He ducked down, not stopping until his lips were hovering above hers. "You're sure?" he demanded, and when she gulped, said:

"Yes."

Their mouths connected with a gentleness that surprised her. He didn't maraud, didn't feast, just tasted. Sampled. Her breath shuddered from her at the delicacy of each caress from his lips, and she had the feeling Devon was a whole other ball of wax to the rest.

It took that one kiss to realize sex with him was going to be pleasure and pain combined.

She reached up to keep him in place, her fingers sliding against his scalp and her nails digging in for further impact. He ignored her, refused to up his pace, to deepen the kiss. He traced his tongue around her Cupid's bow, fluttered it in the tender heart. She sucked in a shuddery breath when the tip tickled along the sensitive inner part and let out a moan when he repeated the action.

"Kiss me," she whispered. "Properly."

His chuckle was cruel. *Enticing*. "I am."

"No," she whined, moaning against his lips once more. "I want you. Need you," she admitted on a whisper.

He smiled, then finally slipped his tongue between hers. She let out a cry as he taunted her again. Sliding his tongue against hers, fluttering here and there, flickering back and forth. Making her tremble. Making her want to beg.

When she'd never wanted to beg ever before. Not like this.

He was giving her what he wanted to give her, not what she needed. She rocked her hips, hoping to drag her pelvis against his. She felt his cock jerk at the move, knew he was hard, knew he was hungry, but his self-control astonished her. Obliterated everything she'd thought she'd known about him.

With a groan, she spread her legs, clasped them around his hips, and dragged him down so their cores clashed. She rode up from beneath, doing as she'd chuckled over earlier—humping him. Trying desperately, to get a reaction from him, and failing.

Overwhelmed, she ceased dragging her nails against his scalp, and moved her fingers down to his neck. She massaged his nape, then trickled the tips down, scraping her nails over the rise and fall of the muscles in his shoulders and waist, and not stopping until she could lift the waistband of his sweatpants and drag them over his ass too. She dug her nails into his butt and wished like hell she could use both hands to urge him into action. But she couldn't, she had to work with what she had available.

She didn't hold back, dug hard into the thick muscle of his glutes, and was rewarded when he pulled away from her mouth and nipped at her bottom lip. Tugging it away from her teeth, he headed down, taking the meat of her chin, biting it. She blinked at the sting but was so grateful that she'd stirred him into action and couldn't find it in herself to care.

He headed further down, relinquishing weight from his hands and steadying himself with his knees as he unbuttoned the flannel jacket of her pajamas. His fingers gave her whispers of sensation as they trailed along her torso like feathers.

Once again, his delicacy was her undoing as those shadowy

caresses had every single inch of her coming to life. She'd never felt so sensitive, so aware of every part of her body thanks to a simple touch against her belly. But of course, his hands were busy, but so was his mouth.

He plied her throat with his lips, teeth, and tongue until she was crying out with the delicious wonder of it.

Nibbling here and there, he sucked down, and would press gentle pecks to the area before trailing his tongue along the sinews of her throat.

At that moment, she felt sure she'd go mad. Every part of her was singing with need and he hadn't even touched her in an overt fashion. Her nipples were like bullets, but he hadn't traced his fingers over them. The scent of her arousal perfumed the air in a way that was close to mortifying. She knew he could feel her juices flowing from her greedy pussy, because the crotch of her pajamas was soaked. Each time he taunted her with a teasing move, she'd rear up to drag her aching cunt along the length of his hard dick. But it wasn't enough. It would never be enough.

Gasping in air, her head rolling from side to side in a way she'd regret later, she felt tears in her eyes as he finally headed down south. With one side of her pajama top open, she knew where he was heading, but he stunned her. Until that moment he'd been careful, gentle. But he surprised the shit out of her by taking the bud of her nipple between his teeth and biting down. Hard.

She shrieked as pain pierced her nipple, and yelled out his name, "Devon!"

He hushed her, and the vibrations to the throbbing nub had her eyes widening, her mouth trembling.

He traced his lips over her belly, bringing the small hairs to attention. Her nerves were on red alert. Small shivers ran up and down the length of her body in response to his touch. She was so achingly aware of her need, every part of her brought to life by him, that the tears burning in her eyes fell without notice.

Another shudder whispered through her when he reached the waistband.

"You have to let go," he directed, pulling at her calves to release the hold she had on him with her thighs. Only because she knew what he was about to do did she obey.

A part of her wasn't certain he'd stay where he was. She felt like he was seducing her, and it made her worry that he'd disappear at any moment.

With a deep breath, she let him go, dreading his next move. Praying to God he wouldn't climb off the bed and head out, math suddenly on his mind. It was then she realized, math had always been on his mind. When he touched her, when he trailed his tongue over her, he was forming symbols. Ones she half recognized from the loathed class that was Trigonometry.

Before the notion could perplex her, he grabbed her waistband and jerked her bottoms down over her hips, ass, and thighs. When the fabric hit her calves, he didn't shrug them off her feet, instead, he used them to keep her legs tied together at the ankle. Then, he grabbed her ankles with one hand, and lifted her legs so they were pointing towards the sky.

Feeling suddenly out on a limb, and not knowing why when she was lying flat on the bed, her hands shot out to either side for stability.

He must have seen this because he whispered, "Point your toes, and keep your legs straight." She complied, watching with nervous eyes as he let go. Still expecting him to bound off the bed, she was relieved when he pushed down his own sweats.

Because his body was hidden by her thighs, she couldn't see him, but she'd felt him. Knew he was thick and long, and her pussy wept with the need for his shaft to fill her. By this point, the small shivers running up and down her form, had turned to shudders of response. If she wasn't careful, she'd end up with cramps in her calves, and have to leap off the damn bed to walk it off.

The amusing thought would normally have had her laughing, but not at this moment. Not when she ached for him.

She felt snow blind. Lost without his touch to ground her. And then, as the thought flashed through her mind, his hand was around her ankles once more, and as he pressed the backs of her calves to his shoulder, she felt the bluntness of his shaft against her wet cunt.

A moan escaped her, sharp and high-pitched with relief. The position clamped her pussy lips together, and the bluntness of his tip had her eyes widening as he pressed it to her gate and notched his cock inside, but Jesus... It felt good.

Better than good.

Heaven.

Barely an inch, and the thickness was more than she felt sure she could stand.

He was big. And she knew she'd thought that about each of them, because they were all far too big for any sane woman, but Devon… He was *thick*.

She gulped, clenched her eyes shut. Once again, not feeling the trickle of tears as they forged a path down her face, she held her breath as slowly, but surely, he made a place for himself deep inside her.

By the time he was all the way in, she was breathing hard. It had been a long time since she'd gone jogging, but this was the best cardio she'd ever had in her life. Her good hand burrowed into the sheets, while the bad one ached with the need to claw at something.

She felt full, so full that she knew with a certainty she'd go mad with it. She stared blindly overhead, eyes popping open when he hit home, but like with everything he'd done so far, Devon stunned her. Short, deep thrusts. The tip of his cock hitting her deep inside, while the thickness of his shaft forged her wide-open.

She felt impaled, and that was the only way she could describe the torture. But she loved it.

"Sweet Jesus," she moaned.

"No, Devon," he corrected gruffly.

On anyone else, that would have been declaration. An arrogant, smug response. To Devon, though, it was a statement of fact. His name wasn't Jesus, but Devon.

How could he do this to her? Make her want to laugh when she felt like her entire world was suddenly experiencing an earthquake?

Her throat closed as laughter tried to spill from her lips, but he fucked the amusement out of her. When those short deep thrusts suddenly became long, slow impalements.

Just as she was gasping for air, he mixed it up. Switching between the two until her body had no choice but to experience what he was willing to give her.

And that was exactly it. Exactly what this was.

His show.

He was fully in control. So dominant in that moment, if she'd had the wherewithal, she would have questioned everything she knew about him. But as it was, she just had to go along with the ride.

And what a ride.

Just when she felt certain she could take no more, his free hand came down to pinch the top of her pussy, holding the bud of her clit captive as he fucked into her.

Electricity flowed from his fingers to her. And like that, she was a goner.

That electricity sparked through her veins, sinking into her muscles, sending them into spasms that fluttered around his shaft.

For the first time since this had begun, he made a noise that was most definitely involuntary. A low, hoarse gasp that was the sweetest, purest music she'd ever heard. As her ears took part in the orgasm too, she soared freely for the first time in weeks. Since the last time one of her men had touched her.

He sent her to the stars and back. Had her spiraling around as supernovas burst behind her eyes. Making her realize that this wasn't sex. This was a fucking opera.

With music and majesty. And math.

The random thought had laughter spilling from her as the sheer joy of the moment overwhelmed her, overtaking everything else, and making her purely, utterly, and irrevocably his.

SEVENTEEN

"WHAT THE FUCK is that woman still doing here?"

Sawyer's lips twitched in response to Sascha's demand. He wasn't the only one amused. Sean had to cough to hide his laughter, before he said, "It was only for last night. I'm going to arrange a hotel room for tonight."

Her nostrils flared as she gritted out, "Good. She's already put a request in for French press coffee with whipped cream, as well as a continental breakfast. I didn't realize we were offering stray cats room for the night."

Kurt chuckled. "Good one, Sascha."

"Stop finding it funny. All of you." She planted her bad hand on her hip and looked set to pull an all-out tantrum as she demanded, "Are you seriously going to help her? After everything she did to Kurt?"

Sawyer clambered to his feet, strode to the door so he could slide an arm around her waist and jerk her into his side. Pressing a kiss to her temple, he teased, "Now, now, don't let jealousy get in the way of being charitable." Not that he blamed her. If anything, he was yanking her chain to see that fire sparkle in her eyes—fuck, the lass was hot when she was angry.

Of the five men, he was the least charitable of the lot of them, so he understood her agitation. He'd have tossed Katrin out on her ear last night. Wicked witches had a tendency of falling on their feet—just like the stray cat she'd likened Katrin to.

She shot him a glower, then pouted. "I can totally be jealous. That woman fucked Kurt. *And* Andrei, damn it. Plus, she's ordering me around like I'm the help." She waved a finger at him. "Don't even say that that's because I *am* the help."

He grabbed her finger, raised it to his mouth, and nipped the tip. "As if I'd dare," he declared dramatically.

She grinned at him. Then it flushed away as though it had never existed, and she glared at him instead. Her defiance had his cock hardening, and considering he knew Devon had been inside her that morning, he wanted to knock the papers off Sean's desk and take her there and then.

She'd feel like fucking heaven... slick and warm and—he stopped his thoughts in their tracks. He couldn't afford to have a hard on with her in this mood. One didn't tempt a Mother Hen intent on defending her flock.

And that was what she was doing—defending her men.

Protecting *them* when they were supposed to be protecting her. Goddammit. Was it any wonder she confused the hell out of him? Made him think and feel shit he'd never felt before?

Before he could freak out, she growled under her breath. "I don't like her," she spat, mostly at him, but at the others too if her equally defiant glare was anything to go by.

Devon snorted. "None of us do."

Rather than throw water onto the flames, Devon's words were more like gasoline. "Then what the fuck is she doing here?" she shrieked.

Sean grimaced. "Andrei is going to look into her accounts. By the sounds of it, her financial consultant has done a pretty good job of clearing her out."

"Seriously?" She bit her lip, and Sawyer hid his grin in her throat as he ducked down and licked a spot where Devon had obviously bitten her earlier. It was pink from his teeth still, but growing dark from having been sucked. Knowing Devon, she'd be covered in hickeys. At his touch, she shivered, whacked him with her good arm, and grumbled, "I've already been tortured once today."

Andrei snickered. "It's always the quiet ones."

"That would make sense. If Devon was quiet. Which he totally isn't," she retorted huffily.

Sean cleared his throat. "To get back to the subject at hand, we're helping as much as we have to to get rid of her."

"Now that is what I want to hear," she stated with a feline smile. Pressing a kiss to Sawyer's cheek, she wiggled out of his arms, and strode across the room to Sean.

He rolled away from the desk so Sascha could take a seat on his lap. She curled her good arm about his neck and snuggled into him. He kissed her cheek and let his hand fall on her stomach.

Sawyer retreated to his armchair and looked over the scene.

Everyone was in Sean's office, having fled here to make plans without the females in the house overhearing. Truth was, they were fortunate she hadn't overheard their previous conversation. If she had, it would have opened a can of worms that none of them were ready to explain.

As he looked at the ease in which Sean and Sascha sat together, an ease she was developing with the five of them, each unit evolving in their own unique way, he'd admit, the sight filled him with warmth.

Sawyer wasn't particularly in touch with his emotions. If anything, of the lot of them, he found it the hardest to open up. There was no particular reason for it. He'd had a good, if poor, childhood. Loving parents, a big extended family that had always shown him affection. Of them all, though he'd had the least growing up where money was concerned, he was the wealthiest when it came down to family.

Sean's parents were snobs. While he and his father got on well, Sean's mother, Deirdre, was dead certain Sean was having a gay relationship with one of them. As a result, she refused to step foot in the house.

Like that was a punishment.

Devon's parents were dead. His father, an officer in the army, was a bastard. He'd beaten Devon's mother, and though he hadn't slit her wrists for her, the psychological torment he'd put the poor woman through was undoubtedly the reason for her suicide. The minute Devon had been of legal age, he'd left his father behind, and hadn't even gone to the man's funeral after he'd died in an insurgent's attack in Baghdad.

Kurt's mother was a pain in the ass. Like Deirdre, the notion she had a gay son was more terrifying than anything else in this world.

She'd set the poor bastard up with Katrin. A punishment no man deserved.

Well, maybe Devon's dad.

Kurt's father and grandfather had been tortured by the Stasi. When the Berlin Wall had come tumbling down, his dad had been released from 'custody', but he'd been beyond fucked up. Though he was still alive, Kurt rarely heard from him. Margritte lived with the man, and probably barely saw him. The man was like a ghost. One left to deal with the haunting of his memories from the horrors he'd endured.

Of them all, Andrei was the worst off. His mother had been the mistress of a high-ranking Bratva Soldier, and he was the result of that relationship. A Brigadier, Andrei's father had immense power in their town. When he'd murdered Andrei's mother, the deed had gone unpunished. Andrei's grandfather, the Pakhan and head of the Bratva division in his town, had learned of his existence and brought a seven-year-old Andrei into a fucked-up home and hearth where blood was spilled on a regular basis, and honor was tied with obeisance.

Though his childhood had been so far out of the norm than anyone could begin to imagine, Andrei loathed his father, but loved his grandfather.

His ties to the Bratva had been working against him of late. Though he was clean, and had no dealings with the Russian Mafia, his name said otherwise. It was why he'd been working with Jacobie.

Andrei, like himself and Devon, enjoyed math. For the three of them, it was their lifeblood. He and Devon worked in different spheres, where Andrei used it to discover market trends. Because Russia wasn't popular at the moment, he'd found it hard to ply his trade. Linking up with Jacobie, he'd worked a miracle. Though he downplayed his recent work, the implications of the software he'd developed with the tech mogul were huge.

As Sawyer contemplated the tableau of fucked-up-ness the five of them represented, he had to wonder what level of batshit Sascha was bringing to the table. She definitely had skeletons in her closet—someone had tried to kill her, after all.

Didn't get much more fucked up than that.

"Why are we all in here anyway?" she grumbled, breaking into his thoughts after she pressed a kiss to Sean's cheek. "We're normally down in the kitchen at this time."

"We weren't sure if the Wicked Witch would go down there, too."

"So, you thought you'd leave me to deal with her?" She scowled. "And we were getting along so well. Expect salt in your coffee today."

Kurt chuckled but reasoned, "Devon said you were out for the count."

"I was. Now I'm not. And considering you were foolish enough to marry her, Kurt, you can come and run interference." Her eyes narrowed. "If the bitch thinks she can look at me like I'm shit on her shoes, she's mistaken."

Though the terminology amused him, the meaning did not. "What did she say?" he demanded, his voice a half growl. He'd put up with so much, but if Katrin was saying shit to Sascha, that was it. She was out on her ass. Designer skirt be damned.

"Just impugned my heritage," came the complaint, but she was still blowing hot air, not genuinely offended so that was something.

"Katrin doesn't like Americans," Kurt murmured, tone apologetic.

"I received that memo loud and clear," she said, rolling her eyes.

"You don't have to make her breakfast, Sascha," Sean said gently, hugging her to him.

"It's my job," she countered.

"Yes, but you're more than the job now, aren't you?"

She cocked a brow at him. "If I wasn't in a position where I could come and sit on your knee, would you have asked me to make breakfast for Katrin?"

He grimaced. "Maybe. But it's different. Not just out of nepotism, either. When she slates you, she slates *us*. We're a package deal."

"The bitch is lucky she got to spend the night," Andrei grumbled, his focus on the cellphone in his hand. The scowl told Sawyer he was reading something serious enough to concern him.

Andrei was a weird bastard.

Sawyer loved him, but that just meant he could embrace the man's oddities rather than be perturbed by him.

After a childhood like his, maybe it made sense that little affected him. Or maybe it was simply his nationality that made him so fucking stoic. All he knew was that a scowl on Andrei's brow was the equivalent to an out-and-out show of rage on another guy.

Considering they'd been discussing Sascha before, and as the topic of her past was very much an ongoing thread of conversation, he decided to leave Andrei to his scowl while she was in the room. The last thing he wanted was to start up a conversation none of them were ready to have with her yet.

Devon, not sensing the undercurrents in the room, murmured, "Lucky isn't the word, Andrei."

"Don't be pedantic," Sawyer stated in a bored tone. Those were three words that were repeated often under this roof.

"I'm not. How can it be lucky when Sean gave her permission to stay here?"

"He's right," Sascha stated, then poked Sean in the shoulder. "You shouldn't have given her permission, Mr. Principal."

Sawyer snorted. "We don't call them that."

She frowned. "What do you call them?"

"Headmasters or headteachers," Sean answered, as he reached for the finger she was using to prod him and pressed a kiss to the tip. "I couldn't see her out on the streets, could I?"

She grunted. "No. But I'll kick her butt out if she maligns the way I make coffee."

"Fair's fair," he teased.

Another huff. "How can she be so poor anyway? Her shoes are like three mortgage payments. And did you see her luggage? It's Vuitton!"

Andrei peered up from his phone. "I'm working on it."

"Working on what?"

Sawyer's brow puckered. "How much do you remember of last night's conversation?"

She rubbed at her temple. "Not a lot by the sounds of it. Mostly that she thinks her hedge fund manager is robbing her?"

"He is," Andrei retorted, shooting her a look.

Interested, Sean asked, "Have you found his location?"

"No. But I'm working on finding the accounts."

Kurt, obviously bored with the financials, stood, and stretched, leaving his armchair vacant. They all had their spots in this room. Only Sascha didn't… but then, she had five laps to choose from, he thought wryly.

"Come on, I shall protect you from the ogress," he told Sascha with a grin.

"Hey, don't have a go at Fiona," she chided. "I liked her. And Shrek too."

Kurt blinked. "You know what I mean."

She grinned. "I like what Sawyer calls her. Devon told me this morning."

"The Wicked Witch of West Germany is the full phrase," he divulged, waggling his eyebrows at her.

She giggled. "Even better. I'll call her that if she pisses me off." She wriggled off Sean's lap after giving him a quick kiss, then strode to Kurt's side. Sliding her arm around his waist, she asked, "Everyone want the usual for breakfast?"

To a chorus of yeses, they left, leaving the room a lot emptier than it had been moments before.

He grimaced at the thought. This sentimentality was growing tedious. It was Sascha's fault, not that she could be blamed for it totally.

Did it disturb him that of all the women they'd shared this way, Sascha was the only one who'd inspired these kinds of weird feelings in him?

Sure, it did.

It concerned him more that someone was willing to kill her by murdering innocent pedestrians, and by blowing up a fucking event hall, though. Concern, he was learning, was a relative concept.

"What were you frowning at?" he asked of Andrei, his thoughts a natural segue to the question.

"Something I was reading about Jacobie."

"What about him?"

"About his ancestry, that's all."

"And you were frowning, because?"

Andrei shrugged. "I didn't realize his family worked for him."

"What does that have to do with anything?" Sean asked.

"I don't know. We worked closely together," Andrei explained, his gaze still on his cell. "Hell, *work*. But he never said anything about that. According to this report, his sister is his PA."

"I'm failing to see a link here."

Andrei peered at him. "There isn't one. I just thought it was odd, that's all."

"If he can keep that secret, what else can he hide?" Devon intoned, as usual, managing to hit the nail on the head while looking totally bored shitless as he did so.

Looking out of the window onto the yard, Devon was staring into the distance. Knowing him, he was probably working through an equation as he sat there. Even after all these years, the way Devon could process shit still astonished him. The man made an onion look one-dimensional.

Andrei nodded at Devon's concise remark. "That's it, exactly."

Sean shrugged. "Let's get back to the matter in hand though, eh? While we know Kurt's keeping her busy?"

Sawyer nodded. "So, Marks still hasn't said a word?" Marks was the guy who'd been hired by only God knew who to murder Sascha.

"No. Nothing since he admitted to his true crime."

Sawyer rubbed his nose. "I still don't get why he confessed to it. It wasn't like the police were even going to arrest him. He braked before impact. It wasn't like he was trying to run her down at that point." Sascha had run into the road to stop a kid, who'd seen something shiny and had charged into oncoming traffic to get it. The car had glanced off her, causing so-called minor injuries that left her with the headaches she was enduring at the moment.

Minor, my ass, Sawyer thought.

Sean rested his head back against the desk chair. "That's just one of the many fucking questions roaming around my brain. We have an American citizen who's lived in the UK for over five years with no issue. Then, she comes and works for us, and suddenly she's the target of some crazy plot.

"A man is hired to mow her down, with the purpose of making it look like a terror attack on the city streets. When that plan is stopped in its tracks because of a little kid running into the street and Sascha rushing off after him to save his butt, rather than regrouping, the driver hands himself into the police. Confesses to his purpose, then stays quiet. Doesn't utter a word. Doesn't even ask for a lawyer, for fuck's sake.

"Two days later, the gala Andrei RSVPed Sascha at, blows up during preparation. But the timer shows it was supposed to blast during Andrei's keynote speech..."

"Are we certain we can't prove they just didn't want Andrei's ass in a million tiny pieces and not Sascha's?"

Andrei blinked. "Thanks, Sawyer. Your concern is touching."

He grinned. "I try my best."

Andrei flipped him the bird, but to Sean, asked, "The dick's right. It can't be coincidence that it was due to explode at that point?"

Sean shrugged. "It doesn't have to be a coincidence. Your keynote speech was when the event hall would have been at its fullest. They'd want maximum collateral damage, not minimum. But the information available to us isn't pointing us in either direction, so again, it's supposition to think they're after you. Sascha too. She'd have been watching your speech in the hall as well.

"All I know is that the reason the bomb exploded hours ahead of schedule, is the reason why they have any evidence to work with. It was a sloppy job."

"Rushed," Sawyer stated with grim certainty. "Like they were in a hurry. Like they'd only just found out Sascha was due to be there."

"But come on, why the fuck would anyone want her dead?" Sean demanded.

On the brink of answering, Devon interrupted. His voice was eerily calm, his gaze staring straight ahead while focused inward too. "Sascha has lived in the UK for a while. But until she came here, she didn't go through an advanced security check, did she?"

"No," Sean replied with a frown. "Nothing too complicated anyway. I don't know how intensive the checks are for American nationals coming to the UK; but it wouldn't be anything like what she went through after she came here."

"Exactly. The background check must have triggered something…" he stated calmly, like he wasn't just blowing their minds. "Her name must have popped up on a radar no one but certain circles were monitoring."

Andrei hissed. "You know how insane that sounds, don't you, Dev?"

Devon shot him a disinterested look. "Isn't it you who often says that the truth is stranger than fiction?"

Andrei snorted. "Does that sound like something I'd say? Kurt's the writer."

Devon wafted a hand. "The rubbish you two say usually blurs together in my mind."

Sawyer chuckled, then laughed harder at Andrei's astonishment. "Just because you're a mathematician doesn't mean you're safe from his jibes," he mocked.

"Apparently so," Andrei retorted. "I don't speak rubbish."

Devon just shrugged. "You do."

Sean cleared his throat. "I'm not certain this conversation is actually helping, guys."

"Isn't it? It certainly cheered me up," Sawyer pointed out with a wide grin. He settled deeper into his armchair like he was settling in for the show.

Sean pulled a face. "Devon, what you're implying… it doesn't bode well."

"Because terror plots *do* bode well?" Devon asked, blandly.

"No, but that's just it. What's going on isn't that. It's just being made to look like it is."

"Exactly. So, it's someone with enough power to be able to keep an eye on certain databases that are supposed to be hack-proof, and who's interested in destabilizing the capital." He blinked. "Now who do we know who's capable of wanting that, and acting upon it?"

Sawyer and Sean looked at one another. "Russia."

Andrei groaned. "Not you two as well."

Sawyer grunted. "It makes sense. Russia's been fucking with everything of late. We all know what they can do with their hackers."

"Yeah, but why the fuck would they be interested in our house-keeper, dammit?"

Sean rubbed his chin. "You don't think it could be to get to you, do you?"

Andrei shook his head. "I'm not a target."

"Maybe you should speak with your grandfather. See what he knows."

"He's not Pakhan anymore," Andrei retorted, switching off his phone and shooting them all an irritated look. "He's old. And ill."

Sean cleared his throat. "So, he may have retired, but he still has the contacts."

"What you really want is for me to talk to my father."

Sawyer grimaced. "We'd never ask that of you, Andrei. You know that."

He firmed his lips, nodding. "Sorry. I was being tetchy."

"Understandable," Sean stated immediately. "But though Vasily has retired now, he'll still know all the right people. Talking to your grandfather might help us cross off a name on the list."

"The reason he's managed to stay alive as long as he has, guys, is because he doesn't ask the wrong questions to the wrong people," came the rueful retort.

"No, but if this plot does involve you, then he'll want to know, won't he? He'll have means of keeping you safe. What if they're trying to use you as a means of getting to him?"

"When he was leader of the Bratva in his town, then yes, that was a distinct possibility. But now? No way. And my bastard father never rose through the ranks like my grandfather. He stayed in his middling position as Brigadier. There's no reason why they'd target me."

"Unless it's because you've been working so close to Jacobie of late."

Devon's remark had the three of them stiffening.

"Fuck," they breathed as one.

"We should talk to Jacobie," Andrei murmured. "See if his security detail has had to handle any similar threats recently."

"Haven't you spoken to him about the bombing?" Sawyer demanded.

"No. He's busy, and I'm busier. I've been trying to create an ethical capitalism manifesto with him."

"Since when were you interested in politics?" Sean demanded with a scowl.

Andrei shrugged. "I've always been interested, but there's never been any point in harvesting it. With my background, I'd never go far."

Sawyer blinked, also surprised at this news. Andrei was the least political person he knew. And he lived in a house full of people totally bored shitless by the everyday humdrum of politics.

They all existed outside of that particular bubble. For a reason. Regular life bored the shit out of them.

"That's why I focused on the economy instead. I can do some good there, at least. Hence the manifesto."

Sean frowned. "You should have mentioned that to me. You know I have friends in the Party."

Andrei grinned. "I'd have come to you at some point, Sean. Don't worry. Your contacts would not have wallowed in vain. But it's been more challenging than I'd anticipated."

To many, that remark would have sounded like a complaint. To the men in the room, they heard the thrill of the challenge in Andrei's tone, and nodded in understanding.

"Can you arrange a meeting with Jacobie? Or, at the very least, his security detail?"

Andrei shrugged. "I can try."

"Do," Sean said softly. "If he tries to avoid you, I'll let some more of my contacts do the talking."

Sawyer snorted. "Ever since MI6 started using you as a consultant, you think you're James-fucking-Bond."

Sean just grinned. "Nah. I prefer mine stirred, not shaken."

Even Devon groaned at that one.

EIGHTEEN

A FEW DAYS LATER, Sawyer entered his and Dev's workroom with a yawn.

Their two bedrooms had a connecting door with this space. Sure, it felt like he never stopped working, but that was one part of his life that he loved. Math wasn't work.

It was everything.

Well, it *used* to be.

A certain American was taking up way too much of his thoughts.

Even in sweats and yoga pants, Sascha was far too sexy for any of their own good.

Peering around the workroom, which not only smelled of Sascha, but had also been invaded by her recently if its tidiness was anything to go by, he asked Devon, "What are you working on?"

They both had desks. His was neat, Devon's wasn't. A mass of paper usually littered the floor, some stacked, other times it was just scattered everywhere. Today, it was in two big heaps—further evidence of Sascha's presence—as well as the fact there was a walkway to the chalkboards that lined the room. His was the one white board, because he hated writing with chalk.

Mathematically, there were a handful of people in the world who could keep up with Devon. Sawyer was one of those few. That didn't lessen Devon's brilliance or heighten Sawyer's self-belief. Keeping up was one thing, actually creating the math Devon could, was another.

Sometimes, Sawyer felt his purpose in life was to ground Devon. To help him reap mathematical miracles and stop him from going off the rails. Some days, that was enough. Other times, it wasn't.

Since he was sixteen, he'd been watching over Devon. It was an honor. One that often grated, yet a duty he'd never recant.

Realizing Devon hadn't answered yet, he repeated himself, "What are you working on?" Seeing Devon was engrossed, he headed over to his friend's half of the room. What he saw, had him snorting.

"Sudoku? You have to be shitting me."

Devon blinked. "What?"

"One of the world's brightest mathematicians can't be engrossed with Sudoku. It's all kinds of wrong."

"I like it," came the stubborn reply.

Sawyer folded his arms across his chest. "Let me guess, this is one of Sascha's ideas."

Devon grinned knowingly. "She said it would help me."

"Help you what?"

"Seem normal."

Sawyer bit back a chuckle. "Would you leap off a cliff if Sascha told you it was a clever idea?"

"She wouldn't do that, would she?" Devon asked, his eyes widening at the prospect.

Sawyer often wondered how it was he could forget how damn literal Devon was, when the man reminded him thousands of times a day.

Grimacing, he stated, "No, Dev. She wouldn't encourage suicide."

"Oh. Phew."

His lips twitched as he took a seat on the corner of Devon's desk. "How long have you been working on that?"

"A few hours." Sawyer peered at the Sudoku square and had to shake his head. Devon had used the puzzle to leapfrog onto one of their current problems. He'd done quite a decent job of it too.

"You weren't supposed to do that with it," he said. "You were just supposed to fill each square with the numbers one to nine."

Devon blinked. "Surely not. That's far too easy."

His grin was lightning quick. "Yes. That's the point." Well, it wasn't, but the point of the puzzle sure as hell wasn't what Devon was doing with it.

Seeing he was about to argue, Sawyer changed the subject. "What's going on? It wasn't Sascha's day today, was it?" Devon allowed Sascha one morning a week to maintain the havoc of the room.

"No. She came in to avoid Katrin."

Sawyer's smile flatlined. "I can't believe that bitch is still here."

"A belief Sascha concurs with if her mumbling was anything to go by."

"You bastards are all soft as shit when it comes to women."

Devon shrugged, erasing a digit as he murmured, "I don't hear her anymore."

"Who? Sascha?"

"No," Devon scoffed. "Of course, I hear her. Her accent does grate from time to time, but I like what she has to say."

"I'm pleased to be such entertainment."

"Ah, the woman herself," Sawyer declared with a grin, looking over his shoulder at the door where she stood pouting.

"My accent grates, Devon?" She strode into the room and planted her hands on her hips.

Seeing he was busy, she peered at his work, then shook her head. "I explained three times how it works, Devon."

Sawyer grinned. "He said it was too easy."

She rolled her eyes. "Devon!"

Her bark stirred Devon's attention. "Sascha? Didn't you go already?"

"I came back."

"Why?"

"To hear my accent being denigrated by you."

"Denigrated? Hardly," he scoffed. "It's particularly pleasing when you go all breathy."

Sawyer nodded, in complete agreement. "And when she cums, that's sexy as fuck, am I right?"

"Definitely."

Sawyer laughed as Sascha's ears turned pink. "The most honest room in all England," she said gruffly. "I don't know why I even come in here."

"Because you signed an NDA agreement," Devon reminded helpfully.

"The other cleaners have too."

"Yes, but they're not as smart as you, and *you* don't understand what any of this is about." Devon frowned. "Plus, we know you won't take pictures and send it to our rivals."

"Since when did you have rivals?" she asked, cocking a brow at him.

"Since forever."

Sawyer grimaced. "Sad, but true. It's all about the math for Dev and me, but that's not true for everyone."

"Sean once told me that some of the problems you've solved, earned you millions of dollars."

Sawyer nodded. "Yep. That's how we got started. Helped pay for this place as a matter of fact."

"Seriously?"

At her gawking, he smirked then winked at her. "Yeah. We're pretty smart." He pointed at Devon. "Of course, he's out-of-this-world smart."

"I'm not an alien," Devon said with a huff.

Sawyer rolled his eyes. "You might as well be with some of the shit you come out with."

"My shit is gold dusted. Well, Sawyer says it is where Andrea was concerned," Devon retorted mildly, his interest in the conversation waning as he went back to the Sudoku.

"Who's Andrea?"

Sawyer smirked at the pique in her voice at the mention of the other woman's name.

"A professor back at Oxford," Sawyer explained with a smile. "She had a crush on him. He could never do a thing wrong, hence the gold-dusted shite. She'd have joined the Dev Fan Club, but the faculty wouldn't have appreciated her fucking one of the star students."

"Plus, I didn't want to fuck her," Devon pointed out. "She had black nails." He shuddered. "They were always chipped too."

Sascha blinked. "That's a problem? When you work in the chaos you do?"

"I think he'd have seen past the chipped nails if Andrea had shaved her pits."

"Ewww, she didn't shave?"

At Sascha's crinkled nose, he had to laugh. "No. She didn't. She was a free spirit."

"Since when do free spirits wear black nail varnish?"

"*Chipped* black nail varnish," Devon corrected with a shudder. "There's a difference. Her fingers always looked bruised."

She rolled her eyes again. "I stand corrected."

"I don't know, but she used to wear tank tops and shit, and you could see the full bush." Sawyer chuckled at the memory. "It was funny as hell watching Dev try to avoid her."

"Funny for you," he said with a scowl.

Sawyer conceded that with a dip of his head. "True." To Sascha, he asked, "Did you come back for a reason?"

"No. I like being in here sometimes."

He blinked. "You do?"

"Yep. It's a restful place to read." He realized then she had papers in her hand. She lifted them. "A manuscript from Kurt," she informed them.

Sawyer smiled. "We'll have to get you an armchair."

"Like in Sean's office?" She bounced on her feet in excitement. "The unofficial meeting grounds of the house?"

Devon snorted. "As long as this doesn't become one too. Only *you're* allowed in here."

"Gotcha," she said with a twinkle in her eye. "I'm blessed."

"Yep," Devon told her. "I think I deserve a kiss for that too."

Her lips widened in a smile. "You deserve one for breathing, handsome."

When he shot Sawyer a smug look, she laughed, swept down to kiss Sawyer first, and before their lips could barely do any kind of tangling, she reached over the desk, the delicious curve of her ass a bitable temptation, to anoint Devon's mouth too.

"No fair. Why did he get one?" Devon grumbled.

She grinned.

"Why was it so damn short?" Sawyer growled, his hand coming up to shape that fine ass of hers. "I'm sure you wear these to torture us."

She peered at him over her shoulder. The coy move shouldn't have amused him, but it did.

"Yoga pants are for exercise," she told him primly. "Can I help it if you think they're for something else?"

She went onto her heels when he slapped her butt gently—well aware of the delicacy of her head—then peered at him over her shoulder. "What was that for?"

"Teasing me."

She smirked. "But I do that every day."

"Hence the spank."

"Sawyer can be quite kinky," Devon advised, his tone that of a professor imparting wisdom onto his students.

"Oh, he can, can he?" she demanded, but Sawyer saw the sparkle in her eyes, and the laughter bubbling from her like water in a fountain.

"I think we should get some work done," he said grandly. Moving from the desk and heading to his.

"Oh, that means it's a good one," she teased. "Come on, Devon. Spill with the gossip."

Devon peered at her over his puzzle. "Gossip? It's fact."

She laughed. "Jesus, Devon, you're too cute sometimes."

His nose wrinkled. "What every man aspires to… *cute*."

Shaking her head, she headed to the spindly office chair that held a stack of papers and files.

Sawyer, seeing this, said, "Wait there, Sascha. I'll go get that armchair from your room. You can use that until we get you another. How's that?"

Her eyes widened. "You don't have to do that."

"I don't have to do anything, but I want to. I want you to be comfortable," he told her simply, and for whatever reason, that had her eyelashes fluttering low to shield her gaze.

"Thank you," she told him breathily as he just nodded at her and headed up to her bedroom.

The conversion had been his idea. It had been a large loft space once used to house the servants who'd worked here, but the last owner had turned it into storage.

Realizing they'd need a live-in housekeeper, Sawyer had told the others it was wise to make the space as pretty as possible… if it was, maybe the housekeeper wouldn't abandon them within the month.

Of course, that hadn't worked.

Before Sascha, they'd gone through housekeepers every four to six weeks.

In fact, when she'd hit the fifth week mark, they'd all been on edge. Dead certain she'd do as the others had—a midnight flit.

Sawyer wasn't sure why they were so bad at keeping staff, just knew that their track record spoke for itself. Sure, Devon wandered around naked from time to time, and Kurt had a habit of exploding in tirades of German that had terrified a couple of the housekeepers, but that wasn't exactly a crime, was it?

Well, the walking around naked might have been, but not the cursing in German.

Sean was relatively normal, Sawyer too. Andrei had a thing about leaving books everywhere, but it wasn't like they shit in the bath and expected the staff to clean it up. Or had raves that destroyed the house on a weekly basis, for God's sake.

As he grabbed the armchair in the corner of her bedroom, beside which was the closet door, he shifted the few items of clean laundry stacked atop it and placed them on the foot of the bed.

Hefting the chair into his arms, he maneuvered out into the hall, and carried the light frame down the stairs.

"We should get you a chair for all the offices," he said as he walked back in, putting the chair closest to the fire. It meant she was furthest away from them, but in winter, when it grew cold, she'd probably appreciate being so near the warmth.

"You don't have to do that," she told him, her cheeks flushing with heat.

"Why not?"

"Sawyer's right. We're all workaholics," Devon murmured. "We spend far too much time in our offices."

"I don't want to intrude. I know if you're busy you need to concentrate."

"I'm sure you do. But you have work of your own too, right? There's no reason why you should do it in that small office downstairs when you could do it here."

"Wouldn't you mind?" she answered Sawyer.

"If you make a lot of noise, yes," Devon replied, honest as ever.

Sawyer snorted. "Ignore him. Of course, we wouldn't mind. We…" He cleared his throat. "We love your company."

Her eyes sparkled. "I love your company, too."

"I should hope so," Devon inserted. "The way we've all been fucking. It would have been a bit peculiar if you'd hated the sight of us."

A quick grin split her cheeks. "You're not wrong, Devon. It would have been peculiar. Bloody peculiar, actually."

Devon cocked a brow. "You sounded just like Sawyer then."

She wrinkled her nose. "I tried to."

"Are you maligning my Scottish brogue?" Sawyer demanded, a fierce scowl twisting his brow—if he'd intended to scare her, it failed.

She giggled.

Fucking giggled.

He rolled his eyes in disgust as she planted her butt in the chair he'd carried down, then tilted her head to the side.

Eying her, he asked, "Something wrong with your neck?"

"You're supposed to kiss me. That was a subtle hint."

Subtle, his ass. "And the lady wants a bluidy kiss tae?" he declared to the room at large.

She shot him a look loaded with heat. "Next time we're in bed, talk like that."

He chuckled, decided to be disobedient and dipped down to kiss her neck, not her cheek. He let his lips trail up to her ear, loving how she shuddered and shivered at the simple touch—God, she was so responsive to him.

To them all.

"Anything you want, lass. I even recite shopping lists upon request," he joked.

She grinned up at him, then shooed him off with her good hand. "Go on. You get cracking. Lord help me if I get accused of making too much noise."

He scoffed at that but traipsed back to his side of the room. Taking a seat, he perused his desk, eyed the admin he'd been handling mostly since Devon had taken up this latest crusade of his.

P vs NP was definitely his baby, not Sawyer's. He was there as a sounding board, and to help develop the solution. All the bright sparks were Devon's ideas. Which, a person might be forgiven for thinking was the case all the time, but the Nobel Prize they'd won four years ago?

Thanks to *Sawyer's* calculations. Not Devon's.

Not that many people knew that or believed it, but Sawyer was secure enough in his own ego to not give a damn.

Sascha cleared her throat as she settled into the seat. He'd thought it was a gesture to grab his attention, but it wasn't. Still, it took hold of his focus anyway.

Jesus, she was beautiful, he thought to himself, studying the curve of her cheek as she bent over the manuscript in her hands. Even without the makeup, without the product in her hair, she was stunning.

Her auburn locks were grouped in a high ponytail that kissed the back of her neck when she moved her head. It was the perfect contrast to her creamy skin, which was pink at the cheeks thanks to their earlier playfulness. The sweep of her eyelashes was ridiculously long, and for some stupid, pathetic reason, he wanted to press his lips to them. Wanted to feel their flutter against his mouth.

He bit his lip to quell the peculiar need and pondered why the other housekeepers had abandoned them when Sascha had done the exact opposite. Had, in fact, seen something in them that had made her want to stay, to become a part of this crazy household.

He tapped the cap of his pen against the desk in a rhythm that would piss Devon off soon if he carried on. But he didn't care. He needed to do something with his hands, and that's what he was doing.

"Mein Gott, was ist…?"

A sudden swell of German roared from the first floor, making the three of them jump with the suddenness of it.

Sascha sat up, turned around to look at him. Devon, save for jolting at the sudden noise, made no other reaction, but Sawyer scowled at the door.

"That bitch had better be out of here soon," he growled.

"You really hate her, don't you?" Sascha queried softly.

"For what she did to Kurt? Sure. For what she did to Andrei, I hate her more."

Her eyes widened, but before she could ask, another wave of pissed off German carried up the stairs. "What's she caterwauling about now?"

"Something about a stain on a bra," Devon said disinterestedly.

What *was* interesting however was the twitch of Sascha's lips. "Oh," was all she said.

His eyes narrowed, then narrowed further when she cleared her throat again—a gesture she made when she was nervous—and settled further into the armchair.

"She's calling you," Devon imparted next as Sawyer watched the charade as part of the audience rather than an active member of the conversation.

"She is? Well, the house isn't that big. I'm sure she'll find me if she needs me," came Sascha's chirpy response.

She wasn't showing fear. Which meant the stain hadn't been an accident she'd tried to cover up. But Sawyer wasn't sure what exactly she *was* showing. Before he could ponder it too much, Katrin exploded through the door.

"Knock first," Devon bellowed, making everyone, save Sawyer, jolt in place. The women gawked at him, but he just said, "I'm trying to work here."

Katrin seethed, brandishing a white silk negligee in her hand. Well, what had once been a white silk negligee, that is.

It wouldn't suit the blonde. It was ice white, and against her coloring would only make her look insipid… not against Sascha's creaminess, however.

Sawyer pursed his lips, then determined when she was better, he'd take her negligee shopping. Just the thought had his cock hardening under the table.

"Is there a reason you've come to disturb us, Katrin?"

His question had her stiffening. "Look at it. Just look at it, would you?" she demanded in German.

"English," Devon roared, making Katrin and Sascha jolt once more. "It's rude when Sascha doesn't speak the language. I shouldn't have to tell you that. Not when you've always tried to instill manners in us."

Sawyer snorted at Devon's astuteness. Most of the time, it had seemed Katrin's petty digs had swept over his head. But nothing did. Not unless he wanted to make it seem that way.

Which was often the case.

There was the time they'd all attended an award ceremony for him and Devon, and Katrin had chided them on their choice of bow tie. Another occasion where she'd asked if Sawyer knew how to use all the right forks at a swank soiree…

Katrin's mouth flatlined when she saw they were going to be no help; although, why she ever thought they would was beyond him.

"This silk negligee cost more than your month's wage," she bit off.

Sascha snorted. "Are you sure the hedge fund manager stole your money and you didn't just spend it all?"

Katrin's eyes widened. "How dare you!"

"Oh, I dare. It's my house, remember? *My* men," Sascha bit back. "You'd better remember that the next time you try and cozy up to Andrei over coffee."

"We were talking about my situation," Katrin declared, her eyes widening as she slammed the silk into her thin chest.

"I'm sure you were. If trying to play footsie with him was part of the investigation, then I'm sure all he'd have to do is look under the fucking table for the culprit." Sascha's jaw flexed as she gritted her teeth.

"So, what? This is a punishment?"

Sascha eyed the negligee with disinterest. "That was a mistake. If you'd not dumped your laundry in with the rest, I'd have been sure to hand wash it. However, I have to take into consideration the fact you're not actually a guest here. More like an unwelcome intrusion, so you should be grateful I did your laundry at all. Badly or not."

Katrin's nostrils flared.

Devon, as usual, threw gas onto the fire by chuckling. "Good one, Sascha."

"I didn't do anything, Devon," Sascha retorted calmly. "Accidents happen, don't they?" she tacked on, her tone as silky as the negligee clutched in the Wicked Witch's hand. She returned her attention to the manuscript on her lap, completely blanking the other woman in the room.

Katrin made an explosive sound under her breath, then spun on her heel and strode out the way she'd come in—*good riddance.*

When the door slammed shut behind the bitch, Sawyer let out a whistle.

"Remind me never to get on your bad side, babe."

Sascha being Sascha, somehow as naïve and naughty as Devon—a terrifying concept—just looked at him and winked.

NINETEEN

"HOW MUCH LONGER IS SHE going to be here?" Sascha grated out.

"I'm still working on the details of her financial situation," Andrei answered, not looking up from his laptop. Perched on his armchair in Sean's room, he looked brooding and mysterious and sexy.

She'd never realized how hot smart guys were until she'd entered this house.

Like Neverland, she'd never get out of this place without changing forever.

"You do get that isn't the answer I wanted, right?"

His lips twitched, and finally, he deigned to look at her over his screen. "Sorry."

"I should think so." She folded her arms across her chest. "I mean, four days? What was her excuse for not going to a hotel today?"

Sean blinked at her, tugged at his shirt collar. "She said she still felt weak."

For the first time in the many weeks she'd been here, Sascha was unsure of her place.

She'd been content with the status quo, just riding through it as they tried to figure out where she fit in. But now? With this bitch here? She was on edge, and she was feeling it.

Why?

If she'd been right at home, felt like this was her place, then she'd have tossed the cow out herself. As it was, she wasn't sure if she had the right to do that, and that uneasiness was pissing her off. Majorly.

With a grumble, she eyed Sean's still tugging fingers and folded her arms across her chest. "Why do you let her get to you?"

He blinked. "What are you talking about?"

"She obviously knows the lifestyle we're electing to lead—is that it? You're afraid she'll tell people if you toss her out on her ass?"

Sean cut a look at Andrei, which was very interesting. He didn't seem the least interested in this conversation. Save for one tiny thing… a little flicker of the muscle at the left side of his mouth. Barely there, and yet, she noticed it. Noticed it because she was looking for it.

Ever since Sawyer had blurted that shit out about Katrin having hurt Kurt, but also Andrei? She'd been super curious.

In fact, super in no way described it. It was eating at her. Eating away at her, because she knew for a fucking fact, that was why the bitch was still here instead of at the Ritz.

Sascha knew this place was great, sheesh. It was like waking up in a period drama some mornings—save for all the intercoms and beeping gadgets Kurt insisted on having working, all at the same time (Alexa and Siri really needed to learn to get on better)—but the Ritz?

Sascha would totally stay the shit out of that place. And considering the guys would be paying Katrin's tab? Sascha wasn't sure why Katrin wasn't leaping at the offer.

Of course, it could be said that she didn't want to put the men out. That she didn't want them to spend a lot of money on her. But that wasn't in the bitch's nature at all. The woman put the Sauer in Sauerkraut. Katrin gave a shit about no one and nothing that didn't begin and end with herself.

"I think it's time you told me why you're putting up with this crap." She firmed her mouth as she stepped deeper into the room, taking the seat opposite Andrei's beside the hearth.

She wasn't sure why this was the unofficial meeting grounds of the house, save for the fact Sean was in it, but that's how it worked. They rarely used the living rooms. The men either worked in their own offices, spent time in here or down in the kitchen with her.

It was a nice room, granted. A thick oatmeal carpet she was glad she didn't have to vacuum, rich wooden paneling on the walls that gave the atmosphere a kind of closeted feeling… like no one could hear whatever was spoken within this room.

There was a painting above the hearth she knew to be a Turner—knew because she'd looked at the signature—and then several armchairs where the men sat when they were here. One for each of them.

Devon's was squashy and over padded, Sawyer's a chunky Chesterfield. Kurt had a sleek leather and chrome number that bounced when he sat on it, and Andrei's was an Axminister, wide and squat, the leather scarred.

She preferred comfort—who didn't?—so usually stole Devon's armchair with its thick cushions when he wasn't in the vicinity.

She plunked her ass down, refusing to budge until she had some answers.

"Andrei?"

Sean's voice wasn't timid—that raspy voice could never be considered in any way weak, but it was quieter than usual. The man could command a room with his voice alone, and in this, there was no difference. Andrei flinched, but shrugged.

"Tell her. It's not a secret."

"Apparently it is if you all felt you had to keep it from me." Despite herself, she was hurt. Hurt that she'd been kept out of the loop.

She bit her lip to stem any silly words from tumbling from her mouth. The last thing she needed was to speak in haste here. It wasn't their fault that she was feeling insecure in her position. Well, it kind of was. But she got the feeling they were as uneasy as she was with Katrin in the house.

The days of ease and comfort in one another's presence seemed in the distant past and the bitch had only been here four days.

"The reason Kurt asked for a divorce was because of Andrei's relationship with Katrin."

Sascha reared back at that. "Huh?"

Sean grimaced, then to Andrei asked, "You sure you wouldn't prefer to answer this?"

Andrei's smile was tight. "You're doing an excellent job so far." He didn't look up from his screen.

Sean sighed. "Though Kurt had invited Andrei into their relationship, it unraveled. Katrin found out she was pregnant, told Andrei it was his, and then when he and Kurt were trying to figure out a way to make it work, she had the baby aborted."

Whatever she'd expected, it hadn't been that.

Her mouth worked for a second as her gaze shot between Andrei and Sean, but no words spilled free.

Her head had been fine this morning, but the astonishment of Sean's revelation had a small ache blossoming at her temples. God, she was sick of the pain, sick of the discomfort. All she wanted to do was fling herself at Andrei, comfort him as best she could but…

In fact, screw it. She rushed across the room, grabbed his laptop, and roughly let it land on the thickly carpeted floor. Before he could do more than jolt in surprise, she was there.

On his lap.

She burrowed her good arm around his neck and pressed her face into his throat. "I am so sorry," she whispered against his skin.

To be told that you were going to be a father, and then for Katrin to do something like that…?

She hated the bitch even more now. Her lips brushed the tender area of his Adam's apple, and she felt a shiver rush through him at the unexpected caress.

He was so fucking stoic sometimes. The kind of guy who hid his agony through cutting remarks and jokes—but he hurt. She knew he did. That baby had meant something to him. It wasn't just an unfortunate accident; nor would it have been for Kurt.

God, she needed to smother him in love too.

That evil bitch needed the opposite. Her right eye twitched as she plotted how to make Katrin suffer. Maybe a pair of blue socks in with her whites? Or laxatives in her coffee…?

No punishment was enough, but Sascha could make her suffer while she was here. And because Katrin was so superficial, only cared about her appearance and her wealth, she was very easy to rile.

"It's okay. It was a long time ago." His tone was soothing, as was the hand that came up to pat her back.

"No. It's not okay. That... Bitch is too kind a word for her."

The laugh he released was shaky. "True." He said something in Russian, something she knew wasn't for Katrin but for her. Before she could ask what he'd said, his lips came to her temple, and he brushed a kiss there. "I have *you* now," he murmured softly, sweetly.

She hadn't expected him to say that. Hadn't expected any of them to make such a sincere and sweet declaration. Considering how insecure she'd been feeling, it was exactly what she needed to hear.

She shuddered against him, loving when his arms came up to wrap around her waist. The comfort wasn't sexual. But it was freely given and warmly accepted.

"You do," she whispered against his throat. She wanted to tack on the word 'always' but wasn't sure if that was too much too soon.

It felt like it to her, but only because of the length of time they'd been together in this way. But wasn't time relative? Did it matter that she'd known them a few short months when it felt like she'd known them forever? Like she was born to be between them, born to be here, to be the softness to their hardness. To bring light to their somber worlds of work?

There was that saying, 'Too smart for your own good'. That epitomized these five. They were all so goddamn brilliant that they barely saw the woods for the trees, and yet she knew that was her role here.

She was their opposite. She brought ease to their world.

Oh, it wasn't a political point of view. Any feminist would weep into their spritzer at such thoughts, but it was how she felt nonetheless.

It was why these past few days she'd felt so disjointed—so out of place. She was all-in where they were concerned, and Katrin's appearance made her feel that wasn't reciprocal.

She hadn't liked the way that made her feel. *Bereft.*

"I'm okay," he told her softly, breaking into her heavy thoughts. "Honestly."

"She's lucky you didn't kick her out and refuse to help her." She couldn't understand why he hadn't.

Andrei shook his head. "This is the last time I will ever help her. She knows that. She's calling in a favor."

Sascha blinked, reared back to stare at him with her arm still wrapped around his neck. "A favor? After what she did to you? To Kurt? To your baby?"

His lips firmed. "Trust me, I wouldn't if I didn't feel obligated."

"Katrin helped Kurt's family, Sascha," Sean said softly.

"She was his wife," came her aggressive retort. "Isn't that what wives do for their husbands?"

Andrei's smile was tight. "If they're tigresses like you."

She huffed. "Don't try to charm me."

He grinned. "But it's so easy."

Poking him in the shoulder, she grumbled, "Don't make me put sugar in your coffee."

"You wouldn't," he mock-gasped. But each time she made him

smile, it grew less wary, softening with the natural amusement he found in the shit she said.

"I would." She shot both men a glower. "How did she help?"

"The *Black Blood* series is based on Kurt's family. You know that, right?"

Her mouth dropped open. "No. I fucking didn't. Holy shit. Are you kidding me? I read the sequel, and he never said anything. Just told me that the main character was real."

Andrei relented enough to say, "There are some secrets that not even you can mine so quickly, Sascha."

She frowned. "What does that mean?"

"This ease we all have with you? It astonishes us as much as I'm sure it perplexes you."

"I-I guess. I don't question it though. It just feels right."

Sean smiled. "Of course, it does, because it is."

"Still, we have lived a lifetime without you. A lifetime can't be shared within the passing of a few months, can it?"

She bit her lip. "No. I guess not."

He reached up, gently swiped his thumb along her mouth, tugging her lip free. "As much as you wish that were not so," he teased, reading her expression correctly, "some things will take time. And all of us, at some point, have been hurt by the women we have cared for. Knowing you're special and different is…" He pursed his lips. "The head and the heart don't always work together on things, you know?"

He sounded so Russian at that moment she wanted to melt.

"I understand," she whispered softly, his words somehow absolving the disappointment she'd felt in Kurt keeping a secret from her.

That bastard Gruber… the horrendous things he'd done had been against Kurt's family?

She flexed her jaw. "How did Katrin help?"

"A journalist caught wind of the fact Kurt's father is a recluse and hasn't left the house since the Berlin Wall came tumbling down and he made it back home."

Her brow puckered. "Why would that be of interest to anyone?"

"Kurt's family were political prisoners, but the articles tried to infer the opposite… that they'd been a part of the Stasi."

Her mouth dropped open. "How the hell did they manage that? Jesus, talk about fake news!"

Sean's mouth curled into a sneer. "They paid people to make it fit." He shrugged. "Katrin helped out. She has clout in Munich, which is where the stories originated. She made the whole thing go away. It was just before the announcement of Kurt winning the Pulitzer. It was perfectly timed to stir up shit."

"He could have lost the prize?" she asked, aghast.

"These things are decided ahead of time, but it might not have helped. Not considering the fact Kurt's book is based on that era."

Her nostrils flared. "I don't have to like her for doing something anyone with any decency would have done." She bit off, "It's not like she wasn't doing it to protect herself too. God forbid her name was dropped to the papers."

Andrei snorted. "You think we're not on the same page?" He rested his hand on her thigh and squeezed gently. "Once this is done, no more favors."

Almost on cue, his cell buzzed—he'd rested it on the armrest where it wobbled precariously thanks to her residence in the armchair.

He pulled a face when he saw the Caller ID. "I need to take that."

She nodded and was grateful when he helped her back onto her feet without her jostling herself too much. The call rang off, but he didn't seem bothered. Instead, he bussed her cheek, and whispered, "Thank you."

"For what?" she asked, her throat thick with emotion.

"For being here."

She blinked at him, smiled a little, then watched as his focus shifted back to the matter at hand. With another kiss to the temple, he connected the call, and was speaking in Russian before he'd even headed out the door.

She watched him go, then turned to Sean who was watching her.

"He'll be okay," he told her softly, seeming to sense where her thoughts had taken her.

"She had an abortion. Without…"

Sean blew out a breath. "I don't mean to sound heartless, but that situation could never have worked out. Not with Katrin for a mom. As soon as I found out, I knew it would only be a matter of time. She's too concerned about stretch marks to give birth."

Because she knew he was right, she conceded his point with a grimace. He wasn't being heartless, just reading the situation correctly.

"Still…"

He held up his hands. "I agree. It was a shitty thing for her to do, but she's capable of far worse."

"Did he want to be a father?"

Sean pursed his lips, watching her as she approached his desk, putting her butt on the edge so she could be nearer him. "Why does that question feel like it's loaded with dynamite?"

She blinked, then shot him a confused smile. "I don't know, because it wasn't lobbed like a grenade."

He grimaced. "Fatherhood… is it something we think about often? No. But I guess when Katrin told Andrei and Kurt what had happened, it did cross our minds."

She shook her head. "How did she even know it was Andrei's? If she was fucking everything with a pulse, I mean?"

Sean sighed. "She said she knew, and I think Andrei wanted to believe her. Because he did, it made the baby his in his mind so…" He shrugged. "The lack of surety about the baby's biological father didn't ease the situation any."

Sean reached out and stroked a finger over her knee.

She tried to ignore the shivers that simple caress triggered. "Do you want to be a dad?" They'd briefly glanced over this topic before, but this news changed things.

"One day, I guess," he admitted.

"Would it…?" She gnawed at the inside of her cheek.

"Would it change the household dynamic?" He cocked a brow at her. "I doubt it. Even with Katrin, the baby would have spent more time here than with her."

"Would you have hired a nanny?"

He nodded. "Of course."

"Communal baby," she teased a little, loving that she could take the somber notes of their conversation away and make him smile.

"Something like that." He eyed her, then with a blown-out breath seemed to sweep away that particular topic of conversation to leapfrog onto a new one. "How are you? Aside from the situation with Katrin, I mean."

She folded her arms across her chest, feeling awkward all of a sudden. "Would you believe me if I said I feel better after this conversation?"

"Probably not, because I'm not sure why you would?" he asked, eyes widening a little in surprise.

She forcibly unfolded her arms, refusing to let him read her body language and think she was tense and uncommunicative—she knew Sean read into shit like that. He and Devon both did. They saw an incredible amount. *Too* much sometimes.

She pressed her fingers to the hand he'd clasped to her knee. "I was feeling insecure."

"You were?" He frowned and sat up straighter in his seat. "Why?"

"Because you weren't throwing her out. I-I would have, but it didn't feel like my place."

"You mean, you didn't feel you had the right? Like this place isn't your home?"

She ducked her head. "Yes."

"And now you do?"

"Not wholly," she admitted. "But Andrei went a huge way to making me feel a lot better."

He tilted his head to the side. "You know if you wanted to kick her out, we wouldn't stop you."

She gawked at him. "You wouldn't?"

"No."

"Then…?" She scowled. "Why didn't you tell me about Andrei? I thought you said this whole thing only worked with honesty between us?"

"And I wasn't lying, but the truth is, Andrei is still very sensitive about that situation. I also told you that I wouldn't share secrets that weren't mine to reveal. Remember?"

She pouted. "I remember."

His smile was small. "Even then, if you had thrown her out without knowing, he'd have backed you. This is your home, Sascha. You should know that by now."

She scowled, folded her arms against her chest again. "I can't throw her out now, can I?"

He chuckled at her scowl. "Well, you can. I'd just ask you to be patient."

"The woman drives me batshit, Sean," she confessed. "I can only be patient for so long."

He beckoned to her by squeezing her knee and murmuring, "Come here." So saying, he scooted back in his chair and she huffed, but shifted to sit on his lap. "She's a piece of work, but it's important to Andrei that he settles this last score."

She pressed her forehead to his cheek, finding it incredible how easy it was to sit on his lap. Hell, to sit on any of their laps.

That was probably why she was feeling so up in the air. The connection she felt to each of them was disconcerting.

It wasn't a normal bond, and yet, it seemed as natural as breathing.

"What are you thinking?" he asked softly as she settled into him.

"That I'm interrupting your work," she lied.

He snorted. "*Liar*. And when you work as much as we do, we can spare a few interruptions."

"Why are you so patient? With all of us?"

The question sprung free without it being possible for her to contain it. His reaction to the outburst was lacking though. He just shrugged, but his finger began to trace a pattern on her thighs. She wished like hell she was wearing her usual skirt so that she'd feel the caress skin to skin without Lycra getting in the way, but beggars couldn't be choosers.

"I'm used to it," he replied after a moment. "It's just how things are here."

"Do you ever feel like it's too much?"

"No. Usually, I enjoy it. It's…" He broke off, and she realized he was settling on a word to describe it. "Different. A change of pace."

"What do you mean?"

He peered down at her. "Are you sure you want to know?"

"Of course." She wanted to know everything. Not even that would be enough.

Andrei was right. She couldn't learn a lifetime's worth of information about five men in the space of a few months, but that didn't mean she didn't want to try. And it sure as hell didn't mean that would stop her from absorbing as much as she could.

"I'm working on a cold case at the moment. A mother came to me to ask me to find the person who kidnapped, raped, tortured, then murdered her eight-year-old daughter." When she froze in his arms, he blew out a shuddery breath. "Yeah… it's intense."

"I-I'm sorry."

"Why are *you* sorry? I don't talk about work because I deal with the shitty side of humanity, Sascha. You can always ask, and I'll always tell you, but you have to prepare yourself for the fact I don't work with stories or numbers… I deal with people. And people are fucked-up." He blew out another breath. "Sometimes, they're less fucked up than usual. Thank Christ. If they were all like this case, then I'd probably go insane."

"Will you catch him?" she asked, feeling for him so intensely at that moment, she didn't know what to do with herself.

That he had to look into something like that… That a poor little girl had to endure such treatment, and that a family had to know how their baby had passed. None of it was right.

Fucked-up didn't even begin to explain how wrong the entire fucking thing was.

"Oh yeah," he gritted out. "I won't stop until I do."

She reached up to cup his cheek. "Good."

His lips twitched. "You don't doubt I'll find him?"

"No. I'm learning that if you say you intend to do something, you'll do it."

He smiled. "Such faith." He tapped her on the nose. "I hope I never disappoint."

"We're all human, Sean. I don't hold you to impossible standards. I just know that you don't say things you don't mean."

He nodded, reached up to cup her chin. "How's your head?"

Banging. "Fine," she told him, opening her lips to kiss the end of his thumb.

"Liar," he sighed softly.

"Nuh-uh," she countered, then with a breathy whisper, added, "Kiss me, Sean."

He swallowed. "Not if your head's aching."

"It's fine. Honestly." She needed him too much at that moment to let him go anywhere, even if it was more of a mental and emotional retreat than a physical one.

He shuddered. "I-I don't want to hurt you, sweetheart."

"You won't. I need you, Sean." She felt desperate for the connection with him. "I always feel better, after…"

His glance dropped down to the swell of her Cupid's bow. His breathing became unsteady, rocky, and under her butt, she felt his cock grow hard and thick.

She shuddered at the pressure, loving how responsive he was to her. They'd barely touched and already his hard on was making itself known.

With a shudder, and refusing to wait any longer, she reached forward. Sliding her arm around his neck, she pulled him down to her, not stopping until their lips were as one.

She shuddered into the kiss. It wasn't their first 'snog' as the Brits called it, nor would it be the last make out session they'd have, but Jesus, it was the most intense.

They breathed into each other's mouths, gifting the other air as they supped and tasted the heat they stirred together. She moaned as his tongue fluttered against hers, feeding the frenzy of the passion flowing inside her. Her nails dug into his shoulder as he nibbled with his lips and teeth, tasting her mouth, exploring every part of her until he'd tasted all she had to give and then some.

With a shudder, she fought back. Seeking his secrets, needing to know all of him, and know that he was hers. They staked claims on one another with that kiss. It was crazy and insane but so perfect, she felt tears burn her eyes with the power of the moment. Deep in her core, the heat swelled and surged, spilling over until it licked at her extremities, until no part of her was free from his caress. He touched her in a single spot, but her body reacted like he had a thousand hands, a thousand mouths, all of them teasing and taunting her in ways that drove her wild.

A shiver whispered through her, and she let out a sharp moan as he pulled his lips from hers to seek the most tender parts of her throat. Her head fell back against the wing of his desk chair, cushioning its fall and supporting it as he raked his teeth along the sensitive flesh.

She squirmed in his lap, loving how each move rubbed along his cock, how each wriggle of her hips would entice and arouse him too.

One hand stayed on her belly, holding her securely in place, but the other came up to the curve of her breast. He didn't do anything with it. Just kept it there. A hot, branding presence that made her shudder harder with longing.

Then, as he nipped at her throat, the hand at her belly sank down, not stopping until it slipped between her thighs. His thumb pressed hard against the crotch of her yoga pants, and though he rubbed over her clit, it wasn't enough. Only skin to skin contact would ever be enough.

"Fuck, you're so wet, Sascha," he gritted out, sucking down against her shoulder as he panted out the words.

She wanted to be mortified but found she couldn't be. He had her exactly where he wanted her, exactly where she wanted to be.

"Fuck me, Sean," she whispered on a gasp. "I need you. I need you inside me."

He groaned. "Your head…"

"Is fine," she repeated, letting her hand come up to scrape along his scalp, holding him in place for a second. "I want this. I want you," she urged throatily.

He let out a sigh that was more explosive than a gust of wind, and she wasn't sure if it was a sound of acquiescence or rejection. She gritted her teeth as the uncertainty overwhelmed her once more. Then, he was helping her off his lap and helping her stand with the desk to the back of her thighs.

Before she could argue, sure he was about to send her away, his hands were at the waistband of her yoga pants and he was tugging them, and her panties, down. She shuddered with the glory of it, the realization that he needed her as desperately as she craved him.

When the pants were hooked down by her knees, his thumbs slid along the inner curve of her thighs. They didn't stop until they were pulling her pussy lips apart, and one thumb slid deeper, coming to a halt only at the entrance.

The barely-there penetration had her pussy clutching the digit, and she whimpered, her head falling back at the teasing touch.

"No," she whimpered, her hands coming up to support her head. "More, more," she demanded, letting her good hand move down to cup his chin.

She felt his smile behind her fingers, but didn't have the wherewithal to chide him, just had to take what he was giving. She loved that about them all. They gave, and she had to take. For the moment. While she was still delicate, they'd get used to this side of her. But when she was back to full working order, they'd get the shock of their lives.

For the moment, she loved their dominance, their willingness to take charge of her body, and give her what it needed. What she needed.

Them.

Any way they'd let her have them.

She moaned when he demanded, "Try to widen your stance."

She complied, managing to find a scant few inches of give in the taut fabric, and was immediately rewarded with his mouth finding her clit. She tilted her head forward to watch, to see his mouth furling around her lips, to watch his tongue explore the secret crevice of her body.

She shuddered, staggering back, thankful when the desk caught her in place. The move widened her legs further, and he went in for the kill, not stopping until she was on tiptoes, her stomach caving in on itself as he fucked her with his tongue, nibbled her clit with his lips, then tested the resilience of her pussy lips with his teeth. Two fingers went inside her, they scissored around, pushing her, testing her. She let out soft whimpers that combined both need and wonder as he prepared her for him.

She whispered, "Come to me," when he got to his feet, and her hands immediately shot out to his fly. Within seconds, his cock was out, and her mouth watered at the sight of the pre-cum bubbling from the tip.

"One day, someday soon," he promised with a growl, knowing her intention, apparently eager for it too as he practically ripped off her yoga pants.

She sighed, then allowed him to push her against the desk. He staggered the move, supporting her until her head was flat against the surface. Then, his cock was there, right between her legs. A thick, blunt presence that made her want to scream with wonder as he began to work himself inside her.

She lifted her legs, clutching them to his hips, and held him close with her calves. Her heels burrowed into his pants-covered ass, and though she longed for a bed, she loved this too.

Having never expected this when she'd walked through the door earlier, she was damn grateful she had. Because Jesus, Sean was finally going to screw her brains out.

She tilted her chin, so she could stare straight into his eyes, and with each inch he conquered, he seemed to lunge deeper into her very soul.

The connection that arced between them was more than she could stand. It made her want to close her eyes, made her want to shut him out, yet at the same time, she wouldn't be happy until all of him was inside all of her.

Her lips trembled as he filled her with him, and then, he grabbed hold of her shoulders, burrowing his hands underneath her back to grip them from behind, and slowly began to thrust.

Deep, measured thrusts.

His hold on her stopped her from moving around too much on the desk, and her head was pretty stationary as he began to fuck her.

Her hips rocked up every time he thrust all the way back in, and she clung to him with everything she could as he retreated, denying her his fullness before he fed his cock back inside her.

Endless whimpers escaped her as throughout the delicious torment, his eyes remained glued to hers.

Words longed to fall from her lips, but this was neither the time nor the place. Not with Katrin down the hall.

Any of her men could have walked in and she would have loved it, but that bitch?

No fucking way.

She had to bite her tongue to stop her emotions from spilling forth, and he seemed to sense that because he dropped his head, letting their mouths connect.

He fucked her lips with his tongue just as he fucked her pussy. Slowly, surely, resolutely.

He claimed her at that moment, letting her know exactly who she belonged to.

The notion should have terrified her, but it didn't. If anything, it was like a livewire soaring through her veins.

She let out a hoarse yell, one he swallowed, as that livewire exploded into a dozen fireworks. She pulled her mouth from his to sink her teeth into his shoulder. The pain was his trigger too. She felt him cum, felt the sluggish pelt of his seed spurt inside her.

It was the *piéce de resistance.*

She dug her heels into his butt as her back soared, strung as tightly as piano wire as the delicious whirling sensations powered through her blood.

He was the leader of this band of not-so-merry-men… and his word was law.

She was his.

Theirs.

Sean had just made it so.

TWENTY

WITH AN UNAPOLOGETIC 'OOPS,' Sascha *accidentally* knocked the bottle of perfume onto the bathroom floor.

When it bounced, she glowered at it, picked it up, and hurled it down.

This time, it smashed, and though she was drowned in two-thousand-dollars-an-ounce tailored scent that smelled like a dying old lady —make that a *rich*, dying old lady—it was more than worth it.

Six. Fucking. Nights.

Six!

Putting up with that bitch was grating on her last nerves, and it wasn't aided by the fact that her doctor's appointment was looming over her. If anything, it made her mood even shittier.

Retreating from the downstairs bath that Katrin had made her own, Sascha headed for the living room where she'd been sleeping ever since her arrival. Opening the door without a knock always pissed the bitch off, so she did it this time and watched the older woman stuffing chocolates into her mouth. Whenever the men even suggested taking her to a hotel, she fainted. Honest to God, swooned.

She'd never seen anything like it in her fucking life, but the woman could collapse on command. Sascha had even squeezed Katrin's earlobe in the hopes of making her yelp and wake up, but no dice.

Yet, Swooning Sally was busily and happily eating chocolates like a trooper!

"I dropped your perfume bottle in the bathroom when I was cleaning it," she said with no apology to her tone. Well aware what she was doing was mean and petty, she didn't care. Sascha hated Katrin with a depth that astonished even her. The bitch had hurt *her* men. For that, Katrin was lucky Sascha was only being petty. "You'll have to clean it yourself. The stench is making my head pound."

Katrin's hand hovered halfway between the box and her mouth. It took that long for her to process Sascha's remark, because from dead silence, a loud shriek formed.

"Do you have any idea how much that scent cost?" she yelled and jumped to her feet in outrage. Considering the merest suggestion of having to move to a hotel had her dropping into a dead faint, her haste was certainly impressive.

Jesus, Sascha *wished* she could move so quickly!

The bitch shot off like a rocket out of the room, elbowing her out of the way as she stormed over to the bathroom. An enraged yell came from within, and Sascha grinned to herself, satisfied with the racket she'd caused. Not that such an explosion of noise was of any interest in this household, of course, she thought, rolling her eyes. Anywhere else, doors would have slammed open, and a stampede of feet would have come running, seeking the source of the shout.

Not here.

A flurry of pissed-off German came next, and she folded her arms against her chest, satisfaction welling in her as she strode out of the living room-cum-patient's ward and headed for the kitchen.

As she carefully walked down the steps, she had to grimace. Katrin's reaction had been so worth the stench, but now, it was kind of fucking with her head.

Another migraine. Great.

She'd have rolled her eyes again, but the pain would be too much.

Hearing footsteps on the stairs as she approached the fridge, she more than expected to see Katrin looming over her, but instead, she saw Sean.

He cocked a brow at her. "Another accident?"

Flaring her eyes wide, she murmured, "I'm clumsy. What can I say?" She turned back to the fridge to hide her satisfied grin.

Call her *petty*, but if Katrin called her a Yankee one more fucking time, she'd do more than smash the bitch's bottle of perfume.

Sean, however, didn't comment, just snorted, headed for the counter, and perched his ass on a stool.

When she turned around with a bottle of water in hand, she saw he was studying her with an intent that made her fidget.

"What?" she asked, passing him the water. He opened the bottle, handed it to her, and she took a sip. Giving it back to him, she watched his throat work as he drank deeply too.

"It's amazing how you've been having so many accidents of late."

She smiled meekly. "I'm concussed."

Another snort. "If that was the reason, I'd have taken you to the ER before now," he grunted. "Next time she pisses you off and you decide to sabotage her shit, don't use my bathroom to do it in? Please?"

His plea had her chuckling. "Stinks like a bitch, right? Quite fitting for her."

"Yeah. But there's no way that smell is going away for a lifetime."

She hid a grin. "Sorry. I couldn't help it. She was dabbing it on her throat this morning, and…"

When she broke off, he cocked a brow at her. "And what?"

She shrugged. "Doesn't matter."

"Sure, it does."

Ducking her head, she sheepishly admitted, "Katrin said Andrei had bought it for her."

"Ah."

She eyed him. "Ah."

"Have you spoken about this with Andrei?"

"No. Of course not." Unease rippled through her. "Why would I? If he did fuck her, that's between him and Kurt. It's also in the past and nothing to do with me."

"All true, and yet, emotions have a funny way of fucking with the truth. You can't help how you feel."

She cleared her throat. "Nope. Guess not."

"I guess I can forgive the stench in my bathroom if she was trying to make you jealous."

She grimaced. "And succeeded at it."

"Well, you succeeded in pissing her off. I think she's trying to cover herself in as much as she can. It must have set Andrei back a fortune if her reaction is anything to go by."

"Are you trying to improve my mood or make it worse?" she gritted out, hating the irrational emotions that were flying through her, and had been doing so for the past week.

She was so over these headaches. So over being incapacitated by them. And so fucking bored of being horny when she had five studs who were more than willing to service her out of her funk.

He grimaced. "Sorry. That was a bit dimwitted of me."

"Ya think?"

He shot her an apologetic look.

"What the fuck were both of them thinking?" she demanded, the words bursting from her. "Sawyer has it right. She's not only the wicked witch, it would be like fucking the deep freeze."

Sean chuckled. "You don't have to convince me. I was never attracted to her."

She eyed him. "Why not? I thought I was just being bitchy."

His chuckle deepened. "She's…" He seemed to struggle to find the words, until he declared, "You're warm, open, giving. She's cold, closed, and a taker. This entire situation sums up Kurt's marriage." He grunted. "That was a fucking nightmare. He spent more time with us than he did with her, but he was constantly sulking. The idiot didn't want her, but he didn't know why."

She blinked. "What did he marry her for? He said it was because of his mom…"

Sean nodded. "It was. Margritte thought he was gay, and shoved Katrin at him. Hell, just because she's not my cup of tea doesn't mean I can't see she's beautiful. He thought with his cock and paid for it."

"Did he really live here a lot?"

Sean grimaced. "Yes. There was a lot of angry German muttering going down. On the plus side, it's how he wrote *Black Blood*. The artist in him must need to suffer to create. He's too happy at the moment."

His words had her perking up. "He is?"

Sean reached over and chucked her under the chin with his pointer finger. "Stop looking for compliments," he teased. Then, shooting her a wink, confessed, "We're all a lot happier. Can't you tell?"

She shrugged. "No comparison. I didn't see you for the miserable bastards you were before I came and brightened up your days."

"True."

"I'm like unicorn farts. I bring glitter and sparkles everywhere I go."

"Don't forget cookies," he added.

"True. Cookies, too."

"Speaking of…?"

She rolled her eyes. "I only put them in the oven ten minutes ago. And they're not cookies today. I wanted some blueberry muffins."

Sean pouted. "But your cookies are the best."

She grinned. "I know. In more ways than one."

"Are you talking dirty to me?" he asked, sounding confused.

She snorted. "Don't spoil it."

"Don't spoil what?"

The tap of more footsteps coming down the stairs broke off their conversation. Spying Sawyer, she immediately asked, "Do you know what a cookie is?"

"Aside from the ones you bake?" he asked, brow quirked. When she nodded, he looked at Sean, huffed. "It's a pussy, man. How can you know so fucking much about humanity and so fucking little, too?"

Sean scowled at him. "Why on earth would they call a pussy a cookie?"

"Because it's loaded with sugar?" she jibed.

"I thought you had sparkles and glitter coming out of every orifice?" he rebuked. "You can't have both."

"True," she conceded with a pout.

"Sparkles and glitter?" Sawyer asked. "What the hell are you two talking about?"

"Mostly Katrin," she replied with a grimace, slipping off her stool to head to the fridge. "You want a protein shake?"

He blinked, ceased leaning on the counter beside Sean, and stood upright. "I'll get it, lass. Sit yourself down."

"I'm not that delicate," she argued, even though she totally was.

He snorted. "Liar."

She narrowed her eyes at him.

Unphased, he pointed to the stool. "Sit."

"Want me to roll over so you can scratch my belly too?" she demanded, complying with a huff.

"You've other more interesting places to scratch, lass."

"Ouch," she mocked. "No nails."

He snorted. "When's that fucking doctor's appointment anyway? I'm tired of seeing that bruised look in your eyes. Makes me want to cosset you, and I'm not a man made for cosseting."

She blinked at that, then cast a quick look at Sean who looked equally stunned. With a quick gulp, she murmured, "It's on Friday."

"Thank God for that. Maybe he can give you better pain meds now?"

She shrugged. "I don't know. I keep thinking I'm getting better then another headache will strike."

"I'll assume the Great Perfume Bottle Break of 2018 hasn't helped your head any?"

His glib question had her lips twitching. "I plead the Fifth."

"You can't plead that over here. We don't have the same constitution," Sean retorted with a chuckle.

"Shit. I knew there was a reason the UK totally sucked ass."

Sawyer grinned but surprised her by not pulling out the fixings for a protein shake, but some juice.

He rarely, if ever, ate sugar, following a strict diet that boggled her brain. Although she'd noticed he'd been growing lax of late. Where before, he'd never touched her cakes or cookies, now, he did.

Sipping straight from the carton, he smacked his lips after.

She glowered at him. "You know how unhygienic that is, right?"

"My lips and everyone else's has been on parts of your body far less hygienic than this juice carton… I think we can deal with germs."

She pulled a face. "That's gross."

He grinned. "Good thing we don't think so."

"I know where I can find some stinky perfume… I also know where you keep your underwear."

As her eyes narrowed, his widened. "You wouldn't dare."

Sean smirked. "I wouldn't test her."

"Fuck. You win." He reached for a glass from the cupboard over the sink and poured himself a drink. "Better?"

"Hardly. The deed is done now." She sighed and shot Sean a look.

He reached over and swiped his thumb along her cheekbone. When his thumb brushed where she was nibbling on her lip, she let her tongue swiped across the blunt end. His eyes darkened. "Minx."

"She can't help it," Sawyer pointed out. "The woman's part vixen."

Sascha cut him a look but couldn't stop the smug grin that curved her lips. "Is that really how you think of me?"

"Aye." He wafted a hand at her as he moved around the counter, a tumbler in his clasp. "You're even more potent in these regular clothes too."

She blinked, peered down at herself with a grimace. With her head the way it had been, she'd barely been putting on anything other than a swipe of gloss on her lips—even that was to stop dry lips, not to look sexy. And her regular clothes consisted of yoga pants and camisoles. Hardly vixen-like wear.

"You think this is sexy?" she asked, astonished by his comment.

"You haven't seen your ass in them," he explained. "Plus, you get the sweetest camel toe." He clutched his heart. "Almost kills me."

She closed her eyes in a mixture of amusement and mortification but couldn't stop the snort from escaping. "You did not just say that?"

"I only speak the truth. Don't I, Sean?"

Her eyes popped open to catch Sean's response. He cleared his throat, looked down at his lap.

"Sean?"

He cleared his throat again. "It's pretty sweet," he mumbled.

"You pervs," she retorted, but the comments actually cheered her up. She'd been feeling like a slug for wearing such boring clothes of late. But she'd wanted comfort over anything else, and these were perfect for that.

Knowing that they liked her dressed for comfort as well as to impress perked her up a treat.

"*Your* pervs," Sawyer retorted, winking at her again.

Sascha huffed out a breath, then peered up at the ceiling when she heard another shriek coming from above. Ducking her head to hide her grin, fingers appeared that forced her to look at them.

"What have you done now?"

Her lips twitched with the need to smile. *Smugly*. "Nothing."

"Jesus. Remind me never to trust that grin again," Sawyer said with a grimace.

She smirked. "That would be very wise of you."

TWENTY-ONE

"THANKS FOR AGREEING to see us, Edward," Andrei murmured as he shook Edward Jacobie's hand. "These are my friends, Sean and Sawyer."

Jacobie's eyes widened in surprise. "Your housemates, too, if I'm not mistaken?"

Andrei shot him a confused frown as Sean and Sawyer shook hands with the man. "How do you know that?"

"Sorry. An invasion of privacy, I know, but my security detail did a check on you before we started working together. I read the file. I was curious about you."

Sawyer shot Sean a look, but he shook his head the slightest eighth of an inch to the left, and Sawyer decided to shut the fuck up.

He wasn't even sure why he was there, except Andrei had said it made sense for Sawyer to show up. If Jacobie was totally unreceptive to answering their questions, they could swiftly turn to business and Sawyer could join in and help sweep things over.

Disinterested in the inane chitchat Andrei and Sean engaged in with the tech mogul, Sawyer looked around the sweet digs.

They were in Surrey, an hour or so away from their home in Kensington. Jacobie's family home was here, and it was an old country pile.

A lot of the old noble estates had either gone to rack and ruin after the First World War, had been turned over to the National Trust who maintained the historical landmarks while opening them to the public, or were owned by the original families who kept them open to the visitors who funded repairs—Jacobie's house was none of those three.

Not that that was completely surprising. The man was a billionaire after all.

When he was in England, this house was his HQ. He had a skyscraper all to himself in London, but according to Andrei, he worked here for the most part.

Sawyer couldn't blame him. The house was not only beautiful, but large; Jacobie's office was the size of a tennis court. A huge plantation desk overlooked a maze in the garden, while large sofas looked onto a hearth so deep and tall, he could probably step inside it with comfort.

The man was overly fond of taxidermy, with dead stag heads on the wall, bears and even a lion on the floor, but these rich bastards usually were, weren't they?

He scrubbed his chin, wondering why being in a high tax bracket meant people forgot about carpeting and started having preference for animal corpses, when a knock sounded at the door.

"Come in," Jacobie hollered.

A maid appeared in a neat black uniform with her hair pulled back in a tight bun. "I've brought coffee, sir," she murmured politely, bowing her head at the tray she was supporting with the flat of one hand.

"Thank you, Maria," Jacobie replied, smiling as she headed past two onyx and gilt statues of boys that guarded the entry way.

She placed the tray on the coffee table separating the seating area where they'd taken up residence. Sean and Andrei were on the sofa, overlooking the hearth, Jacobie was to the left, in an overstuffed armchair, his view took in the door. Sawyer also had an armchair, but he could see out into the yard from his perspective.

Maria neatly tucked her knees together as she approached and bent down to place the tray on the coffee table. Within seconds, she was silently pouring out four cups of coffee.

As the scent of the potent brew perfumed the atmosphere, he asked, "Would it be okay if I used the restroom?"

Knowing Sean and Andrei were shooting him a look, he ignored them. He doubted they believed he needed the bathroom; but they should also have known that if they'd brought him along like a guard dog, he was bound to stray.

"Of course," Jacobie said magnanimously. "Maria will show you to the facilities."

He smiled at the host, then the maid, and got to his feet. Trailing behind her, he shut the living room door, and wandered down a small corridor that led to a large atrium.

Overhead, a kind of old-fashioned skylight illuminated the space. It reminded him of the Crystal Palace. Not neat and sleek like today, but boxy. Still, it retained a charm of its own, because, for its time, it had undoubtedly been innovative.

The central space housed a bank of seating areas. Small clusters that lined the middle, whereas down the wall, there were the usual paraphernalia one found in country piles such as these.

Statues, suits of armor, priceless paintings, ugly portraits of long dead ancestors. He viewed it all with interest, then as they approached the foyer with its large circular table, the table he'd wanted to study alone, he cut a glance at the maid who hadn't spotted his interest.

Taking him down another corridor, she waved a hand toward a door. "Here you are, sir."

"Thanks." He shot her a tight smile.

She bowed her head, and he watched as she retreated, not moving until she'd gone.

Quickly heading inside, he waited by the door, listening for the tap tap of her footsteps to disappear entirely.

When they had, he left the bathroom again, and headed back the way he'd come.

In the foyer, the large maple table gleamed with polish. Old age had taken away some of the definition of the grains, but it still shone with vitality. Atop it, there was a large bouquet of flowers that stunk as he neared, but what interested him, were the frames circling the table.

All shapes and sizes, assorted colors of metal and wood, they framed over a dozen pictures. Old and new.

Some were of sober-faced men, others of laughing children. The one that interested him however was the one he'd spotted the instant he'd walked through the looming double doors of the house.

A woman. Somber-looking. Cheekbones so high they looked carved from marble. Lips so full and pouty, he knew what they felt like against his mouth. Her eyes, the line of her brows—their curve—it was a match too. The still was black and white, so he couldn't make out a hair color, but she wasn't blonde. Nor was she chestnut dark.

Whoever she was, she looked like Sascha.

Or, to be precise, Sascha looked like her.

A hundred years parted the woman he knew and the creature in the still, but he knew that face. Had studied it with the tension of a climax looming. Knew it when it was relaxed from amusement, as laughter spilled from her. When she was angry, sad, stressed, in pain… he'd seen those features in many different guises, and there was no taking away from the fact, the stranger was Sascha's doppelganger.

Reaching for his cell phone and the frame, he quickly snapped a shot of the photo.

Now that she was in his hand, the similarities were enough to have him shaking his head in astonishment.

A text beeped.

Who is that? She and Sascha could be twins.

If Devon saw it, then Sawyer knew his eyes weren't deceiving him.

"My great grandmother," a voice declared from behind him.

He jerked to attention, spinning around, the frame still in his hand.

When he just stared at the new arrival, a woman in jodhpurs and a tight shirt, a Barbour coat hooked over her shoulder, she smiled at him, and with her riding crop, pointed to the frame in his hand. "She's my great-grandmother."

Sawyer cleared his throat. "Oh."

"Is there a reason you just took a photo of her?" she asked, sounding a tad surprised but not suspicious.

He pulled a face. "You caught me. I saw the frame. It's exactly like one I have at home."

She shot him a confused look. "So?"

"I was just showing my partner."

"Okay," she replied with a little laugh when he made no bones about not explaining anything else.

Replacing the photo frame in its original spot, he glanced down at his cell and saw Devon had sent another text.

What the hell is going on?

Quickly, he shot back a message: *Later. I'll explain.*

Shoving his phone back in his pocket, he explained, "I'm with Andrei Kirov?"

Eyes brightening, the woman smiled. "You are? Andrei's become quite the friend. I didn't realize he was coming here today, and I usually coordinate my brother's diary."

"Andrei asked for a meeting a few days ago, but I get the feeling this space just opened up out of nowhere. Andrei got the call two hours ago, and here we are."

Jacobie's sister frowned. "Oh. Well, I've been out riding all morning. It's my day off," she commented.

He smiled, nodded. "A nice day for it."

Her nose wrinkled. "It would have been were it not for a burst of rain last night. Made the ground soggy." She shrugged. "Do you ride, Mr....?"

"Sawyer, please."

"Sawyer," she conceded with a nod. "I'm Louise."

"Pleasure to meet you, Louise."

A demure smile was her only retort, and she held out a hand that was aimed in the general direction of the study he'd just left. "If you'd like me to escort you back to my brother's office?"

"I can probably find my way. I only visited the restroom."

Louise didn't take the bait. "It's no trouble, honestly."

Realizing she had no intention of letting him roam, he allowed himself to be herded. She tapped on the door to her brother's office, but unlike the maid, didn't wait for him to respond.

Shuffling inside, she smiled at her brother. "The wanderer returns."

Jacobie, in the middle of discussing something that had his eyes gleaming with excitement, peered over at his sister. With a glance, he dismissed her.

"Thanks, sis."

Louise's shoulders drooped. "You're welcome. Well, I'll leave you to it," she ended, when Jacobie turned his attention back to Andrei without further ado.

"Great to see you, Lou," Andrei pointed out.

"You too, Andrei." Though her gaze lingered on Sean, when her brother made no attempt to introduce her, she retreated, her jaw clenched with annoyance.

That was the trouble when family worked together, Sawyer thought with a rueful smile as he took a seat in the armchair he'd vacated moments before.

Sometimes, oil and water mixed more cohesively than two siblings.

A TAP SOUNDED at her door. She blinked, placed a paperclip on the page where she was reading, and called out, "Yes?"

When Devon's head popped around the corner, she murmured, "Come in, silly."

He stepped inside, and as was usually the way when one of the men came in here, the large living space shrunk exponentially.

They were all big, but in her rooms, the contrast was never more noticeable.

Wearing jeans and a sweatshirt, she also noticed he was barefoot.

Of all the men, Devon was the least likely to leave the house. She could probably count on one hand how many times he'd gone out in the past month.

Whenever they had business, men in suits with somber expressions either came to the house, or Sawyer went out and dealt with it.

She wasn't sure if he was agoraphobic or just reclusive, or maybe a mixture of the two.

"They're clean," he pointed out as she approached the bed. "Can I get in?"

She blinked at him. "What are clean?"

"My feet. You were looking at them."

She snorted. "I should hope they are. Olga and Agathe were here this morning cleaning."

It was why she'd sequestered herself up here. Now Katrin was at a hotel at last, having figured out she couldn't keep fainting left, right, and center without one of the men trying to call an ambulance, the household was back to normal.

And that alone had her feeling more rested and comfortable.

She was also coming to terms with the fact her appointment with her GP was approaching. Now that first step of making the appointment with the clinic was over with, she'd found her tension had bottomed out, helping with the headaches, and letting her rest a little more easily.

It stunned her how her fear of the doctors had actually put such a pressure on her that it had exacerbated her symptoms, but then, she didn't exactly have the fondest memories of hospitals and clinics. She guessed nobody did, but the times she'd spent there as a child had planted lasting, traumatic memories. Of course, the next hurdle was the appointment itself. She'd think about that when the time came.

The bedsheets rustled as Devon pulled them away from the vacant side of the bed. When he climbed in with her, his head coming to rest on the pillow, he asked, "What are you reading?"

Amused that he was laying down and not sitting up like her, she moved the sheets to the bedside table, and carefully lowered herself down so they were on the same level. "A manuscript of Kurt's. One he wanted me to read."

Devon cocked a brow. "You're blessed."

"I am? Why?" she asked, confused.

"He never lets anyone read his books. Not until he's sent them to his editor."

She couldn't stop the pleasure that flushed through her at Devon's words. "Truly?" she asked softly.

"Truly," he confirmed, closing his eyes, and snuggling into the duvet.

"Wow. I didn't realize he was bestowing some kind of honor on me."

Devon snorted, eyes blinking open. "I wouldn't go that far. Don't tell him I told you. He'll get a bigger head."

Her lips twitched. "Kurt doesn't have a big head."

Devon rolled his eyes. "He takes the artistic temperament too far sometimes."

"And you don't take the reclusive math genius too far, I suppose?" she mocked.

He blinked at her again. "No. Of course not."

The severity of his tone had her snorting. "Seems very one-sided to me," she declared, reaching over to kiss him. "Did he preen when he won the Pulitzer?"

"No."

"Well, how can you say he's big headed then?" she retorted with a huff.

"He used all the paper in the house," Devon replied. "Like we didn't need any at all. It was very rude of him."

She snorted. "You can't be serious?"

"What? He'd never have used all the paper if he hadn't won that award."

"What one has to do with the other, I do not know," she remarked, reaching over to tap his temple. "Your brain is nutty sometimes."

He scowled. "Paper is a precious commodity in this house."

"I'd noticed," she said ruefully. Every week, stacks and stacks of it were delivered to the door.

She had no idea what they did with it. Buying office supplies was something she did, and the quantity of paper never correlated with new ink cartridges in the printer.

"What do you do with it anyway?" she demanded, curiosity driving her.

"Paper?" he asked, and she nodded in reply. "Origami."

Her mouth gaped. "What?"

"It's very calming."

He was serious. Saying that, when wasn't he? She gawked at him. "You do origami?"

He shrugged. "Yes."

"Why have I never seen any?"

"They go on the fire when I'm done."

Her mouth, already gaping, dropped open further. "No fucking way. The next time you make one, I want to see it."

"Why?"

"Because I'm curious, dammit. How did I not know that you liked to do that?"

"Not *like*. Like is too facile a word. It's imperative. I like keeping my hands busy."

She blinked, shaking her head at him as she murmured, "You constantly amaze me, Devon."

"Is that good or bad?" he asked warily.

"Neither. It means I never get bored," came her wry retort.

"That's good. Boredom is bad," he declared, seemingly satisfied by her response.

"What are you doing up here, anyway? I thought you were busy." When she'd popped her head around his door earlier, he'd been so lost in his work, he'd not heard her call his name.

"I knew you'd come," he stated with a huff. "I thought I imagined it."

"Imagined what?"

"Your knocking at the door. But I wasn't sure if my mind was playing tricks on me."

The way the man's brain worked, she wouldn't have been surprised either. Truth was, for all his strengths, Devon was remarkably fragile, too.

Over the weeks, she'd come to see why the others shielded him so much. Something she found herself starting to do.

She reached over to cup his cheek. "It's fine. I just wanted to know if you were hungry."

"I'm sorry. I didn't mean to ignore you."

"You were busy," she said softly, smiling at him. "But you're not now. Do you want to nap?"

He pursed his lips. "Is that a euphemism?"

"No. It's not. Agathe is still down in the kitchen, cleaning up. She said she'd buzz me on the intercom when she was leaving. You can't have your wicked way with me while she's here."

He pouted. "Why not?"

She rolled her eyes and tapped his chin with her finger. He had a butt-chin, and she stroked the dimple in the center of the padding. "Behave."

He winked. "Tell me about why you came to London."

"What about it?" she asked, somewhat surprised by the change in subject.

"What made you come here? How easy it was to get a visa, that kind of thing?"

Eyes flaring wide, she asked, "Why?"

"I'm curious."

And if Devon was anything, it wasn't curious. Not outside of math, anyway.

Suspicious, but wanting to know where he was going with this, she murmured, "I told you already. I came over with a boyfriend."

"You didn't marry though?"

"What? To get a visa?" She huffed. "No way. If it had rested on that, I wouldn't have come. I liked him, and I wanted it to work, but deep down, I knew it wouldn't. Still, it was a chance to come over here. It's always been a dream of mine to visit the UK."

"Why?"

She smiled a little. "My mother visited London when she was younger. She had so many stories about it. When she died, it was always on my bucket list to come here, to see the things she'd seen, to be in the places she'd been."

He frowned. "That's very sentimental."

"Why does that surprise you?" she retorted wryly. "I was a little girl when she passed. Most of her stories became legend to me."

"When my mother died, I was relieved," he whispered quietly.

Stillness overcame her. "Was she ill?"

His eyes had turned inward as they had a habit of doing when his mind was elsewhere. "No."

"Then why were you relieved she'd died?"

"She escaped."

The simple answer had her gulping. "Escaped what?"

"Escaped *whom*. My father. He used to beat her." He closed his eyes. "I can still hear her screams. She tried to leave once. Went without me. I was glad though. I knew she was leaving me behind, but I was just hopeful that she'd escape. That someday, we'd be together again." He shook his head. "It wasn't to be."

"He brought her back?"

"He had contacts in the Military Police." He jerked his chin in the air. "*They* brought her back. The bastards."

She reached over and trailed a finger over the length of his clenched jaw. "I'm so sorry."

"Don't be. I meant it when I said I was relieved for her. There was no escape but death."

"Jesus," she breathed. "How old were you?"

"Eleven."

"Did she…?" She swallowed. "Did she kill herself?"

He nodded.

"W-Who found her?"

"Me."

She sucked in a sharp breath. "Oh, Devon."

"What?" he asked, taking her literally.

Feeling tears prick her eyes, she shook her head. As her hair whispered against the sheets with the movement, she murmured, "Nothing. It doesn't matter." He wouldn't understand the need she had to comfort him, to try to take that pain away… Such an effort would be futile anyway. How could she make *that* better?

Those memories would haunt him for the rest of his life.

"Tell me about your mom," he asked.

She bit her lip as his expression blanked, like he was wiping away the painful memories. Wanting to help him, to soothe his hurt, she did what she could—changed the subject. "She was a nurse."

"She was?" His brows lifted. "How did I not know that?"

She snorted. "I didn't tell you, silly."

"What kind of nurse?"

"Palliative."

"That's a… difficult branch."

Sascha pulled a face. "Agreed. She was very brave. But she loved what she did, even when she lost someone she'd grown close to. She was like that. A giver."

"And she went to the US when she was how old?"

"Early twenties."

"When she was here, did she work?"

She smiled. "When I was a little girl, I just thought she came on an extended vacation. I think that's what my dad believed too. But when I applied for a visa, went through half the process, I learned she had permanent residency over here."

"Your mom was a citizen of Great Britain?" he demanded, eyes widening in response.

"I was shocked too. She had to have worked over here to live here long enough to be a resident, but she always downplayed it." She shrugged—at the time, she'd had so many questions but with her mom long gone, and her relationship with her dad DOA, she'd had to bank her curiosity.

He frowned. "Wait a second. Permanent residency, what does that mean? Was she a citizen or a national?"

"A national. I was surprised. She had an American accent and I thought she'd been raised in Chicago!"

He froze.

"What is it?"

"I-I don't know."

"You're lying to me," she growled, eyes narrowing with her irritation. "What's going on?"

"Have you seen her birth certificate?"

She shook her head. "My dad has all her stuff, and though I was curious at the time, I never asked. Didn't want to upset him or get into a row over it. To be honest, I was just grateful because it made it easier to stay over here without a lot of paperwork." When he fell silent, she asked again, "Devon? Why are you asking all these questions about my mom?"

She was used to him being inquisitive and used to him digging into a topic and never letting go, but the sudden interest in her mom was disconcerting.

His jaw flexed. "I really don't think I should be the one to tell you. Sean, the others… they know better."

Before the last word had left his lips, she screamed, "Kurt!"

Twice more, she hollered his name, and though Devon winced, he didn't move from his spot on the bed.

The sound of footsteps clomping up the staircase was audible, and she winced when the door smashed open.

"Sascha?" Kurt's eyes flared wide when he saw them in bed. "What the hell's wrong?"

"What's going on, Kurt?"

He stared at her blankly. "What are you talking about?"

"Why is it suddenly a big deal that my mother was a national?"

"A national of what?"

"A national of Great Britain," she snapped.

His gaze connected with Devon's, then slowly, he admitted, "We should wait for Sean."

"No. We shouldn't wait for fucking Sean. We should tell me what's going on. Right this goddamn minute. Or I'll go and find Sean myself!"

"He understands the particulars in a way that we don't," Kurt reasoned. "He has access to information he can't share with us."

She swallowed, his tone, his urgency bleeding through to her in a way that freaked her the fuck out. "You're scaring me," she admitted shakily.

"That was never our intention," Devon told her gruffly, his hand coming over to rest against the small of her back. The warmth penetrated the chill that was overtaking her limbs. "If anything, we wanted to protect you."

"From what? Why do I need protecting?" she shrieked, starting to freak out now.

Kurt sighed, looked at Devon again, and stepped toward the bed. As he perched on the side, he kicked up a leg, so he could lean closer to her. "I'll tell you what we know, okay? It isn't much."

"It's more than I do," she snapped. "Something's going on, and if I'm involved, I have a right to know, dammit."

His jaw flexed, but he nodded. "A few hours after you were taken to the hospital, a man walked into a police station, confessed to stalking you with an intent to mowing you down."

She blinked, gaped at him. "You're not being serious?"

"I am."

"He is," Devon confirmed darkly, his fingers pressed into the base of her back, and he palpated the skin, trying to soothe, to remind her of their connection.

Her shoulders sank as she realized they weren't joking. *This wasn't a joke.*

Gulping, she whispered, "Why would anyone target me? Or was it —" She gritted her teeth. "Was *he* just a… stalker?"

Kurt shook his head. "As far as we know, that's not the case. But like I said, Sean isn't telling us everything."

"Why not?"

"Because he signed the Official Secrets Act, Sascha. Some things, he just can't share with us," Kurt explained.

"What happened to the man? Did he explain why he wanted to hurt me?"

"No. He just confessed. Said if you hadn't run into the road, he'd have mowed you down on the sidewalk, and that it was fortune on his side."

She gasped, her hand flying up to her throat. "He'd have killed innocent people to get to me?"

His lips flatlined as he nodded.

"B-But I'm nobody."

"Exactly." Devon curled into an upright position. "You are. But somebody wanted you dead. So, you're not. You understand the dilemma."

A fine tremor took over her body, and she gladly cuddled into Devon when he tugged her against his side.

"W-Why?"

"We don't know," Kurt repeated. "We just know there's something going on that's beyond our ken."

"Sean looked into your father. We figured maybe it was someone with a grudge against him. A criminal he'd put away. But he couldn't find anything like that."

She shook her head. "He worked traffic, then a small beat before he could take the sergeant's exam. He's always had more of an admin role than anything else."

"Yeah. We figured that out too. So, if it wasn't him, and your paternal grandparents were nothing more than a butcher and a home-maker from Phoenix too, then it had to be on your mother's side."

"Her parents died before I was born."

"We know," Kurt stated grimly. "Which meant the person targeting you was because of something you had done or something your mother had.

"Considering you were allowed into the country, we figured it wasn't something you'd done as the regular checks would automatically shoot up a notification if you'd done something illegal, for example. But if you're entitled to be a passport holder because of your mother, then maybe it *is* something you've done," Kurt reasoned, running a hand through his hair, agitating the blond locks and making them fall onto his scowling forehead.

"B-But I'm a housekeeper. That's it. Before this, back in the States, I was in college and I waited tables in a coffee shop. Why would anybody want to hurt me?" she asked, her jaw trembling, making her words stutter.

"That's what we've been trying to figure out," Kurt explained softly, and reaching forward, he pressed his thumb to her chin, and cupped her cheek. "Everything will be okay," he told her. "We'll keep you safe."

"Safe from who?" she exploded. "How can you keep me safe from someone when you don't know who it is?"

Kurt sighed. "I understand you're scared."

"You're damn right I am. Shit, you guys should have told me this before. Why didn't you?"

"You were injured, and then the bombing made things extra tenuous."

She gulped, and her eyes flared wide as she hissed, "You don't think I was the target of the bomb?"

Though he could have dismissed the definite jump to that conclusion, he didn't. And that scared the shit out of her.

What the fuck was going on here? Sascha wailed inwardly.

"We don't know," Kurt answered softly.

Staggering out of the bed, pulling free from their gentle holds on her, she got to her feet and strode from one end of the room to the other. It didn't even matter that she felt sick from the pounding at her temples, it didn't matter that even her goddamn eyeballs were aching. She had to burn off this energy before it burned her.

"This is unreal," she whispered, wrapping her arms around her waist to hug herself.

Devon cleared his throat, drawing her attention to him. He held up his phone, but from the other side of the room, she just saw the picture of a woman.

"Who is it?"

"Sawyer just sent me this picture," Devon explained softly. "You remember the event you and Andrei were attending was because of his work with a tech mogul called Jacobie?"

"The software guy, right?"

Nodding, he continued, "They went to talk to him. Went to see if his security had fielded any major threats recently. We wanted to figure out if you were the target, or if he was."

"So, the bomb might not have been for me?" she demanded, hope lacing her words as she strode forward. But the nearer she walked, the closer the image on his phone was. And the more down the rabbit hole she felt sure she was falling.

She gasped. "Who is that?"

"Sawyer didn't say," Devon murmured, tilting the phone so Kurt could see the screen.

"Jesus. You're her double, Sascha," Kurt whispered, scowling at the screen like he could make sense of what the fuck was going on if he could just make sense of the picture.

"He said he'd explain later."

"Is that photo why you came to see me? Why you were asking questions about my mother?"

He shrugged. "This is… You have to admit, Sascha, it's crazy."

"Crazy?" she squeaked. "It's worse than that! I-I'm the target of a murder plot! The only interesting thing I've done in my life is sleep with you five people." Her eyes widened. "When I woke up in the hospital, I heard one of you asking if Sean was the target… if he'd been hit on purpose."

Kurt shook his head. "It happened once, years ago. It was a tough time. But we know it's got nothing to do with it. Why would the driver confess to intending to hurt you, but not Sean? Who, like the rest of the pedestrians, would have been collateral damage? Plus, if the bomb was for you, Sean was never invited to the ball."

"But Andrei was. M-Maybe this is something to do with him," she reasoned, then clenching her eyes closed, she whispered, "Jesus, I'm trying to backtrack and pin this on one of you." She slammed her hands against her face. "I-I'm sorry. I'm just trying to make sense of this."

Kurt got to his feet, cautiously headed for her. When he was close, he cupped her elbows and tugged her against his chest. "Hey, it's okay."

"N-No, it's not. I don't want this to be about any of you as much as I don't want it to be about me." Her lips quivered as she pressed her forehead against his chest. "I-I care for you guys too much to even think what was just going through my mind."

"Say it how it is, Sascha," Devon stated from his position on the bed.

She turned her head to the side. "What do you mean?"

"Say it how it is," he repeated. "You love us."

"Devon," Kurt barked. "Don't put words in her damn mouth."

She jerked her chin up in the air. "What if I do?" she demanded. "What if these feelings for you *are* love? Isn't that crazy? As crazy as this fucked up situation is?"

Kurt tensed behind her, but he tugged her into his arms again. "It's not insane. We're all falling for you, Sascha. You know that. This house is… it's alive because of you."

She gulped. "That's not enough. You're falling… what if I've *already* fallen?"

Sascha pulled free from his arms and headed for the bed. Devon tried to reach for her, but she evaded his hold to grab his cell phone.

Staring down at the image, she whispered, "This can't be a coincidence."

Devon's eyes turned cold. "There are no such things as coincidences."

Shakily, she ran a hand through her hair. "I need to know who this woman is." So saying, she pressed the 'phone' symbol on the messaging app to connect the call.

"I can't speak now, Dev. I'll call later."

"It's me. I need to know who that woman is."

"Shit. He told you?"

"I asked."

A hiss sounded down the line. "We'll be home shortly."

She heard Sean and Andrei's voices in the background. "No, dammit. I want to know now. Who was she? Why do I fucking look like her?" Sascha gulped because the similarities were more than uncanny.

Aside from the lack of hue to the hair, the strange woman was her spitting image.

"She's Jacobie's great-grandmother."

Sascha's frowned. "I don't understand. How is that possible?"

"I don't know, but Sean's running a background check now."

Before she could say a word, Devon snatched the phone back from her. "Tell him that he needs to grab a hold of the background check the police did on her. She's half-British, Sawyer. Her mother was a national."

"Her mother was English?" Sawyer demanded, his tone so strident, so loud that she could hear him from a short distance.

"Yeah."

"Why the fuck didn't we know this?"

"We never asked," Devon retorted. "Look, just get back here. Sascha's freaking out."

He cut the call, pocketed his phone. "They're on their way."

"I-I knew about the background check, but surely it came up that I was a national too?"

"No. Not so far." He rubbed his chin. "I don't know why that is."

Kurt sighed. "Jesus, when did this all become so complicated?"

Sascha thought back to the image on Devon's phone. "Maybe it always has been, and we just never knew it."

TWENTY-TWO

SEAN STORMED INTO THE HOUSE, Sawyer and Andrei behind him.

That the man was furious, was a given. He'd been given the run around by the people who were in charge of securing the goddamn nation. No wonder he was pissed to have been given half the details on the woman who was living with them.

Hell, Sawyer didn't work with the schmucks, didn't have a relationship with them like Sean did, and *he* was fucked off.

They headed for Sean's office. The lounge would have been more comfortable, but that was their meeting ground. Why change the habit of a lifetime?

Seemed Devon and Kurt were on the same page, because as they strode in, Sascha was curled up in Sean's desk chair, Kurt, and Dev in their usual spots either side of the hearth. Sean strode straight over to Sascha, and before she could do anything stupid like complain, bent down, and tugged her into his arms. He wrapped her up tightly, and bit off, "I know you're mad at us. We kept shit from you, and you're right to be pissed about that, but we did it for your own benefit. You have to believe that. We didn't want to scare you, when we didn't know what the fuck was going on."

"You still don't know what the fuck is going on," she hissed, but she didn't struggle, didn't pull away from him. "Does that mean I'd still be in the dark if Sawyer hadn't seen that picture?"

He shuddered. "I don't know. That picture changes things."

"I know it does. I just don't know how."

Sawyer cleared his throat. "Sascha, I think you need to call your dad."

She pulled away from Sean, peered over his shoulder and caught him with a look. "Why?"

Her tone reminded him of a lost little girl, and it hurt him, so deeply, so intrinsically he felt like he'd been knifed in the gut. The feelings he had for this woman were so far beyond complex that they fucked with his mind. Fucked with everything he thought he knew about himself.

"You know why, sweetheart," he rasped, hating himself for hurting her but knowing she needed to be made to see sense.

"You want me to ask if he's my real dad, don't you?" Her bottom lip trembled and, in her eyes, those beautiful green eyes, he felt himself falling, deeper and deeper into the maelstrom of what she made him feel.

"It's the only thing that makes sense, Sascha," Andrei said softly. He moved away from the door and headed for Sean's desk. Before either of them could move, he approached her from behind, tucked her against his chest, and together, he and Sean embraced her.

Grounded her.

As they would always ground her.

She began to sob in their arms, and the sounds tore at him with great ripping slashes—his heart bleeding.

Helpless, he turned to Devon and Kurt, saw the same torment in their eyes. What he was feeling, they shared. They were in this together. There was no way he could forget that.

Andrei began whispering to her in Russian, and the tsunami of tears slowly ceased overwhelming her.

Grateful, Sawyer cleared his throat. "Sascha, baby." Wet shamrocks peered at him over Sean's shoulder. He strode toward the desk, leaning toward her as he gripped the edge. "We're all here for you, darling."

She swallowed. "Why did they lie to me?"

Sean sighed. "Something's going on, Sascha. Something that goes way beyond anything we can find out."

"W-Why?" she demanded.

Sean let out a deep sigh. "According to the authorities here, your mother's maiden name is not only *not* Natasha Ilsindon, which is what's on your records. Her name was Natalia Theosdottir. She was married to Arthur Jacobie, the grandfather of the man we met today, and..."

"There's more?" she cried. Like what he'd just said wasn't enough to turn her world on its head?

When Sean's mouth worked but no words fell from his lips, Sawyer whispered, "She's listed as dead, Sascha."

"Of course, she is!" she spat, hysteria inches away. "She died when I was nine. Of cancer! In Tucson. A world away from here."

Sawyer shook his head. "No, baby. We're talking about Natalia. Your *birth* mother. She died two months after you were born."

PROTECTED BY THEM

TWENTY-THREE

"HEADACHES ARE NORMAL AFTER A CONCUSSION."

The doctor's tone had Andrei scowling at her, and he was pleased to note that the scowl had her stuttering as she continued, her tone warmer after his silent rebuke, "B-But of course, we'll run some tests."

Sascha sighed, then nudged him in the arm. "Don't let him browbeat you. If they're normal, then that's okay."

"No, it's not okay," Andrei told her grimly. "Do the tests. Expansive ones."

He used the same tone his grandfather, the head of the Bratva, the Russian mafia, in his hometown would have used when talking to his minions.

Satisfied when the woman paled and began typing something on her computer, he turned to Sascha. "This is important."

"I know," she said with an eye roll thrown in. "It's *my* head."

"So why are you complaining?" he asked softly, leaning over to lift her chin up with his pointer finger. When her head was angled just so, he pressed a gentle kiss to her lips.

She sighed against his mouth, making him smile. It still astonished him how she was settling in with the five men she'd only been hired to keep house for.

Her tasks had been to pay the bills, do the laundry, and cook… not *service* Andrei and the rest of his friends in the bedroom.

And yet, it was amazing how things turned out because she was perfect for them.

Perfect.

A word he rarely used. As a statistician, he knew perfect didn't exist. But, in real life, it came in the form of one Ms. Sascha Dubois.

"What are you smirking about?" she grumbled when she pulled away from his kiss.

"Nothing," he said, feigning innocence. She grumbled again, crossed her legs at the ankle, and slouched in the uncomfortable seat in the doctor's office.

She'd been doing that of late, he'd noticed.

She headed into silence rather than diving into a row. Not that she was particularly argumentative, but she had opinions and wasn't afraid to uphold them. Something he admired about her, because in their house, when five geniuses came together, each an expert in their own fields, it would be easy to feel undermined by such intelligence.

But if Sascha felt that, it never came across.

Of course, he conceded, they couldn't exactly start rowing in front of the doctor. Not that he cared either way, but Sascha probably would.

She was still relatively constrained by society's mores. Andrei hadn't been constrained by them for a long time. Too long for him to count.

But, thoughts like that would derail him for a week, so skittering away from them, he asked, "Should she not be engaging in sexual activity?"

The woman, in her thirties, blonde and neat in her white doctor's coat with a smart blouse tucked into high-waisted pants, blushed at his question.

An unusual reaction considering she was a doctor—her unprofessionalism had him scowling again.

"You've been having sex?"

Sascha grimaced. "Look at him. Wouldn't you sleep with him if you had him hanging around all the time?"

The doctor's blush deepened, and Andrei's scowl disappeared as he chuckled. Maybe she wasn't as constrained by society's mores as he feared.

The notion had his lips twitching. "Why, Sascha, you'll embarrass the doctor."

Dr. Gates cleared her throat. "You shouldn't be engaging in any…" Another clearing of her throat. "Strenuous activity."

"Oops."

Andrei sighed. "This is why your concussion isn't getting any better."

"It could well be," the doctor informed her primly—she kept her gaze well averted from him.

Sascha pursed her lips. "I only did it when I was feeling good."

"Yes, then after, you paid the price, I'm sure?" Dr. Gates asked.

She shook her head. "No. I felt better afterward."

"Well," came the brisk retort. "I'm glad you did, but it seems we've cleared up why your headaches aren't improving. If you just rest for a little while longer, I'm certain there will be progress. While there have been studies that suggest the endorphins released after a climax can contribute to pain management, that you're still suffering would imply otherwise. Bouts of heavy activity will only make things worse."

"I can't stay still for the rest of my damn life!" Sascha argued.

"It won't be forever."

"Still," Andrei commanded, "Run the tests."

Dr. Gates swallowed. The nervous act had Sascha elbowing him in the side again. "Of course."

Within the hour, Sascha had been pricked and prodded by needles, had endured an X-ray, and listened to Andrei's fierce demands for an MRI.

All the while, Andrei had waited with her. Only breaking his attention from her if his cell phone buzzed and he had to deal with an important call or message.

Otherwise, he sat there and held her hand, tried to help her relax. She was stuck with so many needles, even he was getting wary of them.

When they left the doctor's office two hours later, she was trembling with fatigue.

The sight concerned him. He wrapped an arm around her shoulder and held her close to his side.

The front of the clinic was a modern monstrosity. Huge red triangular panels that reminded him of blood covered the façade in what he assumed was controlled chaos, not that he could appreciate it.

Even the benches were formed from concrete… cold on the ass, he'd assume, but he steered her to one nonetheless, grateful to be facing away from the crimson façade and onto a small green garden up ahead. It was truly amusing that the weird structure was undoubtedly founded in some bullshit attempt to make the place more soothing for nervous patients.

Andrei had proof that didn't work.

Sascha was nervous. The red monstrosity didn't exactly turn her frown upside down.

"I don't need to sit down," she complained. "I just need to get out of here."

He tutted under his breath, directing her to sit nonetheless. "Just take a minute."

She huffed. "I don't need a minute."

"You don't, huh?" He cocked a brow at her. "Well, what about me? I've watched more blood being pumped out of you than I'd care to see in a lifetime. Maybe my knees are feeling a little unsteady."

She blinked at him, turning her head to gape. "I'm sorry, Andrei, I didn't realize."

Her sudden earnestness had his chest tightening. God, there she was, being perfect again.

He sighed and reached over to cup her cheek. "I don't like to see you ill."

"I'm not ill," she argued. "Just under the weather," she conceded a second later when he scowled at her. "And stop scowling at everyone. I thought Dr. Gates was going to have a coronary, or something. Well, after she stopped crushing on you. Jesus, she was close to drooling. Do you have to be so handsome?" she grumbled.

He snorted dismissively at that. "So prim and fierce, but she melted like butter at my scowl, didn't she?" His tone was laced with the satisfaction he felt. Bullying the doctor wouldn't have been on today's to-do list if the woman had been willing to do her job.

If it made him look like a bastard to everyone else, he'd do it. Just to protect his woman.

Sascha shook her head. "Sometimes, you sound so incredibly Russian."

"That's because I am," he said contentedly.

"I know. I forget sometimes. The accent just fades away into one mass of sexiness," she admitted drily. "Although you were definitely a little harsh. You could have been politer to her."

"Why? She was going to brush us off. You needed the extra tests. Prevention is better than the cure, as the Brits say."

"Apparently not if she wasn't going to run those tests without your Russian scowl prodding her up the ass."

He grunted. "I've been perfecting that scowl. It's been a lifetime in the making."

"I can tell," she said wryly.

That scowl had been under construction since his grandfather had tried to morph him into his Bratva ranks, and he'd had to stand his ground and steer clear from that life path.

Just because he wasn't involved in his grandfather's business, didn't mean he hadn't seen the old man in action.

Seen and learned.

Vasily Kirov could have grown men pissing themselves with little more than a twitch of his brows.

It always amazed him how his grandfather could inspire such terror in… well, everyone. But with Andrei, he was soft as shit.

Rubbing his chin, and thinking that he needed to call the old bastard soon, he murmured, "Do you want to go to that bakery you like in Soho?"

She blinked at him, then grinned. "I'm not five, Andrei."

He frowned. "I'm well aware of this. And very grateful too," he said, with an exaggerated leer at her beautiful breasts. Breasts which were pushing against her V-neck tee like the fabric was a stranglehold and they were desperate for freedom.

"My eyes are up here, buddy," she chided, but he could hear the amusement in her tone. "You have to help me help myself, Andrei. No more looks like that, okay?"

He blinked, confused. "Huh?"

She growled. "How am I supposed to avoid sex when you guys make me think about it all damn day?" She pouted. "I'll go insane before my head heals."

His lips twitched. "I think that might be overstating the issue a tad."

Her tone was glum. "I don't. I've never thought about sex as much in my life. I swear, you've addled my brain. As you're the cause, you have to stop doing whatever it is you do to make me horny. So, no more checking out my boobs, no more feeling me up in the kitchen. I won't make it otherwise."

He had to hide a smile at her sulky retort. "I'm glad to hear we're so irresistible."

Sascha groaned. "Like you don't already know it."

He didn't actually. Though none of them could be considered Hunchback-of-Notre-Dame ugly, they'd never found it easy to date. And Andrei had always assumed that was because they weren't attractive to women.

He knew what he looked like in the mirror, but still... Dating hadn't been fun for any of them. They always seemed to attract the odd ducks who made their lives miserable in the long run. Janna, Katrin—the list wasn't endless but the time they'd wasted on each woman was time they wouldn't get back.

Rubbing his chin again, in contemplation, he murmured, "You really think this?"

She gawked at him, her neck jerking forward as she studied him like a Starbucks' barista trying to translate a coffee order in Klingon. "Wait a minute. You mean you don't know?"

"Don't know what?"

"How fucking gorgeous you are," she shrieked, then immediately grimaced. Lifting a hand, she rubbed her temple and blew out a breath. "You're all tall, and gorgeous, and muscled... Stop me before *I* start drooling."

He preened a little at her foghorn tone. "I think we should definitely go to that bakery now."

"Why?"

"You deserve two rewards. One for stroking my ego, and two for coming here."

She shot him a look, then laughed. "You're nuts."

He shrugged. "Yes. But what are you if you like me anyway?"

"Insane?" she questioned with a quick grin, before she nudged him in the side. "Also, stop making me feel like a dick for wanting you all. I know my own body. I get that you're going to lockdown and be super protective, but I wouldn't have slept with any of you if I'd suffered afterward."

He winced. "We want to look after you."

"And you do." She reached over and kissed his cheek. "Trust me to know what *I* need." As soon as she said the words, she blew out a breath. "Yeah. That's just wishful thinking. I know you're going to drive me nuts. The lot of you," Sascha grumbled as he helped her up to her feet and once again, they walked across the slick gray tarmac to his car.

Of them all, only he and Sean had cars. Mostly because they were the only ones who actually had to leave the damn house for business. Though, granted, they did what they could in their home offices.

Sawyer and Devon, their resident higher-order math geniuses, lived nearly constantly in their rooms. Devon was a hermit, though he wouldn't admit to it. Sawyer wasn't, but he either borrowed Sean's car if necessary or ran to wherever he needed to go—he was a health nut.

Kurt was a writer, and though he definitely wasn't as bad as Devon, he could spend days in the house when the muse struck. He also kept atrocious hours, but then, under their roof, they didn't seem to abide by time zones. GMT, PST, EST… they worked to their own rhythm, one the rest of the world didn't follow.

Someone was always awake. That was a given. Be it Kurt tapping away at his current manuscript, or Devon trying to figure out a formula that would crack a code MI6 needed help with, there was always one vacant bed at three in the morning.

Andrei opened the passenger door and helped slip her inside the low Audi. Sean had a more sensible Maserati sedan, and he realized he should have taken that instead. She had to crouch pretty low to the ground to get into the car, and her head was incredibly sensitive.

Kicking himself for *not* being sensitive, he slid a hand over the side of the car as he appreciated its silken lines.

Like Germans or not, they were good at making two things: money and cars.

He didn't care what Sean had to say about Maseratis. Nothing beat the engineering beauty of the R8 Spyder.

Climbing behind the wheel, he navigated out of the clinic's parking lot and onto the main road.

London, as always, was chaotic. Even now, when it was technically quieter, as everyone was inside their offices for the workday, there was a zip of energy that whizzed through the air. Almost like Tinkerbell spraying magical fairy dust wherever she went, London vibrated with a special energy.

Since meeting Sean, Devon, Kurt, and Sawyer at college in Oxford, he'd never lived outside of the UK. But for his work, he'd traveled the globe.

Madrid, Oslo, New York even… nothing compared in his opinion.

As he veered toward Soho and managed to get stuck in a traffic jam, even though the congestion fees for driving in the city were supposed to reduce traffic, he turned toward Sascha. Had he needed proof she was unwell, she'd just handed it to him on a platter. It was barely approaching lunchtime, and after climbing into the car, she'd rested her head against the window and fallen asleep.

He watched the deep rise and fall of her breasts, and noted her hands were gently open where they rested on her lap, the fingers unfurled and relaxed in a way that told him her sleep wasn't feigned and that she was at peace. Not that she'd have to pretend with him, but he noted the sign anyway.

He let her rest, navigating through London without uttering a peep, though he did lower the volume of the radio, the classical station a soothing drone of instruments.

She needed the sleep. Her love life aside—which admittedly was beyond the pale for most women… five men to one woman were odds most couldn't compute—the rest of her life was also turning into… Well, he wasn't sure what.

His life hadn't been easy. Yes, he'd always had money and a certain semblance of power. Though his family was, to anyone's definition, corrupt to the core, they were high ranking in Russian society, commanded respect and fear from most.

But he'd lost his mother because of his father's stature. Had seen her killed before his very eyes. So, no, life hadn't been easy. Not that it was for anyone, Sascha included.

She'd been purposefully knocked over a few weeks before—hence the concussion and the doctor's visit. A gala she and Andrei had been scheduled to attend had suffered an explosion thanks to a bomb blast… And she'd just learned that her mother wasn't her mother, and her father wasn't her father.

Yes, things were certainly far more complicated than most could handle. Yet, she seemed to be doing just that.

Handling it.

When they'd learned the uncomfortable truth about her parents, the five of them had dreaded sharing the news with her. But a household such as theirs depended on honesty. They'd kept certain things back from her, not out of malice or duplicitousness, but because she'd been recuperating.

Honesty was the only way six people could make a relationship work.

If anyone knew that, it was them. Sacha wasn't the first partner they'd had, after all. But it was amazing how difficult it was to be truthful. Of course, that wasn't on their part, but on the part of women they'd seen in the past.

Pursing his lips, he pulled into a parking space a short walk from the bakery. Fortune on his side, he pondered whether to wake her or to simply grab a selection of pastries. Whenever she came here, she always mentioned it. But she never mentioned what she ate. He realized they'd done her a disservice by never having brought her here before.

They led insular lives. Worlds that revolved around their house in Kensington. But Sascha wasn't like them. She was a firebird. She needed to fly, to go out and explore. If they didn't take that into consideration, they could lose her to that need for flight one day. A notion that disturbed him.

Deeply.

"What's wrong?"

Her voice was gravelly with sleep and made him jolt in surprise; he hadn't realized she'd woken.

He turned to look at her and smiled. "You look better for the nap."

"How long did I sleep?"

"I got caught in traffic near Harvey Nicks," he grimaced. "So, you probably had thirty minutes?"

Her eyes widened. "Wow. I feel like I had longer." She peered around, took note of their surroundings, and smiled. "We're here."

"I promised you cake, didn't I?"

"Donuts are the name of today's game. But what about coffee?" she teased.

"That too. I think I can afford two."

Her grin nearly lit up the car with its beauty, and his heart stuttered at the sight of it. Jesus, she was beautiful. Inside and out.

"You're not supposed to look at me like that anymore. Remember?"

Her voice was more teasing than serious, but he pulled a face nonetheless. "How am I supposed to stop?"

"It's hard being beautiful," she mocked, but jolted in surprise when he reached out to cup her jaw, tilted her head, and then carefully, gently, pressed his lips to hers.

She moaned against his mouth and he swallowed the sound. Loving it, loving her. Everything about her.

Her taste, her touch, her scent.

Her hand came up to cup his cheek, and he wasn't sure if she was trying to push him away, until she moaned again and slipped her tongue between his lips.

He growled under his breath. She was aggressive, this one. Not the kind to lay back and think of England. She was a partner, in all the meanings of the word.

And there came that word again… *perfect*.

Her tongue fucked his mouth, driving him to the brink of his control. She dropped a hand, her fingers stunning him by molding his cock through the folds of his trousers.

"No," he argued, pulling away from her to issue the command.

Her pout had him groaning. "Just my hand. That's it."

"We'll get arrested!" he retorted, but he was amused. She was hungry for him. It was in her eyes, in the dewy perspiration that misted her face. In the way her breasts heaved with each breath.

He let out another growl when her fingers flexed around his shaft again. "Dammit, no, Sascha."

Her mouth pursed into a moue. "Pussy tease."

"I just wanted a kiss!"

Sascha ducked her head, but it was too late, he saw her grin.

He sighed. "You're going to be the death of us."

"Me! Well, I like that," she grumbled. Then, pouting all the more, declared, "If you're going to be mean, then the least you can do is buy me a donut. Two of them."

He grimaced as he adjusted himself.

"Two donuts. Coming up."

IT WAS ALMOST AMUSING WATCHING Andrei in the small bakery.

Managed by a family of Italians who had moved here back in the fifties, the place was authentic. None of the mass chain bullshit.

Everything was baked or prepared fresh, made with honest-to-God food not chemicals, and the coffee was the bomb.

But Andrei, in the small store, was a sight to behold.

He and Sean were the most... Corporate?

Is that the right adjective? she asked herself.

They were usually in suits when they left the house because they had business, more often than not, in the City. If they weren't wearing suits, they were in dress pants with a sweater. Everything shrieking high-end label, mind. Nothing mainstream for her babes, and nothing that didn't have the ability to make her core turn nuclear because of how delicious they were to look at in their sexy formalwear.

That he was wearing a suit now told her he'd be heading for a meeting at some point this afternoon. She was used to that. And at the moment, the last thing she wanted was her own company, so she knew she'd be pestering whoever was at home for some loving.

Well, not some of the good stuff. Just… chitchat, a hug. If she was alone, she'd think, and thinking wasn't good. Not when her past was made up of more lies than a political campaign.

The very foundation of her world was, to put it lightly, bullshit.

"Could this place get any smaller?" he grumbled, breaking into her uncomfortable musings as he placed two mugs on the table. They were brimming with coffee. Freshly percolated. Not from a steam machine.

She wasn't sure why the difference satisfied her. Just that it did. Or maybe it was that it reminded her of home. The diners her father had taken her to for treats, pancakes, or waffles. All while he ate eggs and Canadian bacon and had endlessly topped-off mugs of coffee from waitresses in pink uniforms and white pinnies.

The memory had her smiling, because London was very different in a lot of ways. Staff here wore black pants and a polo shirt blazoned with the *Rossi's* logo on it. Not a pinafore or squeaky white trainers in sight.

She reached for the coffee and took a sip. It was bitter, and all the more reason for her to prefer tea, but the nostalgia always worked against her.

"Your waffles won't be long," he assured her after drinking some of his own coffee.

She'd decided against donuts in the end—not that it would stop her from taking some home. "Are you having anything to eat?"

He shook his head. "Not hungry."

"Did you eat breakfast?" She narrowed her eyes at him. Ever since the accident, she'd been lax with breakfast… dinner, she still made an effort. Sometimes, on the days when her head wasn't hurting too badly, she made enough for two days so that they always had a meal if she wasn't up to cooking the next day.

But breakfast?

Just waking up before nine was becoming a chore.

He shook his head. "I didn't want any."

She pursed her lips, then smiling at the server who placed her plate of waffles before her, complete with macerated cherries, strawberries, and heaps of whipped cream, asked, "Do you have any granola left over from breakfast?"

"Yes, we do."

"Can I have a portion, please?"

Andrei didn't say anything, just sighed when the waiter disappeared to fulfil the order. "You didn't have to do that. I'm quite capable of ordering food for myself."

"Apparently not if you chose not to have anything to eat," she told him primly, then cut into the mountain of sugary carbs with a happy sigh.

Her world might be going around the bend, but there were always carbs to make any shitty day gleam a whole hell of a lot brighter.

TWENTY-FOUR

"DAD?" she asked in surprise.

Eying the clock, she frowned. It was late in Tucson.

"Sweetheart!"

She winced at the bounce to his tone, feeling guilty because she hadn't called him since he'd revealed he'd split up with her least favorite person—her stepmother, Linda.

It was hard to feel pity for him, because she'd never seen the relationship lasting anyway. Which made her feel even guiltier.

Linda had always been a control freak, and though that had probably pleased her father at first, after close to a decade and a half of it, it had to grow stifling. Linda took cleaning to an OCD kind of level.

No one could deal with that forever. Well, not unless they were extremely patient, and her father, for all his good points, certainly wasn't that. If anything, he was the king of impatience.

"I have a surprise for you."

Her eyes widened at the continued chirp in his voice—he sounded positively effervescent. Another first.

Jesus, doing without Linda must be doing him good! she thought.

"Yeah? What surprise is that?" she asked, going along with him.

"I'm here."

"You're here?" She frowned, confused by the statement. "Where's here?"

"Heathrow!"

She almost dropped her phone, and instead of that, sank back into the overlarge sofa in the first-floor lounge.

"You're at Heathrow?"

"I sure am, baby."

"Why didn't you tell me you were coming to visit?"

"I'm telling you now. Anyway, I need an address. Where are you living now?"

She blinked, recited the Kensington address, and murmured, "Just wait there and I'll come and get you."

"No. It's okay. I'm in the taxi anyway. I knew it was Kensington." He said something she didn't catch to the driver; whose Cockney accent came loud and clear over the phone: he wasn't bullshitting.

He *was* here. In London. And only forty goddamn minutes away!

Jesus!

Her mouth worked as she tried to process exactly what the fuck was going on here.

Her dad not only hated traveling, but hated leaving the U.S. As far as she was aware, he didn't even have a passport. Had always said there was too much to see in the States without spending his hard-earned bucks elsewhere.

"I'll see you soon, buttercup!" he almost sang down the line, cutting the call before she could do more than stutter at him.

She looked blindly ahead at the daytime TV trash she'd had on while she was crocheting, then scratched her forehead.

"Where's he going to sleep?"

The question should have been a simple one. But this place wasn't hers. Even if she wasn't sleeping with the bosses, she'd never have been comfortable asking her employers to put up a guest on her behalf.

Still, this was her home. Sean and the others repeatedly told her that. So, it made sense that her father could stay here.

But the only spare bedroom was her own. And if she gave her father that room, then he'd, quite naturally, ask where *she* slept.

Which meant what? Explaining she was sleeping with not one, not two, not even three men, but five? And her employers to boot?

Gulping at the thought of her father decking one of the guys, she scrambled to her feet. Immediately regretting it when her head pounded dully, making her feel faint.

"God, I'm getting pretty fucking tired of this concussion," she grumbled as she stumbled out of the lounge and into the hall.

And oh, boy, what a reminder that was… Her dad still didn't know about the accident. She could hide the concussion, but her damn arm was still in a cast. There was no hiding that, and she had zero intention of freaking him out about the current circumstances.

Not with…

Her throat felt thick as she realized this entire mess had led to the inevitable conclusion that Henry Dubois wasn't actually her father. That neither of the parents she'd loved all her life were biologically hers. So, no, she couldn't handle that confrontation yet. Nor could *he*, considering he'd just been dumped by his wife.

Thoughts heavy, she headed for Sean's office. When she walked in and saw he was on the phone, she half-staggered over to one of the armchairs. Kurt was seated in his, and he smiled in greeting when he looked up from his laptop.

She smiled wanly back, which in turn had him frowning and putting his laptop on the floor. When he made to stand, she held up a hand to stall him.

She should have known one of the others would be in here. For many, the lounge would be the house's meeting point. Either that, or the kitchen. But not here. Sean's office was where the gang all got together.

Sean caught her eye as she rested in the armchair, and she could tell he ended the conversation quicker than intended. His tone shifted from a rumbling baritone to an abrupt, clipped snap. He evenly told the other person on the line that he'd speak to them later and hung up.

"What's wrong?" he immediately asked, leaning forward in his seat where he'd been rocking back and forth.

"Nothing's wrong. Per se."

Kurt rubbed his forehead. "You're going to have to explain that, Sascha. Wrong has taken a different perspective of late."

She grimaced at the truth in his words.

Gulping, she admitted, "My father just called."

"You talked to him about what we found out?" Sean's tone softened with sympathy, and he got to his feet to crouch down before her. Placing his hand on her knee, he squeezed. "Are you okay?"

She winced. She'd known for just over five days now that her father and mother were that in name but not in blood.

The guys had wanted her to speak with her father, ask what the hell was going on, but she'd been putting it off. Finding it too hard to broach the topic. Now, it looked like she wouldn't have a choice. And now, a whole lot of secrets were about to spill forth.

Not just on his end either.

For him to stay here, she'd have to bunk up with one of the men. Not that that was a problem. She spent more time playing musical bedrooms anyway. For her father, on the other hand, problem was an understatement. She highly doubted he'd be okay with the arrangement.

She bit her lip, and Kurt groaned. "You haven't told him, have you?"

Turning to look at him, she ducked her head. "No."

Sean sighed. "Why not?"

"I just… Look, that doesn't matter. He just called me, and he's here."

"Here?" Sean nearly toppled over in his surprise, a reaction that had her giggling. Despite the approaching calamity that was Henry Dubois.

Of them all, Sean was always cool and calm under pressure. To see him nearly fall flat on his ass was more amusing than she could say.

He rolled his eyes at her, then stood so he could perch on the armrest beside her.

"Here as in London?" Kurt clarified.

"Yeah," she gulped. "He's twenty minutes away."

"Wow. That's close."

"Understatement," she corrected. "Where's he going to sleep?"

Sean blinked at her. "Ah."

"Yes. Ah. I really don't want to have this conversation with him. Not yet, anyway. I'd have preferred it if he was five thousand miles away. It would have been a hell of a lot easier."

"You intended to tell him at some point?"

She glowered at Kurt. "That comes as a surprise?"

He held up his hands in surrender. "I don't know why. It just does."

She huffed out a breath then placed her hands on theirs. Covering the one Sean had rested on her lap and squeezing Kurt's tighter. "I'm in this for the long haul," she said softly. "I thought you'd realized that by now."

Sean swallowed. "We… don't like to pressure you."

"And you don't. You never do," she retorted. "If anything, I'm the one who does. Which makes zero sense. Normally women are terrified to make the first move just in case their partner will back off."

"You know it's different for us," Sean countered.

"Yeah, I know. Doesn't make it easier to understand." She pursed her lips, a thought occurring to her. "What happens if you do change your minds though? About me, I mean. About us."

Kurt snorted. "Like that's going to happen."

She scowled at him, trying to do her best 'Andrei' impression. It didn't work. If anything, they just shot each other a look—maybe she looked like she was in pain? Sascha harrumphed at the thought her scowl was unimpressive.

"Nothing is given in this world. I can't take anything for granted. You might change your minds. Things might not work out between us…"

"That's a lot of 'might's," Sean answered softly. "And most of them unnecessary. If that did happen, which I highly doubt, we'd discuss it as our change in feelings happened."

She blinked. "You'd have a group meeting about it, huh?"

He winced. "Not exactly."

"Look, just because I accept this relationship between the six of us doesn't make me perfect. It ticks one of your boxes. Not all of them."

Kurt sighed. "If we aren't showing you, every damn day, how perfect you are for us, then we're the ones who need to be worried. Not you."

Her cheeks turned pink. "Really?"

Sean squeezed her knee, drawing her gaze to his. "Really."

She felt her flush lessen a little, then whispered, "I'm glad."

Kurt blew out a breath. "We'll work on that, but in the meanwhile, we have an issue at hand. Your dad."

She grimaced. "Maybe I should just say I'm sleeping with one of you. Not like he'll approve of that… Sleeping with one of my bosses isn't going to make him think well of me. But at least it's not the whole truth."

Kurt scratched his chin. "How about we say the guest bedroom is Sawyer's? His is the most boring. It could pass for a guest room, maybe? Then, he sleeps with you in the attic, and just has to sneak out on a morning and night."

She pulled a face, wishing that they hadn't converted most of the bedrooms into their offices. They were missing an extra four bedrooms as a result. "That has disaster written all over it, but I prefer it to anything else."

Kurt grinned as he gave her fingers one last squeeze, then got to his feet and headed for the intercom. They were in every room of the house, and she knew he was connecting to Sawyer and Devon's 'Brainiac' room.

"Sawyer?" he said, speaking into the microphone. "Sascha's dad's visiting. You need to clear shit out of your bedroom, so he can sleep in there. You'll have to bunk with Sascha while he's here."

There was a groan on the other end of the line. "How come Sawyer gets to sleep with Sascha?" Devon demanded, his voice as close to a whine as it got.

Her lips twitched. In for a freakin' penny... "Tell him he can. He just has to sneak in and out."

Kurt relayed the message, shooting her a smirk as he did.

"Amazing," Sean murmured wryly.

"What is?"

"How we had no guest bedrooms and now, we have two."

TWENTY-FIVE

ANDREI SIGHED as he bridged his hands together and rested them on his belly.

With endless reams of data in front of him, he should have been in his element.

Instead, the numbers were blurring.

His heart wasn't in it.

For that reason, when his cell buzzed, he answered it rather than ignore it as he would usually have done when he was in the middle of working.

"Fucking hell, Andrei, why haven't you been answering your phone?"

If the screen hadn't told him who was on the other end of the line, the faint Scottish brogue would have. "What's up, Sawyer?"

"Sascha's dad's come for a visit."

His brows rose. "Seriously?"

"Yeah, like I'm going to joke about something like that."

Andrei gawked at nothing in particular as he tried to process a spontaneous visit from a man who was going to be anything but happy about learning his daughter was playing house with five guys.

"What's he doing here?"

"He's visiting. Just landed an hour ago. Anyway, I'm calling to warn you. Devon and I are going to be bunking with Sascha. Henry's going to be sleeping in my room. Don't fuck it up for her by giving the game away."

Andrei blinked. "Okay. Is his reason for being here anything to do with what we learned about her past?"

"Not so far as I can tell. He split up with his wife recently, and I think he's down and putting on a brave face." Sawyer grunted. "Barrel of laughs. But anyway, what time will you be back?"

Andrei had to snort. "You do realize, in the nearly two decades I've known you, that's probably the first time you've ever asked me that."

He didn't have to see the eye roll to know that was what Sawyer was doing. "Sascha's never been a part of our lives before," came the answer. "And her dad has never popped by for a visit. What time?"

He conceded that with a wry smile. "True." He looked at the clock on his desk, down at the sheets before him. "An hour? If traffic's good."

"Traffic's never good," Sawyer groused. "I'll say you'll be here shortly."

Andrei grinned. "Thanks. See you later."

They both cut the call, and Andrei shot the other man in his office a look. "I'll need to leave soon."

Jacobie, Andrei's current business partner, shrugged. "Sure."

Jacobie was a tech whiz that had taken Europe by storm with his recent developments in cryptography. Backed by family money, he'd risen hard and fast, but the pressure wasn't crushing him. If anything, he was flourishing.

Andrei and he were working together on two projects.

The likelihood of a hostile takeover of one of Jacobie's core distribution companies had come to his attention. Something Andrei was helping him avoid. Then, as they'd worked together on that project, they'd come to be friends, and had realized they shared similar mentalities on their view of the world.

Their second project was more of a hobby. Ethical capitalism. They were writing a dissertation on it, with the vague hope in the future they could publish it.

Today, however, Andrei was working on the former issue rather than the latter.

A steel magnate in India had taken a deep interest in Jacobie's activities, going so far as to buy up stock wherever he could in anything Jacobie had invested in.

Narinder Singh was a pain in Jacobie's butt, but he was a joy for Andrei. He did love a good game of chess; he was Russian, after all. And he and Singh had been battling like Grandmasters for months now.

"It's not like Singh's made any recent moves," Jacobie was saying. "You can probably cut down on the amount of time you spend here. I know you hate coming into the office."

Andrei snorted. "That's very short-sighted of you, my friend."

Jacobie's brows rose. "Why is it?"

He had two HQs. One at the family pile in Surrey, one in the heart of the City at Canary Wharf. They met here, and Andrei shared Jacobie's office when they planned strategy. Not only did he not want his own office—schlepping into the City a few times a month was bad enough without formalizing his work with the company—but working in Jacobie's personal office simply made more sense.

They had to work closely together, but more than that, the strategies discussed in here were of a sensitive nature. Jacobie had his room swept for bugs with the frequency of a conspiracy theorist. If anywhere was safe, it was here.

"Just because he hasn't made a move in four months, doesn't mean he isn't planning."

"True," Jacobie ceded. "Wishful thinking on my part. I wish I'd never let the company go public."

"You wouldn't be a billionaire if you hadn't," Andrei pointed out. "And you do like your toys."

Jacobie's grin was swift. "Yeah, there is that."

Andrei shook his head. Jacobie was greedy, but it didn't irritate him as it usually did. If anything, he found it amusing.

Jacobie played games, and because Andrei loved manipulating markets, he could appreciate that in the other man.

He collected his papers together and pushed his chair back from where he worked at the table the board met at in Jacobie's office.

"What do you think Singh's end game is?"

Andrei shrugged. "I don't know." And he really didn't. He'd come across several plays like this in his career, but Singh played with a delicacy he could appreciate.

"We'll never know what he wants. There's no point in questioning it. We just have to make sure we're two steps ahead." He'd have preferred five or more, but that was how good Singh was.

"Do I even want to know your plans?"

Andrei's grin was swift. "*Niet*."

Jacobie just grunted.

There was nothing he could really say to ease Edward's mind. Andrei would be scanning the markets like crazy, looking for any moves, any unusual highs or lows, for potential markers as to Singh's intentions.

Truth was, as great a game as Singh played, he was a traditionalist at heart. He always plowed money into steel. *Always*. That would be Andrei's first point of call when he tried to figure out what the canny bastard was doing but for now, even the call of the game couldn't distract him.

What the hell was Sascha's dad doing here?

Departing with a quick salute, Andrei headed out into the white reception hall. It was sparse and bright, sparkling. It reminded him of Sawyer's room. Only difference was, Sawyer's room was bare because the bastard didn't have an ounce of creativity. This place was bare because it was a design choice.

Shaking his head at the thought, and hiding a grin too, he smiled at the receptionist who was gaping at him. His smile disappeared. "Are you okay?"

The woman's cheeks turned pink. "Of course, sir."

He studied her, then shrugged. "Bye."

Heading for the elevator, he shot another wary smile at the elegant brunette behind the desk, sighed at more owlish blinking, and was relieved when the doors closed with him the only occupant.

Delivered to the garage, he found his Audi in its usual space—there were perks to working in close contact with the head of an international corporation—his space was right beside Jacobie's, next to the elevator bank.

Within ten minutes, he was zooming out into traffic, dashing in and out of the reams of cars on his way home.

As he finagled the traffic jam, earning himself angry beeps from other drivers, he pondered what Sascha's father was doing here. If he'd known his daughter was aware there was no blood tie between them, the reason behind his visit would have made more sense.

Not that blood always mattered when it came to parental relationships, of course. Nor would it for Sascha. Henry Dubois was the only father she'd ever know. The only one she'd ever love.

Love.

Andrei, on the other hand, loathed his father, and though Vasily was his grandfather, a blood connection, he loved the man more than he could say.

As traffic swelled as he passed Paddington, he tapped a few buttons on his dash after calculating the time difference between here and Moscow.

"About time you called," was the grumpy response. "I'm supposed to be the one old enough to have Alzheimer's."

Andrei rolled his eyes then narrowed them as a car whizzed past, almost scraping his side. Hitting the horn, he absentmindedly told his grandfather, "Calls work two ways, you know? You can call me too."

"God knows who'll answer." Vasily knew of, and didn't exactly disapprove of his housemates, but he didn't want to speak to them.

He was well aware, as with most of the household's families, that Vasily thought he was gay and just not willing to come out.

One reason he loved his grandfather though was that as long as neither outright mentioned it, Vasily didn't care.

Considering his grandfather's generation, as well as his less than PC background, that was a huge conciliatory gesture.

Vasily loved him enough to not want to know. If he knew, concrete, then he'd have to act or have an opinion, and he wanted neither.

"Who answers somebody else's cell?" Andrei retorted. "Plus, you know I'm busy."

"You're always busy."

"Like you weren't?" he grunted. "Still are, knowing you. I get your doctor's reports, old man. You're not taking your blood pressure tablets again, are you?"

Silence came down the line. Then a barrage of Russian curses. "I will not have you spying on me through the staff!" the old man declared with all the pomp of a Tsar. Shit, in the eyes of the Bratva, he was.

"I don't need to use the staff to find out what's going on with you," he replied smugly.

"Then who? Who's the spy in my midst?" came the dramatic retort.

"Why would I give up my source? I'd have to be a fool, and we both know, you raised no fool."

"You always were too good with words," Vasily said after a moment's silence.

"And you're probably the only person who'd ever tell me that. Numbers are more my style."

Vasily snorted. "Like I'm unaware of that." He groused, "I don't like how the tablets make me feel."

"Well, they're keeping you around, so you'd better ask for another prescription or get used to it."

"Since when were you so bossy?"

"Since my girlfriend showed me that's the only way to be if you want your own way."

More silence. "Girlfriend?"

His lips twitched. "Yes. She's female. And I'm sleeping with her."

"She lives in the house with you?" He cleared his throat. "In fact, I don't want to know. But this is good news. What's her name?"

"Sascha."

"That's a boy's name," came the suspicious retort.

Andrei snorted. "Only in Russian. She's American."

More Russian curses. "An American? God, you never could do anything the easy way."

He chuckled. "The Cold War happened a long time ago."

"As we've already stated, I didn't raise a fool in you." It went unspoken that he hadn't done such a great job with Andrei's father. "You know very well that things are dicey between our nations."

"Yes, well, when we're in bed, we don't tend to talk about politics."

Vasily's laugh was bawdy, as he'd known it would be. It was probably weird to talk about such things with one's grandfather, and he knew Sascha would probably be mortified, but most topics were an open book with Vasily.

When a man dealt in blood, sex, and money, crass talk was a language that usually greased wheels.

"You're your grandfather's blood, that's for certain." Andrei heard the old bastard rubbing his hands together. "Come on then, tell me what she's like."

"You'd probably think she's gorgeous," he said wryly, as he swept in and out of traffic in a way that would likely earn him a speeding ticket later on. "She looks like Ava Gardner and Rita Hayworth had a baby."

Vasily smacked his lips. "You've good taste, son."

"I know. Plus, she's smart, and she makes the best coffee."

"She's making sure you eat?"

Andrei rolled his eyes. "Not you as well. Henpecking me isn't Bratva style."

"I missed out on my natural calling. Grandfather hen is something I can do without my men questioning my sanity."

Andrei scoffed at that, but conceded, "Yes. She makes sure I eat."

"Then I like her already. When will I meet her?"

He winced. "I don't know."

"You ashamed of me?" The question was said with a mixture of emotions that had Andrei rolling his eyes. Vasily was too arrogant to believe that, but at the same time, if the old bastard had any vulnerability, Andrei knew it was him.

"Of course not. But, she's in a situation."

"What kind of situation?"

"It's complicated."

"Since when was I too feeble minded to handle complicated? I'll have you know I can still keep up with your math talk. Who was it who helped explain most of it to you?"

He wasn't wrong there. If Andrei was a whiz with figures, it was something he'd inherited from Vasily whose talent on that score was truly wasted.

"She was in an accident recently," he said slowly, wondering how to piece all the parts together into some semblance of sense, and wanting his grandfather's input on this shitty situation. "A car ran into her."

Vasily murmured, "On purpose?"

"Yes. But it was an accident."

"Accidentally on purpose?" Vasily snorted. "Impossible."

"A kid ran into the road, she ran after him to save him from being hit by a car. She took the brunt of the crash.

"A couple of hours later, the driver of the car, who'd been cleared of suspicion, walks into the police station and confesses to having targeted Sascha. Had she not crashed into him, he'd been paid to run her down in the street."

"Paid by whom?"

"That's what we're trying to figure out."

"So, the girl has a past."

"No, that's the strangest thing. She doesn't. At least, not on paper. But that's not all. A few days after the crash, we were due to attend a gala. You remember I told you about the economics seminar where I'd been chosen to give the keynote speech?"

"Yes. I remember. You never told me how it went."

"That's because it didn't. That morning, there was a bomb. A lot of staff who were there preparing for the event were killed."

Vasily sucked in a sharp breath. "And you didn't think it best to tell me?"

"I didn't want to worry you. Not until I had more information."

"You'd better have more information," came the grim retort. "I might have the body of an old man, but my brain is sharper than ever."

Wasn't that the damn truth? Andrei grimaced, and said, "Sean's been looking into it, but he found no reason for anyone to target Sascha. She'd been fine, *safe,* until she got into a relationship with me." He was careful to say me, and not us. His grandfather was open minded, but in his eyes, a man had five women to call on, not vice versa.

"Someone's targeting you?" Vasily asked, but his tone was loaded with doubt. "I have tabs kept on you, son. There's been nothing brought to my attention. Certainly nothing that would have an assassination attempt brought against you."

"No. It's her. We found out her parents aren't her real parents."

"Who are they?"

His jaw worked. "Remember I'm working with Jacobie?"

"That idiot boy who sells computers?"

He snorted. "He does more than that and you know it."

"A man who has to hire someone to come up with strategies on his behalf isn't exactly smart."

Andrei's lips twitched. Vasily wasn't wrong. Not exactly. "Surely he's smart for outsourcing to one of the best in the business though?"

"True. I'll give him kudos for that."

Andrei grinned but his grin died a death as he thought about his next words. "Anyway, it's kind of a strange coincidence…"

"You know my opinion on coincidences."

"Yes. I do. Which is what makes even less sense. We have reason to believe Sascha is related to the Jacobies."

Vasily blew out a whistle. "There's definitely no coincidence there. Why do you think they're family?"

"It sounds like a weak link, but the likeness is remarkable—Sawyer saw a photo of Jacobie's great-grandmother. She's the spitting image of

Sascha. It's more than uncanny; it's impossible that they're not related."

Vasily didn't comment on that, just asked, "Didn't you tell me once that Jacobie is old school English? Country pile and everything?"

"Yes."

"Well, there you have it. If she's related to his grandfather, then she's due some of the inheritance."

Andrei nodded, even though he knew his grandfather couldn't see him. "We've been investigating that line of inquiry too."

"It sounds like you've got a real mystery on your hands."

"We do," Andrei said wryly. "Which is why I'm not too keen on the idea of stirring any shit by bringing her to Moscow."

"She'd probably be safer here than there," Vasily pointed out, stung.

Andrei had to wince because, damn him, his grandfather had a point.

TWENTY-SIX

SHE COULD DO THIS. She could. She could sit here with her five lovers and her father, and not want to start giggling. Because yes, her nerves were manifesting in laughter. Just what she needed. The thought had her sniggering into the pot of spaghetti she'd brought up to the boil.

"What's so funny?"

She shot Sawyer a look. "This situation."

His lips twitched. "I thought you'd be panicking. Not laughing your head off."

"This is me panicking," she retorted, to which he shook his head.

"Woman, can you never react normally?" He moved around the counter and kissed her on the forehead. A chaste kiss.

A very un-Sawyer kiss.

She peered around the kitchen, then murmured to him, "Hold that thought."

Heading over to the intercom, she pressed the button to Sawyer's bedroom.

"Dad? I'm in the kitchen. The intercom is over by the door. If you press the green button, that answers me, the red is to mute. I just wanted to let you know that dinner will be ready in twenty minutes."

"Okay, sweetheart," her father said, his voice crackling over the speaker. "I'll see you in twenty. That's enough time for a shower."

Her eyes widened in satisfaction, but she just said, "Great. See you then."

She turned around, and saw Sawyer was watching her. "You told me ten minutes ago that dinner was ready in twenty."

She grinned at his cocked brow. "That's because I have nefarious plans."

His eyes narrowed as he folded his arms across his chest. "Oh no. We've all been warned. No sex for at least a week. And that has nothing to do with your father being under the same roof but everything to do with your concussion."

At that moment, Sascha seriously felt like stomping her foot.

"I need stress relief," she said blandly.

"Then I can massage you again," he retorted, equally as blandly.

She grunted. "I knew I should have asked Devon."

"You thought I'd cave in before the rest of them?"

She pouted. "Not particularly. I just thought I could persuade you. It's been five days since I saw the doctor last. That's almost a week."

"I don't believe you. You want to fuck in the kitchen when your dad is about to come and eat down here?"

When he shook his head at her, she could tell he was both surprised and amused at that. One thing she loved about Sawyer was he was never shocked or disgusted. About anything.

If she'd tried to give him a hand job in the middle of the street like she had with Andrei at the beginning of the week, he'd have let her.

Public be damned—he'd have just taken off his coat to cover his cock and her hand.

His attitude wasn't exactly 'live and let live.' More 'if you don't like me, don't like what I do, then fuck off.'

She wasn't sure if it was a Scottish thing, having only met a few Scots in her life—and knowing him the best—or if it was just a Sawyer thing.

"Can I help it that I have a sex drive?" she complained, folding her arms across her chest. "And I was thinking the garden. Not the kitchen."

For some reason, that had him closing his eyes. He held up a hand. "Stop right there."

She frowned. Then, clutching onto a suspicion that plopped right into her head, she murmured, "Just me and you under the blue sky.

The grass underneath us. The scent of flowers around us as you fuck me…"

He swallowed, his Adam's apple bobbing as he bit off, "Stop it. I'm doing it for your own good."

"But I want you," she whispered, stepping closer, crowding him against the counter.

She pressed her front to his chest, letting their bodies touch from breast to hip where she felt a deliciously thick erection against her belly.

She rocked her hips. "I want you inside me, Sawyer." She reached up on tiptoe then grabbed his bottom lip between her teeth and tugged.

His nostrils flared at the aggressive bite—she hadn't nipped but bitten. His hands shot out to grab her hips, and he pushed her forward against the fridge.

With one hand, he gathered her wrists and placed them above her head.

The move thrilled her. Her eyes widening in delight at having ruptured his control. Breasts heaving as she took quick, panting breaths, she licked her lips as he stared at her. A storm brewing in his eyes.

"You're a pricktease," he accused, his free hand shaping her breasts through her blouse, then dropping down to cup her between the legs. "A dirty, filthy pricktease."

She wasn't sure why, but his gritty tone and the words made her melt inside. Her bottom lip trembled as her core exploded with heat, and she felt sure he could feel her slickness through the layers of her panties and pants.

He pressed his nose against her cheek, running the tip of it along her jaw. As he did, he whispered, "Aren't you, Sascha?"

"Y-Yes," she replied, every part of her quivering now at his sudden dominant hold.

"Say it. Tell me what you are."

She gulped as her pussy started to throb. She could feel the pulse deep inside her core and knew at that moment that he was deep in control. She hadn't ruptured it, she'd just awoken the beast.

"I-I'm a pricktease. A dirty, filthy slut," she whispered and he let out a hiss. "Your dirty, filthy slut."

She wasn't sure why, but the derogatory word that slipped from her lips had her nearly melting in a pool at his feet.

Her pussy pulsed with the need to be filled. By him. All of him. Jesus, all of *them*.

She wanted them so badly at that moment. It was an ache she feared would overtake her senses. Her body answered the call theirs made whenever she was around them, and that call was growing louder and more insistent with each day that passed without one of them inside her.

"I should spank you for calling yourself that," he growled against her throat. Nipping her there, before lashing it with his tongue.

Her eyes widened. "S-Spank?"

"Yes. Paddle your behind," he said with a growl. "You're not a slut."

"I-I am for you," she said on a whimper, her hips rocking against his front, loving the thick bulge between his thighs.

He grabbed her chin, held her head in place. "Look at me," he commanded out of nowhere, and her lashes fluttered open to obey.

He stared at her, a question in his eyes. One she hoped she answered.

In that silent, long look, she knew he was asking if she was speaking ill of herself by calling herself a slut. Or if she was playing, if it was a game that got her hot. His nostrils flared as he realized it was the latter.

"Our dirty slut," he whispered under his breath, his tone like gravel and raspy enough to rake over nerve endings she didn't know she even had.

"If I touched your cunt," he asked, "what would I find?"

She moaned. "I'm wet, Sawyer. So wet. I need you inside me."

"That's not going to happen, baby. Not without doctor's orders."

She licked her lips as desperation struck. "Please. I'm so hungry for you."

He hissed out a breath, then stunned her by dragging her against him. But not for long. He moved back to the counter, then spun away from her. "Bend over," he ordered, and flustered, praying he was about to fuck her, she did. She rested her arms on the marble as she bent over at the waist.

The cold chill of the stone against her overheated skin was a torment in itself, and when he reached around her, began unfastening her fly, then pulled her trousers down to her upper thighs, the chill was a sudden counterpoint to the sheer inferno blazing around her blood.

She was on fire.

A fire only he could quench.

But he didn't touch her. No. She heard rummaging in a drawer, a noise which had her eyes widening and she turned to see what he was doing.

Before she could see what he'd been looking for, a whistle snapped through the air, then a smack. It was strange how she heard it before she felt it, but when she did, she pressed her forehead into the cold counter.

"God," she whimpered on a moan, letting her butt dance a little as the sting of the wooden spoon against her ass spread a fire there.

"You like that?" he said, covering her so she felt his cock prod the area he'd just spanked.

She mewled. "Yes."

"How many do you think you deserve for being my dirty little cocktease?"

She gulped. "I'll cum."

He stilled at that, then chuckled. "I can handle that."

She gulped. "Seven."

"Why seven?"

"I don't know. Just… s-seven," she said with a wriggle of her shoulders.

"I think it should be ten. It's a better, rounder number."

Licking her lips, she nodded. "Okay." Sascha wanted to wince at how breathy her voice was, but it wasn't like she could help it.

This had exploded out of nowhere. From a kiss to Sawyer spanking her with a wooden spoon? Even in her wildest dreams she'd never imagined this happening today. Certainly not with her dad upstairs.

Although, maybe that added an extra thrill to the buzz slaloming around her veins like a bobsled going two hundred miles an hour. Before she could overthink things, the spoon found its aim three more times. She counted under her breath, loving the sting, loving the dance of her hips as she tried to absorb the pain.

When they reached five, he grabbed her butt and murmured, "Keep still."

"But it hurts," she complained.

He rammed his cock into the hot skin of her ass. "You don't think I'm hurting too?"

She whimpered. "I'll try."

"You'll do more than try," he growled roughly, then proceeded to tap her butt again. Five more times. Each one growing progressively harder, creating more of a sting, until she had to grip the counter tight with her fingers, straining them to keep still elsewhere.

She was shuddering when they hit ten, and he stunned her further by slipping the end of the spoon down through the slick folds of her sex, tapping her clit with it, before letting it slide into her greedy, grasping, cock-teasing pussy.

He groaned. "See this, Kurt?"

She jolted, unaware that anyone had even come into the kitchen. Her head popped up, but she had barely a second to process that Kurt was here, Andrei too, when Sawyer pressed against the back of her head, and forced her back down to the counter.

Her cheeks blazoned with embarrassed heat, but the men seemed more intrigued than anything else.

How hadn't she heard them?

Now she knew they were there, she heard their steps, felt them both as they approached her. A hand came up to rub her hot cheek, and she hissed, the muscles in her thighs and calves tensing in response.

"Beautiful," Kurt replied, his voice thick.

Of course, he got off on watching.

Fuck, she really was a pussy tease.

Her stomach muscles clamped down when one of them grabbed the spoon and pulled it out of her. Before she knew what was happening, from the corner of her eye, she saw it held out beside her.

"Suck it clean, dirty girl," Kurt whispered. Her eyes flared at the fire in his face; and she swallowed hard. They watched her tongue dart out, and the way her throat spasmed with each swallow.

He was aroused.

They all were.

She parted her lips and waited for him to press the spoon to her. He thrust it into her mouth, not stopping until she'd tasted herself and the polished wood and had slurped her juices clean of the implement.

A finger appeared at the rim of her cunt. Slender digits, unlike the next one which had calluses. She groaned as they both plunged inside her, rubbing up against each other in a way that had her wondering what it would be like to have two cocks inside her cunt at the same time.

She knew about double vaginal penetration, but they were all too big to fit inside her. But one in her ass as well as her pussy? That was totally workable.

A notion that had her shooting up onto her tiptoes.

From underneath, the spoon appeared, this time, it gently patted her clit. The sting against the tender skin wasn't uncomfortable. If anything, she felt herself soar higher, faster as a result.

As the three of them worked her over, all of them concentrating on her pleasure, she came. Her release was a hoarse cry that she knew would reach the floor above, but she didn't care. She trusted them to cover her up if they heard footsteps and trusted in them to keep her safe from her father's wrath.

She allowed herself to fall into the ecstasy they gifted her, loving the freedom that came with it. The sense of flying and soaring that had her body feeling tension-free.

She gave one last shudder as they pulled away from her, and though she was slightly mortified at having been caught this way, she was too replete to really mind.

Plus, it wasn't like they hadn't seen her in naughty positions before.

Just never with a wooden spoon inside her pussy.

Her cheeks heated, burning hotly against the now-clammy stone.

Hands came up to her waist, and she found herself being urged upright into a standing position.

She blinked as Andrei stepped around her, and as he pressed a kiss to her mouth, his hands went to work on her pants.

He dragged them up to cover her, then fastened her fly. At her back, Sawyer—she knew from his aftershave—acted like a wall for her to use as support. But his hands came up to cup her breasts. His fingers plied the soft mounds, and she knew it was more for his pleasure than hers.

"You'd better sleep naked tonight," he growled in her ear. "That's going to be the only consolation for not being able to get inside that sweet cunt of yours."

She let out a breathy moan.

Kurt chuckled, and she turned to follow the noise, half amused to see he was placing the spoon in the dishwasher. "I'd give her a break. Her father will be down shortly."

Sawyer groused at that, but he stopped touching her breasts, instead, stacked his hands on her hips. "Can you stand?"

"Y-Yes." Of course, she could. If she locked her knees and didn't move for the next ten minutes.

He stepped away but hovered a second to make sure she was okay. Touched, she squeezed his hand as he made to move around the counter. He winked at her.

Kurt stepped closer to her. "How are you feeling?"

There was a wicked sparkle in his eye that had her smiling at him. A dirty secret shared among them that was theirs to know, and for Devon and Sean to ask.

Her answering smile was soft with sleepiness. "Like I could go to bed."

"How's your head?" Andrei asked. "You weren't supposed to touch her, Sawyer."

"And I didn't. Not that way anyway."

Andrei rolled his eyes. "Same difference."

"Guys, come on. I'm fine." And she was. Always had been when they touched her.

Kurt dropped a kiss to her forehead. "I'm glad to hear it."

She turned into him before he left, and he let her hug him, before he wrapped his arms around her.

Sighing in his embrace, she murmured against his shirt, "Why do you always smell good? All of you?"

Kurt snorted. "I wouldn't complain about that if I were you."

"What should we smell of?" Sawyer asked, aggressive as usual. She didn't think he even meant to be, but it was just his tone and his accent.

Like how the Spanish could sound as though they were having a rip-roaring row, and yet, were actually discussing something innocuous—like who forgot to take out the trash.

"I don't know. You just smell perfect."

"Perfect's an adjective I can accept," Kurt teased.

"It's probably a pheromone thing," Devon said as he came down the stairs. For a man who managed to trip head-first into a conversation, he was surprisingly stealthy when he wandered around the house.

The men weren't surprised by his presence—probably because they were used to Devon just popping up. But she was. Surprised, that is.

Grateful her father was a lot more cumbersome on his feet—he was a desk sergeant, rarely saw duty out on the streets where stealth was a requirement—she murmured, "I suppose it could be. For some of you. But all of you?"

He headed for her, then to Kurt, argued, "I want some love too. Move out of the way."

Her lips twitched, and with one last squeeze of her arms, she released Kurt and shuffled into Devon's embrace. "You're such a brat sometimes."

He grinned; she felt the movement of his lips against her cheek. "You have to be in this house. I'd never get any sugar." His nose burrowed into her throat and he hummed under his breath. "You smell good too. Not pheromones, mind. Although, I suppose in a way it is. You smell like sex and mine." He sighed with satisfaction. "Delicious."

She tensed in his arms. "I smell like sex?"

"Ignore him," Kurt ordered. "You don't." He elbowed Devon in the side. "Tell her it's just your super nose."

"Since when did you have a super nose?" she demanded with a scowl.

"Since the Scuba Diving Incident of '97."

She pulled back to stare at him. "The Scuba Diving Incident of '97?"

He grimaced. "Don't ask. Let's just say, an ear infection that led to partial hearing loss in my left ear encouraged me never to go into the sea again."

"He means that too," Andrei remarked as he took a seat at the table. "He won't go near the ocean. Even if it's a city he has to visit for work."

"So, if I wanted to go to Cornwall, you wouldn't go?"

"Do you want to go to Cornwall?" he asked, sounding like she was asking to visit Pluto on a day trip.

She couldn't hide her smile. "I might do. One day. I've never been before, and I've heard it's beautiful."

He heaved out a breath. "With certain encouragement, I'm sure I could be swayed."

Silence fell in the kitchen, and she peered about, demanding, "What?"

Sawyer snorted. "You really are a miracle worker and you don't even know it."

"How's that?" she asked, reaching up to kiss Devon, before tugging free of his arms and getting back to dinner prep.

"For twenty years, we haven't been able to get him near a coastline, Sascha. He just said if you bribe him with sex, he'll go. That never worked before."

Trust Sawyer to come up with phrasing like that.

She rolled her eyes as she stirred the sauce, then moved over to the chopping board and finely sliced some basil leaves she'd picked that morning from the small herb garden she had out in the yard.

"I'm sure that's not true."

"No, it's true," Devon said brightly as he took a seat at the table too. Only the two heads of the table, where she and Sean were seated, as well as the one to her right—her father's place—were empty now.

"It is?" She peered at him. "How come?"

He grinned. "Wouldn't you like to know?"

Her eyes flashed. "I thought we were supposed to be honest with one another."

"We are. But I'm under strict instructions not to discuss anything inflammatory when your father's around, and he's upstairs."

She looked at the ceiling, the move second nature even though it was stupid because it wasn't like she could even see any damn thing.

The faint steps had her grumbling, "Thought you'd lost hearing in one ear."

"Yep, but the other's stronger to compensate, and now I can smell like a perfume maker."

"Bully for you," she retorted. Pointing the spatula at him, she murmured, "Don't think I haven't forgotten this conversation."

"I look forward to having it at a later date."

His smugness had her rolling her eyes. "You're incorrigible."

"But you love me for it."

Their gazes clashed at that. His mocking but earnest nonetheless, hers stunned that he'd breached that particular lover's etiquette when her father was walking down the fucking steps to the kitchen.

Her nostrils flared in outrage, and she glowered at him.

They'd not spoken of love. Not really. For him to do it that way made her want to spank *him* with a spoon too.

"That smells great, Sascha," her father, Henry, murmured as he rounded the corner. His smile wavered as he saw her bosses sitting at the table. "Oh, sorry, I didn't realize we'd all be eating together."

Sascha told him, "We always eat down here."

"You as well?" Henry asked, his brows high in surprise.

"We run a very informal household," Andrei told him, sounding anything but informal.

Henry just blinked. "Oh."

Sascha had to hide a smile because her father didn't like Russians. It was a ridiculous dislike perpetuated by recent events. He could be surprisingly xenophobic when it boiled down to it. A trait she didn't share… considering she was fucking a German, three Brits, and a Russian. Shit, maybe she was running her own, very small version of NATO here.

Although, her version of problem solving was undoubtedly *very* different to NATO's…

Lips curling in a smile, she asked, "You get everything unpacked, dad?" Better to change the subject than to focus on the true oddity of their household.

He would notice more with time. Time was not her friend in this instance.

"Yes, thanks, honey. I had a quick nap and showered up."

"You shouldn't have napped," Devon told him, reaching forward to grab a slice of crusty bread from the wooden board that ran down the center of the table. It was thin, but full—the guys ate so much bread, it was a wonder they didn't all turn into white-sliced loaves.

As he buttered it, he went on, "Your body's natural circadian rhythms have been altered by the flight. Following the time zone you've travelled to is the smarter option if you don't want to be tired throughout the duration of your holiday."

Her father blinked, and she grinned. "He's always like that. Don't mind him."

Kurt cocked a brow as he sipped at the fruity Riesling she'd paired with her dad's favorite pasta dish—Spaghetti Carbonara.

Not that Henry would drink the wine. She'd made sure to grab some beers from the local store a few roads away to satisfy her father's more baser appetites.

Henry wasn't exactly a Guinness drinker. Which was all they had in the house for Sawyer and Kurt's benefit.

"Since when do you know what jet lag does to the body?" Kurt demanded. "You've barely travelled anywhere."

Devon shrugged. "I read."

"Reading isn't the same as doing," Andrei pointed out. "Although, he is right."

"I know he is," Kurt argued. "I'm just saying, he isn't an expert.

Sawyer grumbled, "That's a first. Something Devon isn't an expert in."

"After the Great Snorkeling Incident of '97, I'd say that was a given," she inserted teasingly, making the men laugh and her father look over them with curiosity.

"It wasn't snorkeling, Sascha. It was scuba diving," Devon corrected with a sniff.

She stuck out her tongue then ordered, "Devon, call Sean. Dinner's ready."

"No need. I'm here."

Sean came down the stairs and rounded the corner looking like he'd just walked in off a modelling set. For once, he was in informal wear. A tee-shirt with 'The Smiths' logo on it, and a pair of jeans. He was, as usually was the case, barefoot.

His hair was tousled, the messy waves somehow looking styled to perfection as he headed straight to the kitchen counter where she was working and leaned over for a kiss.

She froze. As did he. And the rest of the diners at the table.

For a second, nobody said anything, and she saw Sean close his eyes in regret, then look at her in apology. "I forgot," he mouthed.

She grimaced, then cleared her throat. With her arm still in a cast, she relied on them to do a lot of the lifting, so saying, she murmured, "Grab the dishes, Sean."

Knowing her cheeks were pink, she moved toward the table and kept her eyes averted from her father's.

As was usually the case, she had a stack of dishes on her setting, and Sean had placed the bowl of Spaghetti Carbonara, complete with raw egg yolk stirred into the deliciously gloopy mix, and enough Parmesano Reggiano to cause a stink, to her left.

Serving up portions, she wished like hell one of the men would speak to cover up Sean's blunder, but they didn't. Not even her father did.

And she didn't dare look at him.

Her eyes caught Sean's as she handed the first dish to Devon, who started passing the dishes down the table. He looked filled with regret, his remorse evident. She gave a tiny headshake, smiling at him a little to tell him she forgave him.

It had been a big thing to ask of them all. Hiding their intimacy was inordinately difficult when they had a tendency of being rather touchy feely.

Truth was, she was surprised she hadn't caved in first.

She loved their affectionate ways. Loved how they greeted her with hugs and kisses when they happened upon her in any room of the house—like they hadn't seen her in a lifetime and needed to reconnect.

It wasn't a habit she wanted to break. No, sirree.

Andrei, thank God, cleared his throat and murmured, "I meant to say. Katrin's situation has been dealt with, Kurt."

Kurt jolted in surprise, almost knocking his wine glass out of his hand. "It is? That was fast!"

Andrei shrugged as he twirled his fork around the spaghetti. "It wasn't too difficult to solve. Not that her bank balance has been restored… Her financial advisor is out of touch because he's living in the Cayman Islands. Well, he was. Now he's just under arrest there."

"What about her money?" Sascha asked as she took a seat, then, realizing her father was in the dark, murmured, "Katrin is Kurt's ex-wife, dad. She came to the house a few weeks ago asking for help."

Andrei pitched in, "Her hedge fund manager had embezzled close to five hundred million euros of his clients' money." He shrugged. "Whether we can recoup the funds is another matter entirely. But I looked into her situation further, and she has about five million tucked away in an old trust fund her maternal grandmother set up for her. She should be okay on that if she economizes."

Her father choked on the sip of beer he'd just taken. "Economizes?"

Sascha grinned. "I know, right? They all live in another stratosphere. But you should have seen her dad. I swear, everything she wore cost at least a thousand dollars."

"Probably more," Kurt said with a grunt. "Economizing isn't in Katrin's nature."

"No. I know. That's why I set her up with a hedge fund manager I trust. Half of it has been reinvested, and that will reinstate her wealth in the long term."

"What are the chances of the authorities getting the money back?"

Andrei shrugged. "Not very high. It was a Ponzi scheme."

Kurt's eyes widened. "I told her to run her investments through you."

Andrei snorted. "She asked, I denied. I didn't want to work with her, Kurt. At the time she was your wife, and I was duty bound to help, but Katrin's a brat. When she came to me, I advised her on who to use. She went with Hans Jorgen when I specifically advised against using him. He was offering far too lucrative returns, and far too consistently."

Her father broke in, "What is it you do exactly? Are you all in finance?"

"No, dad. Just Andrei is in finance."

"Well, I run a lot of different side projects. I play the markets because it's fun, but like Devon and Sawyer, math is my calling."

Henry's eyes widened as he glanced over Devon and Sawyer. "You're into math?"

She giggled. "That's an understatement, dad. They're like Matt Damon in *Good Will Hunting*."

"Technically, they're even smarter than that," Kurt said with a chuckle. "Devon is a prodigy."

"I thought only kids were prodigies."

Sawyer shrugged. "Devon might as well be a kid. He certainly has the self-control of one."

The man in question snorted. "You're only saying that because I beat you at chess this afternoon."

"With a reckless move that made no sense."

Devon just grinned. Smugly. "Worked though, didn't it?"

She cleared her throat, sidestepping the argument she knew was about to happen by inserting, "You remember *Black Blood*? That book that made a splash last year?"

For the first time, she met her father's glance. He nodded. "I remember. Read it too. Damn good book."

"Kurt wrote it."

Her father's mouth dropped open as he turned to stare at Kurt. "You wrote it? You're Kurt Yeller?"

"For my sins," Kurt toasted him.

"Jesus. That's one of my favorite books." He shook his head, disbelief painted onto his features. "Why didn't you tell me sooner?"

She snorted. "And miss out on you being star struck?"

Henry grunted. "Disrespectful as always, girlie."

Sascha just grinned and forked up some of her meal, but he shook his head at her irreverent smile.

"It's a pleasure to meet you, Kurt. I'd have known if Sascha had introduced me with your full names."

Kurt shrugged. "No reason to stand on formality here. This is our home. Sascha's too."

"I can see that," Henry pointed out softly, and his gaze turned into a laser-like beam as he skewered Sean on it. "And you? What is it you do?"

Sean's fork scraped against the china as he murmured, "I'm a criminologist."

That had her father's interest snagged—how couldn't it be when he was a cop? He turned to Sascha, a look in his eyes. She had to hide a smile. "A good one."

Sean frowned, confused by the byplay between father and daughter.

"Dad doesn't reckon much to criminologists."

"Not in the States anyway. They're usually FBI sanctioned, and they come in and muscle in on local cases that our department should be handling, not the Feds."

Sean nodded. "Yes. I've seen how the system works in the States. Been invited over there a time or two for conventions."

"Did you go?" she asked, surprised as he'd never mentioned that before.

"No. I don't like America."

The statement had her freezing in place, dreading what her patriotic father would have to say to that, then Devon broke the ice by snorting. "And I thought *I* was the one who suffered with 'Foot in Mouth' syndrome."

Sean grimaced. "I'm sorry, but it's true. The people are great, but I don't approve of your gun laws, which I'm aware won't make me very popular over there. It's easier for me to stay away than it is to get involved. It's far too easy to make a bad name for yourself in the community I work in, and if that happens, it will destroy the work I can do over here."

Her father pondered that, then nodded. "I can respect a man who stands up for his principles. Better that than a hypocrite."

Though she knew her father had to be suspicious over their relationship after the way Sean had almost kissed her, she also had to reason that her dad was still aware Sean was her boss.

Whether he was being tactful because of that, she wasn't sure.

Kurt cleared his throat. "Europe is a lot more liberal. Is this your first time over here, Henry?"

"Pretty much. Sascha's mother never wanted to leave the States. Said there was too much to see over there, and by the time I married again, I wasn't much interested in travel."

She frowned. "That's sad, dad. There's so much of the world to see."

"I see a lot of it from behind my desk, Sascha. You know that."

"Yeah, but that's all the bad stuff. What about the good?"

He shrugged. "I'm here, aren't I?"

"Only because of the divorce."

"No, because I wanted to see you, and you haven't been back in two years. I know you just started this new job, so I guessed you wouldn't be making your way home any time soon."

Because he'd deduced correctly, she conceded that with a grimace. Truthfully though, work hadn't been the only reason why she'd avoided returning home.

If she hadn't stayed with her father, that would have caused a row, and the last thing she wanted was to share a roof with Linda again.

Almost like her father cottoned on to that, he murmured, "Plus, until recently, you didn't have much reason to come home, did you?"

She winced. "You taught me to be adult about situations that were out of my control, dad."

"And I agreed and understood, even though it saddened me my daughter couldn't come and visit because she knew she'd end up arguing with her stepmother." He reached over and grabbed her hand. As he squeezed it, he murmured, "I'm sorry about that, baby."

Her throat felt thick with emotion. "It's okay, dad."

"No. I knew you didn't like her. I should never have…"

She tightened her hold on his fingers. "What's done is done," she told him softly. "We can move on from that now."

His smile was loaded with a relief she knew went bone deep. In fact, that look alone made her feel lighter inside.

For years, they'd been at crossed purposes. Which now was totally unnecessary. The distance parting them had always caused an ache in her soul.

Before her mother's death, they'd been close. When that relationship had disappeared too, she'd been left grieving for both her parents—in a manner of speaking.

And like that, once those words had been uttered, the tension she'd felt since her father's arrival disappeared.

He'd either disapprove or not of the interplay between her and Sean, but he wouldn't let it get in the way of their relationship.

She saw that, knew that nothing would again. It let her relax. All the internal walls she'd built long ago were just waiting to crumble, because she'd built them out of necessity not desire.

There was nothing more that she wanted than to be close to her father again. As though those internal walls of hers had been a barrier, the storm hovering above them broke, and they relaxed.

It was a damn good meal. Not just because the Carbonara was perfection on a plate, but because father and daughter had accepted the other's olive branch, and peace was on the horizon.

A thought which gave her comfort until she realized the truth of her past would destroy that peace before it had barely any time to develop.

Still, there was no point in thinking about that now.

Not yet, anyway.

TWENTY-SEVEN

"YOU'RE ABOUT to hear a lot of Russian."

Sascha peered over her computer at him, then at the vibrating phone in his hand. "Then you're about to make me very horny."

He smirked, palmed his cell, and murmured, "Two more days."

She grumbled but waved a hand. "Go ahead."

He eyed her as he connected the call, switching to Russian and watching as her eyes dilated while he spoke.

He loved that. Just speaking made her horny… could that make him any more fortunate than he already was?

"Grandfather. Are you well?"

Vasily grumbled. "Do I have to be on my death bed to call you?"

Andrei pulled a face. If any of his lieutenants were aware of how much grumbling Vasily did, they'd totally lose the fear of God they had of him.

"No. But we only spoke the other day."

"I've been digging."

"Digging where?" he asked warily.

"Into your situation."

Andrei scowled. "Why? I didn't tell you to involve you. Just to explain."

"Since when does that matter? If I'm interested, I'm interested. I have the time on my hands, and the connections to find out information you can't discover any other way but via broken fingers."

Andrei sighed, and lifting a hand, pinched the bridge of his nose. "That wasn't necessary."

Vasily cackled. "You never did like spilling blood. But in this instance, you'll be glad I did. I have a name for you."

"A name?"

"Yes. Elizabeth Jacobie."

"Edward Jacobie's mother?" he demanded, sitting up in surprise. "What's she got to do with anything?"

"I had a few people speak to the man behind bars. She's who hired him."

As he processed that, he let out a hiss. "Don't suppose you found out why."

Vasily snorted. "I can't do all the work for you, boy. Although, I'd like to be kept in the loop."

"Why?" he asked warily.

"Because I've seen your Sascha. She does look like Ava Gardner and Rita Hayworth. I'd like to meet her."

"Dirty old bastard," he groused. "She's mine."

Another cackle. "A man can live vicariously, can't he?"

He snorted. "If you expect me to believe Anja is just your nurse, then you really do think I'm a fool."

"A man's bed is his private affair."

"So, what are you doing looking into the woman who occupies my bed then, huh?"

"I was interested. How could I not be? Safe for years in the UK until she goes to your house? Not only that, I was concerned my business enterprises had somehow crossed into your world."

"And they haven't?" He wasn't surprised at his grandfather's concern. Vasily had more fingers in pies than a man with four hands could count. At least two pies per finger.

Minimum.

"No. You weren't the target of that bomb. Nasty business that. Poorly executed."

"Thanks. That poor execution is why I'm still alive."

Vasily just grunted. "You know what I mean. If you're going to do a job, better do it damn well."

"That's back to front logic considering the bomb would have exploded when I was making my speech."

"But it didn't, and you're safe. So, I can afford to be generous." Vasily mumbled something, and Andrei assumed it was to someone in his quarters.

He could easily imagine the huge library where Vasily would be sitting. He'd spent countless hours there as a child.

The place was fit for a Tsar. Which, in his world, Vasily was the equivalent of.

With bookshelves that lined the high walls, making his six-foot length appear miniscule by comparison, his grandfather was surrounded by books. Leather-backed ones, first editions, then gritty paperbacks of the thrillers he loved. High-backed armchairs and sofas sat in clumps around small tables, inviting conversation and the opportunity to read while whoever sat there sipped at bitter coffee or drank shots of vodka. Both of which were, he remembered in amusement, practically on tap.

A coffee, a book, and a game of chess on his antique pedestal board with the marble pieces he'd had smuggled out of China were always on offer in his grandfather's office.

It wasn't just the 'play' side of the library that was beautiful. Vasily's desk had once belonged to a Romanov. The ornate gilt was out of touch and not to Andrei's taste, but it suited Vasily, who was a king to the men under him.

Well, King incumbent.

Supposedly.

Andrei didn't even want to know who was reigning in his grandfather's stead. Didn't even want to know if his grandfather's retirement was 'mock.'

"The bomb was organized by this foolish group I've been reading about," Vasily told him conversationally, like he hadn't just managed to crack two cases that international policing bodies were stumped over.

But then, Vasily had spies everywhere. Information leaked to him through sources that no ordinary policeman would be comfortable using.

Not without fearing a prison sentence himself, anyway.

"Are you going to tell Sean?"

Sean was the only one of his friends his grandfather referred to by name. Mostly out of respect. Sean had helped unravel a criminal organization that had been operating out of Manchester with ties to Chechnya.

Vasily had also been grateful. That organization had been his competition.

"May I?" Andrei asked, tone wary. He rarely imparted the information he received from Vasily. Though Sean would appreciate it, Andrei had to be careful.

Using the information came at a cost, and it was too high if it brought shit to their door. He'd moved from Russia to England to get away from that bullshit. He didn't want to bring it here too.

"Yes. It doesn't clash with any of my concerns."

Yet more proof his grandfather wasn't as retired as he liked to make out.

"So, who is it?"

"They're anti-capitalist idiots, raging against the 1%. And the 1% appertains to ninety percent of the guests at that event. Yourself included."

Relief flushed through him. "So, Sascha wasn't targeted?"

"No. But she's still in danger. I was teasing earlier, but the man hired to hurt her didn't know why she was being targeted. That attempt failed. If another attempt is being planned or is underway, you need to protect your woman."

His woman. Andrei liked the sound of that.

"When this is over, and I know she's safe, I'll bring her to visit you."

Silence pounded down the line, and when Vasily spoke next, his voice had Andrei swallowing with emotion—tears clogged his grandfather's throat. "You will come to Moscow?"

Andrei gnawed at his lip, then studied Sascha whose focus had returned to whatever it was she was doing on her computer.

"Yes."

"It has been a long time, child."

Fifteen years. He'd only returned twice. Once, in his first year of Oxford. After which, he'd decided he could never return unless it was urgent.

The second time had been his grandmother's funeral. That was the kind of urgency he was talking about.

Truth was, Russia was no longer home. He was a proud Russian, but he didn't want to live there. His grandfather's world wasn't one he wanted to inhabit. There was danger there, unnecessary risk. Andrei's gifts didn't lend themselves to that kind of work. He preferred to play with figures, ride the stock market and make it his bitch.

Violence wasn't his way.

Plus, being in Moscow meant being in the same city as his bastard father.

Andrei could just handle sharing a continent. A city was too close and being in the same country was enough to have him still on edge.

"She will be safe over there, yes?"

"Of course. Hurry up and resolve this situation. I wish to see you."

Andrei smiled, then groaned when Vasily tacked on, "It's a dying man's wish."

The melodramatic tone told him everything. "Only the good die young."

Vasily snorted. "Ungrateful wretch."

"I love you too," Andrei teased.

His grandfather scoffed at that, but in English, a language no one in his house would understand, he murmured, "I love you, child." And with that, he cut the call.

Moved, because his grandfather never ceased to stop amazing him, he placed his cell on the desk.

"I spontaneously orgasmed three times," Sascha said blankly, her focus still on the screen.

"Then I appreciate your quiet. My grandfather would have asked what I was doing if he'd thought he heard someone having sex in the background."

Her nose wrinkled as she looked up at him. "Your grandfather? And hey, you talk about sex with him?"

"I talk about everything with him," he replied easily, rocking back in his chair to study her more intently.

This new habit of hers pleased him. Greatly. Not only did she sit in Sean's room, but seemingly at random, she would come and work in one of their offices.

Though she had her own study and room, she preferred to invade theirs. Or, as was the case at the moment, have them invade hers. With her father around for the next ten days, Sean was sleeping in the attic with her.

After he'd gone to kiss her in the kitchen, they'd deemed it wise to play it safe. Sawyer was in Sean's room, and Devon, much to his disgust, had to stay in his own bedroom.

"Everything?" she asked.

"Everything," he confirmed. "He's the one who taught me what sex is." He pulled a face at that conversation. "You don't even want to know how he explained the birds and the bees." Just the memory had him rubbing his temples.

"Now I need to know," she retorted. "If it makes you pull a face like that."

He sighed. "You won't like it, but he meant well."

She frowned. "What did he do?"

"Is your father in the house?"

"No. Why?"

"Where did he go?"

"He wanted to drag me to Buckingham Palace, but I told him I had work to do—not a total lie, thank God."

His lips twitched. "Not a fan of the monarchy?"

"I'm American. I love royalty. It's in my freakin' veins. I'm just not desperate to be caught in the tourist trap, that's all. So, go on. Spill."

"My grandfather is old school. In more ways than you can imagine. He's Bratva. High-ranking, one of the highest in his region. Because of that," he continued, ascertaining that from her lack of surprise, one of the others had shared his family history with her, "He thinks differently than most. Anyway, he had a hooker slip into my room one night. It was a very informative lesson."

"How old were you?"

He grimaced, aware of what her reaction would be. "Thirteen."

"Thirteen?" she shrieked. "You were just a baby!"

He grunted. "Hardly. Plus, I was very happy at the time, I assure you."

"Oh my God, that's all kinds of wrong. A hooker? Jesus, she could have had an STD or anything!"

"I doubt it," he replied wryly. "Vasily's intention was for me to no longer be a virgin. Not to have my cock fall off."

She blinked. "You're totally okay with this, aren't you?"

He knew she wasn't and was sorry for it. Letting out a sigh, he murmured, "Who told you about my past?"

"Kurt."

"Did he explain about my mother?"

"He said…"

When she broke off, hurt in her eyes—hurt for him—he inserted on her behalf, "…that my father killed my mother."

"And that you watched him do it."

He nodded, the pain of those memories alternated between having the power to crush him and to numb him to the extent where he felt nothing for days.

He should really see a shrink. But, the truth was, there was no escaping those images. No amount of talking about it with a trained professional would scrub his mind clean. Sean tried. *Frequently*. And that was the only kind of help he'd accept. But then, Sean was different. He was his brother and sharing those memories with him was more of a purge than a therapy session.

"We don't have to talk about this," she whispered, and he jerked in surprise as he saw she'd moved toward him. Her laptop was on the floor, resting somewhat askew where she'd dumped it moments before.

When she leaned against his desk, he patted his lap, and she immediately rested against him, snuggling into him in a way he'd never imagined wanting.

The other women they'd shared hadn't been like Sascha. Maybe that was why they hadn't worked. They'd been focused on the sex. The thrill. The naughtiness of sleeping with five guys at the same time.

Sascha's interactions with them were… polar. She treated them like individuals. There was a group connection, and a personal one. It made him believe in soul mates. For the first time in his forty-three years, the concept wasn't ridiculous to him.

She fit into their world with the ease of fitting a plug into a socket. Made for them. And damn was it electric.

For the first time, he wanted to believe everything would work out. Rather than dissociate himself from the relationship, aware that hurt would come down the road, he embraced it.

Had decided to do that when Sean had called him, frantic, with news of her accident. For a moment, he'd believed her dead, and the relief that had cascaded through him when he'd learned she was alive, was more than he could describe.

She leaned up to stroke his cheek. "Hey, where'd you go?"

He blinked. "Sorry. I was thinking."

She rubbed her temple against his shoulder. "I meant it. We don't have to talk about this."

"I know you did, but we have to. You have to know all of me, Sascha. The good, the bad, and the ugly."

She sighed. "It won't change anything. You're more than your past."

Her words were bizarrely freeing. "You truly believe that?"

"The past makes us what we are, sure. We wouldn't be standing here today otherwise, would we? But I think that if we condemn people for the mistakes they've made, don't allow ourselves to believe that they're capable of good in the future… Well, it's a pretty hopeless point-of-fucking-view."

"What about murderers and rapists?"

"Some crimes should never be forgiven. But that doesn't mean to say that same person can't do good and can't learn from his past to rectify his future."

"You're an idealist," he said softly, both amused and touched at the realization.

She grimaced. "This isn't about me."

That's where she was wrong. It was all about her.

He cleared his throat. "My mother was my father's mistress. I don't know if it's much better there now, but when I was a child, women aspired to nothing more than that. Being a prostitute was considered a great career opportunity."

She winced. "Every feminist bone in my body just cringed at that."

He chuckled, but there was little amusement to it. "I know. It's not a popular way of thinking, but you have to understand the poverty over there. The extreme divide between the wealthy and the poor." He shrugged. "It is what it is. Mother was happy to be my father's *devushka*. I wasn't ashamed either. I was…" He thought back to those days. "Happy."

They'd had money. Food on the table. A warm house. He'd had toys, unlike many children at school. His clothing had been good quality. They'd known who he was, of course. Or, to be precise, who his grandfather was.

"Father came home drunk that day," he said in a bland tone that was utterly devoid of expression. He could count on one hand how many times he'd told this story. It was one that would never grow easier with the retelling.

"He was angry. Enraged, I suppose. He accused her of cheating on him. Said that she'd been seeing someone else."

"Had she?"

He tensed. "I don't think so. She loved him. I never saw anyone around to indicate she was cheating on the bastard. At any rate, he didn't believe her when she denied it. If anything, her denials seemed to anger him all the more.

"Where we lived, there was only one bedroom. She'd partitioned off a small part of the living room for me to sleep in. It was only the size of a bed, and she'd used blankets, so I could hear everything." He sucked in a deep breath. "Of course, he was moving around like a furious bull. The blankets parted as he moved around."

"You looked?"

"I didn't mean to. I was huddled under my covers, terrified. I didn't like my father. He wasn't interested in me. Didn't seem particularly interested in my mother either, but he visited often so that obviously wasn't true. Whenever he came, I used to go to my room, and I hated the noises that came out of theirs…" He swallowed, bile thickening his throat. "Out of nowhere, a knife appeared in his fist. Like that, she was gone. One minute I saw the glint of metal, the next, there was blood everywhere."

"What did he do? Did he come for you?" she asked quietly, her head tucked underneath his chin.

"No. I doubt he even realized I was there." His laughter was harsh at the very notion. "Mother gave me grandfather's number years before. I don't know whether she realized something might happen to her. Maybe she knew how volatile he was, I don't know. But I found the number in the cake tin where she kept it and called him."

"What did he do?"

"He didn't know about me," he said, laughing a little easier now at the memory. "But I told him his bastard son had gutted my mother, and that I was his blood, and that he needed to come and make her better."

"You knew those words back then?"

He shrugged. "Different world, Sascha."

She gulped. "I guess."

"Anyway, a car came thirty minutes later. I only learned a few years after that it was as fast as he could get there. But I raged at him because she was dead." He raised a hand to cover his mouth as he stared blindly ahead.

Not daring to close his eyes for fear of seeing her as she'd been that day.

"She was so beautiful," he whispered instead. "So delicate and pretty. So smart too. She could have been so much more than his slut."

Sascha reached for his hand. "I'm sorry."

He ignored her. Not out of cruelty but because he wasn't particularly listening. "Vasily came and I kicked him. I punched him. Raged at him like his son had raged at my mama." He huffed out a laugh. "Anyone else would have been struck dead for that. But he just took a look around, made some orders to the men who'd come with him, and gathered me up.

"Before I knew what was happening, my cheek was stinging because he'd slapped me out of my hysteria, and I was being driven in one of the biggest, fanciest cars I'd ever seen."

She seemed to absorb all that, then asked softly, "You love him, don't you? I heard it on the phone."

He blinked, shaken from the spell of the past. "Yes. Of course. He saved me. And he never forgave my father. Vasily couldn't throw him in jail, but he made sure Ivan never rose through the ranks. Ivan didn't have my grandfather's smarts, but heritage alone should have seen him soar to the top. That never happened because of that day."

"Jungle justice."

He nodded. "Probably the only thing that could have hurt Ivan anyway. They view prison differently… It's by no means a blessing, but it's not dreaded either. Not like we dread it."

She cuddled into him and something cold and hard rubbed his throat. "I'm sorry," she said again. "I'm sorry because I don't know what to say to you. I want to make it all better, but I know I can't."

He stilled at her words, touched by them. Touched by her earnest desire to help ease his pain.

He reached for the wrist that was brushing his neck from her gentle clasp on him and felt a heavy bracelet. "This is new," he said softly, surprised because she wore very little jewelry.

She pulled her arm away from his neck and showed him a heavy charm bracelet. "Not new. Not exactly. I just never wear it. It was my mom's."

He rubbed at the heavy gold bracelet complete with dozens of trinkets. "It must be heavy."

Sascha giggled. "It is. Mom was a lot smaller than me too. Her wrists were teeny. It must have weighed her arm down."

"What made you wear it today?" he asked, cocking a brow.

She bit her lip. "I just wanted to feel close to her, I guess." She touched one of the charms, a plain, gold key that was a little larger than the other trinkets. "She loved it, and dad used to buy her a charm whenever we went on vacation. It helps me remember the good times."

He wanted to make some good memories with her; none that were loaded with fears about her safety, concerns about her past... He wanted to make a life with her, he realized. A realization that had a thought popping into his head.

Rubbing another charm, a small book, then fiddling with a piece that looked like the Scottie dog marker on a Monopoly board, he asked, "Would you visit him with me?"

"Your grandfather?" she asked, shocked.

"Yes."

"Do you want me to?"

"I just promised him I'd take you for a visit," he confessed wryly, but it was more than that. He wanted her to see his home, his family, his world. He wanted her to know all of him. Even the shitty side of his past, and the good side too—the loving grandfather who had never, ever given up on him and had supported him throughout his life. "He helped me, and—"

"Helped you how? With what?"

"Ways you don't even want to know," he said ruefully. "And by that, I mean, because you're the daughter of a cop."

She grunted. "Okay. Yeah. Sometimes, TMI is a possibility, I guess."

He tapped her nose with his finger, then anointed the tip with his lips.

"What's going on?"

Sean's voice had them both turning to face him.

"Why?" Andrei asked with a frown.

"Nothing. You just..." Sean shook his head, but it seemed more at himself than at them.

"Sean? Are you okay?"

It wasn't often Andrei saw Sean looking anything other than his usual calm and collected self.

Of them all, Sean was the steadiest. He was strong, solid. Cool under pressure, capable of absorbing a lot of crap from those he loved and handling crises that came as a result.

To see him looking shaken had Andrei frowning with concern.

He watched as Sean came in and leaned against the desk. He pressed his hands to the edge of the table, squeezed tight enough to make his knuckles turn white, and bowing his head between his tensed shoulders, murmured, "One of the cases I'm working on… they found another victim."

"Oh sweetheart, I'm so sorry," Sascha said, scuttling from Andrei's lap and rounding the desk to press close to Sean's side.

She shot him a look, one that he just shrugged in reply to.

Sean worked on several cases at once, and he rarely shared any of the details regarding them.

It was unusual for him to react like this to another victim. Not totally out of the blue, but unique enough that Andrei found himself without words.

"Can we do anything to help?"

He shook his head at her words, then in a flurry of movement, spun on his heel and dragged her against him.

Sascha jumped in surprise, but her generous nature reared its head and she just allowed him to wrap her up in his arms, hold her tight, and lose himself in that generosity.

It was then, as Andrei watched her comfort a man who was closer than a brother, he knew how much he loved her.

The feelings weren't new. They didn't even come as a surprise. But they were real. Very, *very* real. So solid, that his chest felt weighted down with the pressure of his feelings.

So, he said to himself, *this is what love feels like?*

He hid a smile, lest she and Sean think him a total unfeeling prick for gawking and grinning like a loon while Sean had a meltdown, and took a second to allow the sensation of warmth to flush through him.

He'd let Sean deal with his grief, a grief that spoke of the heinousness of what had happened to the victim, and then he'd broach the subject of Elizabeth Jacobie with him.

It was about time they spoke to Henry too, Andrei reckoned.

They needed to resolve this situation, before Sascha found herself in more danger than she already was.

He'd already lost the only other woman he'd loved to violence. He wouldn't lose Sascha too.

And that was a promise. One he made to his seven-year-old self.

TWENTY-EIGHT

"IT'S BEEN A WEEK."

Sean blinked at her from over a sheaf of papers. "Excuse me?"

She propped her hands on her hips. "It's been a week."

"Since what?"

"You know what. My doctor's appointment."

She watched as his lips twitched. "Ah."

"Yes. Ah."

"You're telling me this why?"

"So you can do that weird communication thing you have with the others. I'm not sure if it's Morse Code with your eyelashes or some kind of sigils made with your pasta, but you'd better spread the communiqué around that this girl is back in action."

He coughed. "You need to see the doctor again before you get the all clear."

"I feel better, dammit." And she did. She wasn't just saying that because she was horny.

Which she was. Extremely.

It was like being on a diet and being constantly surrounded by the biggest goddamn cannolis around. Worse; ice cream galore, chips and candy… they were all the bad stuff. Bad stuff she craved with a need that should have astonished her, but she was too busy craving to worry.

Hell, she could worry another time. At the moment, the only thing that was concerning her was her very empty, very needy pussy.

"I'm not going to the doctor's again. Not until it's time to take off my cast."

Sean narrowed his eyes. "That's in, what? Another two weeks."

She grunted. "Trust you to remember that."

"I still can't believe you haven't told your father what happened that day. Why lie to him? Why not tell him everything? Surely he'd want to know?"

Sascha almost stomped her foot at his change of topic. She didn't want to talk about this. She wanted to talk about him. Inside *her*. And if that was avoidance or a delay tactic, then fucking sue her.

If anyone deserved to avoid the shitstorm she was embroiled in, through no fault of her own she might add, it was Sascha goddamn Dubois.

"Because I'm not ready for that conversation. That's why. You know it's way more than just saying I was in an accident. It was easier to tell him I fell, hit my head and broke my arm."

"Why lie about something you're going to have to discuss at some point?"

She pursed her lips. "Why are you changing the subject?"

"Because you're not ready."

"Ready to talk to my dad about my birth mom? No. You've got that damn right. I might never be ready either," she warned with a huff, crossing her arms over her chest.

She no longer had to be gentle with her healing wrist. Not that she could fling it around willy nilly, but she could at least cross her arms now without feeling like it was about to fall off.

Another sign she was on the mend. About goddamn time too. She was sick of not being one hundred percent. Sick of them having to be careful with her. She wanted everything they had to give. And not an ounce less.

"I meant that you're not ready for sex."

"What do you want me to do, dammit? Get a doctor's note?"

He shrugged. "Yes."

She glowered at him, astonished by his reply. "You can't be serious." A statement. Not a question.

"I am. Deadly," he countered.

She watched as he got out of his seat, moved around the desk, then perched his fine behind on the edge. He mimicked her pose—folding his arms across his chest—and murmured, "Why would any of us want to do anything that would harm you?"

"It's not like that," she argued.

"It is. We've already learned we can't trust you to help yourself. You slept with most of us with your head aching. If you lead us to believe that you're doing well, then how are we supposed to judge the truth?

"So, no, I don't believe you when you say you're fine. Because you told us you were fine each time you were with us. So, yes, I need a doctor's note."

She pursed her lips. "This is ridiculous. I felt better after we fucked, dammit! Why does no one believe me?"

He studied her calmly, so calmly she felt flustered and irritable. "Maybe, it *is* ridiculous. But you look after the people you love, don't you? Even when they don't look after themselves."

His words had her freezing in place. Love? God, that changed everything.

"I love you too," she told him softly, her defensive posture slouching into nothingness as she recognized the truth in his words.

It did seem like she was self-sabotaging, she begrudgingly admitted, and the other, *horrendous*, truth was that around them, she *did* have serious control issues. They did something to her. She wasn't even sure what it was, just that when she was around them, she felt this need to connect with them. To be with them.

She'd never felt that driving urge before.

It was so much more than sex. It was a need that was so basic, it would have terrified her if they weren't as in over their heads as she was.

He held out a hand, almost like their thoughts were running parallel. She bit her lip, but let his fingers enfold hers as he pulled her against his chest.

"What's wrong?"

"I'm sorry," she whispered. "I-I… you must think I'm mad. I just don't want to lose you. Any of you."

"Why would you lose us?" he asked, sounding gratifyingly perplexed.

"Because what's the point in being with me if you can't sleep with me?"

He froze, his body overcome with a tension that hurt her. "Is that what you think?"

His voice was like ice, and she winced.

"I-I guess. But it's more than that. I just want to be near you. I hate that these stupid headaches are putting distance between us."

"But they're not."

She peered up at him. "They're not?"

"No. Of course not. Do you think I don't want you? That I don't crave every luscious inch of you?"

She gulped at the heat banked in his stormy blue eyes. "You do?"

"I do," he told her gravely. "We all do. I think we've shown you that in many different ways."

Her cheeks bloomed with heat. Did he know about the wooden spoon?

She didn't have the gall to ask, so instead, whispered, "But… I haven't been able to—"

"And that's life, Sascha. I want you whole and healthy or not at all. Do you understand me? You put your health at risk to sleep with us. We tried—granted, not enough—to hold you back, but we're men. That doesn't excuse us, and I'm fucked off that we couldn't resist you even when it was for your own benefit, but we *will* resist you now. For your own damn good."

She blinked. "But I really do feel better," she told him in a soft voice.

"Then get me the doctor's note to prove it," he retorted. "Anyway, these last few weeks haven't been ideal but look how close we've all knit together. That's what happens when sex isn't involved. Or," he conceded, "not as involved as it could be."

"We have grown close, haven't we?" she mused, pleased by the notion.

"Of course. Each day is a chance to get to know one another better. That hasn't changed with me and the others in the decades I've known them. Every day's a learning curve."

She pursed her lips. "Do you really mean that?"

He sighed. "Since when have you not known me to speak my mind?"

"Never, I guess." She gnawed at the inside of her cheek, then asked, "Will you go on a date with me?"

His eyes widened, then he grinned. "Sure. I've never been asked out on a date before. Where to?"

She gawked at him. "What the hell is wrong with women in this country?"

"What do you mean?"

"You've never been asked out? Are the people with ovaries blind here or something?"

He snorted. "I doubt it. It's just if you don't put yourself in those situations, it's not easy to meet people." He shrugged. "You know how it works."

She grumbled under her breath. "I still think it's weird. But anyway, it's to my gain." Though it made zero sense.

How they'd all failed to be snapped up spoke of a serious lack of brains in the female population of England. In America, these hotties would have been off the shelf since high school.

"Where are you taking me?"

"Do you want to go to the cinema? So we can neck and stuff?" She grinned at the smoky look in his eye, then added, "Post doctor's note. I promise."

He grabbed her hips and pulled her against him. She could feel the bulge of his erection against her belly and loved that it took so little to get him hard.

Hell, who was she kidding?

All of them were the same around her.

No wonder she was horny so much. They made her feel like a sex Goddess. Like she was the sexiest thing on the planet! How could a woman not revel in that? It was damn empowering knowing you had five men who could get hard at the prospect of just kissing you in a darkened cinema hall.

"That sounds perfect."

"I can't imagine it's where you've taken dates in the past."

"No. Restaurants, usually," he told her. "Boring. Do I get to pick the movie?"

"We'll work our way up to restaurants," she chided. "They don't always have to be boring."

"Nothing's boring when you have that twinkle in your eye," he told her with a roguish grin.

"You've just not been eating with the right people. You needed an American to come in and shake things up."

His laughter had him flinging his head back at that. She loved that she could break down his walls, make him act like just a man instead of the criminologist who had more on his plate than most.

The other day, seeing him broken inside at having lost another victim because he had been too slow to catch the murderer? It had done something to her. Twisted her. Something that had already been happening thanks to Andrei's horrible tale of his mother's death.

They'd all been touched, in their own ways, by the depths of depravity. Some of them more than others, but they'd all rallied around and had survived by coming together into this unusual household. One she was grateful to be a part of.

Here, she knew, she could flourish. Just as they had.

She'd found her place, and what a place when the view came with five hunky men, all with cocks that wouldn't goddamn quit.

FINISHING UP IN THE RESTROOM, Sascha didn't return to the kitchen but headed for the front door. Having heard the postman's arrival, she went to grab the letters on the doormat. Riffling through them, she began to sort them in her hand, but as she did, a shadowy figure blocked out some of the light coming in from the inlaid stained glass in the door.

By the blur's diminutive stature, she figured it was a woman. And to save her head from ringing once the doorbell struck, she opened up, a questioning look on her face that immediately turned to one of dislike.

"What are you doing here?" she demanded of Kurt's ex-wife.

A nasty smile played about Katrin Yeller's mouth—it irritated the shit out of Sascha that the bitch still had Kurt's surname.

Call her possessive, but to her, that was wrong on so many levels. The damn woman hadn't been much of a wife when they were married. Why keep the surname now they were divorced?

"I wanted to give my thanks to Andrei and Kurt." She gestured to the gifts she had in her arms. Gifts, Sascha eyed as though they were poisoned snakes.

From this cow, they might as well have been.

"They don't want your thanks." Wasn't that the truth.

This bitch had told Andrei she was pregnant with his child, had let him start making plans with Kurt, and then she'd had an abortion.

As far as Sascha was concerned, any debts the men figured they owed Katrin for having helped keep some of Kurt's family secrets locked away from the press, had been more than paid.

Rather than do the dutiful thing and let the guest into the house, Sascha leaned across the doorway and folded her arms across her chest.

This was *her* house now.

She wasn't here temporarily, nor was she here because this was her place of employment.

It was her home.

Her haven.

And this witch wasn't taking a step inside.

"Aren't you going to let me in?" came the cross demand.

Sascha smiled. *Sweetly*. "No. I see no reason for you to come in. You can always give me the gifts."

"How do I know they'll make it to the men?" Katrin demanded snidely.

Sascha would have been offended, but Katrin was right on the money. "They won't make it anywhere other than the trash." She smiled again. This time, with teeth. "They want nothing from you except for you to disappear. So, go on, piss off."

Katrin's eyes flared wide with outrage. "How dare you speak to me like that? I'll tell Kurt."

She snorted. "Do. Tell him. Oh wait, you won't be able to. He told me he blocked your number, and we both know that if he sees you coming, he'll go in the other direction." She wasn't sure if he *had* blocked her number, but Sascha would make sure that happened today. "You're not wanted here, Katrin. Your gifts and your false praise are unnecessary."

"You think you're so special, don't you?" Katrin spat. "But you're not the first woman to appeal to them. They've had their selection of sluts, but they always, *always* get rid of them once they tire of them. You're no different." A nasty sneer curled her top lip. "Oh, wait, I'm wrong. You *are* different. They make you wash their clothes. What do they call that in English? Value for money?"

If anything, Sascha relaxed at Katrin's words. A week ago, she'd have been hurt and would have tried to hide it, but there was no need. She was secure in her place here. Everything else might be up in the air, but what she had with her quintet was the only solid ground she had.

"I know I'm not their first, but I intend on being their last." She leaned into Katrin's space. "Take your uptight ass, your unwanted gifts, and that stench you call a perfume and get off my property before I call the police."

Katrin narrowed her eyes at her. "You wouldn't dare."

"Try me."

She must have looked serious enough because Katrin just glowered harder then, after a handful of seconds, and with a huff, spun on her four-inched spikes for heels, and stalked down the steps onto the sidewalk.

Sascha watched her head for a smart BMW and didn't stop watching until the Wicked Witch of West Germany—as Sawyer called her—had disappeared from their street.

It was too much to hope that it would be from their lives forever, but for the moment, it was enough.

The fact that Sascha felt secure enough to not only refuse the woman entry, to reject her gifts, and to threaten the police on her if she didn't leave the premises, was a testament to the change in her relationship with her men.

Love made all the difference, she realized. It created a bridge between her and her men where nothing else could. One constructed so strongly, that it would take more than a damn earthquake, or trouble that came in the form of wicked witches, to destroy it.

AS ANDREI SAT at the breakfast counter, he elbowed Devon who was still eating his cereal.

"Where's everyone?"

"Kurt and Sawyer haven't come down yet. Sean and Henry finished earlier. But Sascha went to pee."

"I'm sure she phrased it like that," Andrei said dryly. "You should try not to embarrass the woman who makes your food."

"Why?" He frowned. "You don't think she'd spit on it, do you?"

Andrei couldn't help but roar with laughter at that, and Devon's look of horror as he stared down at what remained of his eggs.

"I heard that, Andrei!" The reprimand came from the staircase. "No, Devon, I won't spit in your food for your inability to follow even the most basic of social customs," she finished sweetly as she returned to the kitchen, placing a small stack of letters on the counter as she did so. "Although, at least I now have a threat worthy of making you tremble in your seat." To Andrei, she murmured, "I suppose I should be grateful he didn't hazard a guess that I'd be having a crap."

Devon blinked, still eying his food with distrust. "Highly unlikely. You used the downstairs bathroom. If you'd used the one in your suite, that's another matter entirely."

Sascha and Andrei groaned at the same time.

Andrei pinched the bridge of his nose. "Jesus, Devon."

"Devon, do I even want to know how you know that?" Sascha demanded, stacking her hands on her hips.

He scowled. "It makes sense, doesn't it? Why would you use the house bathroom rather than your personal one for that? It's just manners."

Her grin was quick. "I have none then it would seem."

Andrei snorted, and Devon looked particularly disturbed. "I'll always use mine from now on," he mumbled under his breath, making Sascha chuckle.

"Are you going to be watching everything I prepare now?"

Devon shrugged. "I usually watch you a lot to be fair. I've never seen you try to spit in our food."

Sascha clucked her tongue. "This isn't a freakin' drive-thru. Why would I spit on your food? If I'm angry at one of you, I'll let you know. You don't have to worry about that."

Her huff had Andrei smirking. "Yes. We know that, don't we, Devon?" he asked rhetorically, elbowing him in the side.

Devon just grunted.

"What would you like for breakfast, Andrei?" Sascha asked him with a smile. She peered over, leaned on the counter, then quickly anointed his lips with a kiss.

"More of that," he teased, holding the back of her head to his so he could taste her further.

Only when she moaned against his lips did he release her. *Her* hand came up to cup the back of *his* head this time, but she only speared her fingers through his hair, making him shiver with delight at her touch.

"When's your next doctor's appointment?"

She chuckled at his rough tone. "Tomorrow."

"Thank God."

"Who's going with you?" Devon asked, completely undisturbed by their making out beside him.

Devon was, as he'd often heard Sawyer call him, an odd duck.

Still, the same could be said for Kurt too. He'd have had the opposite reaction to Devon; undoubtedly, he'd have been panting like a dog at the sight of their hot kiss.

He couldn't say that he hadn't enjoyed Kurt's voyeurism a time or two. Although Katrin had the pussy of a Vagina Dentata—teeth inside to emasculate even the strongest of men—he'd enjoyed being with her and Kurt at the same time.

Each to their own, he supposed ruefully.

Absentmindedly wondering if Sascha would ever be up for something like that, he rubbed his chin as she answered, "Sawyer said he'd come."

"No, I'll come," Devon directed. "He has too much to do tomorrow."

Andrei cocked a brow. "You protecting him?"

"He protects me," Devon said simply.

"Who's protecting who from what?"

"Sawyer's like you. He hates the doctor," Andrei told her, his tone quiet. "Devon doesn't mind; therefore, he's saving Sawyer's butt. Ain't love sweet."

"Don't mock," Sascha retorted, reaching over to kiss Devon.

It was always the quiet ones, Andrei thought drily, when two minutes later, Sascha moved back from Devon's kiss after being tongue-fucked over the breakfast plate.

She staggered back against the cupboard and pressed a hand to her chest.

"Dear God, I'll die before tomorrow."

Devon, of course, didn't look in anyway disturbed by the kiss, but her comment had him sitting up straight. "Do you feel ill?"

That, in turn, had Sascha straightening up. "No. Why?"

Andrei rolled his eyes. "He thinks you were being serious about dying."

She blinked. "Oh, sweetie, no. I just meant I'm so horny I could freakin' burst."

Devon let out a relieved breath. "That's good to know," he said, sounding calmer now.

Andrei eyed him a second, amused as always by how Devon viewed the world.

Of them all, he was the one who had the least problems with women. As was usually the case, they viewed him like Sascha did… calling him 'sweetie' and 'honey'. Almost babying him. But Devon was no baby.

He just had a different way of seeing things.

As one of the two people in the house who could understand Devon's intelligence—the other being Sawyer—rather than just feeling awestruck by it, Andrei could understand Devon's thought processes better than most.

Everything had to have a rational explanation. Nothing *wasn't* founded in logic—double negative be damned.

That logic could tread so deeply into pure theoretical math that it might beggar belief, but it would be there. A thread of reason that few else would understand.

As a result, Devon was the most accepting of this little household of six they had going on. To him, it made perfect sense. So much so that if his parents were alive, he'd be the only one who'd share the truth with them—even though he'd loathed his father before the bastard had died. Devon saw no reason to kowtow to others' sensibilities, and though he often groaned at the man's lack of filter, Andrei was envious of that freedom too.

Everything was so straightforward for Devon. No dithering, no wobbling. Just a straight yes or no.

Andrei was actually surprised Devon had been able to hide the truth from Henry, Sascha's dad. As he saw nothing wrong with their situation, no reason to be ashamed, it therefore computed that there was no reason to hide it from anyone

Andrei realized that for Devon not to have broken Sascha's request that they keep things on the downlow, he was head over heels in love with her.

Which was an interesting concept because, as far as Andrei was aware, he'd never been in love before. They'd all fallen for Janna, but

Devon had been the one who hadn't, and he'd been the least affected by her betrayal.

Not that any of them had realized that until recently, however. They'd treated Devon with kid gloves, worried about him and scared to mention Janna's name… That weird brain of his had pretty much deleted the 'Janna file', however. Leaving the rest of them still smarting over the bitch's betrayal, while he'd been unaffected.

Well, that was before Sascha had come along.

Devon had been the same with even the others who'd shared their lives before. Andrei and the rest had found themselves entangled, then hurting after they left for pastures new, while Devon was quite content to move on. Untouched, unhurt.

It would be easy to think the man a robot, but Andrei knew more than most that the incredible person beside him was flesh and blood.

The notion of Devon being in love made him vow to watch out for his friend. The feelings had to be confusing for someone who'd never known them before. And Devon's reaction to Sascha's unintended declaration that she was about to die, spoke louder than words.

Andrei's supposition that he was head over heels was right on the nose.

"Andrei?" Sascha murmured.

He blinked. "Sorry. Miles away," he murmured when he saw both Devon and Sascha were staring at him in concern.

"Are you okay?"

"Sure," he told her easily. "What were you saying?"

"I was asking what you wanted for breakfast."

"Oh. Did you make some fruit salad this morning?"

She snorted. "When don't I? Devon's a fruit monster. I don't know where he puts it."

"Can I help that it tastes nice?" came Devon's bewildered retort.

Andrei chuckled. "Lies. It's the only sugar Sawyer will let you have, and we both know it."

Sascha tutted. "You've been sleeping better, haven't you, sweetheart?"

Devon blinked. "I sleep."

He had the worst case of insomnia Andrei had ever come across. And he'd been at Oxford. Where people often went without sleep to keep up with their studies. A backward-coming-forward kind of mentality. Without sleep, one couldn't focus. But people had a tendency of panicking under pressure. Devon never did.

He usually did his best work when he hadn't slept in two weeks.

"When was the last time?" Andrei asked, both curious and concerned.

"The last time I slept with Sascha."

The knife in her hand clattered against the board as she dropped it. Aghast, she whispered, "That was ten days ago."

"I know," Devon murmured, sounding quite pleased by how much sleep he'd gotten. "It's been very useful actually. I'm close to cracking that code MI6 sent me." He rubbed his hands together. "It's a very good game."

It was a testimony to how much Devon trusted Sascha that he said as much in front of her.

Sascha, on the other hand, didn't look as relieved by Devon's words. She stepped around the counter and leaned against Devon as she reached up to cup his cheek with her good hand.

"Sweetheart, I thought you were sleeping."

"I am."

Andrei cleared his throat. "How many hours did you get that night, bud?"

"Eight."

Andrei whistled. "That's a lot for him, Sascha."

"A lot?" Sascha squeaked. "I get eight every night. Not every ten days!" She closed her eyes in exasperation, then blew out a breath. "How about we have a nap together this afternoon, huh?"

Devon mumbled, "But I'm not tired."

"No? Well, it will make me feel better if we get some rest."

Devon shot Andrei a confused look, but he just elbowed Devon in the side and said, "I wouldn't complain. Sean's been hogging her ever since he almost kissed her in front of Henry."

"True. But I'm okay, Sascha. I promise."

She swallowed, and Andrei saw how emotional she was at that moment. Her concern was palpable, and Andrei loved her for that. The thought was freeing. This woman loved them in different ways, ways that embraced them in their uniqueness.

To see her caring for Devon though was like a key being turned in a lock.

Sascha carefully cupped Devon's cheek and murmured, "I know you're okay, but you have to get more rest. For me? Promise?"

Though he looked perplexed, he nodded.

She let out a relieved sigh, but Andrei interrupted, "It might not be so easy, Sascha." He grimaced. "It's not as easy as him just getting into bed and sleeping."

"When I get my doctor's note tomorrow, we'll figure out a way, hmm?" she said, staring into Devon's eyes.

His nostrils flared. "That sounds like something I could handle."

She giggled, and Andrei had to hide a grin. "Glad to hear it."

Andrei knocked him in the side with his elbow. "Lucky bastard."

"There's more than enough of me to go around," she said sagely, laughing harder as she skipped around the counter when Andrei made to grab her. "Not in the kitchen, remember?" she chided, but her eyes were dancing. Hell, they looked on the verge of doing the damn salsa.

He let out a growl, then settled back in his seat. Devon watched on like he was Yoda or something, overseeing the events of the crazy people.

When she turned her back on them both to head for the fridge, she asked Devon, "Where's Sawyer?"

"In bed still. We were working late last night."

"I thought you were. I told Sean you were still up at six."

"And how did you know that?" Andrei asked her.

She shrugged. "My arm was itching."

"Your arm was itching?"

Sascha snorted at his bewilderment. "Have you never broken anything before?"

Andrei shook his head, Devon too. Then, he remembered. "A finger, maybe. My nose definitely."

"Ah, well, you don't need casts for them. After a while, they itch like crazy and nothing helps."

"How are you finding sleeping with Sean?" he asked out of curiosity.

"He's a bed hog."

"Janna always used to complain about that," Devon said, and Andrei wanted the floor to open up and swallow them both.

"Jesus, Devon. Really?"

Devon shot him a perplexed look. "What?"

Sascha's lips twitched. "It's okay."

"No," he corrected. "It's not." To Devon, he growled, "It's bad etiquette to talk about an ex with your girlfriend."

"Sascha's not our girlfriend though," Devon pointed out with a logic of his own that Andrei understood, but knew Sascha wouldn't.

He shot her a look, saw the stunned shock on her face before she turned back to the bowl of fruit in her hand and began dishing it out onto a plate for him.

While her back was turned, he knocked Devon with his knee, and jerked his chin at him.

"What?" Devon asked. "I love Sascha. I never loved Janna. Although, she was very good in bed." He pursed his lips. "Gave very good head if I recall. She did this thing with her tongue." He made a move with said appendage. "Remind me to tell you about it sometime, Sascha."

Andrei closed his eyes and wanted another sinkhole to suddenly appear before him.

"God help us, you need a keeper," he bit off.

"I have one. He's called Sawyer."

Sascha turned around to stare at Devon. She narrowed her eyes at him. "You do realize that's like the first proper time you've said you love me? And that you said it at the same time as complimenting another woman's blowjob techniques?"

Devon shrugged. "Don't have to tell you to feel it."

Yet more illogical logic.

Sascha rolled her eyes. "I'd like to hear it from time to time."

"Why?" Dev asked. "Why do you need to know how I feel?"

She rolled her lips inward and Andrei, thanking God, realized she was hiding a smile. "Because I like to know how you feel. And, we're supposed to be honest with one another, aren't we?"

"True," Devon conceded. "I don't want to know if you love me, though."

She scowled at him. "Why the hell not?"

"Just because you say it, doesn't mean you feel it. I prefer you to show me."

She stared at him in confusion, but slowly admitted, "I guess that makes sense."

"My dad used to tell my mother he loved her as he beat the shit out of her. I don't trust the words 'I love you'," Dev said softly as he placed his knife and fork together on his emptied plate. "May I have some fruit, please?"

Sascha gulped. "Sure."

She passed Andrei his breakfast, then went about portioning out some for Devon.

As she placed the dish before him too, she took a seat opposite them, poured herself some coffee then took a sip.

"What constitutes showing you I love you?" she asked quietly.

He paused. "I don't really know. I'll think about it."

Her lips twitched. "Do that." To Andrei, she asked, "And you, Andrei? How do I go about showing you I love you?"

He cleared his throat. "Do you?"

She nodded. Slowly. Her eyes on his. "I do. I love you all. It feels like it's come out of nowhere, but I can't help it. Maybe it's fast, or maybe it's exactly right for us. I don't know."

"How does it make you feel? Insecure?"

She blinked. "No. Of course not."

"Does it make you feel happy?"

Her nod came quicker this time. "Sure, it does."

"Well, then. Doesn't matter how fast it is, how deeply we've fallen." Andrei shrugged. "It just matters that that's how we feel. It's what works for us, Sascha."

She smiled a little. "If you say so."

"I do. And I'm very grateful for the fact you feel so much for us. I know it's quick, and I know that might be difficult for you, because there are more of us…"

She reached over to grab his hand. She placed hers over his knuckles and squeezed. "No. You're easy to love. All of you. It's like you were made for me. The different parts of you fit the different parts of me."

He smiled. "I'm glad."

"Let me just clarify, we're not talking about dicks and pussies here, are we?"

Andrei dropped his head and groaned at Devon. "Devon. Would you fuck off upstairs and quit ruining our moments?"

"What?" he demanded. "'Different parts of you and different parts of me'? How is that not sex related?"

Sascha chuckled. "You're a nut, Devon."

He shook his head. "Three separate psychologists have classified me as sane."

Her mouth dropped open. "Do I even want to know?" she asked warily.

"Probably not," Andrei countered with a snort. Shaking his head, he grumbled, "You know how to ruin the mood."

"I wouldn't worry about it. Sascha likes my irreverence. She'll forgive me," Devon murmured, his faith in her unshakeable.

Sascha groused, "Don't get used to it, Devon. For your worst verbal sins, there's always the threat of saliva in your soup."

It was his turn for his mouth to fall open. He eyed her, snapped his lips shut, then hugged his plate to him.

She winked at Andrei, and not for the first time, he marveled at how goddamn perfect she was.

TWENTY-NINE

"ANY INFORMATION ON ELIZABETH JACOBIE, SEAN?"

Sean took a second to answer as he saved a document on his computer. "Where's Sascha?"

"At the clinic with Devon."

"Getting the note?" Sean sheepishly rubbed his chin. "She suggested it actually. I think I made my point though."

Andrei snickered. "I'm surprised she went through with it."

"I'm surprised she took Devon!"

"True. She must be very horny," he teased, and Sean laughed.

"She isn't the only one. It wasn't easy a floor away. But sharing a damn bed every night?" He groaned like he was in pain.

"I feel for you," Andrei mocked. "Having those curves wrapped around you while you rest… you're an unfortunate man."

Sean grumbled, "I feel your sympathy all the way over here."

"Good. How about this? Recognize this?" Andrei flipped him the bird before he took a seat in his usual armchair. To his right, Kurt's laptop was on the floor, which meant he was working in here. "Where's Kurt?"

"Went for coffee. If you want some, call him."

Andrei nodded, got back on his feet and headed for the intercom. "Kurt? Can you bring me up a mug of coffee too?"

"What am I? A barista?" came the complaint a second later.

"No. Sascha does a better job of it than you. She fills out a skirt nicer."

Kurt huffed. "Fuck off."

"I'm fucking off to my armchair."

Sean shook his head at him. "Ever heard of the phrase, 'you catch more bees with honey than vinegar.'"

"You know you love my acerbic wit," Andrei retorted, completely secure in his place in the world. "Wait until Kurt gets back if you have news on Elizabeth Jacobie."

Sean nodded, but said, "I don't have much."

"Something is better than nothing. Which is what we had before."

"True. It would help if Sascha spoke to her father about her past. But she won't."

"You can't blame her," Andrei countered. "Would you want that particular conversation with your father?" He paused. "Actually, yes. I'd like to know that the bastard and I didn't share DNA."

Sean wrinkled his nose. "You're different. Devon too."

"I think Sawyer's the only one who really gets on with his parents."

Sean sighed. "Probably. At least mine are vaguely normal. I can deal with their being homophobes as long as they leave me alone."

"As long as who leaves who alone?" Kurt asked, coming into the room with a tray in his hands.

"All you need is an apron and you'd make a perfect waiter, Kurt," Andrei remarked drily.

"Do you want hot coffee tossed over you? It can be arranged."

"Someone's been taking advice from Sascha. She's rather a fan of guerrilla warfare, isn't she?"

Kurt just grunted but didn't deny it. The amused sparkle in his eye told Andrei exactly what Kurt thought of Sascha's antics... "So, who do we want to leave us alone?"

"Our parents. Well, my grandfather." Andrei rubbed his chin. He guessed he really should go sooner rather than later to Moscow.

He loved the old bastard to death, but at eighty-nine, only God knew how long Vasily had left on this earth.

A notion that had his chest pinching a little.

"I like my mother when she isn't interfering. Father is... well, mostly in a world of his own. I barely know him. I can't complain though. I'd prefer an overprotective mother hen and disinterested father to what you and Devon had to put up with," Kurt said simply, pouring out three mugs of coffee, which he handed out to Andrei and Sean before he took a seat with his own mug in hand.

Andrei sighed. "He told her yesterday about what happened, you know?"

Kurt swore under his breath as he spilled coffee on his lap.

"You deserved that for threatening me with it," Andrei teased, but Kurt ignored him.

"Devon told Sascha about his father?"

Andrei stared into the pool of black liquid as though it had all the answers. "Some of what happened. Told her he loved her too."

Sean cleared his throat. "Is anyone else stunned shitless that he did all that without Sawyer being there? I'll assume he wasn't?"

"No. It was just the three of us. He said that he didn't want her to tell him she loved him. Said he didn't believe in the words because his father would tell his mother that as he beat her."

Sean let out a hiss. "Anybody else glad that bastard's dead?"

Andrei nodded grimly. Devon was decidedly odd, but he was odder still because of his past.

Andrei too.

They were products of their environment. They'd become more than their pasts, granted. Their intelligence taking them onto a whole other sphere, but when it boiled down to it, they were who they were because of what they'd seen.

Devon's mother had killed herself rather than endure her husband's wrath anymore. Andrei's mother had been murdered before his eyes. Sean had viewed endless crime scenes. Kurt knew way too much about Stasi torture techniques. And Sawyer? Well, hell, he was the most normal of the lot of them.

"It's a wonder we aren't more fucked up than we are." Andrei's sigh was bone deep.

Kurt snorted. "We'll be the judges of that."

"Ha. Ha," he mocked, but he hid a smirk. "Anyway, less of that. Elizabeth Jacobie."

Sean nodded, apparently comfortable with the change in topic. "Well, aside from the fact she's Jacobie's mother, that's all we have on her officially. She doesn't have a record, and there are no ties between her and Sascha. When I said we have less than nothing, I meant it."

"So why did Vasily say she paid the driver to mow Sascha down?" Andrei questioned, doubt in his voice. "He wouldn't be wrong about that. You know how Vasily works. People don't lie to him when he wants answers."

Sean held up a hand. "I don't want to know."

Andrei grunted. Neither did he, truth be told. "Be grateful he's on our side not against us."

"I am. Every damn day."

Kurt broke in and asked, "Every time we've mentioned the Jacobies, Sascha has never seemed like she knows them. Intimately, I mean."

"That's because she doesn't. Jacobie's famous. Why wouldn't she know *his* name? But they don't run in the same circles, do they? I'll assume she's never worked for him?" Andrei asked, directing the question at Sean.

He shook his head. "I thought of that. But no, she's worked for three families since her move to the UK. A diplomat's family who was transferred to the Middle East—we know them, Andrew Kent and his brats, plus that psycho he calls a wife. Remember how she used to stalk Devon at Oxford?" When they just grimaced, remembering the small entourage Devon had back in college, Sean carried on, "Then there's a Marchioness, and the other, a businesswoman in Mayfair."

"Could the Jacobies have crossed paths with the Marchioness? They're both families of the nobility, after all."

Kurt thought about that a second. "Maybe, but that doesn't mean she'd cross paths with Edward's mother, for God's sake. Sascha told me once that with her other employers, they pretty much wanted her not to be seen or heard."

"Yeah, I remember her saying how she was pleased we didn't want her to be über formal." Sean rapped his knuckles against his desk. "Vasily's intel has definitely raised more questions than it's answered."

Andrei grimaced. "She needs to talk to her father."

Sean nodded. "I know."

"We should discuss it with her."

Kurt took a sip of coffee. "No. You have to leave it to her to decide."

"She's in danger, Kurt," Andrei argued.

"You think I don't know that?"

"She has to get this dealt with before the shitstorm resurfaces. I'm not willing to lose her to some crazy bitch."

Kurt sat forward. "I know. But pushing Sascha won't do any good.

Surely you can see that? She'll only be pressed so far before she snaps. Do you really want that?"

Andrei shook his head. "Of course not, but at the same time…" He sighed. "Look, I know you want to tread carefully around her, Kurt. It's natural. We don't want to lose her. But there are times when she's going to push our buttons and we're going to push hers. It's life. We can't avoid those scenarios for fear she'll walk out."

"He's right, Kurt," Sean said softly.

"I know he is, dammit, but are you willing to lose her over this?"

"We'll lose her anyway if that nutcase gets her hands on Sascha," Andrei said grimly.

Kurt flinched, then pursed his lips. "There's an alternative."

"There is?" Andrei asked.

"We speak to Henry. Now. He's upstairs."

Andrei scowled at him. "In what world is that a better idea than Sascha talking to her father herself?"

"She obviously isn't going to do it," Kurt argued.

"How do you know?" Andrei demanded. "That isn't how we told her we'd work. We never said if she wasn't quick enough, we'd do shit behind her back." His scowl hardened. "Henry isn't going anywhere for at least five more days. Give her the time, and show her the fucking respect to let her handle this shit herself."

Silence fell at his words, and Andrei was surprised at the vehemence within them too. He caught Sean's glance, saw the other man was eying him like he was a different person, and hell, maybe he was.

Maybe she'd made him different.

Better.

"You're the one who normally pushes for action," Sean said softly.

And that was true. Andrei was a product of his past, of the environment in which he'd been raised.

Things happened quickly in the mafia. It was part and parcel of the territory. If they hung around, deals went awry or broke up, disintegrating like they'd never existed in the first place. If an informant wasn't handled immediately, then the repercussions could be dire. For the informant, and the man's family.

Sex was on tap. Drugs too, if that was a man's poison of choice. If not, vodka and caviar were on hand. It was a 'live hard and die fast' culture. One he'd had no choice but to absorb as he'd been raised around that lifestyle. His grandmother had been a more grounding influence. She wasn't suited to the life of being a Pakhan's wife, and tended to live out of the city, about half an hour away.

Andrei had lived with her unless his grandfather had sent for him, which he'd done often. Especially when he'd realized Andrei's intelligence. The brains that had bypassed Vasily's son, had been given in double doses to his grandchild. When he'd known that, Andrei had visited more and more often. Not so Vasily could integrate him into the Bratva lifestyle but, Andrei knew, because Vasily enjoyed dealing with an equal. A bizarre concept but even at eleven, Andrei had beaten his grandfather at chess.

A miracle in itself.

Vasily, though untested, had the chess smarts of a Grandmaster.

He ran his hands through his hair, and murmured, "She deserves us to be at our best. For us to be on our A game. Not running around behind her back."

"Even if it's for her own good?" Kurt asked, somewhat askance.

"Even then. I'd prefer to tell her we were considering going behind her back first, then letting that be the trigger. I don't want to fuck this up, guys. And she's by no means a sure deal. I fucking love her. If she leaves…"

"You don't think I feel the same?" Sean spat, for the first time losing his cool as he sat forward in his seat, tension throbbing through him. "You think she hasn't tossed my world on its head and made me question every fucking thing I know about myself?" He gritted his jaw. "I thought I was falling for the others, but I didn't realize until her that I've never known what it is to feel this way before.

"The shitty fact is, she's in danger. This fucking woman, who seems to be a stranger, has put some kind of goddamn hit out on her. I'd prefer to lose her than for her to die because we didn't act."

Kurt's voice was soft. "We need to talk to her."

Andrei cut him a look. "Kurt's right. We need to get this out in the open."

Sean nodded, a little less tense now they'd both bared their feelings for her. "I agree."

"So do I."

The voice had their heads nearly spinning on their necks.

Seeing Henry in the doorway, as one, they grimaced.

Sean cleared his throat. "Henry. I thought you were upstairs."

"I was until I heard you rowing." He shrugged. "It's in my nature to investigate." He sent them each a look, his shrewd eyes narrowing as he took them all in at a glance. "I knew something funny was going on the day I arrived here. Did you know I'd actually reserved a hotel room? I never expected Sascha's bosses to put me up. But who was I to argue when she presumed I'd be staying with you? More time with her, I figured. As well as thinking you were obviously generous in nature."

Andrei shot him a tight smile. "We want her to be happy."

"Yeah. I saw that too. Thought it was good of you. That you were great bosses, didn't want to lose her and appreciated her enough to go the extra mile. But it's more than that, isn't it?"

Kurt cleared his throat. "Sascha's happiness is very important to us, Henry. We're concerned for her."

"I heard. I just can't figure out why." He tilted his head to the side as he stepped into the room. "Someone care to explain it to me?"

Sean shook his head. "It isn't our place."

"No? Well, if my daughter figured it was important enough then she should have told me herself, shouldn't she? And anything that concerns her safety is imperative to me. So, tell me what's going on, and we can pretend this conversation never happened."

Andrei's jaw flexed. "I won't go behind her back."

"You're not. I overheard, loud and clear." He crossed his arms over his chest—the man wasn't going anywhere. "That you aren't willing to address the issue without her consent, I appreciate. But I'm her father, and I want to know what it is you have going on here. With Sascha in particular. What is she to you?"

And how do we answer that? Andrei thought, an uncomfortable clenching in his chest making him sit upright.

Kurt, however, seemed to have it all in hand, because quite accurately, and very succinctly, he murmured, "She's everything."

THIRTY

"YOU KNOW I want to climb you like a staircase, right?"

Sawyer snorted as he pulled out of the doctor's clinic, but Devon beat him to it with, "That's literally impossible, Sascha. You really should try to be more accurate."

"I'll eat a dictionary," she retorted. "Later. Now, I need one of you, or both of you, to screw me senseless."

Tension filled the car, and she saw them flash each other a glance in the rear-view mirror.

"What?" she demanded, confused when they didn't say anything, just looked at one another.

"Nothing," Sawyer said, his brogue suddenly very thick and noticeable.

She shuffled in her seat, knowing she'd have more luck with Devon. He couldn't be discreet if he tried.

"Devon?"

He kept his gaze trained on his knees. "Yes?"

"What's going on?"

"Going on with what?"

She huffed. "Okay. That's it. Stop the car."

Sawyer's head whipped around to face her. "What?"

"Stop the car!"

He scowled at her but pulled into the nearest loading bay. The instant he set the brake, his hand whipped out to lock the doors.

She scowled at him. "What? Did you think I was going to leap out or something?"

"I don't know. I was making sure. This isn't exactly the best area." He eyed the streets with a scowl, then turned to her. "Why did you want me to pull over?"

"Because you're being weird. Weirder than usual," she corrected, jerking her thumb in Devon's direction. "What did I say? You were laughing before I mentioned wanting to screw you both."

He cleared his throat, and simultaneously, Devon shuffled in the backseat.

"There you go again, dammit. What's up with the fidgeting and throat clearing?" She narrowed her eyes at him. "We're supposed to be honest with each other. That's like the rule, isn't it?" When all else failed, she knew if she fell back on that, it would make them cave in.

"There's honest and there's honest, Sascha," Sawyer said gruffly.

"Well, I want very honest."

Silence fell, then Devon began to speak but Sawyer shot him a quelling look. "Shut up, Devon. If anyone's going to explain this, it's me. The last thing we need is your tongue out on the loose."

"No, he's going in the right direction," she retorted. "Devon? What's going on?"

"We haven't done that. In a long time. That's all."

She blinked in confusion. "Done what?"

He scowled. "Fucked someone together."

Blinking harder, she felt her cheeks heat. "Oh."

Sawyer glanced at her. "Oh?"

It was her turn to clear her throat. "I didn't mean it like that."

Sawyer groaned. "Are you kidding me?"

She couldn't help but giggle at his pained groan. "Nope, I'm not. But that's very good to know." She cut Devon a glance, saw he was equally as confused, then asked, "So, it's something you haven't done for a long time, but you're amenable to the idea?"

Sawyer shrugged. "Up to you. Now, can we get out of this area before someone steals Sean's hubcaps?"

She peered around. "It doesn't look that bad to me."

"Trust the native, Yankee," he retorted.

"I'm not a Yankee. If anything, I'm from the South. Don't you know your geography?" she teased.

He wafted a hand. "You're all gun-toting nutcases."

"But you're cute with it, Sascha," Devon pointed out kindly.

"Gee, thanks," she replied, amused by them both. "And yes, you can get us out of this rotten neighborhood, although I think you're being a snob. Not everyone can live in Kensington, you know?"

"I was raised on one of the roughest council estates in Glasgow, Sascha. Trust me, I know what's rotten and what isn't."

She knew council estates were the British equivalent of 'Section A' housing. They were kind of grim over here. All pre-fabricated buildings that stemmed from post-war utilitarianism.

Well, that was the estates and not the tower blocks. A few of which had been in the news thanks to arson attacks and fires starting that engulfed the buildings.

"So, back on topic, would you?"

"Would we what?"

"Don't make out like you don't know what I'm talking about," she said crossly.

Devon murmured, "I would. Sawyer's the squeamish one."

"Just because I didn't appreciate having your balls in my face doesn't make me squeamish," Sawyer retorted, making Sascha burst out laughing.

"I really shouldn't want the details, but I totally do."

Sawyer grumbled. "I don't want to talk about it."

"If that's what you're into, Sascha," Devon said, ever helpful, "Kurt or Andrei would probably be very accommodating."

"What about you?" she asked, peering over into the backseat to spear him with a glance.

He grinned. "I'm game. Sawyer's very sensitive about his balls."

The man in question growled. "What man isn't? And it wasn't my balls that were hanging low for all to see. I love you like a brother, know more about you than anyone bloody else, but that's something I don't need to know about you."

Sascha grinned. "You're cute when you're riled up."

He growled again. "You're purposely pissing me off, and I was going to take you somewhere nice..." His lips pursed in a very masculine pout. "Might not bother now."

She cocked a brow. "Where were you thinking?"

"Harrods."

Her eyes widened in interest. "What for?"

"Those sweets you like," he said gruffly. "Don't know if I'll bother now."

Her eyes sparkled at his grouchy tone—her Scot could be all bluster sometimes. "Don't be mean."

"Mean? You're the ones being mean to me!"

"I did tell you how much I love it when you go all Scottish on me, right?"

"I'm Scottish all the time," he said proudly. "One hundred percent and proud."

"He's very proud of being Scottish," Devon inserted wryly. Although, knowing him, he didn't mean it that way.

She bit back a smile. "I think I deserve sweets," she commented out of the blue, suddenly getting a craving for the fancy schmancy noisettes she'd discovered months ago.

"I deserve a lot of things. Suffered through that visit to the doctors for you, didn't I?" Sawyer remarked.

Devon leaned between the headrests and peered at them both. "You didn't have to come. I said I'd go with her."

"I'm not letting you drive her anywhere," Sawyer scoffed, raising his brows as he looked at Devon in his mirror. "I'd like you both back in one piece at the end of the day."

Sensing an argument was approaching, Sascha quickly repeated, "I deserve sweets after having to ask that snooty bitch of a doctor for a note to prove I can have sex again. What do you think, Devon? Don't you think I deserve them?"

"The woman wants sweets, Sawyer. So that's what we'll give her. Harrods, here we come," he declared, ignoring Sawyer's grunt.

As did she. She clapped her hands together, loving how they treated her, and ready and raring to enjoy her new favorite, atrociously expensive, in no way junk, junk food.

Sascha wasn't joking—if anyone deserved some carbs, it was her. After an uncomfortable conversation with the doctor, yet another round of blood tests *and* a pee sample, she'd been relieved as hell to make it out of the clinic with some fluids still inside her.

Not least because Sawyer had looked like he was on the brink of puking every time they'd stuck her with a needle. God love him.

Hell, God love them all!

She knew *she* did. How couldn't she? When they treated her like a damn queen.

Her other relationships hadn't been particularly healthy. Both of her exes had tried to control her through her self-esteem issues and had used her naivete to do so. They'd watched her food, commented on whatever she ate, making her look like a fatso if she ever had anything that wasn't green or fat free…

But her men? They loved her curves, her ripe generous form. They encouraged it. Andrei had taken her to that bakery after her last appointment at the doctor's. And now Harrods for sweets? Talk about being indulged.

As ever, warmth filled her at their generosity. It went more than just with their money, because hell, sweets from Harrods cost a fortune. But with themselves, they were open and giving, warm and kind.

How could she not love them? Love everything they gave her?

The answer was, it was impossible not to.

ANDREI FOUND them in a lingerie department.

The hallowed halls were rife with people. Japanese tourists were taking selfies, sneaking them here and there as they darted about the store. Women, with the ubiquitous green and gold-logoed bags, strode on extremely high heels as they headed from the upper shopping store to the food market.

Sawyer had given him a head's up when he'd texted after their location—intending to meet up with them.

Having divulged the reality of Sascha's situation, not only with the five of them but the accident that was no accident, to Henry, he was feeling surprisingly shaken up.

It was probably to his detriment that she managed to rattle him the way she did. But the truth was, talking about Elizabeth Jacobie, hearing the truth of her past from her father's life? It had scared him.

She was in danger.

Even here, in one of the city's most indulgent tourist hotspots, who knew what Elizabeth Jacobie was capable of? She'd already hired someone to mow down Sascha and a bunch of innocent bystanders. Why not here? Why not target Sascha in this place too?

Sawyer had told him he'd intended to treat her by stopping by the luxury department store, and it was ridiculous to feel like his presence could do anything to keep her safe. Sean had been with her that day on Regent's Street, and he hadn't been able to keep her in one piece. Why should three of them do the trick?

Still, when he saw them, the unease and distress that had been knotted tightly in his chest unraveled as he saw her chuckling at something Devon said when she held up a teddy against her form.

"Please tell me you're buying ten of those in all our favorite colors?"

"Andrei!" Sascha cried, grinning at the sight of him. She dropped the teddy uncaringly, flinging herself into his arms like she hadn't seen him for days.

The uncomplicated affection was almost more than he could stand. He loved how she gave so much to him; it opened up the closed spaces he'd locked away for his own protection. Even more than that, she didn't make him fear the repercussions of having those spaces freed after so many years of being shut away.

"What are you doing here?" she demanded with a wide grin as she pressed a kiss to his lips.

He shrugged. "The promise of your lips and some sweets. How could I resist?"

Sawyer shot him a look that told him he knew something was going on, and that he'd expect to be told about it shortly. Devon, as ever, was oblivious and yet, mindful. The two contradictions only made sense where he was concerned.

He undoubtedly knew that Andrei's presence meant something, but at the same time, deemed it beyond his attention when Sascha was dashing between them with lacy bits of nothing in her hands.

"I told them I have enough lingerie," she was telling him, a reprimand to her tone.

"Can a woman have too much lingerie?"

"That's what I said," Sawyer retorted.

"You got me here on the pretense of sweets," she chided.

"The sweets were for you. This is for us," he said, no small amount of satisfaction edging his tone.

She chuckled, then reached up to pat his chin.

Surrounded by the three of them, she looked petite.

In her own way, she was statuesque. Ripe and curvy, and tall for a woman at around five-eight, with her limbs toned but round.

Between them however, she was tiny.

Sawyer and Devon were nearer six-five than six feet, and he wasn't exactly small at six-two. Plus, they were built. Even Devon worked out when his insomnia grew too bad or math fucked with his brain so that he couldn't reason his way out of the hole he found himself in.

It was almost amusing to note that they looked like her bodyguards. If only they could protect her as well.

"Have you gone for sweets yet?" Andrei asked.

She snorted. "As if. They hustled me up here before I even had a chance to pout."

Sawyer folded his arms across his chest. "The only way you'll get any man shopping is if you come into this department."

"Or the shoe department," Devon inserted, his fingers flipping through garters. He shot her a quick grin. "You look more fuckable than usual in heels, Sascha. I miss you not cleaning up in them actually."

Her smile turned naughty as she tapped the cast still protecting her wrist. "When this bad boy's off, normal service will be resumed." She turned to him. "Speaking of, Andrei. I've been assured that if I want you and…" She licked her lips. "*Someone* else to entertain me, you'll accommodate me."

Andrei froze, and then shot Sawyer a look, well aware that Devon would be little to no help. "Excuse me?"

She pressed herself against him, and he was almost ashamed to feel his cock twitch as her scent filled his senses, pervading the air he breathed.

"I think you know what I'm talking about."

He gulped in astonishment. "You'd want that?" Fuck, how did she perfect perfection?

"I didn't think I would," she confessed, "but when they mentioned it by accident, I was intrigued."

"How do you mention something like that by accident?" he demanded hoarsely, his gaze darting between his friends.

"A misunderstanding," Sawyer confessed gruffly. "Now she won't stop talking about it."

Andrei had to hide a laugh. Sawyer still hadn't gotten over fucking a woman at the same time as Devon and getting Devon's balls slapped in his face.

He raised a hand and with a finger, trailed it along the edge of her jaw. "Yes."

She blinked. "Yes, what?"

"If that's what you want, I'm game."

A sigh escaped her, and it was breathy and excited and aroused and, of course, perfect.

"Really?"

He nodded, his lips twitching. "Have you ever had anal sex?"

Her eyes widened. "A long time ago."

"We'll stop off and buy some lube," he promised. "Did you like it?"

She nodded. "Oh God, is this really happening?"

"It can if you want it, sweetheart."

Catching her teeth between her bottom lip, the tips of her fingers curled into his chest, scratching him through his shirt as she whispered, "I do. I really do."

He pressed a kiss to her forehead. "Then that's what will happen." To Devon, he asked, "You game?"

Devon smirked. "What do you think?"

Andrei pulled back. "You got the doctor's note, right?"

"Yeah, and she thought it was damn strange when I not only turned up with two different men at my side but had to ask for a note from her to say normal activities could be resumed." She rolled her eyes. "Sean owes me. Big time."

"To be fair, we all needed to know that you're healthier enough for that side of things, Sascha. You should have been honest with us before and told us you weren't ready," Sawyer murmured, ever fair.

She pouted. "I was ready. At the time."

He rolled his eyes. "And that really reassures me. How can we look after you if you don't look after yourself?"

Andrei hadn't touched her since before the accident, but the others had. He knew they were all mad at themselves for having taken her when they'd learned from the doctor she shouldn't have been doing anything more strenuous than lifting a coffee cup.

He understood their self-loathing. When a woman gave the green light, it was difficult to think that she'd sabotage herself in the long run.

Which she totally had, which meant she couldn't be trusted.

He reached up to thumb her bottom lip, tugging it down and away from her teeth. "You need a keeper, baby girl."

She smiled at him, then let out another breathy sigh. "Are you willing to apply for the job?"

His grin was slow in coming but burned hotly nonetheless. "There are five positions on offer, and I took one when you first hired on with us."

She bobbed up onto tiptoe then murmured, "That's what I like to hear."

Grabbing his hand, then Sawyer's, she tugged them both. "Devon, stop fingering the lingerie. You've better things to finger later," she said, sotto voce, but the delight in her tone had Andrei hiding a grin. "We need to buy sweets."

Andrei chuckled. How had she done this? He'd come with a heavy, fear-filled heart. Now, he felt lighter, more at ease. *Happy*.

She screwed with his mind, he realized. But then, wasn't that what happiness was?

After the bleakness of before, the exuberance of her joy was like a beacon of light. He had no choice but to answer the call and to follow the light to her.

"You heard the lady, guys," he said with a wry chuckle.

And so, sweets they went to buy.

THIRTY-ONE

"YOU'RE HAPPY HERE."

Sascha spun around in surprise at her father's voice. The guys had, rather disappointingly, dispersed to their various corners of the house when they'd arrived back from Harrods. Andrei had taken a call, and Devon had suffered an epiphany that required Sawyer's help too.

Which meant all that talk of anal had been exactly that.

Talk.

Still, there was no time for pouting, or even thinking of sex. Not when her father was in the vicinity.

"Hey! You mean, England?"

He shook his head, then after taking a step toward the breakfast counter, he hesitated. "Well, England too. But I actually meant here. With Sean, Devon, Sawyer, Kurt, and Andrei." He grimaced. "The *five* dwarves."

"Oh." A frown flashed over her brow. "Yeah. I am. Why?"

He shrugged. "Nothing. I'm just happy to see it, that's all. I never really got your job, Sascha. Didn't always make a lot of sense to me—why you'd want to be a housewife for a bunch of people you weren't related to." He shrugged. "Still don't get it, if I'm being honest, but I can see it makes you happy, and that's what matters."

She'd been seeing a different side to her dad since he'd come to the UK. Whether time and distance or the divorce were behind those changes, she wasn't sure. Sascha just knew that she liked this less arrogant side of her father.

He wasn't as bullish, which meant she didn't want to scream when she was around him.

"They make me happy," she said carefully, well aware that the phrasing she used was off. But it was the truth. She saw no reason to lie about that. It wasn't like she was blurting out their 'secret.' "They've all got their quirks, and they're a pleasure to look after."

Her dad eyed her askance, then asked, "You got any of that cake from yesterday leftover?"

She blinked. "Sure. Want some coffee too?"

"If some's going."

"It always is. Usually three kinds," she teased. "How the other half live, eh?"

He snorted. "Other half… thought I was going to have a heart attack when Kurt was talking about his ex that first night. Then Andrei saying the five million she had left was basically small fry." He shook his head. "Different world."

"You got that right." One that, by way of her relationship with them, she lived in now.

She reached for the china cake stand and lifted the glass dome off it. Using the cake slice she grabbed from the drawer, she portioned off a big piece, and placed it on a plate she'd readied a moment ago. With that in hand, she replaced the glass dome, grabbed a fork, and placed the dish in front of her father.

"What's this again?" he asked as he cut off a piece with his fork.

"It's a cake I found when I was travelling in Spain. It's called St. John's cake. It's all almonds and gorgeousness."

Her dad snorted. "Almonds and gorgeousness, huh? That a word?"

"It is in my vocabulary."

He grinned, watched her as she poured them both a mug of coffee, then asked, "Does he treat you right?"

Internally, she winced. "Sean? Yeah. He does." They all did.

"Good." He cleared his throat. "I wasn't too happy about you being with your boss. You know how I feel about that."

"I do," she replied, then shrugged. "But it's what I want, and I make my own decisions."

"I've been reading into his cases."

"You have?" she asked, brows high.

"Yeah. I know how to work a tablet, Sascha," he said with some disgust that had her chuckling.

"He's famous over here. Lots of nasty cases. He lost another victim the other day. It cut him up."

"I can imagine. I saw details in the paper." He cleared his throat. "Also saw details about you being knocked over. Then, I thought, that couldn't be, you know? My only daughter would have told me something like that. Right?" He lifted his fingers to his mouth and pinched his bottom lip. "I mean, why the hell would you keep something like that from me? I'm your goddamn father, Sascha. I have a right to know that you're okay."

Sascha froze with one mug in her hand. She closed her eyes, inwardly swore at the newspapers that had only covered the fact she'd been in a crash because she was working for Sean, then decided there was nothing to do but to confess.

Big time.

Fuck.

She'd been hoping to put this conversation off for a while. She knew the guys didn't want to. Knew they wanted answers. Answers that would explain why someone had been paid to mow her and a lot of innocent pedestrians down, but that meant confronting her father about a tale he'd never meant to share.

Considering how he preached about honesty above all else, that meant the story was a doozy. And, though it wasn't like her to bury her head in the sand, she just… Well, at the moment, it was more than she could handle.

Placing the mug in front of him, she returned for her own, then hiked up onto the stool opposite him.

Time to come clean. "Yeah. I was knocked over by a car."

He grunted, kept his head low, gazed trained on his dish. "Why didn't you tell me in the first place? I assume that's how you really broke your arm? Not in a fall like you told me."

She pursed her lips. "Yes. But you're not going to like what I have to say."

"Any world where my daughter gets hurt, I'm not going to like. Doesn't mean I don't want to hear it. Spill."

She eyed him, so gruff and braw. He was a handsome man, her dad. Still straight-backed, broad shouldered, lean-hipped. He ate what he wanted and didn't have a paunch because he went jogging every day.

His chestnut hair was still mostly chestnut, with salt and pepper sprinkled at his temples. He was heavily lined though. Years of scowling at the perps dragged into his precinct, she assumed.

His nose was strong, his jaw stubborn. His eyebrows arched so he looked perpetually pissed off.

As a kid, she'd thought he was always angry with her, until her mom had explained that he always looked like that. A teasing remark which had made her dad grunt over his breakfast until he'd sighed happily as her mom stroked her fingers over his creased brow.

She could remember that scene as easily as breathing. Sascha had been five, and she'd known she was loved and had known that her parents loved her. More than that, they'd loved one another.

Such security was precious. She saw that now. Especially when compared to Andrei, whose security hadn't been… Jesus, optimal wasn't the word.

"Stop gawking and get on with it, Sascha. I want to know what's going on."

She pursed her lips and then came clean, "Someone paid the driver to knock me down. It was only happenstance that it didn't work out that way. I saw a kid run into the road, and I got knocked over when I went to grab him. But later on, the driver went to the cops and told them he'd been paid to hurt me."

Her father's scowl deepened, and he pushed his plate away. "Ex-boyfriend?"

"No. We don't know who." She stared down at her mug and let both fingers of her good, and bad, hand curl around its warmth. Suddenly feeling very cold inside, she carried on, "Sean investigated, pulled some strings, but all he's been able to find out is that I was adopted at birth."

Silence fell at her words, a silence so deep it felt like a chasm had opened up between her and her father.

She peered over at him, saw the desolation on his face, and swallowed. *Hard.*

"Your mother never wanted you to know."

"It doesn't matter to me," she immediately said, her good hand snapping out, reaching for his. But he pulled away.

Pain lashed at her.

"She didn't want you to know for your own good," he said robotically. "Then, it never mattered, because you were ours."

"Of course, I was. I still am."

His jaw worked, and his green eyes blazed with fire. "He must have pulled a hell of a lot of strings to have found that out."

She shrugged, surprisingly at ease with his fury. "There was a lot going on. He was thorough."

"That's more than fucking thorough." His nostrils flared.

"Who are my birth parents?" she asked softly. A part of her wanted to know, but another part genuinely wasn't interested. He was her father, and Natasha had been the best mother a child could wish for. Sascha's only regret was that her mom wasn't around. Not to explain this, but because Sascha missed her. Dreadfully. Regret had her throat closing as she whispered, "Sean and the others seem to think they're the reason I've been targeted. That it's something to do with my past."

Henry went to shake his head, then he gritted his jaw. "Your birth parents were murdered, Sascha. When you were barely a few months old."

His words choked her. "Murdered?"

He nodded. Grimly. The coffee cup scraped against the marble counter as he fiddled with the handle. "I'm not going to lie. When your mom told me the real story, I thought she was nuts. It sounded like something out of an Agatha Christie novel. And she was scared. So scared that she wouldn't be able to keep you safe. In the end, that's pretty much why I believed her."

"Explain," Sascha urged softly.

He ran his finger around the rim of his cup. "Where to start?" he asked, more to himself than her she figured.

"At the beginning. Why was mom a citizen here?"

He cocked a brow. "That's the easy part. She was born near Moscow, but her family moved here when she was still a baby. England was her home."

"Why did she have an American accent?" she demanded.

"She faked it. Didn't want you to know about her past." A chuckle escaped him, and she sensed it surprised him. "You should have heard it at first. Sounded like something from *South Park*." He shook his head. "She got better over time."

"So, she was Russian by birth but an English citizen?" Sascha prompted, wanting to stay on track because she needed answers.

"Yeah. So, your birth father was this Lord or something. An Earl, I think. Well, Nat trained as a nurse here, and started working for this Earl. She liked him. Said the man played spectacular chess.

"He was really old though, and he pissed off his family by marrying his nursemaid who was about forty years his junior. That was why they hired your mom; he'd married one of his carers. Anyway, it caused a stink, but they humored him I think because they thought he wouldn't last that long and, if I remember rightly, Nat said the inheritance was indentured. It wasn't like her marrying him meant she'd get half his fortune. It's not like that over here with estates. At least, not as far as I'm aware."

She nodded. "I understand." She'd read way too much Jane Austen not to.

Indentured estates passed onto blood heirs. Not upstart women who married into the family.

"So, everything was okay until your birth mom announced she was pregnant. Your birth father fell sick, and she did too. By the sounds of it, she almost lost you a few times, but she managed to carry you to term. She died as a result of birthing complications though. Your mom said it was murder. That the complications happened 'for a reason.'" He tagged quote marks around that, using his fingers to get the point home.

Stunned into silence, Sascha just sat there and absorbed the story she'd never wanted to hear.

Pain? Was that what she was feeling?

She wasn't sure.

It felt like a very, very bad cramp. It started in her stomach and was taking over her torso until she wanted to curl up to stem the pain.

She didn't know the people who had birthed her, whose genetics made up her own, and yet, the emotional numbness that spread through her was like the same poison that had murdered those people who were her parents by blood.

Her dad cleared his throat. "Your birth father realized what was happening too late to save your mother but was in time to save you. He had your records wiped clean; I have no idea how. But obviously, he had money, so that helped.

"By this point, he suspected his other carer was having an affair with his daughter-in-law, and that they were working together to hurt them. Natasha said that after your birth mother died, he knew you wouldn't be safe. He liked her, and she said they'd connected a lot because he asked her to play chess with him.

"When things grew desperate and he knew he was dying, he arranged with Natasha to care for you, arranged residency for you both in the States, gave her money to come to America, and told her to never let you know who your family was."

She swallowed, trying desperately not to puke. "It would be useful, for Sean's investigation, if we knew my original surname." Her words were raspy as she continued, "If Natasha told you, that is."

"She did. You were baptized here. That should still be on public record at the church, I imagine… Lady Eloisa Jacobie." He shot her a pained look that held a curious hint of defiance considering his next words. "That's your real name, Sascha."

Her mouth trembled as she processed the tale he'd just spun. But that was the problem. It wasn't a tale. It was real. That was her past. Her history.

She got to her feet and did the only thing she could do at that moment.

Run.

LOVED BY THEM

THIRTY-TWO

THE KEYS WERE in her hand before she knew what was happening.

From the kitchen, there was silence. Her father wasn't shouting after her. Wasn't even calling her name. He'd dropped the bombshell of the century moments before, and was seemingly content for her to just run off.

It shouldn't have stung. It really shouldn't have, not when she was the one running away, but it did.

A frenzy was whipping and stirring in her head with the force of a twister. It was nothing to the migraines she'd been enduring since she'd been hit by a damn car, but she feared she'd reached her breaking point.

Sascha Dubois was made of strong stuff, but after learning the truth of her heritage, enough was enough.

Though she wanted to slam the door to the five-story Kensington villa, Sascha knew it would have the men who lived within its hallowed walls flocking to her.

Not only were those men her employers, they were more. They were her lovers.

She loved them, and as far as she could figure out, they loved her. Some had told her, others were watchful of their tongues. But love didn't have to be spoken to be felt. To be shown.

That thought was grounding, and that sensation brought with it relief because in the whole amount of crazy that was going down, they were there to keep her balanced.

The rest of her life might as well have been up in the air, but *they* weren't. They were solid.

Real.

Still, for all her strength, her hands and knees were shaking as she almost fell down the five steps that led to the front door.

Normally, the grand entrance, even after all these months of living here, had the power to stun her with its magnificence, but that was of no interest to her now as she staggered down the steps. Her Cadillac was her final destination.

It was a beacon of normalcy in this swanky zip code. A bright bolt of retro pizazz amid the exclusive sports cars and high-end sedans. It stuck out like a sore thumb, so when she looked at it, she couldn't fail to see the man standing beside it too.

Devon.

Her bright bolt of *mathematical* pizazz.

He was slouched against the car, resting his arms on the roof. They were folded there, and he'd pressed his chin to them to prop his head up as he watched her scurry towards him.

She came to an abrupt halt at the sight of him beside her vehicle. Of course, that had to be in the middle of the road, didn't it?

A car purred to a stop in front of her; the driver glaring at her then tooting his horn as she started in surprise, realizing the dumbass place she'd decided to put on the brakes was in the center of the goddamn street.

Apparently, she had a death wish where cars were concerned.

Mouthing sorry, she ducked in between the cars to hit the sidewalk, then carried on walking toward her Caddy.

A lack of parking was a major issue here. The residences had been constructed in a time where a two-car family wasn't exactly a 'thing'. That meant the streets had permits, and she had to park her beloved Baby outside and uncovered.

"What are you doing out here, Devon?" she asked somberly. It was probably the first time since she'd moved into their home that she wasn't excited to see one of the five best boyfriends a girl could ever have.

She didn't want to talk to any of them, and that was a testament to how addled her brain was. She wasn't sure what she wanted, but getting out of here was imperative.

"I'm here for you," he said simply, but nothing about Devon was simple.

He was a math genius. And even that was an understatement. A Nobel Prize winner, a code cracker for MI6, there was no ordinary title that fit this man, because he was anything but ordinary.

"I-I need to get out of here."

He nodded. "I understand."

She winced. "I doubt that."

"I heard." His grimace said it all. "I eavesdropped, I'm afraid. Sorry about that."

"That's unlike you to say sorry," she murmured absentmindedly. And it was the truth.

He rarely apologized. Not because he was a douche, but because he just... Well, *didn't*.

There was always a reason behind his actions, and that reason was always logical and rational. Which meant there was no need for him to apologize because his actions were well thought out and, therefore, reasonable.

Yeah, it could be hard being with a man like that. One who saw everything in such stark lines of black and white. Gray didn't exist for Devon. It wasn't even on the color spectrum for him.

"If I'd wanted privacy, then I guess we should have gone to another room," she justified on his behalf, and when he nodded, knew that was how he justified eavesdropping, too.

It was a good thing he was gorgeous, and sweet—it was the sweetness that got to her most—because otherwise, he'd be so goddamn irritating, she'd have wanted to slap his face all the time.

But gorgeous he was with his inky black hair and come-to-bed eyes. His strong form was usually covered in ratty jeans that showcased his taut ass to perfection, and old tees that were washed and better washed, but were soft, and clung to his stomach and arms.

She'd never known a man to wear the clothes of a beggar and somehow still look like a prince.

Shaking her head at the lofty thought, she murmured, "I need a time-out."

"I know where to go," he reasoned.

"I-I need to be alone, Devon."

He shook his head. "That's the last thing you need, Sascha darling."

Her eyes widened at the term of endearment. The others called her pet names, but Devon rarely did unless he was parroting them.

Sometimes, it was like living with a robot. The way he processed things, she could be forgiven for likening him to highly advanced AI, but every now and then, he reminded her he was flesh and blood. Usually in the bedroom. Her core clenched at the too few memories she had of him in that way.

A concussion had put a stop to her love life. Which was really fucking irritating when she had five sex Gods all ready and willing to *service* her at just a word.

She almost pouted, and then realized how ridiculous that was when her father's revelation was still being processed by her lagging reserves.

"Get in," she whispered as she unlocked Baby's doors, another car's presence on the side of the road prompting her to move or be run over. *Again*.

He climbed inside as she settled behind the wheel. With the door closed and her no longer moving, the chill of the day hit her, and she realized she hadn't worn a coat. But clothes had been the last thing on her mind when she'd stormed out of the house.

The interior of the car was as vintage as could be. Almost like stepping back into another era. But it was chilly and damp from the miserable day outside. And without anything covering her arms, she had no choice but to start the engine for some heat. Mere moments before, she'd wanted nothing more than to run away, but now? Here, with him, she just wanted to sit there with her head on the wheel and pretend the last hour had never happened.

Silence filled the cab when the heat came on at last. Both of them quiet, not exactly speechless, just hesitant to speak.

Sascha stared blindly ahead at the car in front of her. Rain spattered against her windshield and the vehicle in front's back window, making rivulets spout down the curvy backside of the canary yellow sports car.

Devon jerked her attention from the riveting display before her; "Sascha? Would you like me to drive?"

Her lips twitched, and it relieved her that she could feel amusement at a time when she was so overloaded with numbness, even tears were far away. "You just want to get your hands on Baby."

Pathetic, but she'd nicknamed the car years before when her father had given her the Cadillac in the vain hope she wouldn't wreck this one as she'd wrecked the others she'd driven after getting her license.

The vintage vehicle had indeed inspired caution in her driving. Getting even so little as a scratch would have infuriated her after she'd saved up for months to get a custom paint job to take the once-rickety vehicle back to its original colors.

"Well, I *would* like to drive it, but at the same time, I'm not sure we're going to get far if you keep staring at the wheel instead of steering it."

She sighed. "When aren't you rational, Devon?"

"Probably never. There's always a rational response to everything."

"There is? What about my situation?" she asked softly, deciding to do as she wanted—rest her forehead on the wheel. Rolling on her forehead so she could look at him rather than at nothing, she waited for his answer.

He shrugged. "It's a relief to know there's a reason for someone targeting you. It was chaos before, Sascha," he told her somewhat earnestly. "We knew you were in danger, but had no idea why. At least now, it makes sense. And where there's sense, there's comfort."

"There is?" she asked, a bitter laugh falling from her lips. "So why don't I feel comforted?"

"Because you're still processing. You've lived a lie, Sascha. But it was a kind lie," he argued. "I wish I'd led a kind lie rather than dealt with the bitter truth of reality."

She frowned. "You really mean that?"

He blinked, his surprise at her questioning him evident. "I really do."

"Why though? Everything I know, it's all… nothing was real."

He shook his head. "Of course, it was real. If anything, you've had more love showered on you as a result of the truth, Sascha. A man, dying, gave his everything to wipe out your identity to protect you. A woman, hired as an employee, gave *her* everything to take you from all she knew to another country.

"There, she married a man who was bound by the law to keep you safe. You were sheltered from the day you were born. Cosseted by love from a family you didn't know, and then embraced by a new one who chose to love you. Because, from everything you've told me about your mom, she loved you."

Sascha's bottom lip trembled as she nodded. "She did."

"She did nothing out of pity or avarice, did she?"

She closed her eyes to blank out the resolve in his face. There was no hiding from Devon. The truth was his haven, and when you were with him, you had no choice but to embrace it too.

"She loved me," Sascha confirmed, because he was right.

Whoever she'd been to Sascha upon her birth, Natasha had dedicated herself to her adopted child.

Never missing a school play, never failing to soothe a hurt, and never missing a single night to tuck her into bed. Only death had altered her dedication, and even Sascha in her weak state of mind couldn't fault her mom for that. Because there were only two labels that fit Natasha Dubois—wife to Henry, mother to Sascha.

"And your father…he took on that responsibility, Sascha," Devon continued, his voice inexorable. Were she in a different mood, she would have hated him for his calm deliberation, but in this, she knew he was making her realize that the truth didn't have to hurt so badly. "He loved your mother and you. Never letting your past come out and always protecting you."

"I wonder why he let me move to England," she whispered raggedly. "It must have been the last place he wanted me to go." Then, she admitted after sucking in a breath, "Not that I'd have let him change my mind. Even when I realized something weird was going on because my visa wasn't a requirement, I didn't care. I wanted to come here, so I came here. Never questioning, like a stupid bitch, just being grateful that I didn't have to worry about too much crazy admin."

"You weren't talking to him when you moved?"

She shook her head. "He didn't approve of my boyfriend. Thought he was flaky, and he was right. But that didn't matter at the time." She let out a shaky breath. "I was so mad at him, I didn't even ask about mom's past. About why I'd never known she had an English passport. Then, over the years, we spoke so little, and my life changed and became even busier that it didn't matter. I was just grateful not to have to worry about a visa to stay here."

Devon murmured, "You were myopic."

She flinched. "Ouch."

He shrugged. "Most young people are."

"I can't imagine you were short-sighted even when you were a bratty ten-year-old," she retorted, a little stung by the harshness of his opinion—not that it was delivered cruelly. Anything but. He'd spoken with his usual blandness. A lack of tone that somehow was all the more evocative for it.

"I had Sawyer from when I was fourteen. Then, I met the others at university. They saved me from short-sightedness. They were my protectors," he mused, a vague smile curling about his lips as he stared ahead, seeing a world she could only begin to imagine.

One where math ruled, not the heart.

Well, not until she'd come along and ruffled up their worlds.

"How did you meet Sawyer?" she asked softly, curious to know more from his point of view.

"You really want to talk about this now?" he asked, cocking a brow.

She nodded. "I don't want to think about what's happening."

He pursed his lips. "Let's go to that coffee shop you like. Rossi's?"

She shot him a surprised look. "Are you sure?"

"Wouldn't have said it if I wasn't."

"Devon, it's okay. We can stay here."

"I know we can. But we don't have to," came his calm response. By not a flicker of his expression did he reveal that this would be the second time in close to thirty days that he'd left the house.

This afternoon, they'd gone to the clinic for her to get the all clear, and after, to Harrods.

Two trips out after a month's reclusiveness was mind boggling to her.

Devon sighed, but the sound wasn't impatient. "What's wrong, Sascha? Why aren't we moving?"

"A-Aren't you feeling nervous?" she asked, gesturing to the house. "You hardly ever leave this place."

He shrugged. "So? It's by choice, not because I'm tied to my chair."

"I know that," she retorted with a huff. "I just mean… you don't have to do anything that makes you uneasy for my sake."

"If there was anyone I'd risk anything for, it's you, Sascha," he told her simply, seemingly unaware of the power he gave her with that one statement. Her heart fluttered in her chest as he continued, "I don't like people, so I stay at home. You, however, don't wish to stay at home, so we'll go somewhere you're comfortable."

She blinked dazedly at him, then admitted on a whisper, "Devon?" When his attention was aimed her way, she carried on, "I love you."

Had she not been studying him, she'd have failed to see the tiny response of his eyelids growing heavy as a result of her soft declaration.

"You know my feelings go beyond that. But," he said on a sigh, pressing a hand to her knee, "I love you too. Now, drive before the cavalry comes. When dinner isn't served, they'll all come out looking for you."

She bit her lip. "Maybe we should just stay here."

"No. You ran out for a reason. Let's stick with your original instinct. It's good to trust in them. You needed out, so out we'll go."

She gnawed at her bottom lip with her teeth, then nodded and set the car into gear.

The low purr of the engine soothed something inside her. When she was out on the road, the tightness in her chest eased. He was right. She did need to get away. Not from the men, per se. Not even from her father. But the house. It was her base here, and she needed a break from it. Just a breather.

Devon was silent as they drove into central London, darting here and there as she took a shortcut that would take her to her favorite café in the city.

It was close to five, and the streets were crammed with pedestrians heading for the underground. Roads heralded gleaming black taxis, which swerved to collect new fares, the vehicles' solid bodies more like a tank than a streamlined car. Businessmen and women in sharp suits and carrying expensive briefcases walked amongst beggars sleeping against doorways, and buskers singing out their souls for the price of a chocolate bar.

It was a sight that never failed to energize her, to revitalize her. But it was one she knew that Londoners failed to appreciate.

This was their life, after all.

Only an outsider could enjoy it and find pleasure in the frenetic energy zipping around the streets.

When they reached Rossi's, she found a space and parked. When she rounded the car to meet up with Devon, he reached for her hand as they checked out oncoming traffic, and together, darted to the other side.

Rossi's had a rush on. People seeking coffee and a small snack for the journey home after a long workday meant the line was crazy, but she headed into the seating area, where armchairs and low tables were a welcome respite for her.

She liked it here. Had found it on her first week in London all those years ago, and she'd watched it transform from what the Brits knew as a greasy spoon—purveyor of everything fried to the masses—to a smart and snazzy coffee shop that served the best waffles this side of the Atlantic.

Their hands tucked inside one another's, she dragged Devon deeper into the café. Her favorite table was in the corner, and it looked out onto the road.

When she reached it, she froze, coming to a halt at the sight before her. Her favorite spot seated three, at the most. But six armchairs had been dragged together, clustered around a table, with Sean, Andrei, Kurt, and Sawyer its occupant.

Looking smart and sexy, unruffled even as they dove into plates of triangle-cut sandwiches, there was a panini thrown in amid the mix here and there, and a dish of salad that was being ignored. They even had a whole Victoria sponge cake in the center, with a tray of tea amid the chaos.

Devon shot her a look as he pressed his hand to the base of her spine. The warmth acted as a shield against unnecessary hurts, which only strengthened as he told her, "You never have to be alone now, Sascha."

Though she'd wanted that when she'd left the house, solitude and a chance to catch her breath, seeing them here had tears burning her eyes. Devon raised their joined hands to his lips, and in a gesture that stunned her, pressed his mouth to her knuckles.

She tightened her fingers around his, and then whispered, "How did they know?"

"We said we'd meet here," he told her easily.

"You shepherded me here," she said, a little accusatorily.

His smile was, of course, unapologetic. "You needed us. You just didn't need to be at the house."

Before she could do more than bite her lip, Sawyer called out, "Lass, if you want some of this food, you'd best get here now before Kurt scoffs the lot."

She had to stop biting her bottom lip then, because a smile instantly appeared when Kurt bitched, "You've eaten twice as much as me."

Devon tugged her forward, ignoring the bickering as he bulldozed through it. "You're safe with us, Sascha."

She let out a shuddery breath, knowing that to be the complete and utter truth.

SAWYER EYED him as he carved out a piece of cake for himself. "You won't sleep if you eat that."

"I don't sleep anyway," he retorted, a child-like glee filling him at the sight of the huge slice of jam and cream sandwiched between two pillowy sponge cakes.

Sugar, Sawyer had decided years ago, was Devon's enemy. It was the reason he was rude and antisocial, why he had insomnia and... Well, the list went on.

Sugar was the root of all sins to the man he considered a brother, and because Sawyer had it hard enough keeping Devon on the straight and narrow, he usually ceded to the bland saccharine-sweetened crap Sawyer handed him.

Not today, though.

Sawyer grumbled at his reply, but Sascha's hand came to rest on his knee. She kneaded the muscles of his thigh. "We'll get you to sleep tonight."

That meant she'd sleep with him.

Triumph roared through him, and it startled Devon to realize that her gentle touch, her soft words, meant more to him than wading through his current workload.

The notion had his head jerking to the side in surprise. She noticed, of course, her gaze catching his, and her fingers tightening on his thigh.

He placed the plate on the table, and with his left hand, grabbed hers. When their fingers knit together, something inside him settled, and he forked up the cake, letting the first bite go to her rather than him.

Her lips curved in a soft smile as she opened her mouth, and he carefully placed the tines between her teeth. Most men wouldn't find feeding her to be as dangerous as strolling across a minefield, but most men didn't have Devon's attention span.

Watching her eat had uncomfortable things happening below his waist, but he was used to that in her presence. Even recently, though she'd stopped wearing her tight pencil skirts, Sascha in yoga pants packed the same punch as the porn stars in the flicks he and Sawyer had watched as horny teenagers. So he ignored his burgeoning erection as he focused on not scratching her with the fork.

Sean cleared his throat. "Devon."

He blinked. "Yes?"

"Control yourself."

Sawyer snorted. "Like that was ever going to work. Since when does telling him to behave get him to behave?"

"Control myself how?" Devon scowled. "I'm not a dog."

"Wish you were. Dogs are obedient."

Andrei chuckled, pointed at Devon's lap. "We're in the window seat, Dev. Kids are around. They don't need to see your hard on."

"My fly is zipped," he retorted, peering down at the admittedly large bulge as he stuck the fork upright in the cake. "It's not like they can see anything. Plus, they shouldn't be looking at my crotch if they don't want to see a penis."

Sascha coughed out a laugh and covered her mouth. "How do you do it?"

"How do I do what?" he asked, perplexed. His eyes bugged as a thought came to him. "Get an erection?" *Did she not know?* he thought, wildly.

She snickered then blew out a deep breath as she fingered a few crumbs on the plate in front of her. "No, silly. Make me laugh when I feel like the whole world is going to hell. Nothing is what it was before I met you guys. I'm not even Sascha anymore. I'm this Eloisa chick."

He blinked at her somber statement, then racked his brain. "Why's the world going to hell?" Had he missed something in the news? It wouldn't be the first time, nor would it be the last. Still, even when he missed important bulletins, life had a habit of carrying on around him. Wasn't like it needed his input for that to happen.

Sean sighed. "Devon, for God's sake. Get with the program. Someone's tried to hurt her."

"Not hurt," Andrei corrected grimly. "Kill her. She's entitled to be shaky."

Sawyer elbowed Andrei in the side. "Great going, arsehole."

Sascha shook her head. "He's right, Sawyer. There's no point in prettying it up. My life now belongs in a Martina Cole novel. It's official."

Kurt snorted. "That's Andrei's life."

Andrei frowned. "Who's Martina Cole?"

"She writes novels about gangland London."

The Russian growled. "I'm not in a gang."

"No. Your grandfather just runs one of the biggest Bratva organizations in Russia," Sawyer retorted, but his voice was low.

"That's him. Not me. And he's retired now."

Like that made it better.

Sascha bit her lip. "We really need to not mention that in front of my dad. You know, the cop?"

Sean stifled a grin. "Don't worry. We won't."

We.

That one word had him settling down inside. It always had. Probably always would.

When he'd heard Henry talking to Sascha, her father explaining the truth of her past, Devon had known, instinctively, that she'd run.

Strange how he'd known that when he rarely understood people. He just knew that he'd run when he'd found his mom lying in the bathroom, her wrists sliced from the base of her hand to her forearm—so there was no mistaking that her attempt wasn't a cry for help.

It had been no attempt at all.

He'd found her that way and had run. And run and run.

Why wouldn't Sascha?

Her mother had been murdered. Her father, too, and she'd been shuffled off to America by a member of the staff. And now, she was back in London, where her biological father's family had discovered her existence once more... A family who apparently wanted her dead.

"Do we think Edward knows anything about her?" Sean asked, out of the blue. Almost like his thoughts were on track with Devon's, which was an impossibility.

If anyone could keep up with Devon, it was Sawyer, and even he was usually a few steps behind.

Devon's brain was like the Victoria sponge cake. Layers within layers. Each one individually processing a subject that mattered.

The thickness of the layer represented how much attention he gave something.

Rather pleased at the analogy, he was determined to use it on Sascha when she tried to understand how his brain worked.

He wasn't sure why she wanted to know, but she asked him odd questions. Queries that told him she wanted to understand him, and because no one had ever wanted to do that before, he wanted to please her in return.

"I doubt it," Andrei said roughly. "At least, I hope not. Why would Edward know about Sascha?"

A few days after Sascha had been knocked over by a car, she and Andrei had been due to attend a gala where Andrei was the keynote speaker. Edward Jacobie, a recent client of Andrei's as well as the founder of a tech company that had taken over the globe, a man who was also Sascha's nephew now her ancestry was known, had been invited to introduce Andrei to the masses.

That gala had never happened thanks to a bomb blast. The capital was still reeling from the terrorist attack.

"How much time was there between you RSVP'ing the event with Sascha as your guest and her being targeted?"

Devon's words cut through the conversation like the knife had sliced through the cake.

Sean sighed. "He has a point."

"When doesn't he?" Kurt grumbled.

Andrei ran a hand through his hair, disheveling the white blonde locks he kept neatly cut close to his head. "I RSVP'd the night before the accident."

"Edward Jacobie's security teams would be in the know of all the changes to the guest list." Devon shrugged. "It's their job to know these things and to run security checks."

"But he's a billionaire, dammit. Why would he be interested in Sascha?"

"Because his mother's a murderer?" Kurt said dryly. "That's a nasty family secret. People have killed to cover up smaller secrets."

"Have you met Elizabeth Jacobie?" Devon asked Andrei, who shook his head.

"I've met Louisa, his sister, but only because she's his PA. I only realized she was his sister recently."

Devon nodded, remembering that conversation—Andrei had been displeased by the idea he hadn't known Louisa's real identity.

"She's a shadow," Sawyer said softly, stirring milk into his tea, making the silver spoon tinkle against the porcelain.

"What do you mean?" Sean asked, frowning at Sawyer.

He, Andrei, and Sawyer had visited Jacobie's home and had discovered their first tie between Sascha and the Jacobie family—a black and white photograph of a woman who was the spitting image of their partner. A woman they'd come to learn was Sascha's grandmother.

"Didn't you notice when we were there? Jacobie dismissed her. She didn't like it. She drooped at the dismissal."

"She's a PA. She's supposed to be in the background," Kurt argued, slouching back in his armchair.

Sawyer shrugged. "Maybe. But she doesn't have to like it, does she?"

Sascha blew out a breath. "This is all very informative, but what do we do?"

Devon blinked in surprise at the odd question. "Sean's called the police, Sascha."

"He has?" She gawked at him. "Why didn't you say?"

"Wasn't it obvious?" Devon asked. "One of the family is a murderer, and the others are undoubtedly involved in the conspiracy. Why wouldn't we involve the police?"

Sascha raised shaky hands to her forehead. Rubbing at her temple, she asked, "So, they're in custody now?"

"Have been since this afternoon." Kurt shot Sean and Andrei a look, but Devon knew why.

Henry had explained the situation to them first before he'd told Sascha.

"They're probably out on bail by now," Sascha said bitterly. "That's even if they've been charged."

Sean shook his head. "I'd have heard. Plus, they're under investigation," Sean corrected Kurt. "The police are investigating the murders of your parents, Sascha, and also trying to determine if anyone aside from Elizabeth Jacobie is involved."

"Like her daughter," Sawyer inserted gruffly.

"That means shit," she snapped. "I'm in as much danger as I was before. With no proof, there's no way they can arrest them."

"Your dad gave us some," Sean said softly.

Sascha gasped. "What?"

He shrugged. "We talked about this with him earlier. He overheard us discussing your situation, and demanded to know what was going on."

"W-What evidence?" she asked, her bottom lip trembling.

"You don't want to know, Sascha," Kurt said softly, reaching over to squeeze her hand.

"That's where you're wrong," she snapped, pulling her hand away. "I need to know. You've kept this from me. All of it. Kept me out of the loop, and if anyone should have known what the fuck was going on, it's me!"

Her voice was raised, enough for a silence to permeate the still busy coffee shop, and for all eyes to turn their way. She positively vibrated with the tension strumming through her, and Devon gently squeezed her fingers, wanting her to know he was there for her.

When she made no other outbursts, disinterest soon followed from the café's patrons. But, all the while, Sascha's eyes had been caught by Sean's. The two of them were staring at one another like they had a line of electricity connecting them, one that couldn't be ruptured.

"Tell me," she said softly, when the regular hush of the café returned.

"There's a safety deposit box with files in it. Your biological father stored the information there in case you were ever in danger again."

She rubbed her head once more. "Why has this crazy woman targeted me again? I was no threat to her."

"Sweetheart," Sawyer told her softly, his brogue thick. "You don't seem to be understanding the gravity of the situation. When you were born, you became an heir to the Jacobie estate. That estate was used to fund Edward Jacobie's corporation—that's public knowledge. Everyone says he had a silver spoon in his mouth from birth, and they're not wrong. But that means, whatever percentage the family plowed into his business, half is yours."

She swallowed thickly. "B-But…"

"It's worth billions, Sascha," Andrei filled in gently. "There are a billion reasons why Elizabeth Jacobie would find your existence a threat."

"But she didn't know it was me! I have a different name! My dad said I was called Eloisa Jacobie. There couldn't be more of a difference between that and Sascha Dubois."

Devon tutted. "Sascha, you saw that picture the other day, sweetheart. That's your grandmother, remember?"

"You look like doppelgangers," Kurt said softly. "A basic security check from Jacobie's team would get your picture. Anyone in the family would see the likeness. How could they not?"

"That photo was in the entry way of the house, Sascha. Seeing her and seeing you? There's no mistaking the familial connection. Or, at least, there's every reason to investigate further," he amended softly.

Sascha raised her free hand, which had fallen into her lap, and covered her eyes. "I'm a housekeeper. I never wanted to be anything else."

"And you don't have to be anything else either," Devon said, tugging at their still united hands. "You just have to be ours."

She swallowed, peeped at him. "You mean that?"

He stared at her blankly. "Of course, I do." When didn't he mean what he said?

What was the point of words otherwise?

The tiniest smile had her lips curling out of the utter misery of moments before. "When don't you mean what you say?" she asked, mirroring his thoughts.

Kurt softly whispered, "Do you forgive us? We were only trying to protect you."

"Seems like people have been trying to protect me since I was baby," she mumbled, sending them all a look. Then, her jaw worked, but she continued, "Thank you."

The tension that had ratcheted up among them at her outburst slowly began to dissipate.

"How did my dad know he'd need to give us the location of the safety deposit box?"

"He didn't," Andrei said softly. "Know, that is."

"But he must have brought the key with him."

"He told us of the charm bracelet your mother always wore. The key was one of the charms."

Her eyes rounded. "The key—the biggest charm. I always fiddled with it."

Andrei murmured, "I saw you wearing it last week, and when your father mentioned it, knew where you kept it."

"This is insane," she breathed. The notion that this conspiracy was the epicenter of her world, was more mind blowing than she knew how to deal with.

Devon murmured, "It isn't, Sascha."

"How can you say that?" she cried softly.

"Insane is the opposite of sane. We're all very sane people."

She gawked at him then pleaded, "Don't be so literal, Devon. Can't you see how messed up this situation is?"

"Of course. But it's not insane."

Sawyer sighed. "Don't be pedantic."

"But I'm right," he argued. "Insanity is a sickness of the mind. How can a situation be insane?"

"I think I'm going mad," Sascha whispered, more to herself than anyone else. She pulled her hand from his and got to her feet. "I-I need to go."

Andrei hissed at Devon. "Now look what you've done!"

Kurt stood, and as she made to sidestep them, grabbed her and tugged her into his arms. Devon watched, with a frown, as she struggled in his hold.

"It's okay, Sascha. Everything will be okay."

"You don't know that," she snapped, then sagged in his arms as he just held her tighter. Devon watched as she pressed her forehead to Kurt's chest. "You don't know that," she repeated.

"I don't. But I know that we'll keep you safe, because we love you. No one will hurt you. Ever again. We won't let them."

"Now that's the truth," Devon said, pleased by Kurt's declaration.

Everyone shot him a glower save for Sascha who was still burrowing fiercely into Kurt's arms. Devon just shrugged, reached for his cake, and took a bite.

THIRTY-THREE

THE TICKER TAPE at the bottom of the screen was an endless stream of 'Breaking News.' So much so, Sascha stared more at that than the screen and the newscasters discussing her life.

She'd seen more pictures of herself on the TV than she had in a lifetime, and she knew it had to be a so-called friend who'd sold her out.

Bastard.

Considering her social media accounts were set to private, the broadcasters had somehow managed to haul dozens of images from there regardless of her settings. They couldn't have done that without help from someone she knew.

Sean was talking about suing because her anonymity was a thing of the past. Privacy itself was a suddenly laughable concept in the face of how much of her world was now public knowledge. He'd spouted something about her human rights having been violated, but it was like locking the stable door after the horse had bolted.

Her face was out there now.

What was done, was done. She'd just been violated in yet another way.

Sascha knew she should probably be grateful that they hadn't figured out her relationship with her bosses was so much more than just work-related. Because if they had, Sascha felt certain such salaciousness would have had them salivating. Chomping at the bit for more of the juicy details.

When sunlight suddenly penetrated the dark lounge, she winced, then sat up. She had the TV on and earphones in her ears. Coldplay was singing about how things were all yellow, while she contemplated how her relatively ordinary life had gone down the crapper.

She peered at the window and saw Kurt was there. Dragging the curtains open wider, the sunlight pierced her eyes as she let the light touch her for the first time in three days. She'd holed up in here after they'd returned from Rossi's, and she'd barely moved since except for bathroom breaks and to grab another tub of ice cream.

Wallowing?

Maybe. She wasn't sure what she was doing if she was being honest. Processing seemed to be a better description, she figured, but processing what? Nothing had changed. Not really.

She was still the same woman she'd always been, except the past made a mockery of that, which was a block she had to overcome.

She was safe. That was all that mattered. The danger had passed. But that didn't stop her from feeling endangered. From feeling like her very sense of self was in peril.

Tugging her ear buds out, she asked, "What are you doing?"

Kurt shrugged. "I'm coming to sit with you."

She blinked. "Why?"

"Because I miss you."

The words had her throat tightening. Through the madness of what was happening, their love was the only beacon that shone brightly enough through the gloom.

"I miss you too."

He cut her a look. "Then you won't mind me sitting with you."

"I stink," she told him bluntly.

He shrugged. "I've played rugby. You can't stink worse than a bunch of wet, sweaty, mud-covered guys."

Her nose wrinkled. "Wanna bet?"

His lips twitched. "I'll stick to the other side of the sofa if it makes you feel better."

Glumly wishing she'd taken the enormous step of showering this morning, she nodded. "Okay."

They were in the lounge with the two L seater sofas, which were brought together to create an open-ended square. She was closer to the windows than the door, and he took the seat closest to the exit—downwind from her, she noted with relief.

Peering at him as he seated himself, she realized he'd brought a carrier bag in with him. "What's in the bag?"

"Those sweets you like. Plus some donuts and other things."

She couldn't stop the smile that curled about her lips. "You brought me junk food?"

His nose wrinkled. "Thought it might make you happy."

She grinned and sat upright. For the first time in days, she felt a snap of excitement as she clapped her hands together. "Show me."

He laughed at her glee, and she felt her cheeks pinken in response.

She was comfort eating in the worst way, but it charmed the hell out of her that he was enabling. She could diet another day. Worry about her ass and thighs when it didn't feel like the world was caving in on her, when her past wasn't a web of lies. For now, there were donuts.

He tossed her the bag and she burrowed through it, eyes widening with excitement at the vast array of candy he'd brought her.

"You buy out the corner shop?" she teased.

He winked. "Anything for my lady."

A giggle escaped her. "This is better than slaying my dragons, although…" Her giggle died and she tensed a little. "You all did that too, didn't you?"

Kurt sighed, made to sit up to come comfort her, but when she stiffened, inwardly cringing about how she had to stink, he grunted under his breath and sat back again.

"Don't think about that. Let's not watch anymore of this crap," he told her, sounding so German in that moment she wanted to laugh again. The rigid and harsh tones exacerbated the command in his words. "I don't know why you're watching the news anyway!" he argued. "Sean would tell you anything you needed to know."

"I don't really want to know anything," she replied, fingers deep in candy wrappers.

"Then why do you have it on?"

"I don't know," she said with a shrug. "It's background noise."

He sighed. "I'll never understand women."

"Good thing. I don't want to be understood. Just accept me for who I am, and that's good enough for me." She pondered her own words a second, then slowly murmured, "Although, I guess even I don't know who I am at the moment, so maybe it's a harder task than I'd give you credit for."

"You haven't changed, Sascha," Kurt argued, a deeply set scowl crossing his handsome brow.

"Haven't I? Everything about me has, Kurt. I'm not even called Sascha, am I? I'm Eloisa."

He sat up, and gritting his teeth declared, "I'll hold my breath. I'm not sitting across the room from you."

She wrinkled her nose. "I stink!" she protested.

"Then get a shower," he countered as he took a seat next to her, not stopping until she was tucked snugly in the corner unit of the sofa, her other side tightly pressed to him.

She sighed as he lifted an arm and curled it around her shoulders. "I will. Soon."

His lips twitched as he pressed them to her temple. "Soon, huh?"

She peered up at him. "I don't know what's wrong with me, Kurt," she admitted sadly. "I just… I don't seem to be able to get my feet back under me again. It's knocked me for a loop and I'm not sure how to carry on."

"You take one breath, then another, and another. Life has a habit of forcing us to carry on whether we want it to or not, Sascha." He kissed her again, letting his mouth linger as he peppered little kisses on the crown of her head. "Plus, you're safe now. That's all that matters. You have time to come to terms with what's been happening."

She gnawed at the inside of her cheek as she pulled out the pack of donuts he'd bought her. "Where did you get these from?"

"Rossi's," he admitted, his attention on the TV.

"You went to Soho for me?"

"I did," he said with a smirk. "I braved the traffic for you and everything."

"You deserve a really huge kiss once I'm showered." *And when she'd brushed her teeth.*

He barked out a laugh. "I'll hold you to that."

"In the meantime, have a donut."

"You'll share?" he asked, brows high.

"With you. My bringer of donuts. But don't tell anyone else. They'll expect me to be generous too." She held out the sweet treat and placed it against his mouth. When he took a large bite, she pulled it back, and was careful to bite where he had, and take a chunk of it for herself.

Humming under her breath, she chewed as the sugar fix went no small way to soothing her fluctuating moods.

So wrong, but so damn good!

"Is it true?" she asked after a moment, when the ticker tape on the screen revealed that Elizabeth Jacobie had been charged for conspiracy to commit murder and two counts of murder to boot—Sascha's parents.

Kurt nodded. "It's true. They have her dead to rights, as Sean says."

"The evidence my dad knew about helped, huh?"

Another nod.

"What kind of evidence was it, Kurt?"

"Some photographs."

"Of who?"

"The guy Elizabeth Jacobie hired to run you down… With her. Together. In the act, as it were." He blew out a breath. "Proof that the drugs she'd been dosing your parents with were paid for by her. Stuff like that."

She shoved a donut in her mouth. *'Stuff like that'*. Just a little thing like conspiracy…

"Where is Dad?" she asked, blowing out a breath as she decided to change the topic. "Is he still here?" He'd been due to leave two days ago, but as he hadn't come in and said farewell, she wasn't sure if he'd stayed or gone.

"Around."

Nobody had braved the front room for more than a few moments at a time. When she slept, they'd come in, tuck blankets around her, lower the volume on the TV or move her phone away from her clutching hands so she could rest a little easier.

Sometimes, they woke her but she kept her eyes closed. Curious as to what they'd do.

Sawyer had pressed a gentle kiss to her lips and told her to, "Sleep safe, lass." Devon had brushed his fingers over her forehead, smoothing her hair away before he nearly took her ear off by pulling the ear buds out—tenderness wasn't his strong suit, she realized. But he'd tried.

They all were. Trying, that is.

She was being selfish, she knew. But dealing with this situation was…

Kurt was right, she realized on a sigh. Just taking one breath, and letting another ebb and flow, was the way to get a handle on this.

"What about the others? Were Edward and Louisa involved?" she asked softly.

"Louisa helped. She's the elder child. Seems she remembered your being born. When the security team sent your picture as part of the updated guest list to the event…"

"So, Devon was right. That did trigger everything?"

"Yeah. Damn him. He needs to not be right every time."

Her grin flashed, and she let out a huffed breath which died as she asked, "What about Edward?"

"Edward had no idea."

"Just the sister-in-law and niece from hell then, huh?" She pursed her lips. "I bet Andrei's relieved about that. I know they've been working together on some project or other."

"Yeah. He is. Edward is… as you can imagine, cut up about it. He wants to meet you. Talk with you."

She stiffened in his arms. "I have nothing to talk to him about."

"You have a lot to talk to him about," Kurt corrected. "Pulling the wool over your eyes isn't going to help, Sascha. You don't have to talk to him now, but you have to gird yourself for the fact a conversation is coming. You own a sizeable chunk of his corporation. For that alone, he'll need to speak with you. Either you do it now, on an informal setting, or it will start off with the attorneys getting involved."

She turned her face to the side and pressed it against his arm. He wore a soft Henley, so her features rubbed against the brushed cotton. He smelled like man, soap, and a minty freshness that told her he'd brushed his teeth recently.

She could scent deodorant, but no aftershave, and as she'd felt the little prickles against her skin, knew the reason for that was he hadn't shaved.

Considering she'd only seen him clean shaven, it was unusual to feel those bristles against her forehead.

"I can't."

"You can," he told her firmly. "You will. But the time and place are yours to decide."

She let out a shuddery breath, dread filling her at the prospect of meeting Jacobie. *Her fucking nephew*. When did that even happen?

Deciding that was a thought process she couldn't handle, she blurted out, "Have reporters come to the house?"

"They camped out for a few days but Sawyer told them you'd moved out. They left shortly after. Plus, Edward sent some of his goons to help corral them. They cleared off the day after you holed up in here."

"Have there been any whispers about us?"

He shook his head. "That would probably be bigger news than what happened with your family, Sascha," he said gruffly. "We're all too famous for our own good." He let out a sigh. "I'm sorry, *Liebchen*."

She pulled her lip between her teeth. "It's not your fault."

"No, but I wish there was something I could do to make things right for you."

She let out a shuddery breath as she asked herself exactly what it would take for things to be right again. But then, wasn't it true that the five men were her 'right?' Not one part of her questioned her place here. This was home. Between these five men, with them, under them, among them.

"I love you, Kurt."

He tensed a little, then murmured, "*Ich liebe dich auch*."

She burrowed against him. "That had better mean I love you."

"It does," he said around a laugh.

"Good." Their love grounded her, she realized, and that was what she needed more than anything. To feel the earth firmly beneath her feet.

His hold on her tightened. "The others are worried."

She blinked at his gruff tone. He was worried too. Not just the others, she realized. "Why are they?"

"Well, aside from the basics, they're concerned you'll go."

"I won't go," she said immediately, so bluntly that his tension eased some. She felt him sink deeper into the cushioned sofa. "You were worried too?" she stated, making it less of a question.

"Hard not to be. You pulled away."

"Not from you," she argued, although there was no fire to his words. No hint of accusation. "From this," she stated, motioning at the screen. "I'm a housekeeper," she repeated, as she'd repeated so many times these past few days she was getting sick of hearing her own voice uttering those words. "I wasn't made for this."

"You were. Circumstances made it so you weren't," he countered.

She gnawed at her lip. "Maybe. Regardless, the only thing that's stopping me from going nuts is you lot."

When she made to sit up, he dragged her back. "It's okay," he told her. "Relax. There's no rush."

"I don't want you thinking I want out," she snapped. "That's the last thing I want. I want to be closer if anything, dammit." Her nostrils flared. "I just… I've brought a lot of shit to your door, Kurt. I'll admit, I wasn't sure how you'd feel about that. I know how Devon feels about publicity, and Andrei too. You all live as under the radar as much as you can."

He sighed. "'As much' being the operative words there. We're used to scrutiny. We're just worried about you." He waved a hand, motioning at the pit she'd created for herself over the last few days. A blanket fort complete with crinkling wrappers of eaten candy. "You handle Devon on a regular basis without freaking out… No one does that save from you and Sawyer. So, all this, it just isn't like you. Not that you're not entitled to have a meltdown. In whichever room you want."

She couldn't help it. She laughed. "Would you like me to have my meltdown in your bedroom?"

"It would be a different kind of meltdown," he immediately countered, smirking but not in a way that made her want to hit him in the side.

Then, she admitted on a sigh, "You're probably right. About that, as well as the fact it takes a lot to ruffle my feathers." She pressed her hand to his chest, and asked, "What do I do, Kurt?" Peering up at him, she saw him look deep into her eyes, those baby blues of his making her, as he'd said, melt.

"We formulate a plan of action. Together. Then we act on it."

It sounded so reasonable. So rational… she had to frown at him. "Did Devon come up with that one?"

Almost as though the words brought him to her, the door opened and Devon peered around it.

When he saw Kurt sitting with her, his shoulders dropped in surprise. "You're awake," he said, eyes widening as he stepped into the mess she'd made of the once neat living room.

He waded through an ocean of junk food wrappers, and perched his fine ass on the coffee table.

Reaching for her hand, he asked, "How are you doing?"

"I'm fine," she said softly. "How are you?"

He peered at her a second. "Well, I'm not sure. Sawyer said that when women say they're fine, they're not. But when men say it, they are." He rubbed his chin. "*I* am fine, but Sawyer also says that women are contradictory. Do you hate me for being fine when you're not?"

She gawked at him, but Kurt beat her to it. He groaned. "Goddammit, Devon, do you have to make a mess of everything?" He swore in German, which made her pat his chest in commiseration.

Devon just shrugged. "I don't want to hurt her feelings by being okay when she's suffering," he reasoned. "Although," he continued, rubbing his chin again. "I don't like how unhappy you are. Also, you smell, which isn't good because you always smell great."

Sascha bit her lip to hide her grin. "You do realize you're digging your own grave here, baby, don't you?"

Devon reared back. "I'm not dead. Why would I need a grave?" His eyes widened in distress.

"Sarcasm, Devon," she heaved out around a laugh.

"The lowest form of wit," he tapered off.

"Yeah. Well, I'm the queen of the lowest form, then. But, anyway, I'm not mad. I'm used to you being offensive. And of course, I'm not upset that you're doing okay. I'm glad you are, but am also appreciative of the fact you aren't happy when I'm unhappy."

Shit, that was a mouthful.

He frowned, studying her. "Do you want some good news?"

"There is some?"

He shrugged. "You still look beautiful even though you haven't washed your hair in three days."

Kurt let out another groan and he kicked out his foot to nail Devon in the shin. "Shut up while you're ahead, idiot."

Sascha just shook her head. "What the hell have I gotten myself in to with you guys, huh?"

It was a question she didn't mind asking herself… a question she'd spend the rest of her life answering.

If they let her.

THIRTY-FOUR

SEAN JOLTED to a halt on the staircase, and behind him, Devon nearly toppled into him.

"What's wrong?" he complained, grunting at the impact and managing, barely, to keep Sean upright.

"Sascha?" Sean asked, completely ignoring Devon as he strode into the kitchen. "Are you okay?"

Devon peered over at the stove where Sascha was standing, seeming semi-normal. Which he didn't trust. One thing he loved about Sascha was the fact she wasn't normal. The fact that she radiated a bland pleasantness that hid an inner core of snark.

He decided to approach with caution.

Sascha was…

A breath of fresh air.

That was the only way he knew how to describe her. She was everything they'd never really known they needed. But more than that, she was what Devon needed. Around her, he didn't feel like a freak show.

Kurt, Andrei, Sawyer, and Sean treated him like a brother, as well as the friend and confidante they all were to one another. Whenever they'd shared a lover in the past, Devon had usually been the one to bring the woman into the fold, but he'd always felt like some kind of experiment. As though they got off on his brain and his smarts but not the man himself. Sascha didn't make him feel like that.

She enjoyed his tongue… and not just for what he could do with it. But most of the time, for what he had to say.

He didn't anger her or irritate her. Sure, there were times when she *did* sigh over his lack of filter, but that was nothing. It hurt less than when Sawyer whacked him in the side.

The worst that it got was that he exasperated her. But he could handle that. He thought she could too.

"You don't have to cook," Sean was saying. "We could have ordered in again."

But Sascha was shaking her head. "No, it's time things went back to normal."

There was that word again.

Normal.

Devon pursed his lips. "Is this a trick?"

Sascha turned to look at him. "Why would you think that?"

"I'm not sure." He flashed through all the logical and rational explanations as to why she'd be standing here, looking her regular put-together self, when hours before, she'd been a ragged, scruffy mess on the sofa. She'd spoken to Kurt, but Kurt couldn't organize a piss up in a brewery, never mind drag Sascha out of her hump with a pow-wow.

There was no logical explanation, he realized, his eyes widening in terror at the prospect.

She seemed to sense his panic however, because she froze, mid-sentence, and asked instead, "Devon? What's wrong?"

His throat felt tight as he bit off, "Nothing."

She shook her head. "You're lying. Tell me what's wrong."

"I don't understand," he said softly, which had her scowling and shooting Sean a look.

"Don't understand what?"

"Why you're here. It doesn't make sense."

She tilted her head to the side. "Does it have to make sense?" she asked softly, her tone gentling. Did she understand his panic? Could she feel his concern as he stumbled around trying to figure out why she'd gone from one extreme to the other in hardly any time at all.

"Y-yes," he said, sounding choked. "Of course, it has to make sense."

Sean's hand appeared on Devon's shoulder. "It's okay, Devon."

"No, it's not." There had to be a reason.

Logic had to explain this away. How could it not? If it didn't, then that meant chaos could overshadow his world.

And when chaos reigned, so did the blackness.

It would overtake everything. Staining every aspect of his existence, drowning and suffocating every beautiful thing.

Sascha.

What was more beautiful than Sascha?

A hand slapped at his back. "Snap out of it," Sawyer said gruffly, the force behind the slap shoving him forward a good two steps.

The jolt had him sucking in a sharp breath. Staring at Sawyer like the lifeline he was, he murmured, "It doesn't make sense."

"What's wrong with him?" he heard Sascha ask in the background, but he wasn't certain who she was talking to.

Sean was close to him, but his mouth wasn't moving. Sawyer was there, looking into his eyes, that impatient purse to his lips one Devon recognized, though in his gaze was the love he knew Sawyer felt for him.

Sawyer had been the first person to love him.

His mom had been too terrified of his father to spare much attention for her gifted son. She'd had too many things to do to please her husband. Too many endless chores, tasks that had to be done just so to satisfy the man's endless need to maintain control over his family.

Only when Sawyer had appeared, had Devon known love. And even as it had warmed him, he'd felt the same panic as he experienced now. Love was chaos.

But because of Sawyer, he could reason it away. Loving Sascha hadn't brought this chaotic deluge of fears. But loving the others had, back when he'd been in his early days at college.

"Devon, it's okay. I told you before that women make no sense." His bluntness had him sucking in a deep breath.

Devon cast Sascha a glance. "Is he right?"

The strain in his tone had Sascha stilling in place. There was the exasperation he was used to seeing, but it was aimed at Sawyer instead of Devon.

He blinked at the sight. "Sascha?" he asked hoarsely.

She gritted her teeth, mumbled under her breath, "I'll get you back for that, Sawyer," then to Devon murmured softly, "He's right, sweetheart. Women don't make sense."

Her words had him sagging with relief. If both Sawyer and Sascha said it was so, and the others were nodding—he realized Kurt and Andrei had made an appearance—then it had to be true.

They wouldn't lie to him.

He almost fell into the seat at the dining table as he watched the others get into their regular dining routine.

Sascha still had a cast on her arm so Kurt hovered around her, grabbing the heavy pots as she served up something that smelled like Shepherd's Pie. But he wasn't hungry. If anything, his stomach was still enduring the riotous calamity of panic.

Another hand came to his shoulder and squeezed. Recognizing Sawyer's scent, he turned his head to the side to watch as his best friend ducked down, and asked, "You okay?"

Devon blinked. "I'm better."

"What happened?" came the quiet question.

"She went from being…" He frowned. "Well, how she was in the living room. To being normal again. But nothing has changed. There's no reason for her to be back to normal."

Sawyer sighed. "I've told you, Devon. Humans aren't like robots. Sometimes we just get over stuff."

"I don't."

"You're not a robot, but you're a close descendant," he teased, but Devon didn't mind. He never did when Sawyer teased him. He only ever recognized the tone—the Scottish brogue turned into a rumbly burr when he was joking.

"So, she's okay?"

Sawyer peered over at the woman who had taken over their home and their hearts. He studied her for a long while, then sighed. "I doubt it. She's probably putting on a brave face."

Before Devon could feel the panic rise once more, Sawyer's grip on his shoulder tightened. "But that's what a lot of people do. It's just a coping mechanism. Getting on with ordinary, everyday chores helps them get back into the swing of things. But don't keep mentioning it. She already looks like she wants to castrate me."

Devon gulped. "You think she would."

Laughter hung heavy in Sawyer's eyes. "I wouldn't put it past her."

When Devon cupped himself, Sawyer hooted out a laugh. "It's okay, buddy. Yours are safe."

"What's safe?" Andrei asked, cocking a brow at them. "Or don't I want to know?"

Devon swallowed. "Sawyer thinks Sascha might castrate us."

A silence fell heavily over the table.

"I doubt my daughter's that brave, considering she knows it's against the law."

Devon shot Henry a look over his shoulder. "Sawyer said she would. Sawyer doesn't lie."

Henry rolled his eyes. "I don't know how you put up with him," he grumbled as he approached the counter where Sascha was working.

Laughter, as it had with Sawyer's comment, was brimming on her lips, and she shrugged at her father's words. "You get used to it."

"I'm a him. Not an it," Devon complained.

"You're a mixture of both," Kurt retorted, taking a seat opposite him, and winking as he did.

Devon never understood why a wink was supposed to take the bite away from a joke, but they all did it, which meant, as usual, he was the odd one out. Still, he placed his attention back on Sascha, watching as her father eyed her a second. She tilted her head to the side, presenting her cheek, and Henry kissed it.

"Take a seat at the table," she directed him and her father obeyed. Taking the additional seat next to Devon's right, because he always had Sascha on his left.

Always.

"Andrei? Could you grab the dish of vegetables?" Sascha asked, her accented voice still having the power to strip Devon bare. Even if it only involved her asking his friend to bring a dish of food to the table.

He watched as she moved away from the stove, her cheeks flushed from a mixture of the heat and exertion from cooking, as well as amusement at the conversation she'd just been a part of. He knew the latter was the truth because her eyes were sparking merrily as they hadn't done in days.

Thinking about what had her so depressed only hours before, he shoved thoughts aside and tried to focus on the P vs NP problem that was going to further cement his and Sawyer's names in the annals of math history.

The money didn't matter, neither did the status. But a man's reputation never died. It was one way to stay truly immortal, and though

Devon didn't want to live forever, he wanted his surname to live on. His mother's maiden name. What he'd reverted to after he'd been of legal age. Cutting all ties with his bastard father. The one way he could truly snub him, and do so forever, was to shine a light on his poor, weak mother's name and completely disintegrate his father's legacy into dust.

Thoughts of that nature settled him somewhat, as did the calculation he ran through as he watched Sascha dish out the meal. He'd been right. It was Shepherd's Pie. And though he'd loathed the concoction at school, he wasn't sure how she did it, but it was one of his favorite meals now. Rich and buttery potatoes, and well-seasoned, rich and juicy beef, with vegetables so crisp yet perfectly tender; he loved when she prepared it.

Eagerly waiting for his portion, he grabbed the dish from her hand, which startled her into laughing.

"You never said you liked Shepherd's Pie, Devon. It wasn't on that little guidebook that you gave me at the start. If it was, I'd make it more often than I do," she commented softly as she took a seat, running her hands down her luscious ass to smooth out her skirt before she did so.

"I didn't tell you?" He was sure he had. But then, sometimes, he was sure he'd said something but actually hadn't.

There were whole conversations with Sascha that had never been uttered aloud, arguments with Andrei and Sawyer that would never hear the light of day but had been fully fleshed out in his mind.

He scratched his forehead. "I meant to."

She smiled. "You're too cute."

His nose wrinkled. "Thanks."

Her smile morphed into laughter. "You're welcome." As she reached for the wine Kurt had poured mere moments ago, she took a sip and murmured, "I wanted to thank you all for being so patient with me."

Though the knives and forks continued scraping against the porcelain—the whole house grateful Sascha was cooking again and they didn't have to endure more takeout—they all focused on her as they ate.

"We weren't being patient with you," Sean reasoned. "It isn't about being patient."

She bit her bottom lip in that way she had which made Devon want to slip his tongue along the curve to soothe the ache. "You know what I mean."

"I do. But it isn't necessary," Sean immediately replied. Shooting her a warning glance, he continued, "Gratitude isn't necessary. You've been through a lot these past two months."

She let out a sigh and slumped against the chair. As she did, he saw her blouse, tight fitting and clinging to her curves, gape open, revealing the pouting flesh of one of her tits.

His mouth salivated at the sight. And it had nothing to do with buttery mashed potatoes and rich beef gravy.

Though she'd been more relaxed since her accident, he'd grown accustomed to seeing her in the tight pencil skirts she favored and the close-fitting blouses that somehow managed to hide and show everything in equal parts.

"Has it really only been eight weeks?" she asked no one in particular.

"Technically, closer to seven," Devon murmured softly, watching as she hid behind the fall of auburn hair she let cascade over her face.

He loved her hair. It was straight, but she did something to it that made it wave around her shoulders and reminded him of the black and white movies he'd watched with his grandparents back in the day.

In fact, everything about Sascha screamed old world Hollywood glamor. He could picture her back then, with the pillbox hats and stocky heels. She wore the retro look so well that he often wasn't sure if there was a Hollywood star dining with them.

Sawyer elbowed him, a sign he knew to mean 'shut up.' Devon rolled his eyes, used to the silent reprimand.

"Dad, there's something I need to tell you."

The table froze, well, apart from him. He watched as all the knives and forks were held in place for a good five seconds as the occupants processed her words.

Devon shot her a look, saw a resolution on her face that had him tilting his head to the side in curiosity.

"You do?" Henry asked cautiously, placing his cutlery on the plate as though preparing himself for a heavy blow.

Sascha gulped, then whispered, "You're not going to like it, but it's my choice and my decision. I can do anything I want to with my life, and…" She clenched her eyes closed, admitting, "Sean isn't my only boyfriend."

Devon had to admit, he hadn't been expecting that.

Kurt let out a shaky sigh beside him, and Sawyer looked as though he'd eaten a brick.

"What do you mean?" Henry asked softly, but Devon got the feeling he was relieved. Like he'd been expecting her to say something else, but as she hadn't, he could breathe easier.

"They're not just my bosses," she whispered, eyes popping open. From shy timidity to glaring self-righteousness, she was a ferocious tigress that got him so hard, his cock ached.

Fuck, the zipper on his fly would tear his dick in two if she didn't stop with the sexy ferocity.

"You're..." Henry clenched his jaw. "...seeing *all* of them? I knew something strange was going down but—"

She nodded, gritting her jaw too. "Yes. And if you don't like it, you know where the door is."

Sean cleared his throat. "That's not necessary, Sascha."

"Yes," she snapped, her gaze ensnaring Sean's in the tempestuous fire flickering around her irises. "It is. You're mine. All of you are. I refuse to be ashamed of it. God only knows if it will leak to the press, and if it does, it does, but if by some miracle, we sneak through, then I want him to know. You're the most important people in the world to me. The only ones who matter. You love me, and I love you. I refuse to be ashamed about that when it comes to him."

Silence throbbed at her declaration, and Devon, unable to help himself, reached for the hand she had fisted beside her knife and covered it with his own.

He shot Henry a look and stated, "Really, it makes perfect sense, Henry."

Sascha's father eyed him. "What does?"

"Sascha's a very strong woman. A facet of her nature you helped create by raising her the way you did. But she's still a woman."

Sascha narrowed her eyes at him. "Be very careful what you say, Devon."

He blinked at her. "What? It's true. We're all really busy. We have careers that take over our lives, and we can't be with you when you need us. This way, you're safe. You're always with one of us, unless you can be with us as a group like this." He shrugged. "I've never understood why people make such a fuss about it. It makes sense for our household. We'd make a woman miserable if we dated her the regular way. But Sascha's happy. Very happy, aren't you?" he asked her, noticing the exasperation tightening her eyes.

She relented enough to sigh. "Yes. I'm very happy."

"Quit while you're ahead, Dev," Andrei advised.

He shrugged again. "I don't mind being yelled at if it makes everyone realize the importance of what's going on here. She makes us happy, we make her happy. That's the only thing that matters." He waved a dismissive hand. "Right?"

For some reason, that had the tight purse of Henry's lips loosening a little.

In all honesty, Devon figured Henry had worked out the truth anyway. After he'd helped Sean with the Jacobies the way he had, surely Henry had picked up on the fact they had a vested interest in Sascha's safety.

An interest that far surpassed that of employer to employee, or that of close friends. The man was a cop, after all.

He eyed Henry a tad suspiciously, uncertain if he believed the man's umbrage.

Then, shrugging it off, he smiled at Sascha when she flattened her fingers and twisted them in his so they could bridge them.

She let out a relieved sigh and smiled, though the look she shot her father's way dared him to disagree as she stated, "You're right, sweetheart. That's all that matters."

THIRTY-FIVE

EDWARD JACOBIE WAS nothing like the interviews.

At least, he was nothing like the interviews she'd seen of him over the years. The brash executive, with a yuppie-like style in his pin-stripe suits and gleaming shirts, all manicured hands and thirty thousand-dollar watches.

In real life, after the news of his family's sordid past, he looked, in a word, exhausted.

His eyes were rimmed red and dark shadows bulged underneath green irises that were remarkably similar to hers. They'd lightened when they'd first met, and he'd sucked in a sharp breath, as he'd shakily admitted, "It's crazy how much you look like my great-grandmother."

Even now, twenty minutes into their awkward meeting, he kept on looking at her like he was astonished. Which made the already uncomfortable situation so much more discomfiting. But a picture of Sascha's grandmother had been the key to the lock of this mystery.

On a visit to Jacobie's country estate, Sawyer had noticed a picture of a woman who looked like Sascha, right down to the too-big hips constrained by a corset, the high cheekbones, and the same pouty mouth that was 100% sassy attitude. The woman was, as Devon had declared, Sascha's sexy doppelganger. But she guessed that was inaccurate. Sascha looked like the woman, after all.

Their likeness had been the missing link to all the craziness that had been happening of late.

Where before they hadn't been able to understand why anyone would want her dead or hurt, now they did. Jacobie was, after all, Britain's answer to Zuckerberg.

There were a billion reasons why someone would have a problem with her heritage. And a handful of reasons as to why Edward was staring at her like he wasn't sure if she was real or his great-grandmother reincarnate.

She folded her hands on her lap, watching as Andrei and Sean took charge of the conversation on her behalf. Edward had wanted to meet at his Canary Wharf headquarters, but Andrei had refused and had invited him here.

Though Kurt, Devon, and Sawyer weren't in the kitchen, they were about the house somewhere. Hovering, undoubtedly, to make sure she was okay.

Her father had gone out for the morning, well aware of who was visiting today.

She wasn't nervous. Not really. Edward Jacobie might be a big whizz in the City but to her, he was nothing. A nobody. They shared genes by chance. That was it. That meant nothing to her. Even if legally, that wasn't the case.

She shifted in her seat, wishing this meeting was over. Hell, wishing the meeting wasn't necessary, period.

Sean caught her eye and reached over to entwine his fingers with hers. She shot him a strained smile, let him toy with the digits as she played with the handle of her coffee mug.

She wasn't certain how they were talking about business when Edward's mother had planned to kill her. Even Edward's sister had a hand in it.

Suddenly, the strain of the truth had her blurting out, "Why are you here?"

Silence fell at her words, and Sean tightened his hold on her hand when she made to pull away.

"There are things we need to discuss," Edward said, smoothly segueing from their previous discussion to handle her exclamation.

"What? How your family planned to kill me? Little things like that?" she demanded.

He flinched. "That. And other things."

"What other things?"

"Your inheritance," he gritted out.

"You mean, what your sister and mother tried to prevent me from having?" She shook her head. "I want nothing to do with it."

"That's not how it works, sweetheart," Sean pointed out quietly. "You can donate it all to charity, but it's still yours."

"What use is it to me? It's blood money. My whole life's been a lie because his mother was insane enough to…to..." To what? She closed her eyes. "I don't even know what happened."

Andrei elbowed Sean. "Do you know?"

Edward clenched his jaw. "Is this really appropriate?"

"You're innocent in this, aren't you?" Andrei demanded. "Don't you want to know why the fuck your family did what they did?"

"I don't know much," Sean countered. "Because I'm close to Sascha, CID closed ranks on me pretty quickly. They don't want to jeopardize their case; especially not against two very high-profile members of the nobility." He shrugged. "Can't blame them."

"Who's CID?" Sascha questioned, confused by the term.

"They're the detectives in charge of the case."

Andrei asked, "What *do* you know?"

"That Arthur was very happy with his new wife, and happier still with her being pregnant. That your father was in his bad graces, Edward, and that Arthur was looking into changing the way the estate was passed down. Your father had been arrested for drug possession." Sean wriggled his shoulders with unease.

"Arthur wanted to see if that voided the terms of the estate, so he could hand down its entirety to… well, Sascha. Your mother would have lost everything if Arthur died after changing his will. Then, even though the will wasn't changed, the estate would still have split between Sascha and your father, Edward. Hence Arthur's desire to hide Sascha in plain sight."

Edward, gulping, fiddled with his coffee cup. "My father wasn't the best man in the world. He did a lot of stupid things. Apparently, my mother did too." He closed his eyes, burrowing his free thumb and pointer finger into them as though trying to rub away the ache.

She knew how he felt. Though the headaches from the concussion had wound down somewhat after the week of no sex and no strenuous activity, the tension from this situation wasn't exactly easy on her.

To Sascha, he murmured, "According to the information your birth father tucked away in the safe deposit, Elizabeth poisoned your mother. It triggered a premature labor that ultimately killed her. You were lucky to be born."

He turned to Edward. "The man your mother hired to run Sascha down, was actually someone who had helped her before. He's confessed to smothering Arthur and to obtaining the poison that killed your biological mother on Elizabeth's dime, sweetheart. He was one of Arthur's caretakers. It seems they were having an affair."

"Why did he confess?"

"For a lighter sentence," Sean told her softly. "He handed himself in after the accident because Elizabeth doesn't handle mistakes well. His hurting and not killing Sascha had him fearing for his own life."

Though Sean's words had her feeling numb, the tech magnate's hand was shaking as he raised his coffee cup to his lips. The sound of the mug rattling against its dish had Andrei murmuring softly, "I'm sorry, Edward. That can't be easy to hear."

The other man shot him a look. "I'm the one who should be apologizing." His jaw firmed, the skin bleeding white. "She always was a perfectionist. Nothing was ever good enough for her standards." His gaze switched to Sascha, then down to the joined hands where she and Sean were clutching at one another. "I know how important Sascha must be to you—what my mother did was unforgivable, and I can't blame you for passing that hate onto me."

Sascha's shoulders straightened at his statement. Did he know about the men's proclivities?

Hell, it wasn't exactly a secret. One of their first partners, Janna, had sold her story, after all. Although they'd managed to put a clamp on the story, some kind of injunction, news still leaked. And if his security detail was as efficient as it seemed to be, well, Edward *knew*.

"This is too weird," she mumbled under her breath as the desire to escape overwhelmed her utterly. "I don't want to be here." When she made to get to her feet, Sean pulled her to a halt.

"Edward has things he needs to discuss."

"Then get on with it," she snapped. "I don't want to sit here listening to you talk shop for the next forty minutes because it's awkward. There's no way to make this situation any less awkward than it already is. We just have to deal with it quickly so that I can get out of here." She was breathing hard by the time she finished speaking.

Sascha wanted Edward out of her house. *Now*.

It didn't matter that he hadn't had a damn thing to do with any of this mess. He was a reminder, and that was the last thing she needed.

From a briefcase he'd brought with him, Edward drew out several sheets of paper and returned it to the chair. What looked like booklets were spread out on the table before her.

"I'll leave these with you for you to read, Sascha, but basically, they're rundowns of..." He gritted his teeth, and she knew it pained him to carry on, "My attorneys have been investigating the situation ever since news came to light of your relationship to my family.

"My father inherited one-hundred percent of the family fortune. Technically, I should have inherited fifty percent of that, and my sister the other half. However, my father liquidated a large portion of the estate to invest into the company when I was just starting out." His smile was tight and pained as it flashed once more. "At my mother's encouragement. Eighty percent of the estate went into my company. Forty percent of which belonged to you." His nostrils flared. "The remaining twenty percent of the whole estate remained intact to ensure things like maintenance of the family seat, etcetera." He shoved a piece of paper forward. "This is what you're entitled to. Legally." That last word came out a low growl.

She stared down at the digits, unable to credit how many zeroes were there.

Raising a shaky hand, she pressed it to her throat.

"However, I have to..." Edward's jaw worked. "*Plead* with you over this matter. The only way I can give you that amount of money is to withdraw it from the company, but if I do that, I'll destabilize it and leave us wide open for a hostile takeover." His fear of that was evident in the pinpricks of his eyes. "Andrei knows how under siege we are the moment. If I add to the imbalance, it will—. I-I'll transfer forty percent of the family-held stocks to your name immediately. But I'm begging you not to cash them in."

It was a startling moment in Sascha's life to have one of the world's richest and most powerful men pleading with her.

What did that make her?

One of the world's richest and most powerful women?

"I don't want it."

"It's legally yours," Edward said dismissively. "I can't not ensure you receive it, Sascha. You have to claim it or it will wind down and revert to the government." His eyes widened in distress. "That would be disastrous for the company."

Sean held up a hand to stall him. "We need to talk about this alone, Edward."

He stiffened but nodded. For a man who, until last week, had been in utter control of his world, she had to figure having the rug pulled out from under him was something that was happening frequently of late, and he didn't appreciate it.

Edward cleared his throat as he got to his feet. "Sascha," he murmured with a polite nod, and Andrei, rising too, guided him out of the kitchen and the house. On their way out, Andrei pressed a hand to her shoulder and squeezed, trying to imbue some semblance of comfort, she supposed.

It didn't work.

"There's nothing to talk about," she said softly when they were alone, and she could hear faint rumbles of conversation overhead.

Only faint, though. These walls were soundproofed. So much so, she wondered if she was imagining the noise. Hypersensitive because that man was here, on the way out, but still somewhere in her house.

Worse than that was the fact he was working with Andrei on an ongoing project.

A notion that had her skin crawling.

So much of what had happened to her recently, as well as right at the beginning of her life, was encapsulated by a numbness deep inside her. It wasn't overtaking her. Not yet. She believed it couldn't, wouldn't because of the men she had in her life. But the emptiness in her core was disturbing her because she'd never felt like this before.

When her mother had died, the bone deep chill that had pervaded her was the only thing she could liken this current feeling to. Except in this, she was an adult. Without the confusion of a child to worsen the situation.

Now, she had the rationale to understand what was happening, but it was like her brain was closing in on itself to protect everything that made her Sascha Dubois.

"Hey," Sean murmured softly. "Where did you go?"

She blinked at him, then jerked her head to the side, edgy with nerves. "I'm not sure." Sascha stared down at the mug of coffee in front of her. She hadn't touched it; the black liquid still rimmed the brim of the cup. "I don't like him."

"Jacobie? I don't either particularly. Although, the evidence does state he didn't have anything to do with recent events. If that eases things for you." His matter-of-fact tone should have rubbed her up the wrong way, and maybe if it wasn't Sean, it would have done.

But he was always cool. Always calm. And always competent. Managing to get down to the heart of the matter in seconds, to strip everything bare and leave it so she couldn't hide from the truth. She was so tired of the truth, she realized on a sigh. But she was also tired of lies. Which put her right in the middle of a fucked-up situation.

"I don't trust him," she blurted out.

"Then your instincts are right on the nose. He's a shark. A very unhappy one at the moment, though." A short laugh escaped him. "His reaction to having to hand over forty percent of his company was rather enjoyable." He toyed with her fingers. "You're a very wealthy woman, Sascha." He raised her hand, lifted it until he could kiss the tips of her fingers. "I'll be your gigolo."

Because she hadn't expected him to say anything like that, she froze. Then, barked out a laugh.

He grinned at her. "There's my Sascha," he said softly after a moment, letting her laughter fade into a wide smile that immediately wobbled at his words.

"I'm sorry," she whispered, ducking her head.

"Don't be. There's nothing to be sorry for. In fact, I wish you'd stop saying sorry. It makes me feel like…"

She noticed the tension in his jaw and frowned at it. "Makes you feel how?" she prompted.

"Like we're your employers. You'd apologize to employers. Not to your lovers."

She shook her head. "No. I don't think of you as my bosses anymore. I haven't since…" Sascha pulled a face. "You won't like it, but ever since you told me about my mom dying a few months after my birth."

"Jesus, Sascha. It's taken you so long to feel that way?"

She shrugged. "I can't help how I felt. But I don't feel that way anymore. Still, it doesn't mean I shouldn't tell you how much I appreciate your thoughtfulness. Because I do. I'm so grateful for all your support. It's so much more than anything I've ever had, Sean. You have to understand why it's... Why *you* are precious to me."

He accepted her remark with a begrudging smile, then his gaze flickered over to the staircase. He jerked his chin up. "You're going to stop working with him now, aren't you?"

Andrei appeared in her peripheral vision and sighed as he took the seat Edward had just vacated so she was surrounded by her men at her left and right. "Yeah."

She tried not to feel relief at that, but failed.

"It's a shame too. We were getting somewhere, but…" He wriggled his shoulders. "It's never wise to work with the enemy."

"I'm sure your grandfather would disagree," Sean pointed out ruefully.

He grunted. "Very likely. But I'm not him. Although, don't forget, Sascha, he wants to meet you. Maybe a trip out of town will do you good. Get you away from all the shit happening here."

She stared at him, feeling a little surprised at his tone. "Are you okay?"

Maybe the question was out of the blue, but it felt right at that moment. They'd been so concerned about her, wondering if she was okay that she'd been selfish and hadn't asked how they were doing.

Andrei looked angry and Sean, tired. Now she thought about it, Kurt did too. His eyes were worn, rimmed with shadows. Sawyer was his usual pissy self, and Devon was as blunt as ever, but they all wore the strain of the recent past.

How had she not seen that?

Andrei frowned at her. "Of course, I am." He reached for her hand, clenched her fingers. "As long as you are."

The amendment had her swallowing. "You look angry."

He sighed. "Why wouldn't you expect that?"

"I don't know. I just… I'm sorry," she whispered, bowing her head. "I've brought so much crap to your world." Her chin trembled. "I'm as bad as Janna."

Her half-wail had both men straightening in their seats. Andrei used his grip on her hand to tug her up onto her feet. Though she tried to avoid the momentum, he wouldn't let her. His hold was inexorable as he urged her to come around the table and to sit on his lap.

Before moving into this house, the last time she'd sat on anyone's lap was before her mother's death.

She could still remember the wonderfully horrible memory.

In the oncology unit, Natasha had one of those bandannas covering her bald head where once there'd been riotous dark gold curls. Her arms had been frail, bruised and pocked from the needle marks that came as part of her treatment, and seeing her mom's weakness, her fragility, had made Sascha cry. Natasha had tucked Sascha onto her lap and cuddled her into a tight hug.

That was the last time she'd been strong enough to hold her so fiercely.

The memory had her stomach diving and she burrowed her face into the side of Andrei's throat. His clutch on her was just as ferocious as her mom's had been, and God, it felt good. Like what she needed.

"You are nothing like her. Do you hear me?"

His words were a low, seething hiss. She bit her lip, but nodded against him, feeling the clammy kiss of her forehead to his throat as their skin cleaved together.

He shook her a little. "Do you, Sascha? Do you know that?"

His urgency pulled at her, but she had to whisper, "I read the articles. She was a bloodsucker."

She was more than that. Janna had been the first woman they'd ever shared, and she'd used her position in their house to skim information from Devon as well as blackmail the men into keeping their proclivities secret. *Bitch* didn't cut it.

Andrei shook his head. "Janna was hungry for money, Sascha. She had nothing, was loaded with student debt, and saw an easy way out. She was one of those women who had brains and beauty, and rather than use her brains to get anywhere, she preferred to use her beauty." He shrugged. "Each to their own."

"She blackmailed you," she hissed.

"I know she did, and she hurt us in doing so, but you aren't her. You're nothing like her, dammit. You make me happy. You make my heart smile. She didn't care if I ate well or if I didn't sleep enough. She used us for sex, and then when that became too much for her, she disappeared like we meant shit to her.

"Which is exactly it. We meant nothing to her.

"That's not the way of it with you—you love us, and you show us that love every day. Do you hear me? Do you see the difference?" He sounded so Russian at that moment, she couldn't bear it.

Her hand came up to knot in his white blond hair. It was closely shorn to his head, but long enough to spill through her fingers. The silk was delicate against the digits and she held tight to yet another connection. Forging yet another bond.

"You make me happy, and you make my heart smile," she repeated the words, a sigh of relief escaping her as he loosened up a little underneath her.

"Then I never want to hear you talk like that again," he commanded, the sounds of the Baltic making his words harsher, the demand more definite somehow.

"I don't want you to feel trapped," she whispered. "This changes things."

She didn't have to see Sean scowl to know that was exactly what he was doing. "How does it?"

Sascha waved blindly at the documents on the table. "How can *that* not change things?"

"Does it matter to you?"

"No."

"Then why should it matter to us?"

"Because I'm suddenly a fucking billionaire, Sean. How the fuck am I supposed to react? How are you supposed to?" She fisted her hands. "I want things to be how they were."

"They can't be," Andrei told her softly. "Things will never return to how they used to be, but why would you want that? How do you know that all of this didn't have to happen, in the exact way it has, for us to come together as we have?"

She gulped, processed that. "Do you really believe that?"

"I really do," he told her softly.

She peered at Sean who solemnly nodded. She tugged at her bottom lip with her fingers, then sucked in a breath.

If they believed that, then she had to as well.

LATER THAT NIGHT, Sascha climbed into Andrei's bed.

She'd been sleeping in her room with Sean since her Dad arrived in London. When the news had broken about her 'heritage,' dubious though it was, she'd retreated to the lounge.

Why Andrei?

She didn't know. Why choose to sleep with any of them in particular?

Hell, why *be* with any of them in any particular?

She didn't have an internal radar that alerted her when one of them was feeling under the weather or down. She just had to go off what she saw and intuited.

Relationships were complicated. The few she'd been in, had been fucked up from the start. She didn't have healthy ones to look back on. Not to reminisce on or to discern the rights and wrongs of steering a partnership in a good direction. She had five relationships going on here. Five men to comfort and love. To love her and be comforted in return.

When she'd been stuck downstairs in her pit of misery, she hadn't forgotten that. But she hadn't wanted to deal with it either. Somehow, not being alone had been as perilous as having the five men with her.

For the first time, Sascha had had a chance to see what life was like without their intrusion, and she hadn't liked it.

Sure, they'd intruded in some ways. It was their house, after all. The food she'd chowed down, they'd paid for. The sofa she'd been vegging on? Yup, all on their dime. But they'd left her alone for the most part. Popping in here and there, but never discussing anything of import. Never bringing her news. They'd been men.

It sounded bizarre because she was well aware they were of the male variety. But, they hadn't been like women. Hadn't wanted to gossip or verbally slaughter someone on her behalf. They hadn't sat in silence with her as she watched shit T.V.

They'd been there. A presence, but they'd left her to her own devices.

Even now, as she thought about it, as she'd been thinking about it since Kurt had decided to end her vegging out, she realized how life could be with the five of them.

It might not have seemed like groundbreaking stuff, but to her it was. It was a revelation.

They were solid.

Dependable.

Reliable.

Collected.

Calming.

Five adjectives she'd never realized she'd needed her quintet of boyfriends to epitomize, but five adjectives that meant the earth.

They were older than her. That too had been apparent. They were serious at moments, lighthearted at others, but their humor was of a different generation—one that didn't push her out in the dark. If anything, she understood it more.

They weren't men who shared memes on Facebook or funny videos on twitter. Their humor was suave. Like them. Even Devon, with his amazing capacity to say the wrong thing at the wrong time held that kind of charm about him.

Andrei shivered next to her as she cuddled up beside him, and it dragged her from her thoughts.

He'd been angry earlier. It was why she was here now.

"Sascha?" he asked groggily, for the first time realizing he wasn't alone.

Her laugh was low. "Well, it's not Katrin."

He stiffened a second, his muscles tensing, then he rolled over from his side and onto his front.

"Thank God for that," he said, lifting an arm and resting it over her belly. With his face in the pillow, he murmured, "You were joking, weren't you?"

In the faint light of the streetlamp through the window—he never closed his curtains—she could see him lift his head and peer at her with one eye.

Her lips twitched. "Yes."

"Good. Wasn't sure of your mood," he mumbled, half asleep once more.

She blinked at him. Had he thought she was accusing him of something? Was that why he'd been tense at her teasing?

She hid a smile and turned her face into his shoulder. "Night."

He hummed under his breath and whispered something in Russian. She figured it was 'good night' though, so she just let herself relax into his hold.

She wasn't sure how long she slept, but the grim morning light woke her.

It was going to rain. *Again,* she thought glumly, as she peered with squinted eyes out of the bay window.

In the near distance, there was the park, and the branches of the trees already whipped around in a frenzy from the growing wind.

In Tucson, she'd been awoken by blinding light in the mornings if she hadn't closed her shades.

Here?

Yeah, it didn't often work like that.

It was half-dark, meaning it had to be past seven, but earlier than nine when it was properly light.

At her side, Andrei was snuggling into her still. His warmth was welcome because the view from his window made her feel chilly. She cuddled into him in return, letting her foot slide against his calf.

The thin hairs tickled her foot, making her smile lazily as she stroked him there.

"What are you doing?" he asked groggily.

"Petting you," she told him, her voice just as thick with sleep.

"Like a dog?" he asked, somewhat disgustedly. "I'm not a dog."

"What about a cat?"

He huffed, lifted his head to glower at her, and she realized this was the first time she'd seen him properly first thing. She'd never spent the night with him. Or Kurt for that matter.

Guilt throbbed through her at the thought.

Or was she making too big a deal out of this? Men were men, right? They didn't think about things the way women did. And it wasn't like she'd been purposely avoiding them.

Most nights, she'd been with Devon if she'd been with anyone recently, and she knew they didn't mind that at all because Devon's insomnia was borderline dangerous.

Well, to himself, but also, to the world. Some of his work was very important. With consequences that could be devastating if he wasn't fast enough or was too tired to work on whatever was necessary.

When he came to her bed, she knew he didn't sleep the whole night through, but he did doze.

She knew he did. She'd seen him sleeping, and felt as proud as a mother who'd managed to get her terrible-twos-toddler to nap after an eight hour rampage with crayons on the wall and three tantrums in the grocery store.

Andrei, unlike Devon, didn't appear peaceful and rested. He looked groggy and grumpy.

But, to be honest, she quite liked that.

He was one of the most debonair and polished men she'd ever seen. With his slicked-back blond hair, perennially shaved jaw, and his wicked sharp suits? He belonged in a GQ magazine twenty-four-seven.

Here in bed, however, it was another matter entirely. And though he was handsome when he was polished, that was nothing to him half-awake.

His hair was all over the place. A tousled golden mess of wavy locks adorned his head like some kind of skewed crown.

His jaw glinted in the gloomy light as his blond stubble started to come through. It was darker than she'd figured. She had even imagined him being a bit strawberry blond where his beard was concerned, but nope. His beard would be dark blond if he ever let it grow out.

His eyes were shaded with fatigue as he squinted at her, seeming to realize she was studying him.

"You're gorgeous," she pronounced after a few seconds of staring into his eyes.

He snorted, then tugged her closer so he could press his face into the pillow and burrow the rest of it in her hair. "You are."

"Takes one to know one then," she retorted, but she wasn't too surprised that he wasn't horrified at the sight of her without make up.

She'd made breakfast often enough in this state. Had even cooked in front of them without brushing her damn hair, figuring they needed to get used to the sight of her *au naturale* as well as in full-on glamor mode.

No woman was glamorous twenty-four-seven, but men were creatures of habit. Devon, more than most. If she did something long enough, he started to believe that was how it would be forever.

Like the time she'd changed her lipstick and he'd gawked at her in astonishment. Like no other lip color existed save for the one she wore most of the time.

"I don't like it," he'd declared, making the men groan and Sawyer knock him in the side with his elbow. "Red is better than pink, Sascha. Pink reminds me of my grandmother," he'd told her with enough earnestness that she could smile now at the memory.

"What are you smiling about?" Andrei grumbled.

She tilted her head to the side in surprise. "How do you know I'm smiling?"

"Yours is not to question why," he said sleepily. "Share the joke."

She snorted and rolled her eyes, long since accustomed to their coming out with weird shit and expecting her to make sense of it.

"Remember that time I wore pink lipstick?"

He groaned. "And Devon said you looked like his grandmother?"

A laugh escaped her. "Yeah. That time."

"Jesus. I tried to kick him under the table, I swear."

She smirked. "I know. You were all too cute. But then, you generally are when he says some dipshit thing to rile me up."

He laughed, his body shaking beside her. "We're used to it, but we know other people aren't."

"I'm not other people," she reminded him, her toes still stroking his calf.

"No. You're not now. You were then."

She conceded that with a bow of her head, her lips curving in a rueful smile that spoke of how true those words were. "Remember when he told me to have tripe to replenish the blood I lost on my period?"

"We're very lucky you didn't walk out the door right then and there."

A laugh left her. "He's adorable. Even when he's rude."

"Good fucking thing he is," he said gravelly, raw enough that she realized he meant every word. Wasn't just saying it in a trite way.

She placed her hand atop the forearm he'd laid on her belly. "I wouldn't say you were a romantic man, Andrei," she said carefully.

He chuckled. "Is that a complaint, query, or a statement?"

She grinned, amused by his take on her remark. "More like a statement."

"Okay, so I can relax?"

"You can relax," she teased. "I just meant, I wouldn't say you were overly romantic, but this... us... don't you think it feels like fate?"

He went quiet for a second, then he leaned up on his elbow. His eyes were a moody green, shifting a little so they seemed almost turquoise, and she was swept away in them. Caught up in his glance.

A shudder swept through her, and she turned into him fully. With a wish, she magically blinked her clothes away, needing to feel all of him against her. But then when reality carried on, her clothes still on her, she burrowed into his arms.

He only wore briefs, so her face smushed against gorgeous muscle with no T-shirt interrupting. He smelled like her man. And as pathetic as that sounded, it was the truth.

She pressed her mouth to his collarbone and dotted open kisses along the hard line. Her tongue peeped out and trailed along too, tasting him, loving the flavor that burst on her taste buds—him. One-hundred percent Andrei.

She wriggled against him, slipping her hands down to grab his cock and hold it firmly in her grasp.

He moaned, but stayed still, and she smiled, loving that he was lying back in a sleepy haze, letting her maul him like this.

Her fingers tightened around him a second before they slipped underneath the elastic of his boxers and touched skin.

He let out a hiss, one that had victory flushing through her. She whispered, "I need you, Andrei. I always need you."

Where the words came from, she didn't know. But she meant them. She meant every single one of them.

She let her tongue trail down, arching her back so she could flicker it over his nipple. It was already puckered from the brush of morning air, so she nibbled on it delicately, adoring the texture against her lips and tongue.

With one hand gripping his shaft, not moving it, not directing him just holding him firmly, with the other, she splayed her fingers against his muscles, gently pressing and massaging as she went.

He shuddered when she moved around to grab his butt and used her hold to pull him closer against her.

"Do you need me?" she asked, and with any other man—save her five—she'd have felt desperate. Like a pathetic woman needing reassurance.

But this was rhetorical.

They needed her. She knew that. Sometimes, the lines were blurred in her head. Sometimes, she got confused and had to have a reckoning, but she knew they needed her as much as she needed them.

The five of them would always be bound together in ways that would forever exclude her, but she was another tie, another reason to keep them united forever. A woman who would never try to break them apart, to tear their connections asunder. In that, she was what bound them together, she knew, and she loved being at the center of their world.

With a shiver at the delicious thought, she murmured, "I want you inside me."

At her words, he tugged her closer and rolled onto his back. His eyes were still sleepy, the lids heavy as he peered at her through the morning gloom. "Have me," he ordered.

A naughty smile played about her lips. "You willing to lie back and think of England?"

He pondered that a second. "How about I think of Russia?"

She snorted, slapped her free hand to his belly and squeezed his cock harder. When he groaned, she retorted, "Ha *ha*. Very funny."

She spread her legs, grateful she wore a long T-shirt to cover herself and not PJ bottoms. The panties were in the way, but they could work with what she wanted to do.

Straddling him, her knees pinned to his hips, she pulled his cock out from under his boxers and pressed it to her core. "Shit, you're hot," he said with a hiss when she cocked a brow at him in confusion after he mumbled something in Russian.

He rarely spoke it, she realized. Never swore in it like Kurt did in German or mumbled crap under his breath. He always spoke either English or German, never his mother tongue.

From out of nowhere, the need to hear him talk to her that way filled her. The guttural sounds were so different to what she was used to hearing, and they set her pulse alight. Her heart thumped heavily in her ribcage, so hard that she felt certain her chest rattled with the motion.

"Don't speak in English," she ordered. "Only Russian."

He blinked, shrugged. Said something. She moaned as he began to talk to her, the low grunts, the harsh syllables, and the weird intonations... all of them worked a magic on her, made her clit throb and her pussy drip.

She shivered and reached down to pull aside her panties. When his cock brushed her pussy, she moaned and let her hips rock as she started to ride him. Her sex was slippery with juices, her wetness beyond normal as he made her gush with the sound of his voice.

He could be reciting the weather forecast to her and she didn't give a damn.

Just needed to hear this, needed to hear him.

It was raw and crude, even though she didn't have a clue what he was saying. The translation was in the heat in his eyes, the tension on his face, the grip of his fingers on her hips.

He spoke to her with words she didn't know but she understood. He wanted her. Badly. He needed her. Under him, over him. In his life, his world. She shivered, head flying back as the glory of the moment whirled through her.

Every nudge of his dick against her clit had her seeing stars, and she made sure to wiggle her hips from side to side for maximum clit torture.

With a moan, she rocked in a harder, shorter motion. The pressure was exquisite and made her sob out with want.

"Sascha," he said thickly, his voice redolent with his accent, a thousand times stronger than usual. "Stop teasing."

He reverted to Russian, but knew he'd spoken in English to get his point across—a point he reiterated by grinding her down against him with his grasp on her hips mashing their pelvises together.

It should have been painful, but she was so wet and he was so hard, that it was a delicious bite of pleasure.

With a gulp, she arched her hips, thrusting them forward, and as his cock dragged through her folds and found her gate, she shuddered as the tip pierced her entrance. Not enough to enter her, but enough to entice. To make her greedy for him.

To make her ache.

He moved a hand from her ass and slid down to grab his shaft and guide himself into her, telling her things she'd never understand but her senses loved the sound of them anyway.

With a whisper, she murmured, "More. I need more."

She needed him thrusting into her. Needed him to take her, to fuck her.

He seemed to understand because he blinked, then grabbed her hips and murmured in English this time, "Swivel around on me."

She blinked, gulped. Wouldn't it have been easier to climb off him then have him fuck her?

Apparently not, because when she tried to move off his shaft, he kept his grip on her hips tight until she complied and began to swivel around on his cock.

As she did, she let out a breathy gasp. "Oh, Jesus!" The words weren't a benediction but a plea.

Holy hell, the movement had his cock touching places she'd never had touched before. At least, she didn't think they'd been discovered, but he could definitely plant a tiny Russian flag on her pussy because he had her seeing stars again just from cautiously moving on his cock.

When she faced forward in a position she loathed—reverse cowgirl—he stunned her by rearing upward. His hands moved to her belly, and he held her close to him as he rocked forward so they were both on their knees.

Before she could do little more than gasp, he began.

His thrusts were heavy and hard. Rough. As rough and as coarse as the words that spilled from his lips. More guttural intonations that set her blood alight. Made her wish she knew what dirty, filthy things he was telling her as he fucked her. As he rocked her world.

One hand stayed on her waist, the other slid down to caress her clit. Her hands fisted in the bedsheets as she slumped forward, her face pressing into the mattress as he fucked her hard.

Her eyes twitched, then nearly rolled back in her head as she let out a low, sharp scream that was swallowed by the sheets. Her orgasm blindsided her.

Andrei became frenzied at that. His hips ramming into her, his cock an almost bruising presence deep inside. When he burst with his own climax, he dragged her over the edge too.

The dual orgasm was more than she could stand. Her vision wavered at the edges, the lines becoming fuzzy as something in her brain short-circuited. Her nerves flickered and fired with the heat of his release inside her but it was exactly what she needed.

He slumped over her, nearly suffocating her with his bulk.

With his cock still hard inside her, his body a lax weight that pushed her into the sheets, she could finally relax. Her body unwound and uncoiled as the tension slipped from her muscles, replaced with a delirious bonelessness that only one of her men could gift her.

THIRTY-SIX

WHEN SASCHA GLANCED AT HIM, Devon shuffled his feet nervously. His movement, however, further caught her attention because she frowned.

"Devon?"

He sighed. "Yes?"

"What's wrong?"

"Nothing."

A smile curved her lips, and he was happy to see it. She'd been kind of miserable this past week, and her smiles had been few and far between.

Well, not when she was with them.

At the dining table, or in Sean's office, she smiled. She even laughed and teased as she usually did. She cuddled up in bed with him in the night-time, and he knew she wasn't pulling away from the others either, because no one had said anything.

But, in the moments when she was alone, as she was now, she was somber.

The sparkle he'd come to associate with her was missing.

Gone were the times when he'd hear her singing as she baked. The giggles as she listened to an audiobook no longer echoed through the house, or the guffawing laughter as she yelled something at the TV in the lounge…

She was quiet.

Sad.

He didn't like that.

Not at all.

She stared up at him, her head tilted back in a way that had to hurt her neck. Spying that, he ducked down and took a seat on the coffee table beside her.

"There a reason you're looming over me?" she asked, a teasing hint in her voice that made his chest squeeze.

"I wanted to…" He squeezed his eyes shut, then shoved something at her.

"What is it?" she asked, surprised.

"Open it, and you'll see."

He didn't open his eyes, kept them tightly closed but he heard the ripping sounds of paper then peeked out.

She pulled out the thick card, then frowned and shook the envelope so none of the contents remained within its tight clasp.

A happy laugh escaped her at the tiny paper crane that was as flat as could be because of the envelope. With her delicate fingers, she dumped out the paper bird and said, "You remembered!"

When he'd told her that he liked origami, she hadn't believed him. Here was her proof. "I did." Like he ever forgot. Anything. *Literally.*

She grinned, leaned over, even though it meant nearly falling off her comfortably slouched position on the sofa to reach up and give him a kiss. "Thank you." She studied the tiny crane, and asked, "Do you always make them so small?"

He jerked a shoulder. "Makes it feel more difficult."

She blinked. "Can't you ever just do something because it's simple?"

"Where would the fun be in that?"

Her lips curved into a wide grin. "True. 'Lessons From A Genius 101', huh?"

It was his turn to blink. "What?"

"Never mind." She let the little bird sit on the palm of her hand a second, before her attention was drawn to the actual gift within the envelope. Tilting her head to the side as she read, each short paragraph seemed to make her eyes widen further and further. He watched, then started wondering how wide her eyes could flare without getting sore.

As he pondered that, he also wondered if he could make her look that wide-eyed when she was writhing underneath him.

She murmured, "You didn't."

The blanket statement had him frowning. "Didn't what?"

"You totally signed us up for tango lessons?" The bewilderment morphed into surprised glee. "And the first class is tonight?" She slapped her hands against the sofa. "Oh my God, it's in an hour!"

He cleared his throat. "There's a reason for that."

"What reason?" she asked, scuttling to her feet, letting the ball of wool and her knitting needles fall to the mass tangle of blankets she'd had covering her.

"Because I couldn't chicken out then."

She froze, and her expression of gleeful panic softened. She turned to him, cupped his cheek. "Thank you, Devon. I promise, we'll have fun."

He doubted that. But if it would make her smile again, if it would make her happy and make her start singing as she baked, then he'd suffer the torment of the damned and learn to tango.

Ninety minutes later, as he allowed himself to be prodded by the South American dance teacher who seemed to have some kind of fascination with his arse, he kept that thought front and center.

Though he knew the dance was supposed to be sensual, she kept on placing her hands on his hips then rubbing up against him in a way that felt more like an assault than anything else.

"Oh my God, I totally see why you don't go out often," Sascha grumbled, shooting the woman a glare as Susanna hustled off to harass some other dancers.

Even *he* wasn't so blind as to miss the signals his teacher was sending, so he couldn't plead ignorance.

Unfortunately.

"She'll see I'm head over heels for you soon enough," was all he said, trying to be placating, but he didn't think he hit the spot when she grabbed a possessive hold of his hips—exactly where Susanna had, he noted—and began circling her own against him.

The move wasn't made to entice, but was supposed to incite passion between partners, Susanna had declared. "Tango is nothing without passion!" she'd said in her husky voice, the sounds of Argentina rolling through each syllable.

Still, entice or not, Sascha's rocking hips had his cock stiffening which, in turn, had a hectic flush gracing her pearly white cheeks.

"You feel good," she whispered, pressing her chest against his.

"You feel better."

It was the truth, yet she shot him a stunned, but pleased look nonetheless.

With her standing so close to him, practically plastered against his body—not that he was about to complain—he could no longer see his feet.

Which meant he couldn't watch his steps.

Having figured out the pattern to the steps Susanna had been teaching, he calculated the angle of his footwork in correlation to Sascha's, whose steps weren't nearly so precise as his, unfortunately. She made the dance harder to fit to the conformed rhythm he was using at the base of his calculation, but it was worth it to have her bumping and grinding the way she did.

"How do you do that?" Sascha groused ten seconds later as he swept her down the ballroom.

The beginner's dance class was filled with people laughing and joking with their partners as they fumbled the steps and stood on each other's feet. One couple almost toppled over when, in a grand display of exuberance, the guy decided to tip his partner over his forearm and dip her low.

Sascha had hid her giggles by pressing her face into his chest, which made him wish all the other guys would be stupid and fail to calculate the correct angles to keep them upright. Really, it was too easy to figure out the math, so why they weren't doing so was beyond him.

"How do I do what?" Devon asked absentmindedly, his mind sparking at a thousand miles a minute. He imagined exactly where he should place his feet, each visual clue annotated with scrawled working out—his own portable, invisible whiteboard.

"Dance!" Sascha retorted. "Have you seen us? We're dancing like we can do this."

He jerked to a halt. Confusion making him stop. "Shouldn't we be able to do this?"

"Well, let's be correct here. I'm not dancing. You're dragging me along in the tide."

He blinked. "I am?" *Was that bad?*

"Yes. You are." But a smile teased at her lips.

Before he could wonder at the contradiction between her words and her tone, Susanna clapped her hands.

"Class, it's time to learn another step."

The bumbling students groaned at the news, but gathered around the ballroom's perimeter to watch her.

There was a chalkboard at the bottom of the hall where there were notes that made little to no sense to Devon, but everyone else seemed to find the information on it useful.

She didn't add to the notes, however, instead, with eyes as dark as blackcurrants, swooped in on him.

"*Señor*, it's time we show the class the next move."

Beside him, Sascha tensed. But that was nothing to his reaction. "Excuse me?"

Susanna waved a beckoning hand. "Come. Dance with me."

Devon frowned, took a step back. "No."

A shocked silence fell at his rebuttal.

Susanna, huffing, said, "I wish to show them the cross! You are the most talented student. Therefore it makes sense to move onto the next step with you."

Devon shook his head. "No. Sascha's my partner."

Sascha's hand came up to cup his ass. "It's okay, Devon."

He stared down at her. "No. It's not. I'm only here for you." He wasn't sure why she said it was okay when it wasn't. There was a storm in her eyes as she looked over at Susanna.

He grumbled, remembering what Sawyer had said. *"Women never make sense, Dev. Once you remember that, you've got it all under control."*

"You heard him. He doesn't want to dance with you." There was a lilt on the words 'with you', and when he peered down at her, he saw there was a wicked smile on Sascha's face as she huddled in close to him.

Susanna narrowed her eyes at Sascha but swept off and grabbed another victim.

She tossed her head, her hair sweeping over her shoulders as she sultrily stalked around the ballroom with the unsuspecting guy she'd ensnared in her trap, but Devon didn't particularly notice.

He watched her move, watched her feet, then tilted his head with curiosity as he saw the ripe sway of her body as she danced with the beginner. When Sean had told him about Sascha's desire to tango, he'd looked it up online. Seeing that the dance was like sex standing up, he'd been encouraged by the prospect of doing that with Sascha.

He couldn't wait for her to start wriggling and writhing all over him again—there had to be some perks to learning to dance.

The students who were already despairing the new step before they even tried it were on the receiving end of a demand from Susanna to try the move, as she went around each individual pair correcting and advising.

Sascha's eyes were sparkling as she looked at him. "You're a bad, bad man, Devon."

He scowled at her. "I'm not bad."

She grinned, reached up to pat his cheek. "Don't change."

The sudden fervency in her tone had him jolting in place. "I can't change."

"Good." She grabbed his hips again, pulled him against her so his cock, already semi-hard from having her writhing against him, stood to full attention. "Now, show me how to do what she just did."

"Didn't you see it?" he asked, confused.

"Yes. But I saw you doing that thing you do."

"What thing?"

"Where you space out and mathify everything."

"Mathify?" He shook his head. "That isn't a word, Sascha."

She chuckled. "I know, but it's a word in our house. You make everything about math." She pursed her lips. "I have no doubt that you've made some kind of equation to figure out where to put your foot or some crap like that. So, show me what she just did. You can even include sultry come-hither looks."

"I prefer to touch, not to look."

Her eyes flared with interest. "Why, Devon, it would seem we're on the same page."

THIRTY-SEVEN

LAUGHTER TORE from Sascha as they left the ballroom where the tango class had been held, the milonga music still bubbling in her ears after an hour.

The old fifties' dance hall was loaded with such atmosphere, she could almost see the girls in their flared skirts and the teddy boys with their Brylcreemed hair.

Hell, she could practically smell the Brylcreem!

Clapping her hands, she danced away from Devon, then practiced the 8-step move they'd just been working on to shuffle back to him. He eyed her with his usual calm collectedness. She rarely saw him look anything else.

Well, apart from the wide-eyed distaste when he'd glanced the instructor's way.

Sascha had wanted to hoot at his reaction to the sexy *Señorita,* but she'd managed to keep the catty noise in. It had been hard because Susanna had made her attraction to Devon so damn obvious it had been nauseating.

Only *she* had the right to grab a hold of Devon's tight ass and pull him to her. Only she had the right to dance against him like they were having public sex. And it would seem, Devon was in full agreement. A thought that had her grinning with delight.

"You're happy," he said, sounding pleased.

"I'm more than happy," she countered. "I'm ecstatic."

"Because of the lesson?"

He sounded dubious and she could understand that. But the class went far deeper than the surface.

They'd listened to her. Hell, *Devon* had. He'd been the one to take her. When Devon barely noticed anything unless it was spoken to him directly.

More than that, her possessiveness had never really been put to the test because they spent so much time at the house. And recently, when she might have been willing to go on dates with them, she'd had that stupid concussion to deal with.

The headaches still came, but they were easier to manage, and not so debilitating, meaning she had more freedom.

Trouble was, recent events had made that seem impossible. But her picture had been kept out of the papers ever since the news had broken and Devon had begged, stolen or borrowed to have an injunction put in place. So, though only a few weeks had passed, news being what it was—traveling at the speed of light—no one really remembered what she looked like, making her safe. Safe to explore London with her men. Safe to go on dates and do regular stuff.

So yeah, she was happy. And until the status quo changed, she would continue to be. Even then, she'd deal with whatever her current circumstances triggered, because she had her five delicious bosses to look after her.

She cuddled the knowledge to herself.

Sascha knew they hadn't been her bosses for a hell of a long time, had been her men for longer, but the label sent dirty, naughty thoughts Sashaying through her mind like she and Devon had just done across the dance hall.

"Was it just me? Or did we dance up a storm in there?"

His chuckle was low, dark. "We definitely danced up a storm," he teased, making her eyes widen.

She'd expected a serious remark about storm fronts and how dancing would have no negative impact on the climate, but instead, he seemed to be enjoying her amusement and her happiness, enough for him to relax too.

She reached for his hands and jerked him to a halt. She'd worn one of her few dresses—a sweetheart neckline with a pencil skirt, in a dark navy blue with a huge cabbage rose at the left hip that curved over her belly and ass, topping it with a fluffy shrug to cover her shoulders.

He wore his usual disreputable jeans and tee shirt, but he'd dragged on a leather jacket, and especially for the occasion, she thought with a chuckle, shoes. Dark brown loafers that were almost like slippers—totally inappropriate for London's rain-slicked streets.

Not that he seemed to mind.

With their torsos pressed together, their hands gripping the other's tightly, she asked, "What made you do this?"

"I wanted to see you smile."

"Why?"

"Because you've been too sad of late. You're such a happy person," he told her, damn near breaking her heart. "I thought this would make you laugh."

Her smile was slow but loaded with meaning. "You always make me laugh."

"I also make you angry," he said with a sigh. "I'm sorry about that."

"Don't be." She reached up on tiptoe to press a kiss to his lips. "Although, thank you for apologizing. I like it when you make me angry." He gaped at her until she winked. "Don't tell Sawyer."

She curled her arm through his and let him lead her back to Sean's Maserati sedan.

It still astonished her that Sean had a Maserati. Although, he had the boring one, so that kind of fit. Not that Sean was boring. He just wasn't flashy.

If anyone was flashy, it was Andrei. Not in the American way. All white teeth and gold watches. Just… there was something about him that shrieked money. Kurt too. Although, she supposed that fit considering the pair of them had been raised in wealthy families.

Her lips twitched. Comparing Kurt's family with Andrei's would undoubtedly make Kurt's mother have some kind of epileptic seizure. Old money to mafia money… She rolled her eyes. When had her life turned into some kind of Dynasty-esque saga. Seriously, she fully expected Joan Collins to make an appearance in her home any day now.

"What are you thinking?"

"That my life belongs on a soap opera."

"It kind of does when you think about it," Devon said, pursing his lips. "You're the secret baby and secret heiress! You'd be the headlining act."

She grunted. "Thanks. Queen of drama."

"Nah. Your life might be a fuckfest, but you're not."

That had her hiding a grin lest she encourage him. "Fuckfest?" she asked, peering up at him. Sometimes, she felt so goddamn short around them, even in her stacked heels. But now, it made her feel delicate.

And considering delicate could in no way describe a woman with Sascha's tits and or hips, that was a miracle in itself.

"Yeah. You know. A festival of fuck."

"That sounds like some place we should visit."

He pondered that a second, falling quiet. "Isn't that just an orgy?"

"I'm game if you are." The husky words tripped from her lips without a second's thought.

He cast her a look. "You're not ready for an orgy."

"Oh? How would you know?"

"I've been in one," he told her, his tone close to proud.

She snorted. "Why does that not surprise me?" Considering the way Susanna had been drooling over him, it made perfect sense. Especially when she remembered what Sawyer had told her about the math groupies Devon had had around campus when he was at Oxford.

"It shouldn't surprise you, Sascha," he told her somberly. "I wasn't a virgin when I met you."

Biting back a laugh, she told him equally as somberly, "I wasn't either, Devon."

That had him scowling. "I refuse to believe you've been in an orgy."

"And why's that?" she asked, scowling back at him.

"Because you think being with us is scandalous."

Shit. He had a point. "I don't anymore."

"No, but the clue is in the word 'anymore'." He shot her a knowing look. "Don't worry. We'll keep on corrupting you. Slowly but surely, you'll get used to it."

"I'm used to it now," she grumbled, though she wasn't entirely certain why she was grumbling.

He patted her hand and just said, "There, there."

SLIPPING OFF HER HEELS, Sascha let her toes sink into the thickly-piled carpet in the living room. With a sigh of relief to be off them, and scribbling a mental reminder to wear something a little more sensible for the next class, she sank into the sofa. Nestling her ass amid the blankets she'd left in a mess only three hours before, she cuddled back into her favorite position.

That had been a whirlwind.

Exactly what the doctor ordered, she realized with a wide grin. A few gropes, a lot of giggles even if the instructor was a little too hands-on for her liking, and Devon had managed to make that a blast.

If his intention had been to cheer her up, then it had certainly worked.

Before she had a chance to do more than grin dopily, not even switch on the TV, the door opened. Expecting one of her men, she saw her father instead.

It was still kind of weird for Henry to pop up the way he did. She was so used to him being in Tucson and her being in London, that for him to be in her space, came as a surprise.

She really needed to get with the program.

"Hey, Dad," she said with a smile, then patted the seat at her side as she switched on the TV.

"Hey, sweetheart," he replied, shuffling over in his ratty sweats and tee shirt. She could remember him in nothing else—a Patriots fan in Arizona, the one place he didn't have to be ashamed about his team was at home. And considering the guys followed soccer, not football, he was safe from ridicule here.

"What are you watching?"

"I don't know yet," she told him, starting to flick through the guide. "Devon and I just got back in. I'm beat."

"I'll bet." He shot her a look. "How did you like the tango classes?"

"You knew and didn't tell me?" she cried.

Henry laughed. "Heard him plotting earlier in the kitchen." He shook his head. "That boy's a weird one."

She nudged him in the side. "Be nice."

He shrugged. "Not being mean. Just stating the truth. Never been around such an odd ball but hell, he's funny, smart, and rich. What more can a man ask for for his daughter?"

Probably that the funny, smart, and rich guy was the only one in her life. Not the other four who came as part of the package too, she supposed. Not that she said that out loud.

"How was he plotting?" she asked, curious. In his own way, Devon was very decisive. The only time he hadn't been was that night when she'd come out of her stuporous vegging session. He'd looked panicked and flustered at the sight of her in the kitchen when, only hours before, she'd been grungy and in desperate need of a shower and a toothbrush.

Trying to understand his mind would take a lifetime though. There was no use in throwing certain questions around. She could ask Sawyer, of course. Or Sean. Ask why Devon had looked so freaked out at the sight of her cooking, and could only calm when he'd pleaded with her to admit that sometimes, women just made no sense at all…

But the truth was, she *did* have a lifetime to understand him, and saw no reason to ask unnecessary questions that would be resolved with time.

Well, unless it started happening frequently, that is.

Her father curled an arm about her shoulder, jolting her from her musings. "Trying to work up the courage to tell you."

"Why?" she asked, astonished. "It's a gift. It's not like he was giving me bad news."

"God knows how the boy's mind works," Henry said with a grunt, then weaseled, "Let me have the remote, baby."

"My house, my rules," she retorted, throwing back the dictate he'd sworn by throughout her teenage years.

When he shot her a hurt look, as well as a pout, she rolled her eyes. "Don't throw me the puppy dog eyes. I know your game."

"Had to give it a shot," he confessed almost immediately, then pressed his lips to her temple. "How was the class anyway?"

"Kind of disastrous for me. Although Devon rocked at it. He was like a pro within minutes. It was nuts. The teacher kept flirting with him, which was irritating but he totally ignored her when she tried to get him to practice the next part of the lesson with her."

He laughed. "He did? I like him more and more."

"Oh yeah. Devon was all, 'I'm not here with you.' He can be so literal sometimes." Her mouth curved in a warm smile. "I love that about him."

"Anyone who can put that smile on your face, then I like them too." He squeezed her shoulders. "You doing okay, sugar?"

She turned her face into his arm as she confessed, "I could be better, Dad. Things are still crazy."

"They'll get crazier still. The media's been contained so far but it will get worse before it gets better."

She nodded, sighing with the knowledge he was right. "I just want things to be easy again."

"They won't be. How can they, Sascha?" He grunted. "Hell, I should never have let you move back to the UK. All of this would have stayed under wraps."

She snorted. "Like you could have stopped me."

"True," he conceded drily. "You barely gave me any warning at all before you moved. Just said, 'That's it, I'm going to London.' My world about broke when you told me that," he admitted. "I knew I was failing your mom, but I didn't… what could I do? The distance between us was my fault. I know Natasha will never forgive me for it."

Frowning, she huddled against him. "There's no fault to be had, Daddy."

"Sure there is." His sigh was heavy. "When your mom died, Sascha, I just fell apart. I didn't… God, I loved that woman."

Her throat closed at the depth of emotion in his voice. "How did you meet?"

"We didn't lie to you entirely," Henry said ruefully, but his smile was sad. "Her car broke down on a road on my beat. It wasn't the best of areas, and I went to help her. The rest, as they say, is history."

"But she had me by that point. How did she tell you about… everything?"

"She didn't. I thought you were hers." He shrugged. "Thought that for close to three years. It never mattered. I fell for you as soon as I saw you too. You were so fucking beautiful. All big green eyes that used to follow me. You loved my badge. Got to the point where flashing it at you was the only thing that would stop you crying some nights." He shook his head at the memory. "That and the police radio." He reached up to run his knuckles against her hair. "You were a weird kid."

"Makes sense," she told him wryly. "I'm a weirder adult."

"We're all weird, honey," he informed her, his gaze caught by something on the TV. "Anyway, we started dating. I just thought she was a single mom. It didn't bother me. I was just astonished she wanted to date me. She had money when you were a baby. Your…" He cleared his throat. "Biological dad had dumped a lot on her to keep you both safe. She had a decent-ish car, until it broke down, nice house. Lived a good life.

"It was only when we got together properly she stopped depending on it. The money stayed in the bank for your college education and for big expenses. You were my daughter. I was paying as was my right.

"In the end, it was a relief we had the money. Most of her medical expenses were covered by my insurance but she had some final experimental treatments that about wiped out the fund. That's why you had to work through college." He clenched his jaw. "I hated touching that money, but we'd have lost the house otherwise. I'd have lost it to keep her with us, mind, but nothing worked."

She closed her eyes at the memories. As a kid, Sascha hadn't worried about the finances of being sick. Had just been terrified about how ill her mom was. She couldn't begin to comprehend how hard it must have been for her father. Dealing with the terror of losing his wife, as well as worrying about the money, then Sascha too.

She'd been hard on him, she realized. Way too hard as only a grieving kid could be.

"I'm sorry," she said softly.

"What for?" he asked, sounding befuddled.

"I was hard on you. After she died, I mean."

"No. You weren't. You were mourning your mom, sweetheart. It was your right to hate the world." He let out a deep breath, admitting, "I just made you hate it harder by bringing Linda into the picture."

"Why did you?" she asked in a small voice.

"Why do we do anything?" he replied, his tone even but she could hear the self-deprecation buried within. "I was frightened and alone. I had you to take care of, and though it had never mattered to me before, that was because I had your mom. You were looking to me to know shit about periods and the birds and the bees. I was fucking useless.

"I always thought we were close, but when Natasha passed away, I realized we weren't. I wanted you to have that again, and I was stupid and ignorant by even thinking another woman could fill your mom's shoes. Jesus, it went beyond stupidity. I was filling your mom's side of the bed too… Took me fucking ages to get used to her touching me."

When he clenched his jaw, she said, her tone lighter, "I really don't need to hear about you with the stepmom."

He let out a jittery breath. "No. I guess not. TMI, huh?" He tensed at her side. "I just… I wanted to help and made things a thousand times worse."

"Why did you guys split up?" she asked, curious for the first time. Her dad wasn't often in a sharing mood, so she decided to take advantage of the unusual frame of mind.

"Linda was good to me, Sascha. You know that. I tried to give her everything she needed, but…" He shrugged. "I'm surprised she lasted as long as she did. I'm as in love with your mother as I was the first time I saw her.

"A woman can only flog a dead horse for so long before she figures out the horse has gone. And I was gone before I even met Linda."

Sadness filled her, making her throat close. "Oh, Dad. I'm so sorry."

"Don't be, sweetheart. At least I had her for a while. It wasn't long enough, but some people never really know what love is. I do." He jerked his shoulder. "Doesn't stop me from getting lonely. I guess it's just something I'll have to deal with. I'm not going to put another woman through what Linda had to deal with."

Sascha bit her lip. Having always disliked her stepmom, having seen her as trying to fill her mom's shoes—exactly what her dad had wanted and Sascha hadn't—it was difficult to empathize.

But Linda had had a shitty time of it, she saw.

How would she cope with the idea of her men loving Janna still? Of her being a replacement, and a lacking one at that?

Heart sore at the notion, she clung to her father. "You don't have to stay in Tucson, Dad."

He let out a laugh. "'Course I do. It's my home, baby." Henry pressed a kiss to her temple.

She shook her head. "No. Your home is with your family. Now that grandma's passed, you're alone there."

"Where would I go?"

"Here?" Sascha shrugged. "I'm a billionaire, didn't you know? I think I can afford to keep my father in the style he's become accustomed to."

Her words had a bark of laughter escaping him. "Think you can keep me in pork rinds and IPA, huh?"

Her lips twitched. "I figure as much."

Silence fell between them, and though she'd almost expected him to shrug off the offer, he surprised her a few moments later by murmuring, "I'll think about it."

THIRTY-EIGHT

DEVON SAT BACK in the armchair that was his alone. Well, he'd share it with Sascha, but nobody else was allowed to touch it. It was cushioned and cozy, held his ass just right, and cosseted his spine in a way that made him feel like he was in bed.

Sometimes, after Sean had gone to his bedroom, Devon would sneak down here to Sean's study and sleep in the chair. Not that he *had* to sneak. Sean's office was open season, after all. Even when he was working on a case, his blackboard out, with case files pinned to it as he tried to figure out the solution to some psychopath's riddle, he had an open door.

"What's wrong?" Sean asked, not looking up from his computer when Devon had settled in his rightful place.

"Why does anything have to be wrong?" Devon asked with a scowl.

"Because you're not working and it's still only the afternoon?"

Devon rubbed at his chest. There was an ache there, and he wasn't sure why it wouldn't go away.

He'd already looked in his medical encyclopedia on 'how a heart attack starts,' and though he had one of the symptoms, the rest were absent. Not that that gave him much relief.

"Do you think she'll leave us now that she's rich?"

The question popped out of his mouth, and Kurt, who was sitting in his usual spot, came out of his writing daze to demand, "Why would you even think that?"

"Kurt," Sean said gruffly. "Don't be hard on him." To Devon, he murmured, "Tell me your reasoning."

He gnawed at his lip, and worked through the thoughts that had been flooding him these past few days. Since the tango class, Sascha had undoubtedly perked up. She was happier all around. He'd even heard her singing an old Sinatra song down in the kitchen. But... money changed people.

"Janna wanted our money."

"Sascha never has," Kurt countered.

"No, but we didn't think Janna did either, did we? Yet she did."

"Sascha's not avaricious."

"I know that," Devon snapped, aggravated at Kurt's short-sightedness. "But... what's the advantage of being with us if it isn't the money?"

Sean tilted his head to the side. "Have you spoken about this with Sawyer?"

"No."

"Why not?"

Devon shrugged. "He's busy."

"When aren't you both?" Kurt argued.

"True, but I didn't want to talk to him about this. He'd just get angry. I don't want to be yelled at by a pissed-off Scot. Sascha will hear, and she'll get mad at him for shouting at me." He rubbed his chin. "It's easier just to ask you."

A glint appeared in Sean's eye. "Why do you think she'd shout at him for yelling at you?"

He thought about it. "She does that. When Andrei's being sarcastic, she does too."

"She's protective of you," Kurt murmured.

"I suppose so, yes," Devon said, having thought about it some more, and agreeing that was the case.

"Was Janna protective of you?" Sean asked quietly.

"No," he said after a moment's thought. "But Janna was a bitch. The only person she protected was herself."

"Yes, that's true. She was number one in her mind. Do you think Sascha feels that way?"

"No, but we're a lot of work. We're good in bed but she has to put up with our moods and tempers. We work all the time, barely leave the house unless it's for business." He shrugged. "She's young. We're not. If it isn't because we can care for her, and do so well, why stay with us?"

Kurt sighed and pressed the tray with his computer to the floor. "You do know there are several ways to care for someone, don't you, Devon?"

He blinked. "There are?"

"There are," Kurt confirmed.

"But, she looks after us. Not the other way around."

Sean murmured, "Why did we pressure her to go to the doctor's, Devon?"

He frowned. "Because she wasn't going to go without being pushed."

"Why did we do that?"

"Because we wanted to make sure she was healthy."

"Exactly. That's an example of us taking care of her. This shitstorm with her family… would you say it's rattled her?"

"Without a doubt. It's taken two weeks for her to start wearing lipstick again."

"And what have we done to put her at ease?"

Devon pursed his lips. "I spoke with that judge who knew my dad and had them put an injunction out on anyone who printed her name, then you leapfrogged off that and started proceedings against the first paper who released her image."

Sean nodded. "Yeah. What else?"

"Sawyer told those reporters that were sniffing around he'd shove a calculator up their ass if they didn't forget our address." Not that it had worked. Only the injunction had stopped the reporters from swarming around—their having learned of their address thanks to being ratted out by some bastard from the hospital Sascha had been treated at after the accident.

"What else?"

"Andrei's handling Jacobie so she doesn't have to."

Sean's brows rose. "Have we told her any of that?"

"No."

"Why not?"

"Because she doesn't need to know. Plus, I don't think she wants to." He scratched his temple. "I suppose we are caring for her. Should we tell her? If she knows we care maybe she won't leave."

"Why would she leave?" Kurt demanded angrily.

"Because she has billions behind her now, Kurt," he explained patiently—the man wasn't an idiot. Couldn't he see that? "She can do whatever she wants. Be whatever she wants. Go whenever and wherever she wants. Why wouldn't she when the alternative is staying here, cooking for us, and washing our clothes?" He blinked. "Isn't it obvious?"

Sean pinched the bridge of his nose. "Please tell me you haven't spoken about this with Sascha?"

Devon scoffed. "As if I would. She might not want to leave—if I talk about it, it might put the idea in her head."

"Your logic astounds me," Kurt said with a grunt.

"My logic is logical," Devon argued, making the other man shake his head.

"You knock some sense into him," Kurt directed at Sean. "I need coffee."

Devon watched the tension in Kurt's back as he headed out the door. In a white Henley, the muscles in his shoulders were bunched up visibly.

"Why is he so mad?" Devon asked, scowling at Kurt.

"Because you're talking about something none of us want to discuss."

"Even you?" Devon asked, eyes round.

Sean sighed. "Even me. But, at the same time, there's no point in even thinking about this, Devon, never mind discussing it."

"That's only because you don't have an answer," he retorted crossly, folding his arms across his chest as he did. "You and I both know she has the world at her feet now. What's to keep her here?"

"Love."

Devon pursed his lips. "I don't trust love."

"No. And I know you have good reason not to either. But, the way you feel for Sascha… do you have faith in it?"

Devon thought about that. "I don't know that she feels the same way I do."

"That's where the faith part comes in," Sean said with a small smile. "But, the way you feel… let's imagine she feels the same. Would you leave her?"

Technically, Devon had the world at his feet already. But he didn't want to go anywhere other than up to his office or down to the kitchen to sneak whatever it was Sascha had been baking today. The entire house smelled like cinnamon.

She'd introduced him to the spice, and ever since, was fulfilling his new addiction with baked treats.

"We need to be more exciting," he said, instead of directly answering Sean's question.

"That isn't what she wants, Devon. She fell for us even though we're all wed to our work."

"Doesn't matter. If we stick with the status quo, then that just gives her the impression we're settling. I don't want her to feel like that. No one should feel like they're not valued."

Sean grunted. "You do realize that the last two months have been 'boring' because of Sascha, right? There's never not a week where one of us doesn't have some engagement… she can always go with us."

"What do you mean?"

Sean rolled his eyes. "Last month, I had a seminar in Amsterdam. I cancelled it because she was still having those bad migraines. Andrei had that gala. I know you avoid your stockholder meetings, but you could always take her to LA and New York and attend in person.

"Then, we both know Sawyer hasn't gone to visit his family in a while. I'm sure she'd love to see Glasgow, Aberdeen, Edinburgh… and he'd take her. Then Andrei wants to take her to visit his grandfather in Moscow. Kurt has so many PR stunts he can't keep up with them… there's plenty for her to dive into if she wants."

"But does *she* know that?" Devon demanded, stubbornly holding onto the topic. The idea of going to those stockholder meetings of the corporations Sawyer had made him start up was abhorrent. Why wouldn't it be to her? But hell, if she wanted to go, then go they would.

"Does she know what?"

The sound of Sascha's voice had Devon's head whipping around to look at her.

"You look beautiful," he blurted out, not to distract her, but because with the light coming in from the hall at her back, she looked like an angel.

Well, a sexy angel. And really, angels had no business being sexy.

She had fitted trousers on that made him want to check out her ass, and a simple cotton blouse that floated as she walked. Her hair was tucked into a kind of rolled under ponytail, and red paint slicked along her lips. He wondered what it would look like with that red smeared on his cock.

"Thank you, Devon," she told him sweetly, sending a smile his way that had his heart thudding. She stepped aside and he saw Kurt was there with a tray in his hand.

Eying her cast, he asked instead, "When's the pot due to come off?"

"A few days."

He nodded. "I'll go to the hospital with you."

Her lips twitched. "Thank you. But don't think you can distract me." The warmth in her eyes, however, told him exactly how much the offer meant to her.

"You can't," Kurt said gruffly. "Sascha's appointment is on Wednesday at twelve, and you have that online conference. Sawyer and I arranged it already." After Kurt placed the tray on Sean's table, he turned to Sascha. "I'm taking you."

Her grin, when it came, was wicked. "So many kind invitations to go to the doctors. I'll have to be terrified of the grocery store… would that make you come with me too?"

Sean chuckled. "We already told you to go online and have them deliver it here."

She winked. "Only teasing. Anyway, I got another call from them. There's been an opening on Monday. They said they can see me then." She gestured at the tray. "Sawyer doesn't want you having coffee for the next few days, Devon. You're to have chamomile tea. But I've sweetened it with honey and I made your favorite banana bread as a consolation prize."

Devon heaved out a breath. "Jesus H Christ. Chamomile or coffee, I won't sleep."

"He wants you rested for that online meeting," Kurt told him as he poured out a coffee for himself, Sean, and Sascha.

To his right, Sascha was hacking into a banana loaf. She placed a very thick slice on a plate and brought it over to him.

With his legs sprawled, she had room to step between them. Before he knew what she was about, she'd perched on his lap. "Time to eat," she murmured, a twinkle in her eye.

"I know how to eat," he said with a huff.

"You looked like you were going to be mutinous."

"Mutiny and stupidity aren't the same thing, Sascha," he informed her. "I'm mutinous about the coffee, not about the cake."

She snickered. "I stand corrected."

He huffed, but grabbed her as he resituated himself in the armchair and hauled her against his chest. She settled down again, this time more comfortably.

It astonished him how perfectly she fit there. It was right. Everything was when they were together. He pressed his head to her throat, and closing his eyes, murmured, "You smell good again."

"Again?" she asked after a moment's pause. "Did I stink before?"

"No. Well, you did when you were vegging. But you stopped wearing that stuff I like."

"Perfume?" She shook her head. "You're charming in the most bizarre way, Devon. It's a good thing. Otherwise you'd end up with more black eyes than a boxer."

He huffed. "Don't remind me."

"Of what?"

"Of my days pre-Sawyer."

"What do you mean?"

"I was beaten up. All the time."

She pulled back. "You?" Sascha eyed him. "Don't bullshit."

He scowled. "Why would I bullshit about that? I didn't always have a bruiser for a best friend. Before, I was little and loved math and said stuff people didn't like. I was in more fights than Mike Tyson."

"Oh my God! That's terrible!"

He winced at the shriek. Americans really knew how to shriek. Rubbing his ear, he murmured, "It's a fact of life. I'm sure it's the same where you're from."

She gnawed at her bottom lip. "I guess."

He rolled his eyes. "You guess? I'll bet you were popular."

More gnawing. "Maybe."

"Don't worry. I won't hold it against you. Our kids will have some cool genes in them, otherwise there's no hope for them at all."

She froze in his lap. "Kids?"

He stared at her. "Yeah. Kids."

Kurt snorted. "You look like a deer in the headlights, Sascha."

"I feel like one," she said hoarsely, and before Devon could say another word, grabbed the banana bread and shoved it in his mouth.

Whole.
It was either chew or choke.
But it silenced him.
For the moment.

"WHAT'S ALL this bullshit about you thinking Sascha's going to leave now she's rich?"

Devon peered over his shoulder and grimaced when he saw Sawyer looming in the doorway.

"Keep your voice down."

"Why? Because you know if she hears, she'll be angry?"

"Maybe," he said with a grunt. "Look, it doesn't matter. I'm just…" He rubbed his chest. "I like her, Sawyer."

Though the scowl on his friend's face didn't disappear, it softened. His red hair was a tousled mess around his equally red face. From the skintight tee and shorts, it didn't take much to figure out Sawyer had been running.

"I know you do," Sawyer said quietly as he stepped deeper into the room, bringing with him the scent of fresh air and sweat. "But saying shit like that is one way of making sure *she* stops liking *you*."

"Sascha won't stop liking me," he argued. "She loves me." Sean had said so, and she'd told him too. Neither of them were prone to lying.

"Well, then. What's the problem?"

"Money. It changes people."

"Not Sascha. She isn't people. She's ours."

He grunted, and bored with the topic, shoved a file across his desk. "Here. You need to look through this."

"What is it?"

"My solution for P vs NP."

Sawyer's nostrils flared. "You're fucking with me," he said hoarsely, staggering back. He went to sit down, but there was no chair behind him so instead, he toppled to the ground.

Devon jerked upright. "Sawyer? Are you okay?"

"I'm fine," he dismissed, gawking up at him from the floor amid piles of loose paper Devon had flung there as he worked. "You haven't solved it. You couldn't have done it." He gaped at the sheets in his hands.

A little pissed at his friend's lack of faith, he grumbled, "It was easy in the end."

"In the end?" Sawyer bit off. "Jesus Christ, man."

Shrugging, Devon sat back down and reached for a piece of paper which he began to fold.

Wondering if Sascha would like a bouquet of paper roses, he murmured, "It's been easier to think about that than anything else lately."

Sawyer rubbed his knuckles against his forehead. "I-I can't believe it, Devon. You're like… You're going to be as rich as Sascha."

He immediately sniffed. "*We* are."

Sawyer shook his head. "I've barely worked on P vs NP. Aside from checking your workings out."

"We're partners." Devon shot his best friend a look. "You know that."

"But this is…"

"You shared the Nobel prize with me, and we both know that was more yours than mine."

"Because your input was pivotal! My input on this wasn't."

As he folded the paper, he stuck his tongue between his teeth as he worked on getting the lines as straight as possible.

Origami was one of the tools he'd learned as a child to maintain a calmness he rarely felt.

Inside, he was a roiling mess of confusion. Nothing made sense outside of the math, not even Sascha. But she didn't add to the melee, she was like the origami—she calmed him. Brought a peace to his world that otherwise was noisy and messy and disturbing.

"Devon, you're a legend, man."

Sawyer's outburst broke into his concentration, and he scowled at his friend. "You didn't know that already?" Everyone always told him his name would outlive him, didn't they? Wasn't that the definition of a legend?

Laughter burst from his friend. "You're a dick sometimes."

"Only sometimes?" Devon blinked. "I'm doing something wrong."

Sawyer shook his head. "I'm still… I don't even know what to say, Devon."

"You've said plenty. Most of it repetitive and unnecessary." He shot

Sawyer a pointed look. "I'll throw that on the fire before I take sole credit for it."

Sawyer's eyes widened in distress and he dragged the folder against his chest. "You dare, I'll beat you senseless."

Satisfied he'd made his point because Sawyer wouldn't beat him, not after a lifetime of saving him from beatings, he said, "Fine. Then add your name to the credit page."

Sawyer closed his eyes. "Devon, man, it's not right."

"You keep me fucking sane, Sawyer," Devon bit off, suddenly furious at Sawyer's obstinacy. "There would be no solution if it weren't for you. Hell, for that matter, Andrei, Kurt, Sean, and Sascha should all be on there too." His voice rippled with emotion. "I can't do this without you. Any of you. It's too much. The noise is…" He clenched his eyes, hating the moisture that had gathered there but was unable to stop it. "It deafens me. You bring the quiet."

He blew out a breath as the melee of the real world clattered in his ears. It always did. It was there. Waiting to consume him. Except within these walls, he was safe. *They* kept him safe.

"I know, Dev, I know. But…" Sawyer sighed. "If you're sure?"

"Deadly," he retorted decisively.

Sawyer scrubbed a hand through his sweaty hair. "I can't believe you've done it. Jesus, Dev, I'm so fucking proud of you."

Devon shot him a smile. "Thanks, bro."

Silence fell as he returned his attention to the rose he was creating for Sascha, then, Sawyer asked, "Dev?"

"Hmm?"

"Do you remember when we first met?"

Devon huffed. "How could I forget? You didn't like me. Called me an uptight prick."

"You were," Sawyer replied, but he was grinning.

"What about it?"

Though Sawyer would deny his own genius, would compare himself to Devon, he could more than hold his own.

The weekend they'd met had been a gathering where universities had pitched their math programs to a bunch of budding mathematicians who had made enough strides in their own right to garner attention.

Sawyer had won several prizes in America, Devon had already

created an algorithm that had been used at CERN… universities had wanted them in their department.

Sawyer had been the archetypal belligerent teenager. Dressed in scruffy jeans and a sweater that had holes in it because, you know, fashion—Devon rolled his eyes at the memory—and bright white high tops, he'd looked his age and he'd also looked ill at ease. A kid from the wrong side of the Glaswegian tracks, he'd been among some of the greatest, and snootiest, mathematicians around.

Devon, on the other hand, had been disinterested by the universities courting him for the most part. Wearing dress pants and a shirt with shoes so shiny he could have used the leather as a writing surface for chalk, he'd been Sawyer's direct opposite. Apathetic, vaguely curious as to what was happening, and only attending because his father had demanded he go. He'd listened without listening—a talent he'd picked up when his dad was berating him over not being able to run more than two miles.

Devon had known which department he was going to. Which university. The one that would challenge him the most; Oxford. Where Dr. Anderson, one of the world's most highly respected mathematicians, held tenure.

He and Sawyer had been shoved together by way of chance, and had gotten into a discussion over the Riemann hypothesis. That discussion had developed into a pen pal friendship, with them eagerly sending several letters a week as they worked together long distance.

Good times, Devon thought with a smile. The start of a friendship that was without end.

"What about the weekend we met?" Devon asked absentmindedly, his mind on the memory as well as the paper rose he was crafting, and the next challenge on his list: the Navier Stokes Problem.

He did like these *Millennium Problems*. They were his version of a to-do list.

"That was the best weekend of my life."

Devon blinked, then scowled. "What about that weekend we went to Amsterdam?"

Sawyer scoffed. "That was a great weekend for all the wrong reasons, dick." He grunted as he got to his feet, then stacked his hands on his hips. "I'm trying to be nice."

"Why?" Devon asked, scowling at his friend. "Stop it. It's weird."

A blank look settled on Sawyer's face, then he rolled his eyes. "Why do I bother?" he asked.

"Bother doing what?"

"Never mind." His hands fell to his sides, the file in his left. "Amsterdam was good, wasn't it?"

Devon grinned. "Do you remember when Sean ducked into that coffee shop that sold pot to escape the hooker who thought Sean was flirting with him?

"Best pot I've ever had," Devon continued, tone reminiscent. "Sean said he was due to go to Amsterdam for a seminar. If I'd known, I'd have planned to go."

Sawyer's brows rose. "You'd have left London?"

Devon grimaced. "I'm not glued here, you know."

"You have been before." He shrugged. "I guess things change."

"Sascha's being here has changed me," Devon admitted. "I feel..." Hell, what did he feel? At peace?

For the first time in his thirty-eight years, was it insane to admit that's how he felt? Like she turned off the noise? For the first time, enabling him to hear far beyond the chaos circling him? What was it about her that even did that?

She was just a woman. Sure, she was beautiful. And she made love like a porn star—concussion be damned. But...Why her? Why was she so special?

He wanted to ask Sawyer that, discuss the topic, but he knew enough to realize Sawyer would get angry if he talked that way. They were all so scared of saying something to hurt Sascha. Of irritating or angering her.

It surprised him he was the only one who saw that. They didn't exactly tiptoe around her. The men were incapable of that.

Andrei alone, with his wicked sarcasm, could barely keep a civil tongue in his head for more than eight hours straight. Never mind for days or weeks at a time!

Still, there was little use in always being so careful around Sascha. Life, as it had shown them, had a habit of disturbing matters. Of upending them and spreading shit around.

It was then he realized he *would* ask her. Not only ask her why she was special enough to make the noise in his head disappear, but also, why she was going to stay with them even though she was rich enough to live alone and do whatever she wanted.

If she was mad at him, she'd forgive him. He recognized that, and knew that they had to stop pussyfooting around her.

Sawyer stared at him, and Devon sensed he'd been quiet a long time when he met his friend's gaze. "What?" he asked, uncertain what they'd been talking about.

Sawyer rolled his eyes. "Never mind." He slapped the file of papers against his leg. "You still sure about this?"

Devon snorted. "When have I ever been uncertain about math?"

Sawyer shrugged. "This is a doozy, Devon. You know that, right? It changes things."

"No. It doesn't," he said calmly, refusing to accept Sawyer's words. "It changes nothing."

"The patents on this alone are going to be staggering," Sawyer immediately argued. "We're talking about changing the face of encryption as we know it."

Devon eyed him after he scored the paper lightly with a paper knife he kept sharpened for occasions such as these. "Since when do I care about things like that?"

Sawyer sighed. "Dammit, Dev. Don't be obtuse."

"I'm not being obtuse. I just don't care."

"We're going to need to set up another corporation, dammit." He rubbed at his eyes. "Anyway, you have to care. This matters."

"Not to me." Devon's voice turned steely.

"What's going on?" Sascha appeared in the doorway with a mug in her hand.

"Nothing," was Devon's immediate retort, as he shot a quelling glance at his friend. "Why have you changed into a skirt?"

She frowned. "I spilled cake batter onto my trousers earlier. I didn't realize you were back, Sawyer. I'd have brought you tea, too."

Sawyer immediately wrinkled his nose. "The chamomile's for Dev."

Her lips curved in a smile. "I don't know. I think as a sign of solidarity we ought to reduce our caffeine intake."

"I'd like to see you pry coffee out of Andrei's cold dead hands," Devon pointed out. "Because that's the only way you'll get him to stop."

She pouted. "I'm sure if I asked kindly."

"Does being kind make a difference?" Devon asked, genuinely curious.

"It tends to, sweetheart. Yes."

Sawyer snorted. "Kindness and Dev don't go together."

"That's nonsense," came her immediate defense, and Devon had to hide a smile. As unpredictable as Sascha was, in her defense of him, she was resolute. She moved from the doorway to the desk where he was working on her paper rose and placed the mug with the piss-yellow brew next to him. As she pressed a kiss to his temple, she murmured, "Just ignore him. You're very kind. In fact, you're kinder than anyone I know because you don't know you're being kind. It's just instinctive."

Sawyer hooted. "Well, there you have it, Dev. You're the next Mother Teresa."

Sascha glared at him, but Devon ignored their verbal tussle to peer down into the cup. "Do I have to drink this?" he asked, sighing as the floral scent filled the air around him.

"Yes. It helps you sleep," was Sawyer's immediate retort as he perched his ass on the edge of his desk on the other side of the room to Devon's.

"The only thing that helps me sleep is Sascha," Devon pointed out. "You don't make me eat her."

Sascha chuckled. "I wouldn't be averse to that cure. And no, I'm not into cannibalism, Dev," she continued without hesitation, apparently anticipating his next wide-eyed question. "I meant, you can go down on me any day of the week."

He narrowed his eyes. "You mean that?"

"Uh, yeah," she told him with a chuckle. "What kind of fool would I be if I said no to that?"

"How about now?"

"Now?"

Sawyer rubbed his hands together. "I knew the afternoon was missing something."

"Group sex was on the agenda?" she demanded, her brows lifting but not in anger, just amused curiosity.

"Nope, but it always can be," Devon retorted, his hand coming up to palm her ass.

She jumped at his touch, apparently not expecting it. Her hand came up to cup his shoulder.

"What are you doing?"

He grinned at her. "What do you think?"

Before she knew what he was about, he pulled his hand back and slapped her butt. She jolted, jerking upward, then pressed her hand to her behind to cup it.

"Not you as well. Why do you want to keep spanking my poor butt? What did it ever do to you?" she demanded, but a teasing grin curved her lips.

"It torments me," he told her. "Wiggles from side to side, urging me to do naughty, naughty things to it."

Her brow arched. "How naughty?"

He grinned. "Very naughty."

"You had to start this when I was sweaty and needed a shower, Dev," Sawyer grumbled.

Sascha shot him a look. "I don't mind. You smell sexy when you're sweaty."

Sawyer pulled a face. "You say that now."

"True. Just don't shove it in my face, and I'm good. Plus, you don't want your cock anywhere near Devon's if memory serves."

A twinkle sparkled in Devon's eye. "Technically, it was my balls."

"I don't want your meat and veggies anywhere near me," Sawyer argued, "But spit roasting our beauty, I'm never not game for that."

Sascha sputtered, and an interesting flush rose on her chest. She swallowed. "Is that what I think it is?"

"Haven't watched much porn, have you, love?" Sawyer retorted, mock-sweet.

She glowered at him, folded her arms across her chest. "I've watched enough."

"Apparently not. But we'll fill in the gaps in your education," Devon told her, his tone pious.

"I'm so grateful for your expert tutelage," she retorted, then squealed when, in a quick move, he pulled his chair back, grabbed her by the waist and tumbled her over his lap.

Her hair fell in a great auburn cascade, covering his legs and veiling her face. Before she could do little more than shriek, he spanked her behind again, then curved his hand over her ass.

His fingers arched downward between the fabric covering her butt from him, but her pussy was throbbing under his palm as he dug the digits against her heat.

"Devon!" she shrieked. "What the hell do you think you're doing?"

He shot Sawyer a look, then had to chuckle when he saw his best friend was already bare ass naked.

"Someone's ready to rock," he teased. He'd seen Sawyer naked often enough to not be uncomfortable, but Sawyer was a prude in many ways.

"Stop eying up my dick."

His grumble had Sascha ceasing to wriggle on his lap. Instead, she jerked upright, her head turning sharply to the side so she could look over at Sawyer.

Hair spilled over her face and caught in her lashes as she blinked. Devon reached forward and tugged her hair into a loose grip. She gulped at the sight of Sawyer who was now stroking his shaft.

Licking her lips, she whispered, "I thought you were teasing."

Devon pulled her hair back gently, arching her throat in a way that did delicious things to the curve of her spine and her ass.

"When have you known us to tease you when it comes to sex?"

She swallowed. "All the time."

"Do you want this, Sascha, love?" Sawyer asked, his cock in his fist, his hand swift as his hardness swelled in his grasp.

She swallowed. "I want you inside me," she answered, and Sawyer nodded his understanding as well as his agreement.

Devon grabbed the hem of her skirt and jerked it up and over her hips. It was a tight fit, and he heard the pull of some stitches as he acted roughly, lifting the taut fabric over the swells of her body.

When her ass was on show, he groaned. "Do you mean to tell me you've been walking around with no panties on?"

She snickered, her head sinking low now—the strain of her earlier position too much on her neck.

Sawyer groaned. "Holy crap." Silence, a few grunts. "Dev? How wet is she?"

Devon slid his fingers down her core, shuddered at the juices that immediately drenched his hand. "She's wetter than a fucking watermelon."

Laughter erupted from Sascha. "But do I taste as good?"

Devon smacked his lips. "I bet you taste even better." He raised his hand to his mouth and slurped up her juices.

The noises had her rearing up again, this time to look at him. Her eyes, so green and bright, were heavy lidded as she watched him taste her, and as he licked his fingers clean, her eyes focused on his, he spanked her ass once more.

She let out a hiss and closed her eyes, her body jerking in response to the touch.

"I'm not sure I appreciate this tendency you have of spanking me."

"Don't forget to tell us important things like the fact you're not wearing any panties, and you won't need to worry about it."

Her bottom lip popped out at Sawyer's gruff retort.

"Bring her round here," Sawyer demanded, making Devon roll his eyes at the bossy dictate.

He wheeled the chair back, and used momentum to swing his way into the middle of the office.

Papers, as usual, covered every surface—the floor included—but he rolled over them regardless.

His was an organized kind of chaos. Until Sawyer came in and filed everything away, ruining his own filing process.

Now in the center of the room, with her butt on show and no longer partially hidden by the desk shielding her, Sascha wiggled on his lap.

"What are you guys going to do?" she asked, her voice breathy.

"What do you think, lass? Give you what you've been begging for o'course."

She moaned. "I haven't been begging for anything."

Devon let his hand curl over her ass and slip between her legs. "This tells us differently."

Sawyer approached her from the side and let his hands come and tangle with Devon's. "Jesus," he hissed. "I need in her, Dev."

She squeaked. "No! I'm not wet enough. You're too big."

"Music for any man's ears, lass," Sawyer crooned. "But dinnae be worrying," he continued, his brogue making a reappearance. "I'll make it good for you."

She reared up again to look back at him. Her eyes were on his cock, the thick shaft, the purple head—already sheathed in a condom he must have grabbed from his desk drawer. She licked her lips at the sight and whispered, "You won't fit."

"I fit before."

"You're too big," she carried on, but the flush on her cheeks spoke of her arousal. Not her fear or discomfort.

Her words were arousing her.

Women, they could be so bizarre sometimes, Devon thought, rolling his eyes at her.

She got off on dirty talk, he'd realized a while back. But the more she was around them, the more powerful that dirty talk became for her.

Sawyer notched his cock against her pussy, sliding the tip through the copious folds. She let out a moan, dropped her head. Her hands shifted, one going to the floor for support, the other clinging to Devon's calf. "You're so big," she moaned, a breath catching in her throat.

Sawyer slipped the tip into her cunt, and Devon watched the rictus of pleasure on his best friend's face as Sascha's slick heat surrounded his dick.

"Fuck," he gritted out, his head flinging back a second, the sinews standing out thickly on his throat. "She feels like heaven, Dev."

A high-pitched cry escaped her. "Oh God, Sawyer!" she mewled, wriggling her ass, rocking her hips, nearly bucking off Devon's lap.

He grabbed her, held her in place as Sawyer slowly skewered her on his shaft. He was slow at first, because Sascha was right—they were all big men, and they could hurt her if they weren't careful.

When he was all the way inside, the pair of them panted like they'd been in a race. Devon's cock was drenched with pre-cum and the pressure of her on his lap wasn't helping any.

He shot Sawyer a look, one he seemed to understand, and with brute force, he lifted Sascha off Devon's lap and hauled her into the air.

The sudden movement had her shrieking as Sawyer's cock not only filled her at a different angle, but also, the blood was undoubtedly rushing to her head, and she had to be feeling shaky from the sudden shift in position.

They were both panting when Sawyer planted his heels, and with more brute force, lifted her legs apart and high until she was impaled on his cock.

The image blazoned its way into Devon's brain, and the sight had him delving between his fly for his shaft.

He grabbed a tight hold of it, wanked himself off as Sawyer held her there, a captive to his cock.

"For fuck's sake, Devon! What have you done with all the goddamn paper?"

Kurt's voice was like a dash of cold water on the proceedings. They froze as his words traveled up the stairs. The door slammed open, all three of them turning to stare at the new arrival, and Kurt's anger-contorted face turned hot in an instant.

His pupils dilated—Devon saw it even from that distance. And he knew his friend well enough to know Kurt was harder than a goddamn pike.

"Mein Gott, was machst du hier?"

His tone was thick, the words close to inaudible as he stepped further into the room, his eyes glued to Sascha's tender folds being split by Sawyer's thickness.

Before any of them could utter a peep, Kurt approached them, dropped to his knees, and placed his mouth on Sascha's cunt.

The cry she let out was sharp, almost pain-filled. Her hands came up to grip Kurt's hair, her nails scraping against his scalp as Kurt placed his hands under her ass and helped Sawyer keep her upright.

Devon watched his friend slurp her down and fuck her clit senseless with his lips. Her head rolled against Sawyer's shoulder, side to side, an endless moan of ecstasy erupting from her mouth.

She was a creature of passion. So utterly taken by the moment, so enraptured by what they were making her feel, she was glorious with it.

Her beauty had always astonished him, but as he looked on, she was so much more than beautiful.

Devon kept his gaze focused on Kurt's tongue, which he could just see from the side. Kurt's chin was covered in pussy juice, and he made mumbling sounds that had Sascha shrieking with each vibration.

Before she knew what hit, she was keening with an orgasm. Her legs came up, trying to clamp together but Sawyer's hold on her and Kurt's presence was never going to allow that to happen. Instead, she roared with delight at her orgasm, her face contorted with a pleasure so strong, it looked like she was in agony.

Devon's cock pounded away in his fist. His pulse was a heavy, thudding beat he felt echoing in his shaft.

When Kurt pulled back, his mouth slick and unashamedly wet from her pussy, he growled out, "Fuck her, Sawyer."

Sascha whimpered, her head rolling from side to side again as she whispered, "No more, no more."

"Yes, more," Kurt retorted, reaching up to grab her chin, hold her steady as he kissed her, fucking his tongue into her mouth, making her taste herself.

She moaned against his lips, and the sounds were hard wired into Devon's goddamn system. He shuddered at the noises she made, felt his blood pressure surge, and his need with it.

"Put her on the floor, Sawyer," Devon instructed, getting up out of his seat and striding over to the trio in front of him. Even though Kurt was otherwise engaged, tongue fucking Sascha until it looked like she could pass out, his hands came to steady Sawyer too.

As a threesome, they helped Sawyer lower her down to the ground, his cock still firmly embedded inside her.

It was a testament to their strength, sure. But also Sawyer's determination not to leave her pussy.

As Sawyer situated himself on the ground, Kurt, who'd had to let go of Sascha's mouth on the journey down, asked, "Why are you using a condom?"

Sawyer rolled his eyes. "I'm sweaty."

Like that explained everything.

Kurt's perplexed look had Devon hiding a snicker.

"You know he gets anal about being clean before sex."

Sascha's eyes popped open at that. "I didn't know that."

"Can we not have a mother's meeting while you're skewered on my dick, please?" Sawyer ground out, his cheeks turning a pink that had everything to do with mortification and nothing to do with arousal.

Kurt and Devon snickered, but Sascha lifted an arm and curved it around the back of Sawyer's neck. "I think it's sweet," she told him, nipping at Sawyer's jaw, then his throat as he turned his neck to give her better access.

A low grumble sounded in his best friend's throat. "I'm not going inside you dirty," he told her, making her chuckle.

"I'm sorry, I'm sorry," she retorted when he growled at her giggles. "It's just amusing that's all." Then, Sawyer, apparently irritated at being mocked, jolted his hips up and Sascha squeaked. "Not funny, not funny. You're a sex God. A veritable machine."

"A veritable one," Devon retorted, grinning wickedly at the tableau in front of him.

Before she could pass out at whatever moves Sawyer was working on her as he swiveled his hips, Devon stepped forward. "I know a way to shut her up, Sawyer," he pointed out, his cock in his hand.

She peered up at him with a glower. "And what makes you think that will work?"

Devon licked his lips and pressed forward, not stopping until his cock was against her mouth. He painted her Cupid's bow with pre-cum, and crooned, "Taste me, sweetheart."

"Oh fuck," Kurt whispered. "She looks like a fucking dream."

His accent was thick again, so cloying that Devon realized how far gone Kurt was, but he didn't spare him much attention. Just focused on Sascha. On her gimlet stare as she looked into his eyes, fighting his will.

She didn't open her mouth, just looked at him, until finally, she let her tongue peep out and she licked the cum he'd painted on her.

She shivered, but his body clenched down in response to the gentle touch of tongue to lip, his form reacting like she'd stroked his cock from tip to base. Then, like she was at the end of her tether, she reached forward, grabbed his ass and jerked him closer.

Her mouth swallowed him. Well, as much as she was able. He was big, her mouth was small. Still, she slurped him down with as much skill as Kurt had shown on her—none.

This wasn't about skill.

This was about hunger.

A rabid hunger.

She was starved for him, and he felt it in every swirling lick of her tongue around his glans, with every hard suck and fierce swallow.

His head fell back as she sucked him down, giving him everything she had. Then, he felt a cock nudge against his own. He jolted, peering to the side to see Kurt was taking part.

He almost jumped in surprise, because Kurt had a habit of staying out of scenes like this. It was probably a testament to how she fucked with his control, and fucked with his mind, that Kurt was taking part at all.

He usually watched from the sidelines, a hungry zeal to his gaze as he jacked off.

Devon didn't get it. He never had. Kurt got more out of wanking than he did fucking... still, Devon never tried to understand his friends' quirks.

Each to their own, he always figured. He loved sharing a woman. Always had. With Sawyer and Andrei, and Kurt watching.

Sean never got involved. Andrei less, but him and Sawyer had shared a lot. Until the whole 'ball brushing' incident had stopped that in its tracks.

He was too turned on to roll his eyes, but he groaned when a soft hand grabbed his cock and Kurt's, pressed them tightly together before Sascha then attempted to slurp the crowns into her mouth.

He shuddered, his hands turning into fists as he bit off, "Jesus Christ, that feels good."

They never touched each other sexually. If they did, case in point with Sawyer, they usually freaked out. But trust Sascha to break down their boundaries without even a second's thought.

"Fuck," Kurt said, and it seemed he was stuck on repeat as he kept on saying the word over and over. It became thicker as she let go of their shafts, and reached up to tug at their balls, cupping the heavy sacks, rolling them in her palm.

Then, she did the damnedest thing. Burrowed further down, stroked his perineum.

Tensing at her touch, on the brink of refusing her advance, Kurt bit off a flurry of German so fast that in Devon's dazed state, he couldn't understand him.

Whatever it was, he realized she was touching Kurt in the exact same way she was touching Devon.

Her finger rubbed his asshole, gently, lightly. Then she pierced the clenched muscle with just the tip.

He grabbed a hold of his cock unable to help it as cum spewed out of his shaft. He jacked off, not stopping until every ounce of seed had been released from his body.

Then, he realized what he'd done and looked down at her.

She was as stunned as he was. But he'd acted on instinct. Nothing but a blind haze of need and lust and arousal swimming around his system.

"Oh hell," he groaned as he saw her, cum dotted on her face, her mouth and lips and jaw covered in it. It had sunk onto her tits too, leaving glossy pools of seed there.

He dropped to his knees and reached for her mouth, uncaring that she was covered in his cum, just loving the sight of her.

So raw. So primal.

So theirs.

He shuddered as their tongues clashed and he tasted himself and Kurt on her lips. A load moan sounded to his left as he reached up and cupped her tits, rubbing his seed into her flesh. He felt the warm release as Kurt came too, onto Dev's hands and Sascha's breasts.

Behind Sascha, Sawyer's grunting breaths echoed around the room and his gentle rocks turning into heavy thrusts as he almost bounced her on his damn lap.

Through it all, Devon kept a hold of her mouth, then slipped a hand down to her cunt, traced a finger through her folds before he captured her clit.

With a few strokes, she was exactly how he wanted her...

A goner.

THIRTY-NINE

"WELL, Ms. Dubois, I have some good news for you."

The doctor shot her a bland smile, and Sascha wondered if she remembered the time she'd been here with Andrei at her side. Or the last time with Sawyer and Devon acting as her guardians…

They'd been quite pleasant to her, but Andrei hadn't. He'd been stern with the doctor. In fact, he'd been rather rude. She wouldn't have minded though. Better rudeness than being alone. Kurt had been in his writing cave all night, and she'd decided to leave him to his work and be a big girl by going to the doctors herself.

She hated being a big girl sometimes.

"You do?" Sascha answered the woman, shooting her an equally limp smile in return.

"Yes. The scans came back clear. We didn't miss anything during your stay in hospital. You had a nasty concussion, but you're on the mend. And your cast can definitely come off today."

She blinked. "That *is* good news." Sascha was about ready to hack the pot off her arm with a table knife. The itch… sweet Lord, it was worse than her memories of the chicken pox.

"But the reason we called you back in sooner than scheduled is because the blood tests also show that you're pregnant." She gave a tight smile. "It would have been good to know there was a potential for pregnancy—we would have followed safety procedures while you were being X-rayed."

For a second, the world came to a halt. Everything screeched to a stop as the word 'pregnant' reverberated around her head like the doctor had spoken through a loudspeaker that was echoing like a yodeler in the middle of the Austrian Alps.

"Pregnant?" she gasped, eyes flaring wide. "But I'm on the pill." She clung to that statement like the lifeline it apparently wasn't.

"Yes. I'm afraid it failed you," the woman said, not sounding afraid at all.

In fact, the only person afraid here was Sascha.

Pregnant? She couldn't be. Could she?

Well, she'd done a lot of stuff that usually helped make a baby. But…

No.

It couldn't be… *She* couldn't be.

But the doctor seemed to think she was. And she went on and on in the same vein. Spewing a lot of words at Sascha, handing her booklets and brochures, telling her she had to schedule appointments, visit the nurse, do this, this, and this…

Through it all, Sascha just sat there. Gawking. Delirious.

Pregnant?

There was a thing growing inside her?

She gulped at the thought. Hell, this wasn't *Alien*. The thing was a baby.

And that baby was…

Well, the baby had a potential pool of five fathers.

She scratched her head. Who was the dad? In their household, did it matter? Or was it unimportant? Would they mind not knowing who the biological father was? Hell, would they mind being a dad period?

Andrei hadn't, had he? Nor Kurt.

Sean had told her how he and Kurt had worked together to try to make a go of things before Katrin had had an abortion. And Andrei was still hurting over that.

Sean and Devon were dark, Andrei and Kurt blond, with Sawyer coming in as a redhead. If the child was a redhead too, then it was Sawyer's, but blond or brunet? Hell, they'd never figure it out without a DNA test.

"Ms. Dubois?"

The doctor's bark had her jolting in place. "Sorry?"

"I was just saying, if you follow me we'll remove your cast now."

She blinked, then woodenly got to her feet. Following the woman, she sat still as glass as they removed the cast on her arm, and she didn't even have it in her to scratch the faintly damp skin—even though her arm had been itching her for the last two weeks.

The doctor had told her she had options. Abortion, adoption… that was if she didn't want the child.

But she did, didn't she?

There was no reason not to.

Sure, the baby wasn't planned, but… abortion?

No.

With her free hand, she touched her stomach.

This was a definite accident but it was her child, and even though she didn't know who the father was, her baby would have more dads than it knew what to do with. And she was richer than a Saudi Sheikh, dammit. She had more money than she knew what to do with, so, if they all bailed on her, she wouldn't be left destitute and unable to support herself. There was certainly no legitimate reason for her not to see this through.

Being shell-shocked certainly wasn't legitimate.

Still feeling the same way, *shell-shocked*, a half-hour later, she staggered out to the front of the clinic where her taxi was waiting for her. The last five minutes had been a daze of appointments with everyone from the nurse to, she felt certain, the clinic's janitor.

She had more reminders to add to her phone calendar than an amnesia patient.

She slipped into the backseat, the daze of shock upon her as they traveled through a gridlocked Paddington.

Watching the world go by was almost impossible. Her brain was turned inward. Inward to the most intense revelation of her life.

She was going to be a mother.

"KURT?"

Eyes flaring wide at the interruption, Kurt's head reared back. It was too funny the way he responded to her gentle murmur of his name—like she'd fired a damn bullet at him or something.

He took a second to blink, and she saw the haze of the blue light on his eyes from the computer, then he smiled. "Sascha."

The warmth imbued in that gentle curve of his mouth, in her name, had something settling deep inside her.

Kurt was... She didn't know what.

These past few weeks she'd been trying to figure out the bond between them all. Trying to understand why it worked. Because if something this complicated felt simple, she figured it needed dissecting.

Not that the guys felt that way, even with all their smarts, so maybe it was just an inherently female thing to do. To pick apart aspects of a relationship, to moon over some, and gnash one's teeth over others.

"Are you okay?" he asked, stretching his arms overhead, gifting her a rather delicious sight of his triceps tautening and bulking out his biceps.

He was sexy in a professor way. Especially recently, when he'd just had to start wearing reading glasses as he worked.

"I'm fine. I was worried about you," she lied. She'd needed to see him. Sean, the most rational of her men, wasn't around but Kurt, the second rational, was.

She wasn't ready to tell him the news. Wasn't even going to tell him he'd forgotten about her appointment… She just needed to be with him. Needed to clarify some things. Things that were important now she was going to be a—cue gulp—mom.

He frowned. "Why?"

"You've been working for eight hours solid." She shrugged. "You haven't eaten or slept."

She'd been with him the night before and had felt him creep out around three AM.

"You know not to worry," he chided, sliding his chair back and getting to his feet. His strides were easy, languid as he moved toward her. When his hands cupped her face, he bowed his head and pressed their mouths together.

She sighed into the gentle meeting of their lips, felt her own smile appear when he pressed his forehead to hers and his arms slid down to curve around her waist and haul her close.

The hug was unexpected, but all the more pleasant for it. She knew he was almost asleep on his feet, and took advantage of the weakness to stay pressed close to him.

He wasn't that sleepy, his cock prodded her in the belly, but she knew he was comfortable too. The hard on more evolutionary than instinctive.

A thought that had her chuckling.

"Are you laughing at me?" he grumbled, turning his head to the side as he kissed her temple.

"Maybe." She rocked her hips. "You're such a man. Dead on your feet but you can still manage an erection."

"A feat I'm very proud of," he assured her, sounding so very, very German at that moment she wanted to snicker.

"I wondered if you wanted to come and chill with me in the lounge."

He pulled back. "Are you okay?"

"I'm fine." And she was.

Really.

His eyes narrowed at her. "What aren't you telling me?"

She cleared her throat. "Nothing. I just thought it might be nice for you to relax a little before you crash into bed."

When she tried to pinpoint what exactly it was that Kurt brought to their dynamic, the only thing she could verbalize was a sense of ease.

That didn't sound too important, which was totally underselling him. That ease was more... Well, he didn't judge.

It was something she'd picked up on early on but hadn't really let flourish in her mind.

Most guys didn't judge at first, but they changed. Morphed over time. Of course, her five were all very open-minded, but Kurt was the most at peace with himself. With his desires.

She figured that was because he'd had longer to think he was a little weird in bed. Voyeurism wasn't exactly the worst kink in the world, but she knew it had affected his marriage and when that had dissolved, his self-image had suffered.

What had Sawyer told her?

That'd he'd drowned himself in drink for a time?

"Is this about the other day?" he asked softly, almost squinting at her as he peered her way.

She bit her lip. That hadn't been on her mind, not with thoughts of the baby front and center. Still, it did need discussing. "Maybe."

There was no need to pinpoint exactly what it was they were discussing.

Having Devon and Kurt in her mouth, and Sawyer in her pussy, wasn't exactly something they could forget.

She could still feel the slip and slide of Devon's fingers as he caressed her clit while Sawyer slammed into her.

Even now, days later, her mouth watered in reaction and her cunt pulsed with need.

God, she was hungry. So hungry for them. All the time.

That was what concerned her.

She was pregnant now—had been pregnant when that wicked foursome had happened. Moms shouldn't have those kinds of desires. Should they? Or was that just being incredibly naïve? Pregnant woman could be horny too, right?

Probably, she thought, answering her own worries and deciding to Google it later. But she'd never been in a gang bang before. Neither had she been pregnant. She figured she could be as naïve as she wanted.

A shaky sigh escaped her, and he gently walked her forward to the low leather sofa he had in front of an old-fashioned fireplace. The grate wasn't ready for firing up, but the iron gleamed like the night sky and the tiles around it were stark white in contrast.

She peered into the empty hearth as he maneuvered her onto the sofa so she was perched on his lap.

He burrowed his face in her throat and settled his hands at her belly. The move, did he but know it, was surprisingly poignant considering the news she'd received less than two hours earlier.

"Talk to me, Sascha. You know we're supposed to share this kind of thing."

'Supposed to' and this 'kind of thing.' The terminology had her wincing a little, then smiling at her own reaction.

"I told Sawyer to call me a slut," she whispered, the words bursting free.

He stiffened, then immediately relaxed, like he blew out the tension with his exhalation. "Why did you do that?" He paused. "When?"

She gulped. "You remember in the kitchen? With the wooden spoon?"

"How could I forget?" he teased gently, but he squeezed her and nuzzled his jaw against her temple.

His chin was stubbled, and the small gesture scratched, but at that moment, she felt so goddamn cherished, her throat choked.

Was it stupid for her to feel this way? When this man, and the rest of her men, so obviously loved her?

"Sascha?" Kurt prompted softly after a few.

She thought nothing of it at the time, but after what happened the other day...

"You feel like a slut," he stated, tone bland.

She flinched.

"I said 'you feel' like a slut, *Liebchen*, not that you are one. Because you aren't."

A breath escaped her. "I'm not."

"For us, you are. But we're sluts for you, too," he teased a little.

"Why do I accept all this, Kurt?"

"Why are you questioning it now?" She wished she could tell him, but she stuck with a half-truth instead.

She needed to process being pregnant first before she revealed it to them. And that processing had her stress levels shooting through the roof: "Because I just had a foursome in two of my lovers' office!"

Her shriek and the fact she half-jumped off his lap had him shushing her. But, she didn't want to slap him upside the head for such an offense. Instead, she let him soothe her by tugging her closer.

"I thought you were past this. The confusion over being with all of us, I mean."

"I thought so too," she mumbled with a sniff. She was until the prospect of making this work with a baby popped into her head.

"Oh hell, are you crying?" he demanded, sounding utterly aghast at the idea. He didn't turn her chin though so she couldn't look at him, see his horror at her tears.

"I did that with my dad in the house," she confessed on a low whisper. "I-I mustn't have any shame."

Silence fell. "Whose house is this, Sascha?"

She frowned. "Everyone's."

He shook his head—she knew, because his chin, stubble and all, scraped against her temple. The prickling sensation made her eyelashes flutter. "Too vague." When she didn't answer, he murmured, "Say the word."

She knew where he was going with this, but murmured nonetheless, "Yours."

"And why isn't it ours?"

Sascha thought about that then shrugged. "I don't know."

"You're richer than us, Sascha. You make my wealth look like a puddle of piss in the park in comparison to what you'll get when your inheritance comes through..."

"Great imagery there, Kurt," she retorted with a huff.

He just snorted. "You know exactly where I'm going with this."

"So what? Maybe I do." She shrugged. "I can't change the way I feel."

"Would you feel the same if you owned the house? I'm certain we're all quite willing to be your boy toys."

She snorted, and then couldn't withhold her giggle. "You're all older than me," she retorted, peering up at him with squinty eyes.

He wiggled his eyebrows. "Still, I've always wanted to be a toy."

"Can you imagine Devon as my sex slave?"

"His cock would be willing but his brain would get bored."

She laughed. "That sounds about right."

Kurt's eyes crinkled at the sides, making tiny lines appear. He pressed his lips to her temple. "Why are you concerned about something that isn't important anymore?"

"Because if I didn't have that inheritance, I'd still feel this way," she replied, unease unfurling through her. "I-I don't want the money, Kurt. Jacobie said something when I met him, and Sean explained that if I don't take the money, it will revert to the government. So, I understand I have to accept the inheritance, but..." She jerked her chin up. "It's blood money. I don't want it."

He shrugged. "Then don't use it. Or, use it for good." A sigh escaped him and after, he squeezed her again. "You don't understand, Sascha. You don't know what we feel for you if you think that money is important."

"That's not true. I know you care for me," she argued.

Kurt snorted. "Care? That's too paltry a word."

"Paltry, huh?" she couldn't resist teasing.

He grinned. "You know I speak no word of a lie."

Looking up at him, she saw his earnestness and had to sigh. "I know Devon's confused," she confessed. "I know he's worried, too."

Kurt's sigh was as long and as low as hers. "Devon can be remarkably simple when it boils down to it. The man's mind-boggling when it comes to math, and a complete moron with anything else."

"You don't deny it, then?"

"What? That he's confused? No. He went to Sean, and I was there. I also got very angry at him for it."

"Why?"

"Because Devon has this very irritating habit of talking about the things we don't want to hear."

"Like shedding a light on them will make it happen?"

"Something like that. Childish, I suppose, but it's... The way he sees the world? Analyses it?" She nodded. "He's usually hitting the nail on the head, even if it's not exactly in the way he thinks."

She licked her lips, understanding where he was coming from.

"See, in this, he's right again. But he's worried you'll leave because of the money. What he doesn't realize, but is sensing nonetheless, is that you're not sticking with us because of our wealth."

"No," she tried to argue. "It isn't like that."

"Then what's it like, Sascha? You know we love you. You know we'd slay fucking monsters to keep you safe, and would do anything in our power to take out anyone who'd dare hurt you. What more can we do? What more do you need to feel like this is your home? Do you need to buy into the damn thing? Is it as easy as that?"

She gnawed at the inside of her cheek. "That would only be possible because of the blood money. I don't want that tarnishing any aspect of my life with you."

He nodded. "I understand that. So, what? What would make you feel like this place was yours?"

She turned her head and burrowed her face into his shirt. He smelled so good. Like aftershave and mint from the chewing gum he whizzed through whenever he was writing.

His arms were tender about her, but so damn fierce that she knew he was right when he said they were all prepared to slay any monsters on her behalf. Even if they were monsters of her own creation.

He didn't push her to answer. Didn't prod her to talk or to verbalize her feelings.

She was glad for that, because truth was, she was in the dark. Probably as much as he.

She didn't know why the house, their status, and everything that came with it, made her feel apart from them.

Because she was looking after them and was still officially on the payroll?

She needed money somehow, though, didn't she? And she didn't want to get another job or to get someone else to take over.

She was happy looking after the house, and caring for them filled her with a contentment no feminist could possibly understand.

"Maybe there's nothing we can do to make that happen," she started slowly.

"There has to be," he argued. "I refuse for you to feel like you're a second-class citizen in your own damn home."

She shook her head. "I didn't mean it like that. Maybe it's my attitude that needs adjusting. Yours doesn't. None of you seem to think anything about this place and me... You know? Not being home." A thought came to her, and it was like a light shining in the darkness. "Maybe..."

"Maybe?" he prompted a moment later when she fell silent, her throat choking with tears.

"Maybe this isn't home not because of anything wrong with me. Maybe it's because you're all my home. This is just where we lay our head."

He stilled beneath her, and his hands were suddenly fierce around her waist. "Do you really mean that?"

She nodded, and he blew out a shaky breath.

"We'll never let you down, Sascha. You know that, right?"

She let out a little laugh. "Oh, Kurt, of course, you will. I'll let you down too. That's life, isn't it?"

He cursed. "I guess. But I don't have to like it, and I'll kick the man's ass who does hurt you, understand me?"

Her lips curved but the burn in her eyes spoke of her tears at the relief the revelation brought with it.

"I get you," she admitted softly.

"But what about this 'slut' thing?" he asked, prodding at a still sore wound. "I won't have you thinking of yourself that way."

"It's just a change of thought process," she replied. "Most people would think that's what I am for wanting what I do and for being with you all." She shrugged. "I think I need to embrace the fact I am a slut."

"No!" he barked, squeezing her in his embrace. "You're not! And you'd better damn well not!"

She smiled, and for the first time, it wasn't tinged with any of her confusion. "You're saying that like being a slut is a bad thing?"

He frowned. "Isn't it?"

"Perhaps with certain people. But not with us, right? Like you said, I'm yours. Inside these walls and behind our closed front door..."

A laugh escaped him. "Yes. You're right." He licked his lips, nuzzled his nose against her throat, making her squirm in his hands from the ticklish feeling the gesture provoked. "Like I'm a pervert for watching, and Devon is weird for enjoying sharing..."

She reached for his hand and squeezed his fingers. "Exactly."

It settled into place. The relief, the *resolve*. She wasn't a slut. Had no idea where the word had come from when she was in Sawyer's care that day when he'd spanked her ass with a wooden spoon and he, Kurt, and Andrei had made her cum, writhing against the kitchen counter like a bitch in heat.

The words had appeared, popped out to play. Like her subconscious wanted her to think about the way she was viewing herself. How low her mindset had dropped because of her new circumstances.

Good girls weren't raised to be shared by five men. Nor were they raised to enjoy it, to love every moment of what those five could give her, to love them.

She nuzzled her forehead against Kurt's cheek, silently thanking him for being her sounding board as she'd processed her feelings.

Each of her men brought something to the table where she was concerned. Before this, she'd known vaguely what Kurt was, but hadn't been able to put a name to it.

He was her rock. Emotionally.

She thanked him the truest way she knew how, "Kurt?"

He hummed under his breath, and she smiled, knowing his eyes would be closed. He was tired from an all-night marathon session, and she'd just put him through the emotional wringer with their talk.

"I love you."

Tension flooded him, but a second later it had disappeared. "I love you too."

She settled into his arms, knowing full well they'd nap like this. His back to the corner of the sofa, her settled between his legs, his chest to her back.

Feeling loved, safe, and cherished, she allowed herself to relax.

There would be doubts. More would come along the way as she

tumbled headfirst into the maelstrom of emotion they made her feel, a maelstrom that would become clouded with pregnancy hormones. But she couldn't run from them, nor would she be scared.

There was no need to be when she had five men willing to chase her monsters away for her. No need to fear her sexual needs would make her a bad mother. She was who she was. They loved her for that. And so would the child they'd gifted her.

FORTY

THE ONE ADVANTAGE TO MONEY, Devon knew, was it let a person do whatever they wanted. Anything, be it for good or ill, became an option. Accessibility was the downside to wealth. There were no limits when the sky was close to hand.

So, when he overheard Sean telling Sascha a stipend from her inheritance had trickled into her account, he'd been on the alert.

Not for anything bad, per se. She could do whatever the hell she wanted with her money. He didn't care if she never touched it and used his for the rest of her life. Money didn't matter to him.

For himself, money accessed a lifestyle he'd never be able to live otherwise. He was free. Had the liberty to putter on the projects he wanted to concentrate on, needing approval from no one.

Well, he kind of needed it from Sawyer. But he didn't count.

He wanted Sawyer in his life. Sawyer was his sanity sometimes. Sascha too, come to think of it. She slotted into his life, taking up the sentinel position opposite Sawyer. Because of that, because of their hyper-vigilance with him, his own brain tended to slide away from that particular problem.

Some might think him selfish. Unobservant about the important things. But he always made sure his household was well. Always made sure the members weren't ill at ease over something.

With Sascha and Sawyer however, he made doubly sure. It was why he was in Sascha's Cadillac today.

Having watched her make breakfast this morning, he'd sensed her edginess. Had known something wasn't right.

Two days ago, Sean had given her the news. News she'd accepted with a marked lack of interest.

Sean was handling her inheritance for her; well, Sean and Andrei. They were sorting out the accounts she'd need to contain the amount of money coming to her, were arranging her finances so that she was forever protected.

She declared she didn't want to use the money now. But when she realized what it would do, Devon knew that would change.

He didn't begrudge her the hypocrisy. Didn't judge her for suddenly wanting to access what she'd never had. He'd known she'd do it; that her opinion of the blood money would change when she realized the doors it opened. He'd just wanted to circumvent the danger of that. Make sure they weren't suddenly unnecessary because money wasn't a problem anymore.

"Devon?" Sascha mouthed his name as she came to a halt in front of the car.

Her eyes narrowed at him. "What are you doing in there? Again? This is getting to be a damn habit!" she declared, heading to the driver's seat, stacking her hands on her hips and glowering at him through the glass.

"I'm coming with you."

"Where?" she demanded.

"To the prison."

Her mouth worked, and he knew his supposition was correct. A smile played about his lips at how well he'd judged her—she was like Sawyer, surprisingly easy to read.

Sean was the hardest. Then Andrei. They kept themselves to themselves when it came to their emotions. He figured that was because Sean was the epitome of a British man—the stiff upper lip was a shield. And Andrei's past prevented him from being as free with his emotions as he might have been without a murderer for a father, a murder victim for a mother, and a Bratva kingpin for a granddad.

Devon rubbed his chin. "We need to introduce you to Sawyer's parents."

She blinked at him then pulled open the Cadillac door. "What?"

He shrugged. "We've all got weird relationships with our parents. All of us save for Sawyer. They like him, don't care what he does as long as he's happy. Plus, you'll love his mum's Spotted Dick. She makes the custard fresh too. All from scratch." He licked his lips just at the thought.

Cinta had welcomed Devon into her home all those years ago when he'd decided to cut off his father. She'd been his surrogate mum, and Hamish, Sawyer's dad, had also greeted the skinny fifteen-year-old, bringing him into the household with a rough care that still had Devon's chest aching.

"They used to live on one of Glasgow's worst estates," he informed her. "But we managed to get them to move into a nice place two years ago. Sawyer and I won't be terrified about taking you up to see them."

She shook her head. "I don't want to try his mom's Spotted Dick."

He grinned. "Stop being facetious."

She stuck out her tongue. "Okay, I know it's a pudding."

He winked. "If his mum has a spotted dick, then that's her business, but what she bakes in the kitchen isn't anything to scoff at."

She huffed and ducked behind the wheel. "What are you doing here, Devon?"

"I told you. I'm going with you."

"Maybe I didn't want you there, huh? Did that never occur to you? I have five overprotective men willing to knife any dragon who steps in my way, and I chose to handle this alone. What does that tell you?"

"That you're misguided," he informed her softly. "But time will change that."

She let out a huff. "I swear, it's a good thing you're cute."

"I'm not cute," he retorted, his top lip curling up in disgust. Cute was one of her favorite adjectives. "A baby's cute. A damn koala bear is cute. I'm not cute."

She reached over and patted his cheek. "You keep telling yourself that."

She winked when he shot her a glower, but prepared herself for the journey ahead. He eyed her, surprised that she didn't try to make him leave the car—but impressed too. She knew he wasn't budging, and she wasn't wasting her time or energy on making that happen. As she set off, leaving Kensington with all its elegant beauty behind, he murmured, "You look very nice for a visit to prison."

She snorted. "I decided I'm an heiress to a fortune that bitch tried to deny me. I wasn't going to slum it when I met her for the first and last time."

Devon didn't know fashion existed outside of its utilitarian purpose. Sawyer had bought all his clothes at one point, then that task had weeded down to the rest of the men too.

If Sean bought a suit, he'd have his tailor come to the house to measure Devon up once a year.

Kurt tended to buy him jeans, Andrei shoes.

He rubbed his chin, wondering what Sascha would add to the mix that was his wardrobe.

Still, though he didn't give a damn about clothes—would have willingly walked around naked if Sawyer hadn't told him it scared the cleaning women—he knew some viewed it as armor.

Sascha was one of those people.

When she'd first come to work for them, she'd lived in pencil skirts and tight blouses. He'd lived for the moment when the seams would split on either. Wanting to see the lush curves in the flesh.

After she'd been hit by that damn car, she'd taken to wearing more comfortable clothes. Yoga pants, tees.

With the concussion she'd suffered on the mend, she'd switched between both. But today? What she was wearing? It was different.

The black skirt screamed something even Devon recognized—a luxury label—mostly because of his mother's taste in clothes as she'd loved designer wear.

He'd never understood why, when the label was all that mattered, it was worn inside. He'd told his mother once that she should wear her clothes inside out then people would know she was wearing Chanel.

He smiled at the memory of her lovely, tinkling laugh as she cupped his cheek and kissed him there. Bringing with her the scent of honeysuckle and almond blossom. "People know this is Chanel without me having to do that, darling," she'd informed him. "Class always shines through."

"What are you looking at?" Sascha asked, as she took them out of the city.

"You," he told her promptly, finding her more interesting than anything that could be going on outside the car. "You're wearing something new."

"Like I said," she admitted with a shrug. "I wanted to make an impact."

The black sheath dress was simple, but it cut into her body in all the right places. Her ripe breasts were caressed by the fabric, the sweetheart neckline providing a hint at her cleavage, without being over the top.

The skirt came down to her calves and cupped her all the way down. Caressing her body in a way he wished he could. On her feet, she wore heels that would put her more substantial frame at the same height as him. He imagined those heels digging into his ass, and knew Kurt would get a kick out of seeing that happen.

Her jacket was Chanel—his mom had been right. That style spoke louder than words.

"You went shopping," he declared, somewhat disappointedly.

She shot him a look as she overtook an elderly man in an old Peugeot that was rattling down the motorway more by luck than management—the damn thing looked like it was held together with Blu-tack and sellotape.

"Why do you sound disappointed?"

He shrugged. "I'd have liked to have gone."

Her lips twitched. "You're just as bad as Kurt."

He frowned. "I am?"

"You only want to watch me get changed."

"Of course," he replied bluntly. "Don't all men want to see their women getting in and out of tight dresses?"

She chuckled. "When you put it like that, I guess so." She reached over, her hand slipping from the stick shift to squeeze his knee. "You're a sweetheart."

He pursed his lips. "I don't think I can stand your compliments today. Cute and sweetheart? God help me."

She snorted. "I'm paying you back."

"For what?" he demanded, aghast at her cruelty. What thirty-eight year old wanted to be labeled the same adjectives as a goddamn bunny rabbit in a pet window?

"Being a pain," she told him cheerfully.

He heaved out a sigh. "I always am."

"I know. But usually, you charm me out of it." She cocked a brow at him. "How did you know I was going to visit her?"

He shrugged. "Overheard Sean tell you your stipend had come through." He wafted a hand at her change in appearance. "Didn't expect this though. This came as a shock."

She shook her head. "Only this would surprise you but nothing else would."

As she shook her head, he frowned. "What do you mean?"

"You're not surprised I'm visiting my parents' murderer in jail, but my change of style comes as a hammer blow." She snickered. "Don't ever change, Devon."

"You keep saying that," he grunted. "But I can't change. I am who I am."

She laughed, reached over to pat his knee again. Seriously, she was making him feel like a dog or something.

Rolling his eyes, he grumbled, "You're going to see Elizabeth. I fail to understand why, but I knew you would."

"I want to look her in the eye."

"She hasn't confessed," he murmured gently. "Hasn't confessed to any of it. What do you expect to say to her? Or for her to say to you?"

She sighed. "I don't know. I just know I need to go and visit her while the court case against her is built."

"I'm surprised you know where's she jailed."

"I read it on a memo on Sean's desk," she admitted with a wry grimace.

"Why?" he asked, scowling at her deceit. She had to have looked for that memo—no way would Sean have left it floating about for her to find.

She heard his disappointment and shifted in her seat. "She murdered my parents, Devon. Like, *killed* them." Her voice grew thick. "As in stole their lives from them, stole them from me. It's not like a video game or something. She robbed me of knowing them."

"I understand what death means," he retorted. "I understand what murder means too. I fail to understand why you need to get involved with something that can do you nothing but harm. You're going to want answers. She's not going to want to give them to you. It's as simple as that."

She stuck her nose in the air. "I can drop you off at that truck stop and pick you up on the way back."

"What? You're going to dump me at Burger King?"

From a trembling bottom lip to a snickering giggle and in less time than it took to blink. "You don't have to sound so horrified. I'm not leaving you to fend for yourself."

"You are by leaving me there," he almost stuttered. "Jesus, that's just cruel."

Her grin came and went. "Well, shut up then," she advised. "I just need to do this, all right?"

He blew out a breath and settled in for the hour-long ride. She wouldn't be alone... that had to count for something, right?

THE CLANG of doors shutting and being locked—some with honest to God keys, others with automatic locks that clicked into place when a black bubble of a camera, which eyed the world in here like it was an omnipotent blackhead, deigned it—had her jolting each time.

They were in a large, open space. Sick-yellow walls, scuffed green linoleum. Dozens of tables placed at regulation distance from the next.

Several vending machines sat on one wall. One providing food, the other bottled drinks.

Scattered around watching proceedings were guards. They looked pissed off. As pissed off as Devon had been at the notion of Sascha dumping him at a service stop on the highway—or as the Brits called it, *motorway*.

Even though she felt sick from tension, the memory was enough to have her snickering inwardly, which, point of fact, lightened her discomfort. She knew Devon didn't understand what she was doing here. She didn't either so she couldn't expect him to understand it. Just… Sean's news about being able to access some of her inheritance, the fact she was pregnant… it had gotten to her.

Made her *need* to act.

She couldn't mope forever. She had a baby on the way but that didn't stop Sascha from needing closure. She feared it wasn't something she could readily get, but this was as much as she'd find. Seeing the woman who'd changed her world behind bars had to count for something.

Devon, confused or otherwise, was back in the car, sulking because the letter of acceptance for visitation rights didn't include him, and she wouldn't lie, she wished he was in here now.

This place was...Well, she knew it wasn't supposed to be pretty. But with her designer togs, she stuck out like a sore thumb.

Ten women were being visited today. Each of them in grey sweats with a kind of bib on them. Their guests wore cheap labels, scuffed trainers, heavy gold earrings their one luxury.

In her simple but elegant outfit, she might as well have been Godzilla. Not necessarily a negative but it just made her question her reasoning for being here. And she was already doing enough of that.

A buzzer sounded, making her stomach tighten and release. She was the only guest without a corresponding prisoner, so that had to be Elizabeth Jacobie.

One of the automatic doors clicked, the guard on this side of it opened it up to reveal a small woman who looked as out of place in the sweats as would a man three times her size.

She wore them with disdain. It dripped from her features, and Sascha had to wonder exactly how it was that this woman wasn't black and blue. If life in here was anything like 'Orange is the New Black,' then it was a wonder she wasn't favoring one arm or something.

Hell, Sascha, without a grudge to bear, would have wanted to slap that attitude off her face if she could. In here? Where facial expressions were taken with offense, Elizabeth was shouting her disrespect.

Diminutive, more so than she'd expected having seen the woman several times on camera, she barely came to Sascha's chin as she stepped towards her with a grace that spoke of finishing schools.

A guard tailed her, mumbled something in her ear, then retreated to the walls with the other officers when Elizabeth took a seat.

She sat with her spine ramrod straight, her head posed elegantly. Her black hair was starting to show gray at the roots, and her face, so clear and unlined in the pictures, was wrinkled and creased. Her chestnut eyes were veritable storms in her face. Her outrage at being in here evident for all to see.

Sascha sat up straighter, feeling the need to match Elizabeth's pose. She placed her hands on the table and murmured, "I had to spend a lot of money to visit you today."

And she had. She'd used a tidbit of information she'd seen on Sean's desk, and had called the lawyer Sean had hired to protect Sascha's interests through the case. This visit hadn't been long in the making, but the lawyer, who charged through the roof of course, had put in a good few hours work on this.

Sascha, who appreciated value for money, really hoped it was worth it.

"I shall endeavor to be entertaining," Elizabeth retorted, her upper lip curling into a sneer.

"Entertainment isn't required," Sascha replied, her own lips curling… into a smile. "All I had to do was see you in here. Suffering and outraged. Suddenly, I feel quite happy."

The other woman's nostrils flared. "I'd enjoy it for the moment. I'll be out soon. The lawyers will hash this out."

"Perhaps they will, perhaps they won't." Sascha shrugged. "I have as much money as your son now, Elizabeth. And I have nothing to spend it on. Perhaps I should use it to see that you never spend a day outside this place again?" The smile curved into a wicked grin. "That sounds quite satisfying. I'm willing to waste your fortune on it."

Elizabeth's grimace rolled over her features, displaying her hatred on every inch of her face. "Edward always was a weak boy."

"Weakness meaning he didn't have it in him to murder people for money? I'd say that's a good trait to have, not a bad one."

Her eyes flashed. "He's split the inheritance?"

"Yes. And there's just so much money to be enjoyed. All his effort, his hard work… I suppose I should appreciate your murdering my only family and letting him invest it into his business. After all, half of it's mine now." She smirked, rapped her nails against the table. "You really did do the work for me, didn't you?"

Elizabeth's rage was a palpable entity between them. Had they been alone, Sascha knew the older woman would have lashed out. Hit her. As it was, she was holding on to her control with the very edges of her fingertips.

She let out a long, slow breath. "I'm certain the trust will ensure he retains the majority."

"No. He concurred. In fact, he begged me to have the money rather than lose it to the government." Her smile was taunting. "I contemplated that for a while. Thought about letting the blood money you worked so hard for, go to the state.

"Then, I thought about all the things I can buy. All the ways I can waste billions you earned by murder, and which are all mine now thanks to a simple twist of fate." Her lips curved into a gleeful grin that she didn't feel but knew would enrage Elizabeth. "How does it feel to be in sweats?" She patted her dress. "This cost a thousand pounds." A giggle escaped her. "My shoes and bag cost over four. I suppose I should thank you for the new wardrobe, because I have to say, yours certainly could do with a pick me up."

"You can spend money on a new wardrobe, but maybe you should invest in a gastric band. Fat and fashion don't go together, Eloisa," came the woman's sweet retort.

But Sascha wasn't stung by the bitch's words. "Oh, I definitely have too much meat on my bones but I'm quite content to be curvaceous. I wonder if being skinny and old will save you from being someone's bitch?" She tapped her chin in contemplation, then her glee morphed into hatred. "Your failure to confess won't stop this from happening, Elizabeth. I have billions to command, and your son has billions to spend on improving his company image—having a murderess for a mother hasn't been good for his stock portfolio, I'm afraid. I hardly think he'll worry about you wasting away in here. Not when the public know exactly what it is you're in here for.

"I can afford to tie this case up. I don't know how, but I do know people who can help me. Who'll help the justice system forget about you. Push your court dates back, then have them rescheduled... because every day you're in here, I'm happy.

"Every day you're suffering, is a day I'm not. I think it's a smart investment for me to make, sister-in-law."

Elizabeth's nostrils flared. "This country isn't as corrupt as you might think."

"It isn't what you know, it's who. I know a lot of important people, Elizabeth, and your money just gave me the means with which to sign your fate." She got to her feet on her two thousand pounds' worth of designer heels and bent over the table slightly. "My parents couldn't save themselves from you, but I can ensure you pay for what you did.

"Have a nice life, Elizabeth. I certainly intend on enjoying every moment of mine."

She headed off, striding through the tables toward the exit with all the aplomb of a catwalk model.

The guard checked her over then released her to the next segment where another officer and another locked door awaited her.

As more doors separated her from the bitch that had murdered her family, she began to quiver, and with each step, her shaking increased.

She trembled the entire way out of the grim facility and nearly staggered to her car.

The door to her cherry red Caddy opened and before she knew it,

Devon was there, wrapping her up in his arms. As she breathed him in, as she let him comfort her, she accepted what she couldn't change.

Her parents were dead. She'd been raised by two people, however, who couldn't have loved her more. Henry and Natasha hadn't been wealthy, but they'd been rich with love.

No, her life hadn't turned out the way it was supposed to. And she'd never answer to Eloisa Jacobie as was her legal right.

But...

None of that mattered.

Not when Devon's arms were around her, and the rest of her men were at home, waiting on her to get back.

That was all that counted.

FORTY-ONE

SAWYER'S EYES cut to her when she stepped into the kitchen. They were narrowed and intense, which let her know Devon had told him of her visit to the jail, but he was on the phone which gave her a reprieve. She almost headed back up the stairs but she needed to get dinner on.

Sascha wasn't in the mood to be reprimanded, so if they were going to do it... they could do it all at once, she decided. Four lectures, after a fifth from Devon in the car on the way back, was far too much to take in after the day she'd had.

As she stepped toward the units, Sawyer murmured, "Ma, I've got someone I'd like you to meet."

Sascha's head whipped around to stare at Sawyer. "What?" she mouthed.

He just grinned, set the phone on the counter, and pressed 'speaker.'

"Who is it?"

The heavy Scottish accent was so dense, Sascha blinked as she tried to process it.

When she managed to translate, she murmured, "Hi Mrs. Bennett. My name's Sascha."

"She's my girlfriend, Ma," Sawyer said helpfully, spotting that she'd choked when it came to stating exactly who she was.

"Yours or *yours*?"

The distinction mattered to the older woman it would seem. "Ours," he clarified, making Sascha's cheeks heat.

"How long?"

"Nearly three months now."

"That long, huh? You going to bring her up here tae meet us?"

"Aye. Been planning on it but things have been mad of late. Have you seen that nutty bitch on the news? "

"The one who murdered all those toffs?"

"Aye. Those toffs were Sascha's parents."

"Oh lass, I'm so sorry." The tone had softened utterly at Sawyer's revelation. From harsh distrust and vague dislike marred with disapproval to utter apology. "That's terrible. Sawyer'll tell yer; I'm a bit of a gossip hound." Sascha's lips twitched—her pronunciation of hound was more like how-und. "I've been devouring all the nasty things that woman did. It's caused a right ruckus."

Sascha cleared her throat. "I know. It's a pleasure to talk to you though, ma'am. Devon says you're the best purveyor of Spotted Dick this side of the Atlantic."

An embarrassed giggle came down the line. "That boy always manages to make me sound like some kind of porn star."

"Ma!" Sawyer bellowed. "Don't be using porn and yerself in the same sentence."

Sascha grinned, loving how thick his brogue was now, and realizing how he dampened it down when he was home.

"What? He does! Although, what kind of dick is spotted, I don't know. Some kind of venereal disease, I'd bet." There was an interested hum. "Yer Aunty Mavis has shown me this marvelous thing called Wikipedia. Have yer heard of it, Sascha?"

"I have, ma'am."

"Ach, less of the ma'am. If Devon trusts ye enough to talk about pudding with VD then I know I can trust yer tae."

She blinked. "Is that good?" she mouthed at Sawyer who nodded quickly.

"Call me Jacinta."

"Thank you, Jacinta. It's a real pleasure to talk to you. Devon only mentioned you today, actually." She cast a look at Sawyer, who grinned widely, confirming her belief this was no coincidence.

"Ach, that's tae uncanny!" Jacinta boomed, and Sascha blinked.

Tugging at her ear and wishing Jacinta wasn't so hard to understand, she murmured, "I know. I don't really believe in coincidences. Not with this lot."

Jacinta snorted. "Can't blame you. You've got yourself a lass wi' a brain at last, lad."

Sawyer snorted back. "Jessica had a PhD."

"You know how much stock I put in them. I love the lad like he were my own, but Devon's got more PhDs than Alphabet Soup and he can barely survive the week without one of you telling him to get dressed, to eat, or to sleep." A grunt sounded down the line. "You're more like the man's caretaker than his friend when he gets into one of his phases tae."

Sascha grinned. "Devon's getting better."

"He is?" Jacinta sounded surprised. "She's good fer him then?"

Sawyer hummed. "Aye. Actually gets him tae sleep."

"I really dinnae want to know how," his mother replied, a bawdy laugh spilling down the line.

Even though Sascha had had the beginnings of a tension headache since leaving the prison, she couldn't help but smile at the amusement in Jacinta's tone.

"You're probably safer not asking," she admitted.

"I can imagine. Yer must be a busy lass, and there's no mistake."

"Ma!" Sawyer bellowed again. "You'll embarrass her."

"Wasn't that the point?" Sascha whispered with a glower at him.

His grin was unrepentant.

"Ach, she cannae be too weak-livered if she's living with the likes of you. Sean's the most charming of the lot and even he's a bugger from time tae time."

Sascha scratched her forehead. "Isn't bugger...?"

A snort sounded from the opposite end of the kitchen. "No, she doesn't mean I'm into buggery," Sean murmured as he stepped deeper into the room. "Hi, Jacinta. Long time since we've caught up."

"Yer not wrong, lad. I'll call you sometime next week. You want some Tablet sending down?"

"Aw, that's sweet of you, Jacinta. I'd appreciate that."

"Tablet?" Sascha asked, cocking a brow as he headed to the fridge and pulled out a bottle of water.

"It's this type of candy. Very Scottish. You'll like it. It's kind of like fudge with sugar crystals."

"It's one of our traditional foods, lass. I'll send down extra so you can try some."

"Sean's watching his sugar, Ma. He's pre-diabetic."

"Bit a'tablet won't do him nae harm," Jacinta argued.

"It's pure bluidy sugar! How the hell can it nae do him harm?"

"Don't worry, they get like this," Sean assured her, whispering in her ear as he came up behind her and wrapped his arm around her belly.

With a sigh, she sank into him, letting him keep her upright. When he nuzzled his nose into her nape, she relaxed even further.

God, it was good to be home.

"I can have a bit," Sean threw into the mix. "A little of what you fancy does you good," he informed them all, rocking his hips up and nudging her with his dick.

She grinned. "He's not wrong, Sawyer."

"Ye would agree, a'course," Sawyer grumbled.

"Since he went all health nutty on us, he won't even have Cranachan! I hope you're curing him, Sascha. A lad needs sweet stuff from time tae time. It's why he's always so sour now..."

"That kind of attitude is exactly why Da has bluidy angina! There's nothing wrong with being healthy."

A disapproving hum sounded down the line. "It's under control."

"Because I designed that diet fer him," Sawyer said, pouncing on her with a rapid-fire retort that had Sascha blinking.

"Aye. Mebbe." Jacinta huffed. "Do you like blood pudding, lass? I can send you a care package down. Even boy wonder over there likes a bit of blood pudding."

Sawyer grimaced. "Yer have me there, Ma."

"I know I do," Jacinta retorted, sounding satisfied.

Sean snorted. "You'll spend a fortune on shipping if you send that, Jacinta. It'll need to be overnighted."

"The lad puts more money in my bank account than I could have used when he was a bairn and constantly growing out of his trousers." Jacinta scoffed. "I tell yer now, I wish you'd been rich then, Sawyer Bennett. Yer nearly had us out on the streets growing out of your damn clothes the way you did."

Sawyer rolled his eyes. "Like I can help being tall."

"And I'm nae complaining. I just wish you'd been rich back then."

"Sorry to be late to the party," he retorted.

"Jacinta!" Devon's happy yell had them all turning to the staircase where he was bounding down into the kitchen. "I thought I heard your dulcet tones."

Jacinta chuckled, and it sounded like a braying horse. "Yer a charmer, yon lad. And here's me thinking it was Sean who had the silver tongue."

"I do, Jacinta, but only with the right woman."

"Aye. I've heard tell of this, Sean. You'd better be treating the lass right. She's nae had it easy with that wicked bitch doing what she did."

Devon blurted out, "Can you send me some Tablet?"

The interruption had them all chuckling. "We just had this conversation," Sawyer told him when he looked confused—truth was, Devon usually looked confused. It wasn't exactly a new look for him.

"About Tablet?"

"Aye, lad. But dinnae worry, I'll send you some too. Do you want me to bake yer some shortbread and Dundee cake?"

"What about Spotted Dick?"

Jacinta brayed out another laugh, and Sascha had to stifle a giggle —could a laugh sound Scottish? "Aye, I'll send you some of that lad, if you want it."

"You're the best, Cinta," Devon said on a sigh that was positively love struck.

"You'll have to send me the recipe, Jacinta. If it makes him that happy, I'll need to keep a supply in."

"He's not supposed to be having sugar either," Sawyer reminded them all, a gloomy trace to his words.

"A little bit of what yer fancy, as Sean says. Maybe the lad would sleep more if you weren't his Mother Hen."

"How does that work?" Sawyer retorted. "Yer said it yerself, he barely gets dressed without my prodding him sometimes."

"I feel like I'm missing out on something here," Sascha complained. "I've never seen Devon walk around in the buff."

Sean snorted. "We lost our last two housekeepers that way. Said he wasn't decent."

"I like being naked," Devon admitted with an unapologetic shrug.

Jacinta chuckled. "If I dinnae think of you as my own son, lad, I'd be grateful for watching you walk around raw."

Sawyer groaned. "Tae much information, Ma."

"What? I said if he weren't like ma own son."

Sascha pouted. "Well, I'm no prude, Devon. Feel free to wander around raw for me."

Jacinta hooted. "You've got yerselves a live one there, lads."

They all looked at each other, wide, sheepishly amused grins creasing their lips.

"Aye, we do. We'll be visiting soon, Ma, so don't be bankrupting us with shipping costs to send us cakes."

"When?" Jacinta immediately demanded. "I haven't seen yer in a lifetime."

"It was six months ago," Sawyer retorted.

"Six months is six months! Half a year, lad."

"I told you to move down here."

A pshawing noise sounded down the line. "Can you imagine yer Da down South? Jesus on the cross, they barely understand me when I'm visitin'."

"Well, it works both ways. You haven't been to see us either."

"You know that's because of Aunty Mary. She's been ill, lad."

Sawyer huffed. "Three days isn't too long a trip."

"I'm coming for more than three days if I've tae make it all the way down there."

"You fly. It takes less than an hour."

Jacinta just grumbled. "Aye, so why don't you do it tae?"

"You know I don't fly, Cinta," Devon told her, breaking into the cookie jar that was getting mighty short of snacks—a reminder for her to bake more appeared on her mental to-do list.

Jacinta grunted. "Aye, that's true. I guess I'll have tae pop down more often then. But we'll never get your Da down there for more than four nights. You and I both know he hates Cockneys."

It was kind of sweet that Devon and Sawyer came as a package with Sawyer's mother. Sascha felt a rush of warmth for the woman who had taken in an emotionally orphaned young boy and had made him a part of the family.

"Sawyer tells me you've solved that wee puzzle you were working on."

Her biological son snorted. "Wee puzzle totally negates the importance of his breakthrough, Ma."

"Ach, you're always doing something important or other. A woman can't be expected tae understand the nonsense you do." She scoffed as though the idea was close to insanity.

"You solved P vs NP?" Sean asked, the awe in his voice seemed to prick Jacinta's attention.

"It's a big deal, Sean?"

"Well, this is bigger than anything he's done yet," Sawyer retorted in Sean's stead. "Think of a needle in a haystack. Ye with me?"

"Aye. Think I can cope so far," Cinta replied, amused.

"Well, imagine if you made a huge feckin' magnet to cover a haystack the size of the feckin' Earth, just to find that one tiny needle. Devon just did the mathematical equivalent of that."

"And that's good?"

Sawyer grunted. "It's bluidy good."

"I think, knowing Devon, your bank balance will be even more padded out shortly, Jacinta," Sean remarked wryly.

"Nae more money. My lads will just guilt trip me for nae visiting more. These old bones can't travel like they used tae."

Sawyer rolled his eyes but Devon asked, his concern evident, "Why can't they, Jacinta? What's wrong with your bones?"

"They're old, lad. That's explanation enough."

Devon scowled. "Do you need to go to the doctor's again?"

"I went last week I'll have you know."

"Why?"

A mumble sounded down the line, but Devon seemed to catch it as did Sawyer—both of them finding it far easier to catch Jacinta's heavy brogue.

"Fer feck's sake, Ma. Have we got to strap you into a chair and take you to the doctor's ourselves?"

"Yer cannae say anything, Sawyer Bennett. You're just as afeared of doctors as I am."

"I dinnae care. I'm not the one with crazy cholesterol and arthritis."

Sascha twisted in Sean's arms. "Do you have a clue what she said?"

Sean pulled a face. "More from context, I'd hazard a guess she took Hamish to the doctor's, and didn't go for her own appointment. But didn't tell a technical 'untruth' because she had gone to the clinic. For him. If that makes sense."

"Hamish is Sawyer's dad?"

Sean nodded.

Devon's voice was sad. "Jacinta, you lied to us."

"I dinnae," came the indignant response. "I went to the doctor's. I didn't say the doctor checked me over."

"That's a technicality."

"You taught me how important technicalities are, Devon, so dinnae be telling me that. Not when yer used tae have me pulling my hair out on technicalities when you were living here with us."

His cheeks turned pink. "That was different."

"How was it?" More indignation.

"I was eighteen! You're a lot older!"

"Now I'm offended. You can scratch the Dundee cake off your list."

Sascha's lips twitched at their bickering. It wasn't like she could judge. In this household, technicalities were as important as oxygen.

"What did he do, Jacinta?" she asked, breaking into their argument.

"Used to tell me he dinnae have girls up in his bedroom because they were hiding in his closet, so technically they were in the closet not in the bedroom. Then there was the time he got into a fight with that idiot, Jamie Dougan, but it wasnae a real fight because he dinnae use his fists. Just kicked the shit out a'him instead."

Sascha's mouth dropped open. "You kicked someone in a fight?"

Even Sean was surprised. She felt his tension at her back.

"You make it sound bad, Jacinta," Devon reprimanded. "It wasn't as terrible as she makes it sounds."

"He had to go to the hospital!" Jacinta bellowed, with the same force as her son.

"He deserved it," came the stubborn retort.

"That's it, yer see. He deserved it, so that added to the technicalities," she scoffed. "I'm going before I start telling yon lassie all the bad stuff I knows about yous two."

Sascha giggled. "For that reason alone, I'd be looking forward to you coming for a visit, Jacinta. It will be a pleasure to meet you in person."

"Thank you, lass. That's kind of you tae say. Watch out for a package from me. And nae Tablet for Devon. I'm sulking with him." She paused. "Love you all." Then, in a brusque manner that reminded her of Sawyer, Jacinta put down the phone without waiting for a reply.

"Well, that was enlightening."

Sean's rueful comment had her giggling again. She covered her mouth when Devon shot her a look. "Sorry, but he's right."

He elbowed Sawyer in the side. "You were supposed to make her suffer a bit."

Sascha rolled her eyes. "Didn't work out for you, did it? She liked me."

"I wasnae going tae let her tear into you," Sawyer comforted in his usual gruff manner. "Just a little bit."

Sean snorted. "Just a little bit of internal bleeding, Sascha. That cheer you up?"

She peered back at him with a wide grin. "Aye. It does," she mocked in faux-Scottish.

"That's not bad, Sascha," Devon pointed out. "You've a good ear."

"I'm just used to hearing Sawyer bellow it."

"I don't bellow."

Sean snorted. "You bellow."

"I'm feeling the prejudice in this kitchen," Sawyer said, close to pouting. "Anti-Scottish sentiment among ye English pigs."

She chuckled. "I'm Ameri—" Her mouth fell open. Technically, she was English, and his smirk told her he hadn't forgotten. "Will you still feel the prejudice if I make your favorite dinner?" she asked instead.

He squinted at her. "What's the catch?"

Her smile was sickly sweet. "No catch."

"Don't trust her," Devon retorted, gloom lacing his tone.

She smiled. "It's always worth it though, isn't it?"

Sean laughed. "She's got you there."

Sawyer let out a sigh. "Okay. I'll bite."

"Spaghetti and meatballs it is."

She reached down and squeezed the hands Sean had banded around her waist. When he didn't release her, she peered back at him. "Sean?"

"How did it go with Elizabeth?"

Unsurprised Devon had shared her visit with her sister-in-law with the rest of the guys, she shrugged. "I feel better for it."

He caught her chin in his hand, studied her a second. What he saw there had him pursing his lips but otherwise nodding.

"I don't like that you went. I don't like how you found out where she was, and used the lawyer to get you a visitor's pass without us knowing... but you did what you had to do. I understand. Still, don't do it alone again. There's no need."

"Some things have to be done by oneself, Sean," she pointed out softly and rather formally.

"No. Not that. We're here for you. Just like you'd be here for us. If you forget that, the house of cards comes tumbling down."

"He's right," Sawyer said softly. "You should have told us. It's only because this one's a bleedin' Sascha savant that he knew what you were up to."

Her lips curved into a smile though she did feel guilty. Not just for today's visit but for what she wasn't telling them too—there was literally another person in the room and they didn't know it. Yet.

"A 'Sascha savant?'" she teased, rather than think about that.

Sean's eyes were serious as he murmured, "Devon seems to have the best read on you." He patted her chin with his pointer finger. "Remember that the next time you sneak around behind our backs."

She blinked at the reprimand but couldn't find it in herself to be angry. The visit might have been a stupid move. It was certainly unnecessary. Still, she felt better for it. Irrational or not.

She'd seen the woman who'd changed her life forever. Had seen the woman who thought money was her God, and who was willing to kill to attain and secure wealth. Now, she was suffering the torment of the damned in a place where her position in society and her family's wealth meant shit.

"I had to meet her," she said simply.

"And that's fine. You should have done it with one of us at your side."

Sean's lack of ire had her frowning at him, but she just nodded. Then, slightly irritated by his almost paternal tone, she narrowed her eyes at him. "Some things have to be handled on our own, Sean. How could I have gone to that frigging woman with you at my back? Do you think she'd have taken me seriously? She'd have thought I was wet behind the ears and wouldn't have told me anything I needed to know." She blew out a breath, because Elizabeth's words weren't what comforted her now. Seeing her misery *was*. "I've lived a long time without you all. I'm a big girl. I know how to handle myself, and I know that when shit comes to shit, I'm a force to be reckoned with—that's a side of me you haven't seen. When the chips are down, when I'm backed into a corner, I come out fighting."

"But you don't have to," he argued.

"I know, and that's why you think I'm docile. I'm not. But I've felt safe with you, protected. That wildcat hasn't been necessary. I knew you were there, knew you were protecting me. But today, I needed to remind myself that I don't have to hang on you for everything. Some things have to be dealt with alone." And knowing she was pregnant, that need had been all the more imperative.

He pursed his lips at her, and she could tell that though he understood her reasoning, he didn't like it. But he didn't have to like it to accept it. "You're ours, Sascha. Ours to protect and to cherish. Ours to love." Sean said, his tone borderline grim. "It's time you remembered that."

He pressed his mouth to hers; his kiss hard. His anger was bleeding through where it hadn't in his words. When he pulled back, she licked her lips. That side of him didn't perturb her. If anything, it stirred her blood.

Sean was always so calm, so rational. When he'd pushed his tongue into her mouth, stroked hers with his, she'd not hide from the fact it had made her heart skip a beat.

"I know I'm yours," she told him softly, submissively. Because she did. She was his. *Theirs*.

He stared her square in the eye again, not stopping until she ducked her chin in admission. Then, he squeezed her in his hold, kissed her temple, and murmured, "Good."

FORTY-TWO

"I NEED you to visit more, Dad," Sascha murmured as she hugged her father tight.

All around them, Heathrow was a manic welter of people as they waved their loved ones goodbye or peered hopelessly up at screens trying to find their flights.

The hubbub was almost deafening after the peace of the Kensington house, which only confirmed she was definitely adjusting to a quieter, more peaceful existence. Months ago, the chaos of Heathrow would have stirred her blood. Now? It made her cringe and wish she was back home.

"I know, Sascha," he murmured against her cheek, his arms still around her as he held her in a prolonged hug. "I'll visit more."

"Are you really thinking about moving here?" she asked, hope lacing her tone as she pulled back to look up at him.

She'd reconnected with her father during his stay here. It was ironic that learning he wasn't her biological dad had brought them closer, but then, how could it not?

He'd made the choice to protect her, to love her... even though she wasn't his. That was a choice that she could only be grateful for.

"I'm thinking about it," he admitted. "I might put the house up for sale. See what it brings." He nudged her. "Think you can put up with your old man living nearby?"

Her smile was genuine. "I'd love it."

"Not that I'd be able to afford fancy digs like your men's place." He whistled. "I've got used to the swanky life, I'll not lie."

She wrinkled her nose. "The money's there if you need it."

He cocked a brow. "Thought you weren't going to use it."

"I won't. Unless it's for something I need." She shrugged. "I need you close."

His head tilted to the side. His salt-and-pepper hair, shorn pretty close to his head, glinted in the dull overhead light. "What aren't you telling me?"

She wiggled her shoulders. "Nothing. You already know the worst of it, dad. Five guys..."

He narrowed his eyes. "Do we have to have a birds and the bees' kind of conversation?"

Sascha snickered, loving how he tried to sound tough but his cheeks were pink with mortification. "I'm on the pill, dad."

Yeah, that had *really* worked for her. Not that he needed to know that. Yet.

"Good."

"Plus, it's way too early for me to be thinking of something like that. We've only been together less than a year." May God have mercy on her for lying.

Henry squinted at her. "If you'd been together longer, would you?"

"Have a kid with them?"

She nodded, deciding to be honest. "I would. I know it's nuts, but yeah. They make me happy, Dad."

He grunted. "What else can I ask for, I suppose?"

"Aside from not to be a granddad just yet?"

A snort was her answer.

"Please. I'm too young."

She giggled. "You're never too young." Popping up on tiptoe, she kissed his cheek. "Please, don't leave it a long time before you visit again. I-I don't want to go back. I'm happy here."

"Why? Why do you never visit?"

There was a sadness in his eyes that cut her. "I can't explain it. This place just feels like home. And it has nothing to do with them. I felt like it before."

"I guess that's the Brit in you coming out to play."

She shrugged. "Maybe it is. I'm just comfortable here."

"I don't understand it, but I can accept it. Plus, it's easier for me to travel than it is for you. I know you have a lot on your hands. Keeping that kid, Devon, in line has to be worse than a toddler with gripe." He grunted. "How you stand him is beyond me."

"I have four guys to help me," she teased. "He's pretty freakin' awesome and makes me laugh harder than a stand-up comedian most days."

Henry shook his head, obviously perplexed by the notion. "I've heard you giggling at the shit he spews. I don't get it."

She winked. "You don't have to."

He sighed. "True." Squeezing her, he murmured, "I'd better go."

"I love you, Dad."

"I love you, too, pumpkin." He kissed her temple. "I'll call more. I promise."

"I'll make sure you do."

As he pulled away, staring deep into her eyes once more before he stepped back, she felt tears prick her own. Waving at him as he backed up, staring at her still until he turned around and headed toward his check-in gate, she felt the burn and had to lift a shaky hand to rub the tears away.

A hand came down to settle on her shoulder, and she turned into Sean's warm embrace. He'd said he'd wait in the car, but she was grateful he hadn't. She burrowed into his arms, loving how right it felt to be there. How secure and at home it was to be tucked in his embrace.

"You okay, love?" he asked, kissing her temple as her father had just done moments ago.

It was strange how the same gesture could mean something completely different.

Her lips curved and a thought popped into her head, one planted by her father. "I'll be fine," she answered, then, peering up at him, she asked, "If I wanted to get married, how would we do that?"

Whatever he'd expected her to say, it wasn't that. For a second, she had the sheer and utter joy of seeing Sean Hayward completely and utterly speechless. Laughter pealed from her at the sight, and she danced out of his arms, content to let him hover in a field of confusion as she grabbed his hand and tugged him out of the airport.

It was only when she was back in the car that he seemed to find his equilibrium.

"Take the next turn on the left," he said after a few moments of silence. Hell, if she'd known asking that question was a way to have some peace and quiet, she'd have asked before.

She shot him a look. "That will take us into the city."

He nodded. "I know."

"We going somewhere?"

"Yup."

She snorted. "You gonna make me guess our end destination?"

"I'm taking you shopping for clothes."

She stilled. "Why would you do a silly thing like that?"

"Andrei's gala has been rescheduled."

"I thought you'd already bought me a dress for that."

"We have. But you can use that another time. I want to feel you up in a changing room. Like you promised all those weeks ago."

"If I had free hands, I'd be playing my air violins right about now," she teased, prompting him to chuckle.

"I deserve it. It's a hard life I lead," he told her mournfully, laughing when she giggled.

"So, you don't want to buy a new dress, just take advantage of the facilities?"

His hand came to rest on her knee. "Don't you?"

Sascha had to purse her lips to hide a smile. "Maybe."

"What can I do to persuade you?"

"I'm sure you have ways and means."

"More than several, I promise you."

"Good," she purred. "Now, which way are we heading?"

As they drove into Mayfair and the more select boutiques within that area, Sascha sensed in a way how full circle they'd come. The night before she and Sean had gone shopping, that fateful day when she'd been hit by a car and this whole rigmarole had started up, she'd slept with Andrei for the first time.

All those months ago, she'd have been nervous at the idea of shopping in Mayfair. Of the amounts of money being spent on a simple dress. Now?

She wasn't exactly spoiled, but she was used to the way the guys lived. If they wanted something, they got it. If they needed something, they bought it. But, otherwise, they saved.

They had a budget which she managed, and she didn't take advantage of the wealth she had at her fingertips. She didn't exactly coupon cut, but there was no need to pass down a BOGO offer if it was smacking her in the face.

In a way, that budget was her version of normalcy.

In a household with five enormous incomes, it would be easy to lose herself to the wealth, and she had no intention of doing that.

Ever.

"What are you thinking about? I know it's not sex. You've tensed up, and not in a good way."

She smirked as she took the left lane and headed toward Mayfair's heart. "I was thinking about how a few months ago, shopping in Mayfair would have scared me."

He nodded. "I know. Back when we went shopping that first time, I figured I'd start you off in Regent's Street then head over this way. I don't think you'd have liked so much money being spent on something you figured you'd only wear the once."

"You read me right."

"Why doesn't that come as a surprise?"

"Maybe because it's your job to read people?"

He clicked his fingers. "Yeah. There is that. Although, you're harder to read than most."

Her lips twitched, but she recognized that of them all, Sean was the one who spoke least about his work.

She and Kurt could have *Kaffee und Kuchen* at eleven, the German version of brunch with lots of coffee and even more cake, and could discuss his book, his plot, and where he was taking his Pulitzer prize winning series.

Andrei wouldn't necessarily bore her with the details of his position, but he'd tell her which companies were doing well and if he'd made a loss or a win that day. Same went with Devon and Sawyer. She knew they'd been working on P vs NP, and had solved it. She'd even googled it to figure what the fuck it was they'd actually solved, and even with the help of Google, she could barely understand it.

She just knew they were in for a big payday when their work was verified by whoever did that kind of thing, some kind of math body she figured with a board of staff who all wore tweed and had thick heavy frames shielding their eyes from the world.

Although, that wasn't fair. Devon and Sawyer were hunks and they were mathematicians.

Math, with them, could be sexy too. So, while they did explain the basics, and told her what they were working on, Sean rarely did.

A couple of weeks back, he'd broken down when another victim was snatched on a case he was consulting on. She didn't know what had put the shadows in her man's eyes but she wanted to bring light to his world.

The thought urged her to say, "Sean?"

"Yes."

"You know I'm here for you, don't you?"

He stilled. "Of course."

"No. I mean… like with work? Stuff like that?"

"Ah." His hand had been a hot and heavy presence on her thigh since early on in their journey, but now he squeezed it. "I know where you're coming from. Thank you, sweetheart."

She bit her lip. "I really mean it. If you ever need to talk…"

"I don't want to put this on you, Sascha. The stuff I deal with, mostly, are things I don't want any of you to see."

"But you deal with it."

"Yeah, I do, and I wish I didn't have to. I wish I didn't have the knack of being able to see flaws in a crazy man's MO. But I do. So I use it." He squeezed her knee again. "You're here for me, Sascha. In ways you don't even realize."

Her brow puckered. "What do you mean?"

"You bring peace to my world, love." He shrugged. "I can only imagine how trite that sounds, but it's true. You do it for all of us. When you're around, it's like what Devon told me once—you cancel out the noise from the rest of the world."

Her eyes widened. "Is that a good thing?"

"For five men who avoid the world but still get caught up in it? Yeah, that's a good thing. Hell, it's a great thing." His smile was rueful. "Not only that, you make me happy."

"I couldn't have recently. Not only have I been moping, but I had that concussion and everything…"

He shook his head. "Life gets in the way. It always does, and you had reason to mope, love. I wouldn't say you were being self-piteous. You were just coming to terms with a whole new truth. A truth that sucks. The only consolation for me is the fact your parents loved you. That's a huge deal."

"I wish I could talk to my mom, you know? Ask her why she agreed to do what she did."

"It probably started off with money, love. Your biological father was a wealthy man, and he'd have paid her well to get you out of the country. Then, she fell for you, and loved you as her own." He smiled. "That makes my heart happy to know."

Touched because she could hear his genuine earnestness, she rested her hand on his knee after she parked in a small lot.

"Thank you, Sean."

"You don't have to thank me."

"I do." She let out a breath. "I only brought this up because I wanted you to know I'm here for you. You don't talk to any of us about your work, and that can't be good for you."

"I do," he countered, surprising her. "Kurt knows a lot but he doesn't say much. Why do you think he's usually always in my office when I'm there?" He jerked a shoulder. "We bounce ideas of one another."

She blinked. "I'd never have guessed that."

He snorted. "I can see from your surprise you didn't. Still, you don't have to worry about the burden. Kurt shares it. Andrei too if he's not busy working on something." He squeezed her knee. "We're a family. That's what we do."

"I know. I should have realized—"

"Hey, why do you sound embarrassed?"

She bit her lip. "I've only been a part of your lives for a short time. I shouldn't have made out like you were incomplete without me, you know?"

His laughter was joyous; so, even though it kind of hurt he was laughing, the sound was so inoffensive, she just had to stare at him in confusion.

"Sweetheart, we *were* incomplete without you." The gentle sweetness to his words had her blushing.

"I love you, Sean."

He smiled. "I love you too, Sascha."

Then, because things were suddenly feeling pretty heavy and that hadn't been her intention at all, she murmured, "Want to go fuck in a dressing room?"

His eyes lit up. "That sounds like a hell of a lot of fun."

FORTY-THREE

THE END OR IS IT?

LAUGHTER SPILLED from her lips as Andrei tugged her out of the hotel.

They were at the Ritz. The old-world grandeur, even hours later, still had the power to stun her.

Its Art Deco charm and elegance reminded her of Maggie Smith in *Downton Abbey*. It was like, when you stepped into its hallowed walls, you were transported back to a time when London was more than just Europe's banking center, but the center of the Empire.

"Why are we rushing?" she asked, gasping a little as Andrei pulled her along behind him.

With the doormen having lifted their hat to her, she knew they'd be watching them as they rushed ahead—the last thing she needed was a witness to her falling on her ass in these heels.

Heels, Sean had picked for her, and ones she'd dug into his ass as he fucked her against a cubicle mirror.

Cheeks heating at the memory, she tugged Andrei's hand. "Andrei! I can't run in these shoes!"

He paused, jerked them to a halt. She laughed when he pushed her against the wall and put his mouth on hers. His hands came up to cup her face, and she felt her hair tumble out of its gravity-defying topknot and fall between his fingers.

She liked this position. Liked being shoved up against walls as their cocks burrowed into her stomach, their hips pinning her in place.

When Sean had dragged her into the changing room only four days before, she'd mewled with disappointment when he'd expected her to ride him as he sat on the chair within the cubicle.

Because the dressing rooms in the stores he took her to, were as unlike anything found in a regular department store as margarine was to butter.

The space had been as large as her bathroom. With a fancy cheval mirror at all the corners of the room so she could see the different angles of the dress.

She wasn't sure why there was an armchair in there, unless the assistants were used to men coming in and fucking their women in them…

Who knew, maybe that was standard practice in posh retail?

She smoothed her hands along Andrei's tuxedo-covered spine and dug her fingers into his ass as thoughts of what she'd done with Sean riled her up.

"Is this why you dragged me out of there?" she demanded a second later when he let her up for air.

Her lips were bruised from his rough passion, but she loved it. Loved it when they all let loose and didn't worry about her sensitivity. They just unleashed themselves on her.

When Sean had pushed her against the wall, her face against it, she'd loved having him behind her, her back and his chest almost glued together as he fumbled to penetrate her.

He'd been deep at that angle. Had fucked her with short, blunt thrusts that had her eyes clenching tightly shut and nails digging into his hands which, once he was fucking her, he bridged with hers and pinned them to the wall beside her shoulders.

She'd loved the crass words that had spilled from his lips. Had loved the feel of him inside her as he claimed her, roughly.

Because that's how it felt. Each and every time. Like they were claiming her. Individually and as a group. And she fucking loved it.

Needed it, even.

She moaned as Andrei broke into her thoughts by nipping her bottom lip. "It was as boring as I told you it would be, wasn't it?"

She blinked. "Huh? You mean the kiss? Hell no."

His lips curved. "I didn't mean the kiss. I meant the gala. But it's good to know my kisses don't incite snores."

She snorted. "Oh, you mean the event. Yeah, it was kind of dry. Worth it to see you standing up there though, all gorgeous in your tux." She ran her nails along his back, loving the texture of the silk against them. "And your speech wasn't dull."

"It was. I tried not to make it too bland for you, though. Not sure how well it worked. I don't want you to dread coming to these things."

His admission had her arching her hips, nudging his cock as she did. "You could never bore me. I don't necessarily understand what the hell it is you're talking about, but that's neither here nor there." That he wanted her to come with him again, meant the world.

He laughed. "True." Bowing his head, he pressed a gentler kiss to her lips and slithered his tongue along the bottom one.

"I was standing up at that podium, bored out of my brain, just thinking about getting you out of this dress. Sean's the devil sometimes. He knows exactly what gets me hard."

She cocked a brow. "How does he?"

Andrei squeezed her hands in his. "Fishing?"

"Only for clues," she retorted, but she was teasing.

"We all know what gets each other hot. It's like knowing Sawyer hates porridge but eats it four times a week. Or that Devon goes through paper like he's feeding it into a fire."

"Oh hell no. There's a major difference between knowing preferences when it comes to food and when it comes to a sexual partner's wardrobe."

He grinned. "Bull. Devon prefers nudity."

"That comes as no shock," she retorted. "Not after I find out he likes wandering around butt naked."

"He told me you encouraged him to start up again." Andrei rolled his eyes. "Do you know how many members of staff we've lost because of that? We only just started keeping him in jeans."

She laughed. "Well, they were all prudes. I, for one, can't wait for him to revert to type."

He grimaced. "Sawyer likes casual clothes. This kind of gear will get him hot, but he prefers…" Andrei pursed his lips. "You know when we were in the kitchen?"

"And he spanked me with a spoon?" She chuckled. "Yeah. I remember."

"Well. That's his style. Impromptu. Spontaneous. Clothes don't do it for him for that reason."

"What about Sean? What does he like?"

"Want pointers?" Andrei joked, but didn't wait for her to reply. "He likes your usual style actually. Skirts. He's definitely a skirt man. But he also likes a bit of danger. More than most of us."

She smirked. "You mean he likes to fuck in public?" Like she hadn't known that already.

Andrei shrugged. "Yeah. Nothing too crazy though."

Just changing rooms, she thought. That kind of thing. Then, she made a mental note to make out with him in her Caddy at some time in the future.

They could spread out on the backseat and make out old-school style.

A prospect that had her already damp thong getting a hell of a lot damper.

"What about Kurt?"

"Aside from the watching?" She nodded. "I guess if you wear lingerie, he'll follow you around like a puppy for life."

Sascha's laugh was husky. "That's not nice."

He grinned. "Maybe not, but true. He already loves that you let him watch."

She shrugged. "It's hot."

"You're perfect for us," he breathed against her lips, slipping his tongue into her mouth and stroking it with his own.

When she was breathing hard, he murmured, "Then, there's me. I love this get up."

She wore a red sheath dress that would have made Marilyn Monroe a very happy bunny.

It was skin-tight from waist to knee, then flared out into a fishtail that swirled around her heels and allowed her to walk. The shocking red was offset by a darker crimson that started at her waist and, at an angle, bisected the top half while covering her breasts in the darker fabric.

The sweetheart neckline was low, so low, she feared for her nipples. But hell, she felt sexy. Especially with the elbow-length white gloves and strappy silver shoes.

Earlier that evening, Kurt had placed a wrap on her shoulders and had kissed her from shoulder to the top of her glove, declaring her to be: "Perfection."

She smiled at the memory, then smiled harder when she thought how Devon had laid back on her bed, eating an apple, as he watched her struggle into the skintight gown.

He hadn't offered to help. Had simply said, "Pretend I'm not here."

It seemed Devon liked watching too.

She panted against Andrei's lips when he pulled back. "Take me home," she murmured, arching against him. "I want you."

"Not yet. I have a surprise for you."

She blinked. "You do?" Then, a tad more suspiciously, asked, "What kind of surprise?"

"You'll love it," he promised her, finally letting her up and tugging her onto her feet so she could balance in the high heels.

"Is that why we're rushing?"

"Why we *were* rushing, yes. Our kiss was a slight but very necessary detour."

She grinned, loving that he found her so sexy in this get up that he'd just had to kiss her. He'd been remarkably restrained all night, but she'd figured, early on, that was nerves.

Though he always seemed calm and confident, she guessed even calm and confident guys got nervous at speaking in front of their peers. Only when they'd entered the gala had she actually realized how many people were attending tonight.

Christ, she didn't mind public speaking, but even she would have been flustered.

When they reached his car, he opened the door for her and helped her into the passenger seat. Touched as always by his gentlemanly behavior, she waited for him to round the vehicle and climb in.

It was cold. But then, when wasn't it? Even in mid-summer, the nights could be chilly. Thankfully, it hadn't rained for a few days, so the nip in the air wasn't enhanced by damp.

Still, when he turned the heaters on, she shivered with relief.

The amber glow of the streetlights was broken up by the bright glare of headlights, but she was nice and cozy, tucked in the car, with a classical radio station playing very smooth, very pretty pieces.

"You comfortable?" he asked after he directed them out of a nasty gridlock.

"Very," she told him, a touch sleepily.

She'd been tired of late, more so than her workload required. As she pressed her hand to her stomach, she guessed she had a reason why.

She turned her head to look at Andrei, a sleepy smile curving her lips as she saw the stern lines of his handsome face tense up as he swore at a driver who cut him off. It wasn't likely he was the father. But maybe he was. *Did it matter?* Sascha asked herself.

They'd all be the father in the end.

She bit her lip at the thought, wondering if they'd take her news with equanimity or the panic she'd had. The notion, with any other man, would have had her freaking out.

With these five, though, it wasn't too scary. She'd have four more pairs of hands around than most women did…

Still, it was sooner than she'd have liked, but it wasn't like she had a say in things.

"You okay?" Andrei cut her a look. "You're quiet."

"I'm warm, full, and content. Why wouldn't I be quiet?"

He snorted. "You do realize most women are quiet when they're upset about something?"

"Since when have I been most women?"

"Touché," he told her with a grin.

"Where are we going?"

"I told you, it's a surprise."

She huffed. "If you think I haven't realized we're going to the airport, then you're nuts." Hell, she'd only dropped her father off four days ago. What did he think she had? A peanut for a memory?

His grin was fleeting. "Don't spoil it."

"Have you packed for me?"

"Partially. A case is in the trunk. But we'll have to buy clothes there."

"Why?"

"Because it's minus ten there?"

She winced. "I know Scotland is cold, but that cold?"

"Why would I take you to Glasgow? That's for Sawyer to do."

"I was kind of hoping Moscow wasn't the end destination." She grimaced. "I'd prefer somewhere warmer than here."

He snorted. "Sorry, love, it's definitely Moscow we're heading for."

"I'm going to meet your grandfather?" The notion perked her up a little. Andrei loved Vasily, so she was curious about him.

A man who, thanks to his rank, could inspire terror in everyone else, while also having the love of his grandchild... that was a man worthy of meeting.

"What am I going to wear when I get there? I'll freeze."

"Vasily will have a car waiting for us. He said he'd bring furs."

She pulled a face. "Furs?"

He shrugged. "I know. It's not very PETA but they're kind of old school. Furs keep you warm."

"So do fancy-schmancy down coats."

"Okay, well, let me rephrase that. My grandfather is old-fashioned. He'd never bring anything fancy-schmancy when fur works fine. We can always buy better coats if the furs disgust you though."

"If you'd let me in on the trip, I could have prepared for it."

"Where would the fun in that be?"

His eagerness was so boyish that she had to chuckle. "You're right. I'll stop being boring."

He winked at her. "You could never be that, love."

FROM HEATHROW to Sheremetyevo International airport, it was just shy of a four-hour flight. By the time they landed, it was seven AM, pitch black, and freezing.

Sascha seriously wondered if she'd ever been so cold in all her life. The clothes he'd packed into a small carry-on were, of course, insubstantial. Still in her red gown with God only knew how many hoodies on over it, she looked like a homeless person who'd been given a designer dress by a moron of a donor.

She'd traveled first class the first time in her life, and had had more orange juice than was advisable. But, aside from being bone-stirringly cold, she was a happy camper. Until a thought struck her. "Andrei? The others know I'm here, don't they?" she asked, as he led her down the tunnel that would take them from the plane to the terminal.

"What? You think I've kidnapped you or something?" he asked, shooting her a grin. His eyes sparkled with amusement.

"No, dumbass," she retorted, tugging his hand. "But... I just..." She bit her lip, and apparently the look on her face was enough to have him concerned because he tugged her out of the main flow of pedestrian traffic and to the side.

"Hey. What is it? What's wrong?"

"I just..." How did she admit that it was going to be weird not being under the same roof as them tonight? Hell, not just tonight. But for however long they were going to be in Russia.

She plucked at the zipper on her third layer of hoodies, and murmured, "I'll miss them."

The simple statement had his eyes widening, then his smile grew. "I know, love. But my grandfather isn't getting any younger, and he wants to meet you. It won't be for long. I promise."

"No," she argued. "It's not that. I'd love to meet him. It's just, they might miss me too, you know?"

"There's no 'might' about it," he replied. "They will, but yeah, they knew. And they want you to have a great time here."

She smiled. "That's cool. I just didn't... they might have worried, you know? What with everything that's happened recently."

He squeezed her fingers. "They're all very happy you're about to have a whirlwind tour of Russia's capital."

His words, bizarre though it may have been, were almost what she needed. It was like having been given permission to enjoy herself.

It wasn't that she needed permission, of course. But it just lightened her load. The thought of them freaking out about her location, after what Elizabeth had put them through, well, she never wanted them to fear for her again.

Silly, but then, sometimes emotions made fools of everyone.

In her strappy heels and red dress, she'd have stuck out like a sore thumb anywhere. Especially with a man as handsome as Andrei dressed in a tux at her side. Throw in the fact they weren't wearing the right clothes? They received a lot of funny glances, and by the time they made it through passport control, out of the luggage area, and through to the entrance of the airport, she had to stifle her giggles.

Then, she couldn't stifle them anymore when she saw, amid the bustling crowd, a large man. Six feet, maybe closer to seven feet, tall and shrouded in furs… He looked like he was wearing a bear.

She blinked at him, then pointed at Andrei. "I'll assume he's our driver."

A laugh escaped him. "You guessed right. And the little guy beside him? That's Vasily. My *dedushka*."

"*Dedushka* is grandfather?"

He nodded.

"Does he speak English?"

"As good as you or I."

"That's a relief," she admitted quietly, then smiled as they approached the small man who, years down the line, gave her a clue as to how Andrei would age.

A garble of Russian flooded the space between the younger and the older Kirov, and Sascha stood to the side, content to let them reconnect.

She knew Andrei hadn't been back in a long time, and from the tears tracking down Vasily's face, the time and distance had been felt.

She swallowed, feeling the lump in her throat at the sight of such naked and raw love. It touched her, and she pressed a hand to her belly. Subconsciously telling her child that was the kind of family it was being born into.

Vasily's eyes popped open as he hugged his grandson, and he skewered her with his glance. They were as bright as Andrei's and just as canny. His body might be old, his frame withered with age—he was skinny even with a thick fur wrapping him up—but he was as on-the-ball as ever.

He spoke to Andrei, and she heard a lot of, "*Da*s." The Russian for 'yes.'

"Forgive me, child," was his next words in croaky English. "You must be freezing. It would seem my grandson has forgotten how to dress a lady." He motioned at the man to his side who tossed one of the furs at Andrei, then held hers open and gestured for her to slide her arms into the sleeves.

The furs were warm from the man's body as well as the overheated temperature of the airport—well, it wasn't for her, but she could tell the rest of the crowd were comfortable. But then, they weren't wearing designer couture that had no interest in covering a woman or making sure she wasn't freezing to death.

She shuddered with relief to be covered in the voluminous folds and tried not to feel guilty at whatever animal had died to keep her warm. She was definitely anti-fur, but at that moment, when it felt like her extremities were about to go numb. She truly appreciated it.

"I have boots for you both too," Vasily murmured, and in his hand, he had a carrier bag. "Andrei told me your size, and I knew you wouldn't get anything like this over in London." He sniffed his disdain.

"They manage to dress for the cold over there, *dedushka*," Andrei argued as he grabbed the bag and held out the boots for her. He didn't switch his own until she slipped off one of her stupid heels, using him for balance, then tugged on her boot. She didn't even care they were doing this in the middle of a busy concourse. She wanted those heels off and that fur covering her frostbitten toes.

When she'd slid the other one on too, Vasily murmured, "You're a sight for sore eyes though, Sascha. In that red dress?" He whistled. "You remind me of Gilda."

"Gilda?" Her brow puckered, then cleared. "Oh! You mean the Rita Hayworth film?"

Vasily's eyes widened in pleasure. "You watch the classics?"

Andrei laughed as he tugged on his own boots. "You've just made a fan for life."

She grinned sheepishly. "They're a guilty pleasure of mine. Did you see 'Now, Voyager?' That's my favorite."

"With Bette Davis?" Vasily's smile was sad. "*Da*. Many years after it was released however."

"Even guys like my grandfather had to put up with the blockades and sanctions," Andrei explained. "Only after the Soviet Union fell could they access things like that."

She nodded her understanding, then murmured, "Thank you so much for the coats and boots, Vasily. If I may call you that?"

"It's my honor," he replied, grabbing her by the arms and planting a kiss on either cheek. "And you're welcome for the clothes. You must have been freezing."

He was taller than her now she'd dropped the heels, but she could still see the sparkling eyes that reminded her of her lover. His craggy face was lined and wrinkled, and he wore every single one of his years on his skin, but he was a handsome man regardless.

"Andrei is impractical. He always was. Would come home with books and no clothes when I sent him for school things."

She grinned. "Really? Are you going to pass me all the gossip about his most embarrassing years?"

Vasily winked. "Of course." When Andrei groaned, he laughed and the sound was so boisterous, it was contagious. As she giggled, he murmured, "But first, we take you to eat. I'm going to show you one of Moscow's best cafes. You're going to eat breakfast, then you're going to get some sleep."

"Oh! But that's missing the first day."

"There's plenty of time," he told her, patting her hand when he tucked her arm into his and guided her out of the entryway toward the doors.

Behind her, she heard Andrei talking to the man who had carried their coats, and though she felt a little like she'd been thrown to the lions, she didn't really mind.

"You're nervous?"

Vasily's question had her frowning. "No. Not really."

"That's unusual. You know his past, *da*?"

"I do," she admitted.

"So you know what I was?" No shame. No fear littered his voice.

"*Da*," she told him in Russian.

"You're not afraid?"

Maybe she should have been but... "I have faith in Andrei."

Vasily grinned. "Good answer." He patted her hand as he led her to a car that was hovering outside the entrance in a spot that should have had him ticketed in an instant.

Instead, the engine was running. Torrents of steam cascaded out of the fender as the air collided with the frigid cold.

She couldn't see much. It was still dark, and though the streetlamps illuminated the roads and the parking areas, it didn't particularly improve visibility. She couldn't see far ahead, couldn't see if Russia was white with snow in the distance or just frigid with cold.

A man hopped out of the car wrapped in a scarf that covered his nose and opened the passenger seat for them. Vasily held her hand as she slid in, then he came next, followed by Andrei.

The door closed, and then she felt the car shift as coat man and the driver climbed in too.

As the engine started, the warmth hit her, and she snuggled into her cozy coat, wiggling her toes as they started to defrost.

"Cafe Pushkin?" Andrei asked.

Vasily nodded. "Best place. They make the good coffee," he told her.

Andrei reached for her hand. "That means he likes you," he teased. "If he hadn't, he'd have taken you somewhere else."

Vasily scoffed. "Don't tell her all my secrets."

She chuckled, but was content to snuggle against Andrei's side and let the men talk. It was kind of them to stay in English, but she dozed off to the sounds of them reverting to Russian.

When she next awoke, daylight was slipping through the cracks but it was still dark-ish.

"What time is it?" she asked around a yawn.

"Eight," Andrei told her, turning his head to kiss her temple. "You had about twenty minutes' sleep. We're almost there."

She smiled, content to just rest there, leaning against him, until she had to move. Fatigue after the journey was hitting her. She hadn't slept on the plane, had instead messed around on her phone while Andrei read a book he'd packed.

She hated to admit it, but Vasily was probably right to suggest they eat then get some rest.

Now she was here though, she wanted to see the sights. Moscow had never been on her 'to-visit' list but that didn't mean she wasn't about to take full advantage of it.

When they pulled up outside a well-lit street, she peered out onto the sidewalk.

The building was old. Wide, two stories, but beautifully maintained. Bricks the size of A3 paper were stacked perfectly, gray-blue grout separated the yellowy cream tiles, and sash windows that matched the grout gleamed in the still-lit streetlights.

A black and gold sign hovered above the door, which was bracketed by a low cast-iron fence. Above the door, there was a window with a small Juliet balcony lined with balustrades. Grand black lanterns were fixed to the walls, giving the whole place a grandeur that caught her breath.

The cold outside did the same thing. She jerked in shock to go from the warm interior to the bitterness of the street. Andrei laughed as she snuggled against him.

"You don't get used to it," he promised her.

Vasily poopoohed that "Your blood has thinned."

Sascha snorted. "Thinned? London isn't exactly warm."

Andrei murmured, "To him, it is."

"I feel no cold," Vasily declared, fist pumping the air and making Sascha laugh at his antics.

The guy was a mob boss but acted like Popeye post-spinach.

She grinned at the notion as they walked to the entrance, and the door popped open, a smiling man awaiting them.

What happened next had her both bewildered and enchanted as they stepped into what was, Andrei informed her after they took a seat, a nobleman's house that had been transformed into a coffee shop. Sascha had never seen anything like it in her life.

They passed through rooms with ornate bookcases, lined with so many leather-bound volumes she wanted to weep. The moldings on the wall panels were exquisite, the floor beneath her feet a glorious parquet that gleamed with the patina of age and thousands of footsteps.

Old-fashioned lights illuminated the cafe, and were necessary in the gloomy morning light. A huge globe sectioned off one side of the room from another, its wooden and paper decoration made her gasp at the antique.

There were dozens of tables as they passed through rooms. Each organically placed. Beside a bookcase here, next to a window there. They fit in, rather than stand out, amid the ornate fireplaces that flickered with fire, the grand staircases that led to an old-fashioned bar top.

Each room had a different color scheme. Red, blue, cream... they were guided to a green and white room, to a table beside the window where a Grandfather clock ticked merrily away behind them.

"This is amazing," she whispered as she took a seat, still awestruck by how incredible this place was.

Vasily, looking pleased as punch, took a seat as their server held out his arm for the old man's coat. Andrei helped her out of hers too, then passed theirs onto the server. With all the coats piled in his arms, he looked like he was wearing a bear just as Vasily's man had earlier at the airport. Or whatever poor animal had died to keep them warm. A thought that had her grimacing with guilt.

She gawked around as Vasily murmured, "This girl has good taste."

The coffee shop was quite busy. As they'd walked through it, she'd seen dozens of tables filled with hungry mouths waiting to be fed. But in their section, it was dead.

Andrei caught her eye and smiled. "Grandfather doesn't like to be watched when he's eating."

The man's power had her flinching, but Andrei understood as he pressed his hand to her knee and squeezed.

That Vasily had the kind of weight to pull...? Well, that told her 'retired' or not, exactly who she was dealing with.

Vasily huffed. "I don't want someone watching me slurp my coffee. Drink, by the way. I told them to have it waiting."

She peered down at the cups which had indeed been waiting for them. A logo of some sort that reminded her of the mathematical symbol for Pi—which told her she'd been hanging around Devon, Andrei, and Sawyer for way too long—had been dusted into the foam on top of hers. Little pots with white sugar cubes and tablets of what looked like brown sugar had dainty pincers nestled amid them.

Vasily took a sip and sighed. "That's better."

Andrei drank his own black coffee and murmured, "Yes. That is." He grinned, rubbed his hands together after he put the cup down. "It's good to be home."

Vasily mumbled something in Russian that had Andrei biting back, but she knew they were just bickering—something she was used to after living with five men for close to six months.

"Boys, do I have to knock some heads together?"

Her words cut through their friendly ripostes, and Vasily hooted. "She has fire! I like her!"

Andrei rolled his eyes, then murmured, "We're off to a good start then."

Vasily grinned. "Sascha, this is my favorite place. I come here on special occasions so my grandson is teasing. He knows I like you or I wouldn't have brought you here."

"You barely know me!" she retorted a little flustered.

"Any woman who puts that smile on his lips has my approval," he told her with a roguish wink that had her blushing. "Plus, that dress is a sight for an old man's eyes."

"Pervert," Andrei barked from behind his coffee cup.

"I'm not dead, Andrei."

The rueful retort had her snickering as she sipped her incredibly strong coffee. The doctor's warning not to drink caffeine had her stumped for a while, but she took a few more sips then decided enough was enough.

"I can see why it's your favorite place... it's remarkable."

"We're on Tverskoy Boulevard," he informed her. "It opened up in the 18th century and was a popular place for Moscow's elite to stroll around." He beamed a smile. "My favorite poet, Alexander Pushkin, is who it is named for. It is said this area inspired his work."

She blinked. "So this isn't his home?"

"No. But it once was a nobleman's mansion," Andrei murmured.

And so began the most bizarre breakfast she'd ever had. They peppered her with facts about the area as she dined on a meal that was more than just breakfast.

She switched to hot chocolate and munched on honey cake after eating rye blinis with salty slivers of salmon. Andrei fed her tidbits from his plate; poached eggs with a shrimp bisque, and even Vasily let her experience sturgeon caviar for the first time on buckwheat blinis.

It was like no other breakfast she'd had, and all the more amazing for the location.

"You two argue a lot," she murmured, feeling sated and sleepy again after eating a veritable feast of weird flavors for the first meal of the day.

She wasn't sure if it was something she could get into, but technically this was supper as she hadn't really rested yet, right?

Vasily cast her a look. "We don't argue. We debate."

After having heard them discussing an IPO for the past ten minutes, she had to snort. "Debate? You play with words too well, Vasily."

He grinned, displaying teeth that were definitely false and gleamed white in his leathery face. "No one can keep up with me save for this young fool."

Andrei rolled his eyes. "We both know Sean can too."

Vasily wagged his fingers. "You have a point, but not in Russian." To her, he told her, "We speak English for you, but later, when you come to visit my house, we will shout and yell in Russian. You mustn't be scared. It is just our way." A tender smile softened the harsh lines of his face. "His grandmother used to raise hell at us. Said we sounded like we were hollering at one another from the other side of the Berlin Wall."

She saw the glint in his eyes that spoke of tears; for a guy who ran the Bratva, he was free with his emotions. Still, deciding to save an old man's pride, she tilted her head to the side and asked, "We're not staying with you?"

Andrei answered, "No. I want you to stay in the city center."

"Why?"

"Grandfather lives out of the city. I want you to see Moscow."

She blinked. "Oh. Well, next time we visit, I'm fine with staying with Vasily. You don't see him enough as it is."

Andrei's grandfather beamed, and Sascha had more confirmation that she had a new fan.

As they left the cafe, she knew she'd be asking Andrei to bring her here again before they left. The place was magical in that it made her feel like she was back in the 18th century. But, she was very grateful she wasn't... heating in these temperatures? What a bitch.

Shuddering as they stepped out onto the sidewalk, she saw there were two cars waiting for them this time.

Vasily kissed her cheek and told her he'd see her later as he headed for his car, and Andrei guided her to the other.

The instant their door closed, they were swept away, and once again, she was reminded of his grandfather's position. How couldn't she be when everything ran so smoothly?

"He's powerful, isn't he?"

The question didn't seem to surprise her partner. "Yes. He's no longer as involved as he once was, but he has very important friends in the government. He helps them, and they grease the wheels."

Her lips curved. "I like him."

"I'm glad."

His simple answer had her reaching for his hand.

"Thank you for bringing me here."

"You're welcome. I wanted you to have a break."

"Why?"

"You've been through a lot recently."

She cocked a brow at him. "That the only reason?"

"You've had an attempt on your life, endured a concussion for too long, discovered things about your past that would fell anyone... you needed a break."

"Devon and you have worse pasts."

"This isn't a competition," he told her softly. "I wish you hadn't had to go through what you did, *moy meeliy*."

She blinked. "That's the first time you've done that."

"Done what?"

"Called me something in Russian. What does it mean?"

His lips twitched. "That's for me to know and for you to find out."

Snorting, she turned to look out the window and what she saw was both impressive and bleak. It was cold. That was it. Her first impression. It just looked so damn frigid. Then, when she looked past that, she saw the grand buildings, the elegant and huge pieces of architecture that were astonishing to the eye.

If she wasn't used to Tucson and London, the sheer mass of space would have astonished her. Then, after driving around the streets for twenty minutes—a detour for her benefit, she assumed—it started to impress her more and more.

How anything or anyone worked in these temperatures was a feat worthy of Merlin.

As eye-opening as it was, by the time they made it to the hotel, she was dead on her feet. She barely noticed the beautiful 19th century interior, was just grateful there was an elevator.

A porter carried their small bags and opened the doors with flair. She stepped inside, took a quick glance around, and then froze in place.

A smile widened her lips and relief and love came with her delight.

Her men were there.

All of them.

Devon was laying flat out on the bed, a notepad in hand and a pencil tucked behind both ears as well as one in his fingers. Sawyer was slouched on an armchair reading. Kurt sat at a desk, fiendishly writing something on his computer. Sean was working on his laptop too in front of a large, fire-filled hearth.

At the sight of them, so comfortable and at ease, her heart burst with love for them.

Now, she could relax. Now, she could enjoy herself because wherever these five were, she was home. And home was all she needed to handle anything life threw at her.

Even impromptu 'meet the family' visits to Moscow.

Andrei came to a stop behind her, and pulling her hair aside, he pressed a kiss to her throat. "Good to be home?"

She shot him a look, astonished that he'd read her mind. He just smiled, and like that, her world fell into place.

Sascha pressed a hand to her stomach, a smile blossoming on her face at how perfect this moment was. "Guys," she said huskily. "I have something to tell you..."

THEIRS TO CHERISH IS NOW LIVE ON KU!

EXCLUSIVE SCENES

HEY DARLINGS,

I have some behind-the-scenes' snippets for the Quintessence series.

You can find them here: https://dl.bookfunnel.com/ap88c4sc23

Just FYI, at least one of them should be read after you've completed Hers To Hold. <3

Soooo hope you enjoyed the first book in the series. <3

Much love,

Serena

Xoxo

FREE EBOOK ALERT!!

Don't forget to grab your free e-Book!
Secrets & Lies is now free!
https://dl.bookfunnel.com/22rhpk2ng2

Meg's love life was missing a spark until she discovered her need to be dominated. When her fiancé shared the same kink, she thought all her birthdays had come at once, and then she came to learn their relationship was one big fat lie.

Gabe has loved Meg for years, watching her from afar, and always wishing he'd been the one to date her first and not his brother. When he has the chance to have Meg in his bed—even better, tied to it—it's an opportunity he can't refuse.

With disastrous consequences.

Can Gabe make Meg realize she's the one woman he's always wanted? But once secrets and lies have wormed their way into a relationship, is it impossible to establish the firm base of trust needed between lovers, and more importantly, between sub and Sir…?

This story features orgasm control in a BDSM setting.

Secrets & Lies is now free!

https://dl.bookfunnel.com/22rhpk2ng2

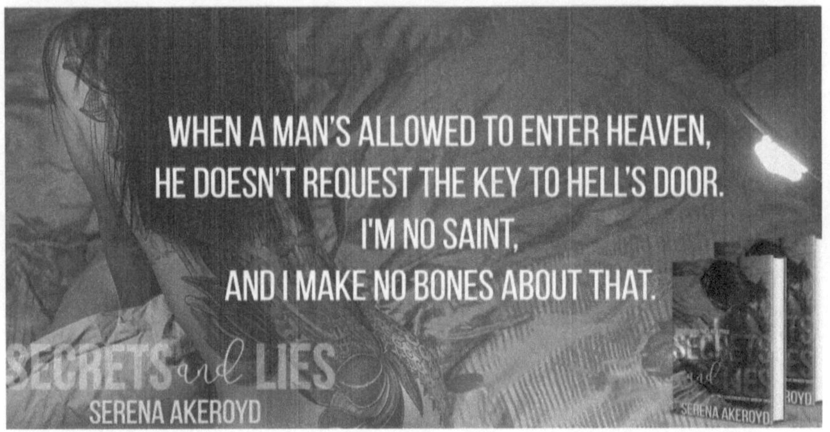

ALSO BY SERENA AKEROYD

For the latest updates, be sure to check out my website!

But, if you'd like to hang out with me and get to know me better, then I'd love to see you in my Diva reader's group where you can find out all the gossip on new releases as and when they happen. You can join here: www.facebook.-com/groups/SerenaAkeroydsDivas. Or, you can always PM or email me. I love to hear from you guys: serenaakeroyd@gmail.com.

Until I see you there or you write me an email or PM, here are more of my books for you to read…

The Five Points' Collection

The Air He Breathes

Filthy Rich

Filthy Dark

The Kingdom of Veronia Collection

Theirs

SATAN'S SINNERS' MC

Nyx

Link

Sin

Dragon Bound

Coven

Leman

Eight Wings Academy

The Ascended

HawkRidge High

Dare You To Love Me

Dare You To Keep Me

Hell's Rebels MC

All Sinner No Saint

The Sex Tape **(Co-written with Helen Scott)**

The Professor

The Caelum Academy

Seven Wishes

Eight Souls

Nine Lives

Naughty Nookie

Sinfully Theirs

Sinfully Mastered

The Gods Are Back In Town

Hotter than Hades

The Sun Revolves Around Apollo

FourWinds

Queen of the Vamps

QUINTESSENCE

Hers To Keep

Theirs To Cherish

Hers To Hold

Anchor Pride Series

Claimed by Caden

McKinnon's Mate

The Corsakis

Three's Never A Crowd

Old Enough to Know Better

The Federation

A Menage Made on Madison

La Belle sans La Bete Series

Menage Material

A Thoroughly Modern Menage

Forever Theirs

Secrets & Lies

The TriAlpha Chronicles

Origin

Trinity

Triskele

Triad

Triumph

Trierna

TriAlpha

Los Lobos

Bound

The Salsang Chronicles (written with Helen Scott)

Stained Egos

Stained Hearts

Stained Minds

Stained Bonds

Stained Souls

www.ingramcontent.com/pod-product-compliance
Lightning Source LLC
Chambersburg PA
CBHW020718310726
48979CB00004B/968
* 9 7 8 1 9 1 5 0 6 2 8 8 8 *